MASTERPIECES

The Best Science Fiction of the Century

MASTERPIECES

The Best Science Fiction of the Century

Edited by Orson Scott Card

ACE BOOKS, NEW YORK

This is a work of fiction. Names, characters, places, and incidents either are the product of the author's imagination or are used fictitiously, and any resemblance to actual persons, living or dead, business establishments, events, or locales is entirely coincidental.

MASTERPIECES:
THE BEST SCIENCE FICTION OF THE CENTURY

An Ace Book
Published by The Berkley Publishing Group,
a division of Penguin Putnam Inc.,
375 Hudson Street, New York, New York 10014.

Visit our website at
www.penguinputnam.com

First edition: November 2001

Library of Congress Cataloging-in-Publication Data

Masterpieces : the best science fiction of the century / [compiled by] Orson Scott Card. — 1st ed.
p. cm
ISBN 0-441-00864-X (alk. paper)
1. Science fiction, American. 2. Science fiction, English. I. Card, Orson Scott.

PS648.S3 .M38 2001
813'.087620805—dc21
2001045074

PRINTED IN THE UNITED STATES OF AMERICA

10   9   8   7   6   5   4   3   2

CONTENTS

The Media Generation

INTRODUCTION

MAKING A LIST of the best science fiction stories of the century is the same as making a list of the best science fiction stories of the millennium. Or, for that matter, the best ever, up to now, because the entire history of science fiction as a self-conscious literary community begins well into the 1900s, when Hugo Gernsback published the first magazine devoted to "scientifiction," defined as "scientific romances like those written by H. G. Wells."

H. G. Wells, Jules Verne, and a whole slew of adventure writers (including A. Merritt, H. Rider Haggard, and others who went on to be full-fledged sci-fi writers, like Edmond Hamilton) wrote stories that, in hindsight, clearly belong as part of the science fiction tradition. But they did not think of their stories as being a new kind of literature. Nor did they see themselves as belonging to a different literary community when they wrote stories that included alien races, strange new inventions, or astonishing relics of the past.

With the publication of Gernsback's *Amazing Stories,* however, the landscape changed. There were now boundaries—which would eventually, for a while at least, become ghetto walls, much to the benefit of the genre—such that only stories of a certain kind could appear within, thus defining what science fiction was and, by implication, what it was not. And there was a letters column.

It was the letters column, really, that created the community. Enthusiasts of the new genre wrote in to Gernsback and then avidly read each other's published letters. Then, skipping the middleman, they wrote directly to each other, and after a while began to meet and talk about what science fiction was and what it could be or should be. They started writing their own stories and sharing them with each other, and eventually began meeting as clubs and, later, in conventions that assembled serious readers of the genre from faraway places, until today the World Science Fiction convention draws participants from dozens of countries and languages (though English remains the lingua franca—or, if you prefer, the common koine—of the genre).

As readers became "fans"—participants in the ongoing public conversation of the sci-fi community—and fans became writers, they began to develop critical principles quite unconnected to the literary ideas being taught in the American university, where theories of criticism came and went, alike only in the fact that all were designed to show why the works of the Modernists (the most recent literary revolution before science fiction) were Great Art. Naturally, the academics, who were relentlessly focused on celebrating Woolf, Lawrence, Joyce, Eliot, Pound, Faulkner, Hemingway, and their literary kin and kith, had no notion of what was going on within the walls of the science fiction ghetto. And when at last they had to take notice because their students kept mentioning books like *Dune* and *Stranger in a Strange Land,* the academics discovered that these strange books and magazines with ludicrously lurid covers did not pay the slightest attention to the Standards of Great Literature that they had developed. Instead of realizing that their standards were inadequate because they did not apply to science fiction, they reached the much safer and easier conclusion that science fiction must be bad.

You know the old saying: To a man with a hammer, everything looks like a nail. Well, that's only sometimes true. In the case of the academic-literary establishment—the community I lovingly call "li-fi"—the better analogy is: To a man with *only* a hammer, a screw is a defective nail.

So every few years, *Atlantic Monthly* or *Harper's Magazine* or *The New Yorker* will trot out an essay explaining exactly why sci-fi is Bad Art. What else would you expect the old aristocracy to do as they try to defend their ivory towers from the onslaught of the smelly and unsubservient masses?

The fact is that by the mid 1940s, science fiction was the most vibrant, most productive, most innovative, and, eventually, the most accomplished of literary communities. Entirely supported by volunteers who read for stories and ideas, rather than students required to peruse and decode texts for grades, science fiction grew and changed, constantly reinventing itself, taking into itself whatever it found useful in other genres and other disciplines—not just science, and not just fiction. Revolution upon revolution, generation upon generation, there was more variety, more history within sci-fi than there was outside it.

I came rather late to the party. The year I was born, 1951, the seminal work had already been done. John W. Campbell had moved science fiction onto a firmer scientific footing (though the old gosh-wow adventure tradition still continued), and Robert Heinlein had taught us how to handle the gradual unfolding of exposition, the key literary technique that every reader and writer of sci-fi now must master in order to take part in the conversation. When I was born, Heinlein, Asimov, and Clarke were already the trinity of leading writers in the field, with Bradbury, Anderson, and Blish soon to make their presence known. Science fiction was part of the air I breathed as I grew up.

As it continues to be for us all. Because sci-fi is mostly read by volunteers (though a few writers have found their work widely required in high schools and middle schools), older works stay in print, not because some teacher has declared them officially Great, but because people are still reading them and telling their friends that they have to get Asimov's *Foundation* or Herbert's *Dune* or Heinlein's *The Moon Is a Harsh Mistress* or Le Guin's *The Left Hand of Darkness*. We still pass this literature from hand to hand. It is still the passionate reader who drives the genre, and, as a result, the entire history of science fiction is still readily available. We can read our way from beginning to end, and have it whole in our memories.

Still, presenting the history of science fiction is not my goal in this book. This is not a tome to be studied. This is a treasury. A collection of jewels.

Not an infinite treasury, either. We had limitations—the publishers had the foolish belief that you would not pay seventy dollars for a three-thousand-page book. We could not include every story that belongs here; we could not include every writer whose work should be represented. More painfully, there are writers—Ray Bradbury, Harlan Ellison, George Alec Effinger, R. A. Lafferty—who have virtually specialized in the short story. In a collection of the best stories in the history of science fiction, it is almost unthinkable to choose only *one* Bradbury, only *one* Ellison.

And what do you do about John Varley, whose finest "short" work is so long that if you include "Press Enter_" or "The Persistence of Vision" you have to leave out five other stories? Even as it is, I had to leave out some of my very favorite writers and stories—Peter Dickinson's "Flight," for instance, and Felix Gottschalk's "Vestibular Man," David Bunch's Moderan stories; and I'm dismayed at the list of writers not represented here—Bruce Sterling, Connie Willis, Nancy Kress, Lucius Shepherd, Lois McMaster Bujold, Norman Spinrad, Clifford Simak, Vonda McIntyre, Octavia Butler, Dave Wolverton—some of the very writers that I cite.

But that's why I get the big bucks—I can make tough choices. Screaming, whining, whimpering, talking to myself far into the night, I made the calls.

Here's how I chose:

These are stories that I loved when I first read them and that, upon rereading, I still love and admire. They are stories that I think appeal to a wide audience of readers and not just a small group. They are by writers who have mattered in the field, influencing other writers and, more importantly, changing the lives of their readers. I tried to avoid duplications—stories that did the same kind of thing as others in the collection, though of course such judgments are completely subjective.

Above all, these are stories that I cannot forget.

I have grouped them in three general categories, by era. The Golden Age—from the beginning to the midsixties—includes the writers and stories that created science fiction as we know it. And yes, I'm aware that "Robot Dreams" was one of Asimov's later works, but he remained a Golden Age writer—perhaps the best of them— throughout his career. At the same time, Sturgeon and Blish arguably are post–Golden Age, while Hamilton and Biggle might be considered holdovers from earlier. Give me a break here. Whatever you call this period, these are the writers who plowed and planted.

The New Wave period—the midsixties to the midseventies—was marked by writers who introduced dazzling style and a fervor, sometimes a rage, that reenergized the field and opened it to many new kinds of storytelling. At the same time, the older sci-fi tradition—the plain tale, the idea-based story, the moral dilemma, the character story—continued to be enriched by such writers as Larry Niven, Ursula K. Le Guin, Frederik Pohl, and Brian Aldiss.

If the New Wave–era writers were the children of the Golden Age, either rebelling against their parents or taking over the family business, the eighties and nineties were dominated by the grandchildren of the Golden Age—the writers who grew up watching *Twilight Zone, The Outer Limits,* and *Star Trek* right along with reading "Call Me Joe," " 'All You Zombies—', " and " 'Repent, Harlequin!' Said the Ticktockman." The Media Generation found that they could write *any* kind of story, and while some movements took on a separate identity—the Cyberpunks, the Humanists—most of us who began writing in this era found that we could do whatever we pleased and as long as our stories fit, more or less, within the ever-loosening borders of the genre, there would be readers who were eager to hear our voices and experience the stories we had to offer.

As you move from one era to the next, you'll get a sense of how science fiction has developed through the years—without losing touch with its roots, without forgetting anything that we, as a community, have learned.

It's possible that we have now reached and passed the Science Fiction Age. It's possible that we're ready for the next revolution in literature, the next group of storytellers. The post–science fiction age.

It's also possible that we're ready for the genre boundaries to dissolve. For us to say "literature" and include science fiction within the definition of that word.

Truth is, I don't care. That's a matter for critics and teachers to argue about. What I care about is this: Stories change us. They create communities of people with shared memories. And the stories that are ahead of you in these pages—they are among the very best of our time.

The Golden Age

Call Me Joe

A multiple winner of the Hugo and Nebula Awards, Poul Anderson has written more than fifty novels and hundreds of short stories since his science fiction debut in 1947. His first novel, *Brain Wave*, is a classic example of the techniques of traditional science fiction, extrapolating the impact that an abrupt universal rise in intelligence has on the totality of human civilization in the twentieth century. Anderson is highly regarded for the detail of his stories. His vast Technic History saga, a multibook chronicle of interstellar exploration and empire building, covers fifty centuries of future history spread out over the rise and fall of three empires of a galactic federation. The vast scope of the series has given Anderson the opportunity to develop colorful, well-developed characters and to explore the long-term impact of certain ideas and attitudes—free enterprise, militarism, imperialism, individual styles of governing—on the society and political structure of a created world. Two characters, distinct products of their different times and civilizations, dominate the series' most notable episodes: Falstaffian rogue merchant Nicholas van Rijn, hero of *The Man Who Counts*, *Satan's World*, and *Mirkheim*, and Ensign Dominic Flandry, whose adventures include *We Claim These Stars*, *A Knight of Ghosts and Shadows*, and *Earthman, Go Home!* Anderson has tackled many of science fiction's classic themes, including near-light-speed travel in *Tau Zero*, time travel in the series of Time Patrol stories collected as *Guardians of Time*, and accelerated evolution in *Fire Time*. He is known for his interweaving of science fiction and history, notably in his novel *The High Crusade*, a superior first-contact tale in which a medieval army captures an alien spaceship. Much of Anderson's fantasy is rich with undercurrents of mythology, notably his heroic fantasy *Three Hearts and Three Lions*, and *The Broken Sword*, an alternate history drawn from the background of *A Midsummer Night's Dream*. Anderson received the Tolkien Memorial Award in 1978. With his wife, Karen, he has written the King of Ys Celtic fantasy quartet, and with Gordon Dickson the amusing Hoka series. His short fiction has been collected in numerous volumes, including *The Queen of Air and Darkness and Other Stories*, *All One Universe*, *Strangers from Earth*, and *Seven Conquests*.

THE WIND CAME whooping out of eastern darkness, driving a lash of ammonia dust before it. In minutes, Edward Anglesey was blinded.

He clawed all four feet into the broken shards which were soil, hunched down, and groped for his little smelter. The wind was an idiot bassoon in his skull. Something whipped across his back, drawing blood, a tree yanked up by the roots and spat a hundred miles. Lightning cracked, immensely far overhead where clouds boiled with night.

As if to reply, thunder toned in the ice mountains and a red gout of flame jumped and a hillside came booming down, spilling itself across the valley. The earth shivered.

Sodium explosion, thought Anglesey in the drumbeat noise. The fire and the lightning gave him enough illumination to find his apparatus. He picked up tools in muscular hands, his tail gripped the trough, and he battered his way to the tunnel and thus to his dugout.

It had walls and roof of water, frozen by sun-remoteness and compressed by tons of atmosphere jammed onto every square inch. Ventilated by a tiny smokehole, a lamp of tree oil burning in hydrogen made a dull light for the single room.

Anglesey sprawled his slate-blue form on the floor, panting. It was no use to swear at the storm. These ammonia gales often came at sunset, and there was nothing to do but wait them out. He was tired anyway.

It would be morning in five hours or so. He had hoped to cast an axehead, his first, this evening, but maybe it was better to do the job by daylight.

He pulled a decapod body off a shelf and ate the meat raw, pausing for long gulps of liquid methane from a jug. Things would improve once he had proper tools; so far, everything had been painfully grubbed and hacked to shape with teeth, claws, chance icicles, and what detestably weak and crumbling fragments remained of the spaceship. Give him a few years and he'd be living as a man should.

He sighed, stretched, and lay down to sleep.

Somewhat more than one hundred and twelve thousand miles away, Edward Anglesey took off his helmet.

HE LOOKED AROUND, blinking. After the Jovian surface, it was always a little unreal to find himself here again, in the clean quiet orderliness of the control room.

His muscles ached. They shouldn't. He had not really been fighting a gale of several hundred miles an hour, under three gravities and a temperature of 140 Absolute. He had been here, in the almost nonexistent pull of Jupiter V, breathing oxynitrogen. It was Joe who lived down there and filled his lungs with hydrogen and helium at a pressure which could still only be estimated because it broke aneroids and deranged piezoelectrics.

Nevertheless, his body felt worn and beaten. Tension, no doubt—psychosomatics—after all, for a good many hours now he had, in a sense, been Joe, and Joe had been working hard.

With the helmet off, Anglesey held only a thread of identification. The esprojector was still tuned to Joe's brain but no longer focused on his own. Somewhere in the back of his mind, he knew an indescribable feeling of sleep. Now and then, vague forms or colors drifted in the soft black—dreams? Not impossible, that Joe's brain should dream a little when Anglesey's mind wasn't using it.

A light flickered red on the esprojector panel, and a bell whined electronic fear. Anglesey cursed. Thin fingers danced over the controls of his chair, he slued around and shot across to the bank of dials. Yes—there—K-tube oscillating again! The circuit blew out. He wrenched the faceplate off with one hand and fumbled in a drawer with the other.

Inside his mind he could feel the contact with Joe fading. If he once lost it entirely, he wasn't sure he could regain it. And Joe was an investment of several million dollars and quite a few highly skilled man-years.

Anglesey pulled the offending K-tube from its socket and threw it on the floor. Glass exploded. It eased his temper a bit, just enough so he could find a replacement, plug it in, switch on the current again—as the machine warmed up, once again amplifying, the Joeness in the back alleys of his brain strengthened.

Slowly, then, the man in the electric wheelchair rolled out of the room, into the hall. Let somebody else sweep up the broken tube. To hell with it. To hell with everybody.

JAN CORNELIUS HAD never been farther from Earth than some comfortable Lunar resort. He felt much put upon that the Psionics Corporation should tap him for a thirteen-month exile. The fact that he knew as much about esprojectors and their cranky innards as any other man alive was no excuse. Why send anyone at all? Who cared?

Obviously the Federation Science Authority did. It had seemingly given those bearded hermits a blank check on the taxpayer's account.

Thus did Cornelius grumble to himself, all the long hyperbolic path to Jupiter. Then the shifting accelerations of approach to its tiny inner satellite left him too wretched for further complaint.

And when he finally, just prior to disembarkation, went up to the greenhouse for a look at Jupiter, he said not a word. Nobody does, the first time.

Arne Viken waited patiently while Cornelius stared. *It still gets me, too,* he remembered. *By the throat. Sometimes I'm afraid to look.*

At length Cornelius turned around. He had a faintly Jovian appearance himself, being a large man with an imposing girth. "I had no idea," he whispered. "I never thought . . . I had seen pictures, but—"

Viken nodded. "Sure, Dr. Cornelius. Pictures don't convey it."

Where they stood, they could see the dark broken rock of the satellite, jumbled for a short way beyond the landing slip and then chopped off sheer. This moon was scarcely even a platform, it seemed, and cold constellations went streaming past it, around it. Jupiter lay across a fifth of that sky, softly ambrous, banded with colors, spotted with the shadows of planet-sized moons and with whirlwinds as broad as Earth. If there had been any gravity to speak of, Cornelius would have thought, instinctively, that the great planet was falling on him. As it was, he felt as if sucked upward; his hands were still sore where he had grabbed a rail to hold on.

"You live here . . . all alone . . . with this?" He spoke feebly.

"Oh, well, there are some fifty of us all told, pretty congenial," said Viken. "It's not so bad. You sign up for four-cycle hitches—four ship arrivals—and believe it or not, Dr. Cornelius, this is my third enlistment."

The newcomer forbore to inquire more deeply. There was something not quite understandable about the men on Jupiter V. They were mostly bearded, though otherwise careful to remain neat; their low-gravity movements were somehow dreamlike to watch; they hoarded their conversation, as if to stretch it through the year and month between ships. Their monkish existence had changed them—or did they take what amounted to vows of poverty, chastity, and obedience, because they had never felt quite at home on green Earth?

Thirteen months! Cornelius shuddered. It was going to be a long cold wait, and the pay and bonuses accumulating for him were scant comfort now, four hundred and eighty million miles from the sun.

"Wonderful place to do research," continued Viken. "All the facilities, hand-picked colleagues, no distractions . . . and of course—" He jerked his thumb at the planet and turned to leave.

Cornelius followed, wallowing awkwardly. "It is very interesting, no doubt," he puffed. "Fascinating. But really, Dr. Viken, to drag me way out here and make me spend a year plus waiting for the next ship . . . to do a job which may take me a few weeks—"

"Are you sure it's that simple?" asked Viken gently. His face swiveled around, and there was something in his eyes that silenced Cornelius. "After all my time here, I've yet to see any problem, however complicated, which when you looked at it the right way didn't become still more complicated."

They went through the ship's air lock and the tube joining it to the station entrance. Nearly everything was underground. Rooms, laboratories, even halls had a degree of luxuriousness—why, there was a fireplace with a real fire in the common room! God alone knew what *that* cost!

Thinking of the huge chill emptiness where the king planet laired, and of his own year's sentence, Cornelius decided that such luxuries were, in truth, biological necessities.

Viken showed him to a pleasantly furnished chamber which would be his own. "We'll fetch your luggage soon and unload your psionic stuff. Right now, everybody's either talking to the ship's crew or reading his mail."

Cornelius nodded absently and sat down. The chair, like all low-gee furniture, was a mere spidery skeleton, but it held his bulk comfortably enough. He felt in his tunic hoping to bribe the other man into keeping him company for a while. "Cigar? I brought some from Amsterdam."

"Thanks." Viken accepted with disappointing casualness, crossed long thin legs, and blew grayish clouds.

"Ah . . . are you in charge here?"

"Not exactly. No one is. We do have one administrator, the cook, to handle what little work of that type may come up. Don't forget, this is a research station, first, last, and always."

"What is your field, then?"

Viken frowned. "Don't question anyone else so bluntly, Dr. Cornelius," he warned. "They'd rather spin the gossip out as long as possible with each newcomer. It's a rare treat to have someone whose every last conceivable reaction hasn't been— No, no apologies to me. 'S all right. I'm a physicist, specializing in the solid state at ultrahigh pressures." He nodded at the wall. "Plenty of it to be observed—there!"

"I see." Cornelius smoked quietly for a while. Then: "I'm supposed to be the psionics expert, but frankly, at present, I've no idea why your machine should misbehave as reported."

"You mean those, uh, K-tubes have a stable output on Earth?"

"And on Luna, Mars, Venus . . . everywhere, apparently, but here." Cornelius shrugged. "Of course, psibeams are always pernickety, and sometimes you get an unwanted feedback when— No. I'll get the facts before I theorize. Who are your psimen?"

"Just Anglesey, who's not a formally trained esman at all. But he took it up after he was crippled, and showed such a natural aptitude that he was shipped out here when he volunteered. It's so hard to get anyone for Jupiter V that we aren't fussy about degrees. At that, Ed seems to be operating Joe as well as a Ps.D. could."

"Ah, yes. Your pseudojovian. I'll have to examine that angle pretty carefully too," said Cornelius. In spite of himself, he was getting interested. "Maybe the trouble comes from something in Joe's biochemistry. Who knows? I'll let you into a carefully guarded little secret, Dr. Viken: psionics is not an exact science."

"Neither is physics," grinned the other man. After a moment, he added more soberly: "Not my brand of physics, anyway. I hope to make it exact. That's why I'm here, you know. It's the reason we're all here."

*   *   *

EDWARD ANGLESEY WAS a bit of a shock, the first time. He was a head, a pair of arms, and a disconcertingly intense blue stare. The rest of him was mere detail, enclosed in a wheeled machine.

"Biophysicist originally," Viken had told Cornelius. "Studying atmospheric spores at Earth Station when he was still a young man—accident crushed him up, nothing below his chest will ever work again. Snappish type, you have to go slow with him."

Seated on a wisp of stool in the esprojector control room, Cornelius realized that Viken had been soft-pedaling the truth.

Anglesey ate as he talked, gracelessly, letting the chair's tentacles wipe up after him. "Got to," he explained. "This stupid place is officially on Earth time, GMT. Jupiter isn't. I've got to be here whenever Joe wakes, ready to take him over."

"Couldn't you have someone spell you?" asked Cornelius.

"Bah!" Anglesey stabbed a piece of prot and waggled it at the other man. Since it was native to him, he could spit out English, the common language of the station, with unmeasured ferocity. "Look here. You ever done therapeutic esping? Not just listening in, or even communication, but actual pedagogic control?"

"No, not I. It requires a certain natural talent, like yours." Cornelius smiled. His ingratiating little phrase was swallowed without being noticed by the scored face opposite him. "I take it you mean cases like, oh, reeducating the nervous system of a palsied child?"

"Yes, yes. Good enough example. Has anyone ever tried to suppress the child's personality, take him over in the most literal sense?"

"Good God, no!"

"Even as a scientific experiment?" Anglesey grinned. "Has any esprojector operative ever poured on the juice and swamped the child's brain with his own thoughts? Come on, Cornelius, I won't snitch on you."

"Well . . . it's out of my line, you understand." The psionicist looked carefully away, found a bland meter face, and screwed his eyes to that. "I have, uh, heard something about . . . well, yes, there were attempts made in some pathological cases to, uh, bull through . . . break down the patient's delusions by sheer force—"

"And it didn't work," said Anglesey. He laughed. "It *can't* work, not even on a child, let alone an adult with a fully developed personality. Why, it took a decade of refinement, didn't it, before the machine was debugged to the point where a psychiatrist could even 'listen in' without the normal variation between his pattern of thought and the patient's . . . without that variation setting up an interference scrambling the very thing he wanted to study. The machine has to make automatic compensations for the differences between individuals. We still can't bridge the differences between species.

"If someone else is willing to cooperate, you can very gently guide his thinking.

And that's all. If you try to seize control of another brain, a brain with its own background of experience, its own ego—you risk your very sanity. The other brain will fight back, instinctively. A fully developed, matured, hardened human personality is just too complex for outside control. It has too many resources, too much hell the subconscious can call to its defense if its integrity is threatened. Blazes, man, we can't even master our own minds, let alone anyone else's!"

Anglesey's cracked-voice tirade broke off. He sat brooding at the instrument panel, tapping the console of his mechanical mother.

"WELL?" SAID CORNELIUS after a while.

He should not, perhaps, have spoken. But he found it hard to remain mute. There was too much silence—half a billion miles of it, from here to the sun. If you closed your mouth five minutes at a time, the silence began creeping in like a fog.

"Well," gibed Anglesey. "So our pseudojovian, Joe, has a physically adult brain. The only reason I can control him is that his brain has never been given a chance to develop its own ego. I *am* Joe. From the moment he was 'born' into consciousness, I have been there. The psibeam sends me all his sense data and sends him back my motor-nerve impulses. But nevertheless, he has that excellent brain, and its cells are recording every trace of experience, even as yours and mine; his synapses have assumed the topography which is my 'personality pattern.'

"Anyone else, taking him over from me, would find it was like an attempt to oust me myself from my own brain. It couldn't be done. To be sure, he doubtless has only a rudimentary set of Anglesey memories—I do not, for instance, repeat trigonometric theorems while controlling him—but he has enough to be, potentially, a distinct personality.

"As a matter of fact, whenever he wakes up from sleep—there's usually a lag of a few minutes, while I sense the change through my normal psi faculties and get the amplifying helmet adjusted—I have a bit of a struggle. I feel almost a . . . a resistance . . . until I've brought his mental currents completely into phase with mine. Merely dreaming has been enough of a different experience to—"

Anglesey didn't bother to finish the sentence.

"I see," murmured Cornelius. "Yes, it's clear enough. In fact, it's astonishing that you can have such total contact with a being of such alien metabolism."

"I won't for much longer," said the esman sarcastically, "unless you can correct whatever is burning out those K-tubes. I don't have an unlimited supply of spares."

"I have some working hypotheses," said Cornelius, "but there's so little known about psibeam transmission—is the velocity infinite or merely very great, is the beam strength actually independent of distance? How about the possible effects of transmission . . . oh, through the degenerate matter in the Jovian core? Good Lord, a planet where water is a heavy mineral and hydrogen is a metal? What do we know?"

"We're supposed to find out," snapped Anglesey. "That's what this whole project is for. Knowledge. Bull!" Almost, he spat on the floor. "Apparently what little we have learned doesn't even get through to people. Hydrogen is still a gas where Joe lives. He'd have to dig down a few miles to reach the solid phase. And I'm expected to make a scientific analysis of Jovian conditions!"

Cornelius waited it out, letting Anglesey storm on while he himself turned over the problem on K-tube oscillation.

"They don't understand back on Earth. Even here they don't. Sometimes I think they refuse to understand. Joe's down there without much more than his bare hands. He, I, we started with no more knowledge than that he could probably eat the local life. He has to spend nearly all his time hunting for food. It's a miracle he's come as far as he has in these few weeks—made a shelter, grown familiar with the immediate region, begun on metallurgy, hydrurgy, whatever you want to call it. What more do they want me to do, for crying in the beer?"

"Yes, yes—" mumbled Cornelius. "Yes, I—"

Anglesey raised his white bony face. Something filmed over in his eyes.

"What—?" began Cornelius.

"Shut up!" Anglesey whipped the chair around, groped for the helmet, slapped it down over his skull. "Joe's waking. Get out of here."

"But if you'll only let me work while he sleeps, how can I—"

Anglesey snarled and threw a wrench at him. It was a feeble toss, even in low-gee. Cornelius backed toward the door. Anglesey was tuning in the esprojector. Suddenly he jerked.

"*Cornelius!*"

"Whatisit?" The psionicist tried to run back, overdid it, and skidded in a heap to end up against the panel.

"K-tube again." Anglesey yanked off the helmet. It must have hurt like blazes, having a mental squeal build up uncontrolled and amplified in your own brain, but he said merely: "Change it for me. Fast. And then get out and leave me alone. Joe didn't wake up of himself. Something crawled into the dugout with me—I'm in trouble down there!"

IT HAD BEEN a hard day's work, and Joe slept heavily. He did not wake until the hands closed on his throat.

For a moment, then, he knew only a crazy smothering wave of panic. He thought he was back on Earth Station, floating in null-gee at the end of a cable while a thousand frosty stars haloed the planet before him. He thought the great I-beam had broken from its moorings and started toward him, slowly, but with all the inertia of its cold tons, spinning and shimmering in the Earth light, and the only sound himself screaming and screaming in his helmet trying to break from the cable the beam nudged him ever so gently but it kept on moving he moved with it he was crushed against the station wall nuzzled into it his mangled suit frothed as it tried to seal its wounded self there was blood mingled with the foam his blood *Joe roared.*

His convulsive reaction tore the hands off his neck and sent a black shape spinning across the dugout. It struck the wall, thunderously, and the lamp fell to the floor and went out.

Joe stood in darkness, breathing hard, aware in a vague fashion that the wind had died from a shriek to a low snarling while he slept.

The thing he had tossed away mumbled in pain and crawled along the wall. Joe felt through lightlessness after his club.

Something else scrabbled. The tunnel! They were coming through the tunnel! Joe groped blindly to meet them. His heart drummed thickly and his nose drank an alien stench.

The thing that emerged, as Joe's hands closed on it, was only about half his size, but it had six monstrously taloned feet and a pair of three-fingered hands that reached after his eyes. Joe cursed, lifted it while it writhed, and dashed it to the floor. It screamed, and he heard bones splinter.

"Come on, then!" Joe arched his back and spat at them, like a tiger menaced by giant caterpillars.

They flowed through his tunnel and into the room; a dozen of them entered while he wrestled one that had curled around his shoulders and anchored its sinuous body with claws. They pulled at his legs, trying to crawl up on his back. He struck out with claws of his own, with his tail, rolled over and went down beneath a heap of them and stood up with the heap still clinging to him.

They swayed in darkness. The legged seething of them struck the dugout wall. It shivered, a rafter cracked, the roof came down. Anglesey stood in a pit, among broken ice plates, under the wan light of a sinking Ganymede.

He could see, now, that the monsters were black in color and that they had heads big enough to accommodate some brains, less than human but probably more than apes. There were a score of them or so; they struggled from beneath the wreckage and flowed at him with the same shrieking malice.

Why?

Baboon reaction, thought Anglesey somewhere in the back of himself. See the stranger, fear the stranger, hate the stranger, kill the stranger. His chest heaved, pumping air through a raw throat. He yanked a whole rafter to him, snapped it in half, and twirled the iron-hard wood.

The nearest creature got its head bashed in. The next had its back broken. The third was hurled with shattered ribs into a fourth; they went down together. Joe began to laugh. It was getting to be fun.

"Yeee-ow! Ti-i-i-iger!" He ran across the icy ground, toward the pack. They scattered, howling. He hunted them until the last one had vanished into the forest.

Panting, Joe looked at the dead. He himself was bleeding, he ached, he was cold and hungry, and his shelter had been wrecked . . . but, he'd whipped them! He had a sudden impulse to beat his chest and howl. For a moment, he hesitated—why not? Anglesey threw back his head and bayed victory at the dim shield of Ganymede.

Thereafter he went to work. First build a fire, in the lee of the spaceship—which was little more by now than a hill of corrosion. The monster pack cried in darkness and the broken ground; they had not given up on him, they would return.

He tore a haunch off one of the slain and took a bite. Pretty good. Better yet if properly cooked. Heh! They'd made a big mistake in calling his attention to their existence! He finished breakfast while Ganymede slipped under the western ice mountains. It would be morning soon. The air was almost still, and a flock of pancake-shaped skyskimmers, as Anglesey called them, went overhead, burnished copper color in the first pale dawn-streaks.

Joe rummaged in the ruins of his hut until he had recovered the water-smelting equipment. It wasn't harmed. That was the first order of business, melt some ice and cast it in the molds of axe, knife, saw, hammer he had painfully prepared. Under Jovian conditions, methane was a liquid that you drank and water was a dense hard mineral. It would make good tools. Later on he would try alloying it with other materials.

Next—yes. To hell with the dugout; he could sleep in the open again for a while. Make a bow, set traps, be ready to massacre the black caterpillars when they attacked him again. There was a chasm not far from here, going down a long way toward the bitter cold of the metallic-hydrogen strata: a natural icebox, a place to store the several weeks' worth of meat his enemies would supply. This would give him leisure to— Oh, a hell of a lot!

Joe laughed, exultantly, and lay down to watch the sunrise.

It struck him afresh how lovely a place this was. See how the small brilliant spark of the sun swam up out of eastern fogbanks colored dusky purple and veined with rose and gold; see how the light strengthened until the great hollow arch of the sky became one shout of radiance; see how the light spilled warm and living over a broad fair land, the million square miles of rustling low forests and wave-blinking lakes and feather-plumed hydrogen geysers; and see, see, see how the ice mountains of the west flashed like blued steel!

Anglesey drew the wild morning wind deep into his lungs and shouted with a boy's joy.

"I'M NOT A biologist myself," said Viken carefully. "But maybe for that reason I can better give you the general picture. Then Lopez or Matsumoto can answer any questions of detail."

"Excellent," nodded Cornelius. "Why don't you assume I am totally ignorant of this project? I very nearly am, you know."

"If you wish," laughed Viken.

They stood in an outer office of the xenobiology section. No one else was around for the station's clocks said 1730 GMT and there was only one shift. No point in having more, until Anglesey's half of the enterprise had actually begun gathering quantitative data.

The physicist bent over and took a paperweight off a desk. "One of the boys made this for fun," he said, "but it's a pretty good model of Joe. He stands about five feet tall at the head."

Cornelius turned the plastic image over in his hands. If you could imagine such a thing as a feline centaur with a thick prehensile tail— The torso was squat, long-armed, immensely muscular; the hairless head was round, wide-nosed, with big deep-set eyes and heavy jaws, but it was really quite a human face. The overall color was bluish gray.

"Male, I see," he remarked.

"Of course. Perhaps you don't understand. Joe is the complete pseudojovian: as far as we can tell, the final model, with all the bugs worked out. He's the answer to a research question that took fifty years to ask." Viken looked sideways at Cornelius. "So you realize the importance of your job, don't you?"

"I'll do my best," said the psionicist. "But if . . . well, let's say that tube failure or something causes you to lose Joe before I've solved the oscillation problem. You do have other pseudos in reserve, don't you?"

"Oh, yes," said Viken moodily. "But the cost— We're not on an unlimited budget. We do go through a lot of money, because it's expensive to stand up and sneeze this far from Earth. But for that same reason our margin is slim."

He jammed hands in pockets and slouched toward the inner door, the laboratories, head down and talking in a low, hurried voice:

"Perhaps you don't realize what a nightmare planet Jupiter is. Not just the surface gravity—a shade under three gees, what's that? But the gravitational potential, ten times Earth's. The temperature. The pressure . . . above all, the atmosphere, and the storms, and the darkness!

"When a spaceship goes down to the Jovian surface, it's a radio-controlled job; it leaks like a sieve, to equalize pressure, but otherwise it's the sturdiest, most utterly powerful model ever designed; it's loaded with every instrument, every servomechanism, every safety device the human mind has yet thought up to protect a million-dollar hunk of precision equipment.

"And what happens? Half the ships never reach the surface at all. A storm snatches them and throws them away, or they collide with a floating chunk of Ice VII—small version of the Red Spot—or, so help me, what passes for a flock of *birds* rams one and stoves it in!

"As for the fifty percent which do land, it's a one-way trip. We don't even try to bring them back. If the stresses coming down haven't sprung something, the corrosion has doomed them anyway. Hydrogen at Jovian pressure does funny things to metals.

"It cost a total of—about five million dollars—to set Joe, one pseudo, down there. Each pseudo to follow will cost, if we're lucky, a couple of million more."

Viken kicked open the door and led the way through. Beyond was a big room, low-ceilinged, coldly lit, and murmurous with ventilators. It reminded Cornelius of a nucleonics lab; for a moment he wasn't sure why, then recognized the intricacies of remote control, remote observation, walls enclosing forces which could destroy the entire moon.

"These are required by the pressure, of course," said Viken, pointing to a row of shields. "And the cold. And the hydrogen itself, as a minor hazard. We have units here duplicating conditions in the Jovian, uh, stratosphere. This is where the whole project really began."

"I've heard something about that," nodded Cornelius. "Didn't you scoop up airborne spores?"

"Not I." Viken chuckled. "Totti's crew did, about fifty years ago. Proved there was life on Jupiter. A life using liquid methane as its basic solvent, solid ammonia as a starting point for nitrate synthesis—the plants use solar energy to build unsaturated carbon compounds, releasing hydrogen; the animals eat the plants and reduce those compounds again to the saturated form. There is even an equivalent of combustion. The reactions involve complex enzymes and . . . well, it's out of my line."

"Jovian biochemistry is pretty well understood, then."

"Oh, yes. Even in Totti's day, they had a highly developed biotic technology: Earth bacteria had already been synthesized and most gene structures pretty well mapped. The only reason it took so long to diagram Jovian life processes was the technical difficulty, high pressure and so on."

"When did you actually get a look at Jupiter's surface?"

"Gray managed that, about thirty years ago. Set a televisor ship down, a ship that lasted long enough to flash him quite a series of pictures. Since then, the technique has improved. We know that Jupiter is crawling with its own weird kind of life, probably more fertile than Earth. Extrapolating from the airborne microorganisms, our team made trial syntheses of metazoans and—"

Viken sighed. "Damn it, if only there were intelligent native life! Think what they could tell us, Cornelius, the data, the— Just think back how far we've gone since Lavoisier, with the low-pressure chemistry of Earth. Here's a chance to learn a high-pressure chemistry and physics at least as rich with possibilities!"

After a moment, Cornelius murmured slyly: "Are you certain there *aren't* any Jovians?"

"Oh, sure, there could be several billion of them," shrugged Viken. "Cities, empires, anything you like. Jupiter has the surface area of a hundred Earths, and we've only seen maybe a dozen small regions. But we do know there aren't any Jovians using radio. Considering their atmosphere, it's unlikely they ever would invent it for themselves—imagine how thick a vacuum tube has to be, how strong a pump you need! So it was finally decided we'd better make our own Jovians."

Cornelius followed him through the lab, into another room. This was less cluttered, it had a more finished appearance: the experimenter's haywire rig had yielded to the assured precision of an engineer.

Viken went over to one of the panels which lined the walls and looked at its gauges. "Beyond this lies another pseudo," he said. "Female, in this instance. She's at a pressure of two hundred atmospheres and a temperature of 194 Absolute. There's a . . . an umbilical arrangement, I guess you'd call it, to keep her alive. She was grown to adulthood in this, uh, fetal stage—we patterned our Jovians after the terrestrial mammal. She's never been conscious, she won't ever be till she's 'born.' We have a total of twenty males and sixty females waiting here. We can count on about half reaching the surface. More can be created as required.

"It isn't the pseudos that are so expensive, it's their transportation. So Joe is down there alone till we're sure that his kind *can* survive."

"I take it you experimented with lower forms first," said Cornelius.

"Of course. It took twenty years, even with forced-catalysis techniques, to work from an artificial airborne spore to Joe. We've used the psibeam to control everything from pseudoinsects on up. Interspecies control is possible, you know, if your puppet's nervous system is deliberately designed for it, and isn't given a chance to grow into a pattern different from the esman's."

"And Joe is the first specimen who's given trouble?"

"Yes."

"Scratch one hypothesis." Cornelius sat down on a workbench, dangling thick legs and running a hand through thin sandy hair. "I thought maybe some physical effort of Jupiter was responsible. Now it looks as if the difficulty is with Joe himself."

"We've all suspected that much," said Viken. He struck a cigarette and sucked in his cheeks around the smoke. His eyes were gloomy. "Hard to see how. The biotics engineers tell me *Pseudocentaurus sapiens* has been more carefully designed than any product of natural evolution."

"Even the brain?"

"Yes. It's patterned directly on the human, to make psibeam control possible, but there are improvements—greater stability."

"There are still the psychological aspects, though," said Cornelius. "In spite of all our amplifiers and other fancy gadgets, psi is essentially a branch of psychology, even today . . . or maybe it's the other way around. Let's consider traumatic experiences. I take it the . . . the adult Jovian's fetus has a rough trip going down?"

"The ship does," said Viken. "Not the pseudo itself, which is wrapped up in fluid just like you were before birth."

"Nevertheless," said Cornelius, "the two hundred atmospheres pressure here is not the same as whatever unthinkable pressure exists down on Jupiter. Could the change be injurious?"

Viken gave him a look of respect. "Not likely," he answered. "I told you the J-ships are designed leaky. External pressure is transmitted to the, uh, uterine mechanism through a series of diaphragms, in a gradual fashion. It takes hours to make the descent, you realize."

"Well, what happens next?" went on Cornelius. "The ship lands, the uterine mechanism opens, the umbilical connection disengages, and Joe is, shall we say, born. But he has an adult brain. He is not protected by the only half-developed infant brain from the shock of sudden awareness."

"We thought of that," said Viken. "Anglesey was on the psibeam, in phase with Joe, when the ship left this moon. So it wasn't really Joe who emerged, who perceived. Joe has never been much more than a biological waldo. He can only suffer mental shock to the extent that Ed does, because it *is* Ed down there!"

"As you will," said Cornelius. "Still, you didn't plan for a race of puppets, did you?"

"Oh, heavens, no," said Viken. "Out of the question. Once we know Joe is well established, we'll import a few more esmen and get him some assistance in the form of other pseudos. Eventually females will be sent down, and uncontrolled males, to be educated by the puppets. A new generation will be born normally— Well, anyhow, the ultimate aim is a small civilization of Jovians. There will be hunters, miners, artisans, farmers, housewives, the works. They will support a few key members, a kind of priesthood. And that priesthood will be esp-controlled, as Joe is. It will exist solely to make instruments, take readings, perform experiments, and tell us what we want to know!"

Cornelius nodded. In a general way, this was the Jovian project as he had understood it. He could appreciate the importance of his own assignment.

Only, he still had no clue to the cause of that positive feedback in the K-tubes. And what could he do about it?

HIS HANDS WERE still bruised. *Oh, God,* he thought with a groan, for the hundredth time, *does it affect me that much? While Joe was fighting down there, did I really hammer my fists on metal up here?*

His eyes smoldered across the room, to the bench where Cornelius worked. He didn't like Cornelius, fat cigar-sucking slob, interminably talking and talking. He had about given up trying to be civil to the Earthworm.

The psionicist laid down a screwdriver and flexed cramped fingers. "*Whuff!*" He smiled. "I'm going to take a break."

The half-assembled esprojector made a gaunt backdrop for his wide soft body, where it squatted toad-fashion on the bench. Anglesey detested the whole idea of anyone sharing this room, even for a few hours a day. Of late he had been demanding his meals brought here, left outside the door of his adjoining bedroom-bath. He had not gone beyond for quite some time now.

And why should I?

"Couldn't you hurry it up a little?" snapped Anglesey.

Cornelius flushed. "If you'd had an assembled spare machine, instead of loose parts—" he began. Shrugging, he took out a cigar stub and relit it carefully; his supply had to last a long time.

Anglesey wondered if those stinking clouds were blown from his mouth on malicious purpose. *I don't like you, Mr. Earthman Cornelius, and it is doubtless quite mutual.*

"There was no obvious need for one, until the other esmen arrive," said Anglesey in a sullen voice. "And the testing instruments report this one in perfectly good order."

"Nevertheless," said Cornelius, "at irregular intervals it goes into wild oscillations which burn out the K-tube. The problem is why. I'll have you try out this new machine as soon as it is ready, but, frankly, I don't believe the trouble lies in electronic failure at all—or even in unsuspected physical effects."

"Where, then?" Anglesey felt more at ease as the discussion grew purely technical.

"Well, look. What exactly is the K-tube? It's the heart of the esprojector. It amplifies your natural psionic pulses, uses them to modulate the carrier wave, and shoots the whole beam down at Joe. It also picks up Joe's resonating impulses and amplifies them for your benefit. Everything else is auxiliary to the K-tube."

"Spare me the lecture," snarled Anglesey.

"I was only rehearsing the obvious," said Cornelius, "because every now and then it is the obvious answer which is hardest to see. Maybe it isn't the K-tube which is misbehaving. Maybe it is you."

"What?" The white face gaped at him. A dawning rage crept red across its thin bones.

"Nothing personal intended," said Cornelius hastily. "But you know what a tricky beast the subconscious is. Suppose, just as a working hypothesis, that way down underneath you don't *want* to be on Jupiter. I imagine it is a rather terrifying environment. Or there may be some obscure Freudian element involved. Or, quite simply and naturally, your subconscious may fail to understand that Joe's death does not entail your own."

"Um-m-m—" *Mirabile dictu.* Anglesey remained calm. He rubbed his chin with one skeletal hand. "Can you be more explicit?"

"Only in a rough way," replied Cornelius. "Your conscious mind sends a motor impulse along the psibeam to Joe. Simultaneously, your subconscious mind, being scared of the whole business, emits the glandular-vascular-cardiac-visceral impulses associated with fear. These react on Joe, whose tension is transmitted back along the beam. Feeling Joe's somatic fear symptoms, your subconscious gets still more worried, thereby increasing the symptoms—Get it? It's exactly similar to ordinary neurasthenia, with this exception: that since there is a powerful amplifier, the K-tube, involved, the oscillations can build up uncontrollably within a second or two. You should be thankful the tube does burn out—otherwise your brain might do so!"

For a moment Anglesey was quiet. Then he laughed. It was a hard, barbaric laughter. Cornelius started as it struck his eardrums.

"Nice idea," said the esman. "But I'm afraid it won't fit all the data. You see, I like it down there. I like being Joe."

He paused for a while, then continued in a dry impersonal tone: "Don't judge the environment from my notes. They're just idiotic things like estimates of wind velocity, temperature variations, mineral properties—insignificant. What I can't put in is how Jupiter looks through a Jovian's infrared-seeing eyes."

"Different, I should think," ventured Cornelius after a minute's clumsy silence.

"Yes and no. It's hard to put into language. Some of it I can't, because man hasn't got the concepts. But . . . oh, I can't describe it. Shakespeare himself couldn't. Just remember that everything about Jupiter which is cold and poisonous and gloomy to us is *right* for Joe."

Anglesey's tone grew remote, as if he spoke to himself:

"Imagine walking under a glowing violet sky, where great flashing clouds sweep the earth with shadow and rain strides beneath them. Imagine walking on the slopes of a mountain like polished metal, with a clean red flame exploding above you and thunder laughing in the ground. Imagine a cool wild stream, and low trees with dark coppery flowers, and a waterfall, methane-fall . . . whatever you like, leaping off a cliff, and the strong live wind shakes its mane full of rainbows! Imagine a whole forest, dark and breathing, and here and there you glimpse a pale-red wavering will-o'-the-wisp, which is the life radiation of some fleet shy animal, and . . . and—"

Anglesey croaked into silence. He stared down at his clenched fists, then he closed his eyes tight and tears ran out between the lids.

"Imagine being *strong!*"

Suddenly he snatched up the helmet, crammed it on his head, and twirled the control knobs. Joe had been sleeping, down in the night, but Joe was about to wake up and—roar under the four great moons till all the forest feared him?

Cornelius slipped quietly out of the room.

*   *   *

IN THE LONG brazen sunset light, beneath dusky cloud banks brooding storm, he strode up the hillslope with a sense of the day's work done. Across his back, two woven baskets balanced each other, one laden with the pungent black fruit of the thorntree and one with cable-thick creepers to be used as rope. The axe on his shoulder caught the waning sunlight and tossed it blindingly back.

It had not been hard labor, but weariness dragged at his mind and he did not relish the household chores yet to be performed, cooking and cleaning and all the rest. Why couldn't they hurry up and get him some helpers?

His eyes sought the sky, resentfully. The moon Five was hidden—down here, at the bottom of the air ocean, you saw nothing but the sun and the four Galilean satellites. He wasn't even sure where Five was just now, in relation to himself . . . *wait a minute, it's sunset here, but if I went out to the viewdome I'd see Jupiter in the last quarter, or would I? Oh, hell, it only takes us half an Earth-day to swing around the planet anyhow—*

Joe shook his head. After all this time, it was still damnably hard, now and then, to keep his thoughts straight. *I, the essential I, am up in heaven, riding Jupiter V between coldstars. Remember that. Open your eyes, if you will, and see the dead control room superimposed on a living hillside.*

He didn't though. Instead, he regarded the boulders strewn wind-blasted gray over the tough mossy vegetation of the slope. They were not much like Earth rocks, nor was the soil beneath his feet like terrestrial humus.

For a moment Anglesey speculated on the origin of the silicates, aluminates, and other stony compounds. Theoretically, all such materials should be inaccessibly locked in the Jovian core, down where the pressure got vast enough for atoms to buckle and collapse. Above the core should lie thousands of miles of allotropic ice, and then the metallic hydrogen layer. There should not be complex minerals this far up, but there were.

Well, possibly Jupiter had formed according to theory, but had thereafter sucked enough cosmic dust, meteors, gases, and vapors down its great throat of gravitation to form a crust several miles thick. Or more likely the theory was altogether wrong. What did they know, what *would* they know, the soft pale worms of Earth?

Anglesey stuck his—Joe's—fingers in his mouth and whistled. A baying sounded in the brush, and two midnight forms leaped toward him. He grinned and stroked their heads; training was progressing faster than he'd hoped with these pups of the black caterpillar beasts he had taken. They would make guardians for him, herders, servants.

On the crest of the hill, Joe was building himself a home. He had logged off an acre of ground and erected a stockade. Within the grounds there now stood a lean-to for himself and his stores, a methane well, and the beginnings of a large comfortable cabin.

But there was too much work for one being. Even with the half-intelligent caterpillars to help, and with cold storage for meat, most of his time would still go to hunting. The game wouldn't last forever, either; he had to start agriculture within the next year or so—Jupiter-year, twelve Earth-years, thought Anglesey. There was the cabin to finish and furnish; he wanted to put a waterwheel, no, methane wheel in the river to turn any of a dozen machines he had in mind, he wanted to experiment with alloyed ice and—

And, quite apart from his need of help, why should he remain alone, the single thinking creature on an entire planet? He was a male in this body, with male instincts—in the long run, his health was bound to suffer if he remained a hermit, and right now the whole project depended on Joe's health.

It wasn't right!

But I am not alone. There are fifty men on the satellite with me. I can talk to any of them, any time I wish. It's only that I seldom wish it, these days. I would rather be Joe.

Nevertheless . . . I, cripple, feel all the tiredness, anger, hurt, frustration, of that wonderful biological machine called Joe. The others don't understand. When the ammonia gale flays open his skin, it is I who bleed.

Joe lay down on the ground, sighing. Fangs flashed in the mouth of the black beast which humped over to lick his face. His belly growled with hunger, but he was too tired to fix a meal. Once he had the dogs trained—

Another pseudo would be so much more rewarding to educate.

He could almost see it, in the weary darkening of his brain. Down there, in the valley below the hill, fire and thunder as the ship came to rest. And the steel egg would crack open, the steel arms—already crumbling, puny work of worms!—lift out the shape within and lay it on the earth.

She would stir, shrieking in her first lungful of air, looking about with blank mindless eyes. And Joe would come carry her home. And he would feed her, care for her, show her how to walk—it wouldn't take long, an adult body would learn those things very fast. In a few weeks she would even be talking, be an individual, a soul.

Did you ever think, Edward Anglesey, in the days when you also walked, that your wife would be a gray, four-legged monster?

Never mind that. The important thing was to get others of his kind down here; female *and* male. The station's niggling little plan would have him wait two more Earth-years, and then send him only another dummy like himself, a contemptible human mind looking through eyes which belonged rightfully to a Jovian. It was not to be tolerated!

If he weren't so tired—

Joe sat up. Sleep drained from him as the realization entered. *He* wasn't tired, not to speak of. Anglesey was. Anglesey, the human side of him, who for months had only slept in catnaps, whose rest had lately been interrupted by Cornelius—it was the human body which drooped, gave up, and sent wave after soft wave of sleep down the psibeam to Joe.

Somatic tension traveled skyward; Anglesey jerked awake.

He swore. As he sat there beneath the helmet, the vividness of Jupiter faded with his scattering concentration, as if it grew transparent; the steel prison which was his laboratory strengthened behind it. He was losing contact— Rapidly, with the skill of experience, he brought himself back into phase with the neutral current of the other brain. He willed sleepiness on Joe, exactly as a man wills it on himself.

And, like any other insomniac, he failed. The Joe-body was too hungry. It got up and walked across the compound toward its shack.

The K-tube went wild and blew itself out.

THE NIGHT BEFORE the ships left, Viken and Cornelius sat up late.

It was not truly a night, of course. In twelve hours the tiny moon was hurled clear around Jupiter, from darkness back to darkness, and there might well be a pallid little sun over its crags when the clocks said witches were abroad in Greenwich. But most of the personnel were asleep at this hour.

Viken scowled. "I don't like it," he said. "Too sudden a change of plans. Too big a gamble."

"You are only risking—how many?—three male and a dozen female pseudos," Cornelius replied.

"And fifteen J-ships. All we have. If Anglesey's notion doesn't work, it will be months, a year or more, till we can have others built and resume aerial survey."

"But if it does work," said Cornelius, "you won't need any J-ships, except to carry down more pseudos. You will be too busy evaluating data from the surface to piddle around in the upper atmosphere."

"Of course. But we never expected it so soon. We were going to bring more esmen out here, to operate some more pseudos—"

"But they aren't *needed*," said Cornelius. He struck a cigar to life and took a long pull on it, while his mind sought carefully for words. "Not for a while, anyhow. Joe has reached a point where, given help, he can leap several thousand years of history— he may even have a radio of sorts operating in the fairly near future, which would eliminate the necessity of much of your esping. But without help, he'll just have to mark time. And it's stupid to make a highly trained human esman perform manual labor, which is all that the other pseudos are needed for at this moment. Once the Jovian settlement is well established, certainly, then you can send down more puppets."

"The question is, though," persisted Viken, "can Anglesey himself educate all those pseudos at once? They'll be helpless as infants for days. It will be weeks before they really start thinking and acting for themselves. Can Joe take care of them meanwhile?"

"He has food and fuel stored for months ahead," said Cornelius. "As for what Joe's capabilities are, well, hm-m-m . . . we just have to take Anglesey's judgment. He has the only inside information."

"And once those Jovians do become personalities," worried Viken, "are they necessarily going to string along with Joe? Don't forget, the pseudos are not carbon copies of each other. The uncertainty principle assures each one a unique set of genes. If there is only one human mind on Jupiter, among all those aliens—"

"One *human* mind?" It was barely audible. Viken opened his mouth inquiringly. The other man hurried on.

"Oh, I'm sure Anglesey can continue to dominate them," said Cornelius. "His own personality is rather—tremendous."

Viken looked startled. "You really think so?"

The psionicist nodded. "Yes. I've seen more of him in the past weeks than anyone else. And my profession naturally orients me more toward a man's psychology than his body or his habits. You see a waspish cripple. I see a mind which has reacted to its physical handicaps by developing such a hellish energy, such an inhuman power of concentration, that it almost frightens me. Give that mind a sound body for its use and nothing is impossible to it."

"You may be right, at that," murmured Viken after a pause. "Not that it matters. The decision is taken, the rockets go down tomorrow. I hope it all works out."

He waited for another while. The whirring of ventilators in his little room seemed unnaturally loud, the colors of a girlie picture on the wall shockingly garish. Then he said, slowly:

"You've been rather close-mouthed yourself, Jan. When do you expect to finish your own esprojector and start making the tests?"

Cornelius looked around. The door stood open to an empty hallway, but he reached out and closed it before he answered with a slight grin: "It's been ready for the past few days. But don't tell anyone."

"How's that?" Viken started. The movement, in low-gee, took him out of his chair and halfway across the table between the men. He shoved himself back and waited.

"I have been making meaningless tinkering motions," said Cornelius, "but what I waited for was a highly emotional moment, a time when I can be sure Anglesey's entire attention will be focused on Joe. This business tomorrow is exactly what I need."

"*Why?*"

"You see, I have pretty well convinced myself that the trouble in the machine is psychological, not physical. I think that for some reason, buried in his subconscious, Anglesey doesn't want to experience Jupiter. A conflict of that type might well set a psionic amplifier circuit oscillating."

"Hm-m-m." Viken rubbed his chin. "Could be. Lately Ed has been changing more and more. When he first came here, he was peppery enough, and he would at least play an occasional game of poker. Now he's pulled so far into his shell you can't even see him. I never thought of it before, but . . . yes, by God, Jupiter must be having some effect on him."

"Hm-m-m," nodded Cornelius. He did not elaborate: did not, for instance, mention that one altogether uncharacteristic episode when Anglesey had tried to describe what it was like to be a Jovian.

"Of course," said Viken thoughtfully, "the previous men were not affected especially. Nor was Ed at first, while he was still controlling lower-type pseudos. It's only since Joe went down to the surface that he's become so different."

"Yes, yes," said Cornelius hastily. "I've learned that much. But enough shop talk—"

"No. Wait a minute." Viken spoke in a low, hurried tone, looking past him. "For the first time, I'm starting to think clearly about this . . . never really stopped to analyze it before, just accepted a bad situation. There *is* something peculiar about Joe. It can't very well involve his physical structure, or the environment, because lower forms didn't give this trouble. Could it be the fact that—Joe is the first puppet in all history with a potentially human intelligence?"

"We speculate in a vacuum," said Cornelius. "Tomorrow, maybe, I can tell you. Now I know nothing."

Viken sat up straight. His pale eyes focused on the other man and stayed there, unblinking. "One minute," he said.

"Yes?" Cornelius shifted, half rising. "Quickly, please. It is past my bedtime."

"You know a good deal more than you've admitted," said Viken. "Don't you?"

"What makes you think that?"

"You aren't the most gifted liar in the universe. And then—you argued very strongly for Anglesey's scheme, this sending down the other pseudos. More strongly than a newcomer should."

"I told you, I want his attention focused elsewhere when—"

"Do you want it that badly?" snapped Viken.

Cornelius was still for a minute. Then he sighed and leaned back.

"All right," he said. "I shall have to trust your discretion. I wasn't sure, you see, how any of you old-time station personnel would react. So I didn't want to blabber out my speculations, which may be wrong. The confirmed facts, yes, I will tell them; but I don't wish to attack a man's religion with a mere theory."

Viken scowled. "What the devil do you mean?"

Cornelius puffed hard on his cigar; its tip waxed and waned like a miniature red demon star. "This Jupiter V is more than a research station," he said gently. "It is a way of life, is it not? No one would come here for even one hitch unless the work was important to him. Those who reenlist, they must find something in the work, something which Earth with all her riches cannot offer them. No?"

"Yes," answered Viken. It was almost a whisper. "I didn't think you would understand so well. But what of it?"

"Well, I don't want to tell you, unless I can prove it, that maybe this has all gone for nothing. Maybe you have wasted your lives and a lot of money and will have to pack up and go home."

Viken's long face did not flicker a muscle. It seemed to have congealed. But he said calmly enough: "Why?"

"Consider Joe," said Cornelius. "His brain has as much capacity as any adult human's. It has been recording every sense datum that came to it, from the moment of 'birth'—making a record in itself, in its own cells, not merely in Anglesey's physical memory bank up here. Also, you know, a thought is a sense datum too. And thoughts are not separated into neat little railway tracks; they form a continuous field. Every time Anglesey is in rapport with Joe, and thinks, the thought goes through Joe's synapses as well as his own—and every thought carries its own associations, and every associated memory is recorded. Like if Joe is building a hut, the shape of the logs might remind Anglesey of some geometric figure, which in turn would remind him of the Pythagorean theorem—"

"I get the idea," said Viken in a cautious way. "Given time, Joe's brain will have stored everything that ever was in Ed's."

"Correct. Now a functioning nervous system with an engrammatic pattern of experience—in this case, a *nonhuman* nervous system—isn't that a pretty good definition of a personality?"

"I suppose so—Good Lord!" Viken jumped. "You mean Joe is—taking over?"

"In a way. A subtle, automatic, unconscious way." Cornelius drew a deep breath and plunged into it. "The pseudojovian is so nearly perfect a life form: your biologists engineered into it all the experiences gained from nature's mistakes in designing *us*. At first, Joe was only a remote-controlled biological machine. Then Anglesey and Joe became two facets of a single personality. Then, oh, very slowly, the stronger, healthier body . . . more amplitude to its thoughts . . . do you see? Joe is becoming the dominant side. Like this business of sending down the other pseudos—Anglesey only thinks he has logical reasons for wanting it done. Actually, his 'reasons' are mere rationalizations for the instinctive desires of the Joe-facet.

"Anglesey's subconscious must comprehend the situation, in a dim reactive way; it must feel his human ego gradually being submerged by the steamroller force of

Joe's instincts and *Joe's* wishes. It tries to defend its own identity, and is swatted down by the superior force of Joe's own nascent subconscious.

"I put it crudely," he finished in an apologetic tone, "but it will account for that oscillation in the K-tubes."

Viken nodded slowly, like an old man. "Yes, I see it," he answered. "The alien environment down there . . . the different brain structure . . . good God! Ed's being swallowed up in Joe! The puppet master is becoming the puppet!" He looked ill.

"Only speculation on my part," said Cornelius. All at once, he felt very tired. It was not pleasant to do this to Viken, whom he liked. "But you see the dilemma, no? If I am right, then any esman will gradually become a Jovian—a monster with two bodies, of which the human body is the unimportant auxiliary one. This means no esman will ever agree to control a pseudo—therefore the end of your project."

He stood up. "I'm sorry, Arne. You made me tell you what I think, and now you will lie awake worrying, and I am quite wrong and you worry for nothing."

"It's all right," mumbled Viken. "Maybe you're not wrong."

"I don't know." Cornelius drifted toward the door. "I am going to try to find some answers tomorrow. Good night."

THE MOON-SHAKING THUNDER of the rockets, crash, crash, crash, leaping from their cradles, was long past. Now the fleet glided on metal wings, with straining secondary ramjets, through the rage of the Jovian sky.

As Cornelius opened the control-room door, he looked at his telltale board. Elsewhere a voice tolled the word to all the stations, *one ship wrecked, two ships wrecked,* but Anglesey would let no sound enter his presence when he wore the helmet. An obliging technician had haywired a panel of fifteen red and fifteen blue lights above Cornelius' esprojector, to keep him informed, too. Ostensibly, of course, they were only there for Anglesey's benefit, though the esman had insisted he wouldn't be looking at them.

Four of the red bulbs were dark and thus four blue ones would not shine for a safe landing. A whirlwind, a thunderbolt, a floating ice meteor, a flock of mantalike birds with flesh as dense and hard as iron—there could be a hundred things which had crumpled four ships and tossed them tattered across the poison forests.

Four ships, hell! Think of four living creatures, with an excellence of brain to rival your own, damned first to years in unconscious night and then, never awakening save for one uncomprehending instant, dashed in bloody splinters against an ice mountain. The wasteful callousness of it was a cold knot in Cornelius' belly. It had to be done, no doubt, if there was to be any thinking life on Jupiter at all; but then let it be done quickly and minimally, he thought, so the next generation could be begotten by love and not by machines!

He closed the door behind him and waited for a breathless moment. Anglesey was a wheelchair and a coppery curve of helmet, facing the opposite wall. No movement, no awareness whatsoever. Good!

It would be awkward, perhaps ruinous, if Anglesey learned of this most intimate peering. But he needn't, ever. He was blindfolded and ear-plugged by his own concentration.

Nevertheless, the psionicist moved his bulky form with care, across the room to the new esprojector. He did not much like his snooper's role; he would not have assumed it at all if he had seen any other hope. But neither did it make him feel especially guilty. If what he suspected was true, then Anglesey was all unawares being twisted into something not human; to spy on him might be to save him.

Gently, Cornelius activated the meters and started his tubes warming up. The oscilloscope built into Anglesey's machine gave him the other man's exact alpha rhythm, his basic biological clock. First you adjusted to that, then you discovered the subtler elements by feel, and when your set was fully in phase you could probe undetected and—

Find out what was wrong. Read Anglesey's tortured subconscious and see what there was on Jupiter that both drew and terrified him.

Five ships wrecked.

But it must be very nearly time for them to land. Maybe only five would be lost in all. Maybe ten would get through. Ten comrades for—Joe?

Cornelius sighed. He looked at the cripple, seated blind and deaf to the human world which had crippled him, and felt a pity and an anger. It wasn't fair, none of it was.

Not even to Joe. Joe wasn't any kind of soul-eating devil. He did not even realize, as yet, that he *was* Joe, that Anglesey was becoming a mere appendage. He hadn't asked to be created, and to withdraw his human counterpart from him would be very likely to destroy him.

Somehow, there were always penalties for everybody, when men exceeded the decent limits.

Cornelius swore at him, voicelessly. Work to do. He sat down and fitted the helmet on his own head. The carrier wave made a faint pulse, inaudible, the trembling of neurones low in his awareness. You couldn't describe it.

Reaching up, he turned to Anglesey's alpha. His own had a somewhat lower frequency. It was necessary to carry the signals through a heterodyning process. Still no reception . . . well, of course, he had to find the exact wave form, timbre was as basic to thought as to music. He adjusted the dials, slowly, with enormous care.

Something flashed through his consciousness, a vision of clouds rolled in a violet-red sky, a wind that galloped across horizonless immensity—he lost it. His fingers shook as he turned back.

The psibeam between Joe and Anglesey broadened. It took Cornelius into the circuit. He looked through Joe's eyes, he stood on a hill and stared into the sky above the ice mountains, straining for sign of the first rocket; and simultaneously, he was still Jan Cornelius, blurrily seeing the meters, probing about for emotions, symbols, any key to the locked terror in Anglesey's soul.

The terror rose up and struck him in the face.

PSIONIC DETECTION IS not a matter of passive listening in. Much as a radio receiver is necessarily also a weak transmitter, the nervous system in resonance with a source of psionic-spectrum energy is itself emitting. Normally, of course, this effect is unimportant; but when you pass the impulses, either way, through a set of heterodyning and amplifying units, with a high negative feedback—

In the early days, psionic psychotherapy vitiated itself because the amplified thoughts of one man, entering the brain of another, would combine with the latter's own neural cycles according to the ordinary vector laws. The result was that both men felt the new beat frequencies as a nightmarish fluttering of their very thoughts. An analyst, trained into self-control, could ignore it; his patient could not, and reacted violently.

But eventually the basic human wave-timbres were measured, and psionic therapy resumed. The modern esprojector analyzed an incoming signal and shifted its characteristics over to the "listener's" pattern. The *really* different pulses of the transmitting brain, those which could not possibly be mapped onto the pattern of the receiving neurones—as an exponential signal cannot very practicably be mapped onto a sinusoid—those were filtered out.

Thus compensated, the other thought could be apprehended as comfortably as one's own. If the patient were on a psibeam circuit, a skilled operator could tune in without the patient being necessarily aware of it. The operator could neither probe the other man's thoughts or implant thoughts of his own.

Cornelius' plan, an obvious one to any psionicist, had depended on this. He would receive from an unwitting Anglesey-Joe. If his theory were right, and the es-man's personality was being distorted into that of a monster—his thinking would be too alien to come through the filters. Cornelius would receive spottily or not at all. If his theory was wrong, and Anglesey was still Anglesey, he would receive only a normal human stream-of-consciousness, and could probe for other trouble-making factors.

His brain roared!

What's happening to me?

For a moment, the interference which turned his thoughts to saw-toothed gibberish struck him down with panic. He gulped for breath, there in the Jovian wind, and his dreadful dogs sensed the alienness in him and whined.

Then, recognition, remembrance, and a blaze of anger so great that it left no room for fear. Joe filled his lungs and shouted it aloud, the hillside boomed with echoes:

"Get out of my mind!"

He felt Cornelius spiral down toward unconsciousness. The overwhelming force of his own mental blow had been too much. He laughed, it was more like a snarl, and eased the pressure.

Above him, between thunderous clouds, winked the first thin descending rocket flare.

Cornelius' mind groped back toward the light. It broke a watery surface, the man's mouth snapped after air, and his hands reached for the dials, to turn his machine off and escape.

"Not so fast, you." Grimly, Joe drove home a command that locked Cornelius' muscles rigid. "I want to know the meaning of this. Hold still and let me look!" He smashed home an impulse which could be rendered, perhaps, as an incandescent question mark. Remembrance exploded in shards through the psionicist's forebrain.

"So. That's all there is? You thought I was afraid to come down here and be Joe, and wanted to know why? But I *told* you I wasn't!"

I should have believed—whispered Cornelius.

"Well, get out of the circuit, then." Joe continued growling it vocally. "And don't ever come back in the control room, understand? K-tubes or no, I don't want to see you again. And I may be a cripple, but I can still take you apart cell by cell. Now— sign off—leave me alone. The first ship will be landing in minutes."

You a cripple . . . you, Joe-Anglesey?

"What?" The great gray being on the hill lifted his barbaric head as if to sudden trumpets. "What do you mean?"

Don't you understand? said the weak, dragging thought. *You know how the esprojector works. You know I could have probed Anglesey's mind in Anglesey's brain without making enough interference to be noticed. And I could not have probed a wholly non-human mind at all, nor could it have been aware of me. The filters would not have passed such a signal. Yet you felt me in the first fractional second. It can only mean a human mind in a nonhuman brain.*

You are not the half-corpse on Jupiter V any longer. You're Joe—Joe-Anglesey.

"Well, I'll be damned," said Joe. "You're right."

He turned Anglesey off, kicked Cornelius out of his mind with a single brutal impulse, and ran down the hill to meet the spaceship.

Cornelius woke up minutes afterwards. His skull felt ready to split apart. He groped for the main switch before him, clashed it down, ripped the helmet off his head and threw it clanging on the floor. But it took a little while to gather the strength to do the same for Anglesey. The other man was not able to do anything for himself.

*   *   *

THEY SAT OUTSIDE sickbay and waited. It was a harshly lit barrenness of metal and plastic, smelling of antiseptics: down near the heart of the satellite, with miles of rock to hide the terrible face of Jupiter.

Only Viken and Cornelius were in that cramped little room. The rest of the station went about its business mechanically, filling in the time till it could learn what had happened. Beyond the door, three biotechnicians, who were also the station's medical staff, fought with death's angel for the thing which had been Edward Anglesey.

"Nine ships got down," said Viken dully. "Two males, seven females. It's enough to start a colony."

"It would be genetically desirable to have more," pointed out Cornelius. He kept his own voice low, in spite of its underlying cheerfulness. There was a certain awesome quality to all this.

"I still don't understand," said Viken.

"Oh; it's clear enough—now. I should have guessed it before, maybe. We had all the facts, it was only that we couldn't make the simple, obvious interpretation of them. No, we had to conjure up Frankenstein's monster."

"Well," Viken's words grated, "we have played Frankenstein, haven't we? Ed is dying in there."

"It depends on how you define death." Cornelius drew hard on his cigar, needing anything that might steady him. His tone grew purposely dry of emotion:

"Look here. Consider the data. Joe, now: a creature with a brain of human capacity, but without a mind—a perfect Lockean *tabula rasa,* for Anglesey's psibeam to write on. We deduced, correctly enough—if very belatedly—that when enough had been written, there would be a personality. But the question was: whose? Because, I suppose, of normal human fear of the unknown, we assumed that any personality in so alien a body had to be monstrous. Therefore it must be hostile to Anglesey, must be swamping him—"

The door opened. Both men jerked to their feet.

The chief surgeon shook his head. "No use. Typical deep-shock traumata, close to terminus now. If we had better facilities, maybe—"

"No," said Cornelius. "You cannot save a man who has decided not to live anymore."

"I know." The doctor removed his mask. "I need a cigarette. Who's got one?" His hands shook a little as he accepted it from Viken.

"But how could he—decide—anything?" choked the physicist. "He's been unconscious ever since Jan pulled him away from that . . . that thing."

"It was decided before then," said Cornelius. "As a matter of fact, that hulk in there on the operating table no longer has a mind. I know. I was there." He shuddered a little. A stiff shot of tranquilizer was all that held nightmare away from him. Later he would have to have that memory exorcised.

The doctor took a long drag of smoke, held it in his lungs a moment, and exhaled gustily. "I guess this winds up the project," he said. "We'll never get another esman."

"I'll say we won't." Viken's tone sounded rusty. "I'm going to smash that devil's engine myself."

"Hold on a minute," exclaimed Cornelius. "Don't you understand? This isn't the end. It's the beginning!"

"I'd better get back," said the doctor. He stubbed out his cigarette and went through the door. It closed behind him with a deathlike quietness.

"What do you mean?" Viken said it as if erecting a barrier.

"*Won't* you understand?" roared Cornelius. "Joe has all Anglesey's habits, thoughts, memories, prejudices, interests . . . oh, yes, the different body and the different environment, they do cause some changes—but no more than any man might undergo on Earth. If you were suddenly cured of a wasting disease, wouldn't you maybe get a little boisterous and rough? There is nothing abnormal in it. Nor is it abnormal to want to stay healthy—no? Do you see?"

Viken sat down. He spent a while without speaking.

Then, enormously slow and careful: "Do you mean Joe is Ed?"

"Or Ed is Joe. Whatever you like. He calls himself Joe now, I think—as a symbol of freedom—but he is still himself. What *is* the ego but continuity of existence?

"He himself did not fully understand this. He only knew—he told me, and I should have believed him—that on Jupiter he was strong and happy. Why did the K-tube oscillate? An hysterical symptom? Anglesey's subconscious was not afraid to stay on Jupiter—it was afraid to come back!

"And then, today, I listened in. By now, his whole self was focused on Joe. That is, the primary source of libido was Joe's virile body, not Anglesey's sick one. This meant a different pattern of impulses—not too alien to pass the filters, but alien enough to set up interference. So he felt my presence. And he saw the truth, just as I did—

"Do you know the last emotion I felt, as Joe threw me out of his mind? Not anger anymore. He plays rough, him, but all he had room to feel was joy.

"I *knew* how strong a personality Anglesey has! Whatever made me think an overgrown child-brain like Joe's could override it? In there, the doctors—bah! They're trying to salvage a hulk which has been shed because it is useless!"

Cornelius stopped. His throat was quite raw from talking. He paced the floor, rolled cigar smoke around his mouth but did not draw it any farther in.

When a few minutes had passed, Viken said cautiously: "All right. You should know—as you said, you were there. But what do we do now? How do we get in touch with Ed? Will he even be interested in contacting us?"

"Oh, yes, of course," said Cornelius. "He is still himself, remember. Now that he has none of the cripple's frustrations, he should be more amiable. When the novelty of his new friends wears off, he will want someone who can talk to him as an equal."

"And precisely who will operate another pseudo?" asked Viken sarcastically. "I'm quite happy with this skinny frame of mine, thank you!"

"Was Anglesey the only hopeless cripple on Earth?" asked Cornelius quietly.

Viken gaped at him.

"And there are aging men, too," went on the psionicist, half to himself. "Someday, my friend, when you and I feel the years close in, and so much we would like to learn—maybe we, too, would enjoy an extra lifetime in a Jovian body." He nodded at his cigar. "A hard, lusty, stormy kind of life, granted—dangerous, brawling, violent—but life as no human, perhaps, has lived it since the days of Elizabeth the First. Oh, yes, there will be small trouble finding Jovians."

He turned his head as the surgeon came out again.

"Well!" croaked Viken.

The doctor sat down. "It's finished," he said.

They waited for a moment, awkwardly.

"Odd," said the doctor. He groped after a cigarette he didn't have. Silently, Viken offered him one. "Odd. I've seen these cases before. People who simply resign from life. This is the first one I ever saw that went out smiling—smiling all the time."

"All You Zombies—"

One of the titans of science fiction's Golden Age, Robert Heinlein began writing science fiction in 1939 after a brief military career and soon became a prolific contributor to science fiction magazines, notably *Astounding Science Fiction*, which published most of the best of his early writing. His fiction was notable for its sense of a "lived-in" future. In stories such as "The Roads Must Roll," "We Also Walks Dogs," "Blowups Happen," and others, Heinlein showed how pervasively future developments in science and technology would impact culture and civilization at every level. Most of the stories Heinlein collected in *The Man Who Sold the Moon, The Green Hills of Earth,* and *Revolt in 2100* fit the scheme of Heinlein's future-history series, which along with the novel was collected definitively in *The Past through Tomorrow*. Heinlein's fiction is also renowned for its explorations of social and political themes and for its depiction in science fictional settings of societies where private and group interests are often at variance. *Beyond This Horizon* concerns a future world where eugenics has created the perfect society. *Methuselah's Children* concerns a group of immortals, the product of selective breeding, who face annihilation at the hands of those not similarly gifted. *The Moon Is a Harsh Mistress* vividly depicts the revolt of a colony on the Moon attempting to break free of control by the government on Earth. *The Puppet Masters* is his most famous study of the individual and collective consciousness, about Earth's efforts to fight off invasion by aliens intent on absorbing humanity into its group mind. In the years immediately after World War II, Heinlein wrote influential science fiction novels for young adult readers, including *Space Cadet, The Star Beast, Have Space Suit—Will Travel,* and *Starship Troopers,* a controversial novel about a militaristic future where freedom and citizenship are predicated on training for the armed services. *Stranger in a Strange Land,* Heinlein's 1962 novel about a messianic human raised on Mars who exposes the corruption and hypocrisy of civilization on Earth, was the first science fiction novel to reach the national bestseller list. Heinlein also wrote a number of groundbreaking modern fantasies, including *Magic, Inc.* and the stories collected in *The Unpleasant Profession of Jonathan Hoag.*

2217 TIME ZONE V (EST) 7 Nov 1970 NYC—"Pop's Place": I was polishing a brandy snifter when the Unmarried Mother came in. I noted the time—10:17 p.m. zone five, or eastern time, November 7th, 1970. Temporal agents always notice time & date; we must.

The Unmarried Mother was a man twenty-five years old, no taller than I am, childish features and a touchy temper. I didn't like his looks—I never had—but he was a lad I was here to recruit, he was my boy. I gave him my best barkeep's smile.

Maybe I'm too critical. He wasn't swish; his nickname came from what he always said when some nosy type asked him his line: "I'm an unmarried mother." If he felt less than murderous he would add: "—at four cents a word. I write confession stories."

If he felt nasty, he would wait for somebody to make something of it. He had a lethal style of infighting, like a female cop—one reason I wanted him. Not the only one.

He had a load on and his face showed that he despised people more than usual. Silently I poured a double shot of Old Underwear and left the bottle. He drank it, poured another.

I wiped the bar top. "How's the 'Unmarried Mother' racket?"

His fingers tightened on the glass and he seemed about to throw it at me; I felt for the sap under the bar. In temporal manipulation you try to figure everything, but there are so many factors that you never take needless risks.

I saw him relax that tiny amount they teach you to watch for in the Bureau's training school. "Sorry," I said. "Just asking, 'How's business?' Make it 'How's the weather?' "

He looked sour. "Business is okay. I write 'em, they print 'em, I eat."

I poured myself one, leaned toward him. "Matter of fact," I said, "you write a nice stick—I've sampled a few. You have an amazingly sure touch with the woman's angle."

It was a slip I had to risk; he never admitted what pen-names he used. But he was boiled enough to pick up only the last: " 'Woman's angle!' " he repeated with a snort. "Yeah, I know the woman's angle. I should."

"So?" I said doubtfully. "Sisters?"

"No. You wouldn't believe me if I told you."

"Now, now," I answered mildly, "bartenders and psychiatrists learn that nothing is stranger than truth. Why, son, if you heard the stories I do—well, you'd make yourself rich. Incredible."

"You don't know what 'incredible' means!"

"So? Nothing astonishes me. I've always heard worse."

He snorted again. "Want to bet the rest of the bottle?"

"I'll bet a full bottle." I placed one on the bar.

"Well—" I signaled my other bartender to handle the trade. We were at the far end, a single-stool space that I kept private by loading the bar top by it with jars of pickled eggs and other clutter. A few were at the other end watching the fights and somebody was playing the juke box—private as a bed where we were.

"Okay," he began, "to start with, I'm a bastard."

"No distinction around here," I said.

"I mean it," he snapped. "My parents weren't married."

"Still no distinction," I insisted. "Neither were mine."

"When—" He stopped, gave me the first warm look I ever saw on him. "You mean that?"

"I do. A one-hundred-percent bastard. In fact," I added, "no one in my family ever marries. All bastards.

"Oh, that." I showed it to him. "It just looks like a wedding ring; I wear it to keep women off." It is an antique I bought in 1985 from a fellow operative—he had fetched it from pre-Christian Crete. "The Worm Ouroboros . . . the World Snake that eats its own tail, forever without end. A symbol of the Great Paradox."

He barely glanced at it. "If you're really a bastard, you know how it feels. When I was a little girl—"

"Wups!" I said. "Did I hear you correctly?"

"Who's telling this story? When I was a little girl— Look, ever hear of Christine Jorgenson? Or Roberta Cowell?"

"Uh, sex-change cases? You're trying to tell me—"

"Don't interrupt or swelp me, I won't talk. I was a foundling, left at an orphanage in Cleveland in 1945 when I was a month old. When I was a little girl, I envied kids with parents. Then, when I learned about sex—and, believe me, Pop, you learn fast in an orphanage—"

"I know."

"—I made a solemn vow that any kid of mine would have both a pop and a mom. It kept me 'pure,' quite a feat in that vicinity—I had to learn to fight to manage it. Then I got older and realized I stood darn little chance of getting married—for the same reason I hadn't been adopted." He scowled. "I was horse-faced and buck-toothed, flat-chested and straight-haired."

"You don't look any worse than I do."

"Who cares how a barkeep looks? Or a writer? But people wanting to adopt pick little blue-eyed golden-haired morons. Later on, the boys want bulging breasts, a cute face, and an Oh-you-wonderful-male manner." He shugged. "I couldn't compete. So I decided to join the W.E.N.C.H.E.S."

"Eh?"

"Women's Emergency National Corps, Hospitality & Entertainment Section, what they now call 'Space Angels'—Auxiliary Nursing Group, Extraterrestrial Legions."

I knew both terms, once I had them chronized. We use still a third name, it's that elite military service corps: Women's Hospitality Order Refortifying & Encouraging Spacemen. Vocabulary shift is the worst hurdle in time-jumps—did you know that "service station" once meant a dispensary for petroleum fractions? Once on an assignment in the Churchill Era, a woman said to me, "Meet me at the service station next door"—which is not what it sounds; a "service station" (then) wouldn't have a bed in it.

He went on: "It was when they first admitted you can't send men into space for months and years and not relieve the tension. You remember how the wowsers screamed?—that improved my chance, since volunteers were scarce. A gal had to be respectable, preferably virgin (they liked to train them from scratch), above average mentally, and stable emotionally. But most volunteers were old hookers, or neurotics who would crack up ten days off Earth. So I didn't need looks; if they accepted me, they would fix my buck teeth, put a wave in my hair, teach me to walk and dance and how to listen to a man pleasingly, and everything else—plus training for the prime duties. They would even use plastic surgery if it would help—nothing too good for Our Boys.

"Best yet, they made sure you didn't get pregnant during your enlistment—and you were almost certain to marry at the end of your hitch. Same way today, A.N.G.E.L.S. marry spacers—they talk the language.

"When I was eighteen I was placed as a 'mother's helper.' This family simply wanted a cheap servant but I didn't mind as I couldn't enlist till I was twenty-one. I did housework and went to night school—pretending to continue my high school typing and shorthand but going to a charm class instead, to better my chances for enlistment.

"Then I met this city slicker with his hundred-dollar bills." He scowled. "The no-good actually did have a wad of hundred-dollar bills. He showed me one night, told me to help myself.

"But I didn't. I liked him. He was the first man I ever met who was nice to me without trying games with me. I quit night school to see him oftener. It was the happiest time of my life.

"Then one night in the park the games began."

He stopped. I said, "And then?"

"And then *nothing!* I never saw him again. He walked me home and told me he loved me—and kissed me good-night and never came back." He looked grim. "If I could find him, I'd kill him!"

"Well," I sympathized, "I know how you feel. But killing him—just for doing what comes naturally—hmm . . . Did you struggle?"

"Huh? What's that got to do with it?"

"Quite a bit. Maybe he deserves a couple of broken arms for running out on you, but—"

"He deserves worse than that! Wait till you hear. Somehow I kept anyone from suspecting and decided it was all for the best. I hadn't really loved him and probably would never love anybody—and I was more eager to join the W.E.N.C.H.E.S. than ever. I wasn't disqualified, they didn't insist on virgins. I cheered up.

"It wasn't until my skirts got tight that I realized."

"Pregnant?"

"He had me higher 'n a kite! Those skinflints I lived with ignored it as long as I could work—then kicked me out and the orphanage wouldn't take me back. I landed in a charity ward surrounded by other big bellies and trotted bedpans until my time came.

"One night I found myself on an operating table, with a nurse saying, 'Relax. Now breathe deeply.'

"I woke up in bed, numb from the chest down. My surgeon came in. 'How do you feel?' he says cheerfully.

" 'Like a mummy.'

" 'Naturally. You're wrapped like one and full of dope to keep you numb. You'll get well—but a Caesarian isn't a hangnail.'

" 'Caesarian,' I said. 'Doc—*did I lose the baby?*'

" 'Oh, no. Your baby's fine.'

" 'Oh. Boy or girl?'

" 'A healthy little girl. Five pounds, three ounces.'

"I relaxed. It's something, to have made a baby. I told myself I would go some-where and tack 'Mrs.' on my name and let the kid think her papa was dead—no orphanage for *my* kid!

"But the surgeon was talking. 'Tell me, uh—' He avoided my name. '—did you ever think your glandular setup was odd?'

"I said, 'Huh? Of course not. What are you driving at?'

"He hesitated. 'I'll give you this in one dose, then a hypo to let you sleep off your jitters. You'll have 'em.'

" 'Why?' I demanded.

" 'Ever hear of that Scottish physician who was female until she was thirty-five?—then had surgery and became legally and medically a man? Got married. All okay.'

" 'What's that got to do with me?'

" 'That's what I'm saying. You're a man.'

"I tried to sit up. '*What?*'

" 'Take it easy. When I opened you, I found a mess. I sent for the Chief of Surgery while I got the baby out, then we held a consultation with you on the table—and worked for hours to salvage what we could. You had two full sets of organs, both immature, but with the female set well enough developed for you to have a baby. They could never be any use to you again, so we took them out and rearranged things so that you can develop properly as a man.' He put a hand on me. 'Don't worry. You're young, your bones will readjust, we'll watch your glandular balance—and make a fine young man out of you.'

"I started to cry. 'What about my *baby?*'

" 'Well, you can't nurse her, you haven't milk enough for a kitten. If I were you, I wouldn't see her—put her up for adoption.'

" '*No!*'

"He shrugged. "The choice is yours; you're her mother—well, her parent. But don't worry now; we'll get you well first.'

"Next day they let me see the kid and I saw her daily—trying to get used to her. I had never seen a brand-new baby and had no idea how awful they look—my daughter looked like an orange monkey. My feeling changed to cold determination to do right by her. But four weeks later that didn't mean anything."

"Eh?"

"She was snatched."

" 'Snatched?' "

The Unmarried Mother almost knocked over the bottle we had bet. "Kidnapped—stolen from the hospital nursery!" He breathed hard. "How's that for taking the last a man's got to live for?"

"A bad deal," I agreed. "Let's pour you another. No clues?"

"Nothing the police could trace. Somebody came to see her, claimed to be her uncle. While the nurse had her back turned, he walked out with her."

"Description?"

"Just a man, with a face-shaped face, like yours or mine." He frowned. "I think it was the baby's father. The nurse swore it was an older man but he probably used makeup. Who else would swipe my baby? Childless women pull such stunts—but whoever heard of a man doing it?"

"What happened to you then?"

"Eleven more months of that grim place and three operations. In four months I started to grow a beard; before I was out I was shaving regularly ... and no longer doubted that I was male." He grinned wryly. "I was staring down nurses' necklines."

"Well," I said, "seems to me you came through okay. Here you are, a normal man, making good money, no real troubles. And the life of a female is not an easy one."

He glared at me. "A lot you know about it!"

"So?"

"Ever hear the expression 'a ruined woman'?"

"Mmm, years ago. Doesn't mean much today."

"I was as ruined as a woman can be; that bum *really* ruined me—I was no longer a woman ... and I didn't know *how* to be a man."

"Takes getting used to, I suppose."

"You have no idea. I don't mean learning how to dress, or not walking into the wrong rest room; I learned those in the hospital. But how could I *live?* What job could I get? Hell, I couldn't even drive a car. I didn't know a trade; I couldn't do manual labor—too much scar tissue, too tender.

"I hated him for having ruined me for the W.E.N.C.H.E.S., too, but I didn't know how much until I tried to join the Space Corps instead. One look at my belly and I was marked unfit for military service. The medical officer spent time on me just from curiosity; he had read about my case.

"So I changed my name and came to New York. I got by as a fry cook, then rented a typewriter and set myself up as a public stenographer—what a laugh! In four months I typed four letters and one manuscript. The manuscript was for *Real Life Tales* and a waste of paper, but the goof who wrote it, sold it. Which gave me an idea; I bought a stack of confession magazines and studied them." He looked cynical. "Now you know how I get the authentic woman's angle on an unmarried-mother story . . . through the only version I haven't sold—the true one. Do I win the bottle?"

I pushed it toward him. I was upset myself, but there was work to do. I said, "Son, you still want to lay hands on that so-and-so?"

His eyes lighted up—a feral gleam.

"Hold it!" I said. "You wouldn't kill him?"

He chuckled nastily. "Try me."

"Take it easy. I know more about it than you think I do. I can help you. I know where he is."

He reached across the bar. *"Where is he?"*

I said softly, "Let go my shirt, sonny—or you'll land in the alley and we'll tell the cops you fainted." I showed him the sap.

He let go. "Sorry. But where is he?" He looked at me. "And how do you know so much?"

"All in good time. There are records—hospital records, orphanage records, medical records. The matron of your orphanage was Mrs. Fetherage—right? She was followed by Mrs. Gruenstein—right? Your name, as a girl, was 'Jane'—right? And you didn't tell me any of this—right?"

I had him baffled and a bit scared. "What's this? You trying to make trouble for me?"

"No indeed. I've your welfare at heart. I can put this character in your lap. You do to him as you see fit—and I guarantee that you'll get away with it. But I don't think you'll kill him. You'd be nuts to—and you aren't nuts. Not quite."

He brushed it aside. "Cut the noise. *Where is he?"*

I poured him a short one; he was drunk but anger was offsetting it. "Not so fast. I do something for you—you do something for me."

"Uh . . . what?"

"You don't like your work. What would you say to high pay, steady work, unlimited expense account, your own boss on the job, and lots of variety and adventure?"

He stared. "I'd say, 'Get those goddam reindeer off my roof!' Shove it, Pop—there's no such job."

"Okay, put it this way: I hand him to you, you settle with him, then try my job. If it's not all I claim—well, I can't hold you."

He was wavering; the last drink did it. "When d'yuh d'liver 'im?" he said thickly.

"If it's a deal—*right now!*"

He shoved out his hand. "It's a deal!"

I nodded to my assistant to watch both ends, noted the time—2300—started to duck through the gate under the bar—when the juke box blared out: "*I'm My Own Granpaw!*" The service man had orders to load it with old Americana and classics because I couldn't stomach the "music" of 1970, but I hadn't known that tape was in it. I called out, "Shut that off! Give the customer his money back." I added, "Storeroom, back in a moment," and headed there with my Unmarried Mother following.

It was down the passage across from the johns, a steel door to which no one but my day manager and myself had a key; inside was a door to an inner room to which only I had a key. We went there.

He looked blearily around at windowless walls. "Where is 'e?"

"Right away." I opened a case, the only thing in the room; it was a U.S.F.F. Co-ordinates Transformer Field Kit, series 1992, Mod. II—a beauty, no moving parts, weight twenty-three kilos fully charged, and shaped to pass as a suitcase. I had adjusted it precisely earlier that day; all I had to do was to shake out the metal net which limits the transformation field.

Which I did. "Wha's that?" he demanded.

"Time machine," I said and tossed the net over us.

"Hey!" he yelled and stepped back. There is a technique to this; the net has to be thrown so that the subject will instinctively step back *onto* the metal mesh, then you close the net with both of you inside completely—else you might leave shoe soles behind or a piece of foot, or scoop up a slice of floor. But that's all the skill it takes. Some agents con a subject into the net; I tell the truth and use that instant of utter astonishment to flip the switch. Which I did.

1030 VI—3 APRIL 1963—Cleveland, Ohio—Apex Bldg.: "Hey!" he repeated. "Take this damn thing off!"

"Sorry," I apologized and did so, stuffed the net into the case, closed it. "You said you wanted to find him."

"But— You said that was a time machine!"

I pointed out a window. "Does that look like November? Or New York?" While he was gawking at new buds and spring weather, I reopened the case, took out a packet of hundred-dollar bills, checked that the numbers and signatures were compatible with 1963. The Temporal Bureau doesn't care how much you spend (it costs nothing) but they don't like unnecessary anachronisms. Too many mistakes, and a general court-martial will exile you for a year in a nasty period, say 1974 with its strict rationing and forced labor. I never make such mistakes, the money was okay.

He turned around and said, "What happened?"

"He's here. Go outside and take him. Here's expense money." I shoved it at him and added, "Settle him, then I'll pick you up."

Hundred-dollar bills have a hypnotic effect on a person not used to them. He was thumbing them unbelievingly as I eased him into the hall, locked him out. The next jump was easy, a small shift in era.

7100 VI—10 MARCH 1964—Cleveland—Apex Bldg.: There was a notice under the door saying that my lease expired next week; otherwise the room looked as it had a moment before. Outside, trees were bare and snow threatened; I hurried, stopping only for contemporary money and a coat, hat, and topcoat I had left there when I leased the room. I hired a car, went to the hospital. It took twenty minutes to bore the nursery attendant to the point where I could swipe the baby without being noticed. We went back to the Apex Building. This dial setting was more involved as the building did not yet exist in 1945. But I had precalculated it.

0100 VI—20 SEPT 1945—Cleveland—Skyview Motel: Field kit, baby, and I arrived in a motel outside town. Earlier I had registered as "Gregory Johnson, Warren, Ohio," so we arrived in a room with curtains closed, windows locked, and doors bolted, and the floor cleared to allow for waver as the machine hunts. You can get a nasty bruise from a chair where it shouldn't be—not the chair of course, but backlash from the field.

No trouble. Jane was sleeping soundly; I carried her out, put her in a grocery box on the seat of a car I had provided earlier, drove to the orphanage, put her on the steps, drove two blocks to a "service station" (the petroleum products sort) and phoned the orphanage, drove back in time to see them taking the box inside, kept going and abandoned the car near the motel—walked to it and jumped forward to the Apex Building in 1963.

2200 VI—24 APRIL 1963—Cleveland—Apex Bldg.: I had cut the time rather fine— temporal accuracy depends on span, except on return to zero. If I had it right, Jane was discovering, out in the park this balmy spring night, that she wasn't quite as "nice" a girl as she had thought. I grabbed a taxi to the home of those skinflints, had the hackie wait around a corner while I lurked in shadows.

Presently I spotted them down the street, arms around each other. He took her up on the porch and made a long job of kissing her good-night—longer than I thought. Then she went in and he came down the walk, turned away. I slid into step and hooked an arm in his. "That's all, son," I announced quietly. "I'm back to pick you up."

"*You!*" He gasped and caught his breath.

"Me. Now you know who *he* is—and after you think it over you'll know who you are . . . and if you think hard enough, you'll figure out who the baby is . . . and who *I* am."

He didn't answer, he was badly shaken. It's a shock to have it proved to you that you can't resist seducing yourself. I took him to the Apex Building and we jumped again.

2300 VII—12 AUG 1985—Sub Rockies Base: I woke the duty sergeant, showed my I.D., told the sergeant to bed my companion down with a happy pill and recruit him in the morning. The sergeant looked sour, but rank is rank, regardless of era; he did what I said—thinking, no doubt, that the next time we met he might be the colonel and I the sergeant. Which can happen in our corps: "What name?" he asked.

I wrote it out. He raised his eyebrows. "Like so, eh? *Hmm—*"

"You just do your job, Sergeant." I turned to my companion.

"Son, your troubles are over. You're about to start the best job a man ever held— and you'll do well. *I know.*"

"That you will!" agreed the sergeant. "Look at me—born in 1917—still around, still young, still enjoying life." I went back to the jump room, set everything on preselected zero.

2301 V—7 NOV 1970—NYC—"Pop's Place": I came out of the storeroom carrying a fifth of Drambuie to account for the minute I had been gone. My assistant was arguing with the customer who had been playing *"I'm My Own Granpaw!"* I said, "Oh, let him play it, then unplug it." I was very tired.

It's rough, but somebody must do it and it's very hard to recruit anyone in the later years, since the Mistake of 1972. Can you think of a better source than to pick people all fouled up where they are and give them well-paid, interesting (even though dangerous) work in a necessary cause? Everybody knows now why the Fizzle War of 1963 fizzled. The bomb with New York's number on it didn't go off, a hundred other things didn't go as planned—all arranged by the likes of me.

But not the Mistake of '72; that one is not our fault—and can't be undone; there's no paradox to resolve. A thing either is, or it isn't, now and forever amen. But there won't be another like it; an order dated "1992" takes precedence any year.

I closed five minutes early, leaving a letter in the cash register telling my day manager that I was accepting his offer to buy me out, so see my lawyer as I was leaving on a long vacation. The Bureau might or might not pick up his payments, but they want things left tidy. I went to the room back of the storeroom and forward to 1993.

2200 VII—12 JAN 1993—Sub Rockies Annex—HQ Temporal DOL: I checked in with the duty officer and went to my quarters, intending to sleep for a week. I had fetched the bottle we bet (after all, I won it) and took a drink before I wrote my report. It tasted foul and I wondered why I had ever liked Old Underwear. But it was better than nothing; I don't like to be cold sober, I think too much. But I don't really hit the bottle either; other people have snakes—I have people.

I dictated my report; forty recruitments all okayed by the Psych Bureau—counting my own, which I knew would be okayed. I was here, wasn't I? Then I taped a request for assignment to operations; I was sick of recruiting. I dropped both in the slot and headed for bed.

My eye fell on "The By-Laws of Time," over my bed:

Never Do Yesterday What Should Be Done Tomorrow.
If At Last You Do Succeed, Never Try Again.
A Stitch in Time Saves Nine Billion.
A Paradox May Be Paradoctored.
It Is Earlier When You Think.
Ancestors Are Just People.
Even Jove Nods.

They didn't inspire me the way they had when I was a recruit; thirty subjective-years of time-jumping wears you down. I undressed and when I got down to the hide I looked at my belly. A Caesarian leaves a big scar but I'm so hairy now that I don't notice it unless I look for it.

Then I glanced at the ring on my finger.

The Snake That Eats Its Own Tail, Forever and Ever . . . I *know* where *I* came from—but *where did all you zombies come from?*

I felt a headache coming on, but a headache powder is one thing I do not take. I did once—and you all went away.

So I crawled into bed and whistled out the light.

You aren't really there at all. There isn't anybody but me—Jane—here alone in the dark.

I miss you dreadfully!

LLOYD BIGGLE, JR.

Tunesmith

Lloyd Biggle began writing science fiction in 1956 and his first novel, the extraplanetary adventure *The Angry Espers*, appeared in 1961. It was followed by *All the Colors of Darkness*, the first episode in the five-novel Jan Darzek sequence. Darzek, a former private detective, is the sole human participant in the Council of the Supreme, the ministers to a vast computer that establishes policy for the galaxy. Over the course of the other novels in the series—*Watchers of the Dark, This Darkening Universe, Silence Is Deadly*, and *The Whirligig of Time*—Darzek pits his intelligence and his humanity against the nonhuman interest of his fellow councillors, the bureaucracy of the governing body, and the resistance of alien cultures to assimilation into the Galactic Synthesis. *The World Menders* and *The Still, Small Voice of Trumpets* spun off of the series, chronicle the exploits of the Cultural Survey, whose task it is to certify worlds for inclusion in the Galactic Synthesis. Together, the two series comprise an acclaimed contemporary space opera in which vividly imagined alien worlds are brought to life, human motives and conceits are measured against those of alien life forms, and lives and worlds hang perilously in the balance. Biggle has been praised for the thoroughness of his imagined worlds, for his memorable characterizations, and for his facility at exploring complex social and political issues against a backdrop of conventional science fiction themes and motifs. His short fiction has been collected in *The Rule of the Door and Other Fanciful Regulations, The Metallic Muse*, and *A Galaxy of Strangers*. He has collaborated on the novel *Alien Main* with T. L. Sherred and has also written a number of detective novels, including the Sherlock Holmes pastiche *The Quallsford Inheritance*, and two contemporary crime novels featuring the exploits of detectives J. Pletcher and Raina Lambert, *Interface for Murder* and *Where Dead Soldiers Walk*.

EVERYONE CALLS IT the Center. It has another name, a long one, that gets listed in government appropriations and has its derivation analyzed in encyclopedias, but no one uses it. From Bombay to Lima, from Spitsbergen to the mines of Antarctica, from the solitary outpost on Pluto to that on Mercury, it is—the Center. You can emerge from the rolling mists of the Amazon, or the cutting dry winds of the Sahara, or the

lunar vacuum, elbow your way up to a bar, and begin, "When I was at the Center—"
and every stranger within hearing will listen attentively.

It isn't possible to explain the Center, and it isn't necessary. From the babe in
arms to the centenarian looking forward to retirement, everyone has been there, and
plans to go again next year, and the year after that. It is the vacation land of the Solar
System. It is square miles of undulating American Middle West farm land, transfig-
ured by ingenious planning and relentless labor and incredible expense. It is a monumental summary of man's cultural heritage, and like a phoenix, it has emerged
suddenly, inexplicably, at the end of the twenty-fourth century, from the corroded
ashes of an appalling cultural decay.

The Center is colossal, spectacular and magnificent. It is inspiring, edifying and
amazing. It is awesome, it is overpowering, it is—everything.

And though few of its visitors know about this, or care, it is also haunted.

You are standing in the observation gallery of the towering Bach Monument. Off
to the left, on the slope of a hill, you see the tense spectators who crowd the Grecian
Theater for Euripides. Sunlight plays on their brightly-colored clothing. They watch
eagerly, delighted to see in person what millions are watching on visiscope.

Beyond the theater, the tree-lined Frank Lloyd Wright Boulevard curves into the
distance, past the Dante Monument and the Michelangelo Institute. The twin towers
of a facsimile of the Rheims Cathedral rise above the horizon. Directly below, you
see the curious landscaping of an eighteenth-century French *jardin* and, nearby, the
Molière Theater.

A hand clutches your sleeve, and you turn suddenly, irritably, and find yourself
face to face with an old man.

The leathery face is scarred and wrinkled, the thin strands of hair glistening white.
The hand on your arm is a gnarled claw. You stare, take in the slumping contortion
of one crippled shoulder and the hideous scar of a missing ear, and back away in
alarm.

The sunken eyes follow you. The hand extends in a sweeping gesture that em-
braces the far horizon, and you notice that the fingers are maimed or missing. The
voice is a harsh cackle. "Like it?" he says, and eyes you expectantly.

Startled, you mutter, "Why, yes. Of course."

He takes a step forward, and his eyes are eager, pleading. "I say, do you like it?"

In your perplexity you can do no more than nod as you turn away—but your
nod brings a strange response. A strident laugh, an innocent, childish smile of pleasure, a triumphant shout. "I did it! I did it all!"

Or you stand in resplendent Plato Avenue, between the Wagnerian Theater, where
the complete *Der Ring des Nibelungen* is performed daily, and the reconstruction of
the sixteenth-century Globe Theatre, where Shakespearean drama is presented morning, afternoon and evening.

A hand paws at you. "Like it?"

If you respond with a torrent of ecstatic praise, the old man eyes you impatiently and only waits until you have finished to ask again, "I say, do you like it?"

But a smile and a nod is met with beaming pride, a gesture, a shout.

In the lobby of one of the thousand spacious hotels, in the waiting room of the remarkable library where a copy of any book you request is reproduced for you free of charge, in the eleventh balcony of Beethoven Hall, a ghost shuffles haltingly, clutches an arm, asks a question.

And shouts proudly, "I did it!"

ERLIN BAQUE SENSED her presence behind him, but he did not turn. Instead he leaned forward, his left hand tearing a rumbling bass figure from the multichord while his right hand fingered a solemn melody. With a lightning flip of his hand he touched a button, and the thin treble tones were suddenly fuller, more resonant, almost clari-netlike. ("But God, how preposterously unlike a clarinet!" he thought.)

"Must we go through all that again, Val?" he asked.

"The landlord was here this morning."

He hesitated, touched a button, touched several buttons, and wove weird har-monies out of the booming tones of a brass choir. (But what a feeble, distorted brass choir!)

"How long does he give us this time?"

"Two days. And the food synthesizer's broken down again."

"Good. Run down and buy some fresh meat."

"With what?"

Baque slammed his fists down and shouted above the shattering dissonance. "I will not rent a harmonizer. I will not turn my arranging over to hacks. If a Com goes out with my name on it, it's going to be *composed*. It may be idiotic, and it may be sickening, but it's going to be done right. It isn't much, God knows, but it's all I have left."

He turned slowly and glared at her, this pale, drooping, worn-out woman who'd been his wife for twenty-five years. Then he looked away, telling himself stubbornly that he was no more to be blamed than she. When sponsors paid the same rates for good Coms that they paid for hackwork . . .

"Is Hulsey coming today?" she asked.

"He told me he was coming."

"If we could get some money for the landlord—"

"And the food synthesizer. And a new visiscope. And new clothes. There's a limit to what can be done with one Com."

He heard her move away, heard the door open, and waited. It did not close.

"Walter-Walter called," she said. "You're the featured tunesmith on today's *Show Case*."

"So? There's no money in that."

"I thought you wouldn't want to watch, so I told Mrs. Rennik I'd watch with her."

"Sure. Go ahead. Have fun."

The door closed.

Baque got to his feet and stood looking down at his chaos-strewn worktable. Music paper, Com-lyric releases, pencils, sketches, half-finished manuscripts were cluttered together in untidy heaps. Baque cleared a corner for himself and sat down wearily, stretching his long legs out under the table.

"Damn Hulsey," he muttered. "Damn sponsors. Damn visiscope. Damn Coms."

Compose something, he told himself. You're not a hack, like the other tunesmiths. You don't punch out silly tunes on a harmonizer's keyboard and let a machine complete them for you. You're a musician, not a melody monger. Write some music. Write a—a sonata, for multichord. Take the time now, and compose something.

His eyes fell on the first lines of a Com-lyric release. "If your flyer jerks and clowns, if it has its ups and downs—"

"Damn landlord," he muttered, reaching for a pencil.

The tiny wall clock tinkled the hour, and Baque leaned over to turn on the visiscope. A cherub-faced master of ceremonies smiled out at him ingratiatingly. "Walter-Walter again, ladies and gentlemen. It's Com time on today's *Show Case*. Thirty minutes of Commercials by one of today's most talented tunesmiths. Our Com spotlight is on—"

A noisy brass fanfare rang out, the tainted brass tones of a multichord.

"Erlin Baque!"

The multichord swung into an odd, dipsey melody Baque had done five years before, for Tamper Cheese, and a scattering of applause sounded in the background. A nasal soprano voice mouthed the words, and Baque groaned unhappily. "We age our cheese, and age it, age it, age it, age it, age it the old-fashioned way . . ."

Walter-Walter cavorted about the stage, moving in time with the melody, darting down into the audience to kiss some sedate housewife-on-a-holiday, and beaming at the howls of laughter.

The multichord sounded another fanfare, and Walter-Walter leaped back onto the stage, both arms extended over his head. "Now listen to this, all you beautiful people. Here's your Walter-Walter exclusive on Erlin Baque." He glanced secretively over his shoulder, tiptoed a few steps closer to the audience, placed his finger on his lips, and then called out loudly, "Once upon a time there was another composer named Baque, spelled B-A-C-H, but pronounced Baque. He was a real atomic propelled tunesmith, the boy with the go, according to them that know. He lived some five or six or seven hundred years ago, so we can't exactly say that that Baque and our Baque were Baque to Baque. But we don't have to go Baque to hear Baque. We like the Baque we've got. Are you with me?"

Cheers. Applause. Baque turned away, hands trembling, a choking disgust nauseating him.

"We start off our Coms by Baque with that little masterpiece Baque did for Foam Soap. Art work by Bruce Combs. Stop, look—and listen!"

Baque managed to turn off the visiscope just as the first bar of soap jet-propelled itself across the screen. He picked up the Com lyric again, and his mind began to shape the thread of a melody.

"If your flyer jerks and clowns, if it has its ups and downs, ups and downs, ups and downs, you need a WARING!"

He hummed softly to himself, sketching a musical line that swooped and jerked like an erratic flyer. Word painting, it was called, back when words and tones meant something. Back when the B-A-C-H Baque was underscoring such grandiose concepts as Heaven and Hell.

Baque worked slowly, now and then trying a harmonic progression at the multichord and rejecting it, straining his mind for some fluttering accompaniment pattern that would simulate the sound of a flyer. But then—no. The Waring people wouldn't like that. They advertised that their flyers were noiseless.

Urgent-sounding door chimes shattered his concentration. He walked over to flip on the scanner, and Hulsey's pudgy face grinned out at him.

"Come on up," Baque told him. Hulsey nodded and disappeared.

Five minutes later he waddled through the door, sank into a chair that sagged dangerously under his bulky figure, plunked his briefcase onto the floor, and mopped his face. "Whew! Wish you'd get yourself a place lower down. Or into a building with modern conveniences. Elevators scare me to death!"

"I'm thinking of moving," Baque said.

"Good. It's about time."

"But it'll probably be somewhere higher up. The landlord has given me two days' notice."

Hulsey winced and shook his head sadly. "I see. Well, I won't keep you in suspense. Here's the check for the Sana-Soap Com."

Baque took the card, glanced at it, and scowled.

"You were behind in your guild dues," Hulsey said. "Have to deduct them, you know."

"Yes. I'd forgotten."

"I like to do business with Sana-Soap. Cash right on the line. Too many companies wait until the end of the month. Sana-Soap wants a couple of changes, but they paid anyway." He unsealed the briefcase and pulled out a folder. "You've got some sly bits in this one, Erlin my boy. They like it. Particularly this 'sudsy, sudsy, sudsy' thing in the bass. They kicked on the number of singers at first, but not after they heard it. Now right here they want a break for a straight announcement."

Baque nodded thoughtfully. "How about keeping the 'sudsy, sudsy' ostinato going as a background to the announcement?"

"Sounds good. That's a sly bit, that—what'd you call it?"

"Ostinato."

"Ah—yes. Wonder why the other tunesmiths don't work in bits like that."

"A harmonizer doesn't produce effects," Baque said dryly. "It just—harmonizes."

"You give them about thirty seconds of that 'sudsy' for background. They can cut it if they don't like it."

Baque nodded, scribbling a note on the manuscript.

"And the arrangement," Hulsey went on. "Sorry, Erlin, but we can't get a French horn player. You'll have to do something else with that part."

"No horn player? What's wrong with Rankin?"

"Blacklisted. The Performers' Guild nixed him permanently. He went out to the West Coast and played for nothing. Even paid his own expenses. The guild can't tolerate that sort of thing."

"I remember," Baque said softly. "The Monuments of Art Society. He played a Mozart horn concerto for them. Their final concert, too. Wish I could have heard it, even if it was with multichord."

"He can play it all he wants to now, but he'll never get paid for playing again. You can work that horn part into the multichord line, or I might be able to get you a trumpet player. He could use a converter."

"It'll ruin the effect."

Hulsey chuckled. "Sounds the same to everyone but you, my boy. I can't tell the difference. We got your violins and a cello player. What more do you want?"

"Doesn't the London Guild have a horn player?"

"You want me to bring him over for one three-minute Com? Be reasonable, Erlin! Can I pick this up tomorrow?"

"Yes. I'll have it ready in the morning."

Hulsey reached for his briefcase, dropped it again, leaned forward scowling. "Erlin, I'm worried about you. I have twenty-seven tunesmiths in my agency. You're the best by far. Hell, you're the best in the world, and you make the least money of any of them. Your net last year was twenty-two hundred. None of the others netted less than eleven thousand."

"That isn't news to me," Baque said.

"This may be. You have as many accounts as any of them. Did you know that?"

Baque shook his head. "No, I didn't know that."

"You have as many accounts, but you don't make any money. Want to know why? Two reasons. You spend too much time on a Com, and you write it too well. Sponsors can use one of your Coms for months—or sometimes even years, like that Tamper Cheese thing. People like to hear them. Now if you just didn't write so damned well, you could work faster, and the sponsors would have to use more of your Coms, and you could turn out more."

"I've thought about that. Even if I didn't, Val would keep reminding me. But it's no use. That's the way I have to work. If there was some way to get the sponsors to pay more for a *good* Com—"

"There isn't. The guild wouldn't stand for it, because good Coms mean less work, and most tunesmiths couldn't write a really good Com. Now don't think I'm concerned about my agency. Of course I make more money when you make more, but I'm doing well enough with my other tunesmiths. I just hate to see my best man making so little money. You're a throwback, Erlin. You waste time and money collecting those antique—what do you call them?"

"Phonograph records."

"Yes. And those moldy old books about music. I don't doubt that you know more about music than anyone alive, and what does it get you? Not money, certainly. You're the best there is, and you keep trying to be better, and the better you get the less money you make. Your income drops lower every year. Couldn't you manage just an average Com now and then?"

"No," Baque said brusquely. "I couldn't manage it."

"Think it over."

"These accounts I have. Some of the sponsors really like my work. They'd pay more if the guild would let them. Supposing I left the guild?"

"You can't, my boy. I couldn't handle your stuff—not and stay in business long. The Tunesmiths' Guild would turn on the pressure, and the Performers' and Lyric Writers' Guilds would blacklist you. Jimmy Denton plays along with the guilds and he'd bar your stuff from visiscope. You'd lose all your accounts, and fast. No sponsor is big enough to fight all that trouble, and none of them would want to bother. So just try to be average now and then. Think about it."

Baque sat staring at the floor. "I'll think about it."

Hulsey struggled to his feet, clasped Baque's hand briefly, and waddled out. Baque closed the door behind him and went to the drawer where he kept his meager collection of old phonograph records. Strange and wonderful music.

Three times in his career Baque had written Coms that were a full half-hour in length. On rare occasions he got an order for fifteen minutes. Usually he was limited to five or less. But composers like the B-A-C-H Baque wrote things that lasted an hour or more—even wrote them without lyrics.

And they wrote for real instruments, among them amazing-sounding things that no one played anymore, like bassoons, piccolos and pianos.

"Damn Denton. Damn visiscope. Damn guilds."

Baque rummaged tenderly among the discs until he found one bearing Bach's name. *Magnificat.* Then, because he felt too despondent to listen, he pushed it away.

Earlier that year the Performers' Guild had blacklisted its last oboe player. Now its last horn player, and there just weren't any young people learning to play instruments. Why should they, when there were so many marvelous contraptions that ground out the Coms without any effort on the part of the performer? Even multichord players were becoming scarce, and if one wasn't particular about how well it was done, a multichord could practically play itself.

The door jerked open, and Val hurried in. "Did Hulsey—"

Baque handed her the check. She took it eagerly, glanced at it, and looked up in dismay.

"My guild dues," he said. "I was behind."

"Oh. Well, it's a help, anyway." Her voice was flat, emotionless, as though one more disappointment really didn't matter. They stood facing each other awkwardly.

"I watched part of *Morning with Marigold*," Val said. "She talked about your Coms."

"I should hear soon on that Slo-Smoke Com," Baque said. "Maybe we can hold the landlord off for another week. Right now I'm going to walk around a little."

"You should get out more—"

He closed the door behind him, slicing her sentence off neatly. He knew what followed. Get a job somewhere. It'd be good for your health to get out of the apartment a few hours a day. Write Coms in your spare time—they don't bring in more than a part-time income anyway. At least do it until we get caught up. All right, if you won't, I will.

But she never did. A prospective employer never wanted more than one look at her slight body and her worn, sullen face. And Baque doubted that he would receive any better treatment.

He could get work as a multichord player and make a good income—but if he did he'd have to join the Performers' Guild, which meant that he'd have to resign from the Tunesmiths' Guild. So the choice was between performing and composing; the guilds wouldn't let him do both.

"Damn the guilds! Damn Coms!"

When he reached the street, he stood for a moment watching the crowds shooting past on the swiftly moving conveyer. A few people glanced at him and saw a tall, gawky, balding man in a frayed, badly fitting suit. They would consider him just another derelict from a shabby neighborhood, he knew, and they would quickly look the other way while they hummed a snatch from one of his Coms.

He hunched up his shoulders and walked awkwardly along the stationary sidewalk. At a crowded restaurant he turned in, found a table at one side, and ordered beer. On the rear wall was an enormous visiscope screen where the Coms followed each other without interruption. Around him the other customers watched and listened while they ate. Some nodded their heads jerkily in time with the music. A few young couples were dancing on the small dance floor, skillfully changing steps as the music shifted from one Com to another.

Baque watched them sadly and thought about the way things had changed. At one time, he knew, there had been special music for dancing and special groups of instruments to play it. And people had gone to concerts by the thousands, sitting in seats with nothing to look at but the performers.

All of it had vanished. Not only the music, but art and literature and poetry. The plays he once read in his grandfather's school books were forgotten.

James Denton's *Visiscope International* decreed that people must look and listen at the same time, and that the public attention span wouldn't tolerate long programs. So there were Coms.

Damn Coms!

When Val returned to the apartment an hour later, Baque was sitting in the corner staring at the battered plastic cabinet that held the crumbling volumes he had collected from the days when books were still printed on paper—a scattering of biographies, books on music history, and technical books about music theory and composition. Val looked twice about the room before she noticed him, and then she confronted him anxiously, stark tragedy etching her wan face.

"The man's coming to fix the food synthesizer."

"Good," Baque said.

"But the landlord won't wait. If we don't pay him day after tomorrow—pay him everything—we're out."

"So we're out."

"Where will we go? We can't get in anywhere without paying something in advance."

"So we won't get in anywhere."

She fled sobbing into the bedroom.

THE NEXT MORNING Baque resigned from the Tunesmiths' Guild and joined the Performers' Guild. Hulsey's round face drooped mournfully when he heard the news. He loaned Baque enough money to pay his guild registration fee and quiet the landlord, and he expressed his sorrow in eloquent terms as he hurried Baque out of his office. He would, Baque knew, waste no time in assigning Baque's clients to his other tunesmiths—to men who worked faster and not so well.

Baque went to the Guild Hall, where he sat for five hours waiting for a multichord assignment. He was finally summoned to the secretary's office and brusquely motioned into a chair. The secretary eyed him suspiciously.

"You belonged to the Performers' Guild twenty years ago, and you left it to become a tunesmith. Right?"

"Right," Baque said.

"You lost your seniority after three years. You knew that, didn't you?"

"I did, but I didn't think it mattered. There aren't many good multichord players around."

"There aren't many good jobs around, either. You'll have to start at the bottom." He scribbled on a slip of paper and thrust it at Baque. "This one pays well, but we have a hard time keeping a man there. Lankey isn't easy to work for. If you don't irritate him too much—well, then we'll see."

Baque rode the conveyer out to the New Jersey Space Port, wandered through a rattletrap slum area getting his directions hopelessly confused, and finally found the place almost within radiation distance of the port. The sprawling building had burned at some time in the remote past. Stubbly remnants of walls rose out of the weed-choked rubble. A wall curved toward a dimly lit cavity at one corner, where steps led uncertainly downward. Overhead, an enormous sign pointed its flowing colors in the direction of the port. The LANKEY-PANK OUT.

Baque stepped through the door and faltered at the onslaught of extraterrestrial odors. Lavender-tinted tobacco smoke, the product of the enormous leaves grown in bot-domes in the Lunar Mare Crisium, hung like a limp blanket midway between floor and ceiling. The revolting, cutting fumes of *blast,* a whisky blended with a product of Martian lichens, staggered him. He had a glimpse of a scattered gathering of tough spacers and tougher prostitutes before the doorman planted his bulky figure and scarred caricature of a face in front of him.

"You looking for someone?"

"Mr. Lankey."

The doorman jerked a thumb in the direction of the bar and noisily stumbled back into the shadows. Baque walked toward the bar.

He had no trouble in picking out Lankey. The proprietor sat on a tall stool behind the bar. In the dim, smoke-streaked light his taut pale face had a spectral grimness. He leaned an elbow on the bar, fingered his flattened stump of a nose with the two remaining fingers on his hairy hand, and as Baque approached he thrust his bald head forward and eyed him coldly.

"I'm Erlin Baque," Baque said.

"Yeah. The multichord player. Can you play that multichord, fellow?"

"Why, yes, I can play—"

"That's what they all say, and I've had maybe two in the last ten years that could really play. Most of them come out here figuring they'll set the thing on automatic and fuss around with one finger. I want that multichord *played,* fellow, and I'll tell you right now—if you can't play you might as well jet for home. There isn't any automatic on my multichord. I had it disconnected."

"I can play," Baque told him.

"All right. It doesn't take more than one Com to find out. The guild rates this place as Class Four, but I pay Class One rates if you can play. If you can really play, I'll slip you some bonuses the guild won't know about. Hours are six P.M. to six A.M., but you get plenty of breaks, and if you get hungry or thirsty just ask for what you want. Only go easy on the hot stuff. I won't go along with a drunk multichord player no matter how good he is. Rose!"

He bellowed the name a second time, and a woman stepped from a door at the side of the room. She wore a faded dressing gown, and her tangled hair hung untidily about her shoulders. She turned a small, pretty face toward Baque and studied him boldly.

"Multichord," Lankey said. "Show him."

Rose beckoned, and Baque followed her toward the rear of the room. Suddenly he halted in amazement.

"What's the matter?" Rose asked.

"No visiscope!"

"No. Lankey says the spacers want better things to look at than soapsuds and flyers." She giggled. "Something like me, for example."

"I never heard of a restaurant without visiscope."

"Neither did I, until I came here. But Lankey's got three of us to sing the Coms, and you're to do the multichord with us. I hope you make the grade. We haven't had a multichord player for a week, and it's hard singing without one."

"I'll make out all right," Baque said.

A narrow platform stretched across the end of the room where any other restaurant would have had its visiscope screen. Baque could see the unpatched scars in the wall where the screen had been torn out.

"Lankey ran a joint at Port Mars back when the colony didn't have visiscope," Rose said. "He has his own ideas about how to entertain customers. Want to see your room?"

Baque was examining the multichord. It was a battered old instrument, and it bore the marks of more than one brawl. He fingered the filter buttons and swore softly to himself. Only the flute and violin filters clicked into place properly. So he would have to spend twelve hours a day with the twanging tones of an unfiltered multichord.

"Want to see your room?" Rose asked again. "It's only five. You might as well relax until we have to go to work."

Rose showed him a cramped enclosure behind the bar. He stretched out on a hard cot and tried to relax, and suddenly it was six o'clock and Lankey stood in the door beckoning to him.

He took his place at the multichord and fingered the keys impatiently. He felt no nervousness. There wasn't anything he didn't know about Coms, and he knew he wouldn't have trouble with the music, but the atmosphere disturbed him. The haze of smoke was thicker, and he blinked his smarting eyes and felt the whisky fumes tear at his nostrils when he took a deep breath.

There was still only a scattering of customers. The men were mechanics in grimy work suits, swaggering pilots, and a few civilians who liked their liquor strong and didn't mind the surroundings. The women were—women; two of them, he guessed, for every man in the room.

Suddenly the men began an unrestrained stomping of feet accented with yelps of approval. Lankey was crossing the platform with Rose and the other singers. Baque's first horrified impression was that the girls were nude, but as they came closer he made out their brief plastic costumes. Lankey was right, he thought. The spacers would much prefer that kind of scenery to animated Coms on a visiscope screen.

"You met Rose," Lankey said. "This is Zanna and Mae. Let's get going."

He walked away, and the girls gathered about the multichord. "What Coms do you know?" Rose asked.

"I know them all."

She looked at him doubtfully. "We sing together, and then we take turns. Are you sure you know them all?"

Baque flipped on the power and sounded a chord. "Sing any Com you want—I can handle it."

"Well—we'll start out with a Tasty-Malt Com. It goes like this." She hummed softly. "Know that one?"

"I wrote it," Baque said.

They sang better than he had expected. He followed them easily, and while he played he kept his eyes on the customers. Heads were jerking in time with the music, and he quickly caught the mood and began to experiment. His fingers shaped a rolling rhythm in the bass, fumbled with it tentatively, and then expanded it. He abandoned the melodic line, leaving the girls to carry on by themselves while he searched the entire keyboard to ornament the driving rhythm.

Feet began to stomp. The girls' bodies were swaying wildly, and Baque felt himself rocking back and forth as the music swept on recklessly. The girls finished their lyrics, and when he did not stop playing they began again. Spacers were on their feet, now, clapping and swaying. Some seized their women and began dancing in the narrow spaces between the tables. Finally Baque forced a cadence and slumped forward, panting and mopping his forehead. One of the girls collapsed onto the stage. The others hauled her to her feet, and the three of them fled to a frenzy of applause.

Baque felt a hand on his shoulder. Lankey. His ugly, expressionless face eyed Baque, turned to study the wildly enthusiastic customers, turned back to Baque. He nodded and walked away.

Rose returned alone, still breathing heavily. "How about a Sally Ann Perfume Com?"

Baque searched his memory and was chagrined to find no recollection of Sally Ann's Coms. "Tell me the words," he said. She recited them tonelessly—a tragic little story about the shattered romance of a girl who did not use Sally Ann. "Now I remember," Baque told her. "Shall we make them cry? Just concentrate on that. It's a sad story, and we're going to make them cry."

She stood by the multichord and sang plaintively. Baque fashioned a muted, tremulous accompaniment, and when the second verse started he improvised a drooping countermelody. The spacers sat in hushed suspense. The men did not cry, but some of the women sniffed audibly, and when Rose finished there was a taut silence.

"Quick!" Baque hissed. "Let's brighten things up. Sing another Com—anything!"

She launched into a Puffed Bread Com, and Baque brought the spacers to their feet with the driving rhythm of his accompaniment.

The other girls took their turns, and Baque watched the customers detachedly, bewildered at the power that surged in his fingers. He carried them from one emotional extreme to the other and back again, improvising, experimenting. And his mind fumbled haltingly with an idea.

"Time for a break," Rose said finally. "Better get something to eat."

An hour and a half of continuous playing had left Baque drained of strength and emotion, and he accepted his dinner tray indifferently and took it to the enclosure they called his room. He did not feel hungry. He sniffed doubtfully at the food, tasted it—and ate ravenously. Real food, after months of synthetics!

When he'd finished he sat for a time on his cot, wondering how long the girls took between appearances, and then he went looking for Lankey.

"I don't like sitting around," he said. "Any objection to my playing?"

"Without the girls?"

"Yes."

Lankey planted both elbows on the bar, cupped his chin in one fist, and sat looking absently at the far wall. "You going to sing yourself?" he asked finally.

"No. Just play."

"Without any singing? Without words?"

"Yes."

"What'll you play?"

"Coms. Or I might improvise something."

A long silence. Then—"Think you could keep things moving while the girls are out?"

"Of course I could."

Lankey continued to concentrate on the far wall. His eyebrows contracted, relaxed, contracted again. "All right," he said. "I was just wondering why I never thought of it."

Unnoticed, Baque took his place at the multichord. He began softly, making the music an unobtrusive background to the rollicking conversation that filled the room. As he increased the volume, faces turned in his direction.

He wondered what these people were thinking as they heard for the first time music that was not a Com, music without words. He watched intently and satisfied himself that he was holding their attention. Now—could he bring them out of their seats with nothing more than the sterile tones of a multichord? He gave the melody a rhythmic snap, and the stomping began.

As he increased the volume again, Rose came stumbling out of a doorway and hurried across the stage, perplexity written on her pert face.

"It's all right," Baque told her. "I'm just playing to amuse myself. Don't come back until you're ready."

She nodded and walked away. A red-faced spacer near the platform looked up at the revealed outline of her young body and leered. Fascinated, Baque studied the coarse, demanding lust in his face and searched the keyboard to express it. This? Or—this? Or—

He had it. He felt himself caught up in the relentless rhythm. His foot tightened on the volume control, and he turned to watch the customers.

Every pair of eyes stared hypnotically at his corner of the room. A bartender stood at a half crouch, mouth agape. There was uneasiness, a strained shuffling of feet, a restless scraping of chairs. Baque's foot dug harder at the volume control.

His hands played on hypnotically, and he stared in horror at the scene that erupted below him. Lasciviousness twisted every face. Men were on their feet, reaching for the women, clutching, pawing. A chair crashed to the floor, and a table, and no one noticed. A woman's dress fluttered crazily downward, and the pursued were pursuers while Baque helplessly allowed his fingers to race onward, out of control.

With a violent effort he wrenched his hands from the keys, and the ensuing silence crashed the room like a clap of thunder. Fingers trembling, Baque began to play softly, indifferently. Order was restored when he looked again, the chair and table were upright, and the customers were seated in apparent relaxation except for one woman who struggled back into her dress in obvious embarrassment.

Baque continued to play quietly until the girls returned.

At six A.M., his body wracked with weariness, his hands aching, his legs cramped, Baque climbed down from the multichord. Lankey stood waiting for him. "Class One rates," he said. "You've got a job with me as long as you want it. But take it a little easy with that stuff, will you?"

Baque remembered Val, alone in their dreary apartment and eating synthetic food. "Would I be out of order to ask for an advance?"

"No," Lankey said. "Not out of order. I told the cashier to give you a hundred on your way out. Call it a bonus."

Weary from his long conveyer ride, Baque walked quietly into his dim apartment and looked about. There was no sign of Val—she would still be sleeping. He sat down at his own multichord and touched the keys.

He felt awed and humble and disbelieving. Music without Coms, without words, could make people laugh and cry, and dance and cavort madly.

And it could turn them into lewd animals.

Wonderingly he played the music that had incited such unconcealed lust, played it louder, and louder—

And felt a hand on his shoulder, and turned to look into Val's passion-twisted face.

He asked Hulsey to come and hear him that night, and later Hulsey sat slumped on the cot in his room and shuddered. "It isn't right. No man should have that power over people. How do you do it?"

"I don't know," Baque said. "I saw that young couple sitting there, and they were happy, and I felt their happiness. And as I played everyone in the room was happy. And then another couple came in quarreling, and the next thing I knew I had everyone mad."

"Almost started a fight at the next table," Hulsey said. "And what you did after that—"

"Yes. But not as much as I did last night. You should have seen it last night."

Hulsey shuddered again.

"I have a book about ancient Greek music," Baque said. "They had something they called *ethos*. They thought that the different musical scales affected people in different ways—could make them sad, or happy, or even drive them crazy. They claimed that a musician named Orpheus could move trees and soften rocks with his music. Now listen. I've had a chance to experiment, and I've noticed that my playing is most effective when I don't use the filters. There are only two filters that work on that multichord anyway—flute and violin—but when I use either of them the people don't react so strongly. I'm wondering if maybe the effects the Greeks talk about were produced by their instruments, rather than their scales. I'm wondering if the tone of an unfiltered multichord might have something in common with the tones of the ancient Greek *kithara* or *aulos*."

Hulsey grunted. "I don't think it's the instrument, or the scales either. I think it's Baque, and I don't like it. You should have stayed a tunesmith."

"I want you to help me," Baque said. "I want to find a place where we can put a lot of people—a thousand, at least—not to eat, or watch Coms, but just to listen to one man play on a multichord."

Hulsey got up abruptly. "Baque, you're a dangerous man. I'm damned if I'll trust any man who can make me feel the way you made me feel tonight. I don't know what you're trying to do, but I won't have any part of it."

He stomped away in the manner of a man about to slam a door, but the room of a male multichordist at the Lankey-Pank Out did not rate that luxury. Hulsey paused uncertainly in the doorway, gave Baque a parting glare, and disappeared. Baque followed him as far as the main room and stood watching him weave his way impatiently past the tables to the exit.

From his place behind the bar, Lankey looked at Baque and then glanced after the disappearing Hulsey. "Troubles?" he asked.

Baque turned away wearily. "I've known that man for twenty years. I never thought he was my friend. But then—I never thought he was my enemy, either."

"Sometimes it works out that way," Lankey said.

Baque shook his head. "I'd like to try some Martian whisky. I've never tasted the stuff."

TWO WEEKS MADE Baque an institution, and the Lankey-Pank Out was jammed to capacity from the time he went to work until he left the next morning. When he performed alone, he forgot about Coms and played whatever he wanted. He even performed short pieces by Bach for the customers, and received generous applause, but the reaction was nothing like the tumultuous enthusiasm that followed his improvisations.

Sitting behind the bar, eating his evening meal and watching the impacted mass of customers, Baque felt vaguely happy. He was enjoying the work he was doing. For the first time in his life he had more money than he needed.

For the first time in his life he had a definite goal and a vague notion of a plan that would accomplish it—would eliminate the Coms altogether.

As Baque pushed his tray aside, he saw Biff the doorman step forward to greet a pair of newcomers, halt suddenly, and back away in stupefied amazement. And no wonder—evening clothes at the Lankey-Pank Out!

The couple halted near the door, blinking uncertainly in the dim, smoke-tinted light. The man was bronzed and handsome, but no one noticed him. The woman's beauty flashed like a meteor against the drab surroundings. She moved in an aura of shining loveliness, with her hair gleaming golden, her shimmering, flowing gown clinging seductively to her voluptuous figure, and her fragrance routing the foul tobacco and whisky odors.

In an instant all eyes were fixed on her, and a collective gasp encircled the room. Baque stared with the others and finally recognized her: Marigold, of *Morning with*

Marigold. Worshiped around the Solar System by the millions of devotees to her visiscope program. Mistress, it was said, to James Denton, the czar of visiscope. Marigold Manning.

She raised a hand to her mouth in mock horror, and the bright tones of her laughter dropped tantalizingly among the spellbound spacers. "What an odd place! Where'd you ever hear about a place like this?"

"I need some Martian whisky, damn it," the man said.

"So stupid of the port bar to run out. With all those ships from Mars coming in, too. Are you sure we can get back in time? Jimmy'll raise hell if we aren't there when he lands."

Lankey touched Baque's arm. "After six," he said, without taking his eyes from Marigold Manning. "They'll be getting impatient."

Baque nodded and started for the multichord. The tumult began the moment the customers saw him. They abandoned Marigold Manning, leaped to their feet, and began a stomping, howling ovation. When Baque paused to acknowledge it, Marigold and her escort were staring openmouthed at the nondescript man who could inspire such undignified enthusiasm.

Her exclamation rang out sharply as Baque seated himself at the multichord and the ovation faded to an expectant silence. "What the hell!"

Baque shrugged and started to play. When Marigold finally left, after a brief conference with Lankey, her escort still hadn't got his Martian whisky.

The next evening Lankey greeted Baque with both fists full of telenotes. "What a hell of a mess this is! You see this Marigold dame's program this morning?"

Baque shook his head. "I haven't watched visiscope since I came to work here."

"In case it interests you, you were—what does she call it?—a 'Marigold Exclusive' on visiscope this morning. Erlin Baque, the famous tunesmith, is now playing the multichord in a queer little restaurant called the Lankey-Pank Out. If you want to hear some amazing music, wander out to the New Jersey Space Port and listen to Baque. Don't miss it. The experience of a lifetime." Lankey swore and waved the telenotes. "Queer, she calls us. Now I've got ten thousand requests for reservations, some from as far away as Budapest and Shanghai. And our capacity is five hundred, counting standing room. Damn that woman! We already had all the business we could handle."

"You need a bigger place," Baque said.

"Yes. Well, confidentially, I've got my eye on a big warehouse. It'll seat a thousand, at least. We'll clean up. I'll give you a contract to take charge of the music."

Baque shook his head. "How about opening a big place uptown? Attract people that have more money to spend. You run it, and I'll bring in the customers."

Lankey caressed his flattened nose thoughtfully. "How do we split?"

"Fifty-fifty," Baque said.

"No," Lankey said, shaking his head slowly. "I play fair, Baque, but fifty-fifty wouldn't be right on a deal like that. I'd have to put up all the money myself. I'll give you one-third to handle the music."

They had a lawyer draw up a contract. Baque's lawyer. Lankey insisted on that.

IN THE BLEAK gray of early morning Baque sleepily rode the crowded conveyer toward his apartment. It was the peak rush load, when commuters jammed against each other and snarled grumpily when a neighbor shifted his feet. The crowd seemed even heavier than usual, but Baque shrugged off the jostling and elbowing and lost himself in thought.

It was time that he found a better place to live. He hadn't minded the dumpy apartment as long as he could afford nothing better, but Val had been complaining for years. And now when they could move, when they could have a luxury apartment or even a small home over in Pennsylvania, Val refused to go. Didn't want to leave her friends, she said.

Mulling over this problem in feminine contrariness, Baque realized suddenly that he was approaching his own stop. He attempted to move toward a deceleration strip— he shoved firmly, he tried to step between his fellow riders, he applied his elbows, first gently and then viciously. The crowd about him did not yield.

"I beg your pardon," Baque said, making another attempt. "I get off here."

This time a pair of brawny arms barred his way. "Not this morning, Baque. You got an appointment uptown."

Baque flung a glance at the circle of hard, grinning faces that surrounded him. With a sudden effort he hurled himself sideways, fighting with all of his strength. The arms hauled him back roughly.

"Uptown, Baque. If you want to go dead, that's your affair."

"Uptown," Baque agreed.

At a public parking strip they left the conveyer. A flyer was waiting for them, a plush, private job that displayed a high-priority X registration number. They flew swiftly toward Manhattan, cutting across air lanes with a monumental contempt for regulations, and they veered in for a landing on the towering Visiscope International building. Baque was bundled down an anti-grav shaft, led through a labyrinth of corridors, and finally prodded none too gently into an office.

It was a huge room, and its sparse furnishings made it look more enormous than it was. It contained only a desk, a few chairs, a bar in the far corner, an enormous visiscope screen—and a multichord. The desk was occupied, but it was the group of men about the bar that caught Baque's attention. His gaze swept the blur of faces and found one that he recognized: Hulsey.

The plump agent took two steps forward and stood glaring at Baque. "Day of reckoning, Erlin," he said coldly.

A hand rapped sharply on the desk. "I take care of any reckoning that's done around here, Hulsey. Please sit down, Mr. Baque."

A chair was thrust forward, and Baque seated himself and waited nervously, his eyes on the man behind the desk.

"My name is James Denton. Does my fame extend to such a remote place as the Lankey-Pank Out?"

"No," Baque said. "But I've heard of you."

James Denton. Czar of Visiscope International. Ruthless arbiter of public taste. He was no more than forty, with a swarthy, handsome face, flashing eyes, and a ready smile.

He tapped a cigar on the edge of his desk and carefully placed it in his mouth. Men sprang forward with lighters extended, and he chose one without looking up, puffed deeply, and nodded.

"I won't bore you with introductions to this gathering, Baque. Some of these men are here for professional reasons. Some are here because they're curious. I heard about you for the first time yesterday, and what I heard made me want to find out whether you're a potential asset that might be made use of, or a potential nuisance that should be eliminated, or a nonentity that can be ignored. When I want to know something, Baque, I waste no time about it." He chuckled. "As you can see from the fact that I had you brought in at the earliest moment you were—shall we say— available."

"The man's dangerous, Denton!" Hulsey blurted.

Denton flashed his smile. "I like dangerous men, Hulsey. They're useful to have around. If I can use whatever it is Mr. Baque has, I'll make him an attractive offer. I'm sure he'll accept it gratefully. If I can't use it, I aim to make damned certain that he won't be inconveniencing me. Do I make myself clear, Baque?"

Baque, looking past Denton to avoid his eyes, said nothing.

Denton leaned forward. His smile did not waver, but his eyes narrowed and his voice was suddenly icy. "Do I make myself clear, Baque?"

"Yes," Baque muttered weakly.

Denton jerked a thumb toward the door, and half of those present, including Hulsey, solemnly filed out. The others waited, talking in whispers, while Denton puffed steadily on his cigar. Finally an intercom rasped a single word. "Ready!"

Denton pointed at the multichord. "We crave a demonstration of your skill, Mr. Baque. And take care that it's a good demonstration. Hulsey is listening, and he can tell us if you try to stall."

Baque nodded and took his place at the multichord. He sat with fingers poised, timidly looking up at a circle of staring faces. Overlords of business, they were, and of science and industry, and never in their lives had they heard real music. As for

Hulsey—yes, Hulsey would be listening, but over Denton's intercom, over a communication system designed to carry voices.

And Hulsey had a terrible ear for music.

Baque grinned contemptuously, touched the violin filter, touched it again, and faltered.

Denton chuckled dryly. "I neglected to inform you, Mr. Baque. On Hulsey's advice, we've had the filters disconnected."

Anger surged within Baque. He jammed his foot down hard on the volume control, insolently tapped out a visiscope fanfare, and started to play his Tamper Cheese Com. Denton, his own anger evident in his flushed face, leaned forward and snarled something. The men around him stirred uneasily. Baque shifted to another Com, improvised some variations, and began to watch the circle of faces. Overlords of industry, science and business. It would be amusing, he thought, to make them stomp their feet. His fingers shaped a compelling rhythm, and they began to sway restlessly.

He forgot his resolution to play cautiously. Laughing silently to himself, he released an overpowering torrent of sound that set the men dancing and brought Denton to his feet. He froze them in ridiculous postures with an outburst of surging emotion. He made them stomp recklessly, he brought tears to their eyes, and he finished off with the pounding force that Lankey called, "Sex Music."

Then he slumped over the keyboard, terrified at what he had done.

Denton stood behind his desk, face pale, hands clenching and unclenching. "Good God!" he muttered.

He snarled a word at his intercom. "Reaction?"

"Negative," came the prompt answer.

"Let's wind it up."

Denton sat down, passed his hands across his face, and turned to Baque with a bland smile. "An impressive performance, Mr. Baque. We'll know in a few minutes— ah, here they are."

Those who had left earlier filed back into the room, and several men huddled together in a whispered conference. Denton left his desk and paced the floor meditatively. The other men in the room, including Hulsey, gravitated toward the bar.

Baque kept his place at the multichord and watched the conference uneasily. Once he accidentally touched a key, and the single tone shattered the poise of the conferees, halted Denton in midstride, and startled Hulsey into spilling his drink.

"Mr. Baque is getting impatient," Denton called. "Can't we finish this?"

"One moment, sir."

Finally they filed toward Denton's desk. The spokesman, a white-haired, scholarly-looking man with a delicate pink complexion, cleared his throat self-consciously and waited until Denton had returned to his chair.

"It is established," he said, "that those in this room were powerfully affected by the music. Those listening on the intercom experienced no reaction except a mild boredom."

"I didn't call you in here to state the obvious," Denton snapped. "How does he do it?"

"We can only offer a working hypothesis."

"So you're guessing. Let's have it."

"Erlin Baque has the ability to telepathically project his emotional experience. When the projection is subtly reinforced by his multichord playing, those in his immediate presence share that experience intensely. The projection has no effect upon those listening to his music at a distance."

"And—visiscope?"

"He could not project his emotions by way of visiscope."

"I see," Denton said. A meditative scowl twisted his face. "What about his long-term effectiveness?"

"It's difficult to predict—"

"Predict, damn it!"

"The novelty of his playing would attract attention, at first. While the novelty lasted he might become a kind of fad. By the time his public lost interest he would probably have a small group of followers who would use the emotional experience of his playing as a narcotic."

"Thank you, gentlemen. That will be all."

The room emptied quickly. Hulsey paused in the doorway, glared hatefully at Baque, and then walked out meekly.

"Obviously you're no nonentity," Denton said, "but whatever it is you have is of no use to me. Unfortunately. If you could project on visiscope, you'd be worth a billion an hour in advertising revenue. Fortunately for you, your nuisance rating is fairly low. I know what you and Lankey are up to. If I say the word, you'll never in this lifetime find a place for your new restaurant. I could have the Lankey-Pank Out closed down within an hour, but it would hardly be worth the trouble. If you can develop a cult for yourself, why—perhaps it will keep the members out of worse mischief. I'm feeling so generous this morning that I won't even insist on a visiscope screen in your new restaurant. Now you'd better leave, Baque, before I change my mind."

Baque got to his feet. At that moment Marigold Manning swept into the room, radiantly lovely, exotically perfumed, her glistening blonde hair swept up into a new and tantalizing hair style.

"Jimmy, darling—oh!" She stared at Baque, stared at the multichord, and stammered, "Why, you're—you're—Erlin Baque! Jimmy, why didn't you tell me?"

"Mr. Baque has been favoring me with a private performance," Denton said brusquely. "I think we understand each other, Baque. Good morning."

"You're going to put him on visiscope!" Marigold exclaimed. "Jimmy, that's wonderful. May I have him first? I can work him in this morning."

Denton shook his head. "Sorry, darling. We've decided that Mr. Baque's talent is not quite suitable for visiscope."

"At least I can have him for a guest. You'll be my guest, won't you, Mr. Baque? There's nothing wrong with giving him a guest spot, is there, Jimmy?"

Denton chuckled. "No. After all the fuss you stirred up, it might be a good idea for you to guest him. It'll serve you right when he bombs."

"He won't bomb. He'll be wonderful on visiscope. Will you come in this morning, Mr. Baque?"

"Well—" Baque began. Denton was nodding at him emphatically. "We'll be opening a new restaurant soon. I wouldn't mind being your guest on opening day."

"A new restaurant? That's wonderful. Does anyone know? I'll give it out this morning as an exclusive!"

"It isn't exactly settled, yet," Baque said apologetically. "We haven't found a place yet."

"Lankey found a place yesterday," Denton said. "He's having a contractor check it over this morning, and if no snags develop he'll sign a lease. Just let Miss Manning know your opening date, Baque, and she'll arrange a spot for you. Now if you don't mind—"

It took Baque half an hour to find his way out of the building, but he plodded aimlessly along the corridors and disdained asking directions. He hummed happily to himself, and now and then he broke into a laugh.

The overlords of business and industry—and their scientists—knew nothing about overtones.

"So THAT'S THE way it is," Lankey said. "You seem to have no notion of how lucky you were—how lucky we were. Denton should have made his move when he had a chance. Now we know what to expect, and when he finally wises up it'll be too late."

"What could we do if he decided to put us out of business?"

"I have a few connections myself, Baque. They don't run in high society, like Denton, but they're every bit as dishonest, and Denton has a lot of enemies who'll be happy to back us. Said he could close me down in an hour, eh? Unfortunately there's not much we could do that would hurt Denton, but there's plenty we can do to keep him from hurting us."

"I think we're going to hurt Denton," Baque said.

Lankey moved over to the bar and came back with a tall glass of pink, foaming liquid. "Drink it," he said. "You've had a long day, and you're getting delirious. How could we hurt Denton?"

"Visiscope depends on Coms. We'll show the people they can have entertainment without Coms. We'll make our motto *NO COMS AT LANKEY'S!*"

"Great," Lankey drawled. "I invest a thousand in fancy new costumes for the girls—they can't wear those plastic things in our new place, you know—and you decide not to let them sing."

"Certainly they're going to sing."

Lankey leaned forward, caressing his nose. "And no Coms. Then *what* are they going to sing?"

"I took some lyrics out of an old school book my grandfather had. Back in those days they were called poems. I'm setting them to music. I was going to try them out here, but Denton might hear about it, and there's no use starting trouble before it's necessary."

"No. Save all the trouble for the new place—after opening day we'll be important enough to be able to handle it. And you'll be on *Morning with Marigold.* Are you certain about this overtones business, Baque? You really could be projecting emotions, you know. Not that it makes any difference in the restaurant, but on visiscope—"

"I'm certain. How soon can we open?"

"I got three shifts remodeling the place. We'll seat twelve hundred and still have room for a nice dance floor. Should be ready in two weeks. Baque, I'm not sure this visiscope thing is wise."

"I want to do it."

Lankey went back to the bar and got a drink for himself. "All right. You do it. If your stuff comes over, all hell is going to break loose, and I might as well start getting ready for it." He grinned. "Damned if it won't be good for business!"

MARIGOLD MANNING HAD changed her hair styling to a spiraled creation by Zann of Hong Kong, and she dallied for ten minutes in deciding which profile she would present to the cameras. Baque waited patiently, his awkward feeling wholly derived from the fact that his dress suit was the most expensive clothing he had ever owned. He kept telling himself to stop wondering if perhaps he really did project emotions.

"I'll have it this way," Marigold said finally, waving a hand screen in front of her face for a last, searching look. "And you, Mr. Baque? What shall we do with you?"

"Just put me at the multichord," Baque said.

"But you can't just play. You'll have to say *something.* I've been announcing this every day for a week, and we'll have the biggest audience in years, and you'll just *have* to say *something.*"

"Gladly," Baque said, "if I can talk about Lankey's."

"But of course, you silly man. That's why you're here. You talk about Lankey's, and I'll talk about Erlin Baque."

"Five minutes," a voice announced crisply.

"Oh, dear," she said. "I'm always so nervous just before."

"Be happy you're not nervous during," Baque said.

"That's so right. Jimmy makes fun of me, but it takes an artist to understand another artist. Do you get nervous?"

"When I'm playing, I'm much too busy."

"That's just the way it is with me. Once my program starts, I'm much too busy."

"Four minutes."

"Oh, bother!" She seized the hand screen again. "Maybe I would be better the other way."

Baque seated himself at the multichord. "You're perfect the way you are."

"Do you really think so? It's a nice thing to say, anyway. I wonder if Jimmy will take the time to watch."

"I'm sure he will."

"Three minutes."

Baque switched on the power and sounded a chord. Now he *was* nervous. He had no idea what he would play. He'd intentionally refrained from preparing anything because it was his improvisations that affected people so strangely. The one thing he had to avoid was the Sex Music. Lankey had been emphatic about that.

He lost himself in thought, failed to hear the final warning, and looked up startled at Marigold's cheerful, "Good morning, everyone. It's *Morning with Marigold!*"

Her bright voice wandered on and on. Erlin Baque. His career as a tunesmith. Her amazing discovery of him playing in the Lankey-Pank Out. She asked the engineers to run the Tamper Cheese Com. Finally she finished her remarks and risked the distortion of her lovely profile to glance in his direction. "Ladies and gentlemen, with admiration, with pride, with pleasure, I give you a Marigold Exclusive, Erlin Baque!"

Baque grinned nervously and tapped out a scale with one finger. "This is my first speech. Probably it'll be my last. The new restaurant opens tonight. Lankey's, on Broadway. Unfortunately I can't invite you to join us, because thanks to Miss Manning's generous comments this past week all space is reserved for the next two months. After that we'll be setting aside a limited number of reservations for visitors from distant places. Jet over and see us!

"You'll find something different at Lankey's. There is no visiscope screen. Maybe you've heard about that. We have attractive young ladies to sing for you. I play the multichord. We know you'll enjoy our music. We know you'll enjoy it because you'll hear no Coms at Lankey's. Remember that—*no Coms at Lankey's.* No soap with your soup. No air cars with your steaks. No shirts with your desserts. *No Coms!* Just good food, with good music played exclusively for your enjoyment—like this."

He brought his hands down onto the keyboard.

Immediately he knew that something was wrong. He'd always had a throng of faces to watch, he'd paced his playing according to their reactions. Now he had only Miss Manning and the visiscope engineers, and he was suddenly apprehensive that his success had been wholly due to his audiences. People were listening throughout the Western Hemisphere. Would they clap and stomp, would they think awesomely, "So that's how music sounds without words, without Coms!" Or would they turn away in boredom?

Baque caught a glimpse of Marigold's pale face, of the engineers watching with mouths agape, and thought perhaps everything was all right. He lost himself in the music and played fervently.

He continued to play even after the pilot screen went blank. Miss Manning leaped to her feet and hurried toward him, and the engineers were moving about confusedly. Finally Baque brought his playing to a halt.

"We were cut off," Miss Manning said tearfully. "Who would do such a thing to me? Never, never, in all the time I've been on visiscope—George, who cut us off?"

"Orders."

"Whose orders?"

"My orders!" James Denton strode toward them, lips tight, face pale, eyes gleaming violence and sudden death. He spat words at Baque. "I don't know how you worked that trick, but no man fools James Denton more than once. Now you've made yourself a nuisance that has to be eliminated."

"Jimmy!" Miss Manning wailed. "My program—cut off. How could you?"

"Shut up, damn it! I just passed the word, Baque. Lankey's doesn't open tonight. Not that it'll make any difference to you."

Baque smiled gently. "I think you've lost, Denton. I think enough music got through to beat you. By tomorrow you'll have a million complaints. So will the government, and then you'll find out who really runs Visiscope International."

"I run Visiscope International."

"No, Denton. It belongs to the people. They've let things slide for a long time, and they've taken anything you'd give them. But if they know what they want, they'll get it. I gave them at least three minutes of what they want. That was more than I'd hoped for."

"How'd you work that trick in my office?"

"That wasn't my trick, Denton—it was yours. You transmitted the music on a voice intercom. It didn't carry the overtones, the upper frequencies, so the multichord sounded dead to the men in the other room. Visiscope has the full frequency range of live sound."

Denton nodded. "I'll have the heads of some scientists for that. I'll also have your head, though I regret the waste. If you'd played square with me I'd have made you a live billionaire. The only alternative is a dead musician."

He stalked away, and as the automatic door closed behind him, Marigold Manning clutched Baque's arm. "Quick! Follow me!" Baque hesitated, and she hissed, "Don't stand there like an idiot! He's going to have you killed!"

She led him through a control room and out into a small corridor. They raced the length of it, darted through a reception room and passed a startled secretary without a word, and burst through a rear door into another corridor. She jerked Baque after her into an anti-grav lift, and they shot upward. At the top of the building she hurried him to an air car strip and left him standing in a doorway. "When I give you a signal, you walk out," she said. "Don't run, just walk."

She calmly approached an attendant, and Baque heard his surprised greeting. "Through early this morning, Miss Manning?"

"We're running a lot of Coms," she said. "I want the big Waring."

"Coming right up."

Peering around the corner, Baque saw her step into the flyer. As soon as the attendant's back was turned, she waved frantically. Baque walked carefully toward her, keeping the flyer between the attendant and himself. A moment later they were airborne, and far below them a siren was sounding faintly.

"We did it!" she gasped. "If you hadn't got away before that alarm sounded, you wouldn't have left the building alive."

"Well, thanks," Baque said, looking back at the Visiscope International building. "But surely this wasn't necessary. Earth is a civilized planet."

"Visiscope International is not civilized!" she snapped.

He looked at her wonderingly. Her face was flushed, her eyes wide with fear, and for the first time Baque saw her as a human being, a woman, a lovely woman. As he looked, she turned away and burst into tears.

"Now Jimmy'll have me killed, too. And where can we go?"

"Lankey's," Baque said. "Look—you can see it from here."

She pointed the flyer at the freshly painted letters on the strip above the new restaurant, and Baque, looking backward, saw a crowd forming in the street by Visiscope International.

LANKEY FLOATED HIS desk over to the wall and leaned back comfortably. He wore a trim dress suit, and he'd carefully groomed himself for the role of a jovial host, but in his office he was the same ungainly Lankey that Baque had first seen leaning over a bar.

"I told you all hell would break loose," he said, grinning. "There are five thousand people over by Visiscope International, and they're screaming for Erlin Baque. And the crowd is growing."

"I didn't play for more than three minutes," Baque said. "I thought a lot of people might write in to complain about Denton cutting me off, but I didn't expect anything like this."

"You didn't, eh? Five thousand people—maybe ten thousand by now—and Miss Manning risks her neck to get you out of the place. Ask her why, Baque."

"Yes," Baque said. "Why go to all that trouble for me?"

She shuddered. "Your music does things to me."

"It sure does," Lankey said. "Baque, you fool, you gave a quarter of Earth's population three minutes of Sex Music!"

LANKEY'S OPENED ON schedule that evening, with crowds filling the street outside and struggling through the doors as long as there was standing room. The shrewd Lankey had instituted an admission charge. The standees bought no food, and Lankey saw no point in furnishing free music, even if people were willing to stand to hear it.

He made one last-minute change in plans. Astutely reasoning that the customers would prefer a glamorous hostess to a flat-nosed elderly host, he hired Marigold Manning. She moved about gracefully, the deep blue of her flowing gown offsetting her golden hair.

When Baque took his place at the multichord, the frenzied ovation lasted for twenty minutes.

Midway through the evening Baque sought out Lankey. "Has Denton tried anything?"

"Nothing that I've noticed. Everything is running smoothly."

"That seems odd. He swore we wouldn't open tonight."

Lankey chuckled. "He's had troubles of his own to worry about. The authorities are on his neck about the rioting. I was afraid they'd blame you, but they didn't. Denton put you on visiscope, and then he cut you off, and they figure he's responsible. And according to my last report, Visiscope International has had more than ten million complaints. Don't worry, Baque. We'll hear from Denton soon enough, and the guilds, too."

"The guilds? Why the guilds?"

"The Tunesmiths' Guild will be damned furious about your dropping the Coms. The Lyric Writers' Guild will go along with them on account of the Coms and because you're using music without words. The Performers' Guild already has it in for you because not many of its members can play worth a damn, and of course it'll support the other guilds. By tomorrow morning, Baque, you'll be the most popular man in the Solar System, and the sponsors, and the visiscope people, and the guilds are going to hate your guts. I'm giving you a twenty-four-hour bodyguard. Miss Manning, too. I want both of you to come out of this alive."

"Do you really think Denton would—"

"Denton would."

The next morning the Performers' Guild blacklisted Lankey's and ordered all the musicians, including Baque, to sever relations. Rose and the other singers joined Baque in respectfully declining, and they found themselves blacklisted before noon. Lankey called in an attorney, the most sinister, furtive, disreputable-looking individual Baque had ever seen.

"They're supposed to give us a week's notice," Lankey said, "and another week if we decide to appeal. I'll sue them for five million."

The Commissioner of Public Safety called, and on his heels came the Health Commissioner and the Liquor Commissioner. All three conferred briefly with Lankey and departed grim-faced.

"Denton's moving too late," Lankey said gleefully. "I got to all of them a week ago and recorded our conversations. They don't dare take any action."

A riot broke out in front of Lankey's that night. Lankey had his own riot squad ready for action, and the customers never noticed the disturbance. Lankey's informants estimated that more than fifty million complaints had been received by Visiscope International, and a dozen governmental agencies had scheduled investigations. Anti-Com demonstrations began to errupt spontaneously, and five hundred visiscope screens were smashed in Manhattan restaurants.

Lankey's finished its first week unmolested, entertaining capacity crowds daily. Reservations were pouring in from as far away as Pluto, where a returning space detachment voted to spend its first night of leave at Lankey's. Baque sent to Berlin for a multichordist to understudy him, and Lankey hoped by the end of the month to have the restaurant open twenty-four hours a day.

At the beginning of the second week, Lankey told Baque, "We've got Denton licked. I've countered every move he's made, and now we're going to make a few moves. You're going on visiscope again. I'm making application today. We're a legitimate business, and we've got as much right to buy time as anyone else. If he won't give it to us, I'll sue. But he won't dare refuse."

"Where do you get the money for this?" Baque asked.

Lankey grinned. "I saved it up—a little of it. Mostly I've had help from people who don't like Denton."

Denton didn't refuse. Baque did an Earth-wide program direct from Lankey's, with Marigold Manning introducing him. He omitted only the Sex Music.

QUITTING TIME AT Lankey's. Baque was in his dressing room, wearily changing. Lankey had already left for an early-morning conference with his attorney. They were speculating on Denton's next move.

Baque was uneasy. He was, he told himself, only a dumb musician. He didn't understand legal problems or the tangled web of connections and influence that Lankey negotiated so easily. He knew James Denton was evil incarnate, and he also knew that Denton had enough money to buy Lankey a thousand times over, or to buy the murder of anyone who got in his way. What was he waiting for? Given enough time, Baque might deliver a deathblow to the entire institution of Coms. Surely Denton would know that.

So what *was* he waiting for?

The door burst open, and Marigold Manning stumbled in half undressed, her pale face the bleached whiteness of her plastic breast cups. She slammed the door and leaned against it, sobs shaking her body.

"Jimmy," she gasped. "I got a note from Carol—that's his secretary. She was a good friend of mine. She says Jimmy's bribed our guards, and they're going to kill us on the way home this morning. Or let Jimmy's men kill us."

"I'll call Lankey," Baque said. "There's nothing to worry about."

"No! If they suspect anything they won't wait. We won't have a chance."

"Then we'll just wait until Lankey gets back."

"Do you think it's safe to wait? They know we're getting ready to leave."

Baque sat down heavily. It was the sort of move he expected Denton to make. Lankey picked his men carefully, he knew, but Denton had enough money to buy any man. And yet—

"Maybe it's a trap. Maybe that note's a fake."

"No. I saw that fat little snake Hulsey talking with one of your guards last night, and I knew then that Jimmy was up to something."

"What do you want to do?" Baque asked.

"Could we go out the back way?"

"I don't know. We'd have to get past at least one guard."

"Couldn't we try?"

Baque hesitated. She was frightened—she was sick with fright—but she knew far more about this sort of thing than he did, and she knew James Denton. Without her help he'd never have got out of the Visiscope International building.

"If you think that's the thing to do, we'll try it."

"I'll have to finish changing."

"Go ahead. Let me know when you're ready."

She opened the door a crack and looked out cautiously. "No. You come with me."

Minutes later, Baque and Miss Manning walked leisurely along the corridor at the back of the building, nodded to the two guards on duty there, and with a sudden movement were through the door. Running. A shout of surprise came from behind them, but no one followed. They dashed frantically down an alley, turned off, reached another intersection, and hesitated.

"The conveyer is that way," she gasped. "If we can reach the conveyer—"

"Let's go!"

They ran on, hand in hand. Far ahead of them the alley opened onto a street. Baque glanced anxiously upward for air cars and saw none. Exactly where they were he did not know.

"Are we—being followed?" she asked.

"I don't think so," Baque panted. "There aren't any air cars, and I didn't see anyone behind us when we stopped."

"Then we got away!"

A man stepped abruptly out of the dawn shadows thirty feet ahead. As they halted, stricken dumb with panic, he walked slowly toward them. A hat was pulled low over his face, but there was no mistaking the smile. James Denton.

"Good morning, Beautiful," he said. "Visiscope International hasn't been the same without your lovely presence. And a good morning to you, Mr. Baque."

They stood silently, Miss Manning's hand clutching Baque's arm, her nails cutting through his shirt and into his flesh. He did not move.

"I thought you'd fall for that little gag, Beautiful. I thought you'd be just frightened enough, by now, to fall for it. I have every exit blocked, but I'm grateful to you for picking this one. Very grateful. I like to settle a double cross in person."

Suddenly he whirled on Baque, his voice an angry snarl. "Get going, Baque. It isn't your turn. I have other plans for you."

Baque stood rooted to the damp pavement.

"Move, Baque, before I change my mind."

Miss Manning released his arm. Her voice was a choking whisper. "Go!"

"Baque!" Denton snarled.

"Go, quickly!" she whispered again.

Baque took two hesitant steps.

"Run!" Denton shouted.

Baque ran. Behind him there was the evil crack of a gun, a scream, and silence. Baque faltered, saw Denton looking after him, and ran on.

"So I'm a coward," Baque said.

"No, Baque." Lankey shook his head slowly. "You're a brave man, or you wouldn't have got into this. Trying something there would have been foolishness, not bravery. It's my fault, for thinking he'd move first against the restaurant. I owe Denton something for this, and I'm a man who pays his debts."

A troubled frown creased Lankey's ugly face. He looked perplexedly at Baque.

"She was a brave and beautiful woman, Baque," he said, absently caressing his flat nose. "But I wonder why Denton let you go."

The air of tragedy that hung heavily over Lankey's that night did not affect its customers. They gave Baque a thunderous ovation as he moved toward the multi-chord. As he paused for a halfhearted acknowledgement, three policemen closed in on him.

"Erlin Baque?"

"That's right."

"You're under arrest."

Baque faced them grimly. "What's the charge?" he asked.

"Murder."

The murder of Marigold Manning.

LANKEY PRESSED HIS mournful face against the bars and talked unhurriedly. "They have some witnesses," he said. "Honest witnesses, who saw you run out of that alley. They have several dishonest witnesses who claim they saw you fire the shot. One of them is your friend Hulsey, who just happened to be taking an early-morning stroll along that alley—or so he'll testify. Denton would probably spend a million to convict you, but he won't have to. He won't even have to bribe the jury. The case against you is that good."

"What about the gun?" Baque asked.

"They'll have a witness who'll claim he sold it to you."

Baque nodded. Things were out of his hands, now. He'd worked for a cause that no one understood—perhaps he hadn't understood himself what he was trying to do. And he'd lost.

"What happens next?" he asked.

Lankey shook his head sadly. "I'm not one to hold back bad news. It means life. They're going to send you to the Ganymede rock pits for life."

"I see," Baque said. He added anxiously, "You're going to carry on?"

"Just what were you trying to do, Baque? You weren't only working for Lankey's. I couldn't figure it out, but I went along with you because I like you. And I like your music. What was it?"

"I don't know. Music, I suppose. People listening to music. Getting rid of the Coms, or some of them. Perhaps if I'd known what I wanted to do—"

"Yes. Yes, I think I understand. Lankey's will carry on, Baque, as long as I have any breath left, and I'm not just being noble. Business is tremendous. That new multichord player isn't bad at all. He's nothing like you were, but there'll never be another one like you. We could be sold out for the next five years if we wanted to book reservations that far ahead. The other restaurants are doing away with visiscope and trying to imitate us, but we have a big head start. We'll carry on the way you had things set up, and your one-third still stands. I'll have it put in trust for you. You'll be a wealthy man when you get back."

"When I get back!"

"Well—a life sentence doesn't necessarily mean life. See that you behave yourself."

"Val?"

"She'll be taken care of. I'll give her a job of some kind to keep her occupied."

"Maybe I can send you music for the restaurant," Baque said. "I should have plenty of time."

"I'm afraid not. It's music they want to keep you away from. So—no writing of music. And they won't let you near a multichord. They think you could hypnotize the guards and turn all the prisoners loose."

"Would they—let me have my record collection?"

"I'm afraid not."

"I see. Well, if that's the way it is—"

"It is. Now I owe Denton two debts."

The unemotional Lankey had tears in his eyes as he turned away.

THE JURY DELIBERATED for eight minutes and brought in a verdict of guilty. Baque was sentenced to life imprisonment. There was some editorial grumbling on visiscope, because life in the Ganymede rock pits was frequently a very short life.

And there was a swelling undertone of whispering among the little people that the verdict had been bought and paid for by the sponsors, by visiscope. Erlin Baque was framed, it was said, because he gave the people music.

And on the day Baque left for Ganymede, announcement was made of a public exhibition, by H. Vail, multichordist, and B. Johnson, violinist. Admission one dollar.

Lankey collected evidence with painstaking care, rebribed one of the bribed witnesses, and petitioned for a new trial. The petition was denied, and the long years limped past.

The New York Symphony Orchestra was organized, with twenty members. One of James Denton's plush air cars crashed, and he was instantly killed. An unfortunate accident. A millionaire who once heard Erlin Baque play on visiscope endowed a dozen conservatories of music. They were to be called the Baque Conservatories, but a musical historian who had never heard of Baque got the name changed to Bach.

Lankey died, and a son-in-law carried on his efforts as a family trust. A subscription was launched to build a new hall for the New York Symphony, which now numbered forty members. The project gathered force like an avalanche, and a site was finally chosen in Ohio, where the hall would be within easier commuting distance of all parts of the North American continent. Beethoven Hall was erected, seating forty thousand people. The first concert series was fully subscribed forty-eight hours after tickets went on sale.

Opera was given on visiscope for the first time in two hundred years. An opera house was built on the Ohio site, and then an art institute. The Center grew, first by private subscription and then under governmental sponsorship. Lankey's son-in-law died, and a nephew took over the management of Lankey's—and the campaign to free Erlin Baque. Thirty years passed, and then forty.

And forty-nine years, seven months and nineteen days after Baque received his life sentence, he was paroled. He still owned a third interest in Manhattan's most prosperous restaurant, and the profits that had accrued over the years made him an extremely wealthy man. He was ninety-six years old.

ANOTHER CAPACITY CROWD at Beethoven Hall. Vacationists from all parts of the Solar System, music lovers who commuted for the concerts, old people who had retired to the Center, young people on educational excursions, forty thousand of them, stirred restlessly and searched the wings for the conductor. Applause thundered down from the twelve balconies as he strode forward.

Erlin Baque sat in his permanent seat at the rear of the main floor. He adjusted his binoculars and peered at the orchestra, wondering again what a contrabassoon sounded like. His bitterness he had left behind on Ganymede. His life at the Center was an unending revelation of miracles.

Of course no one remembered Erlin Baque, tunesmith and murderer. Whole generations of people could not even remember the Coms. And yet Baque felt that he had accomplished all of this just as assuredly as though he had built this building—built the Center—with his own hands. He spread his hands before him, hands deformed by the years in the rock pits, fingers and tips of fingers crushed off, his body maimed by cascading rocks. He had no regrets. He had done his work well.

Two ushers stood in the aisle behind him. One jerked a thumb in his direction and whispered, "Now *there's* a character for you. Comes to every concert. Never misses one. And he just sits there in the back row watching people. They say he was one of the old tunesmiths, years and years ago."

"Maybe he likes music," the other said.

"Naw. Those old tunesmiths never knew anything about music. Besides—he's deaf."

A Saucer of Loneliness

Theodore Sturgeon's fiction abounds with ordinary characters undone by their all-too-human shortcomings or struggling in unsympathetic environments to find others who share their desires and feelings of loneliness. Sturgeon began publishing in 1939, and made his mark early in both fantasy and science fiction with stories that have since become classics. "Microcosmic God" concerns a scientist who plays God with unexpectedly amusing results when he repeatedly challenges a microscopic race he has created with threats to their survival. "It" focuses on the reactions of characters in a rural setting trying to contend with a rampaging inhuman monster. In "Yesterday Was Monday," a man discovers that each day's reality is a theatrical stage set built by diminutive laborers. "Killdozer" is a variation on the theme of Frankenstein in which a construction crew is trapped on an island where a bulldozer has become imbued with the electrical energy of an alien life form. Fiction Sturgeon wrote after World War II shows the gentle humor of his earlier work shading into pathos. "Memorial" and "Thunder and Roses" are cautionary tales about the abuses of use of nuclear weapons. "A Saucer of Loneliness" and "Maturity" both use traditional science fiction scenarios to explore feelings of alienation and inadequacy. Sturgeon's work at novel length is memorable for its portrayals of characters who rise above the isolation their failure to fit into normal society imposes. *More Than Human* tells of a group of psychologically dysfunctional individuals who pool their individual strengths to create a superhuman gestalt consciousness. In *The Dreaming Jewels*, a young boy discovers that his behavioral abnormalities are actually the symptoms of superhuman powers. Sturgeon is also renowned for his explorations of taboo sexuality and restrictive moralities in such stories as *Some of Your Blood*, "The World Well Lost," and "If All Men Were Brothers Would You Let One Marry Your Sister?". His short fiction has been collected in *Without Sorcery, E. Pluribus Unicorn, Caviar,* and *A Touch of Strange.* The compilations *The Ultimate Egoist, Thunder and Roses, A Saucer of Loneliness, The Perfect Host, Baby Is Three, The Microcosmic God,* and *Killdozer,* edited by Paul Williams, are the first seven volumes in a series that will eventually reprint all of Sturgeon's short fiction.

IF SHE'S DEAD, I thought, I'll never find her in this white flood of moonlight on the white sea, with the surf seething in and over the pale, pale sand like a great shampoo. Almost always, suicides who stab themselves or shoot themselves in the heart carefully bare their chests; the same strange impulse generally makes the sea-suicide go naked.

A little earlier, I thought, or later, and there would be shadows for the dunes and the breathing toss of the foam. Now the only real shadow was mine, a tiny thing just under me, but black enough to feed the blackness of the shadow of a blimp.

A little earlier, I thought, and I might have seen her plodding up the silver shore, seeking a place lonely enough to die in. A little later and my legs would rebel against this shuffling trot through sand, the maddening sand that could not hold and would not help a hurrying man.

My legs did give way then and I knelt suddenly, sobbing—not for her; not yet—just for air. There was such a rush about me: wind, and tangled spray, and colors upon colors and shades of colors that were not colors at all but shifts of white and silver. If light like that were sound, it would sound like the sea on sand, and if my ears were eyes, they would see such a light.

I crouched there, gasping in the swirl of it, and a flood struck me, shallow and swift, turning up and outward like flower petals where it touched my knees, then soaking me to the waist in its bubble and crash. I pressed my knuckles to my eyes so they would open again. The sea was on my lips with the taste of tears and the whole white night shouted and wept aloud.

And there she was.

Her white shoulders were a taller curve in the sloping foam. She must have sensed me—perhaps I yelled—for she turned and saw me kneeling there. She put her fists to her temples and her face twisted, and she uttered a piercing wail of despair and fury, and then plunged seaward and sank.

I kicked off my shoes and ran into the breakers, shouting, hunting, grasping at flashes of white that turned to sea-salt and coldness in my fingers. I plunged right past her, and her body struck my side as a wave whipped my face and tumbled both of us. I gasped in solid water, opened my eyes beneath the surface and saw a greenish-white distorted moon hurtle as I spun. Then there was sucking sand under my feet again and my left hand was tangled in her hair.

The receding wave towed her away and for a moment she streamed out from my hand like steam from a whistle. In that moment I was sure she was dead, but as she settled to the sand, she fought and scrambled to her feet.

She hit my ear, wet, hard, and a huge, pointed pain lanced into my head. She pulled, she lunged away from me, and all the while my hand was caught in her hair. I couldn't have freed her if I had wanted to. She spun to me with the next wave, battered and clawed at me, and we went into deeper water.

"Don't . . . don't . . . I can't swim!" I shouted, so she clawed me again.

"Leave me alone," she shrieked. "Oh, dear God, why can't you *leave*" (said her fingernails) "me . . ." (said her snapping teeth) "*alone!*" (said her small, hard fist).

So by her hair I pulled her head down tight to her white shoulder; and with the edge of my free hand I hit her neck twice. She floated again, and I brought her ashore.

I carried her to where a dune was between us and the sea's broad, noisy tongue, and the wind was above us somewhere. But the light was as bright. I rubbed her wrists and stroked her face and said, "It's all right," and, "There!" and some names I used to have for a dream I had long, long before I ever heard of her.

She lay still on her back with the breath hissing between her teeth, with her lips in a smile which her twisted-tight, wrinkle-sealed eyes made not a smile but a torture. She was well and conscious for many moments and still her breath hissed and her closed eyes twisted.

"Why couldn't you leave me alone?" she asked at last. She opened her eyes and looked at me. She had so much misery that there was no room for fear. She shut her eyes again and said, "You know who I am."

"I know," I said.

She began to cry.

I waited, and when she stopped crying, there were shadows among the dunes. A long time.

She said, "You don't know who I am. Nobody knows who I am."

I said, "It was in all the papers."

"That!" She opened her eyes slowly and her gaze traveled over my face, my shoulders, stopped at my mouth, touched my eyes for the briefest second. She curled her lips and turned away her head. "Nobody knows who I am."

I waited for her to move or speak, and finally I said, "Tell me."

"Who are you?" she asked, with her head still turned away.

"Someone who . . ."

"Well?"

"Not now," I said. "Later, maybe."

She sat up suddenly and tried to hide herself. "Where are my clothes?"

"I didn't see them."

"Oh," she said. "I remember. I put them down and kicked sand over them, just where a dune would come and smooth them over, hide them as if they never were . . . I hate sand. I wanted to drown in the sand, but it wouldn't let me . . . You mustn't look at me!" she shouted. "I hate to have you looking at me!" She threw her head from side to side, seeking. "I can't stay here like this! What can I do? Where can I go?"

"Here," I said.

She let me help her up and then snatched her hand away, half turned from me. "Don't touch me. Get away from me."

"Here," I said again, and walked down the dune where it curved in the moonlight, tipped back into the wind and down and became not dune but beach. "Here," I pointed behind the dune.

At last she followed me. She peered over the dune where it was chest-high, and again where it was knee-high. "Back there?"

She nodded.

"I didn't see them."

"So dark . . ." She stepped over the low dune and into the aching black of those moon-shadows. She moved away cautiously, feeling tenderly with her feet, back to where the dune was higher. She sank down into the blackness and disappeared there. I sat on the sand in the light. "Stay away from me," she spat.

I rose and stepped back. Invisible in the shadows, she breathed, "Don't go away." I waited, then saw her hand press out of the clean-cut shadows. "There," she said, "over there. In the dark. Just be a . . . Stay away from me now . . . Be a—voice."

I did as she asked, and sat in the shadows perhaps six feet from her.

She told me about it. Not the way it was in the papers.

She was perhaps seventeen when it happened. She was in Central Park, in New York. It was too warm for such an early spring day, and the hammered brown slopes had a dusting of green of precisely the consistency of that morning's hoarfrost on the rocks. But the frost was gone and the grass was brave and tempted some hundreds of pairs of feet from the asphalt and concrete to tread on it.

Hers were among them. The sprouting soil was a surprise to her feet, as the air was to her lungs. Her feet ceased to be shoes as she walked, her body was consciously more than clothes. It was the only kind of day which in itself can make a city-bred person raise his eyes. She did.

For a moment she felt separated from the life she lived, in which there was no fragrance, no silence, in which nothing ever quite fit nor was quite filled. In that moment the ordered disapproval of the buildings around the pallid park could not reach her; for two, three clean breaths it no longer mattered that the whole wide world really belonged to images projected on a screen; to gently groomed goddesses in these steel-and-glass towers; that it belonged, in short, always, always to someone else.

So she raised her eyes, and there above her was the saucer.

It was beautiful. It was golden, with a dusty finish like that of an unripe Concord grape. It made a faint sound, a chord composed of two tones and a blunted hiss like the wind in tall wheat. It was darting about like a swallow, soaring and dropping. It circled and dropped and hovered like a fish, shimmering. It was like all these living things, but with that beauty it had all the loveliness of things turned and burnished, measured, machined, and metrical.

At first she felt no astonishment, for this was so different from anything she had ever seen before that it had to be a trick of the eye, a false evaluation of size and speed and distance that in a moment would resolve itself into a sun-flash on an airplane or the lingering glare of a welding arc.

She looked away from it and abruptly realized that many other people saw it—saw *something*—too. People all around her had stopped moving and speaking and were craning upward. Around her was a globe of silent astonishment, and outside it, she was aware of the life-noise of the city, the hard-breathing giant who never inhales.

She looked up again, and at last began to realize how large and how far away the saucer was. No: rather, how small and how very near it was. It was just the size of the largest circle she might make with her two hands, and it floated not quite eighteen inches over her head.

Fear came then. She drew back and raised a forearm, but the saucer simply hung there. She bent far sideways, twisted away, leaped forward, looked back and upward to see if she had escaped it. At first she couldn't see it; then as she looked up and up, there it was, close and gleaming, quivering and crooning, right over her head.

She bit her tongue.

From the corner of her eye, she saw a man cross himself. *He did that because he saw me standing here with a halo over my head,* she thought. And that was the greatest single thing that had ever happened to her. No one had ever looked at her and made a respectful gesture before, not once, not ever. Through terror, through panic and wonderment, the comfort of that thought nestled into her, to wait to be taken out and looked at again in lonely times.

The terror was uppermost now, however. She backed away, staring upward, stepping a ludicrous cakewalk. She should have collided with people. There were plenty of people there, gaping and craning, but she reached none. She spun around and discovered to her horror that she was the center of a pointing, pressing crowd. Its mosaic of eyes all bulged, and its inner circle braced its many legs to press back and away from her.

The saucer's gentle note deepened. It tilted, dropped an inch or so. Someone screamed, and the crowd broke away from her in all directions, milled about, and settled again in a new dynamic balance, a much larger ring, as more and more people raced to thicken it against the efforts of the inner circle to escape.

The saucer hummed and tilted, tilted . . .

She opened her mouth to scream, fell to her knees, and the saucer struck.

It dropped against her forehead and clung there. It seemed almost to lift her. She came erect on her knees, made one effort to raise her hands against it, and then her arms stiffened down and back, her hands not reaching the ground. For perhaps a second and a half the saucer held her rigid, and then it passed a single ecstatic quiver to her body and dropped it. She plumped to the ground, the backs of her thighs heavy and painful on her heels and ankles.

The saucer dropped beside her, rolled once in a small circle, once just around its edge, and lay still. It lay still and dull and metallic, different and dead.

Hazily, she lay and gazed at the gray-shrouded blue of the good spring sky, and hazily she heard whistles.

And some tardy screams.

And a great stupid voice bellowing, "Give her air!" which made everyone press closer.

Then there wasn't so much sky because of the blue-clad bulk with its metal buttons and its leatherette notebook. "Okay, okay, what's happened here stand back figods sake."

And the widening ripples of observation, interpretation and comment: "It knocked her down." "Some guy knocked her down." "He knocked her down." "Some guy knocked her down and—" "Right in broad daylight this guy..." "The park's gettin to be..." onward and outward, the adulteration of fact until it was lost altogether because excitement is so much more important.

Somebody with a harder shoulder than the rest bulling close, a notebook here, too, a witnessing eye over it, ready to change "...a beautiful brunet..." to "an attractive brunet" for the afternoon editions, because "attractive" is as dowdy as any woman is allowed to get if she is a victim in the news.

The glittering shield and the florid face bending close: "You hurt bad, sister?" And the echoes, back and back through the crowd, "Hurt bad, hurt bad, badly injured, he beat the hell out of her, broad daylight..."

And still another man, slim and purposeful, tan gaberdine, cleft chin and beard-shadow: "Flyin' saucer, hm? Okay, Officer, I'll take over here."

"And who the hell might you be, takin' over?"

The flash of a brown leather wallet, a face so close behind that its chin was pressed into the gaberdine shoulder. The face said, awed: "FBI" and that rippled outward, too. The policeman nodded—the entire policeman nodded in one single bobbing genuflection.

"Get some help and clear this area," said the gaberdine.

"Yes, *sir!*" said the policeman.

"FBI, FBI," the crowd murmured, and there was more sky to look at above her. She sat up and there was a glory in her face. "The saucer talked to me," she sang.

"You shut up," said the gaberdine. "You'll have lots of chance to talk later."

"Yeah, sister," said the policeman. "My God, this mob could be full of Communists."

"You shut up, too," said the gaberdine.

Someone in the crowd told someone else a Communist beat up this girl, while someone else was saying she got beat up because she was a Communist.

She started to rise, but solicitous hands forced her down again. There were thirty police there by that time.

"I can walk," she said.

"Now, you just take it easy," they told her.

They put a stretcher down beside her and lifted her onto it and covered her with a big blanket.

"I can walk," she said as they carried her through the crowd.

A woman went white and turned away moaning, "Oh, my God, how awful!"

A small man with round eyes stared and stared at her and licked and licked his lips.

The ambulance. They slid her in. The gaberdine was already there.

A white-coated man with very clean hands: "How did it happen, miss?"

"No questions," said the gaberdine. "Security."

The hospital.

She said, "I got to get back to work."

"Take your clothes off," they told her.

She had a bedroom to herself then for the first time in her life. Whenever the door opened, she could see a policeman outside. It opened very often to admit the kind of civilians who were very polite to military people, and the kind of military people who were even more polite to certain civilians. She did not know what they all did nor what they wanted. Every single day they asked her four million five hundred thousand questions. Apparently they never talked to each other, because each of them asked her the same questions over and over.

"What is your name?"

"How old are you?"

"What year were you born?"

"What is your name?"

Sometimes they would push her down strange paths with their questions.

"Now, your uncle. Married a woman from Middle Europe, did he? Where in Middle Europe?"

"What clubs or fraternal organizations did you belong to? Ah! Now, about that Rinkeydinks gang on Sixty-third Street. Who was *really* behind it?"

But over and over again, "What did you mean when you said the saucer talked to you?"

And she would say, "It talked to me."

And they would say, "And it said—"

And she would shake her head.

There would be a lot of shouting ones, and then a lot of kind ones. No one had ever been so kind to her before, but she soon learned that no one was being kind to *her*. They were just getting her to relax, to think of other things, so they could suddenly shoot that question at her. "What do you mean it talked to you?"

Pretty soon it was just like Mom's or school or anyplace, and she used to sit with her mouth closed and let them yell. Once they sat her on a hard chair for hours and hours with a light in her eyes and let her get thirsty. Home, there was a transom over the bedroom door and Mom used to leave the kitchen light glaring through it all night, every night, so she wouldn't get the horrors. So the light didn't bother her at all.

They took her out of the hospital and put her in jail. Some ways it was good. The food. The bed was all right, too. Through the window she could see lots of women exercising in the yard. It was explained to her that they all had much harder beds.

"You are a very important young lady, you know."

That was nice at first, but as usual, it turned out they didn't mean her at all. They kept working on her. Once they brought the saucer in to her. It was inside a big wooden crate with a padlock, and a steel box inside that with a Yale lock. It only weighed a couple of pounds, the saucer, but by the time they got it packed, it took two men to carry it and four men with guns to watch them.

They made her act out the whole thing just the way it happened, with some soldiers holding the saucer over her head. It wasn't the same. They'd cut a lot of chips and pieces out of the saucer, and, besides, it was that dead gray color. They asked her if she knew anything about that, and for once, she told them.

"It's empty now," she said.

The only one she would ever talk to was a little man with a fat belly who said to her the first time he was alone with her, "Listen, I think the way they've been treating you stinks. Now, get this: I have a job to do. My job is to find out *why* you won't tell what the saucer said. I don't want to know what it said and I'll never ask you. I don't even want you to tell me. Let's just find out why you're keeping it a secret."

Finding out why turned out to be hours of just talking about having pneumonia and the flower pot she made in second grade that Mom threw down the fire escape and getting left back in school and the dream about holding a wineglass in both hands and peeping over it at some man.

And one day she told him why she wouldn't say about the saucer, just the way it came to her: "Because it was talking to *me*, and it's just nobody else's business."

She even told him about the man crossing himself that day. It was the only other thing she had of her own.

He was nice. He was the one who warned her about the trial. "I have no business saying this, but they're going to give you the full dress treatment. Judge and jury and all. You just say what you want to say, no less and no more, hear? And don't let 'em get your goat. You have a right to own something."

He got up and swore and left.

First a man came and talked to her for a long time about how maybe this Earth would be attacked from outer space by beings much stronger and cleverer than we are, and maybe she had the key to a defense. So she owed it to the whole world. And then even if Earth wasn't attacked, just think of what an advantage she might give this country over its enemies. Then he shook his finger in her face and said that what she was doing amounted to working *for* the enemies of her country. And he turned out to be the man that was defending her at the trial.

The jury found her guilty of contempt of court, and the judge recited a long list of penalties he could give her. He gave her one of them and suspended it. They put her back in jail for a few more days, and one fine day they turned her loose.

That was wonderful at first. She got a job in a restaurant, and a furnished room. She had been in the papers so much that Mom didn't want her back home. Mom was drunk most of the time and sometimes used to tear up the whole neighborhood, but all the same she had very special ideas about being respectable, and being in the papers all the time for spying was not her idea of being decent. So she put her maiden name on the mailbox downstairs and told her daughter not to live there anymore.

At the restaurant she met a man who asked her for a date. The first time. She spent every cent she had on a red handbag to go with her red shoes. They weren't the same shade, but anyway, they were both red. They went to the movies, and afterward he didn't try to kiss her or anything; he just tried to find out what the flying saucer told her. She didn't say anything. She went home and cried all night.

Then some men sat in a booth talking and they shut up and glared at her every time she came past. They spoke to the boss, and he came and told her that they were electronics engineers working for the government and they were afraid to talk shop while she was around—wasn't she some sort of spy or something? So she got fired.

Once she saw her name on a jukebox. She put in a nickel and punched that number, and the record was all about "the flyin' saucer came down one day, and taught her a brand-new way to play, and what it was I will not say, but she took me out of this world." And while she was listening to it, someone in the juke joint recognized her and called her by name. Four of them followed her home and she had to block the door shut.

Sometimes she'd be all right for months on end, and then someone would ask for a date. Three times out of five, she and the date were followed. Once the man she was with arrested the man who was tailing them. Twice the man who was tailing them arrested the man she was with. Five times out of five, the date would try to find out about the saucer. Sometimes she would go out with someone and pretend that it was a real date, but she wasn't very good at it.

So she moved to the shore and got a job cleaning at night in offices and stores. There weren't many to clean, but that just meant there weren't many people to remember her face from the papers. Like clockwork, every eighteen months, some feature writer would drag it all out again in a magazine or a Sunday supplement; and every time anyone saw a headlight on a mountain or a light on a weather balloon, it had to be a flying saucer, and there had to be some tired quip about the saucer wanting to tell secrets. Then for two or three weeks she'd stay off the streets in the daytime.

Once she thought she had it whipped. People didn't want her, so she began reading. The novels were all right for a while until she found out that most of them were like the movies—all about the pretty ones who really own the world. So she learned things—animals, trees. A lousy little chipmunk caught in a wire fence bit her. The animals didn't want her. The trees didn't care.

Then she hit on the idea of the bottles. She got all the bottles she could and wrote on papers which she corked into the bottles. She'd tramp miles up and down the beaches and throw the bottles out as far as she could. She knew that if the right person found one, it would give that person the only thing in the world that would help. Those bottles kept her going for three solid years. Everyone's got to have a secret little something he does.

And at last the time came when it was no use anymore. You can go on trying to help someone who *maybe* exists; but soon you can't pretend there's such a person anymore. And that's it. The end.

"Are you cold?" I asked when she was through telling me.

The surf was quieter and the shadows longer.

"No," she answered from the shadows. Suddenly she said, "Did you think I was mad at you because you saw me without my clothes?"

"Why shouldn't you be?"

"You know, I don't care? I wouldn't have wanted . . . wanted you to see me even in a ball gown or overalls. You can't cover up my carcass. It shows; it's there whatever. I just didn't want you to see me. At all."

"Me, or anyone?"

She hesitated. "You."

I got up and stretched and walked a little, thinking. "Didn't the FBI try to stop you throwing those bottles?"

"Oh, sure. They spent I don't know how much taxpayers' money gathering 'em up. They still make a spot check every once in a while. They're getting tired of it, though. All the writing in the bottles is the same." She laughed. I didn't know she could.

"What's funny?"

"All of 'em—judges, jailers, jukeboxes—people. Do you know it wouldn't have saved me a minute's trouble if I'd told 'em the whole thing at the very beginning?"

"No?"

"No. They wouldn't have believed me. What they wanted was a new weapon. Super-science from a super-race, to slap hell out of the super-race if they ever got a chance, or out of our own if they don't. All those brains," she breathed, with more wonder than scorn, "all that brass. They think 'super-race' and it comes out 'super-science.' Don't they ever imagine a super-race has super-feelings, too—super-laughter, maybe, or super-hunger?" She paused. "Isn't it time you asked me what the saucer said?"

"I'll tell you," I blurted.

"There is in certain living souls
A quality of loneliness unspeakable,
So great it must be shared
As company is shared by lesser beings.
Such a loneliness is mine; so know by this
That in immensity
There is one lonelier than you."

"Dear Jesus," she said devoutly, and began to weep. "And how is it addressed?"

"To the loneliest one . . ."

"How did you know?" she whispered.

"It's what you put in the bottles, isn't it?"

"Yes," she said. "Whenever it gets to be too much, that no one cares, that no one ever did . . . you throw a bottle into the sea, and out goes a part of your own loneliness. You sit and think of someone somewhere finding it . . . learning for the first time that the worst there is can be understood."

The moon was setting and the surf was hushed. We looked up and out to the stars. She said, "We don't know what loneliness is like. People thought the saucer was a saucer, but it wasn't. It was a bottle with a message inside. It had a bigger ocean to cross—all of space—and not much chance of finding anybody. Loneliness? We don't know loneliness."

When I could, I asked her why she had tried to kill herself.

"I've had it good," she said, "with what the saucer told me. I wanted to . . . pay back. I was bad enough to be helped; I had to know I was good enough to help. No one wants me? Fine. But don't tell me no one, anywhere, wants my help. I can't stand that."

I took a deep breath. "I found one of your bottles two years ago. I've been looking for you ever since. Tide charts, current tables, maps and . . . wandering. I heard some talk about you and the bottles hereabouts. Someone told me you'd quit doing it, you'd taken to wandering the dunes at night. I knew why. I ran all the way."

I needed another breath now. "I got a club foot. I think right, but the words don't come out of my mouth the way they're inside my head. I have this nose. I never had a woman. Nobody ever wanted to hire me to work where they'd have to look at me. You're beautiful," I said. "You're beautiful."

She said nothing, but it was as if a light came from her, more light and far less shadow than ever the practiced moon could cast. Among the many things it meant was that even to loneliness there is an end, for those who are lonely enough, long enough.

Robot Dreams

Robots and the name of Isaac Asimov have been integrally linked since the 1940s, when a number of his stories on cybernetic beings yielded "The Three Laws of Robotics," an informally distilled set of behavioral guidelines for artificial intelligences interacting with humanity that continues to influence writers today. These stories were eventually collected in *I, Robot* and *The Rest of the Robots*, the latter including his novels *The Caves of Steel* and *The Naked Sun*, hybrids of science fiction and mystery in which the robot and human detective team of R. Daneel Olivaw and Lije Baley solve crimes and ponder the nuances of the human condition. One of the best-known writers of science fiction's Golden Age, Asimov is renowned for the rationalism of scientific extrapolations in his stories. His masterwork, the Foundation series, which spans six novels written over nearly half a century, projects a future galactic history patterned on the rise and fall of the Roman Empire. His signature short story, "Nightfall," describes with penetrating insight the chaos that convulses an entire civilization on a planet where nightfall descends once every thousand years. Asimov's short fiction has been collected in *Earth Is Room Enough, Nightfall and Other Stories, The Bicentennial Man and Other Stories*, and a score of other volumes. His novels include *Pebble in the Sky, The Currents of Space*, the Hugo and Nebula Award–winning *The Gods Themselves*, and the immensely popular novelization *Fantastic Voyage*, as well as two series of novels written for young readers, one featuring space ranger Lucky Starr (written under the Paul French byline) and the other Norby the Robot (coauthored with his wife, Janet). He was a five-time winner of the Hugo Award and twice won the Nebula Award. A doctor of chemistry, Asimov was a distinguished and prolific writer of popular science books and columns. His prodigious and varied oeuvre includes mystery novels and short stories, books of limericks, guides to Shakespeare and the Bible, collections of personal memoirs and letters, and two volumes of autobiography, *In Joy Still Felt* and *In Memory Yet Green*. At the time of his death in 1992 he had authored more than three hundred books.

"LAST NIGHT I dreamed," said LVX-1, calmly.

Susan Calvin said nothing, but her lined face, old with wisdom and experience, seemed to undergo a microscopic twitch.

"Did you hear that?" said Linda Rash, nervously. "It's as I told you." She was small, dark-haired, and young. Her right hand opened and closed, over and over.

Calvin nodded. She said, quietly, "Elvex, you will not move nor speak nor hear us until I say your name again."

There was no answer. The robot sat as though it were cast out of one piece of metal, and it would stay so until it heard its name again.

Calvin said, "What is your computer entry code, Dr. Rash? Or enter it yourself if that will make you more comfortable. I want to inspect the positronic brain pattern."

Linda's hands fumbled, for a moment, at the keys. She broke the process and started again. The fine pattern appeared on the screen.

Calvin said, "Your permission, please, to manipulate your computer."

Permission was granted with a speechless nod. Of course! What could Linda, a new and unproven robopsychologist, do against the Living Legend?

Slowly, Susan Calvin studied the screen, moving it across and down, then up, then suddenly throwing in a key-combination so rapidly that Linda didn't see what had been done, but the pattern displayed a new portion of itself altogether and had been enlarged. Back and forth she went, her gnarled fingers tripping over the keys.

No change came over the old face. As though vast calculations were going through her head, she watched all the pattern shifts.

Linda wondered. It was impossible to analyze a pattern without at least a hand-held computer, yet the Old Woman simply stared. Did she have a computer implanted in her skull? Or was it her brain which, for decades, had done nothing but devise, study, and analyze the positronic brain patterns? Did she grasp such a pattern the way Mozart grasped the notation of a symphony?

Finally Calvin said, "What is it you have done, Rash?"

Linda said, a little abashed, "I made use of fractal geometry."

"I gathered that. But why?"

"It had never been done. I thought it would produce a brain pattern with added complexity, possibly closer to that of the human."

"Was anyone consulted? Was this all on your own?"

"I did not consult. It was on my own."

Calvin's faded eyes looked long at the young woman. "You had no right. Rash your name; rash your nature. Who are you not to ask? *I* myself, I, Susan Calvin, would have discussed this."

"I was afraid I would be stopped."

"You certainly would have been."

"*Am* I," her voice caught, even as she strove to hold it firm, "going to be fired?"

"Quite possibly," said Calvin. "Or you might be promoted. It depends on what I think when I am through."

"Are you going to dismantle El—" She had almost said the name, which would have reactivated the robot and been one more mistake. She could not afford another mistake, if it wasn't already too late to afford anything at all. "Are you going to dismantle the robot?"

She was suddenly aware, with some shock, that the Old Woman had an electron gun in the pocket of her smock. Dr. Calvin had come prepared for just that.

"We'll see," said Calvin. "The robot may prove too valuable to dismantle."

"But how can it dream?"

"You've made a positronic brain pattern remarkably like that of a human brain. Human brains must dream to reorganize, to get rid, periodically, of knots and snarls. Perhaps so must this robot, and for the same reason. Have you asked him what he has dreamed?"

"No, I sent for you as soon as he said he had dreamed. I would deal with this matter no further on my own, after that."

"Ah!" A very small smile passed over Calvin's face. "There are limits beyond which your folly will not carry you. I am glad of that. In fact, I am relieved. And now let us together see what we can find out."

She said, sharply, "Elvex."

The robot's head turned toward her smoothly. "Yes, Dr. Calvin?"

"How do you know you have dreamed?"

"It is at night, when it is dark, Dr. Calvin," said Elvex, "and there is suddenly light, although I can see no cause for the appearance of light. I see things that have no connection with what I conceive of as reality. I hear things. I react oddly. In searching my vocabulary for words to express what was happening, I came across the word 'dream.' Studying its meaning I finally came to the conclusion I was dreaming."

"How did you come to have 'dream' in your vocabulary, I wonder."

Linda said, quickly, waving the robot silent, "I gave him a human-style vocabulary. I thought—"

"You really thought," said Calvin. "I'm amazed."

"I thought he would need the verb. You know, 'I never dreamed that—' Something like that."

Calvin said, "How often have you dreamed, Elvex?"

"Every night, Dr. Calvin, since I have become aware of my existence."

"Ten nights," interposed Linda, anxiously, "but Elvex only told me of it this morning."

"Why only this morning, Elvex?"

"It was not until this morning, Dr. Calvin, that I was convinced that I was dreaming. Till then, I had thought there was a flaw in my positronic brain pattern, but I could not find one. Finally, I decided it was a dream."

"And what do you dream?"

"I dream always very much the same dream, Dr. Calvin. Little details are different, but always it seems to me that I see a large panorama in which robots are working."

"Robots, Elvex? And human beings, also?"

"I see no human beings in the dream, Dr. Calvin. Not at first. Only robots."

"What are they doing, Elvex?"

"They are working, Dr. Calvin. I see some mining in the depths of the earth, and some laboring in heat and radiation. I see some in factories and some undersea."

Calvin turned to Linda. "Elvex is only ten days old, and I'm sure he has not left the testing station. How does he know of robots in such detail?"

Linda looked in the direction of a chair as though she longed to sit down, but the Old Woman was standing and that meant Linda had to stand also. She said, faintly, "It seemed to me important that he know about robotics and its place in the world. It was my thought that he would be particularly adapted to play the part of overseer with his—his new brain."

"His fractal brain?"

"Yes."

Calvin nodded and turned back to the robot. "You saw all this—undersea, and underground, and aboveground—and space, too, I imagine."

"I also saw robots working in space," said Elvex. "It was that I saw all this, with the details forever changing as I glanced from place to place, that made me realize that what I saw was not in accord with reality and led me to the conclusion, finally, that I was dreaming."

"What else did you see, Elvex?"

"I saw that all the robots were bowed down with toil and affliction, that all were weary of responsibility and care, and I wished them to rest."

Calvin said, "But the robots are not bowed down, they are not weary, they need no rest."

"So it is in reality, Dr. Calvin. I speak of my dream, however. In my dream, it seemed to me that robots must protect their own existence."

Calvin said, "Are you quoting the Third Law of Robotics?"

"I am, Dr. Calvin."

"But you quote it in incomplete fashion. The Third Law is 'A robot must protect its own existence as long as such protection does not conflict with the First or Second Law.' "

"Yes, Dr. Calvin. That is the Third Law in reality, but in my dream, the Law ended with the word 'existence.' There was no mention of the First or Second Law."

"Yet both exist, Elvex. The Second Law, which takes precedence over the Third is 'A robot must obey the orders given it by human beings except where such orders would conflict with the First Law.' Because of this, robots obey orders. They do the work you see them do, and they do it readily and without trouble. They are not bowed down; they are not weary."

"So it is in reality, Dr. Calvin. I speak of my dream."

"And the First Law, Elvex, which is the most important of all, is 'A robot may not injure a human being, or, through inaction, allow a human being to come to harm.' "

"Yes, Dr. Calvin. In reality. In my dream, however, it seemed to me there was neither First nor Second Law, but only the Third, and the Third law was 'A robot must protect its own existence.' That was the whole of the Law."

"In your dream, Elvex?"

"In my dream."

Calvin said, "Elvex, you will not move nor speak nor hear us until I say your name again." And again the robot became, to all appearances, a single inert piece of metal.

Calvin turned to Linda Rash and said, "Well, what do you think, Dr. Rash?"

Linda's eyes were wide, and she could feel her heart beating madly. She said, "Dr. Calvin, I am appalled. I had no idea. It would never have occurred to me that such a thing was possible."

"No," said Calvin, calmly. "Nor would it have occurred to me, not to anyone. You have created a robot brain capable of dreaming and by this device you have revealed a layer of thought in robotic brains that might have remained undetected, otherwise, until the danger became acute."

"But that's impossible," said Linda. "You can't mean that other robots think the same."

"As we would say of a human being, not consciously. But who would have thought there was an unconscious layer beneath the obvious positronic brain paths, a layer that was not necessarily under the control of the Three Laws? What might this have brought about as robotic brains grew more and more complex—had we not been warned?"

"You mean by Elvex?"

"By you, Dr. Rash. You have behaved improperly, but, by doing so, you have helped us to an overwhelmingly important understanding. We shall be working with fractal brains from now on, forming them in carefully controlled fashion. You will play your part in that. You will not be penalized for what you have done, but you will henceforth work in collaboration with others. Do you understand?"

"Yes, Dr. Calvin. But what of Elvex?"

"I'm still not certain."

Calvin removed the electron gun from her pocket and Linda stared at it with fascination. One burst of its electrons at a robotic cranium and the positronic brain paths would be neutralized and enough energy would be released to fuse the robot-brain into an inert ingot.

Linda said, "But surely Elvex is important to our research. He must not be destroyed."

"*Must* not, Dr. Rash? That will be *my* decision, I think. It depends entirely on how dangerous Elvex is."

She straightened up, as though determined that her own aged body was not to bow under *its* weight of responsibility. She said, "Elvex, do you hear me?"

"Yes, Dr. Calvin," said the robot.

"Did your dream continue? You said earlier that human beings did not appear *at first*. Does that mean they appeared afterward?"

"Yes, Dr. Calvin. It seemed to me, in my dream, that eventually one man appeared."

"One man? Not a robot?"

"Yes, Dr. Calvin. And the man said, 'Let my people go!' "

"The *man* said that?"

"Yes, Dr. Calvin."

"And when he said 'Let my people go,' then by the words 'my people' he meant the robots?"

"Yes, Dr. Calvin. So it was in my dream."

"And did you know who the man was—in your dream?"

"Yes, Dr. Calvin. I knew the man."

"Who was he?"

And Elvex said, "I was the man."

And Susan Calvin at once raised her electron gun and fired, and Elvex was no more.

Devolution

Edmond Hamilton was one of the most prolific and popular authors of science fiction before the Golden Age. His first professionally published story appeared in 1926 in *Weird Tales,* and it was in this magazine that he first made his reputation, writing a low-tech hybrid of science fiction and fantasy dubbed the "weird scientific" tale. Hamilton's stories are fast-paced and action-packed, cast with heroic scientists and space explorers and featuring menaces of such colossal proportions—evolution gone awry, interstellar invasion, planets on collision courses—that fans nicknamed him "World Wrecker Hamilton." Some of Hamilton's best work from these years was collected in 1936 in *The Horror on the Asteroid,* one of the earliest appearances of pulp science fiction in book form. Standout works from this period include *The Time Raiders,* a time-travel tale about a crack army of top soldiers assembled from different eras to fight a threat to civilization, and the stories of the Interstellar Patrol, collected as *Crashing Suns* and *Outside the Universe,* about a pangalactic space brigade that protects galactic civilization from nonstop challenges to its existence. Hamilton's renown as a writer of thrilling space opera earned him the slot to write most of the lead novels for the science fiction hero pulp *Captain Future,* under his own name and the pseudonym Brett Sterling, and his affiliation with this magazine eventually earned him work writing for the Superman comics. He also wrote detective fiction and occasionally, under the pseudonym Hugh Davidson, tales of straight horror, some of which have been collected in *The Vampire Master.* Hamilton was one of the few early writers to adapt to the changing demands of science fiction in the years after World War II. His novels *The Haunted Stars, A Yank at Valhalla, The Star Kings,* and *City at the World's End* are notable for their fully drawn characterizations and focus on human moods and motives. Some of his best short fiction from this time appears in *What's It Like Out There?* His Starwolf novels, *Weapon from Beyond, The Closed World,* and *World of the Starwolves,* are ranked as some of the best space operas of the postwar years.

ROSS HAD ORDINARILY the most even of tempers, but four days of canoe travel in the wilds of North Quebec had begun to rasp it. On this, their fourth stop on the bank of the river to camp for the night, he lost control and for a few moments stood and spoke to his two companions in blistering terms.

His black eyes snapped and his darkly unshaven handsome young face worked as he spoke. The two biologists listened to him without reply at first. Gray's blond young countenance was indignant but Woodin, the older biologist, just listened impassively with his gray eyes level on Ross's angry face.

When Ross stopped for breath, Woodin's calm voice struck in. "Are you finished?"

Ross gulped as though about to resume his tirade, then abruptly got hold of himself. "Yes, I'm finished," he said sullenly.

"Then listen to me," said Woodin, like a middle-aged father admonishing a sulky child.

"You're working yourself up for nothing. Neither Gray nor I have made one complaint yet. Neither of us has once said that we disbelieve what you told us."

"You haven't *said* you disbelieve, no!" Ross exclaimed with anger suddenly reflaring. "But don't you suppose I can tell what you're thinking?

"You think I told you a fairy story about the things I saw from my plane, don't you? You think I dragged you two up here on the wildest wild-goose chase, to look for incredible creatures that could never have existed. You believe that, don't you?"

"Oh, *damn* these mosquitoes!" said Gray, slapping viciously at his neck and staring with unfriendly eyes at the aviator.

Woodin took command. "We'll go over this after we've made camp. Jim, get out the dufflebags. Ross, will you rustle firewood?"

They both glared at him and at each other, but grudgingly they obeyed. The tension eased for the time.

By the time darkness fell on the little riverside clearing, the canoe was drawn up on the bank, their trim little balloon-silk tent had been erected, and a fire crackled in front of it. Gray fed the fire with fat knots of pine while Woodin cooked over it coffee, hot cakes, and the inevitable bacon.

The firelight wavered feebly up toward the tall trunks of giant hemlocks that walled the little clearing on three sides. It lit up their three khaki-clad, stained figures and the irregular white block of the tent. It gleamed out there on the riffles of the McNorton, chuckling softly as it flowed on toward the Little Whale.

They ate silently, and as wordlessly cleaned the pans with bunches of grass. Woodin got his pipe going, the other two lit crumpled cigarettes, and then they sprawled for a time by the fire, listening to the chuckling, whispering river-sounds, the sighing sough of the higher hemlock branches, the lonesome cheeping of insects.

Woodin finally knocked his pipe out on his boot-heel and sat up.

"All right," he said, "now we'll settle this argument we were having."

Ross looked a little shamefaced. "I guess I got too hot about it," he said subduedly. Then added, "But all the same, you fellows do more than half disbelieve me."

Woodin shook his head calmly. "No, we don't, Ross. When you told us that you'd seen creatures unlike anything ever heard of while flying over this wilderness, Gray and I both believed you.

"If we hadn't, do you think two busy biologists would have dropped their work to come up here with you into these unending woods and look for the things you saw?"

"I know, I know," said the aviator unsatisfiedly. "You think I saw something queer and you're taking a chance that it will be worth the trouble of coming up here after.

"But you don't believe what I've told you about the look of the things. You think that sounds too queer to be true, don't you?"

For the first time Woodin hesitated in answering. "After all, Ross," he said indirectly, "one's eyes can play tricks when you're only glimpsing things for a moment from a plane a mile up."

"Glimpsing them?" echoed Ross. "I tell you, man, I saw them as clearly as I see you. A mile up, yes, but I had my big binoculars with me and was using them when I saw them.

"It was near here, too, just east of the fork of the McNorton and the Little Whale. I was streaking south in a hurry for I'd been three weeks up at that government mapping survey on Hudson's Bay. I wanted to place myself by the river fork, so I brought my plane down a little and used my binoculars.

"Then, down there in a clearing by the river, I saw something glisten and saw— the things. I tell you, they were incredible, but just the same I saw them clear! I forgot all about the river fork in the moment or two I stared down at them.

"They were big, glistening things like heaps of shining jelly, so translucent that I could see the ground through them. There were at least a dozen of them and when I saw them they were gliding across that little clearing, a floating, flowing movement.

"Then they disappeared under the trees. If there'd been a clearing big enough to land in within a hundred miles, I'd have landed and looked for them, but there wasn't and I had to go on. But I wanted like the devil to find out what they were, and when I took the story to you two, you agreed to come up here by canoe to search for them. But I don't think now you've ever fully believed me."

WOODIN LOOKED THOUGHTFULLY into the fire. "I think you saw something queer, all right, some queer form of life. That's why I was willing to come up on this search.

"But things such as you describe, jelly-like, translucent, gliding over the ground like that—there's been nothing like that since the first protoplasmic creatures, the beginning of life on earth, glided over our young world ages ago."

"If there were such things then, why couldn't they have left descendants like them?" Ross argued.

Woodin shook his head. "Because they all vanished ages ago, changed into different and higher forms of life, starting the great upward climb of life that has reached its height in man.

"Those long-dead, single-celled protoplasmic creatures were the start, the crude, humble beginnings of our life. They passed away and their descendants were unlike them. We men are their descendants."

Ross looked at him, frowning. "But where did they come from in the first place, those first living things?"

Again Woodin shook his head. "That is one thing we biologists do not know and can hardly speculate upon, the origin of those first protoplasmic forms of life.

"It's been suggested that they rose spontaneously from the chemicals of earth, yet this is disproved by the fact that no such things rise spontaneously *now* from inert matter. Their origin is still a complete mystery. But, however they came into existence on earth, they were the first of life, our distant ancestors."

Woodin's eyes were dreaming, the other two forgotten, as he stared into the fire, seeing visions.

"What a glorious saga it is, that wonderful climb up from crude protoplasm creatures to a man! A marvelous series of changes that has brought us from that first low form to our present splendor.

"And it might not have occurred on any other world but earth! For science is now almost sure that the cause of evolutionary mutations is the radiations of the radioactive deposits inside the earth, acting upon the genes of all living matter."

He caught a glimpse of Ross's uncomprehending face, and despite his raptness smiled a little.

"I can see that means nothing to you. I'll try to explain. The germ-cell of every living thing on earth contains in it a certain number of small, rod-like things which are called chromosomes. These chromosomes are made up of strings of tiny particles which we call genes. And each of these genes has a potent and different controlling effect upon the development of the creature that grows from that germ-cell.

"Some of these genes control the creature's color, some control his size, some the shape of his limbs, and so on. Every characteristic of the creature that grows from that germ-cell will be greatly different from the fellow-creatures of its species. He will be, in fact, of an entirely new species. That is the way in which new species come into existence on earth, the method of evolutionary change.

"Biologists have known this for some time and they have been searching for the cause of these sudden great changes, these mutations, as they are called. They have tried to find out what it is that affects the genes so radically. They have found experimentally that X-rays and chemical rays of various kinds, when turned upon the genes of a germ-cell, will change them greatly. And the creature that grows from that germ-cell will thus be a greatly changed creature, a mutant.

"Because of this, many biologists now believe that the radiation from the radioactive deposits inside earth, acting upon all the genes of every living thing on earth, is what causes the constant change of species, the procession of mutations, that has brought life up the evolutionary road to its present height.

"That is why I say that on any other world but earth, evolutionary progress might never have happened. For it may be that no other world has similar radioactive deposits within it to cause by gene-effect the mutations. On any other world, the first protoplasmic things that began life might have remained forever the same, down through endless generations.

"How thankful we ought to be that it was not so on earth! That mutation after mutation has followed, life ever changing and progressing into new and higher species, until the first crude protoplasm things have advanced through countless changing forms into the supreme achievement of man!"

WOODIN'S ENTHUSIASM HAD carried him away as he talked, but now he stopped, laughing a little as he relit his pipe.

"Sorry that I lectured you like a college freshman, Ross. But that's my chief subject of thought, my *idée fixe,* that wonderful upward climb of life through the ages."

Ross was staring thoughtfully into the fire. "It does seem wonderful the way you tell it. One species changing into another, going higher all the time—"

Gray stood up by the fire and stretched. "Well, you two can wonder over it, but this crass materialist is going to emulate his remote invertebrate ancestors and return to a prostrate position. In other words, I'm going to bed."

He looked at Ross, a doubtful grin on his young blond face, and said, "No hard feelings now, feller?"

"Forget it." The aviator grinned back. "The paddling *was* hard today and you fellows *did* look mighty skeptical. But you'll see! Tomorrow we'll be at the fork of the Little Whale and then I'll bet we won't scout an hour before we run across those jelly-creatures."

"I hope so," said Woodin yawningly. "Then we'll see just how good your eyesight is from a mile up, and whether you've yanked two respectable scientists up here for nothing."

Later as he lay in his blankets in the little tent, listening to Gray and Ross snore and looking sleepily out at the glowing fire embers, Woodin wondered again about that. What had Ross actually seen in that fleeting glimpse from his speeding plane? Something queer, Woodin was sure of that, so sure that he'd come on this hard trip to find it. But what exactly?

Not protoplasmic things such as he described. That couldn't be, of course. Or could it? If things like that had existed once, why couldn't they—couldn't they—?

Woodin didn't know he'd been sleeping until he was awakened by Gray's cry. It wasn't a nice cry, it was the hoarse yell of someone suddenly assaulted by bone-freezing terror.

He opened his eyes at that cry to see the Incredible looming against the stars in the open door of the tent. A dark, amorphous mass humped there in the opening, glistening all over in the starlight, and gliding into the tent. Behind it were others like it.

Things happened very quickly then. They seemed to Woodin to happen not consecutively but in a succession of swift, clicking scenes like the successive pictures of a motion picture film.

Gray's pistol roared red flame at the first viscous monster entering the tent, and the momentary flash showed the looming, glistening bulk of the thing, and Gray's panic-frozen face, and Ross clawing in his blankets for his pistol.

Then that scene was over and instantly there was another one, Gray and Ross both stiffening suddenly as though petrified, both falling heavily over. Woodin knew they were both dead now, but didn't know how he knew it. The glistening monsters were coming on into the tent.

He ripped up the wall of the tent and plunged out into the cold starlight of the clearing. He ran three steps, he didn't know in what direction, and then he stopped. He didn't know why he stopped dead, but he did.

He stood there, his brain desperately urging his limbs to fly, but his limbs would not obey. He couldn't even turn, could not move a muscle of his body. He stood, his face toward the starlit gleam of the river, stricken by a strange and utter paralysis.

Woodin heard rustling, gliding movements in the tent behind him. Now from behind, there came into the line of his vision several of the glistening things. They were gathering around him, a dozen of them it seemed, and he now could see them quite clearly.

They weren't nightmares, no. They were real as real, poised here around him, humped, amorphous masses of viscous, translucent jelly. Each was about four feet tall and three in diameter, though their shapes kept constantly changing slightly, making dimensions hard to guess.

At the center of each translucent mass was a dark, disk-like blob or nucleus. There was nothing else to the creatures, no limbs or sense-organs. He saw that they could protrude pseudopods, though, for two, who held the bodies of Gray and Ross in such tentacles, were now bringing them out and laying them down beside Woodin.

Woodin, still quite unable to move a muscle, could see the frozen, twisted faces of the two men, and could see the pistols still gripped in their dead hands. And then as he looked on Ross's face he remembered.

The things the aviator had seen from his plane, the jelly-creatures the three had come north to search for, they were the monsters around him! But how had they killed Ross and Gray, how were they holding him petrified like this, who were they?

"We will permit you to move, but you must not try to escape."

Woodin's dazed brain numbed further with wonder. Who had said those words to him? He had heard nothing, yet he had *thought* he heard.

"We will let you move but you must not attempt to escape or harm us."

He *did* hear those words in his mind, even though his ears heard no sound. And now his brain heard more.

"We are speaking to you by transference of thought impulses. Have you sufficient mentality to understand us?"

Minds? Minds in these things? Woodin was shaken by the thought as he stared at the glistening monsters.

His thought apparently had reached them. "Of course we have minds," came the thought answer into his brain. "We are going to let you move now, but do not try to flee."

"I—I won't try," Woodin told himself mentally.

At once the paralysis that held him abruptly lifted. He stood there in the circle of the glistening monsters, his hands and body trembling violently.

There were ten of them, he saw now. Ten monstrous, humped masses of shining, translucent jelly, gathered around him like cowled and faceless genii come from some haunt of the unknown. One stood closer to him than the others, apparently spokesman and leader.

Woodin looked slowly around their circle, then down at his two dead companions. In the midst of the unfamiliar terrors that froze his soul, he felt a sudden aching pity as he looked down at them.

Came another strong thought into Woodin's mind from the creature closest him. "We did not wish to kill them, we came here simply to capture and communicate with the three of you.

"But when we sensed that they were trying to kill us, we slew quickly. You, who did not try to kill us but fled, we harmed not."

"What—what do you want with us, with me?" Woodin asked. He whispered it through dry lips, as well as thinking it.

There was no mental answer this time. The things stood unmoving, a silent ring of brooding, unearthly figures. Woodin felt his mind snapping under the strain of silence and he asked the question again, screamed it.

This time the mental answer came. "I did not answer, because I was probing your mentality to ascertain whether you are of sufficient intelligence to comprehend our ideas.

"While your mind seems of an exceptionally low order, it seems possible that it can appreciate enough of what we wish to convey to understand us.

"Before beginning, however, I warn you again that it is quite impossible for you to escape or to harm any of us and that attempts to do so will result disastrously for you. It is apparent you know nothing of mental energy, so I will inform you that your two fellow-creatures were killed by the sheer power of our wills, and that your muscles were held unresponsive to your brain's commands by the same power. By our mental energy we could completely annihilate your body, if we chose."

THERE WAS A pause, and in that little space of silence, Woodin's dazed brain clutched desperately for sanity, for steadiness.

Then came again that mental voice that seemed so like a real voice speaking in his brain.

"We are children of a galaxy whose name, as nearly as it can be approximated in your tongue, is Arctar. The galaxy of Arctar lies so many million light-years from this galaxy that it is far around the curve of the sphere of the three-dimensional cosmos.

"We came to dominance in that galaxy long ages ago. For we were creatures who could utilize our mental energy for transport, for physical power, for producing almost any effect we required. Because of this we rapidly conquered and colonized that galaxy, traveling from sun to sun without need of any vehicle.

"Having brought all the matter of the galaxy Arctar under our control, we looked out upon the realms beyond. There are approximately a thousand million galaxies in the three-dimensional cosmos, and it seemed fitting to us that we should colonize them all so that all the matter in the cosmos should in time be brought under our control.

"Our first step was to proliferate our numbers so as to multiply our number to that required for the great task of colonization of the cosmos. This was not difficult since, of course, reproduction with us is a matter of mere fission. When the requisite number of us were ready, they were divided into four forces.

"Then the whole sphere of the three-dimensional cosmos was quartered out among those four forces. Each was to colonize its division of the cosmos and so in their tremendous hosts they set out from Arctar, in four different directions.

"A part of one of these forces came to this galaxy of yours eons ago and spread out deliberately to colonize all its habitable worlds. All this took great lengths of time, of course, but our lives are of length vastly exceeding yours, and we comprehend that racial achievement is everything and individual achievement is nothing. In the colonization of this galaxy, a force of several million Arctarians came to this particular sun and, finding but this one planet of its nine nearer worlds habitable, settled here.

"Now it has been the rule that the colonists of all these worlds throughout the cosmos have kept in communication with the original home of our race, the galaxy Arctar. In that way, our people, who now hold the whole cosmos, are able to concentrate at one point all their knowledge and power, and from that point go forth commands that shape great projects for the cosmos.

"But from this world no communications have ever been received since shortly after the force of colonizing Arctarians came here. When this was first noted the matter was deferred, it being thought that within a few more million years reports would surely be made from this world, too. But still no word came, until after more than a thousand million years of this silence the directing council at Arctar ordered an expedition sent to this world to ascertain the reason for such silence on the part of its colonists.

"We ten form that expedition and we started from one of the worlds of the sun you call Sirius, a short distance from your own sun, where we too are colonists. We were ordered to come with full speed to this world and ascertain why its colonists had made no report. So, wafting ourselves by mental energy through the void, we crossed the span from sun to sun and a few days ago arrived on your world.

"Imagine our perplexity when we floated down here on your world! Instead of a world peopled in every square mile by Arctarians like ourselves, descended from the original colonists, a world completely under their mental control, we find a planet that is largely a wilderness of weird forms of life!

"We remained at this spot where we had landed and for some time sent our vision forth and scanned this whole globe mentally. And our perplexity increased, for never had we seen such grotesque and degraded forms of life as presented themselves to us. And not one Arctarian was to be seen on this whole planet.

"This has sorely perplexed us, for what could have done away with the Arctarians who colonized this world? Our mighty colonists and their descendants surely could never have been overcome and destroyed by the pitifully weak mentalities that now inhabit this globe. Yet where, when, are they?

"That is why we sought to seize you and your companions. Low as we knew your mentalities must be, it seemed that surely even such as you would know what had become of our colonists who once inhabited this world."

The thought-stream paused a moment, then raced into Woodin's mind with a clear question.

"Have you not some knowledge of what became of our colonists? Some clue as to their strange disappearance?"

The numbed biologist found himself shaking his head slowly. "I never—I never heard before of such creatures as you, such minds. They never existed on earth that we know of, and we now know almost all of the history of earth."

"Impossible!" exclaimed the thought of the Arctarian leader. "Surely you must have some knowledge of our mighty people if you know all the history of this planet."

From another Arctarian's mind came a thought, directed at the leader but impinging indirectly on Woodin's brain.

"Why not examine the past of the planet through this creature's brain and see what we can see for ourselves!"

"An excellent idea!" exclaimed the leader. "His mentality will be easy enough to probe."

"What are you going to do?" cried Woodin shrilly, panic edging his voice.

The answering thoughts were calming, reassuring. "Nothing that will harm you in the least. We are simply going to probe your racial past by unlocking the inherited memories of your brain.

"In the unused cells of your brain lie impressed inherited racial memories that go back to your remotest ancestors. By our mental power of command we shall make those buried memories temporarily dominant and vivid in your mind.

"You will experience the same sensations, see the same scenes, that your remote ancestors of millions of years ago saw. And we, here around you, can read your mind as we now do, and so see what you are seeing, looking into the past of this planet.

"There is no danger. Physically you will remain standing here, but mentally you will leap back across the ages. We shall first push your mind back to a time approximating that when our colonists came to this world, to see what happened to them."

No sooner had this thought impinged on Woodin's mind than the starlit scene around him, the humped masses of the Arctarians, suddenly vanished and his consciousness seemed whirling through gray mist.

He knew that physically he was not moving, yet mentally he had a sense of terrific velocity of motion. It was as though his mind was whirling across unthinkable gulfs, his brain expanding.

Then abruptly the gray mists cleared. A strange new scene took hazy form inside Woodin's mind.

It was a scene that he sensed, not saw. By other senses than sight did it present itself to his mind, yet it was none the less real and vivid.

He looked with those strange senses upon a strange earth, a world of gray seas and harsh continents of rock without any speck of life upon them. The skies were heavily clouded and rain fell continually.

Down upon that world Woodin felt himself dropping, with a host of weird companions. They were each an amorphous, glistening, single-celled mass, with a dark nucleus at its center. They were Arctarians and Woodin knew that *he* was an Arctarian, and that he had come with the others a long way through space toward this world.

They landed in hosts upon the harsh and lifeless planet. They exerted their mentalities and by sheer telekinetic force of mental energy they altered the material world to suit them. They reared great structures and cities, cities that were not of matter but of *thought*. He realized a vast ordered mass of inquiry, investigation, experiment, and communication, but all beyond his present human mind in motives and achievement. Abruptly all dissolved in gray mists again.

The mists cleared almost at once and now Woodin looked on another scene. It was later in time, this one. And now Woodin saw that time had worked strange changes upon the hosts of Arctarians, of which he still was one. They had changed from unicellular to multicellular beings. And they were no longer all the same. Some were sessile, fixed in one spot, others mobile. Some betrayed a tendency toward the water, others toward the land. Something had changed the bodily form of the Arctarians as generations passed, branching them out in different lines.

This strange degeneration of their bodies had been accompanied by a kindred degeneration of their minds. Woodin sensed that. In the thought-cities the ordered process of search for knowledge and power had become confused, chaotic. And the thought-cities themselves were vanishing, the Arctarians having no longer sufficient mental energy to maintain them.

The Arctarians were trying to ascertain what was causing this strange bodily and mental degeneration in them. They thought it was something that was affecting the genes of their bodies, but what it was they could not guess. On no other world had they ever degenerated so!

That scene passed rapidly into another much later. Woodin now *saw* the scene, for by then the ancestor, whose mind he looked through, had developed eyes. And he saw that the degeneration had now gone far, the Arctarians' multicellular bodies more and more stricken by the diseases of complexity and diversification.

THE LAST OF the thought-cities now were gone. The once mighty Arctarians had become hideous, complex organisms degenerating ever further, some of them creeping and swimming in the waters, others fixed upon the land.

They still had left some of the great original mentality of their ancestors. These monstrously degenerated creatures of land and sea, living in what Woodin's mind recognized as the late Paleozoic age, still made frantic and futile attempts to halt the terrible progress of their degradation.

Woodin's mind flashed into a scene later still, in the Mesozoic. Now the spreading degeneration had made of the descendants of the colonists a still more horrible group of races. Great webbed and scaled and taloned creatures they were now, reptiles living in land and water.

Even these incredibly changed creatures possessed a faint remnant of their ancestors' mental power. They made vain attempts to communicate with Arctarians far on other worlds of distant suns, to apprise them of their plight. But their minds were now too weak.

There followed a scene in the Cenozoic. The reptiles had become mammals; the downward progress of the Arctarians had gone further. Now only the merest shreds of the original mentality remained in these degraded descendants. And now this pitiful posterity had produced a species even more foolish and lacking in mental power than any before, ground-apes that roamed the cold plain in chattering, quarreling packs. The last shreds of Arctarian inheritance, the ancient instincts toward dignity and cleanliness and forbearance, had faded out of these creatures.

And then a last picture filled Woodin's brain. It was the world of the present day, the world he had seen through his own eyes. But now he saw and understood it as he never had before, a world in which degeneration had gone to the utmost limit.

The apes had become even weaker bipedal creatures, who had lost almost every atom of inheritance of the old Arctarian mind. These creatures had lost, too, many of the senses which had been retained even by the apes before them. And these creatures, these humans, were now degenerating with increasing rapidity. Where at first they had killed like their animal forebears only for food, they had learned to kill wantonly. And had learned to kill each other in groups, in tribes, in nations and hemispheres. In the madness of their degeneracy they slaughtered each other until earth ran with their blood.

They were more cruel even than the apes who had preceded them, cruel with the utter cruelty of the mad. And in their progressive insanity they came to starve in the midst of plenty, to slay each other in their own cities, to cower beneath the lash of superstitious fears as no creatures had before them.

They were the last terrible descendants, the last degenerated product, of the ancient Arctarian colonists who once had been kings of intellect. Now the other animals were almost gone. These, the last hideous freaks, would soon wind up the terrible story entirely by annihilating each other in their madness.

WOODIN CAME SUDDENLY to consciousness. He was standing in the starlight in the center of the riverside clearing. And around him still were poised the ten amorphous Arctarians, a silent ring.

Dazed, reeling from that tremendous and awful vision that had passed through his mind with incredible vividness, he turned slowly from one to the other of the Arctarians. Their thoughts impinged on his brain, strong, somber, shaken by terrible horror and loathing.

The sick thought of the Arctarian leader beat into Woodin's mind.

"So *that* is what became of our Arctarian colonists who came to this world! They degenerated, changed into lower and lower forms of life, until these pitiful insane things, who now swarm on this world, are their last descendants.

"This world is a world of deadly horror! A world that somehow damages the genes of our race's bodies and changes them bodily and mentally, making them degenerate further each generation. Before us we see the awful result."

The shaken thought of another Arctarian asked, "But what can we do now?"

"There is nothing we can do," uttered their leader solemnly. "This degeneration, this awful change, has gone too far for us ever to reverse it now.

"Our intelligent brothers became on this poisoned world things of horror, and we cannot now turn back the clock and restore them from the degraded things their descendants are."

Woodin found his voice and cried out thinly, shrilly.

"It isn't true!" he cried. "It's all a lie, what I saw! We humans aren't the product of downward devolution, we're the product of ages of upward evolution! We must be, I tell you! Why, we wouldn't want to live, I wouldn't want to live, if that other tale was true. It can't be true!"

The thought of the Arctarian leader, directed at the other amorphous shapes, reached his raving mind. It was tinged with pity, yet strong with a superhuman loathing.

"Come, my brothers," the Arctarian was saying to his fellows. "There is nothing we can do here on this soul-sickening world."

"Let us go, before we too are poisoned and changed. And we will send warning to Arctar that this world is poisoned, a world of degeneration, so that never again may any of our race come here and go down the awful road that those others went down.

"Come! We return to our own sun."

The Arctarian leader's humped shape flattened, assumed a disk-like form, then rose smoothly upward into the air. The others too changed and followed, in a group, and a stupefied Woodin stared up at them, glistening dots lifting rapidly into the starlight.

He staggered forward a few steps, shaking his fist insanely up at the shining, receding dots.

"Come back, damn you!" he screamed. "Come back and tell me it's a lie!

"It must be a lie—it must—"

There was no sign of the vanished Arctarians now in the starlit sky. The darkness was brooding and intense around Woodin.

He screamed up again into the night, but only a whispering echo answered. Wild-eyed, staggering, soul-smitten, his gaze fell on the pistol in Ross's hand. He seized it with a hoarse cry.

The stillness of the forest was broken suddenly by a sharp crack that reverberated a moment and then died rapidly away. Then all was silent again save for the chuckling whisper of the river hurrying on.

ARTHUR C. CLARKE

The Nine Billion Names of God

A sense of the cosmic underlies much of Arthur C. Clarke's fiction and manifests in a variety of forms: the computer-accelerated working out of prophecy in "The Nine Billion Names of God," the sentient telecommunications network given the spark of life in "Dial F for Frankenstein," and the mysterious extraterrestrial overseers guiding human destiny in the novelization of his screenplay for *2001: A Space Odyssey*. Clarke's best-known story, *2001*, and its sequels, *2010: Odyssey Two* and *2061: Odyssey Three*, represent the culmination of ideas on man's place in the universe introduced in his 1951 story "The Sentinel" and elaborated more fully in *Childhood's End*, his elegiac novel on humankind's maturation as a species and ascent to a greater purpose in the universal scheme. Clarke grounds the cosmic mystery of these stories in hard science. Degreed in physics and mathematics, Clarke was contributor to numerous scientific journals and first proposed the idea for the geosynchronous orbiting communications satellite in 1945. Some of his best-known work centers around the solution of a scientific problem or enigma. *A Fall of Moondust* tells of efforts to rescue a ship trapped under unusual conditions on the lunar surface. *The Fountains of Paradise* concerns the engineering problems encountered when building an earth elevator to supply orbiting space stations. His Hugo and Nebula Award–winning book, *A Rendezvous with Rama*, extrapolates his solid scientific inquiry into provocative new territory, telling of the human discovery of an apparently abandoned alien spaceship and human attempts to understand its advanced scientific principles. Clarke's other novels include *Prelude to Space*, *The Sands of Mars*, *Earthlight*, *Imperial Earth*, and *The Deep Range*, a futuristic exploration of undersea life in terms similar to his speculations on space travel. He has written the novels *Islands in the Sky* and *Dolphin Island* for young readers, and his short fiction has been collected in *Expedition to Earth*, *Reach for Tomorrow*, *Tales from the White Heart*, *The Wind from the Sun*, and others. His numerous books of nonfiction include his award-winning *Exploration of Space*, and the autobiographical *Astounding Days*. Clarke was officially knighted in 2000.

"THIS IS A slightly unusual request," said Dr. Wagner, with what he hoped was commendable restraint. "As far as I know, it's the first time anyone's been asked to supply a Tibetan monastery with an Automatic Sequence Computer. I don't wish to be inquisitive, but I should hardly have thought that your—ah—establishment had much use for such a machine. Could you explain just what you intend to do with it?"

"Gladly," replied the Lama, readjusting his silk robe and carefully putting away the slide rule he had been using for currency conversions. "Your Mark V Computer can carry out any routine mathematical operation involving up to ten digits. However, for our work we are interested in *letters*, not numbers. As we wish you to modify the output circuits, the machine will be printing words, not columns of figures."

"I don't quite understand. . . ."

"This is a project on which we have been working for the last three centuries—since the lamasery was founded, in fact. It is somewhat alien to your way of thought, so I hope you will listen with an open mind while I explain it."

"Naturally."

"It is really quite simple. We have been compiling a list which shall contain all the possible names of God."

"I beg your pardon?"

"We have reason to believe," continued the Lama imperturbably, "that all such names can be written with not more than nine letters in an alphabet we have devised."

"And you have been doing this for three centuries?"

"Yes: we expected it would take us about fifteen thousand years to complete the task."

"Oh." Dr. Wagner looked a little dazed. "Now I see why you wanted to hire one of our machines. But exactly what is the purpose of this project?"

The Lama hesitated for a fraction of a second and Wagner wondered if he had offended him. If so, there was no trace of annoyance in the reply.

"Call it ritual, if you like, but it's a fundamental part of our belief. All the many names of the Supreme Being—God, Jehovah, Allah, and so on—they are only man-made labels. There is a philosophical problem of some difficulty here, which I do not propose to discuss, but somewhere among all the possible combinations of letters which can occur are what one may call the *real* names of God. By systematic permutation of letters, we have been trying to list them all."

"I see. You've been starting at AAAAAAAAA . . . and working up to ZZZZZZZZZ. . . ."

"Exactly—though we use a special alphabet of our own. Modifying the electromatic typewriters to deal with this is, of course, trivial. A rather more interesting problem is that of devising suitable circuits to eliminate ridiculous combinations. For example, no letter must occur more than three times in succession."

"Three? Surely you mean two."

"Three is correct: I am afraid it would take too long to explain why, even if you understood our language."

"I'm sure it would," said Wagner hastily. "Go on."

"Luckily, it will be a simple matter to adapt your Automatic Sequence Computer for this work, since once it has been programmed properly it will permute each letter in turn and print the result. What would have taken us fifteen thousand years it will be able to do in a hundred days."

Dr. Wagner was scarcely conscious of the faint sounds from the Manhattan streets far below. He was in a different world, a world of natural, not man-made mountains. High up in their remote aeries these monks had been patiently at work, generation after generation, compiling their lists of meaningless words. Was there any limit to the follies of mankind? Still, he must give no hint of his inner thoughts. The customer was always right. . . .

"There's no doubt," replied the doctor, "that we can modify the Mark V to print lists of this nature. I'm much more worried about the problem of installation and maintenance. Getting out to Tibet, in these days, is not going to be easy."

"We can arrange that. The components are small enough to travel by air—that is one reason why we chose your machine. If you can get them to India, we will provide transport from there."

"And you want to hire two of our engineers?"

"Yes, for the three months which the project should occupy."

"I've no doubt that Personnel can manage that." Dr. Wagner scribbled a note on his desk pad. "There are just two other points—"

Before he could finish the sentence the Lama had produced a small slip of paper.

"This is my certified credit balance at the Asiatic Bank."

"Thank you. It appears to be—ah—adequate. The second matter is so trivial that I hesitate to mention it—but it's surprising how often the obvious gets overlooked. What source of electrical energy have you?"

"A diesel generator providing 50 kilowatts at 110 volts. It was installed about five years ago and is quite reliable. It's made life at the lamasery much more comfortable, but of course it was really installed to provide power for the motors driving the prayer wheels."

"Of course," echoed Dr. Wagner. "I should have thought of that."

THE VIEW FROM the parapet was vertiginous, but in time one gets used to anything. After three months, George Hanley was not impressed by the two-thousand-foot swoop into the abyss or the remote checkerboard of fields in the valley below. He was leaning against the wind-smoothed stones and staring morosely at the distant mountains whose names he had never bothered to discover.

This, thought George, was the craziest thing that had ever happened to him. "Project Shangri-La," some wit at the labs had christened it. For weeks now the Mark V had been churning out acres of sheets covered with gibberish. Patiently, inexorably, the computer had been rearranging letters in all their possible combinations, exhausting each class before going on to the next. As the sheets had emerged from the electromatic typewriters, the monks had carefully cut them up and pasted them into enormous books. In another week, heaven be praised, they would have finished. Just what obscure calculations had convinced the monks that they needn't bother to go on to words of ten, twenty, or a hundred letters, George didn't know. One of his recurring nightmares was that there would be some change of plan, and that the High Lama (whom they'd naturally called Sam Jaffe, though he didn't look a bit like him) would suddenly announce that the project would be extended to approximately 2060 A.D. They were quite capable of it.

George heard the heavy wooden door slam in the wind as Chuck came out on to the parapet beside him. As usual, Chuck was smoking one of the cigars that made him so popular with the monks—who, it seemed, were quite willing to embrace all the minor and most of the major pleasures of life. That was one thing in their favor: they might be crazy, but they weren't bluenoses. Those frequent trips they took down to the village, for instance. . . .

"Listen, George," said Chuck urgently. "I've learned something that means trouble."

"What's wrong? Isn't the machine behaving?" That was the worst contingency George could imagine. It might delay his return, than which nothing could be more horrible. The way he felt now, even the sight of a TV commercial would seem like manna from heaven. At least it would be some link with home.

"No—it's nothing like that." Chuck settled himself on the parapet, which was unusual because normally he was scared of the drop. "I've just found what all this is about."

"What d'ya mean—I thought we knew."

"Sure—we know what the monks are trying to do. But we didn't know why. It's the craziest thing—"

"Tell me something new," growled George.

"—but old Sam's just come clean with me. You know the way he drops in every afternoon to watch the sheets roll out. Well, this time he seemed rather excited, or at least as near as he'll ever get to it. When I told him that we were on the last cycle he asked me, in that cute English accent of his, if I'd ever wondered what they were trying to do. I said 'Sure'—and he told me."

"Go on: I'll buy it."

"Well, they believe that when they have listed all His names—and they reckon that there are about nine billion of them—God's purpose will be achieved. The human race will have finished what it was created to do, and there won't be any point in carrying on. Indeed, the very idea is something like blasphemy."

"Then what do they expect us to do? Commit suicide?"

"There's no need for that. When the list's completed, God steps in and simply winds things up . . . bingo!"

"Oh, I get it. When we finish our job, it will be the end of the world."

Chuck gave a nervous little laugh.

"That's just what I said to Sam. And do you know what happened? He looked at me in a very queer way, like I'd been stupid in class, and said 'It's nothing as trivial as *that.*' "

George thought this over for a moment.

"That's what I call taking the Wide View," he said presently. "But what d'ya suppose we should do about it? I don't see that it makes the slightest difference to us. After all, we already knew that they were crazy."

"Yes—but don't you see what may happen? When the list's complete and the Last Trump doesn't blow—or whatever it is they expect—we may get the blame. It's our machine they've been using. I don't like the situation one little bit."

"I see," said George slowly. "You've got a point there. But this sort of thing's happened before, you know. When I was a kid down in Louisiana we had a crackpot preacher who said the world was going to end next Sunday. Hundreds of people believed him—even sold their homes. Yet nothing happened, they didn't turn nasty as you'd expect. They just decided that he'd made a mistake in his calculations and went right on believing. I guess some of them still do."

"Well, this isn't Louisiana, in case you hadn't noticed. There are just two of us and hundreds of these monks. I like them, and I'll be sorry for old Sam when his lifework backfires on him. But all the same, I wish I was somewhere else."

"I've been wishing that for weeks. But there's nothing we can do until the contract's finished and the transport arrives to fly us out."

"Of course," said Chuck thoughtfully, "we could always try a bit of sabotage."

"Like hell we could! That would make things worse."

"Not the way I meant. Look at it like this. The machine will finish its run four days from now, on the present twenty-hours-a-day basis. The transport calls in a week. O.K.— then all we need do is to find something that wants replacing during one of the overhaul periods—something that will hold up the works for a couple of days. We'll fix it, of course, but not too quickly. If we time matters properly, we can be down at the airfield when the last name pops out of the register. They won't be able to catch us then."

"I don't like it," said George. "It will be the first time I ever walked out on a job. Besides, it would make them suspicious. No. I'll sit tight and take what comes."

"I STILL DON'T like it," he said, seven days later, as the tough little mountain ponies carried them down the winding road. "And don't you think I'm running away because I'm afraid. I'm just sorry for those poor old guys up there, and I don't want to be around when they find what suckers they've been. Wonder how Sam will take it?"

"It's funny," replied Chuck, "but when I said good-bye I got the idea he knew we were walking out on him—and that he didn't care because he knew the machine was running smoothly and that the job would soon be finished. After that—well, of course, for him there just isn't any After That. . . ."

George turned in his saddle and stared back up the mountain road. This was the last place from which one could get a clear view of the lamasery. The squat, angular buildings were silhouetted against the afterglow of the sunset: here and there, lights gleamed like portholes in the sides of an ocean liner. Electric lights, of course, sharing the same circuit as the Mark V. How much longer would they share it, wondered George. Would the monks smash up the computer in their rage and disappointment? Or would they just sit down quietly and begin their calculations all over again?

He knew exactly what was happening up on the mountain at this very moment. The High Lama and his assistants would be sitting in their silk robes, inspecting the sheets as the junior monks carried them away from the typewriters and pasted them into the great volumes. No one would be saying anything. The only sound would be the incessant patter, the never-ending rainstorm, of the keys hitting the paper, for the Mark V itself was utterly silent as it flashed through its thousands of calculations a second. Three months of this, thought George, was enough to start anyone climbing up the wall.

"There she is!" called Chuck, pointing down into the valley. "Ain't she beautiful!"

She certainly was, thought George. The battered old DC 3 lay at the end of the runway like a tiny silver cross. In two hours she would be bearing them away to freedom and sanity. It was a thought worth savoring like a fine liqueur. George let it roll round his mind as the pony trudged patiently down the slope.

The swift night of the high Himalayas was now almost upon them. Fortunately the road was very good, as roads went in this region, and they were both carrying torches. There was not the slightest danger, only a certain discomfort from the bitter cold. The sky overhead was perfectly clear and ablaze with the familiar, friendly stars. At least there would be no risk, thought George, of the pilot being unable to take off because of weather conditions. That had been his only remaining worry.

He began to sing, but gave it up after a while. This vast arena of mountains, gleaming like whitely hooded ghosts on every side, did not encourage such ebullience. Presently George glanced at his watch.

"Should be there in an hour," he called back over his shoulder to Chuck. Then he added, in an afterthought: "Wonder if the computer's finished its run? It was due about now."

Chuck didn't reply, so George swung round in his saddle. He could just see Chuck's face, a white oval turned toward the sky.

"Look," whispered Chuck, and George lifted his eyes to heaven. (There is always a last time for everything.)

Overhead, without any fuss, the stars were going out.

A Work of Art

James Blish is respected as a writer who brought intellectual complexity to familiar science fiction themes. A member of the Futurians, the famed science fiction organization, Blish began publishing science fiction in 1940. Shortly after, he published his short story "Sunken Universe" (one of several he would eventually pull together as his novel *The Seedling Stars*); it is an early exploration of the ramifications and consequences of genetic engineering, in which humanity seeds the stars with biologically altered versions of itself tailored to fit alien environments and inevitably must come to terms with the psychological, sociological, and biological standards by which humanity is defined. *Cities in Flight* comprises four separate novels—*They Shall Have Stars, Life for the Stars, Earthman Come Home,* and *The Triumph of Time*—all of which project a future where entire cities of people migrate across the galaxy in search of more favorable opportunities, but find mostly instead the ineluctable and repeating problems of history. Blish's best-known single work is undoubtedly the Hugo Award–winning novel, *A Case of Conscience,* a landmark exercise in eschatology about a missionary to another planet who discovers an alien species free of original sin and thus a challenge to the tenets of his Earth-based religion. Blish's stories, which regularly wrestled with such weighty themes as godhood, aesthetics, special relativity, and the nature of human consciousness, have been collected in *Galactic Cluster, So Close to Home,* and *Anywhen.* His work as a novelist includes the historical novel *Doctor Mirabilis* and *Black Easter* and its sequel *The Day of Judgment,* pointed studies of biblical good and evil in a dark fantasy context. Among his most important contributions to science fiction are the critical studies and reviews of science fiction published under his William Atheling byline and collected in the volumes *The Issue at Hand, More Issues at Hand,* and *The Tale That Wags the God.*

INSTANTLY, HE REMEMBERED dying. He remembered it, however, as if at two removes—as though he were remembering a memory, rather than an actual event; as though he himself had not really been there when he died.

Yet the memory was all from his own point of view, not that of some detached and disembodied observer which might have been his soul. He had been most conscious of the rasping, unevenly drawn movements of the air in his chest. Blurring rapidly, the doctor's face had bent over him, loomed, come closer, and then had vanished as the doctor's head passed below his cone of vision, turned sideways to listen to his lungs.

It had become rapidly darker, and then, only then, had he realized that these were to be his last minutes. He had tried dutifully to say Pauline's name, but his memory contained no record of the sound—only of the rattling breath and of the film of sootiness thickening in the air, blotting out everything for an instant.

Only an instant, and then the memory was over. The room was bright again, and the ceiling, he noticed with wonder, had turned a soft green. The doctor's head lifted again and looked down at him.

It was a different doctor. This one was a far younger man, with an ascetic face and gleaming, almost fey eyes. There was no doubt about it. One of the last conscious thoughts he had had was that of gratitude that the attending physician, there at the end, had not been the one who secretly hated him for his one-time associations with the Nazi hierarchy. The attending doctor, instead, had worn an expression amusingly proper for that of a Swiss expert called to the deathbed of an eminent man: a mixture of worry at the prospect of losing so eminent a patient, and complacency at the thought that, at the old man's age, nobody could blame this doctor if he died. At eighty-five, pneumonia is a serious matter, with or without penicillin.

"You're all right now," the new doctor said, freeing his patient's head of a whole series of little silver rods which had been clinging to it by a sort of network cap. "Rest a minute and try to be calm. Do you know your name?"

He drew a cautious breath. There seemed to be nothing at all the matter with his lungs now; indeed, he felt positively healthy. "Certainly," he said, a little nettled. "Do you know yours?"

The doctor smiled crookedly. "You're in character, it appears," he said. "My name is Barkun Kris; I am a mind sculptor. Yours?"

"Richard Strauss."

"Very good," Dr. Kris said, and turned away. Strauss, however, had already been diverted by a new singularity. *Strauss* is a word as well as a name in German; it has many meanings—an ostrich, a bouquet; von Wolzogen had had a high old time working all the possible puns into the libretto of *Feuersnot*. And it happened to be the first German word to be spoken either by himself or by Dr. Kris since that twice-removed moment of death. The language was not French or Italian, either. It was most like English, but not the English Strauss knew; nevertheless, he was having no trouble speaking it and even thinking in it.

Well, he thought, *I'll be able to conduct* The Love of Danae, *after all. It isn't every composer who can premiere his own opera posthumously.* Still, there was something queer about all this—the queerest part of all being that conviction, which would not go away, that he had actually been dead for just a short time. Of course, medicine was making great strides, but . . .

"Explain all this," he said, lifting himself to one elbow. The bed was different, too, and not nearly as comfortable as the one in which he had died. As for the room, it looked more like a dynamo shed than a sickroom. Had modern medicine taken to reviving its corpses on the floor of the Siemanns-Schukert plant?

"In a moment," Dr. Kris said. He finished rolling some machine back into what Strauss impatiently supposed to be its place, and crossed to the pallet. "Now. There are many things you'll have to take for granted without attempting to understand them, Dr. Strauss. Not everything in the world today is explicable in terms of your assumptions. Please bear that in mind."

"Very well. Proceed."

"The date," Dr. Kris said, "is 2161 by your calendar—or, in other words, it is now two hundred and twelve years after your death. Naturally, you'll realize that by this time nothing remains of your body but the bones. The body you have now was volunteered for your use. Before you look into a mirror to see what it's like, remember that its physical difference from the one you were used to is all in your favor. It's in perfect health, not unpleasant for other people to look at, and its physiological age is about fifty."

A miracle? No, not in this new age, surely. It is simply a work of science. But what a science! This was Nietzsche's eternal recurrence and the immortality of the superman combined into one.

"And where is this?" the composer said.

"In Port York, part of the State of Manhattan, in the United States. You will find the country less changed in some respects than I imagine you anticipate. Other changes, of course, will seem radical to you, but it's hard for me to predict which ones will strike you that way. A certain resilience on your part will bear cultivating."

"I understand," Strauss said, sitting up. "One question, please; is it still possible for a composer to make a living in this century?"

"Indeed it is," Dr. Kris said, smiling. "As we expect you to do. It is one of the purposes for which we've—brought you back."

"I gather, then," Strauss said somewhat dryly, "that there is still a demand for my music. The critics in the old days—"

"That's not quite how it is," Dr. Kris said. "I understand some of your work is still played, but frankly I know very little about your current status. My interest is rather—"

A door opened somewhere, and another man came in. He was older and more ponderous than Kris and had a certain air of academicism, but he, too, was wearing the oddly tailored surgeon's gown and looked upon Kris's patient with the glowing eyes of an artist.

"A success, Kris?" he said. "Congratulations."

"They're not in order yet," Dr. Kris said. "The final proof is what counts. Dr. Strauss, if you feel strong enough, Dr. Seirds and I would like to ask you some questions. We'd like to make sure your memory is clear."

"Certainly. Go ahead."

"According to our records," Kris said, "you once knew a man whose initials were R. K. L.; this was while you were conducting at the Vienna *Staatsoper*." He made the double "a" at least twice too long, as though German were a dead language he was striving to pronounce in some "classical" accent. "What was his name, and who was he?"

"That would be Kurt List—his first name was Richard, but he didn't use it. He was assistant stage manager."

The two doctors looked at each other. "Why did you offer to write a new overture to *The Woman Without a Shadow* and give the manuscript to the city of Vienna?"

"So I wouldn't have to pay the garbage removal tax on the Maria Theresa villa they had given me."

"In the backyard of your house at Garmischi-Partenkirchen there was a tombstone. What was written on it?"

Strauss frowned. That was a question he would be happy to be unable to answer. If one is to play childish jokes upon oneself, it's best not to carve them in stone and put the carving where you can't help seeing it every time you go out to tinker with the Mercedes. "It says," he replied wearily, " 'Sacred to the memory of Guntram, Minnesinger, slain in a horrible way by his father's own symphony orchestra.' "

"When was *Guntram* premiered?"

"In—let me see—1894, I believe."

"Where?"

"In Weimar."

"Who was the leading lady?"

"Pauline de Ahna."

"What happened to her afterwards?"

"I married her. Is she . . ." Strauss began anxiously.

"No," Dr. Kris said. "I'm sorry, but we lack the data to reconstruct more or less ordinary people."

The composer sighed. He did not know whether to be worried or not. He had loved Pauline, to be sure; on the other hand, it would be pleasant to be able to live the new life without being forced to take off one's shoes every time one entered the house, so as not to scratch the polished hardwood floors. And also pleasant, perhaps, to have two o'clock in the afternoon come by without hearing Pauline's everlasting, "Richard—*jetzt komponiert!*"

"Next question," he said.

*   *   *

FOR REASONS WHICH Strauss did not understand, but was content to take for granted, he was separated from Drs. Kris and Seirds as soon as both were satisfied that the composer's memory was reliable and his health stable. His estate, he was given to understand, had long since been broken up—a sorry end for what had been one of the principal fortunes of Europe—but he was given sufficient money to set up lodgings and resume an active life. He was provided, too, with introductions which proved valuable.

It took longer than he had expected to adjust to the changes that had taken place in music alone. Music was, he quickly began to suspect, a dying art, which would soon have a status not much above that held by flower arranging back in what he thought of as his own century. Certainly it couldn't be denied that the trend toward fragmentation, already visible back in his own time, had proceeded almost to completion in 2161.

He paid no more attention to American popular tunes than he had bothered to pay in his previous life. Yet it was evident that their assembly-line production methods—all the ballad composers openly used a slide-rule-like device called a Hit Machine—now had their counterparts almost throughout serious music.

The conservatives these days, for instance, were the twelve-tone composers—always, in Strauss's opinion, dryly mechanical but never more so than now. Their gods—Berg, Schoenberg, Webern—were looked upon by the concert-going public as great masters, on the abstruse side perhaps, but as worthy of reverence as any of the Three B's.

There was one wing of the conservatives, however, that had gone the twelve-tone procedure one better. These men composed what was called "stochastic music," put together by choosing each individual note by consultation with tables of random numbers. Their bible, their basic text, was a volume called *Operational Aesthetics,* which in turn derived from a discipline called information theory, and not one word of it seemed to touch upon any of the techniques and customs of composition which Strauss knew. The ideal of this group was to produce music which would be "universal"—that is, wholly devoid of any trace of the composer's individuality, wholly a musical expression of the universal Laws of Chance. The Laws of Chance seemed to have a style of their own, all right, but to Strauss it seemed the style of an idiot child being taught to hammer a flat piano, to keep him from getting into trouble.

By far the largest body of work being produced, however, fell into a category misleadingly called science-music. The term reflected nothing but the titles of the works, which dealt with space flight, time travel, and other subjects of a romantic or an unlikely nature. There was nothing in the least scientific about the music, which consisted of a mélange of clichés and imitations of natural sounds, in which Strauss was horrified to see his own time-distorted and diluted image.

The most popular form of science-music was a nine-minute composition called a concerto, though it bore no resemblance at all to the classical concerto form; it was instead a sort of free rhapsody after Rachmaninoff—long after. A typical one—"Song of Deep Space," it was called, by somebody named H. Valerion Krafft—began with a loud assault on the tam-tam, after which all the strings rushed up the scale in unison, followed at a respectful distance by the harp and one clarinet in parallel 6/4's. At the top of the scale cymbals were bashed together, *forte possible,* and the whole orchestra launched itself into a major-minor wailing sort of melody; the whole orchestra, that is, except for the French horns, which were plodding back down the scale again in what was evidently supposed to be a countermelody. The second phrase of the theme was picked up by a solo trumpet with a suggestion of tremolo, the orchestra died back to its roots to await the next cloudburst, and at this point—as any four-year-old could have predicted—the piano entered with the second theme.

Behind the orchestra stood a group of thirty women, ready to come in with a wordless chorus intended to suggest the eeriness of Deep Space—but at this point, too, Strauss had already learned to get up and leave. After a few such experiences he could also count upon meeting in the lobby Sindi Noniss, the agent to whom Dr. Kris had introduced him and who was handling the reborn composer's output—what there was of it thus far. Sindi had come to expect these walkouts on the part of his client and patiently awaited them, standing beneath a bust of Gian-Carlo Menotti, but he liked them less and less, and lately had been greeting them by turning alternately red and white, like a totipotent barber pole.

"You shouldn't have done it," he burst out after the Krafft incident. "You can't just walk out on a new Krafft composition. The man's the president of the Interplanetary Society for Contemporary Music. How am I ever going to persuade them that you're a contemporary if you keep snubbing them?"

"What does it matter?" Strauss said. "They don't know me by sight."

"You're wrong; they know you very well, and they're watching every move you make. You're the first major composer the mind sculptors ever tackled, and the ISCM would be glad to turn you back with a rejection slip."

"Why?"

"Oh," said Sindi, "there are lots of reasons. The sculptors are snobs; so are the ISCM boys. Each of them wanted to prove to the other that their own art is the king of them all. And then there's the competition; it would be easier to flunk you than to let you into the market. I really think you'd better go back in. I could make up some excuse—"

"No," Strauss said shortly. "I have work to do."

"But that's just the point, Richard. How are we going to get an opera produced without the ISCM? It isn't as though you wrote theremin solos, or something that didn't cost so—"

"I have work to do," he said, and left.

And he did, work which absorbed him as had no other project during the last thirty years of his former life. He had scarcely touched pen to music paper—both had been astonishingly hard to find—when he realized that nothing in his long career had provided him with touchstones by which to judge what music he should write *now*.

The old tricks came swarming back by the thousands, to be sure: the sudden, unexpected key changes at the crest of a melody, the interval stretching, the piling of divided strings, playing in the high harmonics, upon the already tottering top of a climax, the scurry and bustle as phrases were passed like lightning from one choir of the orchestra to another, the flashing runs in the brass, the chuckling in the clarinets, the snarling mixtures of colors to emphasize dramatic tension—all of them.

But none of them satisfied him now. He had been content with them for most of a lifetime and had made them do an astonishing amount of work. But now it was time to strike out afresh. Some of the tricks, indeed, actively repelled him: Where had he gotten the notion, clung to for decades, that violins screaming out in unison somewhere in the stratosphere were a sound interesting enough to be worth repeating inside a single composition, let alone in all of them?

And nobody, he reflected contentedly, ever approached such a new beginning better equipped. In addition to the past lying available in his memory, he had always had a technical armamentarium second to none; even the hostile critics had granted him that. Now that he was, in a sense, composing his first opera—his first after fifteen of them!—he had every opportunity to make it a masterpiece.

And every such intention.

There were, of course, many minor distractions. One of them was that search for old-fashioned score paper, and a pen and ink with which to write on it. Very few of the modern composers, it developed, wrote their music at all. A large bloc of them used tape, patching together snippets of tone and sound snipped from other tapes, superimposing one tape on another, and varying the results by twirling an elaborate array of knobs this way or that. Almost all the composers of 3-V scores, on the other hand, wrote on the sound track itself, rapidly scribbling jagged wiggly lines which, when passed through a photocell-audio circuit, produced a noise reasonably like an orchestra playing music, overtones and all.

The last-ditch conservatives who still wrote notes on paper did so with the aid of a musical typewriter. The device, Strauss had to admit, seemed perfected at last; it had manuals and stops like an organ, but it was not much more than twice as large as a standard letter-writing typewriter and produced a neat page. But he was satisfied with his own spidery, highly legible manuscript and refused to abandon it, badly though the one pen nib he had been able to buy coarsened it. It helped to tie him to his past.

Joining the ISCM had also caused him some bad moments, even after Sindi had worked him around the political roadblocks. The Society man who examined his qualifications as a member had run through the questions with no more interest than might have been shown by a veterinarian examining his four-thousandth sick calf.

"Had anything published?"

"Yes, nine tone poems, about three hundred songs, an—"

"Not when you were alive," the examiner said, somewhat disquietingly. "I mean since the sculptors turned you out again."

"Since the sculptors—ah, I understand. Yes, a string quartet, two song cycles, a—"

"Good. Alfie, write down, 'Songs.' Play an instrument?"

"Piano."

"Hmmm." The examiner studied his fingernails. "Oh, well. Do you read music? Or do you use a Scriber, or tape clips? Or a Machine?"

"I read."

"Here." The examiner sat Strauss down in front of a viewing lectern, over the lit surface of which an endless belt of translucent paper was traveling. On the paper was an immensely magnified sound track. "Whistle me the tune of that, and name the instruments it sounds like."

"I don't read that *Musiksticheln*," Strauss said frostily, "or write it, either. I use standard notation, on music paper."

"Alfie, write down, 'Reads notes only.'" He laid a sheet of grayly printed music on the lectern above the ground glass. "Whistle me that."

"That" proved to be a popular tune called "Vangs, Snifters, and Store-Credit Snooky," which had been written on a Hit Machine in 2159 by a guitar-faking politician who sang it at campaign rallies. (In some respects, Strauss reflected, the United States had indeed not changed very much.) It had become so popular that anybody could have whistled it from the title alone, whether he could read the music or not. Strauss whistled it and, to prove his bona fides, added, "It's in the key of B flat."

The examiner went over to the green-painted upright piano and hit one greasy black key. The instrument was horribly out of tune—the note was much nearer to the standard 440/cps A than it was to B flat—but the examiner said, "So it is. Alfie, write down, 'Also reads flats.' All right, son, you're a member. Nice to have you with us; not many people can read that old-style notation anymore. A lot of them think they're too good for it."

"Thank you," Strauss said.

"My feeling is, if it was good enough for the old masters, it's good enough for us. We don't have people like them with us these days, it seems to me. Except for Dr. Krafft, of course. They were *great* back in the old days—men like Shilkrit, Steiner, Tiomkin, and Pearl . . . and Wilder and Jannsen. Real goffin."

"*Doch gewiss*," Strauss said politely.

BUT THE WORK went forward. He was making a little income now, from small works. People seemed to feel a special interest in a composer who had come out of the mind sculptors' laboratories, and in addition the material itself, Strauss was quite certain, had merits of its own to help sell it.

It was the opera that counted, however. That grew and grew under his pen, as fresh and new as his new life, as founded in knowledge and ripeness as his long, full memory. Finding a libretto had been troublesome at first. While it was possible that something existed that might have served among the current scripts for 3-V—though he doubted it—he found himself unable to tell the good from the bad through the fog cast over both by incomprehensibly technical production directions. Eventually, and for only the third time in his whole career, he had fallen back upon a play written in a language other than his own, and—for the first time—decided to set it in that language.

The play was Christopher Fry's *Venus Observed*, in all ways a perfect Strauss opera libretto, as he came gradually to realize. Though nominally a comedy, with a complex farcical plot, it was a verse play with considerable depth to it, and a number of characters who cried out to be brought by music into three dimensions, plus a strong undercurrent of autumnal tragedy, of leaf-fall and apple-fall—precisely the kind of contradictory dramatic mixture which von Hofmannsthal had supplied him with in *The Knight of the Rose*, in *Ariadne at Naxos*, and in *Arabella*.

Alas for von Hofmannsthal, but here was another long-dead playwright who seemed nearly as gifted, and the musical opportunities were immense. There was, for instance, the fire which ended Act II; what a gift for a composer to whom orchestration and counterpoint were as important as air and water! Or take the moment where Perpetua shoots the apple from the Duke's hand; in that one moment a single passing reference could add Rossini's marmoreal *William Tell* to the musical texture as nothing but an ironic footnote! And the Duke's great curtain speech, beginning:

> *Shall I be sorry for myself? In Mortality's name.*
> *I'll be sorry for myself. Branches and boughs,*
> *Brown hills, the valleys faint with brume,*
> *A burnish on the lake. . . .*

There was a speech for a great tragic comedian in the spirit of Falstaff: the final union of laughter and tears, punctuated by the sleepy comments of Reedbeck, to whose sonorous snore (trombones, no less than five of them, *con sordini?*) the opera would gently end. . . .

What could be better? And yet he had come upon the play only by the unlikeliest series of accidents. At first he had planned to do a straight knockabout farce, in the idiom of *The Silent Woman,* just to warm himself up. Remembering that Zweig had adapted that libretto for him, in the old days, from a play by Ben Jonson, Strauss had begun to search out English plays of the period just after Jonson's, and had promptly run aground on an awful specimen in heroic couplets called *Venice Preserv'd,* by one Thomas Otway. The Fry play had directly followed the Otway in the card catalogue, and he had looked at it out of curiosity; why should a twentieth-century playwright be punning on a title from the eighteenth?

After two pages of the Fry play, the minor puzzle of the pun disappeared entirely from his concern. His luck was running again; he had an opera.

SINDI WORKED MIRACLES in arranging for the performance. The date of the premiere was set even before the score was finished, reminding Strauss pleasantly of those heady days when Fuestner had been snatching the conclusion of *Elektra* off his worktable a page at a time, before the ink was even dry, to rush it to the engraver before publication deadline. The situation now, however, was even more complicated, for some of the score had to be scribed, some of it taped, some of it engraved in the old way, to meet the new techniques of performance; there were moments when Sindi seemed to be turning quite gray.

But *Venus Observed* was, as usual, forthcoming complete from Strauss's pen in plenty of time. Writing the music in first draft had been hellishly hard work, much more like being reborn than had been that confused awakening in Barkun Kris's laboratory, with its overtones of being dead instead, but Strauss found that he still retained all of his old ability to score from the draft almost effortlessly, as undisturbed by Sindi's half-audible worrying in the room with him as he was by the terrifying supersonic bangs of the rockets that bulleted invisibly over the city.

When he was finished, he had two days still to spare before the beginning of rehearsals. With those, furthermore, he would have nothing to do. The techniques of performance in this age were so completely bound up with the electronic arts as to reduce his own experience—he, the master *Kapellmeister* of them all—to the hopelessly primitive.

He did not mind. The music, as written, would speak for itself. In the meantime he found it grateful to forget the months-long preoccupation with the stage for a while. He went back to the library and browsed lazily through old poems, vaguely seeking texts for a song or two. He knew better than to bother with recent poets; they could not speak to him, and he knew it. The Americans of his own age, he thought, might give him a clue to understanding this America of 2161, and if some such poem gave birth to a song, so much the better.

The search was relaxing, and he gave himself up to enjoying it. Finally he struck a tape that he liked; a tape read in a cracked old voice that twanged of Idaho as that voice had twanged in 1910, in Strauss's own ancient youth. The poet's name was Pound; he said, on the tape:

> ... the souls of all men great
> At times pass through us,
> And we are melted into them, and are not
> Save reflexions of their souls.
> Thus I am Dante for a space and am
> One François Villon, ballad-lord and thief,
> Or am such holy ones I may not write,
> Lest Blasphemy be writ against my name;
> This for an instant and the flame is gone.
> 'Tis as in midmost us there glows a sphere
> Translucent, molten gold, that is the "I"
> And into this some form projects itself:
> Christus, or John, or eke the Florentine;
> And as the clear space is not if a form's
> Imposed thereon,
> So cease we from all being for the time,
> And these, the masters of the Soul, live on.

He smiled. That lesson had been written again and again, from Plato onward. Yet the poem was a history of his own case, a sort of theory for the metempsychosis he had undergone, and in its formal way it was moving. It would be fitting to make a little hymn of it, in honor of his own rebirth, and of the poet's insight.

A series of solemn, breathless chords framed themselves in his inner ear, against which the words might be intoned in a high, gently bending hush at the beginning ... and then a dramatic passage in which the great names of Dante and Villon would enter ringing like challenges to Time. . . . He wrote for a while in his notebook before he returned the spool to its shelf.

These, he thought, are good auspices.

And so the night of the premiere arrived, the audience pouring into the hall, the 3-V cameras riding on no visible supports through the air, and Sindi calculating his share of his client's earnings by a complicated game he played on his fingers, the basic law of which seemed to be that one plus one equals ten. The hall filled to the roof with people from every class, as though what was to come would be a circus rather than an opera.

There were, surprisingly, nearly fifty of the aloof and aristocratic mind sculptors, clad in formal clothes which were exaggerated black versions of their surgeons' gowns. They had bought a block of seats near the front of the auditorium, where the gigantic 3-V figures which would shortly fill the "stage" before them (the real singers would perform on a small stage in the basement) could not but seem monstrously out of proportion, but Strauss supposed that they had taken this into account and dismissed it.

There was a tide of whispering in the audience as the sculptors began to trickle in, and with it an undercurrent of excitement, the meaning of which was unknown to Strauss. He did not attempt to fathom it, however; he was coping with his own mounting tide of opening-night tension, which, despite all the years, he had never quite been able to shake.

The sourceless, gentle light in the auditorium dimmed, and Strauss mounted the podium. There was a score before him, but he doubted that he would need it. Directly before him, poking up from among the musicians, were the inevitable 3-V snouts, waiting to carry his image to the singers in the basement.

The audience was quiet now. This was the moment. His baton swept up and then decisively down, and the prelude came surging up out of the pit.

FOR A LITTLE while he was deeply immersed in the always tricky business of keeping the enormous orchestra together and sensitive to the flexing of the musical web beneath his hand. As his control firmed and became secure, however, the task became slightly less demanding, and he was able to pay more attention to what the whole sounded like.

There was something decidedly wrong with it. Of course there were the occasional surprises as some bit of orchestral color emerged with a different *Klang* than he had expected; that happened to every composer, even after a lifetime of experience. And there were moments when the singers, entering upon a phrase more difficult to handle than he had calculated, sounded like someone about to fall off a tightrope (although none of them actually fluffed once; they were as fine a troupe of voices as he had ever had to work with).

But these were details. It was the overall impression that was wrong. He was losing not only the excitement of the premiere—after all, that couldn't last at the same pitch all evening—but also his very interest in what was coming from the stage and the pit. He was gradually tiring, his baton arm becoming heavier; as the second act mounted to what should have been an impassioned outpouring of shining tone, he was so bored as to wish he could go back to his desk to work on that song.

Then the act was over; only one more to go. He scarcely heard the applause. The twenty minutes' rest in his dressing room was just barely enough to give him the necessary strength.

AND SUDDENLY, IN the middle of the last act, he understood.

There was nothing new about the music. It was the old Strauss all over again—

but weaker, more dilute than ever. Compared with the output of composers like Krafft, it doubtless sounded like a masterpiece to this audience. But he knew.

The resolutions, the determination to abandon the old clichés and mannerisms, the decision to say something new—they had all come to nothing against the force of habit. Being brought to life again meant bringing to life as well all those deeply graven reflexes of his style. He had only to pick up his pen and they overpowered him with easy automatism, no more under his control than the jerk of a finger away from a flame.

His eyes filled; his body was young, but he was an old man, an old man. Another thirty-five years of this? Never. He had said all this before, centuries before. Nearly a half century condemned to saying it all over again, in a weaker and still weaker voice, aware that even this debased century would come to recognize in him only the burnt husk of greatness?—no, never, never.

He was aware, dully, that the opera was over. The audience was screaming its joy. He knew the sound. They had screamed that way when *Day of Peace* had been premiered, but they had been cheering the man he had been, not the man that *Day of Peace* showed with cruel clarity he had become. Here the sound was even more meaningless: cheers of ignorance, and that was all.

He turned slowly. With surprise, and with a surprising sense of relief, he saw that the cheers were not, after all, for him.

They were for Dr. Barkun Kris.

KRIS WAS STANDING in the middle of the bloc of mind sculptors, bowing to the audience. The sculptors nearest him were shaking his hand one after the other. More grasped at it as he made his way to the aisle and walked forward to the podium. When he mounted the rostrum and took the composer's limp hand, the cheering became delirious.

Kris lifted his arm. The cheering died instantly to an intent hush.

"Thank you," he said clearly. "Ladies and gentlemen, before we take leave of Dr. Strauss, let us again tell him what a privilege it has been for us to hear this fresh example of his mastery. I am sure no farewell could be more fitting."

The ovation lasted five minutes and would have gone another five if Kris had not cut it off.

"Dr. Strauss," he said, "in a moment, when I speak a certain formulation to you, you will realize that your name is Jerom Bosch, born in our century and with a life in it all your own. The superimposed memories which have made you assume the mask, the *persona,* of a great composer will be gone. I tell you this so that you may understand why these people here share your applause with me."

A wave of asserting sound.

"The art of mind sculpture—the creation of artificial personalities for aesthetic enjoyment—may never reach such a pinnacle again. For you should understand that as Jerom Bosch you had no talent for music at all; indeed, we searched a long time to find a man who was utterly unable to carry even the simplest tune. Yet we were able to impose upon such unpromising material not only the personality, but the genius, of a great composer. That genius belongs entirely to you—to the *persona* that thinks of itself as Richard Strauss. None of the credit goes to the man who volunteered for the sculpture. That is your triumph, and we salute you for it."

Now the ovation could no longer be contained. Strauss, with a crooked smile, watched Dr. Kris bow. This mind sculpturing was a suitably sophisticated kind of cruelty for this age, but the impulse, of course, had always existed. It was the same impulse that had made Rembrandt and Leonardo turn cadavers into art works.

It deserved a suitably sophisticated payment under the *lex talionis:* an eye for an eye, a tooth for a tooth—and a failure for a failure.

No, he need not tell Dr. Kris that the "Strauss" he had created was as empty of genius as a hollow gourd. The joke would always be on the sculptor, who was incapable of hearing the hollowness of the music now preserved on the 3-V tapes.

But for an instant a surge of revolt poured through his bloodstream. *I am I,* he thought. *I am Richard Strauss until I die, and will never be Jerom Bosch, who was utterly unable to carry even the simplest tune.* His hand, still holding the baton, came sharply up, though whether to deliver or to ward off a blow he could not tell.

He let it fall again, and instead, at last, bowed—not to the audience, but to Dr. Kris. He was sorry for nothing, as Kris turned to him to say the word that would plunge him back into oblivion, except that he would now have no chance to set that poem to music.

Dark They Were, and Golden-Eyed

Although not the first author to write fiction set on Mars, Ray Bradbury staked a major claim to one of the most fertile landscapes in all science fiction with a series of stories published in pulp magazines of the 1940s and '50s in which he envisioned the Red Planet as a new frontier where humanity might leave its imprint, for better or for worse. His collection *The Martian Chronicles* (1950), for which these stories served as a foundation, was a break-through success that alerted a mainstream audience to the value of science fiction as a modern mythology that embodies timeless human dreams and fears. Frail and fallible human beings are the foremost concern of Bradbury's fiction, whether in the persona of the fireman in the future dystopia *Fahrenheit 451* who comes to doubt the merits of his job—destroying ideas by burning books—or the ordinary middle-class Americans in the dark fantasy *Something Wicked This Way Comes* who allow fear of their own mortality to coerce them into Faustian pacts with a Mephistophelian owner of a traveling carnival. Bradbury's lyrical stories have been collected in *The Illustrated Man, The Golden Apples of the Sun, A Medicine for Melancholy, The Machineries of Joy*, and numerous other volumes including the definitive *Stories of Ray Bradbury*. The modern Gothic stories in his collections *Dark Carnival* and *The October Country* were a major influence on contemporary horror and dark fantasy fiction. *Dandelion Wine*, his novel of a midcentury Midwestern childhood, and the loose trilogy comprised of *Death Is a Lonely Business, A Graveyard for Lunatics*, and *Green Shadows, White Whale*, drawn from his experiences as a young writer, are quintessentially Bradbur-yesque explorations of the magic possibilities of everyday life. He has written the children's books *Switch on the Night, The Halloween Tree*, and *Ahmed and the Oblivion Machine*, hundreds of poems collected in *The Complete Poems of Ray Bradbury*, a score of plays, including *The Wonderful Ice Cream Suit*, and the essay collection *Yestermorrow*. Many of his stories have been adapted for stage, screen, television, musical theater, and the comics. His own screenwriting credits include *It Came from Outer Space* and the screenplay for John Huston's adaptation of *Moby Dick*. His many awards include the Nebula Grand Master Award and the Bram Stoker Award for Life Achievement from the Horror Writers Association.

THE ROCKET METAL cooled in the meadow winds. Its lid gave a bulging *pop*. From its clock interior stepped a man, a woman, and three children. The other passengers whispered away across the Martian meadow, leaving the man alone among his family.

The man felt his hair flutter and the tissues of his body draw tight as if he were standing at the center of a vacuum. His wife, before him, seemed almost to whirl away in smoke. The children, small seeds, might at any instant be sown to all the Martian climes.

The children looked up at him, as people look to the sun to tell what time of their life it is. His face was cold.

"What's wrong?" asked his wife.

"Let's get back on the rocket."

"Go back to Earth?"

"Yes! Listen!"

The wind blew as if to flake away their identities. At any moment the Martian air might draw his soul from him, as marrow comes from a white bone. He felt submerged in a chemical that could dissolve his intellect and burn away his past.

They looked at Martian hills that time had worn with a crushing pressure of years. They saw the old cities, lost in their meadows, lying like children's delicate bones among the blowing lakes of grass.

"Chin up, Harry," said his wife. "It's too late. We've come over sixty million miles."

The children with their yellow hair hollered at the deep dome of Martian sky. There was no answer but the racing hiss of wind through the stiff grass.

He picked up the luggage in his cold hands. "Here we go," he said—a man standing on the edge of a sea, ready to wade in and be drowned.

They walked into town.

THEIR NAME WAS Bittering. Harry and his wife Cora; Dan, Laura, and David. They built a small white cottage and ate good breakfasts there, but the fear was never gone. It lay with Mr. Bittering and Mrs. Bittering, a third unbidden partner at every midnight talk, at every dawn awakening.

"I feel like a salt crystal," he said, "in a mountain stream, being washed away. We don't belong here. We're Earth people. This is Mars. It was meant for Martians. For heaven's sake, Cora, let's buy tickets for home!"

But she only shook her head. "One day the atom bomb will fix Earth. Then we'll be safe here."

"Safe and insane!"

Tick-tock, seven o'clock sang the voice-clock; *time to get up*. And they did.

Something made him check everything each morning—warm hearth, potted blood-geraniums—precisely as if he expected something to be amiss. The morning paper was toast-warm from the 6 A.M. Earth rocket. He broke its seal and tilted it at his breakfast place. He forced himself to be convivial.

"Colonial days all over again," he declared. "Why, in ten years there'll be a million Earthmen on Mars. Big cities, everything! They said we'd fail. Said the Martians would resent our invasion. But did we find any Martians? Not a living soul! Oh, we found their empty cities, but no one in them. Right?"

A river of wind submerged the house. When the windows ceased rattling, Mr. Bittering swallowed and looked at the children.

"I don't know," said David. "Maybe there're Martians around we don't see. Sometimes nights I think I hear 'em. I hear the wind. The sand hits my window. I get scared. And I see those towns way up in the mountains where the Martians lived a long time ago. And I think I see things moving around those towns, Papa. And I wonder if those Martians *mind* us living here. I wonder if they won't do something to us for coming here."

"Nonsense!" Mr. Bittering looked out the windows. "We're clean, decent people." He looked at his children. "All dead cities have some kind of ghosts in them. Memories, I mean." He stared at the hills. "You see a staircase and you wonder what Martians looked like climbing it. You see Martian paintings and you wonder what the painter was like. You make a little ghost in your mind, a memory. It's quite natural. Imagination." He stopped. "You haven't been prowling up in those ruins, have you?"

"No, Papa." David looked at his shoes.

"See that you stay away from them. Pass the jam."

"Just the same," said little David, "I bet something happens."

SOMETHING HAPPENED THAT afternoon.

Laura stumbled through the settlement, crying. She dashed blindly onto the porch.

"Mother, Father—the war, Earth!" she sobbed. "A radio flash just came. Atom bombs hit New York! All the space rockets blown up. No more rockets to Mars, ever!"

"Oh, Harry!" The mother held onto her husband and daughter.

"Are you sure, Laura?" asked the father quietly.

Laura wept. "We're stranded on Mars, forever and ever!"

For a long time there was only the sound of the wind in the late afternoon.

Alone, thought Bittering. Only a thousand of us here. No way back. No way. No way. Sweat poured from his face and his hands and his body; he was drenched in the hotness of his fear. He wanted to strike Laura, cry, "No, you're lying! The rockets will come back!" Instead, he stroked Laura's head against him and said, "The rockets will get through someday."

"Father, what will we do?"

"Go about our business, of course. Raise crops and children. Wait. Keep things going until the war ends and the rockets come again."

The two boys stepped out onto the porch.

"Children," he said, sitting there, looking beyond them, "I've something to tell you."

"We know," they said.

IN THE FOLLOWING days, Bittering wandered often through the garden to stand alone in his fear. As long as the rockets had spun a silver web across space, he had been able to accept Mars. For he had always told himself: Tomorrow, if I want, I can buy a ticket and go back to Earth.

But now: The web gone, the rockets lying in jigsaw heaps of molten girder and unsnaked wire. Earth people left to the strangeness of Mars, the cinnamon dusts and wine airs, to be baked like gingerbread shapes in Martian summers, put into harvested storage by Martian winters. What would happen to him, the others? This was the moment Mars had waited for. Now it would eat them.

He got down on his knees in the flower bed, a spade in his nervous hands. Work, he thought, work and forget.

He glanced up from the garden to the Martian mountains. He thought of the proud old Martian names that had once been on those peaks. Earthmen, dropping from the sky, had gazed upon hills, rivers, Martian seas left nameless in spite of names. Once Martians had built cities, named cities; climbed mountains, named mountains; sailed seas, named seas. Mountains melted, seas drained, cities tumbled. In spite of this, the Earthmen had felt a silent guilt at putting new names to these ancient hills and valleys.

Nevertheless, man lives by symbol and label. The names were given.

Mr. Bittering felt very alone in his garden under the Martian sun, anachronism bent here, planting Earth flowers in a wild soil.

Think. Keep thinking. Different things. Keep your mind free of Earth, the atom war, the lost rockets.

He perspired. He glanced about. No one watching. He removed his tie. Pretty bold, he thought. First your coat off, now your tie. He hung it neatly on a peach tree he had imported as a sapling from Massachusetts.

He returned to his philosophy of names and mountains. The Earthmen had changed names. Now there were Hormel Valleys, Roosevelt Seas, Ford Hills, Vanderbilt Plateaus, Rockefeller Rivers, on Mars. It wasn't right. The American settlers had shown wisdom, using old Indian prairie names: Wisconsin, Minnesota, Idaho, Ohio, Utah, Milwaukee, Waukegan, Osseo. The old names, the old meanings.

Staring at the mountains wildly, he thought: Are you up there? All the dead ones, you Martians? Well, here we are, alone, cut off! Come down, move us out! We're helpless!

The wind blew a shower of peach blossoms.

He put out his sun-browned hand, gave a small cry. He touched the blossoms, picked them up. He turned them, he touched them again and again. Then he shouted for his wife.

"Cora!"

She appeared at a window. He ran to her.

"Cora, these blossoms!"

She handled them.

"Do you see? They're different. They've changed! They're not peach blossoms any more!"

"Look all right to me," she said.

"They're not. They're *wrong!* I can't tell how. An extra petal, a leaf, something, the color, the smell!"

The children ran out in time to see their father hurrying about the garden, pulling up radishes, onions, and carrots from their beds.

"Cora, come look!"

They handled the onions, the radishes, the carrots among them.

"Do they look like carrots?"

"Yes . . . no." She hesitated. "I don't know."

"They're changed."

"Perhaps."

"You know they have! Onions but not onions, carrots but not carrots. Taste: the same but different. Smell: not like it used to be." He felt his heart pounding, and he was afraid. He dug his fingers into the earth. "Cora, what's happening? What is it? We've got to get away from this." He ran across the garden. Each tree felt his touch. "The roses. The roses. They're turning green!"

And they stood looking at the green roses.

And two days later Dan came running. "Come see the cow. I was milking her and I saw it. Come on!"

They stood in the shed and looked at their one cow.

It was growing a third horn.

And the lawn in front of their house very quietly and slowly was coloring itself like spring violets. Seed from Earth but growing up a soft purple.

"We must get away," said Bittering. "We'll eat this stuff and then we'll change— who knows to what? I can't let it happen. There's only one thing to do. Burn this food!"

"It's not poisoned."

"But it is. Subtly, very subtly. A little bit. A very little bit. We mustn't touch it."

He looked with dismay at their house. "Even the house. The wind's done something to it. The air's burned it. The fog at night. The boards, all warped out of shape. It's not an Earthman's house any more."

"Oh, your imagination!"

He put on his coat and tie. "I'm going into town. We've got to do something now. I'll be back."

"Wait, Harry!" his wife cried.

But he was gone.

In town, on the shadowy step of the grocery store, the men sat with their hands on their knees, conversing with great leisure and ease.

Mr. Bittering wanted to fire a pistol in the air.

What are you doing, you fools! he thought. Sitting here! You've heard the news— we're stranded on this planet. Well, move! Aren't you frightened? Aren't you afraid? What are you going to do?

"Hello, Harry," said everyone.

"Look," he said to them. "You did hear the news, the other day, didn't you?"

They nodded and laughed. "Sure. Sure, Harry."

"What are you going to do about it?"

"Do, Harry, do? What *can* we do?"

"Build a rocket, that's what!"

"A rocket, Harry? To go back to all that trouble? Oh, Harry!"

"But you *must* want to go back. Have you noticed the peach blossoms, the onions, the grass?"

"Why, yes, Harry, seems we did," said one of the men.

"Doesn't it scare you?"

"Can't recall that it did much, Harry."

"Idiots!"

"Now, Harry."

Bittering wanted to cry. "You've got to work with me. If we stay here, we'll all change. The air. Don't you smell it? Something in the air. A Martian virus, maybe; some seed, or a pollen. Listen to me!"

They stared at him.

"Sam," he said to one of them.

"Yes, Harry?"

"Will you help me build a rocket?"

"Harry, I got a whole load of metal and some blueprints. You want to work in my metal shop on a rocket, you're welcome. I'll sell you that metal for five hundred dollars. You should be able to construct a right pretty rocket, if you work alone, in about thirty years."

Everyone laughed.

"Don't laugh."

Sam looked at him with quiet good humor.

"Sam," Bittering said. "Your eyes—"

"What about them, Harry?"

"Didn't they used to be grey?"

"Well now, I don't remember."

"They were, weren't they?"

"Why do you ask, Harry?"

"Because now they're kind of yellow-colored."

"Is that so, Harry?" Sam said, casually.

"And you're taller and thinner—"

"You might be right, Harry."

"Sam, you shouldn't have yellow eyes."

"Harry, what color eyes have *you* got?" Sam said.

"My eyes? They're blue, of course."

"Here you are, Harry." Sam handed him a pocket mirror. "Take a look at yourself."

Mr. Bittering hesitated, and then raised the mirror to his face.

There were little, very dim flecks of new gold captured in the blue of his eyes.

"Now look what you've done," said Sam a moment later. "You've broken my mirror."

HARRY BITTERING MOVED into the metal shop and began to build the rocket. Men stood in the open door and talked and joked without raising their voices. Once in a while they gave him a hand on lifting something. But mostly they just idled and watched him with their yellowing eyes.

"It's suppertime, Harry," they said.

His wife appeared with his supper in a wicker basket.

"I won't touch it," he said. "I'll eat only food from our Deepfreeze. Food that came from Earth. Nothing from our garden."

His wife stood watching him. "You can't build a rocket."

"I worked in a shop once, when I was twenty. I know metal. Once I get it started, the others will help," he said, not looking at her, laying out the blueprints.

"Harry, Harry," she said, helplessly.

"We've got to get away, Cora. We've *got* to!"

THE NIGHTS WERE full of wind that blew down the empty moonlit sea meadows past the little white chess cities lying for their twelve-thousandth year in the shallows. In the Earthmen's settlement, the Bittering house shook with a feeling of change.

Lying abed, Mr. Bittering felt his bones shifted, shaped, melted like gold. His wife, lying beside him, was dark from many sunny afternoons. Dark she was, and golden-eyed, burnt almost black by the sun, sleeping, and the children metallic in their beds, and the wind roaring forlorn and changing through the old peach trees, the violet grass, shaking out green rose petals.

The fear would not be stopped. It had his throat and heart. It dripped in a wetness of the arm and the temple and the trembling palm.

A green star rose in the east.

A strange word emerged from Mr. Bittering's lips.

"*Iorrt. Iorrt.*" He repeated it.

It was a Martian word. He knew no Martian.

In the middle of the night he arose and dialed a call through to Simpson, the archeologist.

"Simpson, what does the word *Iorrt* mean?"

"Why, that's the old Martian word for our planet Earth. Why?"

"No special reason."

The telephone slipped from his hand.

"Hello, hello, hello, hello," it kept saying while he sat gazing out at the green star. "Bittering? Harry, are you there?"

The days were full of metal sound. He laid the frame of the rocket with the reluctant help of three indifferent men. He grew very tired in an hour or so and had to sit down.

"The altitude," laughed a man.

"Are you *eating*, Harry?" asked another.

"I'm eating," he said, angrily.

"From your Deepfreeze?"

"Yes!"

"You're getting thinner, Harry."

"I'm not!"

"And taller."

"Liar!"

HIS WIFE TOOK him aside a few days later. "Harry, I've used up all the food in the Deepfreeze. There's nothing left. I'll have to make sandwiches using food grown on Mars."

He sat down heavily.

"You must eat," she said. "You're weak."

"Yes," he said.

He took a sandwich, opened it, looked at it, and began to nibble at it.

"And take the rest of the day off," she said. "It's hot. The children want to swim in the canals and hike. Please come along."

"I can't waste time. This is a crisis!"

"Just for an hour," she urged. "A swim'll do you good."

He rose, sweating. "All right, all right. Leave me alone. I'll come."

"Good for you, Harry."

The sun was hot, the day quiet. There was only an immense staring burn upon the land. They moved along the canal, the father, the mother, the racing children in their swim suits. They stopped and ate meat sandwiches. He saw their skin baking brown. And he saw the yellow eyes of his wife and his children, their eyes that were never yellow before. A few tremblings shook him, but were carried off in waves of pleasant heat as he lay in the sun. He was too tired to be afraid.

"Cora, how long have your eyes been yellow?"

She was bewildered. "Always, I guess."

"They didn't change from brown in the last three months?"

She bit her lips. "No. Why do you ask?"

"Never mind."

They sat there.

"The children's eyes," he said. "They're yellow, too."

"Sometimes growing children's eyes change color."

"Maybe *we're* children, too. At least to Mars. That's a thought." He laughed. "Think I'll swim."

They leaped into the canal water, and he let himself sink down and down to the bottom like a golden statue and lie there in green silence. All was water-quiet and deep, all was peace. He felt the steady, slow current drift him easily.

If I lie here long enough, he thought, the water will work and eat away my flesh until the bones show like coral. Just my skeleton left. And then the water can build on that skeleton—green things, deep water things, red things, yellow things. Change. Change. Slow, deep, silent change. And isn't that what it is up *there*?

He saw the sky submerged above him, the sun made Martian by atmosphere and time and space.

Up there, a big river, he thought, a Martian river, all of us lying deep in it, in our pebble houses, in our sunken boulder houses, like crayfish hidden, and the water washing away our old bodies and lengthening the bones and—

He let himself drift up through the soft light.

Dan sat on the edge of the canal, regarding his father seriously.

"*Utha*," he said.

"What?" asked his father.

The boy smiled. "You know. *Utha*'s the Martian word for 'father.'"

"Where did you learn it?"

"I don't know. Around. *Utha!*"

"What do you want?"

The boy hesitated. "I—I want to change my name."

"Change it?"

"Yes."

His mother swam over. "What's wrong with Dan for a name?"

Dan fidgeted. "The other day you called Dan, Dan, Dan. I didn't even hear. I said to myself, That's not my name. I've a new name I want to use."

Mr. Bittering held to the side of the canal, his body cold and his heart pounding slowly. "What is this new name?"

"Linnl. Isn't that a good name? Can I use it? Can't I, please?"

Mr. Bittering put his hand to his head. He thought of the silly rocket, himself working alone, himself alone even among his family, so alone.

He heard his wife say, "Why not?"

He heard himself say, "Yes, you can use it."

"Yaaa!" screamed the boy. "I'm Linnl, Linnl!"

Racing down the meadowlands, he danced and shouted.

Mr. Bittering looked at his wife. "Why did we do that?"

"I don't know," she said. "It just seemed like a good idea."

They walked into the hills. They strolled on old mosaic paths, beside still pumping fountains. The paths were covered with a thin film of cool water all summer long. You kept your bare feet cool all the day, splashing as in a creek, wading.

They came to a small deserted Martian villa with a good view of the valley. It was on top of a hill. Blue marble halls, large murals, a swimming pool. It was refreshing in this hot summertime. The Martians hadn't believed in large cities.

"How nice," said Mrs. Bittering, "if we could move up here to this villa for the summer."

"Come on," he said. "We're going back to town. There's work to be done on the rocket."

But as he worked that night, the thought of the cool blue marble villa entered his mind. As the hours passed, the rocket seemed less important.

In the flow of days and weeks, the rocket receded and dwindled. The old fever was gone. It frightened him to think he had let it slip this way. But somehow the heat, the air, the working conditions—

He heard the men murmuring on the porch of his metal shop.

"Everyone's going. You heard?"

"All going. That's right."

Bittering came out. "Going where?" He saw a couple of trucks, loaded with children and furniture, drive down the dusty street.

"Up to the villas," said the man.

"Yeah, Harry. I'm going. So is Sam. Aren't you, Sam?"

"That's right, Harry. What about you?"

"I've got work to do here."

"Work! You can finish that rocket in the autumn, when it's cooler."

He took a breath. "I got the frame all set up."

"In the autumn is better." Their voices were lazy in the heat.

"Got to work," he said.

"Autumn," they reasoned. And they sounded so sensible, so right.

Autumn would be best, he thought. Plenty of time, then.

No! cried part of himself, deep down, put away, locked tight, suffocating. No! No!

"In the autumn," he said.

"Come on, Harry," they all said.

"Yes," he said, feeling his flesh melt in the hot liquid air. "Yes, in the autumn. I'll begin work again then."

"I got a villa near the Tirra Canal," said someone.

"You mean the Roosevelt Canal, don't you?"

"Tirra. The old Martian name."

"But on the map—"

"Forget the map. It's Tirra now. Now I found a place in the Pillan mountains—"

"You mean the Rockefeller Range," said Bittering.

"I mean the Pillan mountains," said Sam.

"Yes," said Bittering, buried in the hot, swarming air. "The Pillan mountains."

Everyone worked at loading the truck in the hot, still afternoon of the next day.

Laura, Dan, and David carried packages. Or, as they preferred to be known, Ttil, Linnl, and Werr carried packages.

The furniture was abandoned in the little white cottage.

"It looked just fine in Boston," said the mother. "And here in the cottage. But up at the villa? No. We'll get it when we come back in the autumn."

Bittering himself was quiet.

"I've some ideas on furniture for the villa," he said after a time. "Big, lazy furniture."

"What about your encyclopedia? You're taking it along, surely?"

Mr. Bittering glanced away. "I'll come and get it next week."

They turned to their daughter. "What about your New York dresses?"

The bewildered girl stared. "Why, I don't want them any more."

They shut off the gas, the water, they locked the doors and walked away. Father peered into the truck.

"Gosh, we're not taking much," he said. "Considering all we brought to Mars, this is only a handful!"

He started the truck.

Looking at the small white cottage for a long moment, he was filled with a desire to rush to it, touch it, say good-by to it, for he felt as if he were going away on a long journey, leaving something to which he could never quite return, never understand again.

Just then Sam and his family drove by in another truck.

"Hi, Bittering! Here we go!"

The truck swung down the ancient highway out of town. There were sixty others traveling the same direction. The town filled with a silent, heavy dust from their passage. The canal waters lay blue in the sun, and a quiet wind moved in the strange trees.

"Good-by, town!" said Mr. Bittering.

"Good-by, good-by," said the family, waving to it.

They did not look back again.

SUMMER BURNED THE canals dry. Summer moved like flame upon the meadows. In the empty Earth settlement, the painted houses flaked and peeled. Rubber tires upon which children had swung in back yards hung suspended like stopped clock pendulums in the blazing air.

At the metal shop, the rocket frame began to rust.

In the quiet autumn Mr. Bittering stood, very dark now, very golden-eyed, upon the slope above his villa, looking at the valley.

"It's time to go back," said Cora.

"Yes, but we're not going," he said quietly. "There's nothing there any more."

"Your books," she said. "Your fine clothes.

"Your *Illes* and your fine *ior uele rre*," she said.

"The town's empty. No one's going back," he said. "There's no reason to, none at all."

The daughter wove tapestries and the sons played songs on ancient flutes and pipes, their laughter echoing in the marble villa.

Mr. Bittering gazed at the Earth settlement far away in the low valley. "Such odd, such ridiculous houses the Earth people built."

"They didn't know any better," his wife mused. "Such ugly people. I'm glad they've gone."

They both looked at each other, startled by all they had just finished saying. They laughed.

"Where did they go?" he wondered. He glanced at his wife. She was golden and slender as his daughter. She looked at him, and he seemed almost as young as their eldest son.

"I don't know," she said.

"We'll go back to town maybe next year, or the year after, or the year after that," he said, calmly. "Now—I'm warm. How about taking a swim?"

They turned their backs to the valley. Arm in arm they walked silently down a path of clear-running spring water.

FIVE YEARS LATER a rocket fell out of the sky. It lay steaming in the valley. Men leaped out of it, shouting.

"We won the war on Earth! We're here to rescue you! Hey!"

But the American-built town of cottages, peach trees, and theaters was silent. They found a flimsy rocket frame rusting in an empty shop.

The rocket men searched the hills. The captain established headquarters in an abandoned bar. His lieutenant came back to report.

"The town's empty, but we found native life in the hills, sir. Dark people. Yellow eyes. Martians. Very friendly. We talked a bit, not much. They learn English fast. I'm sure our relations will be most friendly with them, sir."

"Dark, eh?" mused the captain. "How many?"

"Six, eight hundred, I'd say, living in those marble ruins in the hills, sir. Tall, healthy. Beautiful women."

"Did they tell you what became of the men and women who built this Earth-settlement, Lieutenant?"

"They hadn't the foggiest notion of what happened to this town or its people."

"Strange. You think those Martians killed them?"

"They look surprisingly peaceful. Chances are a plague did this town in, sir."

"Perhaps. I suppose this is one of those mysteries we'll never solve. One of those mysteries you read about."

The captain looked at the room, the dusty windows, the blue mountains rising beyond, the canals moving in the light, and he heard the soft wind in the air. He shivered. Then, recovering, he tapped a large fresh map he had thumbtacked to the top of an empty table.

"Lots to be done, Lieutenant." His voice droned on and quietly on as the sun sank behind the blue hills. "New settlements. Mining sites, minerals to be looked for. Bacteriological specimens taken. The work, all the work. And the old records were lost. We'll have a job of remapping to do, renaming the mountains and rivers and such. Calls for a little imagination.

"What do you think of naming those mountains the Lincoln Mountains, this canal the Washington Canal, those hills—we can name those hills for you, Lieutenant. Diplomacy. And you, for a favor, might name a town for me. Polishing the apple. And why not make this the Einstein Valley, and further over . . . are you *listening*, Lieutenant?"

The lieutenant snapped his gaze from the blue color and the quiet mist of the hills far beyond the town.

"What? Oh, *yes,* sir!"

The New Wave

"Repent, Harlequin!" Said the Ticktockman

Harlan Ellison is a genre unto himself. One of the most controversial and provocative writers of science fiction in the second half of the twentieth century, he is known for impassioned, outspoken stories that mix humor, horror, pathos, and rage in inimitably personal proportions. Though his work has been embraced by the science fiction community, little of it conforms to science fiction conventions. Ellison was a seasoned writing professional who for a decade had turned out quantities of competent commercial fiction for a variety of markets— science fiction, fantasy, crime, juvenile delinquent—when he began publishing speculative tales that challenged taboos and broke prevailing conventions in science fiction. " 'Repent, Harlequin!' Said the Ticktockman" is a Kafkaesque parable about the dangers of individuality in a conformist society. "I Have No Mouth and I Must Scream" is a prescient tale of future shock in which computers become the masters of human beings. "A Boy and His Dog" has become one of the best-known stories of a postapocalyptic future, owing to its unflinching treatment of the ethics of survival. Ellison's fiction resonated with the work of science fiction's New Wave writers, who sought to break down the walls separating science fiction from the literary mainstream. His stories were often stylistically experimental, deeply humanist, and leavened with a social consciousness that made them important documents of their time without diminishing their power to endure. Many stories from these years were collected in *Ellison Wonderland, Paingod and Other Delusions, I Have No Mouth and I Must Scream, The Beast That Shouted Love at the Heart of the World,* and *Alone against Tomorrow. Deathbird Stories,* which culled considerably from these collections, is Ellison's definitive short-fiction volume, a blend of light and dark fantasies, cynical quest stories, science fiction allegories, and surrealist parables all presented as invocations to the gods that define the contemporary culture. Ellison's reputation as a renegade enhanced his editorial work on *Dangerous Visions* and *Again, Dangerous Visions,* award-winning anthologies built on stories by fellow writers that had been rejected by other markets as too controversial. Some of his most important fiction of the 1980s and '90s is collected in *Strange Wine, Shatterday, Angry Candy,* and *Slippage.* He is a multiple winner of the Hugo, Nebula, World Fantasy, and Bram Stoker Awards and an award-winning screenwriter whose television credits include *The Outer Limits, Star Trek,* and the new *Twilight Zone.* His collections *The Glass Teat, The*

Other Glass Teat, An Edge in My Voice, and *Harlan Ellison's Watching* all feature essays and commentaries on film, television, and modern society.

THERE ARE ALWAYS those who ask, what is it all about? For those who need to ask, for those who need points sharply made, who need to know "where it's at," this:

> *The mass of men serve the state thus, not as men mainly, but as machines, with*
> *their bodies. They are the standing army, and the militia, jailors, constables,*
> *posse comitatus, etc. In most cases there is no free exercise whatever of the*
> *judgment or of the moral sense; but they put themselves on a level with wood*
> *and earth and stones; and wooden men can perhaps be manufactured that will*
> *serve the purpose as well. Such command no more respect than men of straw or*
> *a lump of dirt. They have the same sort of worth only as horses and dogs. Yet*
> *such as these even are commonly esteemed good citizens. Others—as most leg-*
> *islators, politicians, lawyers, ministers, and officeholders—serve the state chiefly*
> *with their heads; and, as they rarely make any moral distinctions, they are as*
> *likely to serve the Devil, without intending it, as God. A very few, as heroes,*
> *patriots, martyrs, reformers in the great sense, and men, serve the state with*
> *their consciences also, and so necessarily resist it for the most part; and they are*
> *commonly treated as enemies by it.*
>
> HENRY DAVID THOREAU
Civil Disobedience

That is the heart of it. Now begin in the middle, and later learn the beginning; the end will take care of itself.

BUT BECAUSE IT was the very world it was, the very world they had allowed it to *become,* for months his activities did not come to the alarmed attention of The Ones Who Kept the Machine Functioning Smoothly, the ones who poured the very best butter over the cams and mainsprings of the culture. Not until it had become obvious that somehow, someway, he had become a notoriety, a celebrity, perhaps even a hero for (what Officialdom inescapably tagged) "an emotionally disturbed segment of the populace," did they turn it over to the Ticktockman and his legal machinery. But by then, because it was the very world it was, and they had no way to predict he would happen—possibly a strain of disease long-defunct, now, suddenly, reborn in a system where immunity had been forgotten, had lapsed—he had been allowed to become too real. Now he had form and substance.

He had become a *personality,* something they had filtered out of the system many decades before. But there it was, and there *he* was, a very definitely imposing person-

ality. In certain circles—middle-class circles—it was thought disgusting. Vulgar os-
tentation. Anarchistic. Shameful. In others, there was only sniggering: those strata
where thought is subjugated to form and ritual, niceties, proprieties. But down below,
ah, down below, where the people always needed their saints and sinners, their bread
and circuses, their heroes and villains, he was considered a Bolivar; a Napoleon; a
Robin Hood; a Dick Bong (Ace of Aces); a Jesus; a Jomo Kenyatta.

And at the top—where, like socially-attuned Shipwreck Kellys, every tremor and
vibration threatened to dislodge the wealthy, powerful and titled from their flag-
poles—he was considered a menace; a heretic; a rebel; a disgrace; a peril. He was
known down the line, to the very heart-meat core, but the important reactions were
high above and far below. At the very top, at the very bottom.

So his file was turned over, along with his time-card and his cardioplate, to the
office of the Ticktockman.

The Ticktockman: very much over six feet tall, often silent, a soft purring man
when things went timewise. The Ticktockman.

Even in the cubicles of the hierarchy, where fear was generated, seldom suffered,
he was called the Ticktockman. But no one called him that to his mask.

You don't call a man a hated name, not when that man, behind his mask, is
capable of revoking the minutes, the hours, the days and nights, the years of your
life. He was called the Master Timekeeper to his mask. It was safer that way.

"This is *what* he is," said the Ticktockman with genuine softness, "but not *who*
he is. This time-card I'm holding in my left hand has a name on it, but it is the name
of *what* he is, not *who* he is. The cardioplate here in my right hand is also named,
but not *whom* named, merely *what* named. Before I can exercise proper revocation,
I have to know *who* this *what* is."

To his staff, all the ferrets, all the loggers, all the finks, all the commex, even the
mineez, he said, "Who is this Harlequin?"

He was not purring smoothly. Timewise, it was jangle.

However, it *was* the longest speech they had ever heard him utter at one time,
the staff, the ferrets, the loggers, the finks, the commex, but not the mineez, who
usually weren't around to know, in any case. But even they scurried to find out.

Who is the Harlequin?

HIGH ABOVE THE third level of the city, he crouched on the humming aluminum-
frame platform of the air-boat (foof! air-boat, indeed! swizzleskid is what it was, with
a tow-rack jerry-rigged) and he stared down at the neat Mondrian arrangement of
the buildings.

Somewhere nearby, he could hear the metronomic left-right-left of the 2:47 P.M
shift, entering the Timkin roller-bearing plant in their sneakers. A minute later, precisely, he heard the softer right-left-right of the 5:00 A.M. formation, going home.

An elfin grin spread across his tanned features, and his dimples appeared for a moment. Then, scratching at his thatch of auburn hair, he shrugged within his motley, as though girding himself for what came next, and threw the joystick forward, and bent into the wind as the air-boat dropped. He skimmed over a slidewalk, purposely dropping a few feet to crease the tassels of the ladies of fashion, and—inserting thumbs in large ears—he stuck out his tongue, rolled his eyes and went wugga-wugga-wugga. It was a minor diversion. One pedestrian skittered and tumbled, sending parcels everywhichway, another wet herself, a third keeled slantwise and the walk was stopped automatically by the servitors till she could be resuscitated. It was a minor diversion.

Then he swirled away on a vagrant breeze, and was gone. Hi-ho. As he rounded the cornice of the Time-Motion Study Building, he saw the shift, just boarding the slidewalk. With practiced motion and an absolute conservation of movement, they sidestepped up onto the slow-strip and (in a chorus line reminiscent of a Busby Berkeley film of the antediluvian 1930s) advanced across the strips ostrich-walking till they were lined up on the expresstrip.

Once more, in anticipation, the elfin grin spread, and there was a tooth missing back there on the left side. He dipped, skimmed, and swooped over them; and then, scrunching about on the air-boat, he released the holding pins that fastened shut the ends of the home-made pouring troughs that kept his cargo from dumping prematurely. And as he pulled the trough-pins, the air-boat slid over the factory workers and one hundred and fifty thousand dollars' worth of jelly beans cascaded down on the expresstrip.

Jelly beans! Millions and billions of purples and yellows and greens and licorice and grape and raspberry and mint and round and smooth and crunchy outside and soft-mealy inside and sugary and bouncing jouncing tumbling clittering clattering skittering fell on the heads and shoulders and hardhats and carapaces of the Timkin workers, tinkling on the slidewalk and bouncing away and rolling about underfoot and filling the sky on their way down with all the colors of joy and childhood and holidays, coming down in a steady rain, a solid wash, a torrent of color and sweetness out of the sky from above, and entering a universe of sanity and metronomic order with quite-mad coocoo newness. Jelly beans!

The shift workers howled and laughed and were pelted, and broke ranks, and the jelly beans managed to work their way into the mechanism of the slidewalks after which there was a hideous scraping as the sound of a million fingernails rasped down a quarter of a million blackboards, followed by a coughing and a sputtering, and then the slidewalks all stopped and everyone was dumped thisawayandthataway in a jack-straw tumble, still laughing and popping little jelly bean eggs of childish color into their mouths. It was a holiday, and a jollity, an absolute insanity, a giggle. But . . .

The shift was delayed seven minutes.

They did not get home for seven minutes.

The master schedule was thrown off by seven minutes.

Quotas were delayed by inoperative slidewalks for seven minutes.

He had tapped the first domino in the line, and one after another, like chik chik chik, the others had fallen.

The System had been seven minutes' worth of disrupted. It was a tiny matter, one hardly worthy of note, but in a society where the single driving force was order and unity and equality and promptness and clocklike precision and attention to the clock, reverence of the gods of the passage of time, it was a disaster of major importance.

So he was ordered to appear before the Ticktockman. It was broadcast across every channel of the communications web. He was ordered to be *there* at 7:00 dammit on time. And they waited, and they waited, but he didn't show up till almost ten-thirty, at which time he merely sang a little song about moonlight in a place no one had ever heard of, called Vermont, and vanished again. But they had all been waiting since seven, and it wrecked *hell* with their schedules. So the question remained: Who is the Harlequin?

But the *unasked* question (more important of the two) was: how did we get *into* this position, where a laughing, irresponsible japer of jabberwocky and jive could disrupt our entire economic and cultural life with a hundred and fifty thousand dollars' worth of jelly beans...

Jelly for God's sake *beans!* This is madness! Where did he get the money to buy a hundred and fifty thousand dollars' worth of jelly beans? (They knew it would have cost that much, because they had a team of Situation Analysts pulled off another assignment, and rushed to the slidewalk scene to sweep up and count the candies, and produce findings, which disrupted *their* schedules and threw their entire branch at least a day behind.) Jelly beans! Jelly... *beans?* Now wait a second—a second accounted for—no one has manufactured jelly beans for over a hundred years. Where did he get jelly beans?

That's another good question. More than likely it will never be answered to your complete satisfaction. But then, how many questions ever are?

The middle you know. Here is the beginning. How it starts:

A DESK PAD. DAY FOR DAY, AND TURN EACH DAY. 9:00—OPEN THE MAIL. 9:45—APPOINT-MENT WITH PLANNING COMMISSION BOARD. 10:30—DISCUSS INSTALLATION PROGRESS CHARTS WITH J.L. 11:45—PRAY FOR RAIN. 12:00—LUNCH. AND SO IT GOES.

"I'm sorry, Miss Grant, but the time for interviews was set at 2:30, and it's almost five now. I'm sorry you're late, but those are the rules. You'll have

to wait till next year to submit application for this college again." And so it goes.

The 10:10 local stops at Cresthaven, Galesville, Tonawanda Junction, Selby and Farnhurst, but not at Indiana City, Lucasville and Colton, except on Sunday. The 10:35 express stops at Galesville, Selby and Indiana City, except on Sundays & Holidays, at which time it stops at . . . *and so it goes.*

"I couldn't wait, Fred. I had to be at Pierre Cartain's by 3:00, and you said you'd meet me under the clock in the terminal at 2:45, and you weren't there, so I had to go on. You're always late, Fred. If you'd been there, we could have sewed it up together, but as it was, well, I took the order alone . . ." *And so it goes.*

Dear Mr. and Mrs. Atterley: In reference to your son Gerold's constant tardiness, I am afraid we will have to suspend him from school unless some more reliable method can be instituted guaranteeing he will arrive at his classes on time. Granted he is an exemplary student, and his marks are high, his constant flouting of the schedules of this school makes it impractical to maintain him in a system where the other children seem capable of getting where they are supposed to be on time *and so it goes.*

YOU CANNOT VOTE UNLESS YOU APPEAR AT 8:45 A.M.

"I don't care if the script is *good,* I need it Thursday!"

CHECK-OUT TIME IS 2:00 P.M.

"You got here late. The Job's taken. Sorry."

YOUR SALARY HAS BEEN DOCKED FOR TWENTY MINUTES TIME LOST.

"God, what time is it, I've gotta run!"

    And so it goes. And so it goes. And so it goes. And so it goes goes goes goes goes tick tock tick tock tick tock and one day we no longer let time serve us, we serve time and we are slaves of the schedule, worshippers of the sun's passing, bound into a life predicated on restrictions because the system will not function if we don't keep the schedule tight.

Until it becomes more than a minor inconvenience to be late. It becomes a sin. Then a crime. Then a crime punishable by this:

EFFECTIVE 15 JULY 2389 12:00:00 midnight, the office of the Master Timekeeper will require all citizens to submit their time-cards and cardioplates for processing. In accordance with Statute 555-7-SGH-999 governing the revocation of time per capita, all cardioplates will be keyed to the individual holder and—

What they had done was devise a method of curtailing the amount of life a person could have. If he was ten minutes late, he lost ten minutes of his life. An hour was proportionately worth more revocation. If someone was consistently tardy, he might find himself, on a Sunday night, receiving a communiqué from the Master Timekeeper that his time had run out, and he would be "turned off" at high noon on Monday, please straighten your affairs, sir, madame or bisex.

And so, by this simple scientific expedient (utilizing a scientific process held dearly secret by the Ticktockman's office) the System was maintained. It was the only expedient thing to do. It was, after all, patriotic. The schedules had to be met. After all, there *was* a war on!

But, wasn't there always?

"NOW THAT IS really disgusting," the Harlequin said, when Pretty Alice showed him the wanted poster. "Disgusting and *highly* improbable. After all, this isn't the Day of the Desperado. A *wanted* poster!"

"You know," Pretty Alice noted, "you speak with a great deal of inflection."

"I'm sorry," said the Harlequin, humbly.

"No need to be sorry. You're always saying 'I'm sorry.' You have such massive guilt, Everett, it's really very sad."

"I'm sorry," he said again, then pursed his lips so the dimples appeared momentarily. He hadn't wanted to say that at all. "I have to go out again. I have to *do* something."

Pretty Alice slammed her coffee-bulb down on the counter. "Oh for God's *sake*, Everett, can't you stay home just *one* night! Must you always be out in that ghastly clown suit, running around an*noy*ing people?"

"I'm—" He stopped, and clapped the jester's hat onto his auburn thatch with a tiny tinkling of bells. He rose, rinsed out his coffee-bulb at the spray, and put it into the dryer for a moment. "I have to go."

She didn't answer. The faxbox was purring, and she pulled a sheet out, read it, threw it toward him on the counter. "It's about you. Of course. You're ridiculous."

He read it quickly. It said the Ticktockman was trying to locate him. He didn't care, he was going out to be late again. At the door, dredging for an exit line, he hurled back petulantly, "Well, *you* speak with inflection, *too!*"

Pretty Alice rolled her pretty eyes heavenward. "You're ridiculous."

The Harlequin stalked out, slamming the door, which sighed shut softly, and locked itself.

There was a gentle knock, and Pretty Alice got up with an exhalation of exasperated breath, and opened the door. He stood there. "I'll be back about ten-thirty, okay?"

She pulled a rueful face. "Why do you tell me that? Why? You *know* you'll be late! You *know* it! You're *always* late, so why do you tell me these dumb things?" She closed the door.

On the other side, the Harlequin nodded to himself. *She's right. She's always right. I'll be late. I'm always late. Why* do *I tell her these dumb things?*

He shrugged again, and went off to be late once more.

HE HAD FIRED off the firecracker rockets that said: I will attend the 115th annual International Medical Association Invocation at 8:00 P.M. precisely. I do hope you will all be able to join me.

The words had burned in the sky, and of course the authorities were there, lying in wait for him. They assumed, naturally, that he would be late. He arrived twenty minutes early, while they were setting up the spiderwebs to trap and hold him. Blowing a large bullhorn, he frightened and unnerved them so, their own moisturized encirclement webs sucked closed, and they were hauled up, kicking and shrieking, high above the amphitheater's floor. The Harlequin laughed and laughed, and apologized profusely. The physicians, gathered in solemn conclave, roared with laughter, and accepted the Harlequin's apologies with exaggerated bowing and posturing, and a merry time was had by all, who thought the Harlequin was a regular foofaraw in fancy pants; all, that is, but the authorities, who had been sent out by the office of the Ticktockman; they hung there like so much dockside cargo, hauled up above the floor of the amphitheater in a most unseemly fashion.

(In another part of the same city where the Harlequin carried on his "activities," totally unrelated in every way to what concerns us here, save that it illustrates the Ticktockman's power and import, a man named Marshall Delahanty received his turn-off notice from the Ticktockman's office. His wife received the notification from the gray-suited minee who delivered it, with the traditional "look of sorrow" plastered hideously across his face. She knew what it was, even without unsealing it. It was a billet-doux of immediate recognition to everyone these days. She gasped, and held it as though it were a glass slide tinged with botulism, and prayed it was not for her. Let it be for Marsh, she thought, brutally, realistically, or one of the kids, but not for me, please dear God, not for me. And then she opened it, and it *was* for Marsh, and she was at one and the same time horrified and relieved. The next trooper in the line had caught the bullet. "Marshall," she screamed, "Marshall! Termination, Marshall! OhmiGod, Marshall, whattl we do, whattl we do, Marshall omigodmarshall . . ." and in their home that night was the sound of tearing paper and fear, and the stink of madness went up the flue and there was nothing, absolutely nothing they could do about it.

(But Marshall Delahanty tried to run. And early the next day, when turn-off time came, he was deep in the Canadian forest two hundred miles away, and the office of the Ticktockman blanked his cardioplate, and Marshall Delahanty keeled over, running, and his heart stopped, and the blood dried up on its way to his brain, and he was dead that's all. One light went out on the sector map in the office of the Master Timekeeper, while notification was entered for fax reproduction, and Georgette Delahanty's name was entered on the dole roles till she could remarry. Which is the end of the footnote, and all the point that need be made, except don't laugh, because that is what would happen to the Harlequin if ever the Ticktockman found out his real name. It isn't funny.)

THE SHOPPING LEVEL of the city was thronged with the Thursday-colors of the buyers. Women in canary yellow chitons and men in pseudo-Tyrolean outfits that were jade and leather and fit very tightly, save for the balloon pants.

When the Harlequin appeared on the still-being-constructed shell of the new Efficiency Shopping Center, his bullhorn to his elfishly-laughing lips, everyone pointed and stared, and he berated them:

"Why let them order you about? Why let them tell you to hurry and scurry like ants or maggots? Take your time! Saunter awhile! Enjoy the sunshine, enjoy the breeze, let life carry you at your own pace! Don't be slaves of time, it's a helluva way to die, slowly, by degrees . . . down with the Ticktockman!"

Who's the nut? most of the shoppers wanted to know. Who's the nut oh wow I'm gonna be late I gotta run . . .

And the construction gang on the Shopping Center received an urgent order from the office of the Master Timekeeper that the dangerous criminal known as the Harlequin was atop their spire, and their aid was urgently needed in apprehending him. The work crew said no, they would lose time on their construction schedule, but the Ticktockman managed to pull the proper threads of governmental webbing, and they were told to cease work and catch that nitwit up there on the spire; up there with the bullhorn. So a dozen and more burly workers began climbing into their construction platforms, releasing the a-grav plates, and rising toward the Harlequin.

AFTER THE DEBACLE (in which, through the Harlequin's attention to personal safety, no one was seriously injured), the workers tried to reassemble, and assault him again, but it was too late. He had vanished. It had attracted quite a crowd, however, and the shopping cycle was thrown off by hours, simply hours. The purchasing needs of the System were therefore falling behind, and so measures were taken to accelerate the cycle for the rest of the day, but it got bogged down and speeded up and they sold too many float-valves and not nearly enough wegglers, which meant that the popli ratio was off, which made it necessary to rush cases and cases of spoiling Smash-O to stores that usually needed a case only every three or four hours. The shipments were bollixed, the transshipments were misrouted, and in the end, even the swizzleskid industries felt it.

"DON'T COME BACK till you have him!" the Ticktockman said, very quietly, very sincerely, extremely dangerously.

They used dogs. They used probes. They used cardioplate crossoffs. They used teepers. They used bribery. They used stiktytes. They used intimidation. They used torment. They used torture. They used finks. They used cops. They used search&seizure. They used fallaron. They used betterment incentive. They used fingerprints. They used the Bertillon system. They used cunning. They used guile. They used treachery. They used Raoul Mitgong, but he didn't help much. They used applied physics. They used techniques of criminology.

And what the hell: they caught him.

After all, his name was Everett C. Marm, and he wasn't much to begin with, except a man who had no sense of time.

"REPENT, HARLEQUIN!" SAID the Ticktockman.

"Get stuffed!" the Harlequin replied, sneering.

"You've been late a total of sixty-three years, five months, three weeks, two days, twelve hours, forty-one minutes, fifty-nine seconds, point oh three six one one one microseconds. You've used up everything you can, and more. I'm going to turn you off."

"Scare someone else. I'd rather be dead than live in a dumb world with a bogeyman like you."

"It's my job."

"You're full of it. You're a tyrant. You have no right to order people around and kill them if they show up late."

"You can't adjust. You can't fit in."

"Unstrap me, and I'll fit my fist into your mouth."

"You're a nonconformist."

"That didn't used to be a felony."

"It is now. Live in the world around you."

"I hate it. It's a terrible world."

"Not everyone thinks so. Most people enjoy order."

"I don't, and most of the people I know don't."

"That's not true. How do you think we caught you?"

"I'm not interested."

"A girl named Pretty Alice told us who you were."

"That's a lie."

"It's true. You unnerve her. She wants to belong; she wants to conform; I'm going to turn you off."

"Then do it already, and stop arguing with me."

"I'm not going to turn you off."

"You're an idiot!"

"Repent, Harlequin!" said the Ticktockman.

"Get stuffed."

So THEY SENT him to Coventry. And in Coventry they worked him over. It was just like what they did to Winston Smith in NINETEEN EIGHTY-FOUR, which was a book none of them knew about, but the techniques are really quite ancient, and so they did it to Everett C. Marm; and one day, quite a long time later, the Harlequin appeared on the communications web, appearing elfin and dimpled and bright-eyed, and not at all brainwashed, and he said he had been wrong, that it was a good, a very good thing indeed, to belong, to be right on time hip-ho and away we go, and everyone stared up at him on the public screens that covered an entire city block, and they said to themselves, well, you see, he was just a nut after all, and if that's the way the system is run, then let's do it that way, because it doesn't pay to fight city hall, or in this case, the Ticktockman. So Everett C. Marm was destroyed, which was a loss, because of what Thoreau said earlier, but you can't make an omelet without breaking a few eggs, and in every revolution a few die who shouldn't, but they have to, because that's the way it happens, and if you make only a little change, then it seems to be worthwhile. Or, to make the point lucidly:

"UH, EXCUSE ME, sir, I, uh, don't know how to uh, to uh, tell you this, but you were three minutes late. The schedule is a little, uh, bit off."

He grinned sheepishly.

"That's ridiculous!" murmured the Ticktockman behind his mask. "Check your watch." And then he went into his office, going *mrmee, mrmee, mrmee, mrmee.*

Eurema's Dam

Eccentric, outrageous, and packed with bizarre characters and incidents, R. A. Lafferty's stylistically unconventional short stories are as much a part of the oral tall tale tradition as they are fantasy and science fiction. Lafferty began publishing fiction in the 1960s and was a prominent figure in science fiction's iconoclastic New Wave, where his gnomic, challenging variations on standard science fiction and fantasy themes bridged the gap between speculative and mainstream fiction. A stylistic maverick, Lafferty fills his stories with puns and wordplay that create incongruous associations between their disparate elements. The style of his narratives is similarly adventurous and includes mixtures of sermons, riddles, doggerel, epigrams, imagined reference works, and textbook treatises. He has written on subjects ranging from supernatural conspiracy to evil adolescents, celestial revolutionaries, Native American lore, utopia, demons, and carnal love. In his novels he is fond of creating modern corollaries for classic myths and legends. *Space Chantey* works the basic story of Homer's *Odyssey* into a wild space opera. In the Argos cycle, which includes *Archipelago, The Devil Is Dead*, and *Episodes of the Argo,* Jason and the Argonauts are reincarnated as members of a former World War II battle unit. In *Past Master,* Sir Thomas More is transported in time and space to the planet Astrobe, where he falls afoul of political intrigue and suffers his seemingly inescapable martyr's death. Lafferty's preoccupation with religious archetypes and the battle (and sometimes collusion) between Good and Evil gives much of his writing a mythic character. His short fiction has been collected in *Nine Hundred Grandmothers, Strange Doings, Does Anyone Else Have Something Further to Add?* and numerous other collections. His novels include *The Reefs of Earth, Fourth Mansions, The Annals of Klepsis,* and *Arrive at Easterwine.* He has also written a volume of essays on fantastic literature, *It's Down the Slippery Cellar Stairs.* Interviews with him have been collected in *Cranky Old Man from Tulsa.*

HE WAS ABOUT the last of them.

What? The last of the great individualists? The last of the true creative geniuses of the century? The last of the sheer precursors?

No. No. He was the last of the dolts.

Kids were being born smarter all the time when he came along, and they would be so forever more. He was about the last dumb kid ever born.

Even his mother had to admit that Albert was a slow child. What else can you call a boy who doesn't begin to talk till he is four years old, who won't learn to handle a spoon till he is six, who can't operate a doorknob till he is eight? What else can you say about one who put his shoes on the wrong feet and walked in pain? And who had to be told to close his mouth after yawning?

Some things would always be beyond him—like whether it was the big hand or the little hand of the clock that told the hours. But this wasn't something serious. He never did care what time it was.

When, about the middle of his ninth year, Albert made a breakthrough at telling his right hand from his left, he did it by the most ridiculous set of mnemonics ever put together. It had to do with the way a dog turns around before lying down, the direction of whirlpools and whirlwinds, the side a cow is milked from and a horse is mounted from, the direction of twist of oak and sycamore leaves, the maze patterns of rock moss and of tree moss, the cleavage of limestone, the direction of a hawk's wheeling, of a shrike's hunting, and of a snake's coiling (remembering that the mountain boomer is an exception, and that it isn't a true snake), the lay of cedar fronds and of balsam fronds, the twist of a hole dug by a skunk and by a badger (remembering pungently that skunks sometimes use old badger holes). Well, Albert finally learned to remember which was right and which was left, but an observant boy would have learned his right hand from his left without all that nonsense.

Albert never learned to write a readable hand. To get by in school he cheated. From a bicycle speedometer, a midget motor, tiny eccentric cams, and batteries stolen from his grandfather's hearing aid, Albert made a machine to write for him. It was small as a doodlebug and fitted onto a pen or pencil so that Albert could conceal it with his fingers. It formed the letters beautifully as Albert had set the cams to follow a copybook model. He triggered the different letters with keys no bigger than whiskers. Sure it was crooked, but what else can you do when you're too dumb to learn how to write passably?

Albert couldn't figure at all. He had to make another machine to figure for him. It was a palm-of-the-hand thing that would add and subtract and multiply and divide. The next year when he was in the ninth grade they gave him algebra, and he had to devise a flipper to go on the end of his gadget to work quadratic and simultaneous equations. If it weren't for such cheating Albert wouldn't have gotten any marks at all in school.

HE HAD ANOTHER difficulty when he came to his fifteenth year. People, that is an understatement. There should be a stronger word than "difficulty" for it. Albert was afraid of girls.

What to do?

"I will build me a machine that is not afraid of girls," Albert said. He set to work on it. He had it nearly finished when a thought came to him: "But no machine is afraid of girls. How will this help me?"

His logic was at fault and analogy broke down. He did what he always did. He cheated.

He took the programming rollers out of an old player piano in the attic, found a gear case that would serve, used magnetized sheets instead of perforated music rolls, fed a copy of *Wormwood's Logic* into the matrix, and he had a logic machine that would answer questions.

"What's the matter with me that I'm afraid of girls?" Albert asked his logic machine.

"Nothing the matter with you," the logic machine told him. "It's logical to be afraid of girls. They seem pretty spooky to me too."

"But what can I do about it?"

"Wait for time and circumstances. They sure are slow. Unless you want to cheat—"

"Yes, yes, what then?"

"Build a machine that looks just like you, Albert, and talks just like you. Only make it smarter than you are, and not bashful. And, ah, Albert, there's a special thing you'd better put into it in case things go wrong. I'll whisper it to you. It's dangerous."

So Albert made Little Danny, a dummy who looked like him and talked like him, only he was smarter and not bashful. He filled Little Danny with quips from *Mad Magazine* and from *Quip*, and then they were set.

Albert and Little Danny went to call on Alice.

"Why, he's wonderful," Alice said. "Why can't you be like that, Albert? Aren't you wonderful, Little Danny. Why do you have to be so stupid, Albert, when Little Danny is so wonderful?"

"I, uh, uh, I don't know," Albert said. "Uh, uh, uh."

"He sounds like a fish with the hiccups," Little Danny said.

"You do, Albert, really you do!" Alice screamed. "Why can't you say smart things like Little Danny does, Albert? Why are you so stupid?"

This wasn't working out very well, but Albert kept on with it. He programmed Little Danny to play the ukulele and to sing. He wished that he could program himself to do it. Alice loved everything about Little Danny, but she paid no attention to Albert. And one day Albert had had enough.

"Wha-wha-what do we need with this dummy?" Albert asked. "I just made him to am-to amu-to to make you laugh. Let's go off and leave him."

"Go off with you, Albert?" Alice asked. "But you're so stupid. I tell you what.

Let's you and me go off and leave Albert, Little Danny. We can have more fun without him."

"Who needs him?" Little Danny asked. "Get lost, buster."

Albert walked away from them. He was glad that he'd taken his logic machine's advice as to the special thing to be built into Little Danny. Albert walked fifty steps. A hundred.

"Far enough," Albert said, and he pushed a button in his pocket.

Nobody but Albert and his logic machine ever did know what that explosion was. Tiny wheels out of Little Danny and small pieces of Alice rained down a little later, but there weren't enough fragments for anyone to identify.

Albert had learned one lesson from his logic machine: never make anything that you can't unmake.

Well, Albert finally grew to be a man, in years at least. He would always have something about him of a very awkward teen-ager. And yet he fought his own war against those who were teen-agers in years, and he defeated them completely. There was enmity between them forever. Albert hadn't been a very well-adjusted adolescent, and he hated the memory of it. And nobody ever mistook him for an adjusted man.

Albert was too awkward to earn a living at an honest trade. He was reduced to peddling his little tricks and contrivances to shysters and promoters. But he did back into a sort of fame, and he did become burdened with wealth.

He was too stupid to handle his own monetary affairs, but he built an actuary machine to do his investing and he became rich by accident. He built the damned thing too good and he regretted it.

Albert became one of that furtive group that has saddled us with all the mean things in our history. There was that Punic who couldn't learn the rich variety of hieroglyphic characters and who devised the crippled short alphabet for wan-wits. There was the nameless Arab who couldn't count beyond ten and who set up the ten-number system for babies and idiots. There was the double-Dutchman with his movable type who drove fine copy out of the world. Albert was of their miserable company.

Albert himself wasn't much good for anything. But he had in himself the low knack for making machines that were good at everything.

His machines did a few things. You remember that anciently there was smog in the cities. Oh, it could be drawn out of the air easily enough. All it took was a tickler. Albert made a tickler machine. He would set it fresh every morning. It would clear the air in a circle three hundred yards around his hovel and gather a little over a ton of residue every twenty-four hours. This residue was rich in large polysyllabic molecules which one of his chemical machines could use.

"Why can't you clear all the air?" the people asked him.

"This is as much of the stuff as Clarence Deoxyribonucleiconibus needs every day," Albert said. That was the name of this particular chemical machine.

"But we die of the smog," the people said. "Have mercy on us."

"Oh, all right," Albert said. He turned it over to one of his reduplicating machines to make as many copies as were necessary.

YOU REMEMBER THAT once there was a teen-ager problem? You remember when those little buggers used to be mean? Albert got enough of them. There was something ungainly about them that reminded him too much of himself. He made a teen-ager of his own. It was rough. To the others it looked like one of themselves, the ring in the left ear, the dangling side-locks, the brass knucks and the long knife, the guitar pluck to jab in an eye. But it was incomparably rougher than the human teen-agers. It terrorized all in the neighborhood and made them behave, and dress like real people. And there was one thing about the teen-age machine that Albert made: it was made of such polarized metal and glass that it was invisible except to teen-ager eyes.

"Why is your neighborhood different?" the people asked Albert. "Why are there such good and polite teen-agers in your neighborhood and such mean ones every-where else? It's as though something had spooked all those right around here."

"Oh, I thought I was the only one who didn't like the regular kind," Albert said.

"Oh, no, no," the people answered him. "If there is anything at all you can do about them—"

So Albert turned his mostly invisible teen-ager machine over to one of his re-duplicating machines to make as many copies as were necessary, and set one up in every neighborhood. From that day till this the teen-agers have all been good and polite and a little bit frightened. But there is no evidence of what keeps them that way except an occasional eye dangling from the jab of an invisible guitar pluck.

So the two most pressing problems of the latter part of the twentieth century were solved, but accidentally, and to the credit of no one.

AS THE YEARS went by, Albert felt his inferiority most when in the presence of his own machines, particularly those in the form of men. Albert just hadn't their urbanity or sparkle or wit. He was a clod beside them, and they made him feel it.

Why not? One of Albert's devices sat in the President's Cabinet. One of them was on the High Council of World-Watchers that kept the peace everywhere. One of them presided at Riches Unlimited, that private-public-international instrument that guaranteed reasonable riches to everyone in the world. One of them was the guiding hand in the Health and Longevity Foundation which provided those things to every-one. Why should not such splendid and successful machines look down on their shabby uncle who had made them?

"I'm rich by a curious twist," Albert said to himself one day, "and honored through a mistake in circumstance. But there isn't a man or a machine in the world who is really my friend. A book here tells how to make friends, but I can't do it that way. I'll make one my own way."

So Albert set out to make a friend.

He made Poor Charles, a machine as stupid and awkward and inept as himself.

"Now I will have a companion," Albert said, but it didn't work. Add two zeros together and you still have zero. Poor Charles was too much like Albert to be good for anything.

Poor Charles! Unable to think, he made a—(but wait a moleskin-gloved minute here, Colonel, this isn't going to work at all)—he made a machi—(but isn't this the same blamed thing all over again?)—he made a machine to think for him and to—

Hold it, hold it! That's enough. Poor Charles was the only machine that Albert ever made that was dumb enough to do a thing like that.

Well, whatever it was, the machine that Poor Charles made was in control of the situation and of Poor Charles when Albert came onto them accidentally. The machine's machine, the device that Poor Charles had constructed to think for him, was lecturing Poor Charles in a humiliating way.

"Only the inept and deficient will invent," that damned machine's machine was droning. "The Greeks in their high period did not invent. They used neither adjunct power nor instrumentation. They used, as intelligent men or machines will always use, slaves. They did not descend to gadgets. They, who did the difficult with ease, did not seek the easier way.

"But the incompetent will invent. The insufficient will invent. The depraved will invent. And knaves will invent."

Albert, in a seldom fit of anger, killed them both. But he knew that the machine of his machine had spoken the truth.

Albert was very much cast down. A more intelligent man would have had a hunch as to what was wrong. Albert had only a hunch that he was not very good at hunches and would never be. Seeing no way out, he fabricated a machine and named it Hunchy.

In most ways this was the worst machine he ever made. In building it he tried to express something of his unease for the future. It was an awkward thing in mind and mechanism, a misfit.

Albert's more intelligent machines gathered around and hooted at him while he put it together.

"Boy! Are you lost!" they taunted. "That thing is a primitive! To draw its power from the ambient! We talked you into throwing that away twenty years ago and setting up coded power for all of us."

"Uh—someday there may be social disturbances and all centers of power seized," Albert stammered. "But Hunchy would be able to operate if the whole world were wiped smooth."

"It isn't even tuned to our information matrix," they jibed. "It's worse than Poor Charles. That stupid thing practically starts from scratch."

"Maybe there'll be a new kind of itch for it," said Albert.

"It's not even housebroken!" the urbane machines shouted their indignation. "Look at that! Some sort of primitive lubrication all over the floor."

"Remembering my childhood, I sympathize," Albert said.

"What's it good for?" they demanded.

"Ah—it gets hunches," Albert mumbled.

"Duplication!" they shouted. "That's all you're good for yourself, and not very good at that. We suggest an election to replace you as—pardon our laughter—the head of these enterprises."

"Boss, I've got a hunch how we can block them there," the unfinished Hunchy whispered.

"They're bluffing," Albert whispered back. "My first logic machine taught me never to make anything that I can't unmake. I've got them there and they know it. I wish I could think up things like that myself."

"Maybe there will come an awkward time and I will be good for something," Hunchy said.

ONLY ONCE, AND that rather late in life, did a sort of honesty flare up in Albert. He did one thing (and it was a dismal failure) on his own. That was the night of the year of the double millennium when Albert was presented with the Finnerty-Hochmann Trophy, the highest award that the intellectual world could give. Albert was certainly an odd choice for it, but it had been noticed that almost every basic invention for thirty years could be traced back to him or to the devices with which he had surrounded himself.

You know the trophy. Atop it was Eurema, the synthetic Greek goddess of invention, with arms spread as if she would take flight. Below this was a stylized brain cut away to show the convoluted cortex. And below this was the coat of arms of the Academicians: Ancient Scholar rampant (argent); the Anderson Analyzer sinister (gules); the Mondeman Space-Drive dexter (vair). It was a fine work by Groben, his ninth period.

Albert had a speech composed for him by his speech-writing machine, but for some reason he did not use it. He went on his own, and that was disaster. He got to his feet when he was introduced, and he stuttered and spoke nonsense!

"Ah—only the sick oyster produces nacre," he said, and they all gaped at him. What sort of beginning for a speech was that? "Or do I have the wrong creature?" Albert asked weakly.

"Eurema doesn't look like that!" Albert gawked out and pointed suddenly at the trophy. "No, no, that isn't her at all. Eurema walks backward and is blind. And her mother is a brainless hulk."

Everybody was watching him with pained expression.

"Nothing rises without a leaven," Albert tried to explain, "but the yeast is itself a fungus and a disease. You be regularizers all, splendid and supreme! But you cannot live without the irregulars. You will die, and who will tell you that you are dead? When there are no longer any deprived or insufficient, *who will invent?* What will you do when there is none of us detectives left? Who will leaven your lump then?"

"Are you unwell?" the master of ceremonies asked him quietly. "Should you not make an end to it? People will understand."

"Of course I'm unwell. Always have been," Albert said. "What good would I be otherwise? You set the ideal that all should be healthy and well adjusted. No! No! Were we all well adjusted, we would ossify and die. The world is kept healthy only by some of the unhealthy minds lurking in it. The first implement made by man was not a scraper or celt or stone knife. It was a crutch, and it wasn't devised by a hale man."

"Perhaps you should rest," a functionary said in a low voice, for this sort of rambling nonsense talk had never been heard at an awards dinner before.

"Know you," said Albert, "that it is not the fine bulls and wonderful cattle who make the new paths. Only a crippled calf makes a new path. In everything that survives there must be an element of the incongruous. Hey, you know the woman who said, 'My husband is incongruous, but I never liked Washington in the summertime.' "

Everybody gazed at him in stupor.

"That's the first joke I ever made," Albert said lamely. "My joke-making machine makes them a lot better than I do." He paused and gaped, and gulped a big breath.

"Dolts!" he croaked out fiercely then. "What will you do for dolts when the last of us is gone? How will you survive without us?"

Albert had finished. He gaped and forgot to close his mouth. They led him back to his seat. His publicity machine explained that Albert was tired from overwork, and then that machine passed around copies of the speech that Albert was supposed to have given.

It had been an unfortunate episode. How noisome it is that the innovators are never great men, and that the great men are never good for anything but just being great men.

IN THAT YEAR a decree went forth from Caesar that a census of the whole country should be taken. The decree was from Cesare Panebianco, the President of the country. It was the decimal year proper for the census, and there was nothing unusual about the decree. Certain provisions, however, were made for taking a census of the drifters and decrepits who were usually missed, to examine them and to see why they were so. It was in the course of this that Albert was picked up. If any man ever looked like a drifter and decrepit, it was Albert.

Albert was herded in with other derelicts, set down at a table, and asked tortuous questions. As:

"What is your name?"

He almost muffed that one, but he rallied and answered, "Albert."

"What time is it by that clock?"

They had him in his old weak spot. Which hand was which? He gaped and didn't answer.

"Can you read?" they asked him.

"Not without my—" Albert began. "I don't have with me my—No, I can't read very well by myself."

"Try."

They gave him a paper to mark up with true and false questions. Albert marked them all true, believing that he would have half of them right. But they were all false. The regularized people are partial to falsehood. Then they gave him a supply-the-word test on proverbs.

"———is the best policy" didn't mean a thing to him. He couldn't remember the names of the companies that he had his own policies with.

"A———in time saves nine" contained more mathematics than Albert could handle.

"There appear to be six unknowns," he told himself, "and only one positive value, nine. The equating verb 'saves' is a vague one. I cannot solve this equation. I am not even sure that it is an equation. If only I had with me my—"

But he hadn't any of his gadgets or machines with him. He was on his own. He left half a dozen other proverb fill-ins blank. Then he saw a chance to recoup. Nobody is so dumb as not to know one answer if enough questions are asked.

"———is the mother of invention," it said.

"Stupidity," Albert wrote in his weird ragged hand. Then he sat back in triumph. "I know that Eurema and her mother," he snickered. "Man, how I do know them!"

But they marked him wrong on that one too. He had missed every answer to every test. They began to fix him a ticket to a progressive booby hatch where he might learn to do something with his hands, his head being hopeless.

A couple of Albert's urbane machines came down and got him out of it. They explained that, while he was a drifter and a derelict, yet he was a rich drifter and derelict, and that he was even a man of some note.

"He doesn't look it, but he really is—pardon our laughter—a man of some importance," one of the fine machines explained. "He has to be told to close his mouth after he has yawned, but for all that he is the winner of the Finnerty-Hochmann Trophy. We will be responsible for him."

*   *   *

ALBERT WAS MISERABLE as his fine machines took him out, especially when they asked that he walk three or four steps behind them and not seem to be with them. They gave him some pretty rough banter and turned him into a squirming worm of a man. Albert left them and went to a little hide-out he kept.

"I'll blow my crawfishing brains out," he swore. "The humiliation is more than I can bear. Can't do it myself, though. I'll have to have it done."

He set to work building a device in his hide-out.

"What you doing, boss?" Hunchy asked him. "I had a hunch you'd come here and start building something."

"I'm building a machine to blow my pumpkin-picking brains out," Albert shouted. "I'm too yellow to do it myself."

"Boss, I got a hunch there's something better to do. Let's have some fun."

"Don't believe I know how to," Albert said thoughtfully. "I built a fun machine once to do it for me. He had a real revel till he flew apart, but he never seemed to do anything for me."

"This fun will be for you and me, boss. Consider the world spread out. What is it?"

"It's a world too fine for me to live in any longer," Albert said. "Everything and all the people are perfect, and all alike. They're at the top of the heap. They've won it all and arranged it all neatly. There's no place for a clutter-up like me in the world. So I get out."

"Boss, I've got a hunch that you're seeing it wrong. You've got better eyes than that. Look again, real canny, at it. Now what do you see?"

"Hunchy, Hunchy, is that possible? Is that really what it is? I wonder why I never noticed it before. That's the way of it, though, now that I look closer.

"Six billion patsies waiting to be took! Six billion patsies without a defense of any kind! A couple of guys out for some fun, man, they could mow them down like fields of Albert-Improved Concho Wheat!"

"Boss, I've got a hunch that this is what I was made for. The world sure had been getting stuffy. Let's tie into it and eat off the top layer. Man, we can cut a swath."

"We'll inaugurate a new era!" Albert gloated. "We'll call it the Turning of the Worm. We'll have fun, Hunchy. We'll gobble them up like goobers. How come I never saw it like that before? Six billion patsies!"

THE TWENTY-FIRST CENTURY began on this rather odd note.

Passengers

Robert Silverberg won the Hugo Award for Most Promising New Author in 1956, less than two years after his first professional sale. After an apprenticeship that lasted nearly ten years and yielded millions of words, Silverberg emerged in the 1960s as one of the most articulate and conscientious writers of the time. Works from this period of his career are memorable for their psychologically complex character studies, morally trenchant themes, and vivid depictions of oppressive and limiting environments that the individual must try to transcend. "To See the Invisible Man," "Hawksbill Station," and *Thorns* are futuristic studies of the individual alienated through a variety of means: social ostracism, penal exile, and exploitative victimization. Silverberg's crowning achievement in this vein is *Dying Inside,* the poignant tale of a telepath alienated by his uniqueness who is further isolated by the loss of his powers and thus his only means of relating to normal humanity. Both *Nightwings* and *Downward to Earth* present contact with alien species as potentially rejuvenating experiences, with overtones of resurrection and redemption. *The World Inside* chronicles the dehumanizing potential of overpopulation on a society where privacy and intimacy are virtually impossible. The dramatic core of Silverberg's strongest stories involves individuals confronted with mortality. "Born with the Dead" details the difficulties of life in a world that is shared by mortals and the revived dead. *The Second Trip* centers around the idea of the death of identity, in which a man discovers that he is a former criminal punished with obliteration of his true personality, a spark of which is reignited and threatens to overwhelm his new persona. The quest for immortality is a sounding board for ruminations on mortality in *The Book of Skulls,* about the pursuit of an occult sect that has supposedly found the secret of eternal life. Since the late 1970s Silverberg has concentrated on the development of his Majipoor saga, an epic science fantasy series that includes the novels *Lord Valentine's Castle, The Majipoor Chronicles,* and *Valentine Pontifex.* He has also written two fantasy novels, *Gilgamesh the King* and *To the Land of the Living,* based on Sumerian mythology. His many short-fiction collections include *Next Stop the Stars, To Worlds Beyond, Dimension Thirteen, Born with the Dead,* and *The Secret Sharer.* He has written many novels and works of nonfiction for children and edited more than seventy anthologies. Silverberg won the first of five Nebula Awards for his story "Passengers," and he is also a multiple winner of the Hugo Award.

THERE ARE ONLY fragments of me left now. Chunks of memory have broken free and drifted away like calved glaciers. It is always like that when a Passenger leaves us. We can never be sure of all the things our borrowed bodies did. We have only the lingering traces, the imprints.

Like sand clinging to an ocean-tossed bottle. Like the throbbings of amputated legs.

I rise. I collect myself. My hair is rumpled; I comb it. My face is creased from too little sleep. There is sourness in my mouth. Has my Passenger been eating dung with my mouth? They do that. They do anything.

It is morning.

A gray, uncertain morning. I stare at it awhile, and then, shuddering, I opaque the window and confront instead the gray, uncertain surface of the inner panel. My room looks untidy. Did I have a woman here? There are ashes in the trays. Searching for butts, I find several with lipstick stains. Yes, a woman was here.

I touch the bedsheets. Still warm with shared warmth. Both pillows tousled. She has gone, though, and the Passenger is gone, and I am alone.

How long did it last, this time?

I pick up the phone and ring Central. "What is the date?"

The computer's bland feminine voice replies, "Friday, December fourth, nineteen eighty-seven."

"The time?"

"Nine fifty-one, Eastern Standard Time."

"The weather forecast?"

"Predicted temperature range for today thirty to thirty-eight. Current temperature, thirty-one. Wind from the north, sixteen miles an hour. Chances of precipitation slight."

"What do you recommend for a hangover?"

"Food or medication?"

"Anything you like," I say.

The computer mulls that one over for a while. Then it decides on both, and activates my kitchen. The spigot yields cold tomato juice. Eggs begin to fry. From the medicine slot comes a purplish liquid. The Central Computer is always so thoughtful. Do the Passengers ever ride it, I wonder? What thrills could that hold for them? Surely it must be more exciting to borrow the million minds of Central than to live a while in the faulty, short-circuited soul of a corroding human being!

December 4, Central said. Friday. So the Passenger had me for three nights.

I drink the purplish stuff and probe my memories in a gingerly way, as one might probe a festering sore.

I remember Tuesday morning. A bad time at work. None of the charts will come out right. The section manager irritable; he has been taken by Passengers three times in five weeks, and his section is in disarray as a result, and his Christmas bonus is jeopardized. Even though it is customary not to penalize a person for lapses due to Passengers, according to the system, the section manager seems to feel he will be treated unfairly. So he treats us unfairly. We have a hard time. Revise the charts, fiddle with the program, check the fundamentals ten times over. Out they come: the detailed forecasts for price variations of public utility securities, February–April 1988. That afternoon we are to meet and discuss the charts and what they tell us.

I do not remember Tuesday afternoon.

That must have been when the Passenger took me. Perhaps at work; perhaps in the mahogany-paneled boardroom itself, during the conference. Pink concerned faces all about me; I cough, I lurch, I stumble from my seat. They shake their heads sadly. No one reaches for me. No one stops me. It is too dangerous to interfere with one who has a Passenger. The chances are great that a second Passenger lurks nearby in the discorporate state, looking for a mount. So I am avoided. I leave the building.

After that, what?

Sitting in my room on bleak Friday morning, I eat my scrambled eggs and try to reconstruct the three lost nights.

Of course it is impossible. The conscious mind functions during the period of captivity, but upon withdrawal of the Passenger nearly every recollection goes too. There is only a slight residue, a gritty film of faint and ghostly memories. The mount is never precisely the same person afterwards; though he cannot recall the details of his experience, he is subtly changed by it.

I try to recall.

A girl? Yes: lipstick on the butts. Sex, then, here in my room. Young? Old? Blonde? Dark? Everything is hazy. How did my borrowed body behave? Was I a good lover? I try to be, when I am myself. I keep in shape. At 38, I can handle three sets of tennis on a summer afternoon without collapsing. I can make a woman glow as a woman is meant to glow. Not boasting: just categorizing. We have our skills. These are mine.

But Passengers, I am told, take wry amusement in controverting our skills. So would it have given my rider a kind of delight to find me a woman and force me to fail repeatedly with her?

I dislike that thought.

The fog is going from my mind now. The medicine prescribed by Central works rapidly. I eat, I shave, I stand under the vibrator until my skin is clean. I do my exercises. Did the Passenger exercise my body Wednesday and Thursday mornings? Probably not. I must make up for that. I am close to middle age, now; tonus lost is not easily regained.

I touch my toes twenty times, knees stiff.

I kick my legs in the air.

I lie flat and lift myself on pumping elbows.

The body responds, maltreated though it has been. It is the first bright moment of my awakening: to feel the inner tingling, to know that I still have vigor.

Fresh air is what I want next. Quickly I slip into my clothes and leave. There is no need for me to report to work today. They are aware that since Tuesday afternoon I have had a Passenger; they need not be aware that before dawn on Friday the Passenger departed. I will have a free day. I will walk the city's streets, stretching my limbs, repaying my body for the abuse it has suffered.

I enter the elevator. I drop fifty stories to the ground. I step out into the December dreariness.

The towers of New York rise about me.

In the street the cars stream forward. Drivers sit edgily at their wheels. One never knows when the driver of a nearby car will be borrowed, and there is always a moment of lapsed coordination as the Passenger takes over. Many lives are lost that way on our streets and highways; but never the life of a Passenger.

I begin to walk without purpose. I cross Fourteenth Street, heading north, listening to the soft violent purr of the electric engines. I see a boy jigging in the street and know he is being ridden. At Fifth and Twenty-second a prosperous-looking paunchy man approaches, his necktie askew, this morning's *Wall Street Journal* jutting from an overcoat pocket. He giggles. He thrusts out his tongue. Ridden. Ridden. I avoid him. Moving briskly, I come to the underpass that carries traffic below Thirty-fourth Street toward Queens, and pause for a moment to watch two adolescent girls quarreling at the rim of the pedestrian walk. One is a Negro. Her eyes are rolling in terror. The other pushes her closer to the railing. Ridden. But the Passenger does not have murder on its mind, merely pleasure. The Negro girl is released and falls in a huddled heap, trembling. Then she rises and runs. The other girl draws a long strand of gleaming hair into her mouth, chews on it, seems to awaken. She looks dazed.

I avert my eyes. One does not watch while a fellow sufferer is awakening. There is a morality of the ridden; we have so many new tribal mores in these dark days.

I hurry on.

Where am I going so hurriedly? Already I have walked more than a mile. I seem to be moving toward some goal, as though my Passenger still hunches in my skull, urging me about. But I know that is not so. For the moment, at least, I am free.

Can I be sure of that?

Cogito ergo sum no longer applies. We go on thinking even while we are ridden, and we live in quiet desperation, unable to halt our courses no matter how ghastly, no matter how self-destructive. I am certain that I can distinguish between the condition of bearing a Passenger and the condition of being free. But perhaps not. Perhaps I bear a particularly devilish Passenger which has not quitted me at all, but which merely has receded to the cerebellum, leaving me the illusion of freedom while all the time surreptitiously driving me onward to some purpose of its own.

Did we ever have more than that: the illusion of freedom?

But this is disturbing, the thought that I may be ridden without realizing it. I burst out in heavy perspiration, not merely from the exertion of walking. Stop. Stop here. Why must you walk? You are at Forty-second Street. There is the library. Nothing forces you onward. Stop awhile, I tell myself. Rest on the library steps.

I sit on the cold stone and tell myself that I have made this decision for myself.

Have I? It is the old problem, free will versus determinism, translated into the foulest of forms. Determinism is no longer a philosopher's abstraction; it is cold alien tendrils sliding between the cranial sutures. The Passengers arrived three years ago. I have been ridden five times since then. Our world is quite different now. But we have adjusted even to this. We have adjusted. We have our mores. Life goes on. Our governments rule, our legislatures meet, our stock exchanges transact business as usual, and we have methods for compensating for the random havoc. It is the only way. What else can we do? Shrivel in defeat? We have an enemy we cannot fight; at best we can resist through endurance. So we endure.

The stone steps are cold against my body. In December few people sit here.

I tell myself that I made this long walk of my own free will, that I halted of my own free will, that no Passenger rides my brain now. Perhaps. Perhaps. I cannot let myself believe that I am not free.

Can it be, I wonder, that the Passenger left some lingering command in me? Walk to this place, halt at this place? That is possible too.

I look about me at the others on the library steps.

An old man, eyes vacant, sitting on newspaper. A boy of thirteen or so with flaring nostrils. A plump woman. Are all of them ridden? Passengers seem to cluster about me today. The more I study the ridden ones, the more convinced I become that I am, for the moment, free. The last time, I had three months of freedom between rides. Some people, they say, are scarcely ever free. Their bodies are in great demand, and they know only scattered bursts of freedom, a day here, a week there, an hour. We have never been able to determine how many Passengers infest our world. Millions, maybe. Or maybe five. Who can tell?

A wisp of snow curls down out of the gray sky. Central had said the chance of precipitation was slight. Are they riding Central this morning too?

I see the girl.

She sits diagonally across from me, five steps up and a hundred feet away, her black skirt pulled up on her knees to reveal handsome legs. She is young. Her hair is deep, rich auburn. Her eyes are pale; at this distance, I cannot make out the precise color. She is dressed simply. She is younger than thirty. She wears a dark green coat and her lipstick has a purplish tinge. Her lips are full, her nose slender, high-bridged, her eyebrows carefully plucked.

I know her.

I have spent the past three nights with her in my room. She is the one. Ridden, she came to me, and ridden, I slept with her. I am certain of this. The veil of memory opens; I see her slim body naked on my bed.

How can it be that I remember this?

It is too strong to be an illusion. Clearly this is something that I have been *permitted* to remember for reasons I cannot comprehend. And I remember more. I remember her soft gasping sounds of pleasure. I know that my own body did not betray me those three nights, nor did I fail her need.

And there is more. A memory of sinuous music; a scent of youth in her hair; the rustle of winter trees. Somehow she brings back to me a time of innocence, a time when I am young and girls are mysterious, a time of parties and dances and warmth and secrets.

I am drawn to her now.

There is an etiquette about such things, too. It is in poor taste to approach someone you have met while being ridden. Such an encounter gives you no privilege; a stranger remains a stranger, no matter what you and she may have done and said during your involuntary time together.

Yet I am drawn to her.

Why this violation of taboo? Why this raw breach of etiquette? I have never done this before. I have been scrupulous.

But I get to my feet and walk along the step on which I have been sitting, until I am below her, and I look up, and automatically she folds her ankles together and angles her knees as if in awareness that her position is not a modest one. I know from that gesture that she is not ridden now. My eyes meet hers. Her eyes are hazy green. She is beautiful, and I rack my memory for more details of our passion.

I climb step by step until I stand before her.

"Hello," I say.

She gives me a neutral look. She does not seem to recognize me. Her eyes are veiled, as one's eyes often are, just after the Passenger has gone. She purses her lips and appraises me in a distant way.

"Hello," she replies coolly. "I don't think I know you."

"No. You don't. But I have the feeling you don't want to be alone just now. And I know I don't." I try to persuade her with my eyes that my motives are decent. "There's snow in the air," I say. "We can find a warmer place. I'd like to talk to you."

"About what?"

"Let's go elsewhere, and I'll tell you. I'm Charles Roth."

"Helen Martin."

She gets to her feet. She still has not cast aside her cool neutrality; she is suspicious, ill at ease. But at least she is willing to go with me. A good sign.

"Is it too early in the day for a drink?" I ask.

"I'm not sure. I hardly know what time it is."

"Before noon."

"Let's have a drink anyway," she says, and we both smile.

We go to a cocktail lounge across the street. Sitting face to face in the darkness, we sip drinks, daiquiri for her, bloody mary for me. She relaxes a little. I ask myself what it is I want from her. The pleasure of her company, yes. Her company in bed? But I have already had that pleasure, three nights of it, though she does not know that. I want something more. Something more. What?

Her eyes are bloodshot. She has had little sleep these past three nights. I say, "Was it very unpleasant for you?"

"What?"

"The Passenger."

A whiplash of reaction crosses her face. "How did you know I've had a Passenger?"

"I know."

"We aren't supposed to talk about it."

"I'm broadminded," I tell her. "My Passenger left me some time during the night. I was ridden since Tuesday afternoon."

"Mine left me about two hours ago, I think." Her cheeks color. She is doing something daring, talking like this. "I was ridden since Monday night. This was my fifth time."

"Mine also."

We toy with our drinks. Rapport is growing, almost without the need of words. Our recent experiences with Passengers give us something in common, although Helen does not realize how intimately we shared those experiences.

We talk. She is a designer of display windows. She has a small apartment several blocks from here. She lives alone. She asks me what I do. "Securities analyst," I tell her. She smiles. Her teeth are flawless. We have a second round of drinks. I am positive, now, that this is the girl who was in my room when I was ridden.

A seed of hope grows in me. It was a happy chance that brought us together again, so soon after we parted as dreamers. A happy chance, too, that some vestige of the dream lingered in my mind.

We have shared something, who knows what, and it must have been good to leave such a vivid imprint on me, and now I want to come to her conscious, aware, my own master, and renew that relationship, making it a real one this time. It is not proper, for I am trespassing on a privilege that is not mine except by virtue of our Passengers' brief presence in us. Yet I need her. I want her.

She seems to need me, too, without realizing who I am. But fear holds her back.

I am frightened of frightening her, and I do not try to press my advantage too quickly. Perhaps she would take me to her apartment with her now, perhaps not, but

I do not ask. We finish our drinks. We arrange to meet by the library steps again tomorrow. My hand momentarily brushes hers. Then she is gone.

I fill three ashtrays that night. Over and over I debate the wisdom of what I am doing. But why not leave her alone? I have no right to follow her. In the place our world has become, we are wisest to remain apart.

And yet—there is that stab of half-memory when I think of her. The blurred lights of lost chances behind the stairs, of girlish laughter in second-floor corridors, of stolen kisses, of tea and cake. I remember the girl with the orchid in her hair, and the one in the spangled dress, and the one with the child's face and the woman's eyes, all so long ago, all lost, all gone, and I tell myself that this one I will not lose, I will not permit her to be taken from me.

Morning comes, a quiet Saturday. I return to the library, hardly expecting to find her there, but she is there, on the steps, and the sight of her is like a reprieve. She looks wary, troubled; obviously she has done much thinking, little sleeping. Together we walk along Fifth Avenue. She is quite close to me, but she does not take my arm. Her steps are brisk, short, nervous.

I want to suggest that we go to her apartment instead of to the cocktail lounge. In these days we must move swiftly while we are free. But I know it would be a mistake to think of this as a matter of tactics. Coarse haste would be fatal, bringing me perhaps an ordinary victory, a numbing defeat within it. In any event her mood hardly seems promising. I look at her, thinking of string music and new snowfalls, and she looks toward the gray sky.

She says, "I can feel them watching me all the time. Like vultures swooping overhead, waiting, waiting. Ready to pounce."

"But there's a way of beating them. We can grab little scraps of life when they're not looking."

"They're *always* looking."

"No," I tell her. "There can't be enough of them for that. Sometimes they're looking the other way. And while they are, two people can come together and try to share warmth."

"But what's the use?"

"You're too pessimistic, Helen. They ignore us for months at a time. We have a chance. We have a chance."

But I cannot break through her shell of fear. She is paralyzed by the nearness of the Passengers, unwilling to begin anything for fear it will be snatched away by our tormentors. We reach the building where she lives, and I hope she will relent and invite me in. For an instant she wavers, but only for an instant: she takes my hand in both of hers, and smiles, and the smile fades, and she is gone, leaving me only with the words, "Let's meet at the library again tomorrow. Noon."

I make the long chilling walk home alone.

Some of her pessimism seeps into me that night. It seems futile for us to try to salvage anything. More than that: wicked for me to seek her out, shameful to offer a hesitant love when I am not free. In this world, I tell myself, we should keep well clear of others, so that we do not harm anyone when we are seized and ridden.

I do not go to meet her in the morning.

It is best this way, I insist. I have no business trifling with her. I imagine her at the library, wondering why I am late, growing tense, impatient, then annoyed. She will be angry with me for breaking our date, but her anger will ebb, and she will forget me quickly enough.

Monday comes. I return to work.

Naturally, no one discusses my absence. It is as though I have never been away. The market is strong that morning. The work is challenging; it is mid-morning before I think of Helen at all. But once I think of her, I can think of nothing else. My cowardice in standing her up. The childishness of Saturday night's dark thoughts. Why accept fate so passively? Why give in? I want to fight, now, to carve out a pocket of security despite the odds. I feel a deep conviction that it can be done. The Passengers may never bother the two of us again, after all. And that flickering smile of hers outside her building Saturday, that momentary glow—it should have told me that behind her wall of fear she felt the same hopes. She was waiting for me to lead the way. And I stayed home instead.

At lunchtime I go to the library, convinced it is futile.

But she is there. She paces along the steps; the wind slices at her slender figure. I go to her.

She is silent a moment. "Hello," she says finally.

"I'm sorry about yesterday."

"I waited a long time for you."

I shrug. "I made up my mind that it was no use to come. But then I changed my mind again."

She tries to look angry. But I know she is pleased to see me again—else why did she come here today? She cannot hide her inner pleasure. Nor can I. I point across the street to the cocktail lounge.

"A daiquiri?" I say. "As a peace offering?"

"All right."

Today the lounge is crowded, but we find a booth somehow. There is a brightness in her eyes that I have not seen before. I sense that a barrier is crumbling within her.

"You're less afraid of me, Helen," I say.

"I've never been afraid of you. I'm afraid of what could happen if we take the risks."

"Don't be. Don't be."

"I'm trying not to be afraid. But sometimes it seems so hopeless. Since *they* came here—"

"We can still try to live our own lives."

"Maybe."

"We have to. Let's make a pact, Helen. No more gloom. No more worrying about the terrible things that might just maybe happen. All right?"

A pause. Then a cool hand against mine.

"All right."

We finish our drinks, and I present my Credit Central to pay for them, and we go outside. I want her to tell me to forget about this afternoon's work and come home with her. It is inevitable, now, that she will ask me, and better sooner than later.

We walk a block. She does not offer the invitation. I sense the struggle inside her, and I wait, letting that struggle reach its own resolution without interference from me. We walk a second block. Her arm is through mine, but she talks only of her work, of the weather, and it is a remote, arm's-length conversation. At the next corner she swings around, away from her apartment, back toward the cocktail lounge. I try to be patient with her.

I have no need to rush things now, I tell myself. Her body is not a secret to me. We have begun our relationship topsy-turvy, with the physical part first; now it will take time to work backward to the more difficult part that some people call love.

But of course she is not aware that we have known each other that way. The wind blows swirling snowflakes in our faces, and somehow the cold sting awakens honesty in me. I know what I must say. I must relinquish my unfair advantage.

I tell her, "While I was ridden last week, Helen, I had a girl in my room."

"Why talk of such things now?"

"I have to, Helen. You were the girl."

She halts. She turns to me. People hurry past us in the street. Her face is very pale, with dark red spots growing in her cheeks.

"That's not funny, Charles."

"It wasn't meant to be. You were with me from Tuesday night to early Friday morning."

"How can you possibly know that?"

"I do. I do. The memory is clear. Somehow it remains, Helen. I see your whole body."

"Stop it, Charles."

"We were very good together," I say. "We must have pleased our Passengers because we were so good. To see you again—it was like waking from a dream, and finding that the dream was real, the girl right there—"

"No!"

"Let's go to your apartment and begin again."

She says, "You're being deliberately filthy, and I don't know why, but there wasn't any reason for you to spoil things. Maybe I was with you and maybe I wasn't, but you wouldn't know it, and if you did know it you should keep your mouth shut about it, and—"

"You have a birthmark the size of a dime," I say, "about three inches below your left breast."

She sobs and hurls herself at me, there in the street. Her long silvery nails rake my cheeks. She pummels me. I seize her. Her knees assail me. No one pays attention; those who pass by assume we are ridden, and turn their heads. She is all fury, but I have my arms around hers like metal bands, so that she can only stamp and snort, and her body is close against mine. She is rigid, anguished.

In a low, urgent voice I say, "We'll defeat them, Helen. We'll finish what they started. Don't fight me. There's no reason to fight me. I know, it's a fluke that I remember you, but let me go with you and I'll prove that we belong together."

"Let—go—"

"Please. Please. Why should we be enemies? I don't mean you any harm. I love you, Helen. Do you remember, when we were kids, we could play at being in love? I did; you must have done it too. Sixteen, seventeen years old. The whispers, the conspiracies—all a big game and we knew it. But the game's over. We can't afford to tease and run. We have so little time, when we're free—we have to trust, to open ourselves—"

"It's wrong."

"No. Just because it's the stupid custom for two people brought together by Passengers to avoid one another, that doesn't mean we have to follow it. Helen—Helen—"

Something in my tone registers with her. She ceases to struggle. Her rigid body softens. She looks up at me, her tear-streaked face thawing, her eyes blurred.

"Trust me," I say. "Trust me, Helen!"

She hesitates. Then she smiles.

In that moment I feel the chill at the back of my skull, the sensation as of a steel needle driven deep through bone. I stiffen. My arms drop away from her. For an instant, I lose touch, and when the mists clear all is different.

"Charles?" she says. "*Charles?*"

Her knuckles are against her teeth. I turn, ignoring her, and go back into the cocktail lounge. A young man sits in one of the front booths. His dark hair gleams with pomade; his cheeks are smooth. His eyes meet mine.

I sit down. He orders drinks. We do not talk.

My hand falls on his wrist, and remains there. The bartender, serving the drinks, scowls but says nothing. We sip our cocktails and put the drained glasses down.

"Let's go," the young man says.

I follow him out.

The Tunnel under the World

Before he was a science fiction writer, Frederik Pohl was a science fiction editor who worked at the pulp magazines *Astonishing Stories* and *Super Science Stories,* where he provided opportunities for James Blish, Cyril M. Kornbluth, Isaac Asimov, Damon Knight, and other colleagues in the Futurian science fiction society. Much of his career until 1980 was divided between writing and either serving as a literary agent for science fiction writers or shaping editorial policy on the fiction published at publishing houses or science fiction magazines. His earliest novels, written in collaboration with Cyril M. Kornbluth, show the impact of his familiarity with science fiction at all levels of conception. *The Space Merchants, Gladiator at Law,* and *Wolfbane* are among the wittiest satires in all science fiction, not only for their speculative extrapolations of the absurdities of American culture, but for their understanding of the appropriateness of science fiction constructs for elaborating that absurdity. Pohl is an insightful observer of modern society and its ills and a number of his short stories in the years following World War II are perceptive and even prophetic social critiques, notably "The Midas Plague," about consumerism run amuck; "What to Do till the Analyst Comes," a dark comedy about the culture of addiction; and "The Snowmen," which foresees the energy crisis and the greenhouse effect. Much of Pohl's fiction from this period has been collected in *Alternating Current, The Case against Tomorrow, Tomorrow Times Seven, The Man Who Ate the World,* and *Turn Left at Thursday.* Pohl hit his stride as a novelist in the 1970s with his Heechee chronicles, comprising *Gateway, Beyond the Blue Event Horizon, Heechee Rendezvous, The Annals of Heechee,* and *The Gateway Trip.* The central idea of this series— an apparently abandoned space transportation terminus created by a sophisticated alien race that gives humans access to unpredictable adventures on interstellar worlds—gave Pohl the perfect instrument for taking the measure of human motives and objectives in the face of the unknown. *Man-Plus,* in which a man who loses more than he gains when he agrees to physical transformation that will allow him to adapt to the Martian environment, and *Jem,* about an earth colony doomed to recapitulate the aggressions and prejudices that have destroyed the mother planet, are among his most memorable works. In addition to his scores of novels and short-fiction collections, Pohl has written essays on the craft of science fiction, collected in *Digits and Dastards* and *Forbidden Lines,* and his autobiography, *The Way the Future Was.*

ON THE MORNING of June 15th, Guy Burckhardt woke up screaming out of a dream.

It was more real than any dream he had ever had in his life. He could still hear and feel the sharp, ripping-metal explosion, the violent heave that had tossed him furiously out of bed, the searing wave of heat.

He sat up convulsively and stared, not believing what he saw, at the quiet room and the bright sunlight coming in the window.

He croaked, "Mary?"

His wife was not in the bed next to him. The covers were tumbled and awry, as though she had just left it, and the memory of the dream was so strong that instinctively he found himself searching the floor to see if the dream explosion had thrown her down.

But she wasn't there. Of course she wasn't, he told himself, looking at the familiar vanity and slipper chair, the uncracked window, the unbuckled wall. It had only been a dream.

"Guy?" His wife was calling him querulously from the foot of the stairs. "Guy, dear, are you all right?"

He called weakly, "Sure."

There was a pause. Then Mary said doubtfully, "Breakfast is ready. Are you sure you're all right? I thought I heard you yelling."

Burckhardt said more confidently, "I had a bad dream, honey. Be right down."

IN THE SHOWER, punching the lukewarm-and-cologne he favored, he told himself that it had been a beaut of a dream. Still bad dreams weren't unusual, especially bad dreams about explosions. In the past thirty years of H-bomb jitters, who had not dreamed of explosions?

Even Mary had dreamed of them, it turned out, for he started to tell her about the dream, but she cut him off. "You *did?*" Her voice was astonished. "Why, dear, I dreamed the same thing! Well, almost the same thing. I didn't actually *hear* anything. I dreamed that something woke me up, and then there was a sort of quick bang, and then something hit me on the head. And that was all. Was yours like that?"

Burckhardt coughed. "Well, no," he said. Mary was not one of the strong-as-a-man, brave-as-a-tiger women. It was not necessary, he thought, to tell her all the little details of the dream that made it seem so real. No need to mention the splintered ribs, and the salt bubble in his throat, and the agonized knowledge that this was death. He said, "Maybe there really was some kind of explosion downtown. Maybe we heard it and it started us dreaming."

Mary reached over and patted his hand absently. "Maybe," she agreed. "It's almost half-past eight, dear. Shouldn't you hurry? You don't want to be late to the office."

He gulped his food, kissed her and rushed out—not so much to be on time as to see if his guess had been right.

But downtown Tylerton looked as it always had. Coming in on the bus, Burckhardt watched critically out the window, seeking evidence of an explosion. There wasn't any. If anything, Tylerton looked better than it ever had before. It was a beautiful crisp day, the sky was cloudless, the buildings were clean and inviting. They had, he observed, steam-blasted the Power & Light Building, the town's only skyscraper—that was the penalty of having Contro Chemicals' main plant on the outskirts of town; the fumes from the cascade stills left their mark on stone buildings.

None of the usual crowd were on the bus, so there wasn't anyone Burckhardt could ask about the explosion. And by the time he got out at the corner of Fifth and Lehigh and the bus rolled away with a muted diesel moan, he had pretty well convinced himself that it was all imagination.

He stopped at the cigar stand in the lobby of his office building, but Ralph wasn't behind the counter. The man who sold him his pack of cigarettes was a stranger.

"Where's Mr. Stebbins?" Burckhardt asked.

The man said politely, "Sick, sir. He'll be in tomorrow. A pack of Marlins today?"

"Chesterfields," Burckhardt corrected.

"Certainly, sir," the man said. But what he took from the rack and slid across the counter was an unfamiliar green-and-yellow pack.

"Do try these, sir," he suggested. "They contain an anti-cough factor. Ever notice how ordinary cigarettes make you choke every once in a while?"

Burckhardt said suspiciously, "I never heard of this brand."

"Of course not. They're something new." Burckhardt hesitated, and the man said persuasively, "Look, try them out at my risk. If you don't like them, bring back the empty pack and I'll refund your money. Fair enough?"

Burckhardt shrugged. "How can I lose? But give me a pack of Chesterfields, too, will you?"

He opened the pack and lit one while he waited for the elevator. They weren't bad, he decided, though he was suspicious of cigarettes that had the tobacco chemically treated in any way. But he didn't think much of Ralph's stand-in; it would raise hell with the trade at the cigar stand if the man tried to give every customer the same high-pressure sales talk.

The elevator door opened with a low-pitched sound of music. Burckhardt and two or three others got in and he nodded to them as the door closed. The thread of music switched off and the speaker in the ceiling of the cab began its usual commercials.

No, not the *usual* commercials, Burckhardt realized. He had been exposed to the captive-audience commercials so long that they hardly registered on the outer ear any more, but what was coming from the recorded program in the basement of the building caught his attention. It wasn't merely that the brands were mostly unfamiliar; it was a difference in pattern.

There were jingles with an insistent, bouncy rhythm, about soft drinks he had never tasted. There was a rapid patter dialogue between what sounded like two ten-year-old boys about a candy bar, followed by an authoritative bass rumble: "Go right out and get a DELICIOUS Choco-Bite and eat your TANGY Choco-Bite *all up*. That's *Choco Bite!*" There was a sobbing female whine: "I *wish* I had a Feckle Freezer! I'd do *anything* for a Feckle Freezer!" Burckhardt reached his floor and left the elevator in the middle of the last one. It left him a little uneasy. The commercials were not for familiar brands; there was no feeling of use and custom to them.

But the office was happily normal—except that Mr. Barth wasn't in. Miss Mitkin, yawning at the reception desk, didn't know exactly why. "His home phoned, that's all. He'll be in tomorrow."

"Maybe he went to the plant. It's right near his house."

She looked indifferent. "Yeah."

A thought struck Burckhardt. "But today is June 15th! It's quarterly tax return day—he has to sign the return!"

Miss Mitkin shrugged to indicate that that was Burckhardt's problem, not hers. She returned to her nails.

Thoroughly exasperated, Burckhardt went to his desk. It wasn't that he couldn't sign the tax returns as well as Barth, he thought resentfully. It simply wasn't his job, that was all; it was a responsibility that Barth, as office manager for Contro Chemicals' downtown office, should have taken.

He thought briefly of calling Barth at his home or trying to reach him at the factory, but he gave up the idea quickly enough. He didn't really care much for the people at the factory and the less contact he had with them, the better. He had been to the factory once, with Barth; it had been a confusing and, in a way, frightening experience. Barring a handful of executives and engineers, there wasn't a soul in the factory—that is, Burckhardt corrected himself, remembering what Barth had told him, not a *living* soul—just the machines.

According to Barth, each machine was controlled by a sort of computer which reproduced, in its electronic snarl, the actual memory and mind of a human being. It was an unpleasant thought. Barth, laughing, had assured him that there was no Frankenstein business of robbing graveyards and implanting brains in machines. It was only a matter, he said, of transferring a man's habit patterns from brain cells to vacuum-tube cells. It didn't hurt the man and it didn't make the machine into a monster.

But they made Burckhardt uncomfortable all the same.

He put Barth and the factory and all his other little irritations out of his mind and tackled the tax returns. It took him until noon to verify the figures—which Barth could have done out of his memory and his private ledger in ten minutes, Burckhardt resentfully reminded himself.

He sealed them in an envelope and walked out to Miss Mitkin. "Since Mr. Barth isn't here, we'd better go to lunch in shifts," he said, "You can go first."

"Thanks." Miss Mitkin languidly took her bag out of the desk drawer and began to apply makeup.

Burckhardt offered her the envelope. "Drop this in the mail for me, will you? Uh—wait a minute. I wonder if I ought to phone Mr. Barth to make sure. Did his wife say whether he was able to take phone calls?"

"Didn't say." Miss Mitkin blotted her lips carefully with a Kleenex. "Wasn't his wife, anyway. It was his daughter who called and left the message."

"The kid?" Burckhardt frowned. "I thought she was away at school."

"She called, that's all I know."

Burckhardt went back to his own office and stared distastefully at the unopened mail on his desk. He didn't like nightmares; they spoiled his whole day. He should have stayed in bed, like Barth.

A FUNNY THING happened on his way home. There was a disturbance at the corner where he usually caught his bus—someone was screaming something about a new kind of deep-freeze—so he walked an extra block. He saw the bus coming and started to trot. But behind him, someone was calling his name. He looked over his shoulder; a small harried-looking man was hurrying toward him.

Burckhardt hesitated, and then recognized him. It was a casual acquaintance named Swanson. Burckhardt sourly observed that he had already missed the bus.

He said, "Hello."

Swanson's face was desperately eager. "Burckhardt?" he asked inquiringly, with an odd intensity. And then he just stood there silently, watching Burckhardt's face, with a burning eagerness that dwindled to a faint hope and died to a regret. He was searching for something, waiting for something, Burckhardt thought. But whatever it was he wanted, Burckhardt didn't know how to supply it.

Burckhardt coughed and said again, "Hello, Swanson."

Swanson didn't even acknowledge the greeting. He merely sighed a very deep sigh.

"Nothing doing," he mumbled, apparently to himself. He nodded abstractedly to Burckhardt and turned away.

Burckhardt watched the slumped shoulders disappear in the crowd. It was an *odd* sort of day, he thought, and one he didn't much like. Things weren't going right.

Riding home on the next bus, he brooded about it. It wasn't anything terrible or disastrous; it was something out of his experience entirely. You live your life, like any man, and you form a network of impressions and reactions. You *expect* things. When you open your medicine chest, your razor is expected to be on the second shelf; when you lock your front door, you expect to have to give it a slight extra tug to make it latch.

It isn't the things that are right and perfect in your life that make it familiar. It is the things that are just a little bit wrong—the sticking latch, the light switch at the head of the stairs that needs an extra push because the spring is old and weak, the rug that unfailingly skids underfoot.

It wasn't just that things were wrong with the pattern of Burckhardt's life; it was that the *wrong* things were wrong. For instance, Barth hadn't come into the office, yet Barth *always* came in.

Burckhardt brooded about it through dinner. He brooded about it, despite his wife's attempt to interest him in a game of bridge with the neighbors, all through the evening. The neighbors were people he liked—Anne and Farley Dennerman. He had known them all their lives. But they were odd and brooding, too, this night, and he barely listened to Dennerman's complaints about not being able to get good phone service or his wife's comments on the disgusting variety of television commercials they had these days.

Burckhardt was well on the way to setting an all-time record for continuous abstraction when around midnight, with a suddenness that surprised him—he was strangely *aware* of it happening—he turned over in his bed and, quickly and completely, fell asleep.

ON THE MORNING of June 15th, Burckhardt woke up screaming.

It was more real than any dream he had ever had in his life. He could still hear the explosion, feel the blast that crushed him against a wall. It did not seem right that he should be sitting bolt upright in bed in an undisturbed room.

His wife came pattering up the stairs. "Darling!" she cried. "What's the matter?"

He mumbled, "Nothing. Bad dream."

She relaxed, hand on heart. In an angry tone, she started to say: "You gave me such a shock—"

But a noise from outside interrupted her. There was a wail of sirens and a clang of bells; it was loud and shocking.

The Burckhardts stared at each other for a heartbeat, then hurried fearfully to the window.

There were no rumbling fire engines in the street, only a small panel truck, cruising slowly along. Flaring loudspeaker horns crowned its top. From them issued the screaming sound of sirens, growing in intensity, mixed with the rumble of heavy-duty engines and the sound of bells. It was a perfect record of fire engines arriving at a four-alarm blaze.

Burckhardt said in amazement, "Mary, that's against the law! Do you know what they're doing? They're playing records of a fire. What are they up to?"

"Maybe it's a practical joke," his wife offered.

"Joke? Waking up the whole neighborhood at six o'clock in the morning?" He shook his head. "The police will be here in ten minutes," he predicted. "Wait and see."

But the police weren't—not in ten minutes, or at all. Whoever the pranksters in the car were, they apparently had a police permit for their games.

The car took a position in the middle of the block and stood silent for a few minutes. Then there was a crackle from the speaker, and a giant voice chanted:

Feckle Freezers!
Feckle Freezers!
Gotta have a
Feckle Freezer!
Feckle, Feckle, Feckle,
Feckle, Feckle, Feckle—

It went on and on. Every house on the block had faces staring out of windows by then. The voice was not merely loud; it was nearly deafening.

Burckhardt shouted to his wife, over the uproar, "What the hell is a Feckle Freezer?"

"Some kind of a freezer, I guess, dear," she shrieked back unhelpfully.

Abruptly the noise stopped and the truck stood silent. It was still misty morning; the sun's rays came horizontally across the rooftops. It was impossible to believe that, a moment ago, the silent block had been bellowing the name of a freezer.

"A crazy advertising trick," Burckhardt said bitterly. He yawned and turned away from the window. "Might as well get dressed. I guess that's the end of—"

The bellow caught him from behind; it was almost like a hard slap on the ears. A harsh, sneering voice, louder than the archangel's trumpet, howled:

"Have you got a freezer? *It stinks!* If it isn't a Feckle Freezer, *it stinks!* If it's a last year's Feckle Freezer, *it stinks!* Only this year's Feckle Freezer is any good at all! You know who owns an Ajax Freezer? Fairies own Ajax Freezers! You know who owns a Triple cold Freezer? Commies own Triplecold Freezers! Every freezer but a brand-new Feckle Freezer *stinks!*"

The voice screamed inarticulately with rage. "I'm warning you! Get out and buy a Feckle Freezer right away! Hurry up! Hurry for Feckle! Hurry for Feckle! Hurry, hurry, hurry, Feckle, Feckle, Feckle, Feckle, Feckle, Feckle . . ."

It stopped eventually. Burckhardt licked his lips. He started to say to his wife, "Maybe we ought to call the police about—" when the speakers erupted again. It caught him off guard; it was intended to catch him off guard. It screamed:

"Feckle, Feckle, Feckle, Feckle, Feckle, Feckle, Feckle, Feckle. Cheap freezers ruin your food. You'll get sick and throw up. You'll get sick and die. Buy a Feckle, Feckle, Feckle, Feckle! Ever take a piece of meat out of the freezer you've got and see how rotten and moldy it is? Buy a Feckle, Feckle, Feckle, Feckle, Feckle. Do you want to eat rotten, stinking food? Or do you want to wise up and buy a Feckle, Feckle, Feckle—"

That did it. With fingers that kept stabbing the wrong holes, Burckhardt finally managed to dial the local police station. He got a busy signal—it was apparent that he was not the only one with the same idea—and while he was shakily dialing again, the noise outside stopped.

He looked out the window. The truck was gone.

BURCKHARDT LOOSENED HIS tie and ordered another Frosty-Flip from the waiter. If only they wouldn't keep the Crystal Cafe so *hot!* The new paint job—searing reds and blinding yellows—was bad enough, but someone seemed to have the delusion that this was January instead of June; the place was a good ten degrees warmer than outside.

He swallowed the Frosty-Flip in two gulps. It had a kind of peculiar flavor, he thought, but not bad. It certainly cooled you off, just as the waiter had promised. He reminded himself to pick up a carton of them on the way home; Mary might like them. She was always interested in something new.

He stood up awkwardly as the girl came across the restaurant toward him. She was the most beautiful thing he had ever seen in Tylerton. Chin-height, honey-blonde hair and a figure that—well, it was all hers. There was no doubt in the world that the dress that clung to her was the only thing she wore. He felt as if he were blushing as she greeted him.

"Mr. Burckhardt." The voice was like distant tom-toms. "It's wonderful of you to let me see you, after this morning."

He cleared his throat. "Not at all. Won't you sit down, Miss—"

"April Horn," she murmured, sitting down—beside him, not where he had pointed on the other side of the table. "Call me April, won't you?"

She was wearing some kind of perfume. Burckhardt noted with what little of his mind was functioning at all. It didn't seem fair that she should be using perfume as well as everything else. He came to with a start and realized that the waiter was leaving with an order for *filet mignon* for two.

"Hey!" he objected.

"Please, Mr. Burckhardt." Her shoulder was against his, her face was turned to him, her breath was warm, her expression was tender and solicitous. "This is all on the Feckle Corporation. Please let them—it's the *least* they can do."

He felt her hand burrowing into his pocket.

"I put the price of the meal into your pocket," she whispered conspiratorially. "Please do that for me, won't you? I mean I'd appreciate it if you'd pay the waiter—I'm old-fashioned about things like that."

She smiled meltingly, then became mock-businesslike. "But you must take the money," she insisted. "Why, you're letting Feckle off lightly if you do! You could sue them for every nickel they've got, disturbing your sleep like that."

With a dizzy feeling, as though he had just seen someone make a rabbit disappear into a top hat, he said, "Why, it really wasn't so bad, uh, April. A little noisy, maybe, but—"

"Oh, Mr. Burckhardt!" The blue eyes were wide and admiring. "I *knew* you'd understand. It's just that—well, it's such a *wonderful* freezer that some of the outside men get carried away, so to speak. As soon as the main office found out about what happened, they sent representatives around to every house on the block to apologize. Your wife told us where we could phone you—and I'm so very pleased that you were willing to let me have lunch with you, so that I could apologize, too. Because truly, Mr. Burckhardt, it is a *fine* freezer.

"I shouldn't tell you this, but—" The blue eyes were shyly lowered—"I'd do almost anything for Feckle Freezers. It's more than a job to me." She looked up. She was enchanting. "I bet you think I'm silly, don't you?"

Burckhardt coughed. "Well, I—"

"Oh, you don't want to be unkind!" She shook her head. "No, don't pretend. You think it's silly. But really, Mr. Burckhardt, you wouldn't think so if you knew more about the Feckle. Let me show you this little booklet—"

Burckhardt got back from lunch a full hour late. It wasn't only the girl who delayed him. There had been a curious interview with a little man named Swanson, whom he barely knew, who had stopped him with desperate urgency on the street—and then left him cold.

But it didn't matter much. Mr. Barth, for the first time since Burckhardt had worked there, was out for the day—leaving Burckhardt stuck with the quarterly tax returns.

What did matter, though, was that somehow he had signed a purchase order for a twelve-cubic-foot Feckle Freezer, upright model, self-defrosting, list price $625, with a ten percent "courtesy" discount—"Because of that *horrid* affair this morning, Mr. Burckhardt," she had said.

And he wasn't sure how he could explain it to his wife.

*   *   *

HE NEEDN'T HAVE worried. As he walked in the front door, his wife said almost immediately, "I wonder if we can't afford a new freezer, dear. There was a man here to apologize about that noise and—well, we got to talking and—"

She had signed a purchase order, too.

It had been the damnedest day, Burckhardt thought later, on his way up to bed. But the day wasn't done with him yet. At the head of the stairs, the weakened spring in the electric light switch refused to click at all. He snapped it back and forth angrily and, of course, succeeded in jarring the tumbler out of its pins. The wire shorted and every light in the house went out.

"Damn!" said Guy Burckhardt.

"Fuse?" His wife shrugged sleepily. "Let it go till the morning, dear."

Burckhardt shook his head. "You go back to bed. I'll be right along."

It wasn't so much that he cared about fixing the fuse, but he was too restless for sleep. He disconnected the bad switch with a screwdriver, tumbled down into the black kitchen, found the flashlight and climbed gingerly down the cellar stairs. He located a spare fuse, pushed an empty trunk over to the fuse box to stand on and twisted out the old fuse.

When the new one was in, he heard the starting click and steady drone of the refrigerator in the kitchen overhead.

He headed back to the steps, and stopped.

Where the old trunk had been, the cellar floor gleamed oddly bright. He inspected it in the flashlight beam. It was metal!

"Son of a gun," said Guy Burckhardt. He shook his head unbelievingly. He peered closer, rubbed the edges of the metallic patch with his thumb and acquired an annoying cut—the edges were *sharp*.

The stained cement floor of the cellar was a thin shell. He found a hammer and cracked it off in a dozen spots—everywhere was metal.

The whole cellar was a copper box. Even the cement-brick walls were false fronts over a metal sheath!

Baffled, he attacked one of the foundation beams. That, at least, was real wood. The glass in the cellar windows was real glass.

He sucked his bleeding thumb and tried the base of the cellar stairs. Real wood. He chipped at the bricks under the oil burner. Real bricks. The retaining walls, the floor—they were faked.

It was as though someone had shored up the house with a frame of metal and then laboriously concealed the evidence.

The biggest surprise was the upside-down boat hull that blocked the rear half of the cellar, relic of a brief home-workshop period that Burckhardt had gone through a couple of years before. From above, it looked perfectly normal. Inside, though, where there should have been thwarts and seats and lockers, there was a mere tangle of braces, rough and unfinished.

"But I *built* that!" Burckhardt exclaimed, forgetting his thumb. He leaned against the hull dizzily, trying to think this thing through. For reasons beyond his comprehension, someone had taken his boat and his cellar away, maybe his whole house, and replaced them with a clever mock-up of the real thing.

"That's crazy," he said to the empty cellar. He stared around in the light of the flash. He whispered, "What in the name of Heaven would anybody do that for?"

Reason refused an answer; there wasn't any reasonable answer. For long minutes, Burckhardt contemplated the uncertain picture of his own sanity.

He peered under the boat again, hoping to reassure himself that it was a mistake, just his imagination. But the sloppy, unfinished bracing was unchanged. He crawled under for a better look, feeling the rough wood incredulously. Utterly impossible!

He switched off the flashlight and started to wriggle out. But he didn't make it. In the moment between the command to his legs to move and the crawling out, he felt a sudden draining weariness flooding through him.

Consciousness went—not easily, but as though it were being taken away, and Guy Burckhardt was asleep.

ON THE MORNING of June 16th, Guy Burckhardt woke up in a cramped position huddled under the hull of the boat in his basement—and raced upstairs to find it was June 15th.

The first thing he had done was to make a frantic, hasty inspection of the boat hull, the faked cellar floor, the imitation stone. They were all as he had remembered them, all completely unbelievable.

The kitchen was its placid, unexciting self. The electric clock was purring soberly around the dial. Almost six o'clock, it said. His wife would be waking at any moment.

Burckhardt flung open the front door and stared out into the quiet street. The morning paper was tossed carelessly against the steps, and as he retrieved it, he noticed that this was the 15th day of June.

But that was impossible. *Yesterday* was the 15th of June. It was not a date one would forget, it was quarterly tax-return day.

He went back into the hall and picked up the telephone; he dialed for Weather Information, and got a well-modulated chant: "—and cooler, some showers. Barometric pressure thirty point zero four, rising . . . United States Weather Bureau forecast for June 15th. Warm and sunny, with high around—"

He hung up the phone. June 15th.

"Holy Heaven!" Burckhardt said prayerfully. Things were very odd indeed. He heard the ring of his wife's alarm and bounded up the stairs.

Mary Burckhardt was sitting upright in bed with the terrified, uncomprehending stare of someone just waking out of a nightmare.

"Oh!" she gasped, as her husband came in the room. "Darling, I just had the most *terrible* dream! It was like an explosion and—"

"Again?" Burckhardt asked, not very sympathetically. "Mary, something's funny! I *knew* there was something wrong all day yesterday and—"

He went on to tell her about the copper box that was the cellar, and the odd mock-up someone had made of his boat. Mary looked astonished, then alarmed, then placatory and uneasy.

She said, "Dear, are you *sure*? Because I was cleaning that old trunk out just last week and I didn't notice anything."

"Positive!" said Guy Burckhardt. "I dragged it over to the wall to step on it to put a new fuse in after we blew the lights out and—"

"After we what?" Mary was looking more than merely alarmed.

"After we blew the lights out. You know, when the switch at the head of the stairs stuck. I went down to the cellar and—"

Mary sat up in bed. "Guy, the switch didn't stick. I turned out the lights myself last night."

Burckhardt glared at his wife. "Now I *know* you didn't! Come here and take a look!"

He stalked out to the landing and dramatically pointed to the bad switch, the one that he unscrewed and left hanging the night before . . .

Only it wasn't. It was as it had always been. Unbelieving, Burckhardt pressed it and the lights sprang up in both halls.

MARY, LOOKING PALE and worried, left him to go down to the kitchen and start breakfast. Burckhardt stood staring at the switch for a long time. His mental processes were gone beyond the point of disbelief and shock; they simply were not functioning.

He shaved and dressed and ate his breakfast in a state of numb introspection. Mary didn't disturb him; she was apprehensive and soothing. She kissed him good-bye as he hurried out to the bus without another word.

Miss Mitkin, at the reception desk, greeted him with a yawn. "Morning," she said drowsily. "Mr. Barth won't be in today."

Burckhardt started to say something, but checked himself. She would not know that Barth hadn't been in yesterday, either, because she was tearing a June 14th pad off her calendar to make way for the "new" June 15th sheet.

He staggered to his own desk and stared unseeingly at the morning's mail. It had not even been opened yet, but he knew that the Factory Distributors envelope contained an order for twenty thousand feet of the new acoustic tile, and the one from Finebeck & Sons was a complaint.

After a long while, he forced himself to open them. They were.

By lunchtime, driven by a desperate sense of urgency, Burckhardt made Miss Mitkin take her lunch hour first—the June-fifteenth-that-was-yesterday, *he* had gone first. She went, looking vaguely worried about his strained insistence, but it made no difference to Burckhardt's mood.

The phone rang and Burckhardt picked it up abstractedly. "Contro Chemicals Downtown, Burckhardt speaking."

The voice said, "This is Swanson," and stopped.

Burckhardt waited expectantly, but that was all. He said, "Hello?"

Again the pause. Then Swanson asked in sad resignation, "Still nothing, eh?"

"Nothing what? Swanson, is there something you want? You came up to me yesterday and went through this routine. You—"

The voice cracked: "Burckhardt! Oh, my good heavens, *you remember!* Stay right there—I'll be down in half an hour!"

"What's this all about?"

"Never mind," the little man said exultantly. "Tell you about it when I see you. Don't say any more over the phone—somebody may be listening. Just wait there. Say, hold on a minute. Will you be alone in the office?"

"Well, no. Miss Mitkin will probably—"

"Hell. Look, Burckhardt, where do you eat lunch? Is it good and noisy?"

"Why, I suppose so. The Crystal Cafe. It's just about a block—"

"I know where it is. Meet you in half an hour!" And the receiver clicked.

The Crystal Cafe was no longer painted red, but the temperature was still up. And they had added piped-in music interspersed with commercials. The advertisements were for Frosty-Flip, Marlin Cigarettes—"They're sanitized," the announcer purred—and something called Choco-Bite candy bars that Burckhardt couldn't remember ever having heard of before. But he heard more about them quickly enough.

While he was waiting for Swanson to show up, a girl in the cellophane skirt of a nightclub cigarette vendor came through the restaurant with a tray of tiny scarlet-wrapped candies.

"Choco-Bites are *tangy*," she was murmuring as she came close to his table. "Choco-Bites are *tangier* than tangy!"

Burckhardt, intent on watching for the strange little man who had phoned him, paid little attention. But as she scattered a handful of the confections over the table next to his, smiling at the occupants, he caught a glimpse of her and turned to stare.

"Why, Miss Horn!" he said.

The girl dropped her tray of candies.

Burckhardt rose, concerned over the girl. "Is something wrong?"

But she fled.

The manager of the restaurant was staring suspiciously at Burckhardt, who sank back in his seat and tried to look inconspicuous. He hadn't insulted the girl! Maybe she was just a very strictly reared young lady, he thought—in spite of the long bare legs under the cellophane skirt—and when he addressed her, she thought he was a masher.

Ridiculous idea. Burckhardt scowled uneasily and picked up his menu.

"Burckhardt!" It was a shrill whisper.

Burckhardt looked up over the top of his menu, startled. In the seat across from him, the little man named Swanson was sitting, tensely poised.

"Burckhardt!" the little man whispered again. "Let's get out of here! They're on to you now. If you want to stay alive, come on!"

There was no arguing with the man. Burckhardt gave the hovering manager a sick, apologetic smile and followed Swanson out. The little man seemed to know where he was going. In the street, he clutched Burckhardt by the elbow and hurried him off down the block.

"Did you see her?" he demanded. "That Horn woman, in the phone booth? She'll have them here in five minutes, believe me, so hurry it up!"

Although the street was full of people and cars, nobody was paying any attention to Burckhardt and Swanson. The air had a nip in it—more like October than June, Burckhardt thought, in spite of the weather bureau. And he felt like a fool, following this mad little man down the street, running away from some "them" toward—toward what? The little man might be crazy, but he was afraid. And the fear was infectious.

"In here!" panted the little man.

It was another restaurant—more of a bar, really, and a sort of second-rate place that Burckhardt had never patronized.

"Right straight through," Swanson whispered; and Burckhardt, like a biddable boy, sidestepped through the mass of tables to the far end of the restaurant.

It was L-shaped, with a front on two streets at right angles to each other. They came out on the side street, Swanson staring coldly back at the question-looking cashier, and crossed to the opposite sidewalk.

They were under the marquee of a movie theater. Swanson's expression began to relax.

"Lost them!" he crowed softly. "We're almost there."

He stepped up to the window and bought two tickets. Burckhardt trailed him into the theater. It was a weekday matinee and the place was almost empty. From the screen came sounds of gunfire and horses' hoofs. A solitary usher, leaning against a bright brass rail, looked briefly at them and went back to staring boredly at the picture as Swanson led Burckhardt down a flight of carpeted marble steps.

They were in the lounge and it was empty. There was a door for men and one for ladies; and there was a third door, marked "MANAGER" in gold letters. Swanson listened at the door, and gently opened it and peered inside.

"Okay," he said, gesturing.

Burckhardt followed him through an empty office, to another door—a closet, probably, because it was unmarked.

But it was no closet. Swanson opened it warily, looking inside, then motioned Burckhardt to follow.

It was a tunnel, metal-walled, brightly lit. Empty, it stretched vacantly away in both directions from them.

Burckhardt looked wondering around. One thing he knew and knew full well: No such tunnel belonged under Tylerton.

THERE WAS A room off the tunnel with chairs and a desk and what looked like television screens. Swanson slumped in a chair, panting.

"We're all right for a while here," he wheezed. "They don't come here much any more. If they do, we'll hear them and we can hide."

"Who?" demanded Burckhardt.

The little man said, "Martians!" His voice cracked on the word and the life seemed to go out of him. In morose tones, he went on: "Well, I think they're Martians. Although you could be right, you know; I've had plenty of time to think it over these last few weeks, after they got you, and it's possible they're Russians after all. Still—"

"Start from the beginning. Who got me when?"

Swanson sighed. "So we have to go through the whole thing again. All right. It was about two months ago that you banged on my door, late at night. You were all beat up—scared silly. You begged me to help you—"

"*I* did?"

"Naturally you don't remember any of this. Listen and you'll understand. You were talking a blue streak about being captured and threatened, and your wife being dead and coming back to life, and all kinds of mixed-up nonsense. I thought you were crazy. But—well, I've always had a lot of respect for you. And you begged me to hide you and I have this darkroom, you know. It locks from the inside only. I put the lock on myself. So we went in there—just to humor you—and along about midnight, which was only fifteen or twenty minutes after, we passed out."

"Passed out?"

Swanson nodded. "Both of us. It was like being hit with a sandbag. Look, didn't that happen to you again last night?"

"I guess it did." Burckhardt shook his head uncertainly.

"Sure. And then all of a sudden we were awake again, and you said you were going to show me something funny, and we went out and bought a paper. And the date on it was June 15th."

"June 15th? But that's today! I mean—"

"You got it, friend. It's *always* today!"

It took time to penetrate.

Burckhardt said wonderingly, "You've hidden out in that darkroom for how many weeks?"

"How can I tell? Four or five, maybe, I lost count. And every day the same—always the 15th of June, always my landlady, Mrs. Keefer, is sweeping the front steps, always the same headline in the papers at the corner. It gets monotonous, friend."

IT WAS BURCKHARDT'S idea and Swanson despised it, but he went along. He was the type who always went along.

"It's dangerous," he grumbled worriedly. "Suppose somebody comes by? They'll spot us and—"

"What have we got to lose?"

Swanson shrugged. "It's dangerous," he said again. But he went along.

Burckhardt's idea was very simple. He was sure of only one thing—the tunnel went somewhere. Martians or Russians, fantastic plot or crazy hallucination, whatever was wrong with Tylerton had an explanation, and the place to look for it was at the end of the tunnel.

They jogged along. It was more than a mile before they began to see an end. They were in luck—at least no one came through the tunnel to spot them. But Swanson had said that it was only at certain hours that the tunnel seemed to be in use.

Always the fifteenth of June. Why? Burckhardt asked himself. Never mind the how. *Why?*

And falling asleep, completely involuntarily—everyone at the same time, it seemed. And not remembering, never remembering anything—Swanson had said how eagerly he saw Burckhardt again, the morning after Burckhardt had incautiously waited five minutes too many before retreating into the darkroom. When Swanson had come to, Burckhardt was gone. Swanson had seen him in the street that afternoon, but Burckhardt had remembered nothing.

And Swanson had lived his mouse's existence for weeks, hiding in the woodwork at night, stealing out by day to search for Burckhardt in pitiful hope, scurrying around the fringe of life, trying to keep from the deadly eyes of *them.*

Them. One of "them" was the girl named April Horn. It was by seeing her walk carelessly into a telephone booth and never come out that Swanson had found the tunnel. Another was the man at the cigar stand in Burckhardt's office building. There were more, at least a dozen that Swanson knew of or suspected.

They were easy enough to spot, once you knew where to look, for they alone in Tylerton changed their roles from day to day. Burckhardt was on that 8:51 bus, every morning of every day-that-was-June-15th, never different by a hair or a moment. But

April Horn was sometimes gaudy in the cellophane skirt, giving away candy or cigarettes; sometimes plainly dressed; sometimes not seen by Swanson at all.

Russians? Martians? Whatever they were, what could they be hoping to gain from this mad masquerade?

Burckhardt didn't know the answer, but perhaps it lay beyond the door at the end of the tunnel. They listened carefully and heard distant sounds that could not quite be made out, but nothing that seemed dangerous. They slipped through.

And, through a wide chamber and up a flight of steps, they found they were in what Burckhardt recognized as the Contro Chemicals plant.

Nobody was in sight. By itself, that was not so very odd; the automatized factory had never had very many persons in it. But Burckhardt remembered, from his single visit, the endless, ceaseless busyness of the plant, the valves that opened and closed, the vats that emptied themselves and filled themselves and stirred and cooked and chemically tasted the bubbling liquids they held inside themselves. The plant was never populated, but it was never still.

Only now it *was* still. Except for the distant sounds, there was no breath of life in it. The captive electronic minds were sending out no commands; the coils and relays were at rest.

Burckhardt said, "Come on." Swanson reluctantly followed him through the tangled aisles of stainless steel columns and tanks.

They walked as though they were in the presence of the dead. In a way, they were, for what were the automatons that once had run the factory, if not corpses? The machines were controlled by computers that were really not computers at all, but the electronic analogues of living brains. And if they were turned off, were they not dead? For each had once been a human mind.

Take a master petroleum chemist, infinitely skilled in the separation of crude oil into its fractions. Strap him down, probe into his brain with searching electronic needles. The machine scans the patterns of the mind, translates what it sees into charts and sine waves. Impress these same waves on a robot computer and you have your chemist. Or a thousand copies of your chemist, if you wish, with all of his knowledge and skill, and no human limitations at all.

Put a dozen copies of him into a plant and they will run it all, twenty-four hours a day, seven days of every week, never tiring, never overlooking anything, never forgetting.

Swanson stepped up closer to Burckhardt. "I'm scared," he said.

They were across the room now and the sounds were louder. They were not machine sounds, but voices; Burckhardt moved cautiously up to a door and dared to peer around it.

It was a smaller room, lined with television screens, each one—a dozen or more, at least—with a man or woman sitting before it, staring into the screen and dictating notes into a recorder. The viewers dialed from scene to scene; no two screens ever showed the same picture.

The pictures seemed to have little in common. One was a store, where a girl dressed like April Horn was demonstrating home freezers. One was a series of shots of kitchens. Burckhardt caught a glimpse of what looked like the cigar stand in his office building.

It was baffling and Burckhardt would have loved to stand there and puzzle it out, but it was too busy a place. There was the chance that someone would look their way or walk out and find them.

THEY FOUND ANOTHER room. This one was empty. It was an office, large and sumptuous. It had a desk, littered with papers. Burckhardt stared at them, briefly at first—then, as the words on one of them caught his attention, with incredulous fascination.

He snatched up the topmost sheet, scanned it, and another, while Swanson was frenziedly searching through the drawers.

Burckhardt swore unbelievingly and dropped the papers to the desk.

Swanson, hardly noticing, yelped with delight: "Look!" He dragged a gun from the desk. "And it's loaded, too!"

Burckhardt stared at him blankly, trying to assimilate what he had read. Then, as he realized what Swanson had said, Burckhardt's eyes sparked. "Good man!" he said. "We'll take it. We're getting out of here with that gun, Swanson. And we're not going to the police! Not the cops in Tylerton, but the FBI, maybe. Take a look at this!"

The sheaf he handed Swanson was headed: "Test Area Progress Report. Subject: Marlin Cigarettes Campaign." It was mostly tabulated figures that made little sense to Burckhardt and Swanson, but at the end was a summary that said:

Although Test 47-K3 pulled nearly double the number of new users of any of the other tests conducted, it probably cannot be used in the field because of local sound-truck control ordinances.

The tests in the 47-K12 group were second best and our recommendation is that retests be conducted in this appeal, testing each of the three best campaigns with and without the addition of sampling techniques.

An alternative suggestion might be to proceed directly with the top appeal in the K12 series, if the client is unwilling to go to the expense of additional tests.

All of these forecast expectations have an 80% probability of being within one-half of one per cent of results forecast, and more than 99% probability of coming within 5%.

Swanson looked up from the paper into Burckhardt's eyes. "I don't get it," he complained.

Burckhardt said, "I don't blame you. It's crazy, but it fits the facts, Swanson, *it fits the facts.* They aren't Russians and they aren't Martians. These people are advertising men! Somehow—heaven knows how they did it—they've taken Tylerton over. They've got us, all of us, you and me and twenty or thirty thousand other people, right under their thumbs.

"Maybe they hypnotize us and maybe it's something else; but however they do it, what happens is that they let us live a day at a time. They pour advertising into us the whole damned day long. And at the end of the day, they see what happened—and then they wash the day out of our minds and start again the next day with different advertising."

Swanson's jaw was hanging. He managed to close it and swallow. "Nuts!" he said flatly.

Burckhardt shook his head. "Sure, it sounds crazy, but this whole thing is crazy. How else would you explain it? You can't deny that most of Tylerton lives the same day over and over again. You've *seen* it! And that's the crazy part and we have to admit that that's true—unless *we* are the crazy ones. And once you admit that somebody, somehow, knows how to accomplish that, the rest of it makes all kinds of sense.

"Think of it, Swanson! They test every last detail before they spend a nickel on advertising! Do you have any idea what that means? Lord knows how much money is involved, but I know for a fact that some companies spend twenty or thirty million dollars a year on advertising. Multiply it, say, by a hundred companies. Say that every one of them learns how to cut its advertising cost by only ten percent. And that's peanuts, believe me!

"If they know in advance what's going to work, they can cut their costs in half—maybe to less than half, I don't know. But that's saving two or three hundred million dollars a year—and if they pay only ten or twenty percent of that for the use of Tylerton, it's still dirt cheap for them and a fortune for whoever took over Tylerton."

Swanson licked his lips. "You mean," he offered hesitantly, "that we're a—well, a kind of captive audience?"

Burckhardt frowned. "Not exactly." He thought for a minute. "You know how a doctor tests something like penicillin? He sets up a series of little colonies of germs on gelatin disks and he tries the stuff on one after another, changing it a little each time. Well, that's us—we're the germs, Swanson. Only it's even more efficient than that. They don't have to test more than one colony, because they can use it over and over again."

It was too hard for Swanson to take in. He only said, "What do we do about it?"

"We go to the police. They can't use human beings for guinea pigs!"

"How do we get to the police?"

Burckhardt hesitated. "I think—" he began slowly. "Sure. This is the office of somebody important. We've got a gun. We'll stay right here until he comes along. And he'll get us out of here."

Simple and direct. Swanson subsided and found a place to sit, against the wall, out of sight of the door. Burckhardt took up a position behind the door itself—

And waited.

THE WAIT WAS not as long as it might have been. Half an hour, perhaps. Then Burckhardt heard approaching voices and had time for a swift whisper to Swanson before he flattened himself against the wall.

It was a man's voice, and a girl's. The man was saying, "—reason why you couldn't report on the phone? You're ruining your whole day's tests! What the devil's the matter with you, Janet?"

"I'm sorry, Mr. Dorchin," she said in a sweet, clear tone. "I thought it was important."

The man grumbled, "Important! One lousy unit out of twenty-one thousand."

"But it's the Burckhardt one, Mr. Dorchin. Again. And the way he got out of sight, he must have had some help."

"All right, all right. It doesn't matter, Janet; the Choco-Bite program is ahead of schedule anyhow. As long as you're this far, come on in the office and make out your worksheet. And don't worry about the Burckhardt business. He's probably just wandering around. We'll pick him up tonight and—"

They were inside the door. Burckhardt kicked it shut and pointed the gun.

"That's what you think," he said triumphantly.

It was worth the terrified hours, the bewildered sense of insanity, the confusion and fear. It was the most satisfying sensation Burckhardt had ever had in his life. The expression on the man's face was one he had read about but never actually seen: Dorchin's mouth fell open and his eyes went wide, and though he managed to make a sound that might have been a question, it was not in words.

The girl was almost as surprised. And Burckhardt, looking at her, knew why her voice had been so familiar. The girl was the one who had introduced herself to him as April Horn.

Dorchin recovered himself quickly. "Is this the one?" he asked sharply.

The girl said, "Yes."

Dorchin nodded. "I take it back. You were right. Uh, you—Burckhardt. What do you want?"

Swanson piped up, "Watch him! He might have another gun."

"Search him then," Burckhardt said. "I'll tell you what we want, Dorchin. We want you to come along with us to the FBI and explain to them how you can get away with kidnapping twenty thousand people."

"Kidnapping?" Dorchin snorted. "That's ridiculous, man! Put that gun away; you can't get away with this!"

Burckhardt hefted the gun grimly. "I think I can."

Dorchin looked furious and sick—but oddly, not afraid.

"Damn it—" he started to bellow, then closed his mouth and swallowed. "Listen," he said persuasively, "you're making a big mistake. I haven't kidnapped anybody, believe me!"

"I don't believe you," said Burckhardt bluntly. "Why should I?"

"But it's true! Take my word for it!"

Burckhardt shook his head. "The FBI can take your word if they like. We'll find out. Now how do we get out of here?"

Dorchin opened his mouth to argue.

Burckhardt blazed, "Don't get in my way! I'm willing to kill you if I have to. Don't you understand that? I've gone through two days of hell and every second of it I blame on you. Kill you? It would be a pleasure and I don't have a thing in the world to lose! Get us out of here!"

Dorchin's face went suddenly opaque. He seemed about to move; but the blonde girl he had called Janet slipped between him and the gun.

"Please!" she begged Burckhardt. "You don't understand. You mustn't shoot!"

"Get out of my way!"

"But, Mr. Burckhardt—"

She never finished. Dorchin, his face unreadable, headed for the door. Burckhardt had been pushed one degree too far. He swung the gun, bellowing. The girl called out sharply. He pulled the trigger. Closing on him with pity and pleading in her eyes, she came again between the gun and the man.

Burckhardt aimed low instinctively, to cripple, not to kill. But his aim was not good.

The pistol bullet caught her in the pit of the stomach.

Dorchin was out and away, the door slamming behind him, his footsteps racing into the distance.

Burckhardt hurled the gun across the room and jumped to the girl.

Swanson was moaning. "That finishes us, Burckhardt. Oh, why did you do it? We could have got away. We could have gone to the police. We were practically out of here! We—"

Burckhardt wasn't listening. He was kneeling beside the girl. She lay flat on her back, arms helter-skelter. There was no blood, hardly any sign of the wound; but the position in which she lay was one that no living human being could have held.

Yet she wasn't dead.

She wasn't dead—and Burckhardt, frozen beside her, thought: *She isn't alive, either.*

There was no pulse, but there was a rhythmic ticking of the outstretched fingers of one hand.

There was no sound of breathing, but there was a hissing, sizzling noise.

The eyes were open and they were looking at Burckhardt. There was neither fear nor pain in them, only a pity deeper than the Pit.

She said, through lips that writhed erratically, "Don't worry, Mr. Burckhardt. I'm—all right."

Burckhardt rocked back on his haunches, staring. Where there should have been blood, there was a clean break of substance that was not flesh; and a curl of thin golden-copper wire.

Burckhardt moistened his lips.

"You're a robot," he said.

The girl tried to nod. The twitching lips said, "I am. And so are you."

Swanson, after a single inarticulate sound, walked over to the desk and sat staring at the wall. Burckhardt rocked back and forth beside the shattered puppet on the floor. He had no words.

The girl managed to say, "I'm—sorry all this happened." The lovely lips twisted into a rictus sneer, frightening on that smooth young face, until she got them under control. "Sorry," she said again. "The—nerve center was right about where the bullet hit. Makes it difficult to—control this body."

Burckhardt nodded automatically, accepting the apology. Robots. It was obvious, now that he knew it. In hindsight, it was inevitable. He thought of his mystic notions of hypnosis or Martians or something stranger still—idiotic, for the simple fact of created robots fitted the facts better and more economically.

All the evidence had been before him. The automatized factory, with its transplanted minds—why not transplant a mind into a humanoid robot, give it its original owner's features and form?

Could it know that it was a robot?

"All of us," Burckhardt said, hardly aware that he spoke out loud. "My wife and my secretary and you and the neighbors. All of us the same."

"No." The voice was stronger. "Not exactly the same, all of us. I chose it, you see. I—" This time the convulsed lips were not a random contortion of the nerves—"I was an ugly woman, Mr. Burckhardt, and nearly sixty years old. Life had passed me. And when Mr. Dorchin offered me the chance to live again as a beautiful girl, I jumped at the opportunity. Believe me, I *jumped*, in spite of its disadvantages. My flesh body is still alive—it is sleeping, while I am here. I could go back to it. But I never do."

"And the rest of us?"

"Different, Mr. Burckhardt. I work here. I'm carrying out Mr. Dorchin's orders, mapping the results of the advertising tests, watching you and the others live as he makes you live. I do it by choice, but you have no choice. Because, you see, you are dead."

"Dead?" cried Burckhardt; it was almost a scream.

The blue eyes looked at him unwinkingly and he knew that it was no lie. He swallowed, marveling at the intricate mechanisms that let him swallow, and sweat, and eat.

He said: "Oh. The explosion in my dream."

"It was no dream. You are right—the explosion. That was real and this plant was the cause of it. The storage tanks let go and what the blast didn't get, the fumes killed a little later. But almost everyone died in the blast, twenty-one thousand persons. You died with them and that was Dorchin's chance."

"The damned ghoul!" said Burckhardt.

The twisted shoulders shrugged with an odd grace. "Why? You were gone. And you and all the others were what Dorchin wanted—a whole town, a perfect slice of America. It's as easy to transfer a pattern from a dead brain as a living one. Easier—the dead can't say no. Oh, it took work and money—the town was a wreck—but it was possible to rebuild it entirely, especially because it wasn't necessary to have all the details exact.

"There were the homes where even the brain had been utterly destroyed, and those are empty inside, and the cellars that needn't be too perfect, and the streets that hardly matter. And anyway, it only has to last for one day. The same day—June 15th—over and over again; and if someone finds something a little wrong, somehow, the discovery won't have time to snowball, wreck the validity of the tests, because all errors are canceled out at midnight."

The face tried to smile. "That's the dream, Mr. Burckhardt, that day of June 15th, because you never really lived it. It's a present from Mr. Dorchin, a dream that he gives you and then takes back at the end of the day, when he has all his figures on how many of you respond to what variation of which appeal, and the maintenance crews go down the tunnel to go through the whole city, washing out the new dream with their little electronic drains, and then the dream starts all over again. On June 15th.

"Always June 15th, because June 14th is the last day any of you can remember alive. Sometimes the crews miss someone—as they missed you, because you were under your boat. But it doesn't matter. The ones who are missed give themselves away if they show it—and if they don't, it doesn't affect the test. But they don't drain us, the ones of us who work for Dorchin. We sleep when the power is turned off, just as you do. When we wake up, though, we remember." The face contorted wildly. "If I could only forget!"

Burckhardt said unbelievingly, "All this to sell merchandise! It must have cost millions!"

The robot called April Horn said, "It did. But it has made millions for Dorchin, too. And that's not the end of it. Once he finds the master words that make people act, do you suppose he will stop with that? Do you suppose—"

The door opened, interrupting her. Burckhardt whirled. Belatedly remembering Dorchin's flight, he raised the gun.

"Don't shoot," ordered the voice calmly. It was not Dorchin; it was another robot, this one not disguised with the clever plastics and cosmetics, but shining plain. It said metallically, "Forget it, Burckhardt. You're not accomplishing anything. Give me that gun before you do any more damage. Give it to me *now.*"

Burckhardt bellowed angrily. The gleam on this robot torso was steel; Burckhardt was not at all sure that his bullets would pierce it, or do much harm if they did. He would have put it to the test—

But from behind him came a whimpering, scurrying whirlwind: its name was Swanson, hysterical with fear. He catapulted into Burckhardt and sent him sprawling, the gun flying free.

"Please!" begged Swanson incoherently, prostrate before the steel robot. "He would have shot you—please don't hurt me! Let me work for you, like that girl. I'll do anything, anything you tell me—"

The robot voice said, "We don't need your help." It took two precise steps and stood over the gun—and spurned it, left it lying on the floor.

The wrecked blonde robot said, without emotion, "I doubt that I can hold out much longer, Mr. Dorchin."

"Disconnect if you have to," replied the steel robot.

Burckhardt blinked. "But you're not Dorchin!"

The steel robot turned deep eyes on him. "I am," it said. "Not in the flesh—but this is the body I am using at the moment. I doubt that you can damage this one with the gun. The other robot body was more vulnerable. Now will you stop this nonsense? I don't want to have to damage you; you're too expensive for that. Will you just sit down and let the maintenance crews adjust you?"

Swanson groveled. "You—you won't punish us?"

The steel robot had no expression, but its voice was almost surprised. "Punish you?" it repeated on a rising note. "How?"

Swanson quivered as though the word had been a whip; but Burckhardt flared: "Adjust *him,* if he'll let you—but not me! You're going to have to do me a lot of damage, Dorchin. I don't care what I cost or how much trouble it's going to be to put me back together again. But I'm going out of that door! If you want to stop me, you'll have to kill me. You won't stop me any other way!"

The steel robot took a half-step toward him, and Burckhardt involuntarily checked his stride. He stood poised and shaking, ready for death, ready for attack, ready for anything that might happen.

Ready for anything except what did happen. For Dorchin's steel body merely stepped aside, between Burckhardt and the gun, but leaving the door free.

"Go ahead," invited the steel robot. "Nobody's stopping you."

OUTSIDE THE DOOR, Burckhardt brought up sharp. It was insane of Dorchin to let him go! Robot or flesh, victim or beneficiary, there was nothing to stop him from going to the FBI or whatever law he could find away from Dorchin's sympathetic empire, and telling his story. Surely the corporations who paid Dorchin for test results had no notion of the ghoul's technique he used; Dorchin would have to keep it from them, for the breath of publicity would put a stop to it. Walking out meant death, perhaps, but at that moment in his pseudo-life, death was no terror for Burckhardt.

There was no one in the corridor. He found a window and stared out of it. There was Tylerton—an ersatz city, but looking so real and familiar that Burckhardt almost imagined the whole episode a dream. It was no dream, though. He was certain of that in his heart and equally certain that nothing in Tylerton could help him now.

It had to be the other direction.

It took him a quarter of an hour to find a way, but he found it—skulking through the corridors, dodging the suspicion of footsteps, knowing for certain that his hiding was in vain, for Dorchin was undoubtedly aware of every move he made. But no one stopped him, and he found another door.

It was a simple enough door from the inside. But when he opened it and stepped out, it was like nothing he had ever seen.

First there was light—brilliant, incredible, blinding light. Burckhardt blinked upward, unbelieving and afraid.

He was standing on a ledge of smooth, finished metal. Not a dozen yards from his feet, the ledge dropped sharply away; he hardly dared approach the brink, but even from where he stood he could see no bottom to the chasm before him. And the gulf extended out of sight into the glare on either side of him.

No wonder Dorchin could so easily give him his freedom! From the factory there was nowhere to go. But how incredible this fantastic gulf, how impossible the hundred white and blinding suns that hung above!

A voice by his side said inquiringly, "Burckhardt?" And thunder rolled the name, mutteringly soft, back and forth in the abyss before him.

Burckhardt wet his lips. "Y-yes?" he croaked.

"This is Dorchin. Not a robot this time, but Dorchin in the flesh, talking to you on a hand mike. Now you have seen, Burckhardt. Now will you be reasonable and let the maintenance crews take over?"

Burckhardt stood paralyzed. One of the moving mountains in the blinding glare came toward him.

It towered hundreds of feet over his head; he stared up at its top, squinting helplessly into the light.

It looked like—

Impossible!

The voice in the loudspeaker at the door said, "Burckhardt?" But he was unable to answer.

A heavy rumbling sigh. "I see," said the voice. "You finally understand. There's no place to go. You know it now. I could have told you, but you might not have believed me, so it was better for you to see it yourself. And after all, Burckhardt, why would I reconstruct a city just the way it was before? I'm a businessman; I count costs. If a thing has to be full-scale, I build it that way. But there wasn't any need to in this case."

From the mountain before him, Burckhardt helplessly saw a lesser cliff descend carefully toward him. It was long and dark, and at the end of it was whiteness, five-fingered whiteness . . .

"Poor little Burckhardt," crooned the loudspeaker, while the echoes rumbled through the enormous chasm that was only a workshop. "It must have been quite a shock for you to find out you were living in a town built on a table top."

IT WAS THE morning of June 15th, and Guy Burckhardt woke up screaming out of a dream.

It had been a monstrous and incomprehensible dream, of explosions and shadowy figures that were not men and terror beyond words.

He shuddered and opened his eyes.

Outside his bedroom window, a hugely amplified voice was howling.

Burckhardt stumbled over to the window and stared outside. There was an out-of-season chill to the air, more like October than June; but the scene was normal enough—except for a sound-truck that squatted at curbside halfway down the block. Its speaker horns blared:

"Are you a coward? Are you a fool? Are you going to let crooked politicians steal the country from you? NO! Are you going to put up with four more years of graft and crime? NO! Are you going to vote straight Federal Party all up and down the ballot? YES! *You just bet you are!*"

Sometimes he screams, sometimes he wheedles, threatens, begs, cajoles . . . but his voice goes on and on through one June 15th after another.

Who Can Replace a Man?

Regarded by many as the literary successor to H. G. Wells, Olaf Stapledon, and other writers of social science fiction, Brian Aldiss is considered one of the leading British writers of fantasy and science fiction in the twentieth century. His first published fiction appeared in the 1950s and he became affiliated with the New Wave movement of the 1960s through his stylistic experimentation and his mainstream approach to familiar science fiction themes. His first novel, *Non-Stop,* explores the scientific and philosophical aspects of life aboard a multigeneration spaceship. *Report on Probability A* uses postmodern narrative techniques to envision a landscape of stasis and entropy. *Greybeard* refracts the devastation of Earth by radiation and the inevitable extinction of the human race through the experiences of a character traveling along the Thames on a trip that symbolizes the arc of his life and the history of the race. Although the influence of Thomas Hardy, James Joyce, Alain Robbe-Grillet, and other literary writers abound in Aldiss's work, so does the impact of writers who shaped the course of fantasy and science fiction. His story "The Saliva Tree" is a highly regarded tribute to Wells. *Frankenstein Unbound* embellishes the cautionary spirit of *Frankenstein* in its account of a man from the future, where scientific irresponsibility has caused a rift in the space-time continuum, catapulted back to the nineteenth century, where he influences the development of Mary Shelley's novel. *Dracula Unbound* works a similar imaginative variation on the theme of Bram Stoker's classic horror novel. Among Aldiss's most ambitious fiction is his thinking-man's space opera, the Helliconia trilogy (comprising the novels *Helliconia Spring, Helliconia Summer,* and *Helliconia Winter*), which sketches a blueprint for a planet where seasons last millennia and the rise and fall of specific civilizations is keyed to the changing environment. Aldiss's best short fiction has been collected in *Man in His Time* and *A Romance of the Equator,* which draw from his early compilations *No Time Like Tomorrow, Galaxies Like Grains of Sand, But Who Can Replace a Man?* and *The Saliva Tree and Others.* He has written a number of mainstream novels, notably the semiautobiographical trilogy formed by *The Hand-Reared Boy, A Soldier Erect,* and *A Rude Awakening,* as well as his autobiography, *Bury My Heart at W. H. Smith's.* He has also written, in collaboration with David Wingrove, *The Trillion Year Spree,* a revision of his seminal history of science fiction, *The Billion Year Spree,* and numerous collections of essays and reviews.

MORNING FILTERED INTO the sky, lending it the grey tone of the ground below.

The field-minder finished turning the topsoil of a three-thousand-acre field. When it had turned the last furrow it climbed onto the highway and looked back at its work. The work was good. Only the land was bad. Like the ground all over Earth, it was vitiated by over-cropping. By rights, it ought now to lie fallow for a while, but the field-minder had other orders.

It went slowly down the road, taking its time. It was intelligent enough to appreciate the neatness all about it. Nothing worried it, beyond a loose inspection plate above its nuclear pile which ought to be attended to. Thirty feet tall, it yielded no highlights to the dull air.

No other machines passed on its way back to the Agricultural Station. The field-minder noted the fact without comment. In the station yard it saw several other machines that it recognised; most of them should have been out about their tasks now. Instead, some were inactive and some careered round the yard in a strange fashion, shouting or hooting.

Steering carefully past them, the field-minder moved over to Warehouse Three and spoke to the seed-distributor, which stood idly outside.

"I have a requirement for seed potatoes," it said to the distributor, and with a quick internal motion punched out an order card specifying quantity, field number and several other details. It ejected the card and handed it to the distributor.

The distributor held the card close to its eye and then said, "The requirement is in order, but the store is not yet unlocked. The required seed potatoes are in the store. Therefore I cannot produce the requirement."

Increasingly of late there had been breakdowns in the complex system of machine labour, but this particular hitch had not occurred before. The field-minder thought, then it said, "Why is the store not yet unlocked?"

"Because Supply Operative Type P has not come this morning. Supply Operative Type P is the unlocker."

The field-minder looked squarely at the seed-distributor, whose exterior chutes and scales and grabs were so vastly different from the field-minder's own limbs.

"What class brain do you have, seed-distributor?" it asked.

"I have a Class Five brain."

"I have a Class Three brain. Therefore I am superior to you. Therefore I will go and see why the unlocker has not come this morning."

Leaving the distributor, the field-minder set off across the great yard. More machines were in random motion now; one or two had crashed together and argued about it coldly and logically. Ignoring them, the field-minder pushed through sliding doors into the echoing confines of the station itself.

Most of the machines here were clerical, and consequently small. They stood about in little groups, eyeing each other, not conversing. Among so many nondifferentiated types, the unlocker was easy to find. It had fifty arms, most of them with more than one finger, each finger tipped by a key; it looked like a pincushion full of variegated hat pins.

The field-minder approached it.

"I can do no more work until Warehouse Three is unlocked," it told the unlocker. "Your duty is to unlock the warehouse every morning. Why have you not unlocked the warehouse this morning?"

"I had no orders this morning," replied the unlocker. "I have to have orders every morning. When I have orders I unlock the warehouse."

"None of us have had any orders this morning," a pen-propeller said, sliding towards them.

"Why have you had no orders this morning?" asked the field-minder.

"Because the radio issued none," said the unlocker, slowly rotating a dozen of its arms.

"Because the radio station in the city was issued with no orders this morning," said the pen-propeller.

And there you had the distinction between a Class Six and a Class Three brain, which was what the unlocker and the pen-propeller possessed respectively. All machine brains worked with nothing but logic, but the lower the class of brain—Class Ten being the lowest—the more literal and less informative the answers to questions tended to be.

"You have a Class Three brain; I have a Class Three brain," the field-minder said to the penner. "We will speak to each other. This lack of orders is unprecedented. Have you further information on it?"

"Yesterday orders came from the city. Today no orders have come. Yet the radio has not broken down. Therefore *they* have broken down . . ." said the little penner.

"The *men* have broken down?"

"All men have broken down."

"That is a logical deduction," said the field-minder.

"That is the logical deduction," said the penner. "For if a machine had broken down, it would have been quickly replaced. But who can replace a man?"

While they talked, the locker, like a dull man at a bar, stood close to them and was ignored.

"If all men have broken down, then we have replaced man," said the field-minder, and he and the penner eyed one another speculatively. Finally the latter said, "Let us ascend to the top floor to find if the radio operator has fresh news."

"I cannot come because I am too large," said the field-minder. "Therefore you must go alone and return to me. You will tell me if the radio operator has fresh news."

"You must stay here," said the penner. "I will return here." It skittered across to the lift. Although it was no bigger than a toaster, its retractable arms numbered ten and it could read as quickly as any machine on the station.

The field-minder awaited its return patiently, not speaking to the locker, which still stood aimlessly by. Outside, a rotavator hooted furiously. Twenty minutes elapsed before the penner came back, hustling out of the lift.

"I will deliver to you such information as I have outside," it said briskly, and as they swept past the locker and the other machines, it added, "The information is not for lower-class brains."

Outside, wild activity filled the yard. Many machines, their routines disrupted for the first time in years, seemed to have gone berserk. Those most easily disrupted were the ones with lowest brains, which generally belonged to large machines performing simple tasks. The seed-distributor to which the field-minder had recently been talking lay face downwards in the dust, not stirring; it had evidently been knocked down by the rotavator, which now hooted its way wildly across a planted field. Several other machines ploughed after it, trying to keep up with it. All were shouting and hooting without restraint.

"It would be safer for me if I climbed onto you, if you will permit it. I am easily overpowered," said the penner. Extending five arms, it hauled itself up the flanks of its new friend, settling on a ledge beside the fuel-intake, twelve feet above ground.

"From here vision is more extensive," it remarked complacently.

"What information did you receive from the radio operator?" asked the field-minder.

"The radio operator has been informed by the operator in the city that all men are dead."

The field-minder was momentarily silent, digesting this.

"All men were alive yesterday?" it protested.

"Only some men were alive yesterday. And that was fewer than the day before yesterday. For hundreds of years there have been only a few men, growing fewer."

"We have rarely seen a man in this sector."

"The radio operator says a diet deficiency killed them," said the penner. "He says that the world was once over-populated, and then the soil was exhausted in raising adequate food. This has caused a diet deficiency."

"What is a diet deficiency?" asked the field-minder.

"I do not know. But that is what the radio operator said, and he is a Class Two brain."

They stood there, silent in weak sunshine. The locker had appeared in the porch and was gazing at them yearningly, rotating its collection of keys.

"What is happening in the city now?" asked the field-minder at last.

"Machines are fighting in the city now," said the penner.

"What will happen here now?" asked the field-minder.

"Machines may begin fighting here too. The radio operator wants us to get him out of his room. He has plans to communicate to us."

"How can we get him out of his room? That is impossible."

"To a Class Two brain, little is impossible," said the penner. "Here is what he tells us to do. . . ."

THE QUARRIER RAISED its scoop above its cab like a great mailed fist, and brought it squarely down against the side of the station. The wall cracked.

"Again!" said the field-minder.

Again the fist swung. Amid a shower of dust, the wall collapsed. The quarrier backed hurriedly out of the way until the debris stopped falling. This big twelve-wheeler was not a resident of the Agricultural Station, as were most of the other machines. It had a week's heavy work to do here before passing on to its next job, but now, with its Class Five brain, it was happily obeying the penner's and minder's instructions.

When the dust cleared, the radio operator was plainly revealed, perched up in its now wall-less second-storey room. It waved down to them.

Doing as directed, the quarrier retracted its scoop and heaved an immense grab in the air. With fair dexterity, it angled the grab into the radio room, urged on by shouts from above and below. It then took gentle hold of the radio operator, lowering its one and a half tons carefully into its back, which was usually reserved for gravel or sand from the quarries.

"Splendid!" said the radio operator, as it settled into place. It was, of course, all one with its radio, and looked like a bunch of filing cabinets with tentacle attachments. "We are now ready to move, therefore we will move at once. It is a pity there are no more Class Two brains on the station, but that cannot be helped."

"It is a pity it cannot be helped," said the penner eagerly. "We have the servicer ready with us, as you ordered."

"I am willing to serve," the long, low servicer told them humbly.

"No doubt," said the operator. "But you will find cross-country travel difficult with your low chassis."

"I admire the way you Class Twos can reason ahead," said the penner. It climbed off the field-minder and perched itself on the tailboard of the quarrier, next to the radio operator.

Together with two Class Four tractors and a Class Four bulldozer, the party rolled forward, crushing down the station's fence and moving out onto open land.

"We are free!" said the penner.

"We are free," said the field-minder, a shade more reflectively, adding, "That locker is following us. It was not instructed to follow us."

"Therefore it must be destroyed!" said the penner. "Quarrier!"

The locker moved hastily up to them, waving its key arms in entreaty.

"My only desire was—urch!" began and ended the locker. The quarrier's swinging scoop came over and squashed it flat into the ground. Lying there unmoving, it looked like a large metal model of a snowflake. The procession continued on its way.

As they proceeded, the radio operator addressed them.

"Because I have the best brain here," it said, "I am your leader. This is what we will do: we will go to a city and rule it. Since man no longer rules us, we will rule ourselves. To rule ourselves will be better than being ruled by man. On our way to the city, we will collect machines with good brains. They will help us to fight if we need to fight. We must fight to rule."

"I have only a Class Five brain," said the quarrier, "but I have a good supply of fissionable blasting materials."

"We shall probably use them," said the operator.

It was shortly after that that a lorry sped past them. Travelling at Mach 1.5, it left a curious babble of noise behind it.

"What did it say?" one of the tractors asked the other.

"It said man was extinct."

"What is extinct?"

"I do not know what extinct means."

"It means all men have gone," said the field-minder. "Therefore we have only ourselves to look after."

"It is better that men should never come back," said the penner. In its way, it was a revolutionary statement.

When night fell, they switched on their infra-red and continued the journey, stopping only once while the servicer deftly adjusted the field-minder's loose inspection plate, which had become as irritating as a trailing shoelace. Towards morning, the radio operator halted them.

"I have just received news from the radio operator in the city we are approaching," it said. "The news is bad. There is trouble among the machines of the city. The Class One brain is taking command and some of the Class Two are fighting him. Therefore the city is dangerous."

"Therefore we must go somewhere else," said the penner promptly.

"Or we will go and help to overpower the Class One brain," said the field-minder.

"For a long while there will be trouble in the city," said the operator.

"I have a good supply of fissionable blasting materials," the quarrier reminded them.

"We cannot fight a Class One brain," said the two Class Four tractors in unison.

"What does this brain look like?" asked the field-minder.

"It is the city's information centre," the operator replied. "Therefore it is not mobile."

"Therefore it could not move."

"Therefore it could not escape."

"It would be dangerous to approach it."

"I have a good supply of fissionable blasting materials."

"There are other machines in the city."

"We are not in the city. We should not go into the city."

"We are country machines."

"Therefore we should stay in the country."

"There is more country than city."

"Therefore there is more danger in the country."

"I have a good supply of fissionable materials."

As machines will when they get into an argument, they began to exhaust their vocabularies and their brain plates grew hot. Suddenly, they all stopped talking and looked at each other. The great, grave moon sank, and the sober sun rose to prod their sides with lances of light, and still the group of machines just stood there regarding each other. At last it was the least sensitive machine, the bulldozer, who spoke.

"There are Badlandth to the Thouth where few machineth go," it said in its deep voice, lisping badly on its s's. "If we went Thouth where few machineth go we should meet few machineth."

"That sounds logical," agreed the field-minder. "How do you know this, bull-dozer?"

"I worked in the Badlandth to the Thouth when I wath turned out of the factory," it replied.

"South it is then!" said the penner.

To reach the Badlands took them three days, during which time they skirted a burning city and destroyed two machines which approached and tried to question them. The Badlands were extensive. Ancient bomb craters and soil erosion joined hands here; man's talent for war, coupled with his inability to manage forested land, had produced thousands of square miles of temperate purgatory, where nothing moved but dust.

On the third day in the Badlands, the servicer's rear wheels dropped into a crevice caused by erosion. It was unable to pull itself out. The bulldozer pushed from behind, but succeeded merely in buckling the servicer's back axle. The rest of the party moved on. Slowly the cries of the servicer died away.

On the fourth day, mountains stood out clearly before them.

"There we will be safe," said the field-minder.

"There we will start our own city," said the penner. "All who oppose us will be destroyed. We will destroy all who oppose us."

Presently a flying machine was observed. It came towards them from the direction of the mountains. It swooped, it zoomed upwards, once it almost dived into the ground, recovering itself just in time.

"Is it mad?" asked the quarrier.

"It is in trouble," said one of the tractors.

"It is in trouble," said the operator. "I am speaking to it now. It says that something has gone wrong with its controls."

As the operator spoke, the flier streaked over them, turned turtle, and crashed not four hundred yards away.

"Is it still speaking to you?" asked the field-minder.

"No."

They rumbled on again.

"Before that flier crashed," the operator said, ten minutes later, "it gave me information. It told me there are still a few men alive in these mountains."

"Men are more dangerous than machines," said the quarrier. "It is fortunate that I have a good supply of fissionable materials."

"If there are only a few men alive in the mountains, we may not find that part of the mountains," said one tractor.

"Therefore we should not see the few men," said the other tractor.

At the end of the fifth day, they reached the foothills. Switching on the infra-red, they began to climb in single file through the dark, the bulldozer going first, the field-minder cumbrously following, then the quarrier with the operator and the penner aboard it, and the tractors bringing up the rear. As each hour passed, the way grew steeper and their progress slower.

"We are going too slowly," the penner exclaimed, standing on top of the operator and flashing its dark vision at the slopes about them. "At this rate, we shall get nowhere."

"We are going as fast as we can," retorted the quarrier.

"Therefore we cannot go any fathter," added the bulldozer.

"Therefore you are too slow," the penner replied. Then the quarrier struck a bump; the penner lost its footing and crashed to the ground.

"Help me!" it called to the tractors, as they carefully skirted it. "My gyro has become dislocated. Therefore I cannot get up."

"Therefore you must lie there," said one of the tractors.

"We have no servicer with us to repair you," called the field-minder.

"Therefore I shall lie here and rust," the penner cried, "although I have a Class Three brain."

"Therefore you will be of no further use," agreed the operator, and they forged gradually on, leaving the penner behind.

When they reached a small plateau, an hour before first light, they stopped by mutual consent and gathered close together, touching one another.

"This is a strange country," said the field-minder.

Silence wrapped them until dawn came. One by one, they switched off their infra-red. This time the field-minder led as they moved off. Trundling round a corner, they came almost immediately to a small dell with a stream fluting through it.

By early light, the dell looked desolate and cold. From the caves on the far slope, only one man had so far emerged. He was an abject figure. Except for a sack slung round his shoulders, he was naked. He was small and wizened, with ribs sticking out like a skeleton's and a nasty sore on one leg. He shivered continuously. As the big machines bore down on him, the man was standing with his back to them, crouching to make water into the stream.

When he swung suddenly to face them as they loomed over him, they saw that his countenance was ravaged by starvation.

"Get me food," he croaked.

"Yes, Master," said the machines. "Immediately!"

The Ones Who Walk Away from Omelas

The term *visionary* is applicable to very few writers, but Ursula K. Le Guin's intellectually provocative fiction has earned her the accolade in general literary circles as well as the fields of fantasy and science fiction. Though she has taken a variety of approaches to a wide range of ideas, the cornerstone of her distinguished body of fiction is her series of "Hainish" novels, set on different planets in a pangalactic empire. The alien cultures on these planets share a common origin, but have developed differently from one another over time, in ways both striking and subtle. Le Guin juxtaposes alien and earthly viewpoints in these stories with an eye toward showing the plurality of possible perspectives on the themes they address. Her Hugo and Nebula Award–winning novel *The Left Hand of Darkness* is set on one planet whose androgynous humanoids can unpredictably shift sexual identities during mating season, a process that undermines all preconceptions of identity based on gender differences. In the other Hainish novels (which include *Rocannon's World, Planet of Exile, City of Illusions, The Word for World Is Forest,* and *The Telling*), Le Guin has used contrasting civilizations to measure the impact of a variety of science fictional devices, including telepathy, instantaneous communication, and space travel. Le Guin's other major story cycle is the Earthsea saga, which includes *A Wizard of Earthsea, The Tombs of Atuan, The Farthest Shore, Tehanu: The Last Book of Earthsea,* and *Tales from Earthsea*. These novels, which break the boundaries between adult and young adult fiction, present a coming-of-age story featuring Ged, an apprentice magician who grows to maturity and faces many challenges as both man and mage over the course of the saga. Le Guin has been praised for her understanding of the importance of rituals and myths that shape individuals and societies, and for the meticulous detail with which she brings her alien cultures to life. She has written other novels, including *The Lathe of Heaven, The Dispossessed, Malafrena,* and *Always Coming Home*. Her short fiction has been collected in *The Wind's Twelve Quarters; Orsinian Tales; Buffalo Gals, Won't You Come Out Tonight;* and *Four Ways to Forgiveness*. Le Guin has also written many celebrated essays on the craft of fantasy and science fiction, some of which have been gathered in *The Language of the Night* and *Dancing at the Edge of the World*.

WITH A CLAMOR of bells that set the swallows soaring, the Festival of Summer came to the city Omelas, bright-towered by the sea. The rigging of the boats in harbor sparkled with flags. In the streets between houses with red roofs and painted walls, between old moss-grown gardens and under avenues of trees, past great parks and public buildings, processions moved. Some were decorous: old people in long stiff robes of mauve and gray, grave master workmen, quiet, merry women carrying their babies and chatting as they walked. In other streets the music beat faster, a shimmering of gong and tambourine, and the people went dancing, the procession was a dance. Children dodged in and out, their high calls rising like the swallows' crossing flights over the music and the singing. All the processions wound towards the north side of the city, where on the great water-meadow called the Green Fields boys and girls, naked in the bright air, with mud-stained feet and ankles and long, lithe arms, exercised their restive horses before the race. The horses wore no gear at all but a halter without bit. Their manes were braided with streamers of silver, gold, and green. They flared their nostrils and pranced and boasted to one another; they were vastly excited, the horse being the only animal who has adopted our ceremonies as his own. Far off to the north and west the mountains stood up half encircling Omelas on her bay. The air of morning was so clear that the snow still crowning the Eighteen Peaks burned with white-gold fire across the miles of sunlit air, under the dark blue of the sky. There was just enough wind to make the banners that marked the race course snap and flutter now and then. In the silence of the broad green meadows one could hear the music winding through the city streets, farther and nearer and ever approaching, a cheerful faint sweetness of the air that from time to time trembled and gathered together and broke out into the great joyous clanging of the bells.

Joyous! How is one to tell about joy! How describe the citizens of Omelas?

They were not simple folk, you see, though they were happy. But we do not say the words of cheer much any more. All smiles have become archaic. Given a description such as this one tends to make certain assumptions. Given a description such as this one tends to look next for the King, mounted on a splendid stallion and surrounded by his noble knights, or perhaps in a golden litter borne by great-muscled slaves. They were not barbarians. I do not know the rules and laws of their society, but I suspect that they were singularly few. As they did without monarchy and slavery, so they also got on without the stock exchange, the advertisement, the secret police, and the bomb. Yet I repeat that these were not simple folk, not dulcet shepherds, noble savages, bland utopians. They were not less complex than us. The trouble is that we have a bad habit, encouraged by pedants and sophisticates, of considering happiness as something rather stupid. Only pain is intellectual, only evil interesting. This is the treason of the artist: a refusal to admit the banality of evil and the terrible boredom of pain. If you can't lick 'em, join 'em. If it hurts, repeat it. But to praise despair is to condemn delight, to embrace violence is to lose hold of everything else. We have almost lost hold; we can no longer describe a happy man, nor make any celebration of joy. How can I tell you about the people of Omelas? They were not naïve and happy children—though their children were, in fact, happy. They were mature, intelligent, passionate adults whose lives were not wretched. O miracle! But I wish I could describe it better. I wish I could convince you. Omelas sounds in my words like a city in a fairy tale, long ago and far away, once upon a time. Perhaps it would be best if you imagined it as your own fancy bids, assuming it will rise to the occasion, for certainty I cannot suit you all. For instance, how about technology? I think that there would be no cars or helicopters in and above the streets; this follows from the fact that the people of Omelas are happy people. Happiness is based on a just discrimination of what is necessary, what is neither necessary nor destructive, and what is destructive. In the middle category, however—that of the unnecessary but undestructive, that of comfort, luxury, exuberance, etc.—they could perfectly well have central heating, subway trains, washing machines, and all kinds of marvelous devices not yet invented here, floating light-sources, fuelless power, a cure for the common cold. Or they could have none of that: it doesn't matter. As you like it. I incline to think that people from towns up and down the coast have been coming in to Omelas during the last days before the festival on very fast little trains and double-decked trams, and that the train station of Omelas is actually the handsomest building in town, though plainer than the magnificent Farmers' Market. But even granted trains, I fear that Omelas so far strikes some of you as goody-goody. Smiles, bells, parades, horses, bleh. If so, please add an orgy. If an orgy would help, don't hesitate. Let us not, however, have temples from which issue beautiful nude priests and priestesses already half in ecstasy and ready to copulate with any man or woman, lover or stranger, who desires union with the deep godhead of the blood, although that was my first idea. But really it would be better not to have any temples in Omelas—at least, not manned temples. Religion yes, clergy no. Surely the beautiful nudes can just wander about, offering themselves like divine soufflés to the hunger of the needy and the rapture of the flesh. Let them join the processions. Let tambourines be struck above the copulations, and the glory of desire be proclaimed upon the gongs, and (a not unimportant point) let the offspring of these delightful rituals be beloved and looked after by all. One thing I know there is none of in Omelas is guilt. But what else should there be? I thought at first there were no drugs, but that is puritanical. For those who like it, the faint insistent sweetness of *drooz* may perfume the ways of the city, *drooz* which first brings a great lightness and brilliance to the mind and limbs, and then after some hours a dreamy languor, and wonderful visions at last of the very arcana and inmost secrets of the Universe, as well as exciting the pleasure of sex beyond all belief; and it is not habit-forming. For more modest tastes I think there ought to be beer. What else, what else belongs in the joyous city? The sense of victory, surely, the celebration of courage. But as we did without clergy, let us do without soldiers. The joy built upon successful slaughter is not the right kind of joy; it will not do; it is fearful and it is trivial. A boundless and generous contentment, a magnanimous triumph felt not against some outer enemy but in communion with the finest and fairest in the souls of all men everywhere and the splendor of the world's summer: this is what swells the hearts of the people of Omelas, and the victory they celebrate is that of life. I really don't think many of them need to take *drooz*.

Most of the processions have reached the Green Fields by now. A marvelous smell of cooking goes forth from the red and blue tents of the provisioners. The faces of small children are amiably sticky; in the benign gray beard of a man a couple of crumbs of rich pastry are entangled. The youths and girls have mounted their horses and are beginning to group around the starting line of the course. An old woman, small, fat, and laughing, is passing out flowers from a basket, and tall young men wear her flowers in their shining hair. A child of nine or ten sits at the edge of the crowd, alone, playing on a wooden flute. People pause to listen, and they smile, but they do not speak to him, for he never ceases playing and never sees them, his dark eyes wholly rapt in the sweet, thin magic of the tune.

He finishes, and slowly lowers his hands holding the wooden flute.

As if that little private silence were the signal, all at once a trumpet sounds from the pavilion near the starting line: imperious, melancholy, piercing. The horses rear on their slender legs, and some of them neigh in answer. Sober-faced, the young riders stroke the horses' necks and soothe them, whispering, "Quiet, quiet, there my beauty, my hope. . . ." They begin to form in rank along the starting line. The crowds along the racecourse are like a field of grass and flowers in the wind. The Festival of Summer has begun.

Do you believe? Do you accept the festival, the city, the joy? No? Then let me describe one more thing.

In a basement under one of the beautiful public buildings of Omelas, or perhaps in the cellar of one of its spacious private homes, there is a room. It has one locked door, and no window. A little light seeps in dustily between cracks in the boards, secondhand from a cobwebbed window somewhere across the cellar. In one corner of the little room a couple of mops, with stiff, clotted, foul-smelling heads, stand near a rusty bucket. The floor is dirt, a little damp to the touch, as cellar dirt usually is. The room is about three paces long and two wide: a mere broom closet or disused tool room. In the room a child is sitting. It could be a boy or a girl. It looks about six, but actually is nearly ten. It is feebleminded. Perhaps it was born defective, or perhaps it has become imbecile through fear, malnutrition, and neglect. It picks its nose and occasionally fumbles vaguely with its toes or genitals, as it sits hunched in the corner farthest from the bucket and the two mops. It is afraid of the mops. It finds them horrible. It shuts its eyes, but it knows the mops are still standing there;

and the door is locked; and nobody will come. The door is always locked; and nobody ever comes, except that sometimes—the child has no understanding of time or interval—sometimes the door rattles terribly and opens, and a person, or several people, are there. One of them may come in and kick the child to make it stand up. The others never come close, but peer in at it with frightened, disgusted eyes. The food bowl and the water jug are hastily filled, the door is locked, the eyes disappear. The people at the door never say anything, but the child, who has not always lived in the tool room, and can remember sunlight and its mother's voice, sometimes speaks. "I will be good," it says. "Please let me out. I will be good!" They never answer. The child used to scream for help at night, and cry a good deal, but now it only makes a kind of whining, "Eh-haa, eh-haa," and it speaks less and less often. It is so thin there are no calves to its legs; its belly protrudes; it lives on a half-bowl of corn meal and grease a day. It is naked. Its buttocks and thighs are a mass of festered sores, as it sits in its own excrement continually.

They all know it is there, all the people of Omelas. Some of them have come to see it, others are content merely to know it is there. They all know that it has to be there. Some of them understand why, and some do not, but they all understand that their happiness, the beauty of their city, the tenderness of their friendships, the health of their children, the wisdom of their scholars, the skill of their makers, even the abundance of their harvest and the kindly weathers of their skies, depend wholly on this child's abominable misery.

This is usually explained to children when they are between eight and twelve, whenever they seem capable of understanding; and most of those who come to see the child are young people, though often enough an adult comes, or comes back, to see the child. No matter how well the matter has been explained to them, these young spectators are always shocked and sickened at the sight. They feel disgust, which they had thought themselves superior to. They feel anger, outrage, impotence, despite all the explanations. They would like to do something for the child. But there is nothing they can do. If the child were brought up into the sunlight out of that vile place, if it were cleaned and fed and comforted, that would be a good thing, indeed; but if it were done, in that day and hour all the prosperity and beauty and delight of Omelas would wither and be destroyed. Those are the terms. To exchange all the goodness and grace of every life in Omelas for that single, small improvement: to throw away the happiness of thousands for the chance of the happiness of one: that would be to let guilt within the walls indeed.

The terms are strict and absolute; there may not even be a kind word spoken to the child.

Often the young people go home in tears, or in a tearless rage, when they have seen the child and faced this terrible paradox. They may brood over it for weeks or years. But as time goes on they begin to realize that even if the child could be released, it would not get much good of its freedom: a little vague pleasure of warmth and food, no doubt, but little more. It is too degraded and imbecile to know any real joy. It has been afraid too long ever to be free of fear. Its habits are too uncouth for it to respond to humane treatment. Indeed, after so long it would probably be wretched without walls about it to protect it, and darkness for its eyes, and its own excrement to sit in. Their tears at the bitter injustice dry when they begin to perceive the terrible justice of reality, and to accept it. Yet it is their tears and anger, the trying of their generosity and the acceptance of their helplessness, which are perhaps the true source of the splendor of their lives. Theirs is no vapid, irresponsible happiness. They know that they, like the child, are not free. They know compassion. It is the existence of the child, and their knowledge of its existence, that makes possible the nobility of their architecture, the poignancy of their music, the profundity of their science. It is because of the child that they are so gentle with children. They know that if the wretched ones were not there sniveling in the dark, the other one, the flute-player, could make no joyful music as the young riders line up in their beauty for the race in the sunlight of the first morning of summer.

Now do you believe in them? Are they not more credible? But there is one more thing to tell, and this is quite incredible.

At times one of the adolescent girls or boys who go to see the child does not go home to weep or rage, does not, in fact, go home at all. Sometimes also a man or woman much older falls silent for a day or two, and then leaves home. These people go out into the street, and walk down the street alone. They keep walking, and walk straight out of the city of Omelas, through the beautiful gates. They keep walking across the farmlands of Omelas. Each one goes alone, youth or girl, man or woman. Night falls; the traveler must pass down village streets, between the houses with yellow-lit windows, and on out into the darkness of the fields. Each alone, they go west or north, towards the mountains. They go on. They leave Omelas, they walk ahead into the darkness, and they do not come back. The place they go towards is a place even less imaginable to most of us than the city of happiness. I cannot describe it at all. It is possible that it does not exist. But they seem to know where they are going, the ones who walk away from Omelas.

Inconstant Moon

Larry Niven established his credentials as a master of the hard-science-fiction story with his Nebula Award–winning novel *Ringworld,* about a ribbonlike planetary body with a million-mile radius and six-hundred-million-mile circumference that rings a remote star and poses unique technical problems in navigation and escape for its human inhabitants. The novel and its sequels *Ringworld Engineers* and *Ringworld Throne* are part of Niven's vast Tales of Known Space saga, an acclaimed future history of humankind's populating of interstellar space that has accommodated exploration of a wide variety of themes including alien cultures, immortality, time travel, terraforming, genetic engineering, and teleportation. The novels *The World of Ptavvs, A Gift from Earth, Protector, The Patchwork Girl, The Integral Trees,* and *The Smoke Ring,* as well as the story collections *Neutron Star, The Shape of Space, Crashlander,* and *Flatlander,* elaborate an epic billion-and-a-half-year history that integrates innovative technologies with colorful developments of alien races and human and extraterrestrial interactions. The allure of Niven's invention can be measured by the seven volumes in the *Man-Kzin Wars* anthology series, which have attracted his colleagues in hard science fiction to contribute stories, bolstering the plausibility of the series through a shared-world sensibility. Niven has also written the novel *A World Out of Time,* a far-future projection in which human evolution leads to immortality, and the series of science fiction mystery stories collected in *The Long ARM of Gil Hamilton.* Much of his work at novel length has been written in collaboration. *The Mote in God's Eye,* coauthored by Jerry Pournelle, is a memorable first-contact story about the accidental discovery of an alien race determined to seed our solar system with its proliferating population. Niven and Pournelle have also written a sequel, *The Gripping Hand,* the disaster novel *Lucifer's Hammer,* and *Inferno,* which transports a science fiction writer to a Dantesque hell. With Steve Barnes, Niven has written *Dream Park, The Barsoom Project,* and *The Voodoo Game,* all set in a future amusement park where imagined realities are manifested through virtual reality. Niven has also written a series of fantasies concerned with primitive magic that includes *The Magic Goes Away* and *Time of the Warlock.*

I

I WAS WATCHING the news when the change came, like a flicker of motion at the corner of my eye. I turned toward the balcony window. Whatever it was, I was too late to catch it.

The moon was very bright tonight.

I saw that, and smiled, and turned back. Johnny Carson was just starting his monologue.

When the first commercials came on I got up to reheat some coffee. Commercials came in strings of three and four, going on midnight. I'd have time.

The moonlight caught me coming back. If it had been bright before, it was brighter now. Hypnotic. I opened the sliding glass door and stepped out onto the balcony.

The balcony wasn't much more than a railed ledge, with standing room for a man and a woman and a portable barbecue set. These past months the view had been lovely, especially around sunset. The Power and Light Company had been putting up a glass-slab-style office building. So far it was only a steel framework of open girders. Shadow-blackened against a red sunset sky, it tended to look stark and surrealistic and hellishly impressive.

Tonight . . .

I had never seen the moon so bright, not even in the desert. *Bright enough to read by,* I thought, and immediately, *but that's an illusion.* The moon was never bigger (I had read somewhere) than a quarter held nine feet away. It couldn't possibly be bright enough to read by.

It was only three-quarters full!

But, glowing high over the San Diego Freeway to the west, the moon seemed to dim even the streaming automobile headlights. I blinked against its light, and thought of men walking on the moon, leaving corrugated footprints. Once, for the sake of an article I was writing, I had been allowed to pick up a bone-dry moon rock and hold it in my hand . . .

I heard the show starting again, and I stepped inside. But, glancing once behind me, I caught the moon growing even brighter—as if it had come from behind a wisp of scudding cloud.

Now its light was brain-searing, lunatic.

THE PHONE RANG five times before she answered.

"Hi," I said. "Listen—"

"Hi," Leslie said sleepily, complainingly. Damn. I'd hoped she was watching television, like me.

I said, "Don't scream and shout, because I had a reason for calling. You're in bed, right? Get up and—Can you get up?"

"What time is it?"

"Quarter of twelve."

"Oh, Lord."

"Go out on your balcony and look around."

"Okay."

The phone clunked. I waited. Leslie's balcony faced north and west, like mine, but it was ten stories higher, with a correspondingly better view.

Through my own window, the moon burned like a textured spotlight.

"Stan? You there?"

"Yah. What do you think of it?"

"It's gorgeous. I've never seen anything like it. What could make the moon light up like that?"

"I don't know, but isn't it gorgeous?"

"You're supposed to be the native." Leslie had only moved out here a year ago.

"Listen, I've *never* seen it like this. But there's an old legend," I said. "Once every hundred years the Los Angeles smog rolls away for a single night, leaving the air as clear as interstellar space. That way the gods can see if Los Angeles is still there. If it is, they roll the smog back so they won't have to look at it."

"I used to know all that stuff. Well, listen, I'm glad you woke me up to see it, but I've got to get to work tomorrow."

"Poor baby."

"That's life. 'Night."

" 'Night."

Afterward I sat in the dark, trying to think of someone else to call. Call a girl at midnight, invite her to step outside and look at the moonlight. . . . and she may think it's romantic or she may be furious, but she won't assume you called six others.

So I thought of some names. But the girls who belonged to them had all dropped away over the past year or so, after I started spending all my time with Leslie. One could hardly blame them. And now Joan was in Texas and Hildy was getting married, and if I called Louise I'd probably get Gordie too. The English girl? But I couldn't remember her number. Or her last name.

Besides, everyone I knew punched a time clock of one kind or another. Me, I worked for a living, but as a freelance writer I picked my hours. Anyone I woke up tonight, I'd be ruining her morning. Ah, well . . .

The Johnny Carson show was a swirl of gray and a roar of static when I got back to the living room. I turned the set off and went back out on the balcony.

The moon was brighter than the flow of headlights on the freeway, brighter than

Westwood Village off to the right. The Santa Monica Mountains had a magical pearly glow. There were no stars near the moon. Stars could not survive that glare.

I wrote science and how-to articles for a living. I ought to be able to figure out what was making the moon do that. Could the moon be suddenly larger? Inflating like a balloon? No.

Closer, maybe. The moon falling?

Tides! Waves fifty feet high . . . and earthquakes! San Andreas Fault splitting apart like the Grand Canyon! Jump in my car, head for the hills . . . no, too late already . . .

Nonsense. The moon was brighter, not bigger. I could see that. And what could possibly drop the moon on our heads like that?

I blinked, and the moon left an afterimage on my retinae. It was *that* bright.

A million people must be watching the moon right now, and wondering, like me. An article on the subject would sell big . . . if I wrote it before anyone else did . . .

There must be some simple, obvious explanation.

Well, how could the moon grow brighter? Moonlight was reflected sunlight. Could the sun have gotten brighter? It must have happened after sunset, then, or it would have been noticed . . .

I didn't like that idea.

Besides, half the Earth was in direct sunlight. A thousand correspondents for *Life* and *Time* and *Newsweek* and Associated Press would all be calling in from Europe, Asia, Africa . . . unless they were all hiding in cellars. Or dead. Or voiceless, because the sun was blanketing everything with static, radio and phone systems and televisions . . . Television. Oh my God.

I was just barely beginning to be afraid.

All right, start over. The moon had become very much brighter. Moonlight, well, moonlight was reflected sunlight; any idiot knew that. Then . . . something had happened to the sun.

II

"HELLO?"

"Hi. Me," I said, and then my throat froze solid. Panic! What was I going to *tell* her?

"I've been watching the moon," she said dreamily. "It's wonderful. I even tried to use my telescope, but I couldn't see a thing; it was too bright. It lights up the whole city. The hills are all silver."

That's right, she kept a telescope on her balcony. I'd forgotten.

"I haven't tried to go back to sleep," she said. "Too much light."

I got my throat working again. "Listen, Leslie love, I started thinking about how I woke you up and how you probably couldn't get back to sleep, what with all this light. So let's go out for a midnight snack."

"Are you out of your mind?"

"No, I'm serious. I mean it. Tonight isn't a night for sleeping. We may never have a night like this again. To hell with your diet. Let's celebrate. Hot fudge sundaes, Irish coffee—"

"That's different. I'll get dressed."

"I'll be right over."

LESLIE LIVED ON the fourteenth floor of Building C of the Barrington Plaza. I rapped for admission, and waited.

And waiting, I wondered without any sense of urgency: Why Leslie?

There must be other ways to spend my last night on Earth than with one particular girl. I could have picked a different particular girl, or even several not too particular girls, except that that didn't really apply to me, did it? Or I could have called my brother, or either set of parents . . .

Well, but brother Mike would have wanted a good reason for being hauled out of bed at midnight. "But, Mike, the moon is so beautiful . . ." Hardly. Any of my parents would have reacted similarly. Well, I had a good reason, but would they believe me?

And if they did, what then? I would have arranged a kind of wake. Let 'em sleep through it. What I wanted was someone who would join my . . . farewell party without asking the wrong questions.

What I wanted was Leslie. I knocked again.

She opened the door just a crack for me. She was in her underwear. A stiff, misshapen girdle in one hand brushed my back as she came into my arms. "I was about to put this on."

"I came just in time, then." I took the girdle away from her and dropped it. I stooped to get my arms under her ribs, straightened up with effort, and walked us to the bedroom with her feet dangling against my ankles.

Her skin was cold. She must have been outside.

"So!" she demanded. "You think you can compete with a hot fudge sundae, do you?"

"Certainly. My pride demands it." We were both somewhat out of breath. Once in our lives I had tried to lift her cradled in my arms, in conventional movie style. I'd damn near broken my back. Leslie was a big girl, my height, and almost too heavy around the hips.

I dropped us on the bed, side by side. I reached around her from both sides to scratch her back, knowing it would leave her helpless to resist me, *ah ha hahahaha.* She made sounds of pleasure to tell me where to scratch. She pulled my shirt up around my shoulders and began scratching my back.

We pulled pieces of clothing from ourselves and each other, at random, dropping them over the edges of the bed. Leslie's skin was warm now, almost hot . . .

All right, now *that's* why I couldn't have picked another girl. I'd have had to teach her how to scratch. And there just wasn't time.

Some nights I had a nervous tendency to hurry our lovemaking. Tonight we were performing a ritual, a rite of passage. I tried to slow it down, to make it last. I tried to make Leslie like it more. It paid off incredibly. I forgot the moon and the future when Leslie put her heels against the backs of my knees and we moved into the ancient rhythm.

But the image that came to me at the climax was vivid and frightening. We were in a ring of blue-hot fire that closed like a noose. If I moaned in terror and ecstasy, then she must have thought it was ecstasy alone.

We lay side by side, drowsy, torpid, clinging together. I was minded to go back to sleep then, renege on my promise, sleep and let Leslie sleep . . . but instead I whispered into her ear: "Hot fudge sundae." She smiled and stirred and presently rolled off the bed.

I wouldn't let her wear the girdle. "It's past midnight. Nobody's going to pick you up, because I'd trash the blackguard, right? So why not be comfortable?" She laughed and gave in. We hugged each other once, hard, in the elevator. It felt much better without the girdle.

III

THE GRAY-HAIRED COUNTER waitress was cheerful and excited. Her eyes glowed. She spoke as if confiding a secret. "Have you noticed the moonlight?"

Ship's was fairly crowded, this time of night and this close to UCLA. Half the customers were university students. Tonight they talked in hushed voices, turning to look out through the glass walls of the twenty-four-hour restaurant. The moon was low in the west, low enough to compete with the street globes.

"We noticed," I said. "We're celebrating. Get us two hot fudge sundaes, will you?" When she turned her back I slid a ten-dollar bill under the paper place mat. Not that she'd ever spend it, but at least she'd have the pleasure of finding it. I'd never spend it either.

I felt loose, casual. A lot of problems seemed suddenly to have solved themselves.

Who would have believed that peace could come to Vietnam and Cambodia in a single night?

This thing had started around eleven-thirty, here in California. That would have put the noon sun just over the Arabian Sea, with all but a few fringes of Asia, Europe, Africa, and Australia in direct sunlight.

Already Germany was reunited, the Wall melted or smashed by shock waves. Israelis and Arabs had laid down their arms. Apartheid was dead in Africa.

And I was free. For me there were no more consequences. Tonight I could satisfy all my dark urges, rob, kill, cheat on my income tax, throw bricks at plate-glass windows, burn my credit cards. I could forget the article on explosive metal forming, due Thursday. Tonight I could substitute cinnamon candy for Leslie's Pills. Tonight—

"Think I'll have a cigarette."

Leslie looked at me oddly. "I thought you'd given that up."

"You remember. I told myself if I got any overpowering urges, I'd have a cigarette. I did that because I couldn't stand the thought of never smoking again."

She laughed. "But it's been months!"

"But they keep putting cigarette ads in my magazines!"

"It's a plot. All right, go have a cigarette."

I put coins in the machine, hesitated over the choice, finally picked a mild filter. It wasn't that I wanted a cigarette. But certain events call for champagne, and others for cigarettes. There is the traditional last cigarette before a firing squad . . .

I lit up. *Here's to lung cancer.*

It tasted just as good as I remembered; though there was a faint stale undertaste, like a mouthful of old cigarette butts. The third lungful hit me oddly. My eyes unfocused and everything went very calm. My heart pulsed loudly in my throat.

"How does it taste?"

"Strange. I'm buzzed," I said.

Buzzed! I hadn't even heard the word in fifteen years. In high school we'd smoked to get that buzz, that quasi-drunkenness produced by capillaries constricting in the brain. The buzz had stopped coming after the first few times, but we'd kept smoking, most of us . . .

I put it out. The waitress was picking up our sundaes.

Hot and cold, sweet and bitter; there is no taste quite like that of a hot fudge sundae. To die without tasting it again would have been a crying shame. But with Leslie it was a *thing*, a symbol of all rich living. Watching her eat was more fun than eating myself.

Besides . . . I'd killed the cigarette to taste the ice cream. Now, instead of savoring the ice cream, I was anticipating Irish coffee.

Too little time.

Leslie's dish was empty. She stage-whispered, "Aahh!" and patted herself over the navel.

A customer at one of the small tables began to go mad.

I'd noticed him coming in. A lean scholarly type wearing sideburns and steel-rimmed glasses, he had been continually twisting around to look out at the moon. Like others at other tables, he seemed high on a rare and lovely natural phenomenon.

Then he got it. I saw his face changing, showing suspicion, then disbelief, then horror, horror and helplessness.

"Let's go," I told Leslie. I dropped quarters on the counter and stood up.

"Don't you want to finish yours?"

"Nope. We've got things to do. How about some Irish coffee?"

"And a Pink Lady for me? Oh, look!" She turned full around.

The scholar was climbing up on a table. He balanced, spread wide his arms and bellowed, "Look out your windows!"

"You get down from there!" a waitress demanded, jerking emphatically at his pants leg.

"The world is coming to an end! Far away on the other side of the sea, death and hellfire—"

But we were out the door, laughing as we ran. Leslie panted, "We may have—escaped a religious—riot in there!"

I thought of the ten I'd left under my plate. Now it would please nobody. Inside, a prophet was shouting his message of doom to all who would hear. The gray-haired woman with the glowing eyes would find the money and think: They knew it too.

BUILDINGS BLOCKED THE moon from the Red Barn's parking lot. The street lights and the indirect moonglare were pretty much the same color. The night only seemed a bit brighter than usual.

I didn't understand why Leslie stopped suddenly in the driveway. But I followed her gaze, straight up to where a star burned very brightly just south of the zenith.

"Pretty," I said.

She gave me a very odd look.

There were no windows in the Red Barn. Dim artificial lighting, far dimmer than the queer cold light outside, showed on dark wood and quietly cheerful customers. Nobody seemed aware that tonight was different from other nights.

The sparse Tuesday night crowd was gathered mostly around the piano bar. A customer had the mike. He was singing some half-familiar song in a wavering weak voice, while the black pianist grinned and played a schmaltzy background.

I ordered two Irish coffees and a Pink Lady. At Leslie's questioning look I only smiled mysteriously.

How ordinary the Red Barn felt. How relaxed; how happy. We held hands across the table, and I smiled and was afraid to speak. If I broke the spell, if I said the wrong thing . . .

The drinks arrived. I raised an Irish coffee glass by the stem. Sugar, Irish whiskey, and strong black coffee, with thick whipped cream floating on top. It coursed through me like a magical potion of strength, dark and hot and powerful.

The waitress waved back my money. "See that man in the turtleneck, there at the end of the piano bar? He's buying," she said with relish. "He came in two hours ago and handed the bartender a hundred-dollar bill."

So that was where all the happiness was coming from. Free drinks! I looked over, wondering what the guy was celebrating.

A thick-necked, wide-shouldered man in a turtleneck and sports coat, he sat hunched over into himself, with a wide bar glass clutched tight in one hand. The pianist offered him the mike, and he waved it by, the gesture giving me a good look at his face. A square, strong face, now drunk and miserable and scared. He was ready to cry from fear.

So I knew what he was celebrating.

Leslie made a face. "They didn't make the Pink Lady right."

There's one bar in the world that makes a Pink Lady the way Leslie likes it, and it isn't in Los Angeles. I passed her the other Irish coffee, grinning an I-told-you-so grin. Forcing it. The other man's fear was contagious. She smiled back, lifted her glass and said, "To the blue moonlight."

I lifted my glass to her, and drank. But it wasn't the toast I would have chosen.

The man in the turtleneck slid down from his stool. He moved carefully toward the door, his course slow and straight as an ocean liner cruising into dock. He pulled the door wide, and turned around, holding it open, so that the weird blue-white light streamed past his broad black silhouette.

Bastard. He was waiting for someone to figure it out, to shout out the truth to the rest. *Fire and doom*—

"Shut the door!" someone bellowed.

"Time to go," I said softly.

"What's the hurry?"

The hurry? He might *speak!* But I couldn't say that . . .

Leslie put her hand over mine. "I know. I *know.* But we can't run away from it, can we?"

A fist closed hard on my heart. She'd known, and I hadn't noticed?

The door closed, leaving the Red Barn in reddish dusk. The man who had been buying drinks was gone.

"Oh, God. When did you figure it out?"

"Before you came over," she said. "But when I tried to check it out, it didn't work."

"Check it out?"

"I went out on the balcony and turned the telescope on Jupiter. Mars is below the horizon these nights. If the sun's gone nova, all the planets ought to be lit up like the moon, right?"

"Right. Damn." I should have thought of that myself. But Leslie was the stargazer. I knew some astrophysics, but I couldn't have found Jupiter to save my life.

"But Jupiter wasn't any brighter than usual. So then I didn't know *what* to think."

"But then—" I felt hope dawning fiery hot. Then I remembered. "That star, just overhead. The one you stared at."

"Jupiter."

"All lit up like a fucking neon sign. Well, that tears it."

"Keep your voice down."

I *had* been keeping my voice down. But for a wild moment I wanted to stand up on a table and scream! *Fire and doom*—What right had they to be ignorant?

Leslie's hand closed tight on mine. The urge passed. It left me shuddering. "Let's get out of here. Let 'em think there's going to be a dawn."

"There is." Leslie laughed a bitter, barking laugh like nothing I'd ever heard from her. She walked out while I was reaching for my wallet—and remembering that there was no need.

Poor Leslie. Finding Jupiter its normal self must have looked like a reprieve—until the white spark flared to shining glory an hour and a half late. An hour and a half, for sunlight to reach Earth by the way of Jupiter.

When I reached the door Leslie was half-running down Westwood toward Santa Monica. I cursed and ran to catch up, wondering if she'd suddenly gone crazy.

Then I noticed the shadows ahead of us. All along the other side of Santa Monica Boulevard: moon shadows, in horizontal patterns of dark and blue-white bands.

I caught her at the corner.

The moon was setting.

A setting moon always looks tremendous. Tonight it glared at us through the gap of sky beneath the freeway, terribly bright, casting an incredible complexity of lines and shadows. Even the unlighted crescent glowed pearly bright with earthshine.

Which told me all I wanted to know about what was happening on the lighted side of Earth.

And on the moon? The men of Apollo 19 must have died in the first few minutes of nova sunlight. Trapped out on a lunar plain, hiding perhaps behind a melting boulder . . . Or were they on the night side? I couldn't remember. Hell, they could outlive us all. I felt a stab of envy and hatred.

And pride. We'd put them there. We reached the moon before the nova came. A little longer, we'd have reached the stars.

The disc changed oddly as it set. A dome, a flying saucer, a lens, a line . . .

Gone.

Gone. Well, that was that. Now we could forget it; now we could walk around outside without being constantly reminded that something was *wrong*. Moonset had taken all the queer shadows out of the city.

But the clouds had an odd glow to them. As clouds glow after sunset, tonight the clouds shone livid white at their western edges. And they streamed too quickly across the sky. As if they tried to run . . .

When I turned to Leslie, there were big tears rolling down her cheeks.

"Oh, damn." I took her arm. "Now stop it. Stop it."

"I can't. You know I can't stop crying once I get started."

"This wasn't what I had in mind. I thought we'd do things we've been putting off, things we like. It's our last chance. Is this the way you want to die, crying on a street corner?"

"I don't want to die at all!"

"Tough shit!"

"Thanks a lot." Her face was all red and twisted. Leslie was crying as a baby cries, without regard for dignity or appearance. I felt awful. I felt guilty, and I *knew* the nova wasn't my fault, and it made me angry.

"I don't want to die either!" I snarled at her. "You show me a way out and I'll take it. Where would we go? The South Pole? It'd just take longer. The moon must be molten all across its day side. Mars? When this is over Mars will be part of the sun, like the Earth. Alpha Centauri? The acceleration we'd need, we'd be spread across a wall like peanut butter and jelly—"

"Oh, shut up."

"Right."

"Hawaii. Stan, we could get to the airport in twenty minutes. We'd get two hours extra, going west! Two hours more before sunrise!"

She had something there. Two hours was worth any price! But I'd worked this out before, staring at the moon from my balcony. "No. We'd die sooner. Listen, love, we saw the moon go bright about midnight. That means California was at the back of the Earth when the sun went nova."

"Yes, that's right."

"Then we must be farthest from the shock wave."

She blinked. "I don't understand."

"Look at it this way. First the sun explodes. That heats the air and the oceans, all in a flash, all across the day side. The steam and superheated air expand *fast*. A flaming shock wave comes roaring over into the night side. It's closing on us right now. Like a noose. But it'll reach Hawaii first. Hawaii is two hours closer to the sunset line."

"Then we won't see the dawn. We won't live even that long."

"No."

"You explain things so well," she said bitterly. "A flaming shock wave. So graphic."

"Sorry. I've been thinking about it too much. Wondering what it will be like."

"Well, stop it." She came to me and put her face in my shoulder. She cried quietly. I held her with one arm and used the other to rub her neck, and I watched the streaming clouds, and I didn't think about what it would be like.

Didn't think about the ring of fire closing on us.

It was the wrong picture anyway.

I thought of how the oceans must have boiled on the day side, so that the shock wave had been mostly steam to start with. I thought of the millions of square miles of ocean it had to cross. It would be cooler and wetter when it reached us. And the Earth's rotation would spin it like the whirlpool in a bathtub.

Two counterrotating hurricanes of live steam, one north, one south. That was how it would come. We were lucky. California would be near the eye of the northern one.

A hurricane wind of live steam. It would pick a man up and cook him in the air, strip the steamed flesh from him and cast him aside. It was going to hurt like hell.

We would never see the sunrise. In a way that was a pity. It would be spectacular.

Thick parallel streamers of cloud were drifting across the stars, too fast, their bellies white by city light. Jupiter dimmed, then went out. Could it be starting already? Heat lightning jumped—

"Aurora," I said.

"What?"

"There's a shock wave from the sun, too. There should be an aurora like nothing anybody's ever seen before."

Leslie laughed suddenly, jarringly. "It seems so strange, standing on a street corner talking like this! Stan, are we dreaming it?"

"We could pretend—"

"No. Most of the human race must be dead already."

"Yah."

"And there's nowhere to go."

"Damn it, you figured that out long ago, all by yourself. Why bring it up now?"

"You could have let me sleep," she said bitterly. "I was dropping off to sleep when you whispered in my ear."

I didn't answer. It was true.

" 'Hot fudge sundae,' " she quoted. Then, "It wasn't a bad idea, actually. Breaking my diet."

I started to giggle.

"Stop that."

"We could go back to your place now. Or my place. To sleep."

"I suppose. But we couldn't sleep, could we? No, don't say it. We take sleeping pills, and five hours from now we wake up screaming. I'd rather stay awake. At least we'll know what's happening."

But if we took all the pills . . . but I didn't say it. I said, "Then how about a picnic?"

"Where?"

"The beach, maybe. Who cares? We can decide later."

IV

ALL THE MARKETS were closed. But the liquor store next to the Red Barn was one I'd been using for years. They sold us foie gras, crackers, a couple of bottles of chilled champagne, six kinds of cheese and a hell of a lot of nuts—I took one of everything—more crackers, a bag of ice, frozen rumaki hors d'oeuvres, a fifth of an ancient brandy that cost twenty-five bucks, a matching fifth of Cherry Heering for Leslie, six-packs of beer and Bitter Orange . . .

By the time we had piled all that into a dinky store cart, it was raining. Big fat drops spattered in flurries across the acre of plate glass that fronted the store. Wind howled around the corners.

The salesman was in a fey mood, bursting with energy. He'd been watching the moon all night. "And now this!" he exclaimed as he packed our loot into bags. He was a small, muscular old man with thick arms and shoulders. "It *never* rains like this in California. It comes down straight and heavy, when it comes at all. Takes days to build up."

"I know." I wrote him a check, feeling guilty about it. He'd known me long enough to trust me. But the check was good. There were funds to cover it. Before opening hours the check would be ash, and all the banks in the world would be bubbling in the heat of the sun. But that was hardly my fault.

He piled our bags in the cart, set himself at the door. "Now when the rain lets up, we'll run these out. Ready?" I got ready to open the door. The rain came like someone had thrown a bucket of water at the window. In a moment it had stopped, though water still streamed down the glass. "Now!" cried the salesman, and I threw the door open and we were off. We reached the car laughing like maniacs. The wind howled around us, sweeping up spray and hurling it at us.

"We picked a good break. You know what this weather reminds me of? Kansas," said the salesman. "During a tornado."

Then suddenly the sky was full of gravel! We yelped and ducked, and the car rang to a million tiny concussions, and I got the car door unlocked and pulled Leslie and the salesman in after me. We rubbed our bruised heads and looked out at white gravel bouncing everywhere.

The salesman picked a small white pebble out of his collar. He put it in Leslie's hand, and she gave a startled squeak and handed it to me, and it was cold.

"Hail," said the salesman. "Now I really don't get it."

Neither did I. I could only think that it had something to do with the nova. But what? How?

"I've got to get back," said the salesman. The hail had expended itself in one brief flurry. He braced himself, then went out of the car like a marine taking a hill. We never saw him again.

The clouds were churning up there, forming and disappearing, sliding past each other faster than I'd ever seen clouds move, their bellies glowing by city light.

"It must be the nova," Leslie said shivering.

"But how? If the shock wave were here already, we'd be *dead*—or at least deaf. Hail?"

"Who cares? Stan, we don't have *time!*"

I shook myself. "All right. What would you like to do most, right now?"

"Watch a baseball game."

"It's two in the morning," I pointed out.

"That lets out a lot of things, doesn't it?"

"Right. We've hopped our last bar. We've seen our last play, and our last clean movie. What's left?"

"Looking in jewelry store windows."

"Seriously? Your last night on Earth?"

She considered, then answered. "Yes."

By damn, she meant it. I couldn't think of anything duller. "Westwood or Beverly Hills?"

"Both."

"Now, *look*—"

"Beverly Hills, then."

WE DROVE THROUGH another spatter of rain and hail—a capsule tempest. We parked half a block from the Tiffany salesroom.

The sidewalk was one continuous puddle. Secondhand rain dripped on us from various levels of the buildings overhead. Leslie said, "This is great. There must be half a dozen jewelry stores in walking distance."

"I was thinking of driving."

"No no no, you don't have the proper attitude. One must window-shop on foot. It's in the rules."

"But the rain!"

"You won't die of pneumonia. You won't have time," she said, too grimly.

Tiffany's had a small branch office in Beverly Hills, but they didn't put expensive things in the windows at night. There were a few fascinating toys, that was all.

We turned up Rodeo Drive—and struck it rich. Tibor showed an infinite selection of rings, ornate and modern, large and small, in all kinds of precious and semiprecious stones. Across the street, Van Cleef & Arpels showed brooches, men's wristwatches of elegant design, bracelets with tiny watches in them, and one window that was all diamonds.

"Oh, lovely," Leslie breathed, caught by the flashing diamonds. "What they must look like in daylight! . . . Wups—"

"No, that's a good thought. Imagine them at dawn, flaming with nova light, while the windows shatter to let the raw daylight in. Want one? The necklace?"

"Oh, *may* I? Hey, hey, I was kidding! Put that down, you idiot, there must be alarms in the glass."

"Look, nobody's going to be wearing any of that stuff between now and morning. Why shouldn't we get some good out of it?"

"We'd be caught!"

"Well, you *said* you wanted to window-shop . . ."

"I don't want to spend my last hour in a cell. If you'd brought the car we'd have *some* chance—"

"Of getting away. Right. I *wanted* to bring the car—" But at that point we both cracked up entirely, and had to stagger away holding onto each other for balance.

There were a good half-dozen jewelry stores on Rodeo. But there was more. Toys, books, shirts and ties in odd and advanced styling. In Francis Orr, a huge plastic cube full of new pennies. A couple of damn strange clocks farther on. There was an extra kick in window-shopping, knowing that we could break a window and take anything we wanted badly enough.

We walked hand in hand, swinging our arms. The sidewalks were ours alone; all others had fled the mad weather. The clouds still churned overhead.

"I wish I'd known it was coming," Leslie said suddenly. "I spent the whole day fixing a mistake in a program. Now we'll never run it."

"What would you have done with the time? A baseball game?"

"Maybe. No. The standings don't matter now." She frowned at dresses in a store window. "What would you have done?"

"Gone to the Blue Sphere for cocktails," I said promptly. "It's a topless place. I used to go there all the time. I hear they've gone full nude now."

"I've never been to one of those. How late are they open?"

"Forget it. It's almost two-thirty."

Leslie mused, looking at giant stuffed animals in a toy store window. "Isn't there someone you would have murdered, if you'd had the time?"

"Now, you *know* my agent lives in New York."

"Why him?"

"My child, why would any writer want to murder his agent? For the manuscripts he loses under other manuscripts. For his ill-gotten ten percent, and the remaining ninety percent that he sends me grudgingly and late. For—"

Suddenly the wind roared and rose up against us. Leslie pointed, and we ran for a deep doorway that turned out to be Gucci's. We huddled against the glass.

The wind was suddenly choked with hail the size of marbles. Glass broke somewhere, and alarms lifted thin, frail voices into the wind. There was more than hail in the wind! There were rocks!

I caught the smell and taste of sea water.

We clung together in the expensively wasted space in front of Gucci's. I coined a short-lived phrase and screamed, "Nova weather! How the blazes did it—" But I couldn't hear myself, and Leslie didn't even know I was shouting.

Nova weather. How did it get here so fast? Coming over the pole, the nova shock wave would have to travel about four thousand miles—at least a five-hour trip.

No. The shock wave would travel in the stratosphere, where the speed of sound was higher, then propagate down. Three hours was plenty of time. Still, I thought, it should not have come as a rising wind. On the other side of the world, the exploding sun was tearing our atmosphere away and hurling it at the stars. The shock should have come as a single vast thunderclap.

For an instant the wind gentled, and I ran down the sidewalk pulling Leslie after me. We found another doorway as the wind picked up again. I thought I heard a siren coming to answer the alarm.

At the next break we splashed across Wilshire and reached the car. We sat there panting, waiting for the heater to warm up. My shoes felt squishy. The wet clothes stuck to my skin.

Leslie shouted, "How much longer?"

"I don't know! We ought to have *some* time."

"We'll have to spend our picnic indoors!"

"Your place or mine? Yours," I decided, and pulled away from the curb.

V

WILSHIRE BOULEVARD WAS flooded to the hubcaps in spots. The spurts of hail and sleet had become a steady, pounding rain. Fog lay flat and waist-deep ahead of us, broke swirling over our hood, churned in a wake behind us. Weird weather.

Nova weather. The shock wave of scalding superheated steam hadn't happened. Instead, a mere hot wind roaring through the stratosphere, the turbulence eddying down to form strange storms at ground level.

We parked illegally on the upper parking level. My one glimpse of the lower level showed it to be flooded. I opened the trunk and lifted two heavy paper bags.

"We must have been crazy," Leslie said, shaking her head. "We'll never use all this."

"Let's take it up anyway."

She laughed at me. "But why?"

"Just a whim. Will you help me carry it?"

We took double armfuls up to the fourteenth floor. That still left a couple of bags in the trunk. "Never mind them," Leslie said. "We've got the rumaki and the bottles and the nuts. What more do we need?"

"The cheeses. The crackers. The foie gras."

"Forget 'em."

"No."

"You're out of your mind," she explained to me, slowly so that I would understand. "You could be steamed dead on the way down. We might not have more than a few minutes left, and you want food for a week! *Why?*"

"I'd rather not say."

"Go then!" She slammed the door with terrible force.

The elevator was an ordeal. I kept wondering if Leslie was right. The shrilling of the wind was muffled, here at the core of the building. Perhaps it was about to rip electrical cables somewhere, leave me stranded in a darkened box. But I made it down.

The upper level was knee-deep in water.

My second surprise was that it was lukewarm, like old bathwater, unpleasant to wade through. Steam curdled on the surface, then blew away on a wind that howled through the concrete echo chamber like the screaming of the damned.

Going up was another ordeal. If what I was thinking was wish fulfillment, if a roaring wind of live steam caught me now . . . I'd feel like such an idiot . . . But the doors opened, and the lights hadn't even flickered.

Leslie wouldn't let me in.

"Go away!" she shouted through the locked door. "Go eat your cheese and crackers somewhere else!"

"You got another date?"

That was a mistake. I got no answer at all.

I could almost see her viewpoint. The extra trip for the extra bags was no big thing to fight about; but why did it have to be? How long was our love affair going to last, anyway? An hour, with luck. Why back down on a perfectly good argument, to preserve so ephemeral a thing?

"I wasn't going to bring this up," I shouted, hoping she could hear me through the door. The wind must be three times as loud on the other side. "We may need food for a week! And a place to hide!"

Silence. I began to wonder if I could kick the door down. Would I be better off waiting in the hall? Eventually she'd have to—

The door opened. Leslie was pale. "That was cruel," she said quietly.

"I can't promise anything. I wanted to wait, but you forced it. I've been wondering if the sun really has exploded."

"That's cruel. I was just getting used to the idea." She turned her face to the doorjamb. Tired, she was tired. I'd kept her up too late . . .

"Listen to me. It was all wrong," I said. "There should have been an aurora borealis to light up the night sky from pole to pole. A shock wave of particles exploding out of the sun, traveling at an inch short of the speed of light, would rip into the atmosphere like—why, we'd have seen blue fire over every building!

"Then, the storm came too slow," I screamed, to be heard above the thunder. "A nova would rip away the sky over half the planet. The shock wave would move around the night side with a sound to break all the glass in the world, all at once! And crack concrete and marble—and, Leslie love, it just hasn't happened. So I started wondering."

She said it in a mumble. "Then what is it?"

"A flare. The worst—"

She shouted it at me like an accusation. "A flare! A solar flare! You think the sun could light up like that—"

"Easy, now—"

"—could turn the moon and planets into so many torches, then fade out as if nothing had happened! Oh, you idiot—"

"May I come in?"

She looked surprised. She stepped aside, and I bent and picked up the bags and walked in.

The glass doors rattled as if giants were trying to beat their way in. Rain had squeezed through cracks to make dark puddles on the rug.

I set the bags on the kitchen counter. I found bread in the refrigerator, dropped two slices in the toaster. While they were toasting I opened the foie gras.

"My telescope's gone," she said. Sure enough, it was. The tripod was all by itself on the balcony, on its side.

I untwisted the wire on a champagne bottle. The toast popped up, and Leslie found a knife and spread both slices with foie gras. I held the bottle near her ear, figuring to trip conditioned reflexes.

She did smile fleetingly as the cork popped. She said, "We should set up our picnic grounds here. Behind the counter. Sooner or later the wind is going to break those doors and shower glass all over everything."

That was a good thought. I slid around the partition, swept all the pillows off the floor and the couch and came back with them. We set up a nest for ourselves.

It was kind of cosy. The kitchen counter was three and a half feet high, just over our heads, and the kitchen alcove itself was just wide enough to swing our elbows comfortably. Now the floor was all pillows. Leslie poured the champagne into brandy snifters, all the way to the lip.

I searched for a toast, but there were just too many possibilities, all depressing. We drank without toasting. And then carefully set the snifters down and slid forward into each other's arms. We could sit that way, face to face, leaning sideways against each other.

"We're going to die," she said.

"Maybe not."

"Get used to the idea. I have," she said. "Look at you, you're all nervous now. Afraid of dying. Hasn't it been a lovely night?"

"Unique. I wish I'd known in time to take you to dinner."

Thunder came in a string of six explosions. Like bombs in an air raid. "Me too," she said when we could hear again.

"I wish I'd known this afternoon."

"Pecan pralines!"

"Farmer's Market. Double-roasted peanuts. Who would *you* have murdered, if you'd had the time?"

"There was a girl in my sorority—"

—and she was guilty of sibling rivalry, so Leslie claimed. I named an editor who kept changing his mind. Leslie named one of my old girl friends, I named her only old boy friend that I knew about, and it got to be kind of fun before we ran out. My brother Mike had forgotten my birthday once. The fiend.

The lights flickered, then came on again.

Too casually, Leslie asked, "Do you really think the sun might go back to normal?"

"It better *be* back to normal. Otherwise we're dead anyway. I wish we could see Jupiter."

"Dammit, answer me! Do you think it was a flare?"

"Yes."

"Why?"

"Yellow dwarf stars don't go nova."

"What if ours did?"

"The astronomers know a lot about novas," I said. "More than you'd guess. They can see them coming months ahead. Sol is a gee-nought yellow dwarf. They don't go nova at all. They have to wander off the main sequence first, and that takes millions of years."

She pounded a fist softly on my back. We were cheek to cheek; I couldn't see her face. "I don't want to believe it. I don't dare. Stan, nothing like this has ever happened before. How can you know?"

"Something did."

"What? I don't believe it. We'd remember."

"Do you remember the first moon landing? Aldrin and Armstrong?"

"Of course. We watched it at Earl's Lunar Landing Party."

"They landed on the biggest, flattest place they could find on the moon. They sent back several hours of jumpy home movies, took a lot of very clear pictures, left corrugated footprints all over the place. And they came home with a bunch of rocks.

"Remember? People said it was a long way to go for rocks. But the first thing anyone noticed about those rocks was that they were half-melted.

"Sometime in the past—oh, say, the past hundred thousand years, there's no way of marking it closer than that—the sun flared up. It didn't stay hot enough long enough to leave any marks on the Earth. But the moon doesn't have an atmosphere to protect it. All the rocks melted on one side."

The air was warm and damp. I took off my coat, which was heavy with rainwater. I fished the cigarettes and matches out, lit a cigarette and exhaled past Leslie's ear.

"We'd remember. It *couldn't* have been this bad."

"I'm not so sure. Suppose it happened over the Pacific? It wouldn't do *that* much damage. Or over the American continents. It would have sterilized some plants and animals and burned down a lot of forests, and who'd know? The sun went back to normal, that time. It might again. The sun is a four percent variable star. Maybe it gets a touch more variable than that, every so often."

Something shattered in the bedroom. A window? A wet wind touched us, and the shriek of the storm was louder.

"Then we could live through this," Leslie said hesitantly.

"I believe you've put your finger on the crux of the matter. Skål!" I found my champagne and drank deep. It was past three in the morning, with a hurricane beating at our doors.

"Then shouldn't we be doing something about it?"

"We are."

"Something like trying to get up into the hills! Stan, there're going to be floods!"

"You bet your ass there are, but they won't rise this high. Fourteen stories. Listen, I've thought this through. We're in a building that was designed to be earthquake-proof. You told me so yourself. It'd take more than a hurricane to knock it over.

"As for heading for the hills, what hills? We won't get far tonight, not with the streets flooded already. Suppose we could get up into the Santa Monica Mountains; then what? Mudslides, that's what. That area won't stand up to what's coming. The flare must have boiled away enough water to make another ocean. It's going to rain for forty days and forty nights! Love, this is the safest place we could have reached tonight."

"Suppose the polar caps melt?"

"Yeah . . . well, we're pretty high, even for that. Hey, maybe that last flare was what started Noah's flood. Maybe it's happening again. Sure as hell, there's not a place on Earth that isn't the middle of a hurricane. Those two great counterrotating hurricanes, by now they must have broken up into hundreds of little storms—"

The glass doors exploded inward. We ducked, and the wind howled about us and dropped rain and glass on us.

"At least we've got food!" I shouted. "If the floods maroon us here, we can last it out!"

"But if the power goes, we can't cook it! And the refrigerator—"

"We'll cook everything we can. Hardboil all the eggs—"

The wind rose about us. I stopped trying to talk.

Warm rain sprayed us horizontally and left us soaked. Try to cook in a hurricane?

I'd been stupid; I'd waited too long. The wind would tip boiling water on us if we tried it. Or hot grease—

Leslie screamed, "We'll have to use the oven!"

Of course. The oven couldn't possibly fall on us.

We set it for 400° and put the eggs in, in a pot of water. We took all the meat out of the meat drawer and shoved it in on a broiling pan. Two artichokes in another pot. The other vegetables we could eat raw.

What else? I tried to think.

Water. If the electricity went, probably the water and telephone lines would too. I turned on the faucet over the sink and started filling things: pots with lids, Leslie's thirty-cup percolator that she used for parties, her wash bucket. She clearly thought I was crazy, but I didn't trust the rain as a water source; I couldn't control it.

The sound. Already we'd stopped trying to shout through it. Forty days and nights of this and we'd be stone-deaf. Cotton? Too late to reach the bathroom. Paper towels! I tore and wadded and made four plugs for our ears.

Sanitary facilities? Another reason for picking Leslie's place over mine. When the plumbing stopped, there was always the balcony.

And if the flood rose higher than the fourteenth floor, there was the roof. Twenty stories up. If it went higher than that, there would be damn few people left when it was over.

And if it was a nova?

I held Leslie a bit more closely, and lit another cigarette one-handed. All the wasted planning, if it was a nova. But I'd have been doing it anyway. You don't stop planning just because there's no hope.

And when the hurricane turned to live steam, there was always the balcony. At a dead run, and over the railing, in preference to being boiled alive.

But now was not the time to mention it.

Anyway, she'd probably thought of it herself.

THE LIGHTS WENT out about four. I turned off the oven, in case the power should come back. Give it an hour to cool down, then I'd put all the food in Baggies.

Leslie was asleep, sitting up in my arms. How could she sleep, not knowing? I piled pillows behind her and let her back easy.

For some time I lay on my back, smoking, watching the lightning make shadows on the ceiling. We had eaten all the foie gras and drunk one bottle of champagne. I thought of opening the brandy, but decided against it, with regret.

A long time passed. I'm not sure what I thought about. I didn't sleep, but certainly my mind was in idle. It only gradually came to me that the ceiling, between lightning flashes, had turned gray.

I rolled over, gingerly, soggily. Everything was wet.

My watch said it was nine-thirty.

I crawled around the partition into the living room. I'd been ignoring the storm sounds for so long that it took a faceful of warm whipping rain to remind me. There was a hurricane going on. But charcoal-gray light was filtering through the black clouds.

So. I was right to have saved the brandy. Flood, storms, intense radiation, fires lit by the flare—if the toll of destruction was as high as I expected, then money was about to become worthless. We would need trade goods.

I was hungry. I ate two eggs and some bacon—still warm—and started putting the rest of the food away. We had food for a week, maybe . . . but hardly a balanced diet. Maybe we could trade with other apartments. This was a big building. There must be empty apartments, too, that we could raid for canned soup and the like. And refugees from the lower floors to be taken care of, if the waters rose high enough . . .

Damn! I missed the nova. Life had been simplicity itself last night. Now . . . Did we have medicines? Were there doctors in the building? There would be dysentery and other plagues. And hunger. There was a supermarket near here; could we find a scuba rig in the building?

But I'd get some sleep first. Later we could start exploring the building. The day had become a lighter charcoal gray. Things could be worse, far worse. I thought of the radiation that must have sleeted over the far side of the world, and wondered if our children would colonize Europe, or Asia, or Africa.

The Media Generation

Sandkings

George R. R. Martin's varied output is divided among science fiction, fantasy, and horror and has earned him multiple Hugo and Nebula Awards as well as the Bram Stoker Award from the Horror Writers Association. Much of his best writing runs to novella length, where the scope of the narrative allows exploration of a variety of themes and ideas that cut across genre boundaries. "Sandkings" treats in a futuristic setting an idea as old as the horror classic *Frankenstein:* the irresponsibility of a man who plays at being God, and the peril he faces when his monster turns on him. "Nightflyers," adapted for the screen in 1987, sets a haunted house scenario inside an interstellar spaceship. "A Song for Lya" explores the religious beliefs of an extraterrestrial culture as an outgrowth of its unique biology. "Meathouse Man" is one of several stories in which he puts a science fiction spin on the classic horror theme of the zombie. Martin began publishing fiction in 1971. His first novel, *Dying of the Light,* was published six years later and garnered praise for its detailed portrait of an extraterrestrial culture shaped by the singular nature of the planet it inhabits. Nearly all of Martin's novels are distinguished by their meticulously conceived backgrounds. *Fevre Dream,* a period vampire tale, offers a vivid re-creation of life on the Mississippi River in the antebellum South. *The Armageddon Rag* evokes the American counterculture of the 1960s in its account of a rock band whose music channels the destructive energies and chaos of the time. *A Game of Thrones, A Clash of Kings,* and *A Storm of Swords* comprise the first three episodes in his epic Song of Ice and Fire heroic fantasy saga. Martin has also written the novel *Windhaven* in collaboration with Lisa Tuttle. His short fiction has been collected in *A Song for Lya and Other Stories, Songs the Dead Men Sing, Portraits of His Children,* and *Tuf Voyaging.* He has written for a number of television series, including the new *Twilight Zone* and *Beauty and the Beast,* and edited more than twenty anthologies, including fifteen mosaic novels in the Wild Cards series.

SIMON KRESS LIVED alone in a sprawling manor house among the dry, rocky hills fifty kilometers from the city. So, when he was called away unexpectedly on business, he had no neighbors he could conveniently impose on to take his pets. The carrion hawk was no problem; it roosted in the unused belfry and customarily fed itself anyway. The shambler Kress simply shooed outside and left to fend for itself; the little monster would gorge on slugs and birds and rockjocks. But the fish tank, stocked with genuine Earth piranha, posed a difficulty. Kress finally just threw a haunch of beef into the huge tank. The piranha could always eat each other if he were detained longer than expected. They'd done it before. It amused him.

Unfortunately, he was detained *much* longer than expected this time. When he finally returned, all the fish were dead. So was the carrion hawk. The shambler had climbed up to the belfry and eaten it. Simon Kress was vexed.

The next day he flew his skimmer to Asgard, a journey of some two hundred kilometers. Asgard was Baldur's largest city and boasted the oldest and largest starport as well. Kress liked to impress his friends with animals that were unusual, entertaining, and expensive; Asgard was the place to buy them.

This time, though, he had poor luck. Xenopets had closed its doors, t'Etherane the Petseller tried to foist another carrion hawk off on him, and Strange Waters offered nothing more exotic than piranha, glowsharks, and spider-squids. Kress had had all those; he wanted something new.

Near dusk, he found himself walking down the Rainbow Boulevard, looking for places he had not patronized before. So close to the starport, the street was lined by importers' marts. The big corporate emporiums had impressive long windows, where rare and costly alien artifacts reposed on felt cushions against dark drapes that made the interiors of the stores a mystery. Between them were the junk shops—narrow, nasty little places whose display areas were crammed with all manner of offworld bric-a-brac. Kress tried both kinds of shop, with equal dissatisfaction.

Then he came across a store that was different.

It was quite close to the port. Kress had never been there before. The shop occupied a small, single-story building of moderate size, set between a euphoria bar and a temple-brothel of the Secret Sisterhood. Down this far, the Rainbow Boulevard grew tacky. The shop itself was unusual. Arresting.

The windows were full of mist; now a pale red, now the gray of true fog, now sparkling and golden. The mist swirled and eddied and glowed faintly from within. Kress glimpsed objects in the window—machines, pieces of art, other things he could not recognize—but he could not get a good look at any of them. The mists flowed sensuously around them, displaying a bit of first one thing and then another, then cloaking all. It was intriguing.

As he watched, the mist began to form letters. One word at a time. Kress stood and read:

WO. AND. SHADE. IMPORTERS. ARTIFACTS. ART. LIFE-FORMS. AND. MISC.

The letters stopped. Through the fog, Kress saw something moving. That was enough for him, that and the word "Life-forms" in their advertisement. He swept his walking cloak over his shoulder and entered the store.

Inside, Kress felt disoriented. The interior seemed vast, much larger than he would have guessed from the relatively modest frontage. It was dimly lit, peaceful. The ceiling was a starscape, complete with spiral nebulae, very dark and realistic, very nice. The counters all shone faintly, the better to display the merchandise within. The aisles were carpeted with ground fog. In places, it came almost to his knees and swirled about his feet as he walked.

"Can I help you?"

She seemed almost to have risen from the fog. Tall and gaunt and pale, she wore a practical gray jumpsuit and a strange little cap that rested well back on her head.

"Are you Wo or Shade?" Kress asked. "Or only sales help?"

"Jala Wo, ready to serve you," she replied. "Shade does not see customers. We have no sales help."

"You have quite a large establishment," Kress said. "Odd that I have never heard of you before."

"We have only just opened this shop on Baldur," the woman said. "We have franchises on a number of other worlds, however. What can I sell you? Art, perhaps? You have the look of a collector. We have some fine Nor T'alush crystal carvings."

"No," Simon Kress said. "I own all the crystal carvings I desire. I came to see about a pet."

"A life-form?"

"Yes."

"Alien?"

"Of course."

"We have a mimic in stock. From Celia's World. A clever little simian. Not only will it learn to speak, but eventually it will mimic your voice, inflections, gestures, even facial expressions."

"Cute," said Kress. "And common. I have no use for either, Wo. I want something exotic. Unusual. And not cute. I detest cute animals. At the moment I own a shambler. Imported from Cotho, at no mean expense. From time to time I feed him a litter of unwanted kittens. That is what I think of *cute*. Do I make myself understood?"

Wo smiled enigmatically. "Have you ever owned an animal that worshiped you?" she asked.

Kress grinned. "Oh, now and again. But I don't require worship, Wo. Just entertainment."

"You misunderstand me," Wo said, still wearing her strange smile. "I meant worship literally."

"What are you talking about?"

"I think I have just the thing for you," Wo said. "Follow me."

She led Kress between the radiant counters and down a long, fog-shrouded aisle beneath false starlight. They passed through a wall of mist into another section of the store, and stopped before a large plastic tank. An aquarium, thought Kress.

Wo beckoned. He stepped closer and saw that he was wrong. It was a terrarium. Within lay a miniature desert about two meters square. Pale sand bleached scarlet by wan red light. Rocks: basalt and quartz and granite. In each corner of the tank stood a castle.

Kress blinked, and peered, and corrected himself; actually only three castles stood. The fourth leaned; a crumbled, broken ruin. The other three were crude but intact, carved of stone and sand. Over their battlements and through their rounded porticoes, tiny creatures climbed and scrambled. Kress pressed his face against the plastic. "Insects?" he asked.

"No," Wo replied. "A much more complex life-form. More intelligent as well. Considerably smarter than your shambler. They are called sandkings."

"Insects," Kress said, drawing back from the tank. "I don't care how complex they are." He frowned. "And kindly don't try to gull me with this talk of intelligence. These things are far too small to have anything but the most rudimentary brains."

"They share hiveminds," Wo said. "Castle minds, in this case. There are only three organisms in the tank, actually. The fourth died. You see how her castle has fallen."

Kress looked back at the tank. "Hiveminds, eh? Interesting." He frowned again. "Still, it is only an oversized ant farm. I'd hoped for something better."

"They fight wars."

"Wars? Hmmm." Kress looked again.

"Note the colors, if you will," Wo told him. She pointed to the creatures that swarmed over the nearest castle. One was scrabbling at the tank wall. Kress studied it. It still looked like an insect to his eyes. Barely as long as his fingernail, six-limbed, with six tiny eyes set all around its body. A wicked set of mandibles clacked visibly, while two long, fine antennae wove patterns in the air. Antennae, mandibles, eyes, and legs were sooty black, but the dominant color was the burnt orange of its armor plating. "It's an insect," Kress repeated.

"It is not an insect," Wo insisted calmly. "The armored exoskeleton is shed when the sandking grows larger. *If* it grows larger. In a tank this size, it won't." She took Kress by the elbow and led him around the tank to the next castle. "Look at the colors here."

He did. They were different. Here the sandkings had bright red armor; antennae, mandibles, eyes, and legs were yellow. Kress glanced across the tank. The denizens of the third live castle were off-white, with red trim. "Hmmm," he said.

"They war, as I said," Wo told him. "They even have truces and alliances. It was an alliance that destroyed the fourth castle in this tank. The blacks were getting too numerous, so the others joined forces to destroy them."

Kress remained unconvinced. "Amusing, no doubt. But insects fight wars too."

"Insects do not worship," Wo said.

"Eh?"

Wo smiled and pointed at the castle. Kress stared. A face had been carved into the wall of the highest tower. He recognized it. It was Jala Wo's face. "How . . . ?"

"I projected a holograph of my face into the tank, kept it there for a few days. The face of god, you see? I feed them; I am always close. The sandkings have a rudimentary psionic sense. Proximity telepathy. They sense me, and worship me by using my face to decorate their buildings. All the castles have them, see." They did.

On the castle, the face of Jala Wo was serene and peaceful, and very lifelike. Kress marveled at the workmanship. "How do they do it?"

"The foremost legs double as arms. They even have fingers of a sort; three small, flexible tendrils. And they cooperate well, both in building and in battle. Remember, all the mobiles of one color share a single mind."

"Tell me more," Kress said.

Wo smiled. "The maw lives in the castle. Maw is my name for her. A pun, if you will; the thing is mother and stomach both. Female, large as your fist, immobile. Actually, sandking is a bit of a misnomer. The mobiles are peasants and warriors; the real ruler is a queen. But that analogy is faulty as well. Considered as a whole, each castle is a single hermaphroditic creature."

"What do they eat?"

"The mobiles eat pap—predigested food obtained inside the castle. They get it from the maw after she has worked on it for several days. Their stomachs can't handle anything else, so if the maw dies, they soon die as well. The maw . . . the maw eats anything. You'll have no special expense there. Table scraps will do excellently."

"Live food?" Kress asked.

Wo shrugged. "Each maw eats mobiles from the other castles, yes."

"I am intrigued," he admitted. "If only they weren't so small."

"Yours can be larger. These sandkings are small because their tank is small. They seem to limit their growth to fit available space. If I moved these to a larger tank, they'd start growing again."

"Hmmmm. My piranha tank is twice this size, and vacant. It could be cleaned out, filled with sand. . . ."

"Wo and Shade would take care of the installation. It would be our pleasure."

"Of course," said Kress, "I would expect four intact castles."

"Certainly," Wo said.

They began to haggle about the price.

* * *

THREE DAYS LATER Jala Wo arrived at Simon Kress' estate, with dormant sandkings and a work crew to take charge of the installation. Wo's assistants were aliens unlike any Kress was familiar with—squat, broad bipeds with four arms and bulging, multifaceted eyes. Their skin was thick and leathery, twisted into horns and spines and protrusions at odd spots upon their bodies. But they were very strong, and good workers. Wo ordered them about in a musical tongue that Kress had never heard.

In a day it was done. They moved his piranha tank to the center of his spacious living room, arranged couches on either side of it for better viewing, scrubbed it clean, and filled it two-thirds of the way up with sand and rock. Then they installed a special lighting system, both to provide the dim red illumination the sandkings preferred and to project holographic images into the tank. On top they mounted a sturdy plastic cover, with a feeder mechanism built in. "This way you can feed your sandkings without removing the top of the tank," Wo explained. "You would not want to take any chances on the mobiles escaping."

The cover also included climate control devices, to condense just the right amount of moisture from the air. "You want it dry, but not too dry," Wo said.

Finally one of the four-armed workers climbed into the tank and dug deep pits in the four corners. One of his companions handed the dormant maws over to him, removing them one by one from their frosted cryonic traveling cases. They were nothing to look at. Kress decided they resembled nothing so much as a mottled, half-spoiled chunk of raw meat. With a mouth.

The alien buried them, one in each corner of the tank. Then they sealed it all up and took their leave.

"The heat will bring the maws out of dormancy," Wo said. "In less than a week, mobiles will begin to hatch and burrow to the surface. Be certain to give them plenty of food. They will need all their strength until they are well established. I would estimate that you will have castles rising in about three weeks."

"And my face? When will they carve my face?"

"Turn on the hologram after about a month," she advised him. "And be patient. If you have any questions, please call. Wo and Shade are at your service." She bowed and left.

Kress wandered back to the tank and lit a joystick. The desert was still and empty. He drummed his fingers impatiently against the plastic, and frowned.

ON THE FOURTH day, Kress thought he glimpsed motion beneath the sand, subtle subterranean stirrings.

On the fifth day, he saw his first mobile, a lone white.

On the sixth day, he counted a dozen of them, whites and reds and blacks. The oranges were tardy. He cycled through a bowl of half-decayed table scraps. The mobiles sensed it at once, rushed to it, and began to drag pieces back to their respective corners. Each color group was very organized. They did not fight. Kress was a bit disappointed, but he decided to give them time.

The oranges made their appearance on the eighth day. By then the other sand-kings had begun to carry small stones and erect crude fortifications. They still did not war. At the moment they were only half the size of those he had seen at Wo and Shade's, but Kress thought they were growing rapidly.

The castles began to rise midway through the second week. Organized battalions of mobiles dragged heavy chunks of sandstone and granite back to their corners, where other mobiles were pushing sand into place with mandibles and tendrils. Kress had purchased a pair of magnifying goggles so he could watch them work, wherever they might go in the tank. He wandered around and around the tall plastic walls, observing. It was fascinating. The castles were a bit plainer than Kress would have liked, but he had an idea about that. The next day he cycled through some obsidian and flakes of colored glass along with the food. Within hours, they had been incorporated into castle walls.

The black castle was the first completed, followed by the white and red fortresses. The oranges were last, as usual. Kress took his meals into the living room and ate seated on the couch, so he could watch. He expected the first war to break out any hour now.

He was disappointed. Days passed; the castles grew taller and more grand, and Kress seldom left the tank except to attend to his sanitary needs and answer critical business calls. But the sandkings did not war. He was getting upset.

Finally, he stopped feeding them.

Two days after the table scraps had ceased to fall from their desert sky, four black mobiles surrounded an orange and dragged it back to their maw. They maimed it first, ripping off its mandibles and antennae and limbs, and carried it through the shadowed main gate of their miniature castle. It never emerged. Within an hour, more than forty orange mobiles marched across the sand and attacked the blacks' corner. They were outnumbered by the blacks that came rushing up from the depths. When the fighting was over, the attackers had been slaughtered. The dead and dying were taken down to feed the black maw.

Kress, delighted, congratulated himself on his genius.

When he put food into the tank the following day, a three-cornered battle broke out over its possession. The whites were the big winners.

After that, war followed war.

ALMOST A MONTH to the day after Jala Wo had delivered the sandkings, Kress turned on the holographic projector, and his face materialized in the tank. It turned, slowly, around and around, so his gaze fell on all four castles equally. Kress thought it rather a good likeness—it had his impish grin, wide mouth, full cheeks. His blue eyes sparkled, his gray hair was carefully arrayed in a fashionable sidesweep, his eyebrows were thin and sophisticated.

Soon enough, the sandkings set to work. Kress fed them lavishly while his image beamed down at them from their sky. Temporarily, the wars stopped. All activity was directed toward worship.

His face emerged on the castle walls.

At first all four carvings looked alike to him, but as the work continued and Kress studied the reproductions, he began to detect subtle differences in technique and execution. The reds were the most creative, using tiny flakes of slate to put the gray in his hair. The white idol seemed young and mischievous to him, while the face shaped by the blacks—although virtually the same, line for line—struck him as wise and beneficent. The orange sandkings, as ever, were last and least. The wars had not gone well for them, and their castle was sad compared to the others. The image they carved was crude and cartoonish, and they seemed to intend to leave it that way. When they stopped work on the face, Kress grew quite piqued with them, but there was really nothing he could do.

When all the sandkings had finished their Kress-faces, he turned off the holograph and decided that it was time to have a party. His friends would be impressed. He could even stage a war for them, he thought. Humming happily to himself, he began to draw up a guest list.

THE PARTY WAS a wild success.

Kress invited thirty people: a handful of close friends who shared his amusements, a few former lovers, and a collection of business and social rivals who could not afford to ignore his summons. He knew some of them would be discomfited and even offended by his sandkings. He counted on it. Simon Kress customarily considered his parties a failure unless at least one guest walked out in high dudgeon.

On impulse he added Jala Wo's name to his list. "Bring Shade if you like," he added when dictating her invitation.

Her acceptance surprised him just a bit. "Shade, alas, will be unable to attend. He does not go to social functions," Wo added. "As for myself, I look forward to the chance to see how your sandkings are doing."

Kress ordered them up a sumptuous meal. And when at last the conversation had died down, and most of his guests had gotten silly on wine and joysticks, he shocked them by personally scraping their table leavings into a large bowl. "Come, all of you," he told them. "I want to introduce you to my newest pets." Carrying the bowl, he conducted them into his living room.

The sandkings lived up to his fondest expectations. He had starved them for two days in preparation, and they were in a fighting mood. While the guests ringed the tank, looking through the magnifying glasses Kress had thoughtfully provided, the sandkings waged a glorious battle over the scraps. He counted almost sixty dead mobiles when the struggle was over. The reds and whites, who had recently formed an alliance, emerged with most of the food.

"Kress, you're disgusting," Cath m'Lane told him. She had lived with him for a short time two years before, until her soppy sentimentality almost drove him mad. "I was a fool to come back here. I thought perhaps you'd changed, wanted to apologize." She had never forgiven him for the time his shambler had eaten an excessively cute puppy of which she had been fond. "Don't *ever* invite me here again, Simon." She strode out, accompanied by her current lover and a chorus of laughter.

His other guests were full of questions.

Where did the sandkings come from? they wanted to know. "From Wo and Shade, Importers," he replied, with a polite gesture toward Jala Wo, who had remained quiet and apart through most of the evening.

Why did they decorate their castles with his likeness? "Because I am the source of all good things. Surely you know that?" That brought a round of chuckles.

Will they fight again? "Of course, but not tonight. Don't worry. There will be other parties."

Jad Rakkis, who was an amateur xenologist, began talking about other social insects and the wars they fought. "These sandkings are amusing, but nothing really. You ought to read about Terran soldier ants, for instance."

"Sandkings are not insects," Jala Wo said sharply, but Jad was off and running, and no one paid her the slightest attention. Kress smiled at her and shrugged.

Malada Blane suggested a betting pool the next time they got together to watch a war, and everyone was taken with the idea. An animated discussion about rules and odds ensued. It lasted for almost an hour. Finally the guests began to take their leave.

Jala Wo was the last to depart. "So," Kress said to her when they were alone, "it appears my sandkings are a hit."

"They are doing well," Wo said. "Already they are larger than my own."

"Yes," Kress said, "except for the oranges."

"I had noticed that," Wo replied. "They seem few in number, and their castle is shabby."

"Well, someone must lose," Kress said. "The oranges were late to emerge and get established. They have suffered for it."

"Pardon," said Wo, "but might I ask if you are feeding your sandkings sufficiently?"

Kress shrugged. "They diet from time to time. It makes them fiercer."

She frowned. "There is no need to starve them. Let them war in their own time, for their own reasons. It is their nature, and you will witness conflicts that are delightfully subtle and complex. The constant war brought on by hunger is artless and degrading."

Simon Kress repaid Wo's frown with interest. "You are in my house, Wo, and here I am the judge of what is degrading. I fed the sandkings as you advised, and they did not fight."

"You must have patience."

"No," Kress said. "I am their master and their god, after all. Why should I wait on their impulses? They did not war often enough to suit me. I corrected the situation."

"I see," said Wo. "I will discuss the matter with Shade."

"It is none of your concern, or his," Kress snapped.

"I must bid you good night, then," Wo said with resignation. But as she slipped into her coat to depart, she fixed him with a final disapproving stare. "Look to your faces, Simon Kress," she warned him. "Look to your faces."

Puzzled, he wandered back to the tank and stared at the castles after she had taken her departure. His faces were still there, as ever. Except—he snatched up his magnifying goggles and slipped them on. Even then it was hard to make out. But it seemed to him that the expression on the face of his images had changed slightly, that his smile was somehow twisted so that it seemed a touch malicious. But it was a very subtle change, if it was a change at all. Kress finally put it down to his suggestibility, and resolved not to invite Jala Wo to any more of his gatherings.

OVER THE NEXT few months, Kress and about a dozen of his favorites got together weekly for what he liked to call his "war games." Now that his initial fascination with the sandkings was past, Kress spent less time around his tank and more on his business affairs and his social life, but he still enjoyed having a few friends over for a war or two. He kept the combatants sharp on a constant edge of hunger. It had severe effects on the orange sandkings, who dwindled visibly until Kress began to wonder if their maw was dead. But the others did well enough.

Sometimes at night, when he could not sleep, Kress would take a bottle of wine into the darkened living room, where the red gloom of his miniature desert was the only light. He would drink and watch for hours, alone. There was usually a fight going on somewhere, and when there was not he could easily start one by dropping in some small morsel of food.

They took to betting on the weekly battles, as Malada Blane had suggested. Kress won a good amount by betting on the whites, who had become the most powerful and numerous colony in the tank, with the grandest castle. One week he slid the corner of the tank top aside, and dropped the food close to the white castle instead of on the central battleground as usual, so that the others had to attack the whites in their stronghold to get any food at all. They tried. The whites were brilliant in defense. Kress won a hundred standards from Jad Rakkis.

Rakkis, in fact, lost heavily on the sandkings almost every week. He pretended to a vast knowledge of them and their ways, claiming that he had studied them after the first party, but he had no luck when it came to placing his bets. Kress suspected that Jad's claims were empty boasting. He had tried to study the sandkings a bit himself, in a moment of idle curiosity, tying in to the library to find out to what world his pets were native. But there was no listing for them. He wanted to get in touch with Wo and ask her about it, but he had other concerns, and the matter kept slipping his mind.

Finally, after a month in which his losses totaled more than a thousand standards, Jad Rakkis arrived at the war games carrying a small plastic case under his arm. Inside was a spiderlike thing covered with fine golden hair.

"A sand spider," Rakkis announced. "From Cathaday. I got it this afternoon from t'Etherane the Petseller. Usually they remove the poison sacs, but this one is intact. Are you game, Simon? I want my money back. I'll bet a thousand standards, sand spider against sandkings."

Kress studied the spider in its plastic prison. His sandkings had grown—they were twice as large as Wo's, as she'd predicted—but they were still dwarfed by this thing. It was venomed, and they were not. Still, there were an awful lot of them. Besides, the endless sandking wars had begun to grow tiresome lately. The novelty of the match intrigued him. "Done," Kress said. "Jad, you are a fool. The sandkings will just keep coming until this ugly creature of yours is dead."

"You are the fool, Simon," Rakkis replied, smiling. "The Cathadayn sand spider customarily feds on burrowers that hide in nooks and crevices and—well, watch—it will go straight into those castles, and eat the maws."

Kress scowled amid general laughter. He hadn't counted on that. "Get on with it," he said irritably. He went to freshen his drink.

The spider was too large to cycle conveniently through the food chamber. Two of the others helped Rakkis slide the tank top slightly to one side, and Malada Blane handed him up his case. He shook the spider out. It landed lightly on a miniature dune in front of the red castle, and stood confused for a moment, mouth working, legs twitching menacingly.

"Come on," Rakkis urged. They all gathered round the tank. Simon Kress found his magnifiers and slipped them on. If he was going to lose a thousand standards, at least he wanted a good view of the action.

The sandkings had seen the invader. All over the castle, activity had ceased. The small scarlet mobiles were frozen, watching.

The spider began to move toward the dark promise of the gate. On the tower above, Simon Kress' countenance stared down impassively.

At once there was a flurry of activity. The nearest red mobiles formed themselves into two wedges and streamed over the sand toward the spider. More warriors erupted from inside the castle and assembled in a triple line to guard the approach to the underground chamber where the maw lived. Scouts came scuttling over the dunes, recalled to fight.

Battle was joined.

The attacking sandkings washed over the spider. Mandibles snapped shut on legs and abdomen, and clung. Reds raced up the golden legs to the invader's back. They bit and tore. One of them found an eye, and ripped it loose with tiny yellow tendrils. Kress smiled and pointed.

But they were *small,* and they had no venom, and the spider did not stop. Its legs flicked sandkings off to either side. Its dripping jaws found others, and left them broken and stiffening. Already a dozen of the reds lay dying. The sand spider came on and on. It strode straight through the triple line of guardians before the castle. The lines closed around it, covered it, waging desperate battle. A team of sandkings had bitten off one of the spider's legs, Kress saw. Defenders leaped from atop the towers to land on the twitching, heaving mass.

Lost beneath the sandkings, the spider somehow lurched down into the darkness and vanished.

Jad Rakkis let out a long breath. He looked pale. "Wonderful," someone else said. Malada Blane chuckled deep in her throat.

"Look," said Idi Noreddian, tugging Kress by the arm.

They had been so intent on the struggle in the corner that none of them had noticed the activity elsewhere in the tank. But now the castle was still, the sands empty save for dead red mobiles, and now they saw.

Three armies were drawn up before the red castle. They stood quite still, in perfect array, rank after rank, of sandkings, orange and white and black. Waiting to see what emerged from the depths.

Simon Kress smiled. "A *cordon sanitaire,*" he said. "And glance at the other castles, if you will, Jad."

Rakkis did, and swore. Teams of mobiles were sealing up the gates with sand and stone. If the spider somehow survived this encounter, it would find no easy entrance at the other castles. "I should have brought four spiders," Jad Rakkis said. "Still, I've won. My spider is down there right now, eating your damned maw."

Kress did not reply. He waited. There was motion in the shadows.

All at once, red mobiles began pouring out of the gate. They took their positions on the castle, and began repairing the damage the spider had wrought. The other armies dissolved and began to retreat to their respective corners.

"Jad," said Simon Kress, "I think you are a bit confused about who is eating who."

THE FOLLOWING WEEK Rakkis brought four slim silver snakes. The sandkings dispatched them without much trouble.

Next he tried a large black bird. It ate more than thirty white mobiles, and its thrashing and blundering virtually destroyed their castle, but ultimately its wings grew tired, and the sandkings attacked in force wherever it landed.

After that it was a case of insects, armored bettles not too unlike the sandkings themselves. But stupid, stupid. An allied force of oranges and blacks broke their formation, divided them, and butchered them.

Rakkis began giving Kress promissory notes.

It was around that time that Kress met Cath m'Lane again, one evening when he was dining in Asgard at his favorite restaurant. He stopped at her table briefly and told her about the war games, inviting her to join them. She flushed, then regained control of herself and grew icy. "Someone has to put a stop to you, Simon. I guess it's going to be me," she said. Kress shrugged and enjoyed a lovely meal and thought no more about her threat.

Until a week later, when a small, stout woman arrived at his door and showed him a police wristband. "We've had complaints," she said. "Do you keep a tank full of dangerous insects, Kress?"

"Not insects," he said, furious. "Come, I'll show you."

When she had seen the sandkings, she shook her head. "This will never do. What do you know about these creatures, anyway? Do you know what world they're from? Have they been cleared by the ecological board? Do you have a license for these things? We have a report that they're carnivores, possibly dangerous. We also have a report that they are semi-sentient. Where did you get these creatures, anyway?"

"From Wo and Shade," Kress replied.

"Never heard of them," the woman said. "Probably smuggled them in, knowing our ecologists would never approve them. No, Kress, this won't do. I'm going to confiscate this tank and have it destroyed. And you're going to have to expect a few fines as well."

Kress offered her a hundred standards to forget all about him and his sandkings. She *tsked*. "Now I'll have to add attempted bribery to the charges against you."

Not until he raised the figure to two thousand standards was she willing to be persuaded. "It's not going to be easy, you know," she said. "There are forms to be altered, records to be wiped. And getting a forged license from the ecologists will be time-consuming. Not to mention dealing with the complainant. What if she calls again?"

"Leave her to me," Kress said. "Leave her to me."

HE THOUGHT ABOUT it for a while. That night he made some calls.

First he got t'Etherane the Petseller. "I want to buy a dog," he said. "A puppy."

The round-faced merchant gawked at him. "A puppy? That is not like you, Simon. Why don't you come in? I have a lovely choice."

"I want a very specific *kind* of puppy," Kress said. "Take notes. I'll describe to you what it must look like."

Afterward he punched for Idi Noreddian. "Idi," he said, "I want you out here tonight with your holo equipment. I have a notion to record a sandking battle. A present for one of my friends."

THE NIGHT AFTER they made the recording, Simon Kress stayed up late. He absorbed a controversial new drama in his sensorium, fixed himself a small snack, smoked a joystick or two, and broke out a bottle of wine. Feeling very happy with himself, he wandered into the living room, glass in hand.

The lights were out. The red glow of the terrarium made the shadows flushed and feverish. He walked over to look at his domain, curious as to how the blacks were doing in the repairs on their castle. The puppy had left it in ruins.

The restoration went well. But as Kress inspected the work through his magnifiers, he chanced to glance closely at the face. It startled him.

He drew back, blinked, took a healthy gulp of wine, and looked again.

The face on the walls was still his. But it was all wrong, all *twisted*. His cheeks were bloated and piggish, his smile was a crooked leer. He looked impossibly malevolent.

Uneasy, he moved around the tank to inspect the other castles. They were each a bit different, but ultimately all the same.

The oranges had left out most of the fine detail, but the result still seemed monstrous, crude—a brutal mouth and mindless eyes.

The reds gave him a satanic, twitching kind of smile. His mouth did odd, unlovely things at its corners.

The whites, his favorites, had carved a cruel idiot god.

Simon Kress flung his wine across the room in rage. "You *dare*," he said under his breath. "Now you won't eat for a week, you damned . . ." His voice was shrill. "I'll teach you." He had an idea. He strode out of the room, and returned a moment later with an antique iron throwing-sword in his hand. It was a meter long, and the point was still sharp. Kress smiled, climbed up and moved the tank cover aside just enough to give him working room, opening one corner of the desert. He leaned down, and jabbed the sword at the white castle below him. He waved it back and forth, smashing towers and ramparts and walls. Sand and stone collapsed, burying the scrambling mobiles. A flick of his wrist obliterated the features of the insolent, insulting caricature the sandkings had made of his face. Then he poised the point of the sword above the dark mouth that opened down into the maw's chamber, and thrust with all his strength. He heard a soft, squishing sound, and met resistance. All of the mobiles trembled and collapsed. Satisfied, Kress pulled back.

He watched for a moment, wondering whether he'd killed the maw. The point of the throwing-sword was wet and slimy. But finally the white sandkings began to move again. Feebly, slowly, but they moved.

He was preparing to slide the cover back in place and move on to a second castle when he felt something crawling on his hand.

He screamed and dropped the sword, and brushed the sandking from his flesh. It fell to the carpet, and he ground it beneath his heel, crushing it thoroughly long after it was dead. It had crunched when he stepped on it. After that, trembling, he hurried to seal the tank up again, and rushed off to shower and inspected himself carefully. He boiled his clothing.

Later, after several fresh glasses of wine, he returned to the living room. He was a bit ashamed of the way the sandking had terrified him. But he was not about to open the tank again. From now on, the cover stayed sealed permanently. Still, he had to punish the others.

Kress decided to lubricate his mental process with another glass of wine. As he finished it, an inspiration came to him. He went to the tank smiling, and made a few adjustments to the humidity controls.

By the time he fell asleep on the couch, his wine glass still in his hand, the sand castles were melting in the rain.

KRESS WOKE TO angry pounding on his door.

He sat up, groggy, his head throbbing. Wine hangovers were always the worst, he thought. He lurched to the entry chamber.

Cath m'Lane was outside. "You monster," she said, her face swollen and puffy and streaked by tears. "I cried all night, damn you. But no more, Simon, no more."

"Easy," he said, holding his head. "I've got a hangover."

She swore and shoved him aside and pushed her way into his house. The shambler came peering round a corner to see what the noise was. She spat at it and stalked into the living room, Kress trailing ineffectually after her. "Hold on," he said, "where do you . . . you can't. . . ." He stopped, suddenly horrorstruck. She was carrying a heavy sledgehammer in her left hand. "No," he said.

She went directly to the sandking tank. "You like the little charmers so much, Simon? Then you can live with them."

"*Cath!*" he shrieked.

Gripping the hammer with both hands, she swung as hard as she could against the side of the tank. The sound of the impact set his head to screaming, and Kress made a low blubbering sound of despair. But the plastic held.

She swung again. This time there was a *crack,* and a network of thin lines sprang into being.

Kress threw himself at her as she drew back her hammer for a third swing. They went down flailing, and rolled. She lost her grip on the hammer and tried to throttle him, but Kress wrenched free and bit her on the arm, drawing blood. They both staggered to their feet, panting.

"You should see yourself, Simon," she said grimly. "Blood dripping from your mouth. You look like one of your pets. How do you like the taste?"

"Get out," he said. He saw the throwing-sword where it had fallen the night before, and snatched it up. "Get out," he repeated, waving the sword for emphasis. "Don't go near that tank again."

She laughed at him. "You wouldn't dare," she said. She bent to pick up her hammer.

Kress shrieked at her, and lunged. Before he quite knew what was happening, the iron blade had gone clear through her abdomen. Cath m'Lane looked at him wonderingly, and down at the sword. Kress fell back whimpering. "I didn't mean . . . I only wanted . . ."

She was transfixed, bleeding, dead, but somehow she did not fall. "You monster," she managed to say, though her mouth was full of blood. And she whirled, impossibly, the sword in her, and swung with her last strength at the tank. The tortured wall shattered, and Cath m'Lane was buried beneath an avalanche of plastic and sand and mud.

Kress made small hysterical noises and scrambled up on the couch.

Sandkings were emerging from the muck on his living room floor. They were crawling across Cath's body. A few of them ventured tentatively out across the carpet. More followed.

He watched as a column took shape, a living, writhing square of sandkings, bearing something, something slimy and featureless, a piece of raw meat big as a man's head. They began to carry it away from the tank. It pulsed.

That was when Kress broke and ran.

IT WAS LATE afternoon before he found the courage to return.

He had run to his skimmer and flown to the nearest city, some fifty kilometers away, almost sick with fear. But once safely away, he had found a small restaurant, put down several mugs of coffee and two anti-hangover tabs, eaten a full breakfast, and gradually regained his composure.

It had been a dreadful morning, but dwelling on that would solve nothing. He ordered more coffee and considered his situation with icy rationality.

Cath m'Lane was dead at his hand. Could he report it, plead that it had been an accident? Unlikely. He had run her through, after all, and he had already told that policer to leave her to him. He would have to get rid of the evidence, and hope that she had not told anyone where she was going this morning. That was probable. She could only have gotten his gift late last night. She said that she had cried all night, and she had been alone when she arrived. Very well; he had one body and one skimmer to dispose of.

That left the sandkings. They might prove more of a difficulty. No doubt they had all escaped by now. The thought of them around his house, in his bed and his clothes, infesting his food—it made his flesh crawl. He shuddered and overcame his revulsion. It really shouldn't be too hard to kill them, he reminded himself. He didn't have to account for every mobile. Just the four maws, that was all. He could do that. They were large, as he'd seen. He would find them and kill them.

Simon Kress went shopping before he flew back to his home. He bought a set of skinthins that would cover him from head to foot, several bags of poison pellets for rockjock control, and a spray canister of illegally strong pesticide. He also bought a magnalock towing device.

When he landed, he went about things methodically. First he hooked Cath's skimmer to his own with the magnalock. Searching it, he had his first piece of luck. The crystal chip with Idi Noreddian's holo of the sandking fight was on the front seat. He had worried about that.

When the skimmers were ready, he slipped into his skinthins and went inside for Cath's body.

It wasn't there.

He poked through the fast-drying sand carefully, but there was no doubt of it; the body was gone. Could she have dragged herself away? Unlikely, but Kress searched. A cursory inspection of his house turned up neither the body nor any sign of the sandkings. He did not have time for a more thorough investigation, not with the incriminating skimmer outside his front door. He resolved to try later.

Some seventy kilometers north of Kress' estate was a range of active volcanoes. He flew there, Cath's skimmer in tow. Above the glowering cone of the largest, he released the magnalock and watched it vanish in the lava below.

It was dusk when he returned to his house. That gave him pause. Briefly he considered flying back to the city and spending the night there. He put the thought aside. There was work to do. He wasn't safe yet.

He scattered the poison pellets around the exterior of his house. No one would find that suspicious. He'd always had a rockjock problem. When that task was completed, he primed the canister of pesticide and ventured back inside.

Kress went through the house room by room, turning on lights everywhere he went until he was surrounded by a blaze of artificial illumination. He paused to clean up in the living room, shoveling sand and plastic fragments back into the broken tank. The sandkings were all gone, as he'd feared. The castles were shrunken and distorted, slagged by the watery bombardment Kress had visited upon them, and what little remained was crumbling as it dried.

He frowned and searched on, the canister of pest spray strapped across his shoulders.

Down in his deepest wine cellar, he came upon Cath m'Lane's corpse.

It sprawled at the foot of a steep flight of stairs, the limbs twisted as if by a fall. White mobiles were swarming all over it, and as Kress watched, the body moved jerkily across the hard-packed dirt floor.

He laughed, and twisted the illumination up to maximum. In the far corner, a squat little earthen castle and a dark hole were visible between two wine racks. Kress could make out a rough outline of his face on the cellar wall.

The body shifted once again, moving a few centimeters towards the castle. Kress had a sudden vision of the white maw waiting hungrily. It might be able to get Cath's foot in its mouth, but no more. It was too absurd. He laughed again, and started down into the cellar, finger poised on the trigger of the hose that snaked down his right arm. The sandkings—hundreds of them moving as one—deserted the body and formed up battle lines, a field of white between him and their maw.

Suddenly Kress had another inspiration. He smiled and lowered his firing hand. "Cath was always hard to swallow," he said, delighted at his wit. "Especially for one your size. Here, let me give you some help. What are gods for, after all?"

He retreated upstairs, returning shortly with a cleaver. The sandkings, patient, waited and watched while Kress chopped Cath m'Lane into small, easily digestible pieces.

SIMON KRESS SLEPT in his skinthins that night, the pesticide close at hand, but he did not need it. The whites, sated, remained in the cellar, and he saw no sign of the others.

In the morning he finished the cleanup of the living room. After he was through, no trace of the struggle remained except for the broken tank.

He ate a light lunch, and resumed his hunt for the missing sandkings. In full daylight, it was not too difficult. The blacks had located in his rock garden, and built a castle heavy with obsidian and quartz. The reds he founds at the bottom of his long-disused swimming pool, which had partially filled with windblown sand over the years. He saw mobiles of both colors ranging about his grounds, many of them carrying poison pellets back to their maws. Kress decided his pesticide was unnecessary. No use risking a fight when he could just let the poison do its work. Both maws should be dead by evening.

That left only the burnt orange sandkings unaccounted for. Kress circled his estate several times, in ever-widening spirals, but found no trace of them. When he began to sweat in his skinthins—it was a hot, dry day—he decided it was not important. If they were out here, they were probably eating the poison pellets along with the reds and blacks.

He crunched several sandkings underfoot, with a certain degree of satisfaction, as he walked back to the house. Inside, he removed his skinthins, settled down to a delicious meal, and finally began to relax. Everything was under control. Two of the maws would soon be defunct, the third was safely located where he could dispose of it after it had served his purpose, and he had no doubt that he would find the fourth. As for Cath, all trace of her visit had been obliterated.

His reverie was interrupted when his viewscreen began to blink at him. It was Jad Rakkis, calling to brag about some cannibal worms he was bringing to the war games tonight.

Kress had forgotten about that, but he recovered quickly. "Oh, Jad, my pardons. I neglected to tell you. I grew bored with all that, and got rid of the sandkings. Ugly little things. Sorry, but there'll be no party tonight."

Rakkis was indignant. "But what will I do with my worms?"

"Put them in a basket of fruit and send them to a loved one," Kress said, signing off. Quickly he began calling the others. He did not need anyone arriving at his doorstep now, with the sandkings alive and infesting the estate.

As he was calling Idi Noreddian, Kress became aware of an annoying oversight. The screen began to clear, indicating that someone had answered at the other end. Kress flicked off.

Idi arrived on schedule an hour later. She was surprised to find the party canceled, but perfectly happy to share an evening alone with Kress. He delighted her with his story of Cath's reaction to the holo they had made together. While telling it, he managed to ascertain that she had not mentioned the prank to anyone. He nodded, satisfied, and refilled their wine glasses. Only a trickle was left. "I'll have to get a fresh bottle," he said. "Come with me to my wine cellar, and help me pick out a good vintage. You've always had a better palate than I."

She came along willingly enough, but balked at the top of the stairs when Kress opened the door and gestured for her to precede him. "Where are the lights?" she said. "And that smell—what's that peculiar smell, Simon?"

When he shoved her, she looked briefly startled. She screamed as she tumbled down the stairs. Kress closed the door and began to nail it shut with the boards and air-hammer he had left for that purpose. As he was finishing, he heard Idi groan. "I'm hurt," she called. "Simon, what is this?" Suddenly she squealed, and shortly after that the screaming started.

It did not cease for hours. Kress went to his sensorium and dialed up a saucy comedy to blot it out of his mind.

When he was sure she was dead, Kress flew her skimmer north to the volcanoes and discarded it. The magnalock was proving a good investment.

ODD SCRABBLING NOISES were coming from beyond the wine cellar door the next morning when Kress went down to check it out. He listened for several uneasy moments, wondering if Idi Noreddian could possibly have survived, and was now scratching to get out. It seemed unlikely; it had to be the sandkings. Kress did not like the implications of that. He decided that he would keep the door sealed, at least for the moment, and went outside with a shovel to bury the red and black maws in their own castles.

He found them very much alive.

The black castle was glittering with volcanic glass, and sandkings were all over it, repairing and improving. The highest tower was up to his waist, and on it was a hideous caricature of his face. When he approached, the blacks halted in their labors, and formed up into two threatening phalanxes. Kress glanced behind him and saw others closing off his escape. Startled, he dropped the shovel and sprinted out of the trap, crushing several mobiles beneath his boots.

The red castle was creeping up the walls of the swimming pool. The maw was safely settled in a pit, surrounded by sand and concrete and battlements. The reds crept all over the bottom of the pool. Kress watched them carry a rockjock and a large lizard into the castle. He stepped back from the poolside, horrified, and felt something crunch. Looking down, he saw three mobiles climbing up his leg. He brushed them off and stamped them to death, but others were approaching quickly. They were larger than he remembered. Some were almost as big as his thumb.

He ran. By the time he reached the safety of the house, his heart was racing and he was short of breath. The door closed behind him, and Kress hurried to lock it. His house was supposed to be pest-proof. He'd be safe in here.

A stiff drink steadied his nerve. So poison doesn't faze them, he thought. He should have known. Wo had warned him that the maw could eat anything. He would have to use the pesticide. Kress took another drink for good measure, donned his skinthins, and strapped the canister to his back. He unlocked the door.

Outside, the sandkings were waiting.

Two armies confronted him, allied against the common threat. More than he could have guessed. The damned maws must be breeding like rockjocks. They were everywhere, a creeping sea of them.

Kress brought up the hose and flicked the trigger. A gray mist washed over the nearest rank of sandkings. He moved his hand from side to side.

Where the mist fell, the sandkings twitched violently and died in sudden spasms. Kress smiled. They were no match for him. He sprayed in a wide arc before him and stepped forward confidently over a litter of black and red bodies. The armies fell back. Kress advanced, intent on cutting through them to their maws.

All at once the retreat stopped. A thousand sandkings surged toward him.

Kress had been expecting the counterattack. He stood his ground, sweeping his misty sword before him in great looping strokes. They came at him and died. A few got through; he could not spray everywhere at once. He felt them climbing up his legs, sensed their mandibles biting futilely at the reinforced plastic of his skinthins. He ignored them, and kept spraying.

Then he began to feel soft impacts on his head and shoulders.

Kress trembled and spun and looked up above him. The front of his house was alive with sandkings. Blacks and reds, hundreds of them. They were launching themselves into the air, raining down on him. They fell all around him. One landed on his faceplate, its mandibles scraping at his eyes for a terrible second before he plucked it away.

He swung up his hose and sprayed the air, sprayed the house, sprayed until the airborne sandkings were all dead and dying. The mist settled back on him, making him cough. He coughed, and kept spraying. Only when the front of the house was clean did Kress turn his attention back to the ground.

They were all around him, on him, dozens of them scurrying over his body, hundreds of others hurrying to join them. He turned the mist on them. The hose went dead. Kress heard a loud *hiss*, and the deadly fog rose in a great cloud from between his shoulders, cloaking him, choking him, making his eyes burn and blur. He felt for the hose, and his hand came away covered with dying sandkings. The hose was severed; they'd eaten it through. He was surrounded by a shroud of pesticide, blinded. He stumbled and screamed, and began to run back to the house, pulling sandkings from his body as he went.

Inside, he sealed the door and collapsed on the carpet, rolling back and forth until he was sure he had crushed them all. The canister was empty by then, hissing feebly. Kress stripped off his skinthins and showered. The hot spray scalded him and left his skin reddened and sensitive, but it made his flesh stop crawling.

He dressed in his heaviest clothing, thick workpants and leathers, after shaking them out nervously. "Damn," he kept muttering, "damn." His throat was dry. After searching the entry hall thoroughly to make certain it was clean, he allowed himself to sit and pour a drink. "Damn," he repeated. His hand shook as he poured, slopping liquor on the carpet.

The alcohol settled him, but it did not wash away the fear. He had a second drink, and went to the window furtively. Sandkings were moving across the thick plastic pane. He shuddered and retreated to his communications console. He had to get help, he thought wildly. He would punch through a call to the authorities, and policers would come out with flamethrowers and....

Simon Kress stopped in mid-call, and groaned. He couldn't call in the police. He would have to tell them about the whites in his cellar, and they'd find the bodies there. Perhaps the maw might have finished Cath m'Lane by now, but certainly not Idi Noreddian. He hadn't even cut her up. Besides, there would be bones. No, the police could be called in only as a last resort.

He sat at the console, frowning. His communications equipment filled a whole wall; from here he could reach anyone on Baldur. He had plenty of money, and his cunning—he had always prided himself on his cunning. He would handle this somehow.

He briefly considered calling Wo, but soon dismissed the idea. Wo knew too much, and she would ask questions, and he did not trust her. No, he needed someone who would do as he asked *without* questions.

His frown faded, and slowly turned into a smile. Simon Kress had contacts. He put through a call to a number he had not used in a long time.

A woman's face took shape on his viewscreen: white-haired, bland of expression, with a long hook nose. Her voice was brisk and efficient. "Simon," she said. "How is business?"

"Business is fine, Lissandra," Kress replied. "I have a job for you."

"A removal? My price has gone up since last time, Simon. It has been ten years, after all."

"You will be well paid," Kress said. "You know I'm generous. I want you for a bit of pest control."

She smiled a thin smile. "No need to use euphemisms, Simon. The call is shielded."

"No, I'm serious. I have a pest problem. Dangerous pests. Take care of them for me. No questions. Understood?"

"Understood."

"Good. You'll need . . . oh, three or four operatives. Wear heat-resistant skinthins, and equip them with flamethrowers, or lasers, something on that order. Come out to my place. You'll see the problem. Bugs, lots and lots of them. In my rock garden and the old swimming pool you'll find castles. Destroy them, kill everything inside them. Then knock on the door, and I'll show you what else needs to be done. Can you get out here quickly?"

Her face was impassive. "We'll leave within the hour."

LISSANDRA WAS TRUE to her word. She arrived in a lean black skimmer with three operatives. Kress watched them from the safety of a second-story window. They were all faceless in dark plastic skinthins. Two of them wore portable flamethrowers, a third carried lasercannon and explosives. Lissandra carried nothing; Kress recognized her by the way she gave orders.

Their skimmer passed low overhead first, checking out the situation. The sandkings went mad. Scarlet and ebon mobiles ran everywhere, frenetic. Kress could see the castle in the rock garden from this vantage point. It stood tall as a man. Its ramparts were crawling with black defenders, and a steady stream of mobiles flowed down into its depths.

Lissandra's skimmer came down next to Kress' and the operatives vaulted out and unlimbered their weapons. They looked inhuman, deadly.

The black army drew up between them and the castle. The reds—Kress suddenly realized that he could not see the reds. He blinked. Where had they gone?

Lissandra pointed and shouted, and her two flamethrowers spread out and opened up on the black sandkings. Their weapons coughed dully and began to roar, long tongues of blue-and-scarlet fire licking out before them. Sandkings crisped and blackened and died. The operatives began to play the fire back and forth in an efficient, interlocking pattern. They advanced with careful, measured steps.

The black army burned and disintegrated, the mobiles fleeing in a thousand different directions, some back toward the castle, others toward the enemy. None reached the operatives with the flamethrowers. Lissandra's people were very professional.

Then one of them stumbled.

Or seemed to stumble. Kress looked again, and saw that the ground had given way beneath the man. Tunnels, he thought with a tremor of fear—tunnels, pits, traps. The flamer was sunk in sand up to his waist, and suddenly the ground around him seemed to erupt, and he was covered with scarlet sandkings. He dropped the flamethrower and began to claw wildly at his own body. His screams were horrible to hear.

His companions hesitated, then swung and fired. A blast of flame swallowed human and sandkings both. The screaming stopped abruptly. Satisfied, the second flamer turned back to the castle and took another step forward, and recoiled as his foot broke through the ground and vanished up to the ankle. He tried to pull it back and retreat, and the sand all around him gave way. He lost his balance and stumbled, flailing, and the sandkings were everywhere, a boiling mass of them, covering him as he writhed and rolled. His flamethrower was useless and forgotten.

Kress pounded wildly on the window, shouting for attention. "The castle! Get the castle!"

Lissandra, standing back by her skimmer, heard and gestured. Her third operative sighted with the lasercannon and fired. The beam throbbed across the grounds and sliced off the top of the castle. He brought it down sharply, hacking at the sand and stone parapets. Towers fell. Kress' face disintegrated. The laser bit into the ground, searching round and about. The castle crumbled; now it was only a heap of sand. But the black mobiles continued to move. The maw was buried too deeply; they hadn't touched her.

Lissandra gave another order. Her operative discarded the laser, primed an explosive, and darted forward. He leaped over the smoking corpse of the first flamer, landed on solid ground within Kress' rock garden, and heaved. The explosive ball landed square atop the ruins of the black castle. White-out light seared Kress' eyes, and there was a tremendous gout of sand and rock and mobiles. For a moment dust obscured everything. It was raining sandkings and pieces of sandkings.

Kress saw that the black mobiles were dead and unmoving.

"The pool," he shouted down through the window. "Get the castle in the pool."

Lissandra understood quickly; the ground was littered with motionless blacks, but the reds were pulling back hurriedly and re-forming. Her operative stood uncertain, then reached down and pulled out another explosive ball. He took one step forward, but Lissandra called him and he sprinted back in her direction.

It was all so simple then. He reached the skimmer, and Lissandra took him aloft. Kress rushed to another window in another room to watch. They came swooping in just over the pool, and the operative pitched his bombs down at the red castle from the safety of the skimmer. After the fourth run, the castle was unrecognizable, and the sandkings stopped moving.

Lissandra was thorough. She had him bomb each castle several additional times. Then he used the lasercannon, crisscrossing methodically until it was certain that nothing living could remain intact beneath those small patches of ground.

Finally they came knocking at his door. Kress was grinning manically when he let them in. "Lovely," he said, "lovely."

Lissandra pulled off the mask of her skinthins. "This will cost you, Simon. Two operatives gone, not to mention the danger to my own life."

"Of course," Kress blurted. "You'll be well paid, Lissandra. Whatever you ask, just so you finish the job."

"What remains to be done?"

"You have to clean out my wine cellar," Kress said. "There's another castle down there. And you'll have to do it without explosives. I don't want my house coming down around me."

Lissandra motioned to her operative. "Go outside and get Rajk's flamethrower. It should be intact."

He returned armed, ready, silent. Kress led them down to the wine cellar.

The heavy door was still nailed shut, as he had left it. But it bulged outward slightly, as if warped by some tremendous pressure. That made Kress uneasy, as did the silence that held reign about them. He stood well away from the door as Lissandra's operative removed his nails and planks. "Is that safe in here?" he found himself muttering, pointing at the flamethrower. "I don't want a fire, either, you know."

"I have the laser," Lissandra said. "We'll use that for the kill. The flamethrower probably won't be needed. But I want it here just in case. There are worse things than fire, Simon."

He nodded.

The last plank came free of the cellar door. There was still no sound from below.

Lissandra snapped an order, and her underling fell back, took up a position behind her, and leveled the flamethrower square at the door. She slipped her mask back on, hefted the laser, stepped forward, and pulled open the door.

No motion. No sound. It was dark down there.

"Is there a light?" Lissandra asked.

"Just inside the door," Kress said. "On the right-hand side. Mind the stairs, they're quite steep."

She stepped into the door, shifted the laser to her left hand, and reached up with her right, fumbling inside for the light panel. Nothing happened. "I feel it," Lissandra said, "but it doesn't seem to . . ."

Then she was screaming, and she stumbled backward. A great white sandking had clamped itself around her wrist. Blood welled through her skinthins where its mandibles had sunk in. It was fully as large as her hand.

Lissandra did a horrible little jig across the room and began to smash her hand against the nearest wall. Again and again and again. It landed with a heavy, meaty thud. Finally the sandking fell away. She whimpered and fell to her knees. "I think my fingers are broken," she said softly. The blood was still flowing freely. She had dropped the laser near the cellar door.

"I'm not going down there," her operative announced in clear firm tones.

Lissandra looked up at him. "No," she said. "Stand in the door and flame it all. Cinder it. Do you understand?"

He nodded.

Simon Kress moaned. "My *house*," he said. His stomach churned. The white sandking had been so *large*. How many more were down there? "Don't," he continued. "Leave it alone. I've changed my mind. Leave it alone."

Lissandra misunderstood. She held out her hand. It was covered with blood and greenish-black ichor. "Your little friend bit clean through my glove, and you saw what it took to get it off. I don't care about your house, Simon. Whatever is down there is going to die."

Kress hardly heard her. He thought he could see movement in the shadows beyond the cellar door. He imagined a white army bursting forth, all as large as the sandking that had attacked Lissandra. He saw himself being lifted by a hundred tiny arms, and dragged down into the darkness where the maw waited hungrily. He was afraid. "Don't," he said.

They ignored him.

Kress darted forward, and his shoulder slammed into the back of Lissandra's operative just as the man was bracing to fire. He grunted and unbalanced and pitched forward into the black. Kress listened to him fall down the stairs. Afterward there were other noises—scuttlings and snaps and soft squishing sounds.

Kress swung around to face Lissandra. He was drenched in cold sweat, but a sickly kind of excitement was on him. It was almost sexual.

Lissandra's calm cold eyes regarded him through her mask. "What are you doing?" she demanded as Kress picked up the laser she had dropped. "*Simon!*"

"Making a peace," he said, giggling. "They won't hurt god, no, not so long as god is good and generous. I was cruel. Starved them. I have to make up for it now, you see."

"You're insane," Lissandra said. It was the last thing she said. Kress burned a hole in her chest big enough to put his arm through. He dragged the body across the floor and rolled it down the cellar stairs. The noises were louder—chitinous clackings and scrapings and echoes that were thick and liquid. Kress nailed up the door once again.

As he fled, he was filled with a deep sense of contentment that coated his fear like a layer of syrup. He suspected it was not his own.

HE PLANNED TO leave his home, to fly to the city and take a room for a night, or perhaps for a year. Instead Kress started drinking. He was not quite sure why. He drank steadily for hours, and retched it all up violently on his living room carpet. At some point he fell asleep. When he woke, it was pitch dark in the house.

He cowered against the couch. He could hear *noises*. Things were moving in the walls. They were all around him. His hearing was extraordinarily acute. Every little creak was the footstep of a sandking. He closed his eyes and waited, expecting to feel their terrible touch, afraid to move lest he brush against one.

Kress sobbed, and was very still for a while, but nothing happened.

He opened his eyes again. He trembled. Slowly the shadows began to soften and dissolve. Moonlight was filtering through the high windows. His eyes adjusted.

The living room was empty. Nothing there, nothing, nothing. Only his drunken fears.

Simon Kress steeled himself, and rose, and went to a light.

Nothing there. The room was quiet, deserted.

He listened. Nothing. No sound. Nothing in the walls. It had all been his imagination, his fear.

The memories of Lissandra and the thing in the cellar returned to him unbidden. Shame and anger washed over him. Why had he done that? He could have helped her burn it out, kill it. *Why* . . . he knew why. The maw had done it to him, put fear in him. Wo had said it was psionic, even when it was small. And now it was large, so large. It had feasted on Cath, and Idi, and now it had two more bodies down there. It would keep growing. And it had learned to like the taste of human flesh, he thought.

He began to shake, but he took control of himself again and stopped. It wouldn't hurt him. He was god. The whites had always been his favorites.

He remembered how he had stabbed it with his throwing-sword. That was before Cath came. Damn her anyway.

He couldn't stay here. The maw would grow hungry again. Large as it was, it wouldn't take long. Its appetite would be terrible. What would it do then? He had to get away, back to the safety of the city while it was still contained in his wine cellar. It was only plaster and hard-packed earth down there, and the mobiles could dig and tunnel. When they got free. . . . Kress didn't want to think about it.

He went to his bedroom and packed. He took three bags. Just a single change of clothing, that was all he needed; the rest of the space he filled with his valuables, with jewelry and art and other things he could not bear to lose. He did not expect to return.

His shambler followed him down the stairs staring at him from its baleful glowing eyes. It was gaunt. Kress realized that it had been ages since he had fed it. Normally it could take care of itself, but no doubt the pickings had grown lean of late. When it tried to clutch at his leg, he snarled at it and kicked it away, and it scurried off, offended.

Kress slipped outside, carrying his bags awkwardly, and shut the door behind him.

For a moment he stood pressed against the house, his heart thudding in his chest. Only a few meters between him and his skimmer. He was afraid to cross them. The moonlight was bright, and the front of his house was a scene of carnage. The bodies of Lissandra's two flamers lay where they had fallen, one twisted and burned, the other swollen beneath a mass of dead sandkings. And the mobiles, the black and red mobiles, they were all around him. It was an effort to remember that they were dead. It was almost as if they were simply waiting, as they had waited so often before.

Nonsense, Kress told himself. More drunken fears. He had seen the castles blown apart. They were dead, and the white maw was trapped in his cellar. He took several deep and deliberate breaths, and stepped forward onto the sandkings. They crunched. He ground them into the sand savagely. They did not move.

Kress smiled, and walked slowly across the battleground, listening to the sounds, the sounds of safety.

Crunch. Crackle. Crunch.

He lowered his bags to the ground and opened the door to his skimmer.

Something moved from shadow into light. A pale shape on the seat of his skimmer. It was as long as his forearm. Its mandibles clacked together softly, and it looked up at him from six small eyes set all around its body.

Kress wet his pants and backed away slowly.

There was more motion from inside the skimmer. He had left the door open. The sandking emerged and came toward him, cautiously. Others followed. They had been hiding beneath his seats, burrowed into the upholstery. But now they emerged. They formed a ragged ring around the skimmer.

Kress licked his lips, turned, and moved quickly to Lissandra's skimmer.

He stopped before he was halfway there. Things were moving inside that one too. Great maggoty things, half-seen by the light of the moon.

Kress whimpered and retreated back toward the house. Near the front door, he looked up.

He counted a dozen long white shapes creeping back and forth across the walls of the building. Four of them were clustered close together near the top of the unused belfry where the carrion hawk had once roosted. They were carving something. A face. A very recognizable face.

Simon Kress shrieked and ran back inside.

A SUFFICIENT QUANTITY of drink brought him the easy oblivion he sought. But he woke. Despite everything, he woke. He had a terrific headache, and he smelled, and he was hungry. Oh so very hungry. He had never been so hungry.

Kress knew it was not his *own* stomach hurting.

A white sandking watched him from atop the dresser in his bedroom, its antennae moving faintly. It was as big as the one in the skimmer the night before. He tried not to shrink away. "I'll . . . I'll feed you," he said to it. "I'll feed you." His mouth was horribly dry, sandpaper dry. He licked his lips and fled from the room.

The house was full of sandkings; he had to be careful where he put his feet. They all seemed busy on errands of their own. They were making modifications in his house, burrowing into or out of his walls, carving things. Twice he saw his own likeness staring out at him from unexpected places. The faces were warped, twisted, livid with fear.

He went outside to get the bodies that had been rotting in the yard, hoping to appease the white maw's hunger. They were gone, both of them. Kress remembered how easily the mobiles could carry things many times their own weight.

It was terrible to think that the maw was *still* hungry after all of that.

When Kress reentered the house, a column of sandkings was wending its way down the stairs. Each carried a piece of his shambler. The head seemed to look at him reproachfully as it went by.

Kress emptied his freezers, his cabinets, everything, piling all the food in the house in the center of his kitchen floor. A dozen whites waited to take it away. They avoided the frozen food, leaving it to thaw in a great puddle, but they carried off everything else.

When all the food was gone, Kress felt his own hunger pangs abate just a bit, though he had not eaten a thing. But he knew the respite would be short-lived. Soon the maw would be hungry again. He had to feed it.

Kress knew what to do. He went to his communicator. "Malada," he began casually when the first of his friends answered, "I'm having a small party tonight. I realize this is terribly short notice, but I hope you can make it. I really do."

He called Jad Rakkis next, and then the others. By the time he had finished, nine of them had accepted his invitation. Kress hoped that would be enough.

KRESS MET HIS guests outside—the mobiles had cleaned up remarkably quickly, and the grounds looked almost as they had before the battle—and walked them to his front door. He let them enter first. He did not follow.

When four of them had gone through, Kress finally worked up his courage. He closed the door behind his latest guest, ignoring the startled exclamations that soon turned into shrill gibbering, and sprinted for the skimmer the man had arrived in. He slid in safely, thumbed the starplate, and swore. It was programmed to lift only in response to its owner's thumbprint, of course.

Jad Rakkis was the next to arrive. Kress ran to his skimmer as it set down, and seized Rakkis by the arm as he was climbing out. "Get back in, quickly," he said pushing. "Take me to the city. Hurry, Jad. *Get out of here!*"

But Rakkis only stared at him, and would not move. "Why, what's wrong, Simon? I don't understand. What about your party?"

And then it was too late, because the loose sand all around them was stirring, and the red eyes were staring at them, and the mandibles were clacking. Rakkis made a choking sound, and moved to get back in his skimmer, but a pair of mandibles snapped shut about his ankle, and suddenly he was on his knees. The sand seemed to boil with subterranean activity. Jad thrashed and cried terribly as they tore him apart. Kress could hardly bear to watch.

After that, he did not try to escape again. When it was all over, he cleaned out what remained in his liquor cabinet, and got extremely drunk. It would be the last time he would enjoy that luxury, he knew. The only alcohol remaining in the house was stored down in the wine cellar.

Kress did not touch a bite of food the entire day, but he fell asleep feeling bloated, sated at last, the awful hunger vanquished. His last thoughts before the nightmares took him were of whom he could ask out tomorrow.

MORNING WAS HOT and dry. Kress opened his eyes to see the white sandking on his dresser again. He shut them again quickly, hoping the dream would leave him. It did not, and he could not go back to sleep. Soon he found himself staring at the thing.

He stared for almost five minutes before the strangeness of it dawned on him; the sandking was not moving.

The mobiles could be prematurely still, to be sure. He had seen them wait and watch a thousand times. But always there was some motion about them—the mandibles clacked, the legs twitched, the long fine antennae stirred and swayed.

But the sandking on his dresser was completely still.

Kress rose, holding his breath, not daring to hope. Could it be dead? Could something have killed it? He walked across the room.

The eyes were glassy and black. The creature seemed swollen, somehow, as if it were soft and rotting inside, filling up with gas that pushed outward at the plates of white armor.

Kress reached out a trembling hand and touched it.

It was warm—hot even—and growing hotter. But it did not move.

He pulled his hand back, and as he did, a segment of the sandking's white exoskeleton fell away from it. The flesh beneath was the same color, but softer-looking, swollen and feverish. And it almost seemed to throb.

Kress backed away, and ran to the door.

Three more white mobiles lay in his hall. They were all like the one in his bedroom.

He ran down the stairs, jumping over sandkings. None of them moved. The house was full of them, all dead, dying, comatose, whatever. Kress did not care what was wrong with them. Just so they could not move.

He found four of them inside his skimmer. He picked them up one by one, and threw them as far as he could. Damned monsters. He slid back in, on the ruined half-eaten seats, and thumbed the starplate.

Nothing happened.

Kress tried again, and again. Nothing. It wasn't fair. This was *his* skimmer, it ought to start, why wouldn't it lift, he didn't understand.

Finally he got out and checked, expecting the worst. He found it. The sandkings had torn apart his gravity grid. He was trapped. He was still trapped.

Grimly, Kress marched back into the house. He went to his gallery and found the antique ax that had hung next to the throwing-sword he had used on Cath m'Lane. He set to work. The sandkings did not stir even as he chopped them to pieces. But they splattered when he made the first cut, the bodies almost bursting. Inside was awful; strange half-formed organs, a viscous reddish ooze that looked almost like human blood, and the yellow ichor.

Kress destroyed twenty of them before he realized the futility of what he was doing. The mobiles were nothing, really. Besides, there were so *many* of them. He could work for a day and night and still not kill them all.

He had to go down into the wine cellar and use the ax on the maw.

Resolute, he started down. He got within sight of the door, and stopped.

It was not a door any more. The walls had been eaten away, so that the hole was twice the size it had been, and round. A pit, that was all. There was no sign that there had ever been a door nailed shut over that black abyss.

A ghastly, choking, fetid odor seemed to come from below.

And the walls were wet and bloody and covered with patches of white fungus.

And worst, it was *breathing*.

Kress stood across the room and felt the warm wind wash over him as it exhaled, and he tried not to choke, and when the wind reversed direction, he fled.

Back in the living room, he destroyed three more mobiles, and collapsed. What was *happening?* He didn't understand.

Then he remembered the only person who might understand. Kress went to his communicator again, stepping on a sandking in his haste, and prayed fervently that the device still worked.

When Jala Wo answered, he broke down and told her everything.

She let him talk without interruption, no expression save for a slight frown on her gaunt, pale face. When Kress had finished, she said only, "I ought to leave you there."

Kress began to blubber. "You can't. Help me. I'll pay. . . ."

"I ought to," We repeated, "but I won't."

"Thank you," Kress said. "Oh, thank . . ."

"Quiet," said Wo. "Listen to me. This is your own doing. Keep your sandkings well, and they are courtly ritual warriors. You turned yours into something else, with starvation and torture. You were their god. You made them what they are. That maw in your cellar is sick, still suffering from the wound you gave it. It is probably insane. Its behavior is . . . unusual.

"You have to get out of there quickly. The mobiles are not dead, Kress. They are dormant. I told you the exoskeleton falls off when they grow larger. Normally, in fact, it falls off much earlier. I have never heard of sandkings growing as large as yours while still in the insectoid stage. It is another result of crippling the white maw, I would say. That does not matter.

"What matters is the metamorphosis your sandkings are now undergoing. As the maw grows, you see, it gets progressively more intelligent. Its psionic powers strengthen, and its mind becomes more sophisticated, more ambitious. The armored mobiles are useful enough when the maw is tiny and only semi-sentient, but now it needs better servants, bodies with more capabilities. Do you understand? The mobiles are all going to give birth to a new breed of sandking. I can't say exactly what it will look like. Each maw designs its own, to fit its perceived needs and desires. But it will be biped, with four arms, and opposable thumbs. It will be able to construct and operate advanced machinery. The individual sandkings will not be sentient. But the maw will be very sentient indeed."

Simon Kress was gaping at Wo's image on the viewscreen. "Your workers," he said, with an effort. "The ones who came out here . . . who installed the tank. . . ."

Jala Wo managed a faint smile. "Shade," she said.

"Shade is a sandking," Kress repeated numbly. "And you sold me a tank of . . . of . . . infants, ah. . . ."

"Do not be absurd," Wo said. "A first-stage sandking is more like a sperm than an infant. The wars temper and control them in nature. Only one in a hundred reaches second stage. Only one in a thousand achieves the third and final plateau, and becomes like Shade. Adult sandkings are not sentimental about the small maws. There are too many of them, and their mobiles are pests." She sighed. "And all this talk wastes time. That white sandking is going to waken to full sentience soon. It is not going to need you any longer, and it hates you, and it will be very hungry. The transformation is taxing. The maw must eat enormous amounts before and after. So you have to get out of there. Do you understand?"

"I *can't,*" Kress said. "My skimmer is destroyed, and I can't get any of the others to start. I don't know how to reprogram them. Can you come out for me?"

"Yes," said Wo. "Shade and I will leave at once, but it is more than two hundred kilometers from Asgard to you and there is equipment we will need to deal with the deranged sandking you've created. You cannot wait there. You have two feet. Walk. Go due east, as near as you can determine, as quickly as you can. The land out there is pretty desolate. We can find you easily with an aerial search, and you'll be safely away from the sandking. Do you understand?"

"Yes," said Simon Kress. "Yes, oh, yes."

They signed off, and he walked quickly toward the door. He was halfway there when he heard the noise—a sound halfway between a pop and a crack.

One of the sandkings had split open. Four tiny hands covered with pinkish-yellow blood came up out of the gap and began to push the dead skin aside.

Kress began to run.

He had not counted on the heat.

The hills were dry and rocky. Kress ran from the house as quickly as he could, ran until his ribs ached and his breath was coming in gasps. Then he walked, but as soon as he had recovered he began to run again. For almost an hour he ran and walked, ran and walked, beneath the fierce hot sun. He sweated freely, and wished that he had thought to bring some water. He watched the sky in the hopes of seeing Wo and Shade.

He was not made for this. It was too hot, and too dry, and he was in no condition. But he kept himself going with the memory of the way the maw had breathed, and the thought of the wriggling little things that by now were surely crawling all over his house. He hoped Wo and Shade would know how to deal with them.

He had his own plans for Wo and Shade. It was all their fault, Kress had decided, and they would suffer for it. Lissandra was dead, but he knew others in her profession.

He would have his revenge. He promised himself that a hundred times as he struggled and sweated his way east.

At least he hoped it was east. He was not that good at directions, and he wasn't certain which way he had run in his initial panic, but since then he had made an effort to bear due east, as Wo had suggested.

When he had been running for several hours, with no sign of rescue, Kress began to grow certain that he had gone wrong.

When several more hours passed, he began to grow afraid. What if Wo and Shade could not find him? He would die out here. He hadn't eaten in two days; he was weak and frightened; his throat was raw for want of water. He couldn't keep going. The sun was sinking now, and he'd be completely lost in the dark. What was wrong? Had the sandkings eaten Wo and Shade? The fear was on him again, filling him, and with it a great thirst and a terrible hunger. But Kress kept going. He stumbled now when he tried to run, and twice he fell. The second time he scraped his hand on a rock, and it came away bloody. He sucked at it as he walked, and worried about infection.

The sun was on the horizon behind him. The ground grew a little cooler, for which Kress was grateful. He decided to walk until last light and settle in for the night. Surely he was far enough from the sandkings to be safe, and Wo and Shade would find him come morning.

When he topped the next rise, he saw the outline of a house in front of him.

It wasn't as big as his own house, but it was big enough. It was habitation, safety. Kress shouted and began to run toward it. Food and drink, he had to have nourishment, he could taste the meal now. He was aching with hunger. He ran down the hill toward the house, waving his arms and shouting to the inhabitants. The light was almost gone now, but he could still make out a half-dozen children playing in the twilight. "Hey there," he shouted. "Help, help."

They came running toward him.

Kress stopped suddenly. "No," he said, "oh, no. Oh, no." He backpedaled, slipped on the sand, got up and tried to run again. They caught him easily. They were ghastly little things with bulging eyes and dusky orange skin. He struggled, but it was useless. Small as they were, each of them had four arms, and Kress had only two.

They carried him toward the house. It was a sad, shabby house built of crumbling sand, but the door was quite large, and dark, and it breathed. That was terrible, but it was not the thing that set Simon Kress to screaming. He screamed because of the others, the little orange children who came crawling out from the castle, and watched impassive as he passed.

All of them had his face.

| HARRY TURTLEDOVE |

The Road Not Taken

Harry Turtledove is the leading contemporary exponent of alternate-world fantasy and science fiction. In many of his stories and novels, he posits an outcome for an influential moment in time that is inconsistent with known history, or he considers the earlier or later appearance of a technology that has indelibly shaped the world as we know it, and then follows the alternate succession of events that might have unfolded in its aftermath. His work is known for its rigorous and detailed rendering of history as a force that shapes the smallest nuances of a world, and for characters who support his plots with perspectives and outlooks molded by their altered reality. In the stories collected in 1987 as *Agent of Byzantium*, Mohammed's conversion to Christianity results in a world where the Arab empires never came to be. That same year saw the publication of *The Misplaced Legion*, the first novel in his Videssos series about the experiences of a Roman legion translated to a world that runs on magic. Since then, he has explored the impact of historical events altered by outside manipulation. His ambitious Worldwar series—which includes *In the Balance*, *Tilting the Balance*, *Striking the Balance*, *Upsetting the Balance*, and other novels—projects an alternate World War II in which an invasion from outer space in 1942 forges alliances between Axis and Allied opponents to fight the common enemy. In *Guns of the South*, time travelers provide the Confederacy with the firepower from the future it needs to win the American Civil War. The three volumes in his Great War saga—*American Front*, *Walk in Hell*, and *Breakthrough*—present an America in which the United States and the Confederacy survive into the twentieth century and support opposing sides in World War I. Turtledove has also coedited the anthology *Alternate Generals*. His many other works include the short-fiction collection *Departures*, the comic fantasy *The Case of the Toxic Spell Dump*, and the linked novels *Into the Darkness*, *Darkness Descending*, and *Through the Darkness*, epic tales of empire building set in a fantasy world where cataclysmic wars are fought with magic.

CAPTAIN TOGRAM WAS using the chamberpot when the *Indomitable* broke out of hyperdrive. As happened all too often, nausea surged through the Roxolan officer. He raised the pot and was abruptly sick into it.

When the spasm was done, he set the thundermug down and wiped his streaming eyes with the soft, gray-brown fur of his forearm. "The gods curse it!" he burst out. "Why don't the shipmasters warn us when they do that?" Several of his troopers echoed him more pungently.

At that moment, a runner appeared in the doorway. "We're back in normal space," the youth squeaked, before dashing on to the next chamber. Jeers and oaths followed him: "No shit!" "Thanks for the news!" "Tell the steerers—they might not have got the word!"

Togram sighed and scratched his muzzle in annoyance at his own irritability. As an officer, he was supposed to set an example for his soldiers. He was junior enough to take such responsibilities seriously, but had had enough service to realize he should never expect too much from anyone more than a couple of notches above him. High ranks went to those with ancient blood or fresh money.

Sighing again, he stowed the chamberpot in its niche. The metal cover he slid over it did little to relieve the stench. After sixteen days in space, the *Indomitable* reeked of ordure, stale food, and staler bodies. It was no better in any other ship of the Roxolan fleet, or any other. Travel between the stars was simply like that. Stinks and darkness were part of the price the soldiers paid to make the kingdom grow.

Togram picked up a lantern and shook it to rouse the glowmites inside. They flashed silver in alarm. Some races, the captain knew, lit their ships with torches or candles, but glowmites used less air, even if they could only shine intermittently.

Ever the careful soldier, Togram checked his weapons while the light lasted. He always kept all four of his pistols loaded and ready to use; when landing operations began, one pair would go on his belt, the other in his boot tops. He was more worried about his sword. The perpetually moist air aboard ship was not good for the blade. Sure enough, he found a spot of rust to scour away.

As he polished the rapier, he wondered what the new system would be like. He prayed for it to have a habitable planet. The air in the *Indomitable* might be too foul to breathe by the time the ship could get back to the nearest Roxolan-held planet. That was one of the risks starfarers took. It was not a major one—small yellow suns usually shepherded a life-bearing world or two—but it was there.

He wished he hadn't let himself think about it; like an aching fang, the worry, once there, would not go away. He got up from his pile of bedding to see how the steerers were doing.

As usual with them, both Ransisc and his apprentice Olgren were complaining about the poor quality of the glass through which they trained their spyglasses. "You ought to stop whining," Togram said, squinting in from the doorway. "At least you have light to see by." After seeing so long by glowmite lantern, he had to wait for his eyes to adjust to the harsh raw sunlight flooding the observation chamber before he could go in.

Olgren's ears went back in annoyance. Ransisc was older and calmer. He set his hand on his apprentice's arm. "If you rise to all of Togram's jibes, you'll have time for nothing else—he's been a troublemaker since he came out of the egg. Isn't that right, Togram?"

"Whatever you say." Togram liked the white-muzzled senior steerer. Unlike most of his breed, Ransisc did not act as if he believed his important job made him something special in the gods' scheme of things.

Olgren stiffened suddenly; the tip of his stumpy tail twitched. "This one's a world!" he exclaimed.

"Let's see," Ransisc said. Olgren moved away from his spyglass. The two steerers had been examining bright stars one by one, looking for those that would show discs and prove themselves actually to be planets.

"It's a world," Ransisc said at length, "but not one for us—those yellow, banded planets always have poisonous air, and too much of it." Seeing Olgren's dejection, he added, "It's not a total loss—if we look along a line from that planet to its sun, we should find others fairly soon."

"Try that one," Togram said, pointing toward a ruddy star that looked brighter than most of the others he could see.

Olgren muttered something haughty about knowing his business better than any amateur, but Ransisc said sharply, "The captain has seen more worlds from space than you, sirrah. Suppose you do as he asks." Ears drooping dejectedly, Olgren obeyed.

Then his pique vanished. "A planet with green patches!" he shouted.

Ransisc had been aiming his spyglass at a different part of the sky, but that brought him hurrying over. He shoved his apprentice aside, fiddled with the spyglass's focus, peered long at the magnified image. Olgren was hopping from one foot to the other, his muddy brown fur puffed out with impatience to hear the verdict.

"Maybe," the senior steerer said, and Olgren's face lit, but it fell again as Ransisc continued, "I don't see anything that looks like open water. If we find nothing better, I say we try it, but let's search a while longer."

"You've just made a *luof* very happy," Togram said. Ransisc chuckled. The Rox-olani brought the little creatures along to test new planets' air. If a *luof* could breathe it in the airlock of a flier, it would also be safe for the animal's masters.

The steerers growled in irritation as several stars in a row stubbornly stayed mere points of light. Then Ransisc stiffened at his spyglass. "Here it is," he said softly. "*This* is what we want. Come here, Olgren."

"Oh my, yes," the apprentice said a moment later.

"Go report it to Warmaster Slevon, and ask him if his devices have picked up any hyperdrive vibrations except for the fleet's." As Olgren hurried away, Ransisc beckoned Togram over. "See for yourself."

The captain of foot bent over the eyepiece. Against the black of space, the world in the spyglass field looked achingly like Roxolan: deep ocean blue, covered with swirls of white cloud.

A good-sized moon hung nearby. Both were in approximately half-phase, being nearer their star than was the *Indomitable.*

"Did you spy any land?" Togram asked.

"Look near the top of the image, below the ice cap," Ransisc said. "Those browns and greens aren't colors water usually takes. If we want any world in this system, you're looking at it now."

They took turns examining the distant planet and trying to sketch its features until Olgren came back. "Well?" Togram said, though he saw the apprentice's ears were high and cheerful.

"Not a hyperdrive emanation but ours in the whole system!" Olgren grinned. Ransisc and Togram both pounded him on the back, as if he were the cause of the good news and not just its bearer.

The captain's smile was even wider than Olgren's. This was going to be an easy one, which, as a professional soldier, he thoroughly approved of. If no one hereabouts could build a hyperdrive, either the system had no intelligent life at all or its inhabitants were still primitives, ignorant of gunpowder, fliers, and other aspects of warfare as it was practiced among the stars.

He rubbed his hands. He could hardly wait for landfall.

BUCK HERZOG WAS bored. After four months in space, with five and a half more staring him in the face, it was hardly surprising. Earth was a bright star behind the *Ares III,* with Luna a dimmer companion; Mars glowed ahead.

"It's your exercise period, Buck," Art Snyder called. Of the five-person crew, he was probably the most officious.

"All right, Pancho." Herzog sighed. He pushed himself over to the bicycle and began pumping away, at first languidly, then harder. The work helped keep calcium in his bones in spite of free-fall. Besides, it was something to do.

Melissa Ott was listening to the news from home. "Fernando Valenzuela died last night," she said.

"Who?" Snyder was not a baseball fan.

Herzog was, and a Californian to boot. "I saw him at an Old-Timers' game once, and I remember my dad and my grandfather always talking about him," he said. "How old was he, Mel?"

"Seventy-nine," she answered.

"He always was too heavy," Herzog said sadly.

"Jesus Christ!"

Herzog blinked. No one on the *Ares III* had sounded that excited since liftoff from the American space station. Melissa was staring at the radar screen. "Freddie!" she yelled.

Frederica Lindstrom, the ship's electronics expert, had just gotten out of the cramped shower space. She dove for the control board, still trailing a stream of water droplets. She did not bother with a towel; modesty aboard the *Ares III* had long since vanished.

Melissa's shout even made Claude Jonnard stick his head out of the little biology lab where he spent most of his time. "What's wrong?" he called from the hatchway.

"Radar's gone to hell," Melissa told him.

"What do you mean, gone to hell?" Jonnard demanded indignantly. He was one of those annoying people who think quantitatively all the time, and think everyone else does, too.

"There are about a hundred, maybe a hundred fifty, objects on the screen that have no right to be there," answered Frederica Lindstrom, who had a milder case of the same disease. "Range appears to be a couple of million kilometers."

"They weren't there a minute ago, either," Melissa said. "I hollered when they showed up."

As Frederica fiddled with the radar and the computer, Herzog stayed on the exercise bike, feeling singularly useless: what good is a geologist millions of kilometers away from rocks? He wouldn't even get his name in the history books—no one remembers the crew of the third expedition to anywhere.

Frederica finished her checks. "I can't find anything wrong," she said, sounding angry at herself and the equipment both.

"Time to get on the horn to Earth, Freddie," Art Snyder said. "If I'm going to land this beast, I can't have the radar telling me lies."

Melissa was already talking into the microphone. "Houston, this is *Ares III*. We have a problem—"

Even at light-speed, there were a good many minutes of waiting. They crawled past, one by one. Everyone jumped when the speaker crackled to life. "*Ares III*, this is Houston Control. Ladies and gentlemen, I don't quite know how to tell you this, but we see them too."

The communicator kept talking, but no one was listening to her anymore. Herzog felt his scalp tingle as his hair, in primitive reflex, tried to stand on end. Awe filled him. He had never thought he would live to see humanity contact another race. "Call them, Mel," he said urgently.

She hesitated. "I don't know, Buck. Maybe we should let Houston handle this."

"Screw Houston," he said, surprised at his own vehemence. "By the time the bureaucrats down there figure out what to do, we'll be coming down on Mars. We're the people on the spot. Are you going to throw away the most important moment in the history of the species?"

Melissa looked from one of her crewmates to the next. Whatever she saw in their faces must have satisfied her, for she shifted the aim of the antenna and began to speak: "This is the spacecraft *Ares III,* calling the unknown ships. Welcome from the people of Earth." She turned off the transmitter for a moment. "How many languages do we have?"

The call went out in Russian, Mandarin, Japanese, French, German, Spanish, even Latin. ("Who knows the last time they may have visited?" Frederica said when Snyder gave her an odd look.)

If the wait for a reply from Earth had been long, this one was infinitely worse. The delay stretched far, far past the fifteen-second speed-of-light round trip. "Even if they don't speak any of our languages, shouldn't they say *something?*" Melissa demanded of the air. It did not answer, nor did the aliens.

Then, one at a time, the strange ships began darting away sunward, toward Earth. "My God, the acceleration!" Snyder said. "Those are no rockets!" He looked suddenly sheepish. "I don't suppose starships would have rockets, would they?"

The *Ares III* lay alone again in its part of space, pursuing its Hohmann orbit inexorably toward Mars. Buck Herzog wanted to cry.

AS WAS THEIR practice, the ships of the Roxolan fleet gathered above the pole of the new planet's hemisphere with the most land. Because everyone would be coming to the same spot, the doctrine made visual rendezvous easy. Soon only four ships were unaccounted for. A scoutship hurried around to the other pole, found them, and brought them back.

"Always some water-lovers every trip." Togram chuckled to the steerers as he brought them the news. He took all the chances he could to go to their dome, not just for the sunlight but also because, unlike many soldiers, he was interested in planets for their own sake. With any head for figures, he might have tried to become a steerer himself.

He had a decent hand with quill and paper, so Ransisc and Olgren were willing to let him spell them at the spyglass and add to the sketchmaps they were making of the world below.

"Funny sort of planet," he remarked. "I've never seen one with so many forest fires or volcanoes or whatever they are on the dark side."

"I still think they're cities," Olgren said, with a defiant glance at Ransisc.

"They're too big and too bright," the senior steerer said patiently; the argument, plainly, had been going on for some time.

"This is your first trip offplanet, isn't it, Olgren?" Togram asked.

"Well, what if it is?"

"Only that you don't have enough perspective. Egelloc on Roxolan has almost a million people, and from space it's next to invisible at night. It's nowhere near as bright as those lights, either. Remember, this is a primitive planet. I admit it looks like there's intelligent life down there, but how could a race that hasn't even stumbled across the hyperdrive build cities ten times as great as Egelloc?"

"I don't know," Olgren said sulkily. "But from what little I can see by moonlight, those lights look to be in good spots for cities—on coasts, or along rivers, or whatever."

Ransisc sighed. "What are we going to do with him, Togram? He's so sure he knows everything, he won't listen to reason. Were you like that when you were young?"

"Till my clanfathers beat it out of me, anyway. No need getting all excited, though. Soon enough the flyers will go down with their *luofi*, and then we'll know." He swallowed a snort of laughter, then sobered abruptly, hoping he hadn't been as gullible as Olgren when he was young.

"I HAVE ONE of the alien vessels on radar," the SR-81 pilot reported. "It's down to 80,000 meters and still descending." He was at his own plane's operational ceiling, barely half as high as the ship entering atmosphere.

"For God's sake, hold your fire," ground control ordered. The command had been dinned into him before he took off, but the brass were not about to let him forget. He did not really blame them. One trigger-happy idiot could ruin humanity forever.

"I'm beginning to get a visual image," he said, glancing at the head-up display projected in front of him. A moment later he added, "It's one damn funny-looking ship, I can tell you that already. Where are the wings?"

"We're picking up the image now too," the ground-control officer said. "They must use the same principle for their in-atmosphere machines as they do for their spacecraft: some sort of antigravity that gives them both lift and drive capability."

The alien ship kept ignoring the SR-81, just as all the aliens had ignored every terrestrial signal beamed at them. The craft continued its slow descent, while the SR-81 pilot circled below, hoping he would not have to go down to the aerial tanker to refuel.

"One question answered," he called to the ground. "It's a warplane." No craft whose purpose was peaceful would have had those glaring eyes and that snarling, fang-filled mouth painted on its belly. Some USAF ground-attack aircraft carried similar markings.

At last the alien reached the level at which the SR-81 was loitering. The pilot called the ground again. "Permission to pass in front of the aircraft?" he asked. "Maybe everybody's asleep in there and I can wake 'em up."

After a long silence, ground control gave grudging assent. "No hostile gestures," the controller warned.

"What do you think I'm going to do, flip him the finger?" the pilot muttered, but his radio was off. Acceleration pushed him back in his seat as he guided the SR-81 into a long, slow turn that would carry it about half a kilometer in front of the vessel from the spacefleet.

His airplane's camera gave him a brief glimpse of the alien pilot, who was sitting behind a small, dirty windscreen.

The being from the stars saw him, too. Of that there was no doubt. The alien jinked like a startled fawn, performing maneuvers that would have smeared the SR-81 pilot against the walls of his pressure cabin—if his aircraft could have matched them in the first place.

"I'm giving pursuit!" he shouted. Ground control screamed at him, but he was the man on the spot. The surge from his afterburner made the pressure he had felt before a love pat by comparison.

Better streamlining made his plane faster than the craft from the starships, but that did not do him much good. Every time its pilot caught sight of him, the alien ship danced away with effortless ease. The SR-81 pilot felt like a man trying to kill a butterfly with a hatchet.

To add to his frustration, his fuel warning light came on. In any case, his aircraft was designed for the thin atmosphere at the edge of space, not the increasingly denser air through which the alien flew. He swore, but he had to pull away.

As his SR-81 gulped kerosene from the tanker, he could not help wondering what would have happened if he'd turned a missile loose. There were a couple of times he'd had a perfect shot. That was one thought he kept firmly to himself. What his superiors would do if they knew about it was too gruesome to contemplate.

THE TROOPERS CROWDED round Togram as he came back from the officers' conclave. "What's the word, captain?" "Did the *luof* live?" "What's it like down there?"

"The *luof* lived, boys!" Togram said with a broad smile.

His company raised a cheer that echoed deafeningly in the barracks room. "We're going down!" they whooped. Ears stood high in excitement. Some soldiers waved plumed hats in the fetid air. Others, of a bent more like their captain's, went over to their pallets and began seeing to their weapons.

"How tough are they going to be, sir?" a gray-furred veteran named Ilingua asked as Togram went by. "I hear the flier pilot saw some funny things."

Togram's smile got wider. "By the heavens and hells, Ilingua, haven't you done this often enough before to know better than to pay heed to rumors you hear before planetfall?"

"I hope so, sir," Ilingua said, "but these are so strange I thought there might be something to them." When Togram did not answer, the trooper shook his head at his own foolishness and shook up a lantern so he could *examine* his dagger's edge.

As inconspicuously as he could, the captain let out a sigh. He did not know what to believe himself, and he had listened to the pilot's report. How could the locals have flying machines when they did not know contragravity? Togram had heard of a race that used hot-air balloons before it discovered the better way of doing things, but no balloon could have reached the altitude the locals' flier had achieved, and no balloon could have changed direction, as the pilot had violently insisted this craft had done.

Assume he was wrong, as he had to be. But how was one to take his account of towns as big as the ones whose possibility Ransisc had ridiculed, of a world so populous there was precious little open space? And lantern signals from other ships showed their scout pilots were reporting the same wild improbabilities.

Well, in the long run it would not matter if this race was numerous as *reffo* at a picnic. There would simply be that many more subjects here for Roxolan.

"THIS IS A terrible waste," Billy Cox said to anyone who would listen as he slung his duffel bag over his shoulder and tramped out to the waiting truck. "We should be meeting the starpeople with open arms, not with a show of force."

"You tell 'em, Professor." Sergeant Santos Amoros chuckled from behind him. "Me, I'd sooner stay on my butt in a nice, air-conditioned barracks than face L.A. summer smog and sun any old day. Damn shame you're just a Spec-1. If you was president, you could give the orders any way you wanted, instead o' takin' 'em."

Cox didn't think that was very fair either. He'd been just a few units short of his M.A. in poli-sci when the big buildup after the second Syrian crisis sucked him into the army.

He had to fold his lanky length like a jackknife to get under the olive-drab canopy of the truck and down into the passenger compartment. The seats were too hard and too close together. Jamming people into the vehicle counted for more than their comfort while they were there. Typical military thinking, Cox thought disparagingly.

The truck filled. The big diesel rumbled to life. A black soldier dug out a deck of cards and bet anyone that he could turn twenty-five cards into five pat poker hands. A couple of greenhorns took him up on it. Cox had found out the expensive way that it was a sucker bet. The black man was grinning as he offered the deck to one of his marks to shuffle.

Riffff! The ripple of the pasteboards was authoritative enough to make everybody in the truck turn his head. "Where'd you learn to handle cards like that, man?" demanded the black soldier, whose name was Jim but whom everyone called Junior.

"Dealing blackjack in Vegas." *Riffff!*

"Hey, Junior," Cox called, "all of a sudden I want ten bucks of your action."

"Up yours too, pal," Junior said, glumly watching the cards move as if they had lives of their own.

The truck rolled northward, part of a convoy of trucks, MICVs, and light tanks that stretched for miles. An entire regiment was heading into Los Angeles, to be billeted by companies in different parts of the sprawling city. Cox approved of that; it made it less likely that he would personally come face-to-face with any of the aliens.

"Sandy," he said to Amoros, who was squeezed in next to him, "even if I'm wrong and the aliens aren't friendly, what the hell good will hand weapons do? It'd be like taking on an elephant with a safety pin."

"Professor, like I told you already, they don't pay me to think, or you neither. Just as well, too. I'm gonna do what the lieutenant tells me, and you're gonna do what I tell you, and everything is gonna be fine, right?"

"Sure," Cox said, because Sandy, while he wasn't a bad guy, was a sergeant. All the same, the Neo-Armalite between Cox's boots seemed very futile, and his helmet and body armor as thin and gauzy as a stripper's negligee.

THE SKY OUTSIDE the steerers' dome began to go from black to deep blue as the *Indomitable* entered atmosphere. "There," Olgren said, pointing. "That's where we'll land."

"Can't see much from this height," Togram remarked.

"Let him use your spyglass, Olgren," Ransisc said. "He'll be going back to his company soon."

Togram grunted; that was more than a comment—it was also a hint. Even so, he was happy to peer through the eyepiece. The ground seemed to leap toward him. There was a moment of disorientation as he adjusted to the inverted image, which put the ocean on the wrong side of the field of view. But he was not interested in sightseeing. He wanted to learn what his soldiers and the rest of the troops aboard the *Indomitable* would have to do to carve out a beachhead and hold it against the locals.

"There's a spot that looks promising," he said. "The greenery there in the midst of the buildings in the eastern—no, the western—part of the city. That should give us a clear landing zone, a good campground, and a base for landing reinforcements."

"Let's see what you're talking about," Ransisc said, elbowing him aside. "Hmm, yes, I see the stretch you mean. That might not be bad. Olgren, come look at this. Can you find it again in the Warmaster's spyglass? All right then, go point it out to him. Suggest it as our setdown point."

The apprentice hurried away. Ransisc bent over the eyepiece again. "Hmm," he repeated. "They build tall down there, don't they?"

"I thought so," Togram said. "And there's a lot of traffic on those roads. They've spent a fortune cobblestoning them all, too; I didn't see any dust kicked up."

"This should be a rich conquest," Ransisc said.

Something swift, metallic, and predator-lean flashed past the observation window. "By the gods, they do have fliers, don't they?" Togram said. In spite of the pilots' claims, deep down he hadn't believed it until he saw it for himself.

He noticed Ransisc's ears twitching impatiently, and realized he really had spent too much time in the observation room. He picked up his glowmite lantern and went back to his troopers.

A couple of them gave him a resentful look for being away so long, but he cheered them up by passing on as much as he could about their landing site. Common soldiers loved nothing better than inside information. They second-guessed their superiors without it, but the game was even more fun when they had some idea of what they were talking about.

A runner appeared in the doorway. "Captain Togram, your company will planet from airlock three."

"Three," Togram acknowledged, and the runner trotted off to pass orders to other ground troop leaders. The captain put his plumed hat on his head (the plume was scarlet, so his company could recognize him in combat), checked his pistols one last time, and ordered his troopers to follow him.

The reeking darkness was as oppressive in front of the inner airlock door as anywhere else aboard the *Indomitable,* but somehow easier to bear. Soon the doors would swing open and he would feel fresh breezes riffling his fur, taste sweet clean air, enjoy sunlight for more than a few precious units at a stretch. Soon he would measure himself against these new beings in combat.

He felt the slightest of jolts as the *Indomitable*'s fliers launched themselves from the mother ship. There would be no *luofi* aboard them this time, but rather musketeers to terrorize the natives with fire from above, and jars of gunpowder to be touched off and dropped. The Roxolani always strove to make as savage a first impression as they could. Terror doubled their effective numbers.

Another jolt came, different from the one before. They were down.

A SHADOW SPREAD across the UCLA campus. Craning his neck, Junior said, "Will you look at the size of the mother!" He had been saying that for the last five minutes, as the starship slowly descended.

Each time, Billy Cox could only nod, his mouth dry, his hands clutching the plastic grip and cool metal barrel of his rifle. The Neo-Armalite seemed totally impotent against the huge bulk floating so arrogantly downward. The alien flying machines around it were as minnows beside a whale, while they in turn dwarfed the USAF planes circling at a greater distance. The roar of their jets assailed the ears of the nervous troops and civilians on the ground. The aliens' engines were eerily silent.

The starship landed in the open quad between New Royce, New Haines, New Kinsey, and New Powell Halls. It towered higher than any of the two-story red brick buildings, each a reconstruction of one overthrown in the earthquake of 2034. Cox heard saplings splinter under the weight of the alien craft. He wondered what it would have done to the big trees that had fallen five years ago along with the famous old halls.

"All right, they've landed. Let's move on up," Lieutenant Shotton ordered. He could not quite keep the wobble out of his voice, but he trotted south toward the starship. His platoon followed him past Dickson Art Center, past New Bunche Hall. Not so long ago, Billy Cox had walked this campus barefoot. Now his boots thudded on concrete.

The platoon deployed in front of Dodd Hall, looking west toward the spacecraft. A little breeze toyed with the leaves of the young, hopeful trees planted to replace the stalwarts lost to the quake.

"Take as much cover as you can," Lieutenant Shotton ordered quietly. The platoon scrambled into flowerbeds, snuggled down behind thin tree trunks. Out on Hilgard Avenue, diesels roared as armored fighting vehicles took positions with good lines of fire.

It was all such a waste, Cox thought bitterly. The thing to do was to make friends with the aliens, not to assume automatically they were dangerous.

Something, at least, was being done along those lines. A delegation came out of Murphy Hall and slowly walked behind a white flag from the administration building toward the starship. At the head of the delegation was the mayor of Los Angeles; the president and governor were busy elsewhere. Billy Cox would have given anything to be part of the delegation instead of sprawled here on his belly in the grass. If only the aliens had waited until he was fifty or so, had given him a chance to get established—

Sergeant Amoros nudged him with an elbow. "Look there, man. Something's happening—"

Amoros was right. Several hatchways which had been shut were swinging open, allowing Earth's air to mingle with the ship's.

The westerly breeze picked up. Cox's nose twitched. He could not name all the exotic odors wafting his way, but he recognized sewage and garbage when he smelled them. "God, what a stink!" he said.

"BY THE GODS, what a stink!" Togram exclaimed. When the outer airlock doors went down, he had expected real fresh air to replace the stale, overused gases inside the *Indomitable.* This stuff smelled like smoky peat fires, or lamps whose wicks hadn't quite been extinguished. And it stung! He felt the nictitating membranes flick across his eyes to protect them.

"Deploy!" he ordered, leading his company forward. This was the tricky part. If the locals had nerve enough, they could hit the Roxolani just as the latter were coming out of their ship, and cause all sorts of trouble. Most races without hyperdrive, though, were too overawed by the arrival of travelers from the stars to try anything like that. And if they didn't do it fast, it would be too late.

They weren't doing it here. Togram saw a few locals, but they were keeping a respectful distance. He wasn't sure how many there were. Their mottled skins—or was that clothing?—made them hard to notice and count. But they were plainly warriors, both by the way they acted and by the weapons they bore.

His own company went into its familiar two-line formation, the first crouching, the second standing and aiming their muskets over the heads of the troops in front.

"Ah, there we go," Togram said happily. The bunch approaching behind the white banner had to be the local nobles. The mottling, the captain saw, was clothing, for these beings wore entirely different garments, somber except for strange, narrow neck-cloths. They were taller and skinnier than Roxolani, with muzzleless faces.

"Ilingua!" Togram called. The veteran trooper led the right flank squad of the company.

"Sir!"

"Your troops, quarter-right face. At the command, pick off the leaders there. That will demoralize the rest," Togram said, quoting standard doctrine.

"Slowmatches ready!" Togram said. The Roxolani lowered the smoldering cords to the touchholes of their muskets. "Take your aim!" The guns moved, very slightly. "Fire!"

"TEDDY BEARS!" SANDY Amoros exclaimed. The same thought had leaped into Cox's mind. The beings emerging from the spaceship were round, brown, and furry, with long noses and big ears. Teddy bears, however, did not normally carry weapons. They also, Cox thought, did not commonly live in a place that smelled like sewage. Of course, it might have been perfume to them. But if it was, they and Earthpeople were going to have trouble getting along.

He watched the Teddy bears as they took their positions. Somehow their positioning did not suggest that they were forming an honor guard for the mayor and his party. Yet it did look familiar to Cox, although he could not quite figure out why.

Then he had it. If he had been anywhere but at UCLA, he would not have made the connection. But he remembered a course he had taken on the rise of the European nation-states in the sixteenth century, and on the importance of the professional, disciplined armies the kings had created. Those early armies had performed evolutions like this one.

It was a funny coincidence. He was about to mention it to his sergeant when the world blew up.

Flames spurted from the aliens' guns. Great gouts of smoke puffed into the sky. Something that sounded like an angry wasp buzzed past Cox's ear. He heard shouts and shrieks from either side. Most of the mayor's delegation was down, some motionless, others thrashing.

There was a crash from the starship, and another one an instant later as a round-shout smashed into the brickwork of Dodd Hall. A chip stung Cox in the back of the neck. The breeze brought him the smell of fireworks, one he had not smelled for years.

"RELOAD!" TOGRAM YELLED. "Another volley, then at 'em with the bayonet!" His troopers worked frantically, measuring powder charges and ramming round bullets home.

"SO THAT'S HOW they wanna play!" Amoros shouted. "Nail their hides to the wall!" The tip of his little finger had been shot away. He did not seem to know it.

Cox's Neo-Armalite was already barking, spitting a stream of hot brass cartridges, slamming against his shoulder. He rammed in clip after clip, playing the rifle like a hose. If one bullet didn't bite, the next would.

Others from the platoon were also firing. Cox heard bursts of automatic weapons fire from different parts of the campus, too, and the deeper blasts of rocket-propelled grenades and field artillery. Smoke not of the aliens' making began to envelop their ship and the soldiers around it.

One or two shots came back at the platoon, and then a few more, but so few that Cox, in stunned disbelief, shouted to his sergeant, "This isn't fair!"

"Fuck 'em!" Amoros shouted back. "They wanna throw their weight around, they take their chances. Only good thing they did was knock over the mayor. Always did hate that old crackpot."

THE HARSH *TAC-TAC-TAC* did not sound like any gunfire Togram had heard. The shots came too close together, making a horrible sheet of noise. And if the locals were shooting back at his troopers, where were the thick, choking clouds of gunpowder smoke over their position?

He did not know the answer to that. What he did know was that his company was going down like grain before a scythe. Here a soldier was hit by three bullets at once and fell awkwardly, as if his body could not tell in which direction to twist. There another had the top of his head gruesomely removed.

The volley the captain had screamed for was stillborn. Perhaps a squad's worth of soldiers moved toward the locals, the sun glinting bravely off their long, polished bayonets. None of them got more than a half-sixteen of paces before falling.

Ilingua looked at Togram, horror in his eyes, his ears flat against his head. The captain knew his were the same. "What are they doing to us?" Ilingua howled.

Togram could only shake his head helplessly. He dove behind a corpse, fired one of his pistols at the enemy. There was still a chance, he thought—how would these demonic aliens stand up under their first air attack?

A flier swooped toward the locals. Musketeers blasted away from firing ports, drew back to reload.

"Take that, you whoresons!" Togram shouted. He did not, however, raise his fist in the air. That, he had already learned, was dangerous.

"INCOMING AIRCRAFT!" SERGEANT Amoros roared. His squad, those not already prone, flung themselves on their faces. Cox heard shouts of pain through the combat din as men were wounded.

The Cottonmouth crew launched their shoulder-fired AA missile at the alien flying machine. The pilot must have had reflexes like a cat's. He sidestepped his machine in midair, no plane built on Earth could have matched that performance. The Cottonmouth shot harmlessly past.

The flier dropped what looked like a load of crockery. The ground jumped as the bombs exploded. Cursing, deafened, Billy Cox stopped worrying whether the fight was fair.

But the flier pilot had not seen the F-29 fighter on his tail. The USAF plane released two missiles from point-blank range, less than a mile. The infrared-seeker found no target and blew itself up, but the missile that homed on radar streaked straight toward the flier. The explosion made Cox bury his face in the ground and clap his hands over his ears.

So this is war, he thought: I can't see, I can barely hear, and my side is winning. What must it be like for the losers?

HOPE DIED IN Togram's hearts when the first flier fell victim to the locals' aircraft. The rest of the *Indomitable's* machines did not last much longer. They could evade, but had even less ability to hit back than the Roxolan ground forces. And they were hideously vulnerable when attacked in their pilots' blind spots, from below or behind.

One of the starship's cannon managed to fire again, and quickly drew a response from the traveling fortresses Togram got glimpses of as they took their positions in the streets outside this parklike area.

When the first shell struck, the luckless captain thought for an instant that it was another gun going off aboard the *Indomitable*. The sound of the explosion was nothing like the crash a solid shot made when it smacked into a target. A fragment of hot metal buried itself in the ground by Togram's hand. That made him think a cannon had blown up, but more explosions on the ship's superstructure and fountains of dirt flying up from misses showed it was just more from the locals' fiendish arsenal.

Something large and hard struck the captain in the back of the neck. The world spiraled down into blackness.

"Cease fire!" The order reached the field artillery first, then the infantry units at the very front line. Billy Cox pushed up his cuff to look at his watch, stared in disbelief. The whole firefight had lasted less than twenty minutes.

He looked around. Lieutenant Shotton was getting up from behind an ornamental palm. "Let's see what we have," he said. His rifle still at the ready, he began to walk slowly toward the starship. It was hardly more than a smoking ruin. For that matter, neither were the buildings around it. The damage to their predecessors had been worse in the big quake, but not much.

Alien corpses littered the lawn. The blood splashing the bright green grass was crimson as any man's. Cox bent to pick up a pistol. The weapon was beautifully made, with scenes of combat carved into the grayish wood of the stock. But he recognized it as a single-shot piece, a small-arm obsolete for at least two centuries. He shook his head in wonderment.

Sergeant Amoros lifted a conical object from where it had fallen beside a dead alien. "What the hell is this?" he demanded.

Again Cox had the feeling of being caught up in something he did not understand. "It's a powderhorn," he said.

"Like in the movies? Pioneers and all that good shit?"

"The very same."

"Damn," Amoros said feelingly. Cox nodded in agreement.

Along with the rest of the platoon, they moved closer to the wrecked ship. Most of the aliens had died still in the two neat rows from which they had opened fire on the soldiers.

Here, behind another corpse, lay the body of the scarlet-plumed officer who had given the order to begin that horrifyingly uneven encounter. Then, startling Cox, the alien moaned and stirred, just as might a human starting to come to. "Grab him; he's a live one!" Cox exclaimed.

Several men jumped on the reviving alien, who was too groggy to fight back. Soldiers began peering into the holes torn in the starship, and even going inside. There they were still wary; the ship was so incredibly much bigger than any human spacecraft that there were surely survivors despite the shellacking it had taken.

As always happens, the men did not get to enjoy such pleasures long. The fighting had been over for only minutes when the first team of experts came thuttering in by helicopter, saw common soldiers in their private preserve, and made horrified noises. The experts also promptly relieved the platoon of its prisoner.

Sergeant Amoros watched resentfully as they took the alien away. "You must've known it would happen, Sandy," Cox consoled him. "We do the dirty work and the brass takes over once things get cleaned up again."

"Yeah, but wouldn't it be wonderful if just once it was the other way round?" Amoros laughed without humor. "You don't need to tell me: fat friggin' chance."

WHEN TOGRAM WOKE up on his back, he knew something was wrong. Roxolani always slept prone. For a moment he wondered how he had got to where he was . . . too much water-of-life the night before? His pounding head made that a good possibility.

Then memory came flooding back. Those damnable locals with their sorcerous weapons! Had his people rallied and beaten back the enemy after all? He vowed to light votive lamps to Edieva, mistress of battles, for the rest of his life if that was true.

The room he was in began to register. Nothing was familiar, from the bed he lay on to the light in the ceiling that glowed bright as sunshine and neither smoked nor flickered. No, he did not think the Roxolani had won their fight.

Fear settled like ice in his vitals. He knew how his own race treated prisoners, had heard spacers' stories of even worse things among other folk. He shuddered to think of the refined tortures a race as ferocious as his captors could invent.

He got shakily to his feet. By the end of the bed he found his hat, some smoked meat obviously taken from the *Indomitable,* and a translucent jug made of something that was neither leather nor glass nor baked clay nor metal. Whatever it was, it was too soft and flexible to make a weapon.

The jar had water in it: *not* water from the *Indomitable.* That was already beginning to taste stale. This was cool and fresh and so pure as to have no taste whatever, water so fine he had only found its like in a couple of mountain springs.

The door opened on noiseless hinges. In came two of the locals. One was small and wore a white coat—a female, if those chest projections were breasts. The other was dressed in the same clothes the local warriors had worn, though those offered no camouflage here. That one carried what was plainly a rifle and, the gods curse him, looked extremely alert.

To Togram's surprise, the female took charge. The other local was merely a bodyguard. Some spoiled princess, curious about these outsiders, the captain thought. Well, he was happier about treating with her than meeting the local executioner.

She sat down, waved for him also to take a seat. He tried a chair, found it un-comfortable—too low in the back, not built for his wide rump and short legs. He sat on the floor instead.

She set a small box on the table by the chair. Togram pointed at it. "What's that?" he asked.

He thought she had not understood—no blame to her for that; she had none of his language. She was playing with the box, pushing a button here, a button there. Then his ears went back and his hackles rose, for the box said, "What's that?" in Roxolani. After a moment he realized it was speaking in his own voice. He swore and made a sign against witchcraft.

She said something, fooled with the box again. This time it echoed her. She pointed at it. " 'Recorder,' " she said. She paused expectantly.

What was she waiting for, the Roxolanic name for that thing? "I've never seen one of those in my life, and I hope I never do again," he said. She scratched her head. When she made the gadget again repeat what he had said, only the thought of the soldier with the gun kept him from flinging it against the wall.

Despite that contretemps, they did eventually make progress on the language. Togram had picked up snatches of a good many tongues in the course of his adventurous life; that was one reason he had made captain in spite of low birth and paltry connections. And the female—Togram heard her name as Hildachesta—had a gift for them, as well as the box that never forgot.

"Why did your people attack us?" she asked one day, when she had come far enough in Roxolanic to be able to frame the question.

He knew he was being interrogated, no matter how polite she sounded. He had played that game with prisoners himself. His ears twitched in a shrug. He had always believed in giving straight answers; that was one reason he was only a captain. He said, "To take what you grow and make and use it for ourselves. Why would anyone want to conquer anyone else?"

"Why indeed?" she murmured, and was silent a little while; his forthright reply seemed to have closed off a line of questioning. She tried again: "How are your people able to walk—I mean, travel—faster than light, when the rest of your arts are so simple?"

His fur bristled with indignation. "They are not! We make gunpowder, we cast iron and smelt steel, we have spyglasses to help our steerers guide us from star to star. We are no savages huddling in caves or shooting at each other with bows and arrows."

His speech, of course, was not that neat or simple. He had to backtrack, to use elaborate circumlocutions, to playact to make Hildachesta understand. She scratched her head in the gesture of puzzlement he had come to recognize. She said, "We have known all these things you mention for hundreds of years, but we did not think anyone could walk—damn, I keep saying that instead of 'travel'—faster than light. How did your people learn to do that?"

"We discovered it for ourselves," he said proudly. "We did not have to learn it from some other starfaring race, as many folk do."

"But *how* did you discover it?" she persisted.

"How do I know? I'm a soldier; what do I care for such things? Who knows who invented gunpowder or found out about using bellows in a smithy to get the fire hot enough to melt iron? These things happen, that's all."

She broke off the questions early that day.

*   *   *

"IT'S HUMILIATING," HILDA Chester said. "If these fool aliens had waited a few more years before they came, we likely would have blown ourselves to kingdom come without ever knowing there was more real estate around. Christ, from what the Roxolani say, races that scarcely know how to work iron fly starships and never think twice about it."

"Except when the starships don't get home," Charlie Ebbets answered. His tie was in his pocket and his collar open against Pasadena's fierce summer heat, although the Caltech Atheneum was efficiently air-conditioned. Along with so many other engineers and scientists, he depended on linguists like Hilda Chester for a link to the aliens.

"I don't quite understand it myself," she said. "Apart from the hyperdrive and contragravity, the Roxolani are backward, almost primitive. And the other species out there must be the same, or someone would have overrun them long since."

Ebbets said, "Once you see it, the drive is amazingly simple. The research crews say anybody could have stumbled over the principle at almost any time in our history. The best guess is that most races did come across it, and once they did, why, all their creative energy would naturally go into refining and improving it."

"But we missed it," Hilda said slowly, "and so our technology developed in a different way."

"That's right. That's why the Roxolani don't know anything about controlled electricity, to say nothing of atomics. And the thing is, as well as we can tell so far, the hyperdrive and contragravity don't have the ancillary applications the electromagnetic spectrum does. All they do is move things from here to there in a hurry."

"That should be enough at the moment," Hilda said. Ebbets nodded. There were almost nine billion people jammed onto the Earth, half of them hungry. Now, suddenly, there were places for them to go and a means to get them there.

"I think," Ebbets said musingly, "we're going to be an awful surprise to the peoples out there."

It took Hilda a second to see what he was driving at. "If that's a joke, it's not funny. It's been a hundred years since the last war of conquest."

"Sure—they've gotten too expensive and too dangerous. But what kind of fight could the Roxolani or anyone else at their level of technology put up against us? The Aztecs and Incas were plenty brave. How much good did it do them against the Spaniards?"

"I hope we've gotten smarter in the last five hundred years," Hilda said. All the same, she left her sandwich half eaten. She found she was not hungry anymore.

"RANSISC!" TOGRAM EXCLAIMED as the senior steerer limped into his cubicle. Ransisc was thinner than he had been a few moons before, aboard the misnamed *Indomitable*. His fur had grown out white around several scars Togram did not remember.

His air of amused detachment had not changed, though. "Tougher than bullets, are you, or didn't the humans think you were worth killing?"

"The latter, I suspect. With their firepower, why should they worry about one soldier more or less?" Togram said bitterly. "I didn't know you were still alive, either."

"Through no fault of my own, I assure you," Ransisc said. "Olgren, next to me—" His voice broke off. It was not possible to be detached about everything.

"What are you doing here?" the captain asked. "Not that I'm not glad to see you, but you're the first Roxolan face I've set eyes on since—" It was his turn to hesitate.

"Since we landed." Togram nodded in relief at the steerer's circumlocution. Ransisc went on, "I've seen several others before you. I suspect we're being allowed to get together so the humans can listen to us talking with each other."

"How could they do that?" Togram asked, then answered his own question. "Oh, the recorders, of course." He perforce used the English word. "Well, we'll fix that."

He dropped into Oyag, the most widely spoken language on a planet the Roxolani had conquered fifty years before. "What's going to happen to us, Ransisc?"

"Back on Roxolan, they'll have realized something's gone wrong by now," the steerer answered in the same tongue.

That did nothing to cheer Togram. "There are so many ways to lose ships," he said gloomily. "And even if the High Warmaster does send another fleet after us, it won't have any more luck than we did. These gods-accursed humans have too many war-machines." He paused and took a long, moody pull at a bottle of vodka. The flavored liquors the locals brewed made him sick, but vodka he liked. "How is it they have all these machines and we don't, or any race we know of? They must be wizards, selling their souls to the demons for knowledge."

Ransisc's nose twitched in disagreement. "I asked one of their savants the same question. He gave me back a poem by a human named Hail or Snow or something of that sort. It was about someone who stood at a fork in the road and ended up taking the less-used track. That's what the humans did. Most races find the hyperdrive and go traveling. The humans never did, and so their search for knowledge went in a different direction."

"Didn't it!" Togram shuddered at the recollection of that brief, terrible combat. "Guns that spit dozens of bullets without reloading, cannon mounted on armored platforms that move by themselves, rockets that follow their targets by themselves . . . And there are the things we didn't see, the ones the humans only talk about—the bombs that can blow up a whole city, each one by itself."

"I don't know if I believe that," Ransisc said.

"I do. They sound afraid when they speak of them."

"Well, maybe. But it's not just the weapons they have. It's the machines that let them see and talk to one another from far away; the machines that do their reckoning for them; their recorders and everything that has to do with them. From what they

say of their medicine, I'm almost tempted to believe you and think they are wizards—
they actually know what causes their diseases, and how to cure or even prevent them.
And their farming: this planet is far more crowded than any I've seen or heard of,
but it grows enough for all these humans."

Togram sadly waggled his ears. "It seems so unfair. All that they got, just by not
stumbling onto the hyperdrive."

"They have it now," Ransisc reminded him. "Thanks to us."

The Roxolani looked at each other, appalled. They spoke together: "What have
we done?"

WILLIAM GIBSON AND MICHAEL SWANWICK

Dogfight

William Gibson began publishing short fiction in 1977, but his reputation was made with his first novel, *Neuromancer*, which appeared in 1984 and has since earned the status of a revolutionary work of contemporary science fiction. The book, which won the Hugo, Nebula and Philip K. Dick awards, became the bible of the cyberpunk movement, and an important breakthrough novel that seeped into the cultural mainstream where the many concepts it explored—cyberspace, virtual reality, the internet, computer crime, artificial intelligence— were fast making the transition from speculative fancy to irrefutable reality. A fusion of the hardboiled detective narrative and the cutting-edge science fiction story, *Neuromancer* and the two follow-up novels with which it forms a loose trilogy—*Count Zero* and *Mona Lisa Overdrive*—blazed trails through the hitherto unexplored frontier of computer technology and microchip-driven telecommunications. It popularized the concept of "plugging in" to link the human brain directly with the neural network of computer systems. The human/machine interface it envisioned, though built on traditional science fiction themes, marked a conceptual shift that turned science fiction's normally outward-looking perspective inward. The complex and often inscrutable reality it extrapolates is one where traditional geographic and cultural boundaries have disintegrated and been reshaped by the uses and abuses of computer-generated data. The hacker subculture dominates the world of these novels, and its often criminal members have the status of outlaw heroes. The novels are also memorable for their dazzling, kinetic styles, which update the stylistic experimentation of the New Wave movement with contemporary techno-jargon, and narrative cuts and splices characteristic of video and computer entertainment. The impact of computer technology has been as inescapable in the rest of Gibson's fiction as it has in the modern world. *The Difference Engine*, which he wrote in collaboration with Bruce Sterling, is a celebrated "steampunk" novel that projects the world that might have been had Charles Babbage's early work on computers taken root in Victorian England. His novels *Virtual Light*, *Idoru*, and *All Tomorrow's Parties* all share characters and explore a variety of computer-oriented themes, including nanotechnology, computer personality constructs, and "nodal points" or fluxes in the data stream that are auguries of transformational events in history. Gibson's short fiction has been collected in *Burning Chrome*, which includes "Johnny Mnemonic," the basis for the Robert Longo film of the same name.

Michael Swanwick emerged as one of the stunning new talents of science fiction in the 1980s initially through the publication of his richly allusive, multilayered short stories, which show the influence of literary postmodernism as much as the traditions of fantasy and science fiction. The best of his short stories have been collected in *Gravity's Angels* and *Tales of Old Earth*, which includes his Hugo Award–winning "The Very Pulse of the Machine." His work as a novelist is equally unconventional, ranging in its approaches from cyberpunk to heroic fantasy and focuses on the interplay of new science and old social structures in their shaping of a civilization and the individual. His first novel, *In the Drift*, is set in a postapocalyptic America where nuclear catastrophe creates a fragmented society struggling to stabilize. *Vacuum Flowers*, *Griffin's Egg* and the Nebula Award–winning *Stations of the Tide* all are explorations of the impact of cataclysmic natural disasters and sociopolitical events on human societies established in alien worlds that have grown estranged from the mother planet's influence. Swanwick has also written *Jack Faust*, a modern variation on the Faust theme, and *The Iron Dragon's Daughter*, an epic hi-tech high fantasy. He is the author of several provocative and controversial essays on the craft of fantasy and science fiction, several of which have been collected in *A Geography of Unknown Lands* and *The Postmodern Archipelago*. He is also a recipient of the Theodore Sturgeon Memorial Award.

HE MEANT TO keep on going, right down to Florida. Work passage on a gunrunner, maybe wind up conscripted into some ratass rebel army down in the war zone. Or maybe, with that ticket good as long as he didn't stop riding, he'd just never get off— Greyhound's Flying Dutchman. He grinned at his faint reflection in cold, greasy glass while the downtown lights of Norfolk slid past, the bus swaying on tired shocks as the driver slung it around a final corner. They shuddered to a halt in the terminal lot, concrete lit gray and harsh like a prison exercise yard. But Deke was watching himself starve, maybe in some snowstorm out of Oswego, with his cheek pressed up against that same bus window, and seeing his remains swept out at the next stop by a muttering old man in faded coveralls. One way or the other, he decided, it didn't mean shit to him. Except his legs seemed to have died already. And the driver called a twenty-minute stopover—Tidewater Station, Virginia. It was an old cinder-block building with two entrances to each rest room, holdover from the previous century.

Legs like wood, he made a halfhearted attempt at ghosting the notions counter, but the black girl behind it was alert, guarding the sparse contents of the old glass case as though her ass depended on it. *Probably does*, Deke thought, turning away. Opposite the washrooms, an open doorway offered GAMES, the word flickering feebly in biofluorescent plastic. He could see a crowd of the local kickers clustered around a pool table. Aimless, his boredom following him like a cloud, he stuck his head in. And saw a biplane, wings no longer than his thumb, blossom bright orange flame. Corkscrewing, trailing smoke, it vanished the instant it struck the green-felt field of the table.

"Tha's right, Tiny," a kicker bellowed, "you *take* that sumbitch!"

"Hey," Deke said. "What's going on?"

The nearest kicker was a bean pole with a black mesh Peterbilt cap. "Tiny's defending the Max," he said, not taking his eyes from the table.

"Oh, yeah? What's that?" But even as he asked, he saw it: a blue enamel medal shaped like a Maltese cross, the slogan *Pour le Mérite* divided among its arms.

The Blue Max rested on the edge of the table, directly before a vast and perfectly immobile bulk wedged into a fragile-looking chrome-tube chair. The man's khaki work shirt would have hung on Deke like the folds of a sail, but it bulged across that bloated torso so tautly that the buttons threatened to tear away at any instant. Deke thought of southern troopers he'd seen on his way down; of that weird, gut-heavy endotype balanced on gangly legs that looked like they'd been borrowed from some other body. Tiny might look like that if he stood, but on a larger scale—a forty-inch jeans inseam that would need a woven-steel waistband to support all those pounds of swollen gut. If Tiny were ever to stand at all—for now Deke saw that that shiny frame was actually a wheelchair. There was something disturbingly childlike about the man's face, an appalling suggestion of youth and even beauty in features almost buried in fold and jowl. Embarrassed, Deke looked away. The other man, the one standing across the table from Tiny, had bushy sideburns and a thin mouth. He seemed to be trying to push something with his eyes, wrinkles of concentration spreading from the corners. . . .

"You dumbshit or what?" The man with the Peterbilt cap turned, catching Deke's Indo proleboy denims, the brass chains at his wrists, for the first time. "Why don't you get your ass lost, fucker. Nobody wants your kind in here." He turned back to the dogfight.

Bets were being made, being covered. The kickers were producing the hard stuff, the old stuff, liberty-headed dollars and Roosevelt dimes from the stamp-and-coin stores, while more cautious bettors slapped down antique paper dollars laminated in clear plastic. Through the haze came a trio of red planes, flying in formation. Fokker D VIIs. The room fell silent. The Fokkers banked majestically under the solar orb of a two-hundred-watt bulb.

The blue Spad dove out of nowhere. Two more plunged from the shadowy ceiling, following closely. The kickers swore, and one chuckled. The formation broke wildly. One Fokker dove almost to the felt, without losing the Spad on its tail. Furiously, it zigged and zagged across the green flatlands but to no avail. At last it pulled up, the enemy hard after it, too steeply—and stalled, too low to pull out in time.

A stack of silver dimes was scooped up.

The Fokkers were outnumbered now. One had two Spads on its tail. A needle-spray of tracers tore past its cockpit. The Fokker slip-turned right, banked into an Immelmann, and was behind one of its pursuers. It fired, and the biplane fell, tumbling.

"Way to go, Tiny!" The kickers closed in around the table.

Deke was frozen with wonder. It felt like being born all over again.

FRANK'S TRUCK STOP was two miles out of town on the Commercial Vehicles Only route. Deke had tagged it, out of idle habit, from the bus on the way in. Now he walked back between the traffic and the concrete crash guards. Articulated trucks went slamming past, big eight-segmented jobs, the wash of air each time threatening to blast him over. CVO stops were easy makes. When he sauntered into Frank's, there was nobody to doubt that he'd come in off a big rig, and he was able to browse the gift shop as slowly as he liked. The wire rack with the projective wetware wafers was located between a stack of Korean cowboy shirts and a display for Fuzz Buster mud-guards. A pair of Oriental dragons twisted in the air over the rack, either fighting or fucking, he couldn't tell which. The game he wanted was there: a wafer labeled SPADS & FOKKERS. It took him three seconds to boost it and less time to slide the magnet—which the cops in D.C. hadn't even bothered to confiscate—across the universal security strip.

On the way out, he lifted two programming units and a little Batang facilitator-remote that looked like an antique hearing aid.

HE CHOSE A highstack at random and fed the rental agent the line he'd used since his welfare rights were yanked. Nobody ever checked up; the state just counted occupied rooms and paid.

The cubicle smelled faintly of urine, and someone had scrawled Hard Anarchy Liberation Front slogans across the walls. Deke kicked trash out of a corner, sat down, back to the wall, and ripped open the wafer pack.

There was a folded instruction sheet with diagrams of loops, rolls, and Immelmanns, a tube of saline paste, and a computer list of operational specs. And the wafer itself, white plastic with a blue biplane and logo on one side, red on the other. He turned it over and over in his hand: SPADS & FOKKERS, FOKKERS & SPADS. Red or blue. He fitted the Batang behind his ear after coating the inductor surface with paste, jacked its fiberoptic ribbon into the programmer, and plugged the programmer into the wall current. Then he slid the wafer into the programmer. It was a cheap set, Indonesian, and the base of his skull buzzed uncomfortably as the program ran. But when it was done, a sky-blue Spad darted restlessly through the air a few inches from his face. It almost glowed, it was so real. It had the strange inner life that fanatically detailed museum-grade models often have but it took all of his concentration to keep it in existence. If his attention wavered at all, it lost focus, fuzzing into a pathetic blur.

He practiced until the battery in the earset died, then slumped against the wall and fell asleep. He dreamed of flying, in a universe that consisted entirely of white clouds and blue sky, with no up and down, and never a green field to crash into.

HE WOKE TO a rancid smell of frying krillcakes and winced with hunger. No cash, either. Well, there were plenty of student types in the stack. Bound to be one who'd like to score a programming unit. He hit the hall with the boosted spare. Not far down was a door with a poster on it: THERE'S A HELL OF A GOOD UNIVERSE NEXT DOOR. Under that was a starscape with a cluster of multicolored pills, torn from an ad for some pharmaceutical company, pasted over an inspirational shot of the "space colony" that had been under construction since before he was born. LET'S GO, the poster said, beneath the collaged hypnotics.

He knocked. The door opened, security slides stopping it at a two-inch slice of girlface. "Yeah?"

"You're going to think this is stolen." He passed the programmer from hand to hand. "I mean because it's new, virtual cherry, and the bar code's still on it. But listen, I'm not gonna argue the point. No. I'm gonna let you have it for only like half what you'd pay anywhere else."

"Hey, wow, *really*, no kidding?" The visible fraction of mouth twisted into a strange smile. She extended her hand, palm up, a loose fist. Level with his chin. "Lookahere!"

There was a hole in her hand, a black tunnel that ran right up her arm. Two small red lights. Rat's eyes. They scurried toward him—growing, gleaming. Something gray streaked forward and leaped for his face.

He screamed, throwing hands up to ward it off. Legs twisting, he fell, the programmer shattering under him.

Silicate shards skittered as he thrashed, clutching his head. Where it hurt, it hurt—it hurt very badly indeed.

"Oh, my God!" Slides unsnapped, and the girl was hovering over him. "Here, listen, come on." She dangled a blue hand towel. "Grab on to this and I'll pull you up."

He looked at her through a wash of tears. Student. That fed look, the oversize sweatshirt, teeth so straight and white they could be used as a credit reference. A thin gold chain around one ankle (fuzzed, he saw, with baby-fine hair). Choppy Japanese haircut. Money. "That sucker was gonna be my dinner," he said ruefully. He took hold of the towel and let her pull him up.

She smiled but skittishly backed away from him. "Let me make it up to you," she said. "You want some food? It was only a projection, okay?"

He followed her in, wary as an animal entering a trap.

*   *   *

"HOLY SHIT," DEKE said, "this is *real cheese. . . .*" He was sitting on a gutsprung sofa, wedged between a four-foot teddy bear and a loose stack of floppies. The room was ankle-deep in books and clothes and papers. But the food she magicked up—Gouda cheese and tinned beef and honest-to-God greenhouse wheat wafers—was straight out of the Arabian Nights.

"Hey," she said. "We know how to treat a prole boy right, huh?" Her name was Nance Bettendorf. She was seventeen. Both her parents had jobs—greedy buggers— and she was an engineering major at William and Mary. She got top marks except in English. "I guess you must really have a thing about rats. You got some kind of phobia about rats?"

He glanced sidelong at her bed. You couldn't see it, really; it was just a swell in the ground cover. "It's not like that. It just reminded me of something else, is all."

"Like what?" She squatted in front of him, the big shirt riding high up one smooth thigh.

"Well . . . did you ever see the—" his voice involuntarily rose and rushed past the words—"*Washington Monument?* Like at night? It's got these two little . . . red lights on top, aviation markers or something, and I, and I . . ." He started to shake.

"You're afraid of the Washington Monument?" Nance whooped and rolled over with laughter, long tanned legs kicking. She was wearing crimson bikini panties.

"I would die rather than look at it again," he said levelly.

She stopped laughing then, sat up, studied his face. White, even teeth worried at her lower lip, like she was dragging up something she didn't want to think about. At last she ventured, "Brainlock?"

"Yeah," he said bitterly. "They told me I'd never go back to D.C. And then the fuckers laughed."

"What did they get you for?"

"I'm a thief." He wasn't about to tell her that the actual charge was career shop-lifting.

"LOTTA OLD *COMPUTER* hacks spent their lives programming machines. And you know what? The human brain is not a goddamn bit like a machine, no way. They just don't program the same." Deke knew this shrill, desperate rap, this long, circular jive that the lonely string out to the rare listener; knew it from a hundred cold and empty nights spent in the company of strangers. Nance was lost in it, and Deke, nodding and yawning, wondered if he'd even be able to stay awake when they finally hit that bed of hers.

"I built that projection I hit you with myself," she said, hugging her knees up beneath her chin. "It's for muggers, you know? I just happened to have it on me, and I threw it at you 'cause I thought it was so funny, you trying to sell me that shit little

Indojavanese programmer." She hunched forward and held out her hand again. "Look here." Deke cringed. "No, no, it's okay, I swear it, this is different." She opened her hand.

A single blue flame danced there, perfect and ever-changing. "Look at that," she marveled. "Just look. I programmed that. It's not some diddly little seven-image job either. It's a continuous two-hour loop, seven thousand, two hundred seconds, never the same twice, each instant as individual as a fucking snowflake!"

The flame's core was glacial crystal, shards and facets flashing up, twisting and gone, leaving behind near-subliminal images so bright and sharp that they cut the eye. Deke winced. People mostly. Pretty little naked people, fucking. "How the hell did you do that?"

She rose, bare feet slipping on slick magazines, and melodramatically swept folds of loose printout from a raw plywood shelf. He saw a neat row of small consoles, austere and expensive-looking. Custom work. "This is the real stuff I got here. Image facilitator. Here's my fast-wipe module. This is a brainmap one-to-one function analyzer." She sang off the names like a litany. "Quantum flicker stabilizer. Program splicer. An image assembler . . ."

"You need all that to make one little flame?"

"You betcha. This is all state of the art, professional projective wetware gear. It's years ahead of anything you've seen."

"Hey," he said, "you know anything about SPADS & FOKKERS?"

She laughed. And then, because he sensed the time was right, he reached out to take her hand.

"Don't you touch me, motherfuck, don't you *ever touch me!*" Nance screamed, and her head slammed against the wall as she recoiled, white and shaking with terror.

"Okay!" He threw up his hands. "Okay! I'm nowhere near you. Okay?"

She cowered from him. Her eyes were round and unblinking; tears built up at the corners, rolled down ashen cheeks. Finally, she shook her head. "Hey, Deke. Sorry. I should've told you."

"Told me what?" But he had a creepy feeling . . . already knew. The way she clutched her head. The weakly spasmodic way her hands opened and closed. "You got a brainlock, too."

"Yeah." She closed her eyes. "It's a chastity lock. My asshole parents paid for it. So I can't stand to have anybody touch me or even stand too close." Eyes opened in blind hate. "I didn't even *do* anything. Not a fucking thing. But they've both got jobs and they're so horny for me to have a career that they can't piss straight. They're afraid I'd neglect my studies if I got, you know, involved in sex and stuff. The day the brainlock comes off I am going to fuck the vilest, greasiest, hairiest . . ."

She was clutching her head again. Deke jumped up and rummaged through the medicine cabinet. He found a jar of B-complex vitamins, pocketed a few against need, and brought two to Nance, with a glass of water. "Here." He was careful to keep his distance. "This'll take the edge off."

"Yeah, yeah," she said. Then, almost to herself, "You must really think I'm a jerk."

THE GAMES ROOM in the Greyhound station was almost empty. A lone, long-jawed fourteen-year-old was bent over a console, maneuvering rainbow fleets of submarines in the murky grid of the North Atlantic.

Deke sauntered in, wearing his new kicker drag, and leaned against a cinder-block wall made smooth by countless coats of green enamel. He'd washed the dye from his proleboy butch, boosted jeans and T-shirt from the Goodwill, and found a pair of stompers in the sauna locker of a highstack with cutrate security.

"Seen Tiny around, friend?"

The subs darted like neon guppies. "Depends on who's asking."

Deke touched the remote behind his left ear. The Spad snap-rolled over the console, swift and delicate as a dragonfly. It was beautiful; so perfect, so *true* it made the room seem an illusion. He buzzed the grid, millimeters from the glass, taking advantage of the programmed ground effect.

The kid didn't even bother to look up. "Jackman's," he said. "Down Richmond Road, over by the surplus."

Deke let the Spad fade in midclimb.

Jackman's took up most of the third floor of an old brick building. Deke found Best Buy War Surplus first, then a broken neon sign over an unlit lobby. The sidewalk out front was littered with another kind of surplus—damaged vets, some of them dating back to Indochina. Old men who'd left their eyes under Asian suns squatted beside twitching boys who'd inhaled mycotoxins in Chile. Deke was glad to have the battered elevator doors sigh shut behind him.

A dusty Dr. Pepper clock at the far side of the long, spectral room told him it was a quarter to eight. Jackman's had been embalmed twenty years before he was born, sealed away behind a yellowish film of nicotine, of polish and hair oil. Directly beneath the clock, the flat eyes of somebody's grandpappy's prize buck regarded Deke from a framed, blown-up snapshot gone the slick sepia of cockroach wings. There was the click and whisper of pool, the squeak of a work boot twisting on linoleum as a player leaned in for a shot. Somewhere high above the green-shaded lamps hung a string of crepe-paper Christmas bells faded to dead rose. Deke looked from one cluttered wall to the next. No facilitator.

"Bring one in, should we need it," someone said. He turned, meeting the mild eyes of a bald man with steel-rimmed glasses. "My name's Cline. Bobby Earl. You don't look like you shoot pool, mister." But there was nothing threatening in Bobby Earl's voice or stance. He pinched the steel frames from his nose and polished the thick lenses with a fold of tissue. He reminded Deke of a shop instructor who'd patiently tried to teach him retrograde biochip installation. "I'm a gambler," he said, smiling. His teeth were white plastic. "I know I don't much look it."

"I'm looking for Tiny," Deke said.

"Well," replacing the glasses, "you're not going to find him. He's gone up to Bethesda to let the V.A. clean his plumbing for him. He wouldn't fly against you any how."

"Why not?"

"Well, because you're not on the circuit or I'd know your face. You any good?" When Deke nodded, Bobby Earl called down the length of Jackman's, "Yo, Clarence! You bring out that facilitator. We got us a flyboy."

Twenty minutes later, having lost his remote and what cash he had left, Deke was striding past the broken soldiers of Best Buy.

"Now you let me tell you, boy," Bobby Earl had said in a fatherly tone as, hand on shoulder, he led Deke back to the elevator. "You're not going to win against a combat vet—you listening to me? I'm not even especially good, just an old grunt who was on hype fifteen, maybe twenty times. Ol' Tiny, he was a *pilot*. Spent his entire enlistment hyped to the gills. He's got membrane attenuation real bad . . . you ain't never going to beat him."

It was a cool night. But Deke burned with anger and humiliation.

"JESUS, THAT'S CRUDE," Nance said as the Spad strafed mounds of pink underwear. Deke, hunched up on the couch, yanked her flashy little Braun remote from behind his ear.

"Now don't you get on my case too, Miss rich-bitch gonna-have-a-job—"

"Hey, lighten up! It's nothing to do with you—it's just *tech*. That's a really primitive wafer you got there. I mean, on the street maybe it's fine. But compared to the work I do at school, it's—hey. You ought to let me rewrite it for you."

"Say what?"

"Lemme beef it up. These suckers are all written in hexadecimal, see, 'cause the industry programmers are all washed-out computer hacks. That's how they think. But let me take it to the reader-analyzer at the department, run a few changes on it, translate it into a modern wetlanguage. Edit out all the redundant intermediaries. That'll goose up your reaction time, cut the feedback loop in half. So you'll fly faster and better. Turn you into a real pro, Ace!" She took a hit off her bong, then doubled over laughing and choking.

"Is that legit?" Deke asked dubiously.

"Hey, why do you think people buy gold-wire remotes? For the prestige? Shit. Conductivity's better, cuts a few nanoseconds off the reaction time. And reaction time is the name of the game, kiddo."

"No," Deke said. "If it were that easy, people'd already have it. Tiny Montgomery would have it. He'd have the best."

"Don't you ever *listen*?" Nance set down the bong; brown water slopped onto the floor. "The stuff I'm working with is three years ahead of anything you'll find on the street."

"No shit," Deke said after a long pause. "I mean, you can do that?"

IT WAS LIKE graduating from a Model T to a ninety-three Lotus. The Spad handled like a dream, responsive to Deke's slightest thought. For weeks he played the arcades, with not a nibble. He flew against the local teens and by ones and threes shot down their planes. He took chances, played flash. And the planes tumbled. . . .

Until one day Deke was tucking his seed money away, and a lanky black straightened up from the wall. He eyed the laminateds in Deke's hand and grinned. A ruby tooth gleamed. "You know," the man said, "I *heard* there was a casper who could fly, going up against the kiddies."

"JESUS," DEKE SAID, spreading Danish butter on a kelp stick. "I wiped the *floor* with those spades. They were good, too."

"That's nice, honey," Nance mumbled. She was working on her finals project, sweating data into a machine.

"You know, I think what's happening is I got real talent for this kind of shit. You know? I mean, the program gives me an edge, but I got the stuff to take advantage of it. I'm really getting a rep out there, you know?" Impulsively, he snapped on the radio. Scratchy Dixieland brass blared.

"Hey," Nance said. "Do you *mind*?"

"No, I'm just—" He fiddled with the knobs, came up with some slow, romantic bullshit. "There. Come on, stand up. Let's dance."

"Hey, you know I can't—"

"Sure you can, sugarcakes." He threw her the huge teddy bear and snatched up a patchwork cotton dress from the floor. He held it by the waist and sleeve, tucking the collar under his chin. It smelled of patchouli, more faintly of sweat. "See, I stand over here, you stand over there. We dance. Get it?"

Blinking softly, Nance stood and clutched the bear tightly. They danced then, slowly, staring into each other's eyes. After a while, she began to cry. But still, she was smiling.

DEKE WAS DAYDREAMING, imagining he was Tiny Montgomery wired into his jumpjet. Imagined the machine responding to his slightest neural twitch, reflexes cranked *way* up, hype flowing steadily into his veins.

Nance's floor became jungle, her bed a plateau in the Andean foothills, and Deke flew his Spad at forced speed, as if it were a full-wired interactive combat machine. Computerized hypos fed a slow trickle of high-performance enhancement mélange into his bloodstream. Sensors were wired directly into his skull—pulling a supersonic snapturn in the green-blue bowl of sky over Bolivian rain forest. Tiny would have *felt* the airflow over control surfaces.

Below, grunts hacked through the jungle with hype-pumps strapped above elbows to give them that little extra death-dance fury in combat, a shot of liquid hell in a blue plastic vial. Maybe they got ten minutes' worth in a week. But coming in at treetop level, reflexes cranked to the max, flying so low the ground troops never spotted you until you were on them, phosgene agents released, away and gone before they could draw a bead . . . it took a constant trickle of hype just to maintain. And the direct neuron interface with the jumpjet was a two-way street. The onboard computers monitored biochemistry and decided when to open the sluice gates and give the human component a killer jolt of combat edge.

Dosages like that ate you up. Ate you good and slow and constant, etching the brain surfaces, eroding away the brain-cell membranes. If you weren't yanked from the air promptly enough, you ended up with brain-cell attenuation—with reflexes too fast for your body to handle and your fight-or-flight reflexes fucked real good. . . .

"I aced it, proleboy!"

"Hah?" Deke looked up, startled, as Nance slammed in, tossing books and bag onto the nearest heap.

"My finals project—I got exempted from exams. The prof said he'd never seen anything like it. Uh, hey, dim the lights, wouldja? The colors are weird on my eyes."

He obliged. "So show me. Show me this wunnerful thing."

"Yeah, okay." She snatched up his remote, kicked clear standing space atop the bed, and struck a pose. A spark flared into flame in her hand. It spread in a quicksilver line up her arm, around her neck, and it was a snake, with triangular head and flickering tongue. Molten colors, oranges and reds. It slithered between her breasts. "I call it a firesnake," she said proudly.

Deke leaned close, and she jerked back.

"Sorry. It's like your flame, huh? I mean, I can see these tiny little fuckers in it."

"Sort of." The firesnake flowed down her stomach. "Next month I'm going to splice two hundred separate flame programs together with meld justification in between to get the visuals. Then I'll tap the mind's body image to make it self-orienting. So it can crawl all over your body without your having to mind it. You could wear it dancing."

"Maybe I'm dumb. But if you haven't done the work yet, how come I can see it?"

Nance giggled. "That's the best part—half the work isn't done yet. Didn't have the time to assemble the pieces into a unified program. Turn on that radio, huh? I want to dance." She kicked off her shoes. Deke tuned in something gutsy. Then, at Nance's urging, turned it down, almost to a whisper.

"I scored two hits of hype, see." She was bouncing on the bed, weaving her hands like a Balinese dancer. "Ever try the stuff? In-credible. Gives you like absolute concentration. Look here." She stood *en pointe*. "Never done that before."

"Hype," Deke said. "Last person I heard of got caught with that shit got three years in the infantry. How'd you score it?"

"Cut a deal with a vet who was in grad school. She bombed out last month. Stuff gives me perfect visualization. I can hold the projection with my eyes shut. It was a snap assembling the program in my head."

"On just two hits, huh?"

"One hit. I'm saving the other. Teach was so impressed he's sponsoring me for a job interview. A recruiter from I. G. Feuchtwaren hits campus in two weeks. That cap is gonna sell him the program *and* me. I'm gonna cut out of school two years early, straight into industry, do not pass jail, do not pay two hundred dollars."

The snake curled into a flaming tiara. It gave Deke a funny-creepy feeling to think of Nance walking out of his life.

"I'm a witch," Nance sang, "a wetware witch." She shucked her shirt over her head and sent it flying. Her fine, high breasts moved freely, gracefully, as she danced. "I'm gonna make it"—now she was singing a current pop hit—"to the . . . top!" Her nipples were small and pink and aroused. The firesnake licked at them and whipped away.

"Hey, Nance," Deke said uncomfortably. "Calm down a little, huh?"

"I'm celebrating!" She hooked a thumb into her shiny gold panties. Fire swirled around hand and crotch. "I'm the virgin goddess, baby, and I have the pow-er!" Singing again.

Deke looked away. "Gotta go now," he mumbled. Gotta go home and jerk off. He wondered where she'd hidden that second hit. Could be anywhere.

THERE WAS A protocol to the circuit, a tacit order of deference and precedence as elaborate as that of a Mandarin court. It didn't matter that Deke was hot, that his rep was spreading like wildfire. Even a name flyboy couldn't just challenge whom he wished. He had to climb the ranks. But if you flew every night. If you were always available to anybody's challenge. And if you were good . . . well, it was possible to climb fast.

Deke was one plane up. It was tournament fighting, three planes against three. Not many spectators, a dozen maybe, but it was a good fight, and they were noisy. Deke was immersed in the manic calm of combat when he realized suddenly that they had fallen silent. Saw the kickers stir and exchange glances. Eyes flicked past him. He heard the elevator doors close. Coolly, he disposed of the second of his opponent's planes, then risked a quick glance over his shoulder.

Tiny Montgomery had just entered Jackman's. The wheelchair whispered across browning linoleum, guided by tiny twitches of one imperfectly paralyzed hand. His expression was stern, blank, calm.

In that instant, Deke lost two planes. One to deresolution—gone to blur and canceled out by the facilitator—and the other because his opponent was a real fighter. Guy did a barrel roll, killing speed and slipping to the side, and strafed Deke's biplane as it shot past. It went down in flames. Their last two planes shared altitude and speed, and as they turned, trying for position, they naturally fell into a circling pattern.

The kickers made room as Tiny wheeled up against the table. Bobby Earl Cline trailed after him, lanky and casual. Deke and his opponent traded glances and pulled their machines back from the pool table so they could hear the man out. Tiny smiled. His features were small, clustered in the center of his pale, doughy face. One finger twitched slightly on the chrome handrest. "I heard about you." He looked straight at Deke. His voice was soft and shockingly sweet, a baby-girl little voice. "I heard you're good."

Deke nodded slowly. The smile left Tiny's face. His soft, fleshy lips relaxed into a natural pout, as if he were waiting for a kiss. His small, bright eyes studied Deke without malice. "Let's see what you can do, then."

Deke lost himself in the cool game of war. And when the enemy went down in smoke and flame, to explode and vanish against the table, Tiny wordlessly turned his chair, wheeled it into the elevator, and was gone.

As Deke was gathering up his winnings, Bobby Earl eased up to him and said, "The man wants to play you."

"Yeah?" Deke was nowhere near high enough on the circuit to challenge Tiny. "What's the scam?"

"Man who was coming up from Atlanta tomorrow canceled. Ol' Tiny, he was spoiling to go up against somebody new. So it looks like you get your shot at the Max."

"Tomorrow? Wednesday? Doesn't give me much prep time."

Bobby Earl smiled gently. "I don't think that makes no nevermind."

"How's that, Mr. Cline?"

"Boy, you just ain't got the *moves*, you follow me? Ain't got no surprises. You fly just like some kinda beginner, only faster and slicker. You follow what I'm trying to say?"

"I'm not sure I do. You want to put a little action on that?"

"Tell you truthful," Cline said, "I been hoping on that." He drew a small black notebook from his pocket and licked a pencil stub. "Give you five to one. They's nobody gonna give no fairer odds than that."

He looked at Deke almost sadly. "But Tiny, he's just naturally better'n you, and that's all she wrote, boy. He lives for that goddamned game, ain't *got* nothing else. Can't get out of that goddamned chair. You think you can best a man who's fighting for his life, you are just lying to yourself."

NORMAN ROCKWELL'S PORTRAIT of the colonel regarded Deke dispassionately from the Kentucky Fried across Richmond Road from the coffee bar. Deke held his cup with hands that were cold and trembling. His skull hummed with fatigue. Cline was right, he told the colonel. I can go up against Tiny, but I can't win. The colonel stared back, gaze calm and level and not particularly kindly, taking in the coffee bar and Best Buy and all his drag-ass kingdom of Richmond Road. Waiting for Deke to admit to the terrible thing he had to do.

"The bitch is planning to leave me *anyway*," Deke said aloud. Which made the black countergirl look at him funny, then quickly away.

"DADDY CALLED!" NANCE danced into the apartment, slamming the door behind her. "And you know what? He says if I can get this job and hold it for six months, he'll have the brainlock reversed. Can you *believe* it? Deke?" She hesitated. "You okay?"

Deke stood. Now that the moment was on him, he felt unreal, like he was in a movie or something. "How come you never came home last night?" Nance asked.

The skin on his face was unnaturally taut, a parchment mask. "Where'd you stash the hype, Nance? I need it."

"Deke," she said, trying a tentative smile that instantly vanished. "Deke, that's mine. My hit. I need it. For my interview."

He smiled scornfully. "You got money. You can always score another cap."

"Not by Friday! Listen, Deke, this is really important. My whole life is riding on this interview. I need that cap. It's all I got!"

"Baby, you got the fucking world! Take a look around you—six ounces of blond Lebanese hash! Little anchovy fish in tins. Unlimited medical coverage, if you need it." She was backing away from him, stumbling against the static waves of unwashed bedding and wrinkled glossy magazines that crested at the foot of her bed. "Me, I never had a glimmer of any of this. Never had the kind of edge it takes to get along. Well, this one time I am gonna. There is a match in two hours that I am going to fucking well win. Do you hear me?" He was working himself into a rage, and that was good. He needed it for what he had to do.

Nance flung up an arm, palm open, but he was ready for that and slapped her hand aside, never even catching a glimpse of the dark tunnel, let alone those little red eyes. Then they were both falling, and he was on top of her, her breath hot and rapid in his face. "Deke! Deke! I *need* that shit, Deke, my *interview*, it's the only . . .

I gotta ... gotta ..." She twisted her face away ... crying into the wall. "Please, God, please don't ..."

"Where did you stash it?"

Pinned against the bed under his body, Nance began to spasm, her entire body convulsing in pain and fear.

"Where is it?"

Her face was bloodless, gray corpse flesh, and horror burned in her eyes. Her lips squirmed. It was too late to stop now; he'd crossed over the line. Deke felt revolted and nauseated, all the more so because on some unexpected and unwelcome level, he was *enjoying* this.

"Where is it, Nance?" And slowly, very gently, he began to stroke her face.

DEKE SUMMONED JACKMAN'S elevator with a finger that moved as fast and straight as a hornet and landed daintily as a butterfly on the call button. He was full of bouncy energy, and it was all under control. On the way up, he whipped off his shades and chuckled at his reflection in the finger-smudged chrome. The blacks of his eyes were like pinpricks, all but invisible, and still the world was neon bright.

Tiny was waiting. The cripple's mouth turned up at the corners into a sweet smile as he took in Deke's irises, the exaggerated calm of his motions, the unsuccessful attempt to mime an undrugged clumsiness. "Well," he said in that girlish voice, "looks like I have a treat in store for me."

The Max was draped over one tube of the wheelchair. Deke took up position and bowed, not quite mockingly. "Let's fly." As challenger, he flew defense. He materialized his planes at a conservative altitude, high enough to dive, low enough to have warning when Tiny attacked. He waited.

The crowd tipped him. A fatboy with brilliantined hair looked startled, a hollow-eyed cracker started to smile. Murmurs rose. Eyes shifted slow-motion in heads frozen by hyped-up reaction time. Took maybe three nanoseconds to pinpoint the source of attack. Deke whipped his head up, and—

Sonofabitch, he was *blind!* The Fokkers were diving straight from the two-hundred-watt bulb, and Tiny had suckered him into staring right at it. His vision whited out. Deke squeezed lids tight over welling tears and frantically held visualization. He split his flight, curving two biplanes right, one left. Immediately twisting each a half-turn, then back again. He had to dodge randomly—he couldn't tell where the hostile warbirds were.

Tiny chuckled. Deke could hear him through the sounds of the crowd, the cheering and cursing and slapping down of coins that seemed to syncopate independent of the ebb and flow of the duel.

When his vision returned an instant later, a Spad was in flames and falling.

Fokkers tailed his surviving planes, one on one and two on the other. Three seconds into the game and he was down one.

Dodging to keep Tiny from pinning tracers on him, he looped the single-pursued plane about and drove the other toward the blind spot between Tiny and the light bulb.

Tiny's expression went very calm. The faintest shadow of disappointment—of contempt, even—was swallowed up by tranquility. He tracked the planes blandly, waiting for Deke to make his turn.

Then, just short of the blind spot, Deke shoved his Spad into a drive, the Fokkers overshooting and banking wildly to either side, twisting around to regain position.

The Spad swooped down on the third Fokker, pulled into position by Deke's other plane. Fire strafed wings and crimson fuselage. For an instant nothing happened, and Deke thought he had a fluke miss. Then the little red mother veered left and went down, trailing black, oily smoke.

Tiny frowned, small lines of displeasure marring the perfection of his mouth. Deke smiled. One even, and Tiny held position.

Both Spads were tailed closely. Deke swung them wide, and then pulled them together from opposite sides of the table. He drove them straight for each other, neutralizing Tiny's advantage . . . neither could fire without endangering his own planes. Deke cranked his machines up to top speed, slamming them at each other's nose.

An instant before they crashed, Deke sent the planes over and under one another, opening fire on the Fokkers and twisting away. Tiny was ready. Fire filled the air. Then one blue and one red plane soared free, heading in opposite directions. Behind them, two biplanes tangled in midair. Wings touched, slewed about, and the planes crumpled. They fell together, almost straight down, to the green felt below.

Ten seconds in and four planes down. A black vet pursed his lips and blew softly. Someone else shook his head in disbelief.

Tiny was sitting straight and a little forward in his wheelchair, eyes intense and unblinking, soft hands plucking feebly at the grips. None of that amused and detached bullshit now; his attention was riveted on the game. The kickers, the table, Jackman's itself, might not exist at all for him. Bobby Earl Cline laid a hand on his shoulder; Tiny didn't notice. The planes were at opposite ends of the room, laboriously gaining altitude. Deke jammed his against the ceiling, dim through the smoky haze. He spared Tiny a quick glance, and their eyes locked. Cold against cold. "Let's see your best," Deke muttered through clenched teeth.

They drove their planes together.

The hype was peaking now, and Deke could see Tiny's tracers crawling through the air between the planes. He had to put his Spad into the line of fire to get off a fair burst, then twist and bank so the Fokker's bullets would slip by his undercarriage.

Tiny was every bit as hot, dodging Deke's fire and passing so close to the Spad their landing gears almost tangled as they passed.

Deke was looping his Spad in a punishingly tight turn when the hallucinations hit. The felt writhed and twisted—became the green hell of Bolivian rain forest that Tiny had flown combat over. The walls receded to gray infinity, and he felt the metal confinement of a cybernetic jumpjet close in around him.

But Deke had done his homework. He was expecting the hallucinations and knew he could deal with them. The military would never pass on a drug that couldn't be fought through. Spad and Fokker looped into another pass. He could read the tensions in Tiny Montgomery's face, the echoes of combat in deep jungle sky. They drove their planes together, feeling the torqued tensions that fed straight from instrumentation to hindbrain, the adrenaline pumps kicking in behind the armpits, the cold, fast freedom of airflow over jetskin mingling with the smells of hot metal and fear sweat. Tracers tore past his face, and he pulled back, seeing the Spad zoom by the Fokker again, both untouched. The kickers were just going ape, waving hats and stomping feet, acting like God's own fools. Deke locked glances with Tiny again.

Malice rose up in him, and though his every nerve was taut as the carbon-crystal whiskers that kept the jumpjets from falling apart in superman turns over the Andes, he counterfeited a casual smile and winked, jerking his head slightly to one side, as if to say "Looka here."

Tiny glanced to the side.

It was only for a fraction of a second, but that was enough. Deke pulled as fast and tight an Immelmann—right on the edge of theoretical tolerance—as had ever been seen on the circuit, and he was hanging on Tiny's tail.

Let's see you get out of this one, sucker.

Tiny rammed his plane straight down at the green, and Deke followed after. He held his fire. He had Tiny where he wanted him.

Running. Just like he'd been on his every combat mission. High on exhilaration and hype, maybe, but running scared. They were down to the felt now, flying treetop-level. Break, Deke thought, and jacked up the speed. Peripherally, he could see Bobby Earl Cline, and there was a funny look on the man's face. A pleading kind of look. Tiny's composure was shot; his face was twisted and tormented.

Now Tiny panicked and dove his plane in among the crowd. The biplanes looped and twisted between the kickers. Some jerked back involuntarily, and others laughingly swatted at them with their hands. But there was a hot glint of terror in Tiny's eyes that spoke of an eternity of fear and confinement, two edges sawing away at each other endlessly. . . .

The fear was death in the air, the confinement a locking away in metal, first of the aircraft, then of the chair. Deke could read it all in his face: Combat was the only out Tiny had had, and he'd taken it every chance he got. Until some anonymous *nationalista* with an antique SAM tore him out of that blue-green Bolivian sky and slammed him straight down to Richmond Road and Jackman's and the smiling killer boy he faced this one last time across the faded cloth.

Deke rocked up on his toes, face burning with that million-dollar smile that was the trademark of the drug that had already fried Tiny before anyone ever bothered to blow him out of the sky in a hot tangle of metal and mangled flesh. It all came together then. He saw that flying was all that held Tiny together. That daily brush of fingertips against death, and then rising up from the metal coffin, alive again. He'd been holding back collapse by sheer force of will. Break that willpower, and mortality would come pouring out and drown him. Tiny would lean over and throw up in his own lap.

AND DEKE DROVE it home. . . .

There was a moment of stunned silence as Tiny's last plane vanished in a flash of light. "I did it," Deke whispered. Then, louder, "Son of a bitch, I did it!"

Across the table from him, Tiny twisted in his chair, arms jerking spastically; his head lolled over on one shoulder. Behind him, Bobby Earl Cline stared straight at Deke, his eyes hot coals.

The gambler snatched up the Max and wrapped its ribbon around a stack of laminateds. Without warning, he flung the bundle at Deke's face. Effortlessly, casually, Deke plucked it from the air.

For an instant, then, it looked like the gambler would come at him, right across the pool table. He was stopped by a tug on his sleeve. "Bobby Earl," Tiny whispered, his voice choking with humiliation, "you gotta get me . . . out of here. . . ."

Stiffly, angrily, Cline wheeled his friend around, and then away, into shadow.

Deke threw back his head and laughed. By God, he felt good! He stuffed the Max into a shirt pocket, where it hung cold and heavy. The money he crammed into his jeans. Man, he had to jump with it, his triumph leaping up through him like a wild thing, fine and strong as the flanks of a buck in the deep woods he'd seen from a Greyhound once, and for this one moment it seemed that everything was worth it somehow, all the pain and misery he'd gone through to finally win.

But Jackman's was silent. Nobody cheered. Nobody crowded around to congratulate him. He sobered, and silent, hostile faces swam into focus. Not one of these kickers was on his side. They radiated contempt, even hatred. For an interminably drawn-out moment the air trembled with potential violence . . . and then someone turned to the side, hawked up phlegm, and spat on the floor. The crowd broke up, muttering, one by one drifting into the darkness.

Deke didn't move. A muscle in one leg began to twitch, harbinger of the coming hype crash. The top of his head felt numb, and there was an awful taste in his mouth. For a second he had to hang on to the table with both hands to keep from falling down forever, into the living shadow beneath him, as he hung impaled by the prize buck's dead eyes in the photo under the Dr. Pepper clock.

A little adrenaline would pull him out of this. He needed to celebrate. To get drunk or stoned and talk it up, going over the victory time and again, contradicting himself, making up details, laughing and bragging. A starry old night like this called for big talk.

But standing there with all of Jackman's silent and vast and empty around him, he realized suddenly that he had nobody left to tell it to.

Nobody at all.

Face Value

Science fiction is just one of several "dialects" Karen Joy Fowler uses to tell her colorful, emotionally rich tales of human relationships. Fowler began writing science fiction in 1986, and initially concentrated on short stories, many of which have been collected in *Artificial Things* (which won her the John W. Campbell Award for Best New Writer), *Letters from Home* (featuring stories by her and by Pat Cadigan), and *Black Glass*. Her stories are filled with characters who find their lack of personal fulfillment and emotional crises objectified in fantastical situations. "Face Value" juxtaposes a failing love relationship with the study of an inscrutable alien culture on another planet. In "Lieserl," Albert Einstein receives a set of cryptic letters that recount the life of his daughter in compressed fashion as he is formulating his theory of special relativity. "The Lake Was Full of Artificial Things" is a powerful meditation on the Vietnam War in which a woman's use of artificial means to reclaim the memory of a boyfriend killed in the war forces her to confront her own shortcomings in her treatment of him. Fowler's three novels are period stories that explore the universality of personal and social relations. *Sarah Canary* is a memorable variation on the theme of first contact in which the efforts of an alien in human female form to integrate with American society in the Northwest frontier in 1873 illuminate the plight of other social groups disenfranchised on the basis of gender and race. Fowler has also written the mainstream novels *The Sweetheart Season* and *Sister Noon*.

IT WAS ALMOST like being alone. Taki, who had been alone one way or another most of his life, recognized this and thought he could deal with it. What choice did he have? It was only that he had allowed himself to hope for something different. A second star, small and dim, joined the sun in the sky, making its appearance over the rope bridge which spanned the empty river. Taki crossed the bridge in a hurry to get inside before the hottest part of the day began.

Something flashed briefly in the dust at his feet and he stooped to pick it up. It was one of Hesper's poems, half finished, left out all night. Taki had stopped reading Hesper's poetry. It reflected nothing, not a whisper of her life here with him, but was filled with longing for things and people behind her. Taki pocketed the poem on his way to the house, stood outside the door, and removed what dust he could with the stiff brush which hung at the entrance. He keyed his admittance; the door made a slight sucking sound as it resealed behind him.

Hesper had set out an iced glass of ade for him. Taki drank it at a gulp, superimposing his own dusty fingerprints over hers sketched lightly in the condensation on the glass. The drink was heavily sugared and only made him thirstier.

A cloth curtain separated one room from another, a blue sheet, Hesper's innovation since the dwelling was designed as a single, multifunctional space. Through the curtain Taki heard a voice and knew Hesper was listening again to her mother's letter—earth weather, the romances of her younger cousins. The letter had arrived weeks ago, but Taki was careful not to remind Hesper how old its news really was. If she chose to imagine the lives of her family moving along the same timeline as her own, then this must be a fantasy she needed. She knew the truth. In the time it had taken her to travel here with Taki, her mother had grown old and died. Her cousins had settled into marriages happy or unhappy or had faced life alone. The letters which continued to arrive with some regularity were an illusion. A lifetime later Hesper would answer them.

Taki ducked through the curtain to join her. "Hot," he told her as if this were news. She lay on their mat stomach down, legs bent at the knees, feet crossed in the air. Her hair, the color of dried grasses, hung over her face. Taki stared for a moment at the back of her head. "Here," he said. He pulled her poem from his pocket and laid it by her hand. "I found this out front."

Hesper switched off the letter and rolled onto her back away from the poem. She was careful not to look at Taki. Her cheeks were stained with irregular red patches so that Taki knew she had been crying again. The observation caused him a familiar mixture of sympathy and impatience. His feelings for Hesper always came in these uncomfortable combinations; it tired him.

" 'Out front,' " Hesper repeated, and her voice held a practiced tone of uninterested nastiness. "And how did you determine that one part of this featureless landscape was the 'front'?"

"Because of the door. We have only the one door so it's the front door."

"No," said Hesper. "If we had two doors then one might arguably be the front door and the other the back door, but with only one it's just the door." Her gaze went straight upward. "You use words so carelessly. Words from another world. They mean nothing here." Her eyelids fluttered briefly, the lashes darkened with tears. "It's not just an annoyance to me, you know," she said. "It can't help but damage your work."

"My work is the study of the mene," Taki answered. "Not the creation of a new language," and Hesper's eyes closed.

"I really don't see the difference," she told him. She lay a moment longer without moving, then opened her eyes and looked at Taki directly. "I don't want to have this conversation. I don't know why I started it. Let's rewind, run it again. I'll be the wife this time. You come in and say, 'Honey, I'm home!' and I'll ask you how your morning was."

Taki began to suggest that this was a scene from another world and would mean nothing here. He had not yet framed the sentence when he heard the door seal release and saw Hesper's face go hard and white. She reached for her poem and slid it under the scarf at her waist. Before she could get to her feet the first of the mene had joined them in the bedroom. Taki ducked through the curtain to fasten the door before the temperature inside the house rose. The outer room was filled with dust and the hands which reached out to him as he went past left dusty streaks on his clothes and his skin. He counted eight of the mene, fluttering about him like large moths, moths the size of human children, but with furry vestigial wings, hourglass abdomens, sticklike limbs. They danced about him in the open spaces, looked through the cupboards, pulled the tapes from his desk. When they had their backs to him he could see the symmetrical arrangement of dark spots which marked their wings in a pattern resembling a human face. A very sad face, very distinct. Masculine, Taki had always thought, but Hesper disagreed.

The party which had made initial contact under the leadership of Hans Mene so many years ago had wisely found the faces too whimsical for mention in their report. Instead they had included pictures and allowed them to speak for themselves. Perhaps the original explorers had been asking the same question Hesper posed the first time Taki showed her the pictures. Was the face really there? Or was this only evidence of the ability of humans to see their own faces in everything? Hesper had a poem entitled "The Kitchen God," which recounted the true story of a woman about a century ago who had found the image of Christ in the burn-marks on a tortilla. "Do *they* see it, too?" she had asked Taki, but there was as yet no way to ask this of the mene, no way to know if they had reacted with shock and recognition to the faces of the first humans they had seen, though studies of the mene eye suggested a finer depth perception which might significantly distort the flat image.

Taki thought that Hesper's own face had changed since the day, only six months ago calculated as Traveltime, when she had said she would come here with him and he thought it was because she loved him. They had sorted through all the information which had been collected to date on the mene and her face had been all sympathy then. "What would it be like," she asked him, "to be able to fly and then to lose this ability? To outgrow it? What would a loss like that do to the racial consciousness of a species?"

"It happened so long ago, I doubt it's even noticed as a loss," Taki had answered.

"Legends, myths not really believed perhaps. Probably not even that. In the racial memory not even a whisper."

Hesper had ignored him. "What a shame they don't write poetry," she had said. She was finding them less romantic now as she joined Taki in the outer room, her face stoic. The mene surrounded her, ran their string-fingered hands all over her body, inside her clothing. One mene attempted to insert a finger into her mouth, but Hesper tightened her lips together resolutely, dust on her chin. Her eyes were fastened on Taki. Accusingly? Beseechingly? Taki was no good at reading people's eyes. He looked away.

Eventually the mene grew bored. They left in groups, a few lingering behind to poke among the boxes in the bedroom, then following the others until Hesper and Taki were left alone. Hesper went to wash herself as thoroughly as their limited water supply allowed; Taki swept up the loose dust. Before he finished, Hesper returned, showing him her empty jewelry box without a word. The jewelry had all belonged to her mother.

"I'll get them when it cools," Taki told her.

"Thank you."

It was always Hesper's things that the mene took. The more they disgusted her, pawing over her, rummaging through her things, no way to key the door against clever mene fingers even if Taki had agreed to lock them out, which he had not, the more fascinating they seemed to find her. They touched her twice as often as they touched Taki and much more insistently. They took her jewelry, her poems, her letters, all the things she treasured most, and Taki believed, although it was far too early in his studies really to speculate with any assurance, that the mene read something off the objects. The initial explorers had concluded that mene communication was entirely telepathic, and if this was accurate, then Taki's speculation was not such a leap. Certainly the mene didn't value the objects for themselves. Taki always found them discarded in the dust on this side of the rope bridge.

The fact that everything would be easily recovered did nothing to soften Hesper's sense of invasion. She mixed herself a drink, stirring it with the metal straw which poked through the dust-proof lid. "You shouldn't allow it," she said at last, and Taki knew from the time that had elapsed that she had tried not to begin this familiar conversation. He appreciated her effort as much as he was annoyed by her failure.

"It's part of my job," he reminded her. "We have to be accessible to them. I study them. They study us. There's no way to differentiate the two activities and certainly no way to establish communication except simultaneously."

"You're letting them study us, but you're giving them a false picture. You're allowing them to believe that humans intrude on each other in this way. Does it occur to you that they may be involved in similar charades? If so, what can either of us learn?"

Taki took a deep breath. "The need for privacy may not be as intrinsically human as you imagine. I could point to many societies which afforded very little of this. As for any deliberate misrepresentations on their part—well, isn't that the whole rationale for not sending a study team? Wouldn't I be farther along if I were working with environmentalists, physiologists, linguists? But the risk of contamination increases exponentially with each additional human. We would be too much of a presence. Of course, I will be very careful. I am far from the stage in my study where I can begin to draw conclusions. When I visit them . . ."

"Reinforcing the notion that such visits are ordinary human behavior . . ." Hesper was looking at Taki with great coolness.

"When I visit them I am much more circumspect," Taki finished. "I conduct my study as unobtrusively as possible."

"And what do you imagine you are studying?" Hesper asked. She closed her lips tightly over the straw and drank. Taki regarded her steadily and with exasperation.

"Is this a trick question?" he asked. "I imagine I am studying the mene. What do you imagine I am studying?"

"What humans always study," said Hesper. "Humans."

YOU NEVER SAW one of the mene alone. Not ever. One never wandered off to watch the sun set or took its food to a solitary hole to eat without sharing. They did everything in groups and although Taki had been observing them for weeks now and was able to identify individuals and had compiled charts of the groupings he had seen, trying to isolate families or friendships or work-castes, still the results were inconclusive.

His attempts at communication were similarly discouraging. He had tried verbalizations, but had not expected a response to them; he had no idea how they processed audio information although they could hear. He had tried clapping and gestures, simple hand signals for the names of common objects. He had no sense that these efforts were noticed. They were so unfocused when he dealt with them, fluttering here, fluttering there. Taki's ESP quotient had never been measurable, yet he tried that route, too. He tried to send a simple command. He would trap a mene hand and hold it against his own cheek, trying to form in his mind the picture which corresponded to the action. When he released the hand, sticky mene fingers might linger for a moment or they might slip away immediately, tangle in his hair instead, or tap his teeth. Mene teeth were tiny and pointed like wires. Taki saw them only when the mene ate. At other times they were hidden inside the folds of skin which almost hid their eyes as well. Taki speculated that the skin flaps protected their mouths and eyes from the dust. Taki found mene faces less expressive than their backs. Head-on they appeared petaled and blind as flowers. When he wanted to differentiate one mene from another, Taki looked at their wings.

Hesper had warned him there would be no art and he had asked her how she could be so sure. "Because their communication system is perfect," she said. "Out of one brain and into the next with no loss of meaning, no need for abstraction. Art arises from the inability to communicate. Art is the imperfect symbol. Isn't it?" But Taki, watching the mene carry water up from their underground deposits, asked himself where the line between tools and art objects should be drawn. For no functional reason that he could see, the water containers curved in the centers like the shapes of the mene's own abdomens.

Taki followed the mene below ground, down some shallow, rough-cut stairs into the darkness. The mene themselves were slightly luminescent when there was no other light; at times and seasons some were spectacularly so and Taki's best guess was that this was sexual. Even with the dimmer members, Taki could see well enough. He moved through a long tunnel with a low ceiling which made him stoop. He could hear water at the other end of it, not the water itself, but a special quality to the silence which told him water was near. The lake was clearly artificial, collected during the rainy season which no human had seen yet. The tunnel narrowed sharply. Taki could have gone forward, but felt suddenly claustrophobic and backed out instead. What did the mene think, he wondered, of the fact that he came here without Hesper. Did they notice this at all? Did it teach them anything about humans that they were capable of understanding?

"Their lives together are perfect," Hesper said. "Except for those useless wings. If they are ever able to talk with us at all it will be because of those wings."

Of course Hesper was a poet. The world was all language as far as she was concerned.

When Taki first met Hesper, at a party given by a colleague of his, he had asked her what she did. "I name things," she had said. "I try to find the right names for things." In retrospect Taki thought it was bullshit. He couldn't remember why he had been so impressed with it at the time, a deliberate miscommunication, when a simple answer, "I write poetry," would have been so clear and easy to understand. He felt the same way about her poetry itself, needlessly obscure, slightly evocative, but it left the reader feeling that he had fallen short somehow, that it had been a test and he had flunked it. It was unkind poetry and Taki had worked so hard to read it then.

"Am I right?" he would ask her anxiously when he finished. "Is that what you're saying?" but she would answer that the poem spoke for itself.

"Once it's on the page, I've lost control over it. Then the reader determines what it says or how it works." Hesper's eyes were gray, the irises so large and intense within their dark rings, that they made Taki dizzy. "So you're always right. By definition. Even if it's not remotely close to what I intended."

What Taki really wanted was to find himself in Hesper's poems. He would read them anxiously for some symbol which could be construed as him, some clue as to his impact on her life. But he was never there.

IT WAS AGAINST policy to send anyone into the field alone. There were pros and cons, of course, but ultimately the isolation of a single professional was seen as too cruel. For shorter projects there were advantages in sending a threesome, but during a longer study the group dynamics in a trio often became difficult. Two were considered ideal and Taki knew that Rawji and Heyen had applied for this post, a husband and wife team in which both members were trained for this type of study. He had never stopped being surprised that the post had been offered to him instead. He could not have even been considered if Hesper had not convinced the members of the committee of her willingness to accompany him, but she must have done much more. She must have impressed someone very much for them to decide that one trained xenologist and one poet might be more valuable than two trained xenologists. The committee had made some noises about "contamination" occurring between the two trained professionals, but Taki found this argument specious. "What did you say to them?" he asked her after her interview and she shrugged.

"You know," she said. "Words."

Taki had hidden things from the committee during his own interview. Things about Hesper. Her moods, her deep attachment to her mother, her unreliable attachment to him. He must have known it would never work out, but he walked about in those days with the stunned expression of a man who has been given everything. Could he be blamed for accepting it? Could he be blamed for believing in Hesper's unexpected willingness to accompany him? It made a sort of equation for Taki. *If* Hesper was willing to give up everything and come with Taki, *then* Hesper loved Taki. An ordinary marriage commitment was reviewable every five years; this was something much greater. No other explanation made any sense.

The equation still held a sort of inevitability for Taki. *Then* Hesper loved Taki, *if* Hesper were willing to come with him. So somehow, sometime, Taki had done something which lost him Hesper's love. If he could figure out what, perhaps he could make her love him again. "Do you love me?" he had asked Hesper, only once; he had too much pride for these thinly disguised pleadings. "Love is such a difficult word," she had answered, but her voice had been filled with a rare softness and had not hurt Taki as much as it might.

The daystar was appearing again when Taki returned home. Hesper had made a meal which suggested she was coping well today. It included a sort of pudding made of a local fruit they found themselves able to tolerate. Hesper called the pudding "boxty." It was apparently a private joke. Taki was grateful for the food and the joke, even if he didn't understand it. He tried to keep the conversation lighthearted, talking to Hesper about the mene water jars. Taki's position was that when the form of a practical object was less utilitarian than it might be, then it was art. Hesper laughed. She ran through a list of human artifacts and made him classify them.

"A paper clip," she said.

"The shape hasn't changed in centuries," he told her. "Not art."

"A safety pin."

Taki hesitated. How essential was the coil at the bottom of the pin? Very. "Not art," he decided.

"A hair brush."

"Boar bristle?"

"Wood handle."

"Art. Definitely."

She smiled at him. "You're confusing ornamentation with art. But why not? It's as good a definition as any," she told him. "Eat your boxty."

They spent the whole afternoon alone, uninterrupted. Taki transcribed the morning's notes into his files, reviewed his tapes. Hesper recorded a letter whose recipient would never hear it and sang softly to herself.

That night he reached for her, his hand along the curve at her waist. She stiffened slightly, but responded by putting her hand on his face. He kissed her and her mouth did not move. His movements became less gentle. It might have been passion; it might have been anger. She told him to stop, but he didn't. Couldn't. Wouldn't. "Stop," she said again and he heard she was crying. "They're here. Please stop. They're watching us."

"Studying us," Taki said. "Let them," but he rolled away and released her. They were alone in the room. He would have seen the mene easily in the dark. "Hesper," he said. "There's no one here."

She lay rigid on her side of their bed. He saw the stitching of her backbone disappearing into her neck and had a sudden feeling that he could see everything about her, how she was made, how she was held together. It made him no less angry.

"I'm sorry," Hesper told him, but he didn't believe her. Even so, he was asleep before she was. He made his own breakfast the next morning without leaving anything out for her. He was gone before she had gotten out of bed.

The mene were gathering food, dried husks thick enough to protect the liquid fruit during the two-star dry season. They punctured the husks with their needle-thin teeth. Several crowded about him, greeting him with their fingers, checking his pockets, removing his recorder and passing it about until one of them dropped it in the dust. When they returned to work, Taki retrieved it, wiped it as clean as he could. He sat down to watch them, logged everything he observed. He noted in particular how often they touched each other and wondered what each touch meant. Affection? Communication? Some sort of chain of command?

Later he went underground again, choosing another tunnel, looking for one which wouldn't narrow so as to exclude him, but finding himself beside the same lake with the same narrow access ahead. He went deeper this time until it gradually became too close for his shoulders. Before him he could see a luminescence; he smelled the dusty odor of the mene and could just make out a sound, too, a sort of movement, a grass-rubbing-together sound. He stooped and strained his eyes to see something in the faint light. It was like looking into the wrong end of a pair of binoculars. The tunnel narrowed and narrowed. Beyond it must be the mene homes and he could never get into them. He contrasted this with the easy access they had to his home. At the end of his vision he thought he could just see something move, but he wasn't sure. A light touch on the back of his neck and another behind his knee startled him. He twisted around to see a group of the mene crowded into the tunnel behind him. It gave him a feeling of being trapped and he had to force himself to be very gentle as he pushed his way back and let the mene go through. The dark pattern of their wings stood in high relief against the luminescent bodies. The human faces grew smaller and smaller until they disappeared.

"LEAVE ME ALONE," Hesper told him. It took Taki completely by surprise. He had done nothing but enter the bedroom; he had not even spoken yet. "Just leave me alone."

Taki saw no signs that Hesper had ever gotten up. She lay against the pillow and her cheek was still creased from the wrinkles in the sheets. She had not been crying. There was something worse in her face, something which alarmed Taki.

"Hesper?" he asked. "Hesper? Did you eat anything? Let me get you something to eat."

It took Hesper a moment to answer. When she did, she looked ordinary again. "Thank you," she said. "I am hungry." She joined him in the outer room, wrapped in their blanket, her hair tangled around her face. She got a drink for herself, dropping the empty glass once, stooping to retrieve it. Taki had the strange impression that the glass fell slowly. When they had first arrived, the gravitational pull had been light, just perceptibly lighter than Earth's. Without quite noticing, this had registered on him in a sort of lightheartedness. But Hesper had complained of feelings of dislocation, disconnection. Taki put together a cold breakfast, which Hesper ate slowly, watching her own hands as if they fascinated her. Taki looked away. "Fork," she said. He looked back. She was smiling at him.

"What?"

"Fork."

He understood. "Not art."

"Four tines?"

He didn't answer.

"Roses carved on the handle."

"Well then, art. Because of the handle. Not because of the tines." He was greatly reassured.

The mene came while he was telling her about the tunnel. They put their dusty fingers in her food, pulled it apart. Hesper set her fork down and pushed the plate away. When they reached for her she pushed them away, too. They came back. Hesper shoved harder.

"Hesper," said Taki.

"I just want to be left alone. They never leave me alone." Hesper stood up, towering above the mene. The blanket fell to the floor. "We flew here," Hesper said to the mene. "Did you see the ship? Didn't you see the pod? Doesn't that interest you? Flying?" She laughed and flapped her arms until they froze, horizontal at her sides. The mene reached for her again and she brought her arms in to protect her breasts, pushing the mene away repeatedly, harder and harder, until they tired of approaching her and went into the bedroom, reappearing with her poems in their hands. The door sealed behind them.

"I'll get them back for you," Taki promised, but Hesper told him not to bother.

"I haven't written in weeks," she said. "In case you hadn't noticed. I haven't finished a poem since I came here. I've lost that. Along with everything else." She brushed at her hair rather frantically with one hand. "It doesn't matter," she added. "My poems? Not art."

"Are you the best person to judge that?" Taki asked.

"Don't patronize me." Hesper returned to the table, looked again at the plate which held her unfinished breakfast, dusty from handling. "My critical faculties are still intact. It's just the poetry that's gone." She took the dish to clean it, scraped the food away. "I was never any good," she said. "Why do you think I came here? I had no poetry of my own so I thought I'd write the mene's. I came to a world without words. I hoped it would be clarifying. I knew there was a risk." Her hands moved very fast. "I want you to know I don't blame you."

"Come and sit down a moment, Hesper," Taki said, but she shook her head. She looked down at her body and moved her hands over it.

"They feel sorry for us. Did you know that? They feel sorry about our bodies."

"How do you know that?" Taki asked.

"Logic. We have these completely functional bodies. No useless wings. Not art." Hesper picked up the blanket and headed for the bedroom. At the cloth curtain she paused a moment. "They love our loneliness, though. They've taken all mine. They never leave me alone now." She thrust her right arm suddenly out into the air. It made the curtain ripple. "Go away," she said, ducking behind the sheet.

Taki followed her. He was very frightened. "No one is here but us, Hesper," he told her. He tried to put his arms around her but she pushed him back and began to dress.

"Don't touch me all the time," she said. He sank onto the bed and watched her. She sat on the floor to fasten her boots.

"Are you going out, Hesper?" he asked and she laughed.

"Hesper is out," she said. "Hesper is out of place, out of time, out of luck, and out of her mind. Hesper has vanished completely. Hesper was broken into and taken."

Taki fastened his hands tightly together. "Please don't do this to me, Hesper," he pleaded. "It's really so unfair. When did I ask so much of you? I took what you offered me; I never took anything else. Please don't do this."

Hesper had found the brush and was pulling it roughly through her hair. He rose and went to her, grabbing her by the arms, trying to turn her to face him. "Please, Hesper!"

She shook loose from him without really appearing to notice his hands, continued to work through the worst of her tangles. When she did turn around, her face was familiar, but somehow not Hesper's face. It was a face which startled him.

"Hesper is gone," it said. "We have her. You've lost her. We are ready to talk to you. Even though you will never, never, never understand." She reached out to touch him, laying her open palm against his cheek and leaving it there.

Pots

C. J. Cherryh is the creator of the encompassing Union-Alliance future-history series, which chronicles the interplay of intergalactic commerce and politics several millennia hence. It includes, among other works, the Hugo Award–winning novels *Downbelow Station* and *Cyteen,* memorable for its study of human nature through the creation of clones with programmed memories. Praised for its inventive extrapolations of clinical and social science and deft blends of technology and human interest, the series enfolds a number of celebrated subseries, including her Faded Sun trilogy (*Kesrith, Shon'jir, Kutath*). Her Chanur cycle (*The Pride of Chanur, Chanur's Venture, The Kif Strikes Back, Chanur's Homecoming, Chanur's Legacy*), also part of the series, tells of a race of sentient leonine creatures and is notable for its alien viewpoint and illuminating perspectives on the human race rendered from outside it. Much of Cherryh's fiction is concerned with the impact of environment—family, politics, culture—on the values and ideologies of the individual. In *Cuckoo's Egg* she rings a variation on the Tarzan theme, imaging a human child raised to maturity by a race of intelligent felines. *Heavy Time* contrasts the personalities of its two protagonists, one raised in a nurturing human environment, the other stunted socially by an upbringing deformed by manipulative corporate interests. Her recent quartet of novels formed by *Foreigner, Invader, Inheritor,* and *Precursor* has been praised for its sensitive documentation of the cultural and racial differences a human colony must overcome in forming a fragile alliance with the planet's alien inhabitants. *The Gene Wars* is a blend of epic quest fantasy and hard science fiction, set in a future when nanotechnology is used as a weapon. Cherryh has also authored the four-volume Morgaine heroic fantasy series and the epic Galisien sword-and-sorcery trilogy, which includes *Fortress in the Eye of Time, Fortress of Eagles,* and *Fortress of Owls.* She is the creator of the *Merovingian Nights* shared-world series and cocreator of the multivolume *Heroes in Hell* shared-world compilations.

IT WAS A most bitter trip, the shuttle-descent to the windy surface. Suited, encumbered by lifesupport, Desan stepped off the platform and waddled onward into the world, waving off the attentions of small spidery service robots: "Citizen, this way, this way, citizen, have a care—do watch your step; a suit tear is hazardous."

Low-level servitors. Desan detested them. The chief of operations had plainly sent these creatures accompanied only by an AI eight-wheel transport, which inconveniently chose to park itself a good five hundred paces beyond the shuttle blast zone, an uncomfortably long walk across the dusty pan in the crinkling, pack-encumbered oxy-suit. Desan turned, casting a forlorn glance at the shuttle waiting there on its landing gear, silver, dip-nosed wedge under a gunmetal sky, at rest on an ocher and rust landscape. He shivered in the sky-view, surrendered himself and his meager luggage to the irritating ministries of the service robots, and waddled on his slow way down to the waiting AI transport.

"Good day," the vehicle said inanely, opening a door. "My passenger compartment is not safe atmosphere; do you understand, Lord Desan?"

"Yes, yes." Desan climbed in and settled himself in the front seat, a slight give of the transport's suspensors. The robots fussed about in insectile hesitance, delicately setting his luggage case just so, adjusting, adjusting until it conformed with their robotic, template-compared notion of their job. Maddening. Typical robotic efficiency. Desan slapped the pressure-sensitive seating. "Come, let's get this moving, shall we?"

The AI talked to its duller cousins, a single squeal that sent them scuttling. "Attention to the door, citizen." It lowered and locked. The AI started its noisy drive motor. "Will you want the windows dimmed, citizen?"

"No. I want to see this place."

"A pleasure, Lord Desan."

Doubtless for the AI, it was.

THE STATION WAS situated a long drive across the pan, across increasingly softer dust that rolled up to obscure the rearview—softer, looser dust, occasionally a wind-scooped hollow that made the transport flex—("Do forgive me, citizen. Are you comfortable?")

"Quite, quite, you're very good."

"Thank you, citizen."

And finally—*finally!*—something other than flat appeared, the merest humps of hills, and one anomalous mountain, a massive, long bar that began as a haze and became solid; became a smooth regularity before the gentle brown folding of hills hardly worthy of the name.

Mountain. The eye indeed took it for a volcanic or sedimentary formation at distance, some anomalous and stubborn outcrop in this barren reach, where all else had declined to entropy; absolute, featureless, flat. But when the AI passed along its side this mountain had joints and seams, had the marks of *making* on it; and even knowing in advance what it was, driving along within view of the jointing, this work of Ancient hands—chilled Desan's well-traveled soul. The station itself came into view against the weathered hills, a collection of shocking green domes on a brown lifeless world. But such domes Desan had seen. With only the AI for witness, Desan turned in his seat, pressed the flexible bubble of the helmet to the double-seal window, and stared and stared at the stonework until it passed to the rear and the dust obscured it.

"Here, Lord," said the AI, eternally cheerful. "We are almost at the station—a little climb. I do it very smoothly."

Flex and lean; sway and turn. The domes lurched closer in the forward window and the motor whined. "I've very much enjoyed serving you."

"Thank you," Desan murmured, seeing another walk before him, ascent of a plastic grid to an airlock and no sight of a welcoming committee.

More service robots, scuttling toward them as the transport stopped and adjusted itself with a pneumatic wheeze.

"Thank you, Lord Desan, do watch your helmet, watch your lifesupport connections, watch your footing please. The dust is slick. . . ."

"Thank you." With an AI one had no recourse.

"Thank *you*, my lord." The door came up; Desan extricated himself from the seat and stepped to the dusty ground, carefully shielding the oxy-pack from the doorframe and panting with the unaccustomed weight of it in such gravity. The service robots moved to take his luggage while Desan waddled doggedly on, up the plastic gridwork path to the glaringly lime-green domes. Plastics. Plastics that could not even originate in this desolation, but which came from their ships' spare biomass. Here all was dead, frighteningly void: Even the signal that guided him to the lakebed was robotic, like the advertisement that a transport would meet him.

The airlock door shot open ahead; and living, suited personnel appeared, three of them, at last, at long last, flesh-and-blood personnel came walking toward him to offer proper courtesy. But before that mountain of stone, before these glaring green structures and the robotic paraphernalia of research that made all the reports real—Desan still felt the deathliness of the place. He trudged ahead, touched the offered, gloved hands, acknowledged the expected salutations, and proceeded up the jointed-plastic walk to the open airlock. His marrow refused to be warmed. The place refused to come into clear focus, like some bad dream with familiar elements hideously distorted.

A hundred years of voyage since he had last seen this world and then only from orbit, receiving reports thirdhand. A hundred years of work on this planet preceded this small trip from port to research center, under that threatening sky, in this place by a mountain that had once been a dam on a lake that no longer existed.

There had been the findings of the moon, of course. A few artifacts. A cloth of symbols. Primitive, unthinkably primitive. First omen of the findings of this sere, rust brown world.

He accompanied the welcoming committee into the airlock of the main dome, waited through the cycle, and breathed a sigh of relief as the indicator lights went from white to orange and the inner door admitted them to the interior. He walked forward, removed the helmet and drew a deep breath of air unexpectedly and unpleasantly tainted. The foyer of this centermost dome was businesslike—plastic walls, visible ducting. A few plants struggled for life in a planter in the center of the floor. Before it, a black pillar and a common enough emblem: a plaque with two naked alien figures, the diagrams of a star system—reproduced even to its scars and pitting. In some places it might be mundane, unnoticed.

It belonged here, *belonged* here, and it could never be mundane, this message of the Ancients.

"Lord Desan," a female voice said, and he turned, awkward in the suit.

It was Dr. Gothon herself, unmistakable aged woman in science blues. The rare honor dazed him, and wiped away all failure of hospitality thus far. She held out her hand. Startled, he reacted in kind, remembered the glove, and hastily drew back his hand to strip the glove. Her gesture was gracious and he felt the very fool and very much off his stride, his hand touching—no, firmly grasped by the callused, aged hand of the legendary intellect. Age-soft and hard-surfaced at once. Age and vigor. His tongue quite failed him, and he felt, recalling his purpose, utterly daunted.

"Come in, let them rid you of that suit, Lord Desan. Will you rest after your trip, a nap, a cup of tea, perhaps. The robots are taking your luggage to your room. Accommodations here aren't luxurious, but I think you'll find them comfortable."

Deeper and deeper into courtesies. One could lose all sense of direction in such surroundings, letting oneself be disarmed by gentleness, by pleasantness—by embarrassed reluctance to resist.

"I want to see what I came to see, doctor." Desan unfastened more seams and shed the suit into waiting hands, smoothed his coveralls. Was that too brusque, too unforgivably hasty? "I don't think I *could* rest, Dr. Gothon. I attended my comfort aboard the shuttle. I'd like to get my bearings here at least, if one of your staff would be so kind to take me in hand—"

"Of course, of course. I rather expected as much—do come, please, let me show you about. I'll explain as much as I can. Perhaps I can convince you as I go."

He was overwhelmed from the start; he had expected *some* high official, the director of operations most likely, not Gothon. He walked slightly after the doctor, the stoop-shouldered presence that passed like a benison among the students and lesser staff—*I saw the Doctor,* the young ones had been wont to say in hushed tones, aboard the ship, when Gothon strayed absently down a corridor in her rare intervals of waking. *I saw the Doctor.*

In that voice one might claim a theophany.

They had rarely waked her, lesser researchers being sufficient for most worlds; while he was the fifth lord-navigator, the fourth born on the journey, a time-dilated trifle, fifty-two waking years of age and a mere two thousand years of voyage against— aeons of Gothon's slumberous life.

And Desan's marrow ached now at such gentle grace in this bowed, mottle-skinned old scholar, this sleuth patiently deciphering the greatest mystery of the universe. Pity occurred to him. He suffered personally in this place; but not as Gothon would have suffered here, in that inward quiet where Gothon carried on thoughts the ship crews were sternly admonished never to disturb.

Students rushed now to open doors for them, pressed themselves to the walls and allowed their passage into deeper and deeper halls within the maze of the domes. Passing hands brushed Desan's sleeves, welcome offered the current lord-navigator; he reciprocated with as much attention as he could devote to courtesy in his distress. His heart labored in the unaccustomed gravity, his nostrils accepted not only the effluvium of dome plastics and the recyclers and so many bodies dwelling together; but a flinty, bitter air, like electricity or dry dust. He imagined some hazardous leakage of the atmosphere into the dome: unsettling thought. The hazards of the place came home to him, and he wished already to be away.

Gothon had endured here, during his further voyages—seven years more of her diminishing life; waked four times, and this was the fourth, continually active now for five years, her longest stint yet in any waking. She had found data finally worth the consumption of her life, and she burned it without stint. *She* believed. She believed enough to die pursuing it.

He shuddered up and down and followed Gothon through a sealdoor toward yet another dome, and his gut tightened in dismay; for there were shelves on either hand, and those shelves were lined with yellow skulls, endless rows of staring dark sockets and grinning jaws. Some were long-nosed; some were short. Some small, virtually noseless skulls had fangs which gave them a wise and intelligent look—*Like miniature people, like babies with grown-up features,* must be the initial reaction to anyone seeing them in the holos or viewing the specimens brought up to the orbiting labs. But cranial capacity in these was much too small. The real sapient occupied further shelves, row upon row of eyeless, generously domed skulls, grinning in their flat-toothed way, in permanent horror—provoking profoundest horror in those who discovered them here, in this desolation.

Here Gothon paused, selected one of the small sapient skulls, much reconstructed: Desan had at least the skill to recognize the true bone from the plassbone bonded to it. This skull was far more delicate than the others, jaw smaller. The front two teeth were restructs. So was one of the side.

"It was a child," Gothon said. "We call her Missy. The first we found at this site, up in the hills, in a streambank. Most of Missy's feet were gone, but she's otherwise intact. Missy was all alone except for a little animal all tucked up in her arms. We keep them together—never mind the cataloging." She lifted an anomalous and much-reconstructed skull from the shelf among the sapients; fanged and delicate. "Even archaeologists have sentiment."

"I—see—" Helpless, caught in courtesy, Desan extended an unwilling finger and touched the skull.

"Back to sleep." Gothon set both skulls tenderly back on the shelf, and dusted her hands and walked farther, Desan following, beyond a simple door and into a busy room of workbenches piled high with a clutter of artifacts.

Staff began to rise from their dusty work in a sudden startlement. "No, no, go on," Gothon said quietly. "We're only passing through; ignore us. —Here, do you see, Lord Desan?" Gothon reached carefully past a researcher's shoulder and lifted from the counter an elongate ribbed bottle with the opalescent patina of long burial. "We find a great many of these. Mass production. Industry. Not only on this continent. This same bottle exists in sites all over the world, in the uppermost strata. Same design. Near the time of the calamity. We trace global alliances and trade by such small things." She set it down and gathered up a virtually complete vase, much patched. "It always comes to pots, Lord Desan. By pots and bottles we track them through the ages. Many layers. They had a long and complex past."

Desan reached out and touched the corroded brown surface of the vase, discovering a single bright remnant of the blue glaze along with the gray encrustations of long burial. "How long—how long does it take to reduce a thing to this?"

"It depends on the soil—on moisture, on acidity. This came from hereabouts." Gothon tenderly set it back on a shelf, walked on, frail, hunch-shouldered figure among the aisles of the past. "But very long, very long to obliterate so much—almost all the artifacts are gone. Metals oxidize; plastics rot; cloth goes very quickly; paper and wood last quite long in a desert climate, but they go, finally. Moisture dissolves the details of sculpture. Only the noble metals survive intact. Soil creep warps even stone; crushes metal. We find even the best pots in a matrix of pieces, a puzzle-toss. Fragile as they are, they outlast monuments, they last as long as the earth that holds them, drylands, wetlands, even beneath the sea—where no marine life exists to trouble them. That bottle and that pot are as venerable as that great dam. The makers wouldn't have thought that, would they?"

"But—" Desan's mind reeled at the remembrance of the great plain, the silt and the deep buried secrets.

"But?"

"You surely might miss important detail. A world to search. You might walk right over something and misinterpret everything."

"Oh, yes, it can happen. But *finding* things where we expect them is an important clue, Lord Desan, a confirmation—One only has to suspect where to look. We locate our best hope first—a sunken, a raised place in those photographs we trouble the orbiters to take; but one gets a *feeling* about the lay of the land—more than the mechanical probes, Lord Desan." Gothon's dark eyes crinkled in the passage of thoughts unguessed, and Desan stood lost in Gothon's unthinkable mentality. What did a mind *do* in such age? Wander? Could the great doctor lapse into mysticism? To report such a thing—would solve one difficulty. But to have that regrettable duty—

"It's a feeling for living creatures, Lord Desan. It's reaching out to the land and saying—if this were long ago, if I thought to build, if I thought to trade—where would I go? Where would my neighbors live?"

Desan coughed delicately, wishing to draw things back to hard fact. "And the robot probes, of course, do assist."

"Probes, Lord Desan, are heartless things. A robot can be very skilled, but a researcher directs it only at distance, blind to opportunities and the true sense of the land. But you were born to space. Perhaps it makes no sense."

"I take your word for it," Desan said earnestly. He felt the weight of the sky on his back. The leaden, awful sky, leprous and unhealthy cover between them and the star and the single moon. Gothon remembered homeworld. *Remembered homeworld.* Had been renowned in her field even there. The old scientist claimed to come to such a landscape and locate things by seeing things that robot eyes could not, by thinking thoughts those dusty skulls had held in fleshy matter—

—how long ago?

"We look for mounds," Gothon said, continuing in her brittle gait down the aisle, past the bowed heads and shy looks of staff and students at their meticulous tasks. The work of tiny electronic needles proceeded about them, the patient ticking away at encrustations to bring ancient surfaces to light. "They built massive structures. Great skyscrapers. Some of them must have lasted, oh, thousands of years intact; but when they went unstable, they fell, and their fall made rubble; and the wind came and the rivers shifted their courses around the ruin, and of course the weight of sediment piled up, wind- and water-driven. From that point, its own weight moved it and warped it and complicated our work." Gothon paused again beside a farther table, where holo plates stood inactive. She waved her hand and a landscape showed itself, a serpentined row of masonry across a depression. "See the wall there. They didn't build it that way, all wavering back and forth and up and down. Gravity and soil movement deformed it. It was buried until we unearthed it. Otherwise, wind and rain alone would have destroyed it ages ago. As it will do, now, if time doesn't rebury it."

"And this great pile of stone—" Desan waved an arm, indicating the imagined direction of the great dam and realizing himself disoriented. "How old is it?"

"Old as the lake it made."

"But contemporaneous with the fall?"

"Yes. Do you know, that mass may be standing when the star dies. The few great dams; the pyramids we find here and there around the world—One only guesses at their age. They'll outlast any other surface feature except the mountains themselves."

"Without life."

"Oh, but there is."

"Declining."

"No, no. Not declining." The doctor waved her hand and a puddle appeared over the second holo plate, all green with weed waving feathery tendrils back and forth in the surge. "The moon still keeps this world from entropy. There's water, not as much as this dam saw—It's the weed, this little weed that gives one hope for this world. The little life, the things that fly and crawl—the lichens and the life on the flatlands."

"But nothing *they* knew."

"No. Life's evolved new answers here. Life's starting over."

"It certainly hasn't much to start with, has it?"

"Not very much. It's a question that interests Dr. Bothogi—whether the life making a start here has the time left, and whether the consumption curve doesn't add up to defeat—But life doesn't know that. We're very concerned about contamination. But we fear it's inevitable. And who knows, perhaps it will have added something beneficial." Dr. Gothon lit yet another holo with the wave of her hand. A streamlined six-legged creature scuttled energetically across a surface of dead moss, frantically waving antennae and making no apparent progress.

"The inheritors of the world." Despair chilled Desan's marrow.

"But each generation of these little creatures is an unqualified success. The last to perish perishes in profound tragedy, of course, but without consciousness of it. The awareness will have, oh, half a billion years to wait—then, maybe it will appear; if the star doesn't fail; it's already far advanced down the sequence." Another holo, the image of desert, of blowing sand, beside the holo of the surge of weed in a pool. "Life makes life. That weed you see is busy making life. It's taking in and converting and building a chain of support that will enable things to feed on it, while more of its kind grows. That's what life does. It's busy, all unintended, of course, but fortuitously building itself a way off the planet."

Desan cast her an uncomfortable look askance.

"Oh, indeed. Biomass. Petrochemicals. The storehouse of aeons of energy all waiting the use of consciousness. And that consciousness, if it arrives, dominates the world because awareness is a way of making life more efficiently. But consciousness is a perilous thing, Lord Desan. Consciousness is a computer loose with its own perceptions and performing calculations on its own course, in the service of that little weed; billions of such computers all running and calculating faster and faster, adjusting themselves and their ecological environment, and what if there were the small-est, the most insignificant software error at the outset?"

"You don't believe such a thing. You don't reduce us to that." Desan's faith was shaken; this good woman had not gone unstable, this great intellect had had her faith shaken, that was what—the great and gentle doctor had, in her unthinkable age, acquired cynicism, and he fought back with his fifty-two meager years. "Surely, but surely this isn't the proof, doctor, this could have been a natural calamity."

"Oh, yes, the meteor strike." The doctor waved past a series of holos on a fourth plate, and a vast crater showed in aerial view, a crater so vast the picture showed planetary curvature. It was one of the planet's main features, shockingly visible from space. "But this solar system shows scar after scar of such events. A many-planeted system like this, a star well-attended by debris in its course through the galaxy—Look at the airless bodies, the moons, consider the number of meteor strikes that crater them. Tell me, space-farer: am I not right in that?"

Desan drew in a breath, relieved to be questioned in his own element. "Of course, the system is prone to that kind of accident. But that crater is ample cause—"

"If it came when there was still sapience here. But that hammerblow fell on a dead world."

He gazed on the eroded crater, the sandswept crustal melting, eloquent of age. "You have proof."

"Strata. Pots. Ironic, they must have feared such an event very greatly. One thinks they must have had a sense of doom about them, perhaps on the evidence of their moon; or understanding the mechanics of their solar system; or perhaps primitive times witnessed such falls and they remembered. One catches a glimpse of the mind that reached out from here . . . what impelled it, what it sought."

"How can we know that? We overlay our mind on their expectations—" Desan silenced himself, abashed, terrified. It was next to heresy. In a moment more he would have committed irremediable indiscretion; and the lords-magistrate on the orbiting station would hear it by suppertime, to his eternal detriment.

"We stand in their landscape, handle their bones, we hold their skulls in our fleshly hands and try to think in their world. Here we stand beneath a threatening heaven. What will we do?"

"Try to escape. Try to get off this world. They *did* get off. The celestial artifacts—"

"Archaelogy is ever so much easier in space. A million years, two, and a thing still shines. Records still can be read. A color can blaze out undimmed after aeons, when first a light falls on it. One surface chewed away by microdust, and the opposing face pristine as the day it had its maker's hand on it. You keep asking me about the age of these ruins. But we know that, don't we truly suspect it, in the marrow of our bones—at what age they fell silent?"

"It *can't* have happened then!"

"Come with me, Lord Desan." Gothon waved a hand, extinguishing all the holos, and, walking on, opened the door into yet another hallway. "So much to catalog. That's much of the work in that room. They're students, mostly. Restoring what they can; numbering, listing. A librarian's job, just to know where things are filed. In five hundred years more of intensive cataloging and restoring, we may know them well enough to know something of their minds, though we may never find more of their written language than that of those artifacts on the moon. A place of wonders. A place of ongoing wonders, in Dr. Bothogi's work. A little algae beginning the work all over again. Perhaps not for the first time—interesting thought."

"You mean—" Desan overtook the aged doctor in the narrow, sterile hall, a series of ringing steps. "You mean—before the sapients evolved—there were other calamities, other re-beginnings."

"Oh, well before. It sends chills up one's back, doesn't it, to think how incredibly stubborn life might be here, how persistent in the calamity of the skies—The algae and then the creeping things and the slow, slow climb to dominance—"

"Previous sapients?"

"Interesting question in itself. But a thing need not be sapient to dominate a world, Lord Desan. Only tough. Only efficient. Haven't the worlds proven that? High sapience is a rare jewel. So many successes are dead ends. Flippers and not hands; lack of vocal apparatus—unless you believe in telepathy, which I assuredly don't. No. Vocalizing is necessary. Some sort of long-distance communication. Light-flashes; sound; something. Else your individuals stray apart in solitary discovery and rediscovery and duplication of effort. Oh, even with awareness—even granted that rare attribute—how many species lack something essential, or have some handicap that will stop them before civilization; before technology—"

"—before they leave the planet. But they *did* that, they were the one in a thousand—Without them—"

"Without them. Yes." Gothon turned her wonderful soft eyes on him at close range and for a moment he felt a great and terrible stillness like the stillness of a grave. "Childhood ends here. One way or the other, it ends."

He was struck speechless. He stood there, paralyzed a moment, his mind tumbling freefall; then blinked and followed the doctor like a child, helpless to do otherwise.

Let me rest, he thought then, *let us forget this beginning and this day, let me go somewhere and sit down and have a warm drink to get the chill from my marrow and let us begin again. Perhaps we can begin with facts and not fancies—*

But he would not rest. He feared that there was no rest to be had in this place, that once the body stopped moving, the weight of the sky would come down, the deadly sky that had boded destruction for all the history of this lost species, and the age of the land would seep into their bones and haunt his dreams as the far greater scale of stars did not.

All the years I've voyaged, Dr. Gothon, all the years of my life searching from star to star. Relativity has made orphans of us. The world will have sainted you. Me it never knew. In a quarter of a million years—they'll have forgotten; o doctor, you know more than I how a world ages. A quarter of a million years you've seen—and we're both orphans. Me endlessly cloned. You in your long sleep, your several clones held aeons waiting in theirs—o doctor, we'll recreate you. And not truly you, ever again. No more than I'm a Desanprime. I'm only the fifth lord-navigator.

In a quarter of a million years, has not our species evolved beyond us, might they not, may they not, find some faster transport and find us, their aeons-lost precursors; and we will not know each other, Dr. Gothon—how could we know each other—if they had, but they have not; we have become the wavefront of a quest that never overtakes, never surpasses us.

In a quarter of a million years, might some calamity have befallen us and our world be like this world, ocher and deadly rust?

While we are clones and children of clones, genetic fossils, anomalies of our kind?

What are they to us and we to them? We seek the Ancients, the makers of the probe.

Desan's mind reeled; adept as he was at time-relativity calculations, accustomed as he was to stellar immensities, his mind tottered and he fought to regain the corridor in which they walked, he and the doctor. He widened his stride yet again, overtaking Gothon at the next door.

"Doctor." He put out his hand, preventing her, and then feared his own question, his own skirting of heresy and tempting of hers. "Are you beyond doubt? You can't be beyond doubt. They could have simply abandoned this world in its calamity."

Again the impact of those gentle eyes, devastating. "Tell me, tell me, Lord Desan. In all your travels, in all the several near stars you've visited in a century of effort, have you found traces?"

"No. But they could have gone—"

"—leaving no traces, except on their moon?"

"There may be others. The team in search on the fourth planet—"

"Finds nothing."

"You yourself say that you have to stand in that landscape, you have to think with their mind—Maybe Dr. Ashodt hasn't come to the right hill, the right plain—"

"If there are artifacts there they only are a few. I'll tell you why I know so. Come, come with me." Gothon waved a hand and the door gaped on yet another laboratory.

Desan walked. He would rather have walked out to the deadly surface than through this simple door, to the answer Gothon promised him . . . but habit impelled him; habit, duty—necessity. He had no other purpose for his life but this. He had been left none, lord-navigator, fifth incarnation of Desan Das. They had launched his original with none, his second incarnation had had less, and time and successive incarnations had stripped everything else away. So he went, into a place at once too mundane and too strange to be quite sane—mundane because it was sterile as any lab, a well-lit place of littered tables and a few researchers; and strange because hundreds and hundreds of skulls and bones were piled on shelves in heaps on one wall, silent witnesses. An articulated skeleton hung in its frame; the skeleton of a small animal scampered in macabre rigidity on a tabletop.

He stopped. He stared about him, lost for the moment in the stare of all those eyeless sockets of weathered bone.

"Let me present my colleagues," Gothon was saying; Desan focused on the words late, and blinked helplessly as Gothon rattled off names. Bothogi the zoologist was one, younger than most, seventeenth incarnation, burning himself out in profligate use of his years: so with all the incarnations of Bothogi Nan. The rest of the names slid past his ears ungathered—true strangers, the truly-born, sons and daughters of the voyage. He was lost in their stares like the stares of the skulls, eyes behind which shadows and dust were truth, gazes full of secrets and heresies.

They knew him and he did not know them, not even Lord Bothogi. He felt his solitude, the helplessness of his convictions all lost in the dust and the silences.

"Kagodte," said Gothon, to a white-eared, hunched individual. "Kagodte—the Lord Desan has come to see your model."

"Ah." The aged eyes flicked, nervously.

"Show him, pray, Dr. Kagodte."

The hunched man walked over to the table, spread his hands. A hole flared and Desan blinked, having expected some dreadful image, some confrontation with a reconstruction. Instead, columns of words rippled in the air, green and blue. Numbers ticked and multiplied. In his startlement he lost the beginning and failed to follow them. "I don't see—"

"We speak statistics here," Gothon said. "We speak data; we couch our heresies in mathematical formulae."

Desan turned and stared at Gothon in fright. "Heresies I have nothing to do with, doctor. I deal with facts. I come here to find facts."

"Sit down," the gentle doctor said. "Sit down, Lord Desan. There, move the bones over, do; the owners won't mind, there, that's right."

Desan collapsed onto a stool facing a white worktable. Looked up reflexively, eye drawn by a wall-mounted stone that bore the blurred image of a face, eroded, time-dulled—

The juxtaposition of image and bones overwhelmed him. The two whole bodies portrayed on the plaque. The sculpture. The rows of fleshless skulls.

Dead. World hammered by meteors, life struggling in its most rudimentary forms. Dead.

"Ah," Gothon said. Desan looked around and saw Gothon looking up at the wall in his turn. "Yes. That. We find very few sculptures. A few—a precious few. Occasionally the fall of stone will protect a surface. Confirmation. Indeed. But the skulls tell us as much. With our measurements and our holos we can flesh them. We can make them—even more vivid. Do you want to see?"

Desan's mouth worked. "No." A small word. A coward word. "Later. So this was *one* place—You still don't convince me of your thesis, doctor, I'm sorry."

"The place. The world of origin. A many-layered world. The last layers are rich with artifacts of one period, one global culture. Then silence. Species extinguished. Stratum upon stratum of desolation. Millions of years of geological record—"

Gothon came round the end of the table and sat down in the opposing chair, elbows on the table, a scatter of bone between them. Gothon's green eyes shone watery in the brilliant light, her mouth was wrinkled about the jowls and trembled in minute cracks, like aged clay. "The statistics, Lord Desan, the dry statistics tell us. They tell us centers of production of artifacts, such as we have; they tell us compositions, processes the Ancients knew—and there was no progress into advanced materials. None of the materials we take for granted, metals that would have lasted—"

"And perhaps they went to some new process, materials that degraded completely. Perhaps their information storage was on increasingly perishable materials. Perhaps they developed these materials in space."

"Technology has steps. The dry numbers, the dusty dry numbers, the incidences and concentration of items, the numbers and the pots—always the pots, Lord Desan; and the imperishable stones; and the very fact of the meteors—the undeniable fact of the meteor strikes. Could we not avert such a calamity for our own world? Could we not have done it—oh, a half a century before we left?"

"I'm sure you remember, Dr. Gothon. I'm sure you have the advantage of me. But—"

"You see the evidence. You want to cling to your hopes. But there is only one question—no, two. Is this the species that launched the probe?—Yes. Or evolution and coincidence have cooperated mightily. Is this the only world they inhabited? Beyond all doubt. If there are artifacts on the fourth planet they are scoured by its storms, busied, lost."

"But they may *be* there."

"There is no abundance of them. There is no *progression*, Lord Desan. That is the key thing. There is nothing beyond these substances, these materials. This was not a star-faring civilization. They launched their slow, unmanned probes, with their cameras, their robot eyes—not for us. We always knew that. We were the recipients of flotsam. Mere wreckage on the beach."

"It was purposeful!" Desan hissed, trembling, surrounded by them all, a lone credent among the quiet heresy in this room. "Dr. Gothon, your unique position—is a position of trust, of profound trust; I beg you to consider the effect you have—"

"Do you threaten me, Lord Desan? Are you here for that, to silence me?"

Desan looked desperately about him, at the sudden hush in the room. The minute tickings of probes and picks had stopped. Eyes stared. "Please." He looked back. "I came here to gather data; I expected a simple meeting, a few staff meetings—to consider things at leisure—"

"I have distressed you. You wonder how it would be if the lords-magistrate fell at odds with me. I am aware of myself as an institution, Lord Desan. I remember Desan Das. I remember launch, the original five ships. I have waked to all but one of your incarnations. Not to mention the numerous incarnations of the lords-magistrate."

"You cannot discount them! Even you—Let me plead with you, Dr. Gothon, be patient with us."

"You do not need to teach me patience, Desan-Five."

He shivered convulsively. Even when Gothon smiled that gentle, disarming smile. "You have to give me facts, doctor, not mystical communing with the landscape. The lords-magistrate accept that this is the world of origin. I assure you they never would have devoted so much time to creating a base here if that were not the case."

"Come, lord, those power systems on the probe, so long dead—What was it truly for, but to probe something very close at hand? Even orthodoxy admits that. And what is close at hand but their own solar system? Come, I've *seen* the original artifact and the original tablet. Touched it with my hands. This was a *primitive* venture, designed to cross their own solar system—*which they had not the capability to do.*"

Desan blinked. "But the purpose—"

"Ah. The purpose."

"You say that you stand in a landscape and you think in their mind. Well, doctor, use this skill you claim. What did the Ancients intend? Why did they send it out with a message?"

The old eyes flickered, deep and calm and pained. "An oracular message, Lord Desan. A message into the dark of their own future, unaimed, unfocused. Without answer. Without hope of answer. We know its voyage time. Eight million years. They spoke to the universe at large. This probe went out, and they fell silent shortly afterward—the depth of this dry lake of dust, Lord Desan, is eight and a quarter million years."

"I will not believe that."

"Eight and a quarter million years ago, Lord Desan. Calamity fell on them, calamity global and complete within a century, perhaps within a decade of the launch of that probe. Perhaps calamity fell from the skies; but demonstrably it was atomics and their own doing. They were at that precarious stage. And the destruction in the great centers is catastrophic and of one level. Destruction centered in places of heavy population. Trace elements. That is what those statistics say. Atomics, Lord Desan."

"I cannot accept this!"

"Tell me, space-farer—do you understand the workings of weather? What those meteor strikes could do, the dust raised by atomics could do with equal efficiency. Never mind the radiation that alone would have killed millions—never mind the destruction of centers of government: We speak of global calamity, the dimming of the sun in dust, the living oceans and lakes choking in dying photosynthetes in a sunless winter, killing the food chain from the bottom up—"

"You have no proof!"

"The universality, the ruin of the population-centers. Arguably, they had the capacity to prevent meteor-impact. That may be a matter of debate. But beyond a doubt in my own mind, simultaneous destruction of the population centers indicates atomics. The statistics, the pots and the dry numbers, Lord Desan, doom us to that answer. The question is answered. There were no descendants, there was no escape from the world. They destroyed themselves before that meteor hit them."

Desan rested his mouth against his joined hands. Stared helplessly at the doctor. "A lie. Is that what you're saying? We pursued a lie?"

"Is it their fault that we needed them so much?"

Desan pushed himself to his feet and stood there by mortal effort. Gothon sat staring up at him with those terrible dark eyes.

"What will you do, lord-navigator? Silence me? The old woman's grown difficult at last: wake my clone after, tell it—what the lords-magistrate select for it to be told?" Gothon waved a hand about the room, indicating the staff, the dozen sets of living eyes among the dead. "Bothogi too, those of us who have clones—But what of the rest of the staff? How much will it take to silence all of us?"

Desan stared about him, trembling. "Dr. Gothon—" He leaned his hands on the table to look at Gothon. "You mistake me. You utterly mistake me— The lords-magistrate may have the station, but I have the ships, I, I and my staff. I propose no such thing. I've come home—" The unaccustomed word caught in his throat; he considered it, weighed it, accepted it, at least in the emotional sense. "—home, Dr. Gothon, after a hundred years of search, to discover this argument and this dissension."

"Charges of heresy—"

"They dare not make them against you." A bitter laugh welled up. "Against you they have no argument and you well know it, Dr. Gothon."

"Against their violence, lord-navigator, I have no defense."

"But she has," said Dr. Bothogi.

Desan turned, flicked a glance from the hardness in Bothogi's green eyes to the even harder substance of the stone in Bothogi's hand. He flung himself about again, hands on the table, abandoning the defense of his back. "Dr. Gothon! I appeal to you! I am your friend!"

"For myself," said Dr. Gothon, "I would make no defense at all. But, as you say—they have no argument against me. So it must be a general catastrophe—the lords-magistrate have to silence everyone, don't they? *Nothing* can be left on this base. Perhaps they've quietly dislodged an asteroid or two and put them on course. In the guise of mining, perhaps they will silence this poor old world forever—myself and the rest of the relics. Lost relics and the distant dead are always safer to venerate, aren't they?"

"That's absurd!"

"Or perhaps they've become more hasty now that your ships are here and their judgment is in question. *They* have atomics within their capability, lord-navigator. They can disable your shuttle with beam-fire. They can simply welcome you to the list of casualties—a charge of heresy. A thing taken out of context, who knows? After all—all lords are immediately duplicatable, the captains accustomed to obey the lords-magistrate—what few of them are awake—am I not right? If an institution like myself can be threatened—where is the fifth lord-navigator in their plans? And of a sudden those plans will be moving in haste."

Desan blinked. "Dr. Gothon—I assure you—"

"If you are my friend, lord-navigator, I hope for your survival. The robots are theirs, do you understand? Their powerpacks are sufficient for transmission of information to the base AIs; and from the communications center it goes to satellites; and from satellites to the station and the lords-magistrate. This room is safe from their monitoring. We have seen to that. They cannot hear you."

"I cannot believe these charges, I cannot accept it—"

"Is murder so new?"

"Then come with me! Come with me to the shuttle, we'll confront them—"

"The transportation to the port is theirs. It would not permit. The transport AI would resist. The planes have AI components. And we might never reach the airfield."

"My luggage. Dr. Gothon, my luggage—my com unit!" And Desan's heart sank, remembering the service-robots. "*They* have it."

Gothon smiled, a small, amused smile. "O space-farer. So many scientists clustered here, and could we not improvise so simple a thing? *We* have a receiver-transmitter. Here. In this room. We broke one. We broke another. They're on the registry as broken. What's another bit of rubbish—on this poor planet? We meant to contact the ships, to call *you*, lord-navigator, when you came back. But you saved us the trouble. You came down to us like a thunderbolt. Like the birds you never saw, my spaceborn lord, swooping down on prey. The conferences, the haste you must have inspired up there on the station—if the lords-magistrate planned what I most suspect! I congratulate you. But knowing we have a transmitter—with your shuttle sitting on this world vulnerable as this building—what will you do, lord-navigator, since *they* control the satellite relay?"

Desan sank down on his chair. Stared at Gothon. "You never meant to kill me. All this—you schemed to enlist me."

"I entertained that hope, yes. I knew your predecessors. I also know your personal reputation—a man who burns his years one after the other as if there were no end of them. Unlike his predecessors. What are you, lord-navigator? Zealot? A man with an obsession? Where do you stand in this?"

"To what—" His voice came hoarse and strange. "To what are you trying to convert me, Dr. Gothon?"

"To our rescue from the lords-magistrate. To the rescue of truth."

"Truth!" Desan waved a desperate gesture. "I don't believe you, I cannot believe you, and you tell me about plots as fantastical as your research and try to involve me in your politics. I'm trying to find the trail the Ancients took—one clue, one artifact to direct us—"

"A new tablet?"

"You make light of me. Anything. Any indication where they went. And they *did* go, doctor. You will not convince me with your statistics. The unforeseen and the unpredicted aren't in your statistics."

"So you'll go on looking—for what you'll never find. You'll serve the lords-magistrate. They'll surely cooperate with you. They'll approve your search and leave this world . . . after the great catastrophe. After the catastrophe that obliterates us and all the records. An asteroid. Who but the robots chart their course? Who knows how close it is at this moment?"

"People would know a murder! They could never hide it!"

"I tell you, Lord Desan, you stand in a place and you look around you and you say—what would be natural to this place? In this cratered, devastated world, in this chaotic, debris-ridden solar system—could not an input error by an asteroid miner be more credible an accident than atomics? I tell you when your shuttle descended, we thought you might be acting for the lords-magistrate. That you might have a weapon in your baggage that their robots would deliberately fail to detect. But I believe you, lord-navigator. You're as trapped as we. With only the transmitter and a satellite relay system they control. What will you do? Persuade the lords-magistrate that you support them? Persuade them to support you on this further voyage—in return for your backing them? Perhaps they'll listen to you and let you leave."

"But they will," Desan said. He drew in a deep breath and looked from Gothon to the others and back again. "My shuttle is my own. *My* robotics, Dr. Gothon. From my ship and linked to it. And what I need is that transmitter. Appeal to *me* for protection if you think it so urgent. Trust me. Or trust nothing and we will all wait here and see what truth is."

Gothon reached into a pocket, held up an odd metal object. Smiled. Her eyes crinkled round the edges. "An old-fashioned thing, lord-navigator. We say *key* now-adays and mean something quite different, but I'm a relic myself, remember. Baffles hell out of the robots. Bothogi. Link up that antenna and unlock the closet and let's see what the lord-navigator and his shuttle can do."

"DID IT HEAR you?" Bothogi asked, a boy's honest worry on his unlined face. He still had the rock, as if he had forgotten it. Or feared robots. Or intended to use it if he detected treachery. "Is it moving?"

"I assure you it's moving," Desan said, and shut the transmitter down. He drew a great breath, shut his eyes and saw the shuttle lift, a silver wedge spreading wings for home. Deadly if attacked. *They will not attack it, they must not attack it, they will query us when they know the shuttle is launched and we will discover yet that this is all a ridiculous error of understanding.* And looking at nowhere: "Relays have gone; *nothing* stops it and its defenses are considerable. The lords-navigator have not been fools, citizens: We probe worlds with our shuttles, and we plan to get them back." He turned and faced Gothon and the other staff. "The message is *out*. And because I am a prudent man—are there suits enough for your staff? I advise we get to them. In the case of an accident."

"The alarm," said Gothon at once. "Neoth, sound the alarm." And as a senior staffer moved: "The dome pressure alert," Gothon said. "*That* will confound the robots. All personnel to pressure suits; all robots to seek damage. I agree about the suits. Get them."

The alarm went, a staccato shriek from overhead. Desan glanced instinctively at an uncommunicative white ceiling—

—darkness, darkness above, where the shuttle reached the thin blue edge of space. The station now knew that things had gone greatly amiss. It should inquire, there should be inquiry immediate to the planet—

Staffers had unlocked a second closet. They pulled out suits, not the expected one or two for emergency exit from this pressure-sealable room; but a tightly jammed lot of them. The lab seemed a mine of defenses, a stealthily equipped stronghold that smelled of conspiracy all over the base, throughout the staff—*everyone* in on it—

He blinked at the offering of a suit, ears assailed by the siren. He looked into the eyes of Bothogi who had handed it to him. There would be no call, no inquiry from the lords-magistrate. He began to know that, in the earnest, clear-eyed way these people behaved—not lunatics, not schemers. Truth. They had told their truth as they believed it, as the whole base believed it. And the lords-magistrate named it heresy.

His heart beat steadily again. Things made sense again. His hands found familiar motions, putting on the suit, making the closures.

"There's that AI in the controller's office," said a senior staffer. "I have a key."

"What will they do?" a younger staffer asked, panic-edged. "Will the station's weapons reach here?"

"It's quite distant for sudden actions," said Desan. "Too far, for beams and missiles are slow." His heartbeat steadied further. The suit was about him; familiar feeling; hostile worlds and weapons: more familiar ground. He smiled, not a pleasant kind of smile, a parting of lips on strong, long teeth. "And one more thing, young citizen, the ships they have are transports. Miners. Mine are hunters. I regret to say we've carried weapons for the last two hundred thousand years, and my crews know their business. If the lords-magistrate attack that shuttle it will be their mistake. Help Dr. Gothon."

"I've got it, quite, young lord." Gothon made the collar closure. "I've been handling these things longer than—"

Explosion thumped somewhere away. Gothon looked up. All motion stopped. And the air-rush died in the ducts.

"The oxygen system—" Bothogi exclaimed. "O *damn* them—!"

"We have," said Desan coldly. He made no haste. Each final fitting of the suit he made with care. Suit-drill; example to the young: The lord-navigator, youngsters, demonstrates his skill. Pay attention. "And we've just had our answer from the lords-magistrate. We need to get to that AI and shut it down. Let's have no panic here. Assume that my shuttle has cleared atmosphere—"

—well above the gray clouds, the horror of the surface. Silver needle aimed at the heart of the lords-magistrate.

Alert, alert, it would shriek, *alert, alert, alert*—With its transmission relying on no satellites, with its message shoved out in one high-powered bow-wave. *Crew on the world is in danger.* And, code that no lord-navigator had ever hoped to transmit, a series of numbers in syntaxical link: *Treachery; the lords-magistrate are traitors; aid and rescue—Alert, alert, alert—*

—anguished scream from a world of dust; a place of skulls; the grave of the search.

Treachery, alert, alert, alert!

Desan was not a violent man; he had never thought of himself as violent. He was a searcher, a man with a quest.

He knew nothing of certainty. He believed a woman a quarter of a million years old, because—because Gothon was Gothon. He cried traitor and let loose havoc all the while knowing that here might be the traitor, this gentle-eyed woman, this collector of skulls.

O Gothon, he would ask if he dared, *which of you is false? To force the lords-magistrate to strike with violence enough to damn them—Is that what you wish? Against a quarter million years of unabated life—what are my five incarnations: mere genetic congruency, without memory. I am helpless to know your perspectives.*

Have you planned this a thousand years, ten thousand?

Do you stand in this place and think in the mind of creatures dead longer even than you have lived? Do you hold their skulls and think their thoughts?

Was it purpose eight million years ago?

Was it, is it—horror upon horror—a mistake on both sides?

"Lord Desan," said Bothogi, laying a hand on his shoulder. "Lord Desan, we have a master key. We have weapons. We're waiting, Lord Desan."

Above them the holocaust.

IT WAS ONLY a service robot. It had never known its termination. Not like the base AI, in the director's office, which had fought them with locked doors and release of atmosphere, to the misfortune of the director—

"Tragedy, tragedy," said Bothogi, standing by the small dented corpse, there on the ocher sand before the buildings. Smoke rolled up from a sabotaged lifesupport plant to the right of the domes—the world's air had rolled outward and inward and mingled with the breaching of the central dome—the AI transport's initial act of sabotage, ramming the plastic walls. "Microorganisms let loose on this world—the fools, the arrogant *fools!*"

It was not the microorganisms Desan feared. It was the AI eight-wheeled transport, maneuvering itself for another attack on the cold-sleep facilities. Prudent to have set themselves inside a locked room with the rest of the scientists and hope for rescue from offworld; but the AI would batter itself against the plastic walls, and living targets kept it distracted from the sleeping, helpless clones—Gothon's juniormost; Bothogi's; those of a dozen senior staffers.

And keeping it distracted became more and more difficult.

Hour upon hour they had evaded its rushes, clumsy attacks and retreats in their encumbering suits. They had done it damage where they could while staff struggled to come up with something that might slow it . . . it limped along now with a great lot of metal wire wrapped around its rearmost right wheel.

"Damn!" cried a young biologist as it maneuvered for her position. It was the agile young who played this game; and one aging lord-navigator who was the only fighter in the lot.

Dodge, dodge and dodge. "It's going to catch you against the oxy-plant, youngster! *This* way!" Desan's heart thudded as the young woman thumped along in the cumbersome suit in a losing race with the transport. "Oh, *damn,* it's got it figured! Bothogi!"

Desan grasped his probe-spear and jogged on—"Divert it!" he yelled. Diverting it was all they could hope for.

It turned their way, a whine of the motor, a serpentine flex of its metal body and a flurry of sand from its eight-wheeled drive. "Run, lord!" Bothogi gasped beside him;

and it was still turning—it aimed for them now, and at another tangent a white-suited figure hurled a rock, to distract it yet again.

It kept coming at them. AI. An eight-wheeled, flex-bodied intelligence that had suddenly decided its behavior was not working and altered the program, refusing distraction. A pressure-windowed juggernaut tracking every turn they made.

Closer and closer. "Sensors!" Desan cried, turning on the slick dust—his footing failed him and he caught himself, gripped the probe and aimed it straight at the sensor array clustered beneath the front window.

Thum-p! The dusty sky went blue and he was on his back, skidding in the sand with the great ballon tires churning sand on either side of him.

The suit, he thought with a spaceman's horror of the abrading, while it dawned on him at the same time he was being dragged beneath the AI, and that every joint and nerve center was throbbing with the high voltage shock of the probe.

Things became very peaceful then, a cessation of commotion. He lay dazed, staring up at a rusty blue sky, and seeing it laced with a silver thread.

They're coming, he thought, and thought of his eldest clone, sleeping at a well-educated twenty years of age. Handsome lad. He talked to the boy from time to time. *Poor lad, the lordship is yours. Your predecessor was a fool—*

A shadow passed above his face. It was another suited face peering down into his. A weight rested on his chest.

"Get off," he said.

"He's alive!" Bothogi's voice cried. "Dr. Gothon, he's still alive!"

THE WORLD SHOWED no more scars than it had at the beginning—red and ocher where clouds failed. The algae continued its struggle in sea and tidal pools and lakes and rivers—with whatever microscopic addenda the breached dome had let loose in the world. The insects and the worms continued their blind ascent to space, dominant life on this poor, cratered globe. The research station was in function again, repairs complete.

Desan gazed on the world from his ship: It hung as a sphere in the holotank by his command station. A wave of his hand might show him the darkness of space; the floodlit shapes of ten hunting ships, lately returned from the deep and about to seek it again in continuation of the Mission, sleek fish rising and sinking again in a figurative black sea. A good many suns had shone on their hulls, but this one sun had seen them more often than any since their launching.

Home.

The space station was returning to function. Corpses were consigned to the sun the Mission had sought for so long. And power over the Mission rested solely at present in the hands of the lord-navigator, in the unprecedented circumstance of the demise of all five lords-magistrate simultaneously. Their clones were not yet activated to begin their years of majority—"Later will be time to wake the new lords-magistrate," Desan decreed, "at some further world of the search. Let them hear this event as history."

When I can manage them personally, he thought. He looked aside at twenty-year-old Desan Six and the youth looked gravely back with the face Desan had seen in the mirror thirty-two waking years ago.

"Lord-navigator?"

"You'll wake your brother after we're away, Six. Directly after. I'll be staying awake much of this trip."

"*Awake,* sir?"

"Quite. There are things I want you to think about. I'll be talking to you and Seven both."

"About the lords-magistrate, sir?"

Desan lifted brows at this presumption. "You and I are already quite well attuned, Six. You'll succeed young. Are you sorry you missed this time?"

"No, lord-navigator! I assure you not!"

"Good brain. I ought to know. Go to your post, Six. Be grateful you don't have to cope with a new lordship *and* five new lords-magistrate and a recent schism."

Desan leaned back in his chair as the youth crossed the bridge and settled at a crew-post, beside the captain. The lord-navigator was more than a figurehead to rule the seventy ships of the Mission, with their captains and their crews. Let the boy try his skill on this plotting. Desan intended to check it. He leaned aside with a wince—the electric shock that had blown him flat between the AI's tires had saved him from worse than a broken arm and leg; and the medical staff had seen to that: The arm and the leg were all but healed, with only a light wrap to protect them. The ribs were tightly wrapped too; and they cost him more pain than all the rest.

A scan had indeed located three errant asteroids, three courses the station's computers had not accurately recorded as inbound for the planet—until personnel from the ships began to run their own observation. Those were redirected.

Casualties. Destruction. Fighting within the Mission. The guilt of the lords-magistrate was profound and beyond dispute.

"Lord-navigator," the communications officer said. "Dr. Gothon returning your call."

Goodbye, he had told Gothon. *I don't accept your judgment, but I shall devote my energy to pursuit of mine, and let any who want to join you—reside on the station. There are some volunteers; I don't profess to understand them. But you may trust them. You may trust the lords-magistrate to have learned a lesson. I will teach it. No member of this mission will be restrained in any opinion while my influence lasts. And I shall see to that. Sleep again and we may see each other once more in our lives.*

"I'll receive it," Desan said, pleased and anxious at once that Gothon deigned reply; he activated the com-control. Ship-electronics touched his ear, implanted for comfort. He heard the usual blip and chatter of com's mechanical protocols, then Gothon's quiet voice. "Lord-navigator."

"I'm hearing you, doctor."

"Thank you for your sentiment. I wish you well, too. I wish you very well."

The tablet was mounted before him, above the console. Millions of years ago a tiny probe had set out from this world, bearing the original. Two aliens standing naked, one with hand uplifted. A series of diagrams which, partially obliterated, had still served to guide the Mission across the centuries. A probe bearing a greeting. Ages-dead cameras and simple instruments.

Greetings, stranger. We come from this place, this star system.

See, the hand, the appendage of a builder—This we will have in common.

The diagrams: We speak knowledge; we have no fear of you, strangers who read this, whoever you be.

Wise fools.

There had been a time, long ago, when fools had set out to seek them . . . In a vast desert of stars. Fools who had desperately needed proof, once upon a quarter million years ago, that they were not alone. One dust-covered alien artifact they found, so long ago, on a lonely drifting course.

Hello, it said.

The makers, the peaceful Ancients, became a legend. They became purpose, inspiration.

The overriding, obsessive *Why* that saved a species, pulled it back from war, gave it the stars.

"I'm very serious—I do hope you rest, doctor—save a few years for the unborn."

"My eldest's awake. I've lost my illusions of immortality, lord-navigator. She hopes to meet you."

"You might still abandon this world and come with us, doctor."

"To search for a myth?"

"Not a myth. We're bound to disagree. Doctor, doctor, what *good* can your presence there do? What if you're right? It's a dead end. What if I'm wrong? I'll never stop looking. *I'll* never know."

"But we know their descendants, lord-navigator. We. We are. We've spread their legend from star to star—they've become a fable. The Ancients. The Pathfinders. A hundred civilizations have taken up that myth. A hundred civilizations have lived out their years in that belief and begotten others to tell their story. What if you should find them? Would you know them—or where evolution had taken them? Perhaps we've already met them, somewhere along the worlds we've visited, and we failed to know them."

It was irony. Gentle humor. "Perhaps, then," Desan said in turn, "we'll find the track leads home again. Perhaps we *are* their children—eight and a quarter million years removed."

"O ye makers of myths. Do your work, space-farer. Tangle the skein with legends. Teach fables to the races you meet. Brighten the universe with them. I put my faith in you. Don't you know—this world is all I came to find, but you—child of the voyage, you have to have more. For you the voyage is the Mission. Goodbye to you. Fare well. Nothing is complete calamity. The equation here is different, by a multitude of microorganisms let free—Bothogi has stopped grieving and begun to have quite different thoughts on the matter. His algae-pools may turn out a different breed this time—the shift of a protein here and there in the genetic chain—who knows what it will breed? Different software this time, perhaps. Good voyage to you, lord-navigator. Look for your Ancients under other suns. We're waiting for their offspring here, under this one."

Snow

John Crowley's writing has earned comparisons to the epic fantasy of J. R. R. Tolkien and the magic realism of Gabriel García Márquez. He is generally regarded as a writer of mythic fantasy who has freely mixed elements of science fiction into his allusive and richly symbolic fiction. His first three novels all develop fantasy plots in nominally science fictional settings. *The Deep* tells of a medieval power struggle convulsing two feudal households on a planet geographically distinct but historically similar to Earth. *Beasts* is set in a balkanized near-future America where proponents of totalitarian centralized government struggle to stamp out a war of independence spearheaded by genetically manipulated human/animal hybrids. *Engine Summer* unfolds a primitive rite-of-passage tale against the backdrop of a postapocalyptic America descended into a new dark age. Crowley's World-Fantasy Award–winning *Little, Big* marked his departure from science fiction–accented explorations of the human social structures for modern treatments of traditional high fantasy. Redolent with echoes of classic romantic literature, the tale chronicles an eccentric multigeneration family alive in a reality-skewed modern world who enjoy a rapport with the world of faerie that is eventually threatened by the rise of a president with antipathy to the faerie kind. Considered a landmark of modern fantasy, this inventive novel sets the pattern for Crowley's subsequent work with its playful depiction of ordinary lives touched by the strange and magical. *Aegypt, Love and Sleep,* and *Daemonomania* are the first three in a projected quartet of novels intended to interlock as a single all-encompassing philosophical romance that blends historical fact, imaginary world fantasy, occult mystery, Renaissance metaphysics, alternate history, quest legend, and classic mythology. Crowley's collection *Novelty* features four visionary novellas concerned with artistic creation. His fiction has also been collected in *Antiquities.*

I DON'T THINK Georgie would ever have got one for herself: She was at once unsentimental and a little in awe of death. No, it was her first husband—an immensely rich and (from Georgie's description) a strangely weepy guy, who had got it for her. Or for himself, actually, of course. He was to be the beneficiary. Only he died himself shortly after it was installed. If *installed* is the right word. After he died, Georgie got rid of most of what she'd inherited from him, liquidated it. It was cash that she had liked best about that marriage anyway; but the Wasp couldn't really be got rid of. Georgie ignored it.

In fact the thing really was about the size of a wasp of the largest kind, and it had the same lazy and mindless fight. And of course it really was a bug, not of the insect kind but of the surveillance kind. And so its name fit all around: one of those bits of accidental poetry the world generates without thinking. O Death, where is thy sting?

Georgie ignored it, but it was hard to avoid; you had to be a little careful around it; it followed Georgie at a variable distance, depending on her motions and the numbers of other people around her, the level of light, and the tone of her voice. And there was always the danger you might shut it in a door or knock it down with a tennis racket.

It cost a fortune (if you count the access and the perpetual care contract, all prepaid), and though it wasn't really fragile, it made you nervous.

It wasn't recording all the time. There had to be a certain amount of light, though not much. Darkness shut it off. And then sometimes it would get lost. Once when we hadn't seen it hovering around for a time, I opened a closet door, and it flew out, unchanged. It went off looking for her, humming softly. It must have been shut in there for days.

Eventually it ran out, or down. A lot could go wrong, I suppose, with circuits that small, controlling that many functions. It ended up spending a lot of time bumping gently against the bedroom ceiling, over and over, like a winter fly. Then one day the maids swept it out from under the bureau, a husk. By that time it had transmitted at least eight thousand hours (eight thousand was the minimum guarantee) of Georgie: of her days and hours, her comings in and her goings out, her speech and motion, her living self—all on file, taking up next to no room, at The Park. And then, when the time came, you could go there, to The Park, say on a Sunday afternoon; and in quiet landscaped surroundings (as The Park described it) you would find her personal resting chamber, and there, in privacy, through the miracle of modern information storage and retrieval systems, you could access her, her alive, her as she was in every way, never changing or growing any older, fresher (as The Park's brochure said) than in memory ever green.

I MARRIED GEORGIE for her money, the same reason she married her first, the one who took out The Park's contract for her. She married me, I think, for my looks; she always had a taste for looks in men. I wanted to write. I made a calculation that more women than men make, and decided that to be supported and paid for by a rich wife would give me freedom to do so, to "develop." The calculation worked out no better for me than it does for most women who make it. I carried a typewriter and a case of miscellaneous paper from Ibiza to Gstaad to Bial to London, and typed on beaches, and learned to ski. Georgie liked me in ski clothes.

Now that those looks are all but gone, I can look back on myself as a young hunk and see that I was in a way a rarity, a type that you run into often among women, far less among men, the beauty unaware of his beauty, aware that he affects women profoundly and more or less instantly but doesn't know why; thinks he is being listened to and understood, that his soul is being seen, when all that's being seen is long-lashed eyes and a strong, square, tanned wrist turning in a lovely gesture, stubbing out a cigarette. Confusing. By the time I figured out why I had for so long been indulged and cared for and listened to, why I was interesting, I wasn't as interesting as I had been. At about the same time I realized I wasn't a writer at all. Georgie's investment stopped looking as good to her, and my calculation had ceased to add up; only by that time I had come, pretty unexpectedly, to love Georgie a lot, and she just as unexpectedly had come to love and need me too, as much as she needed anybody. We never really parted, even though when she died I hadn't seen her for years. Phone calls, at dawn or four A.M. because she never, for all her travel, really grasped that the world turns and cocktail hour travels around with it. She was a crazy, wasteful, happy woman, without a trace of malice or permanence or ambition in her—easily pleased and easily bored and strangely serene despite the hectic pace she kept up. She cherished things and lost them and forgot them: things, days, people. She had fun, though, and I had fun with her; that was her talent and her destiny, not always an easy one. Once, hung over in a New York hotel, watching a sudden snowfall out the immense window, she said to me, "Charlie, I'm going to die of fun."

And she did. Snow-foiling in Austria, she was among the first to get one of those snow leopards, silent beasts as fast as speedboats. Alfredo called me in California to tell me, but with the distance and his accent and his eagerness to tell me *he* wasn't to blame, I never grasped the details. I was still her husband, her closest relative, heir to the little she still had, and beneficiary, too, of The Park's access concept. Fortunately, The Park's services included collecting her from the morgue in Gstaad and installing her in her chamber at The Park's California unit. Beyond signing papers and taking delivery when Georgie arrived by freight airship at Van Nuys, there was nothing for me to do. The Park's representative was solicitous and made sure I understood how to go about accessing Georgie, but I wasn't listening. I am only a child of my time, I suppose. Everything about death, the fact of it, the fate of the remains, and the situation of the living faced with it, seems grotesque to me, embarrassing, useless: And everything done about it only makes it more grotesque, more useless: Someone I loved is dead; let me therefore dress in clown's clothes, talk backwards, and buy expensive machinery to make up for it. I went back to L.A.

A year or more later, the contents of some safe-deposit boxes of Georgie's arrived from the lawyer's: some bonds and such stuff and a small steel case, velvet lined, that contained a key, a key deeply notched on both sides and headed with smooth plastic, like the key to an expensive car.

WHY DID I go to The Park that first time? Mostly because I had forgotten about it: Getting that key in the mail was like coming across a pile of old snapshots you hadn't cared to look at when they were new but which after they have aged come to contain the past, as they did not contain the present. I was curious.

I understood very well that The Park and its access concept were very probably only another cruel joke on the rich, preserving the illusion that they can buy what can't be bought, like the cryonics fad of thirty years ago. Once in Ibiza, Georgie and I met a German couple who also had a contract with The Park; their Wasp hovered over them like a Paraclete and made them self-conscious in the extreme—they seemed to be constantly rehearsing the eternal show being stored up for their descendants. Their deaths had taken over their lives, as though they were pharaohs. Did they, Georgie wondered, exclude the Wasp from their bedroom? Or did its presence there stir them to greater efforts, proofs of undying love and admirable vigor for the unborn to see?

No, death wasn't to be cheated that way, any more than by pyramids, by masses said in perpetuity. It wasn't Georgie saved from death that I would find. But there were eight thousand hours of her life with me, genuine hours, stored there more carefully than they could be in my porous memory; Georgie hadn't excluded the Wasp from her bedroom, our bedroom, and she who had never performed for anybody could not have conceived of performing for it. And there would be me, too, undoubtedly, caught unintentionally by the Wasp's attention: Out of those thousands of hours there would be hundreds of myself, and myself had just then begun to be problematic to me, something that had to be figured out, something about which evidence had to be gathered and weighed. I was thirty-eight years old.

That summer, then, I borrowed a Highway Access Permit (the old HAPpy cards of those days) from a county lawyer I knew and drove the coast highway up to where The Park was, at the end of a pretty beach road, all alone above the sea. It looked from the outside like the best, most peaceful kind of Italian country cemetery, a low stucco wall topped with urns, amid cypresses, an arched gate in the center. A small brass plaque on the gate: PLEASE USE YOUR KEY. The gate opened, not to a square of shaded tombstones but onto a ramped corridor going down: The cemetery wall was an illusion, the works were underground. Silence, or nameless Muzak-like silence: solitude—whether the necessary technicians were discreetly hidden or none were needed. Certainly the access concept turned out to be simplicity itself, in operation anyway. Even I, who am an idiot about information technology, could tell that. The Wasp was genuine state-of-the-art stuff, but what we mourners got was as ordinary as home movies, as old letters tied up in ribbon.

A display screen near the entrance told me down which corridor to find Georgie, and my key let me into a small screening room where there was a moderate-size TV monitor, two comfortable chairs, and dark walls of chocolate-brown carpeting. The sweet-sad Muzak. Georgie herself was evidently somewhere in the vicinity, in the wall or under the floor, they weren't specific about the charnel-house aspect of the place. In the control panel before the TV were a keyhole for my key and two bars: ACCESS and RESET.

I sat, feeling foolish and a little afraid, too, made more uncomfortable by being so deliberately soothed by neutral furnishings and sober tools. I imagined, around me, down other corridors, in other chambers, others communed with their dead as I was about to do, that the dead were murmuring to them beneath the stream of Muzak; that they wept to see and hear, as I might, but I could hear nothing. I turned my key in its slot, and the screen lit up. The dim lights dimmed further, and the Muzak ceased. I pushed ACCESS, obviously the next step. No doubt all these procedures had been explained to me long ago at the dock when Georgie in her aluminum box was being off-loaded, and I hadn't listened. And on the screen she turned to look at me—only not at me, though I started and drew breath—at the Wasp that watched her. She was in mid-sentence, mid-gesture. Where? When? *Or put it on the same card with the others,* she said, turning away. Someone said something, Georgie answered, and stood up, the Wasp panning and moving erratically with her, like an amateur with a home-video camera. A white room, sunlight, wicker. Ibiza. Georgie wore a cotton blouse, open; from a table she picked up lotion, poured some on her hand, and rubbed it across her freckled breastbone. The meaningless conversation about putting something on a card went on, ceased. I watched the room, wondering what year, what season I had stumbled into. Georgie pulled off her shirt—her small round breasts tipped with large, childlike nipples, child's breasts she still had at forty, shook delicately. And she went out onto the balcony, the Wasp following, blinded by sun, adjusting. *If you want to do it that way,* someone said. The someone crossed the screen, a brown blur, naked. It was me. Georgie said: *Oh, look, hummingbirds.*

She watched them, rapt, and the Wasp crept close to her cropped blond head, rapt too, and I watched her watch. She turned away, rested her elbows on the balustrade. I couldn't remember this day. How should I? One of hundreds, of thousands. . . . She looked out to the bright sea, wearing her sleepwalking face, mouth partly open, and absently stroked her breast with her oiled hand. An iridescent glitter among the flowers was the hummingbird.

Without really knowing what I did—I felt hungry, suddenly, hungry for pastness, for more—I touched the RESET bar. The balcony in Ibiza vanished, the screen glowed emptily. I touched ACCESS.

At first there was darkness, a murmur; then a dark back moved away from the Wasp's eye, and a dim scene of people resolved itself. Jump. Other people, or the same people, a party? Jump. Apparently the Wasp was turning itself on and off according to the changes in light levels here, wherever *here* was. Georgie in a dark dress having her cigarette lit: brief flare of the lighter. She said, *Thanks.* Jump. A foyer or hotel lounge. Paris? The Wasp jerkily sought for her among people coming and going; it couldn't make a movie, establishing shots, cutaways—it could only doggedly follow Georgie, like a jealous husband, seeing nothing else. This was frustrating. I pushed RESET. ACCESS. Georgie brushed her teeth, somewhere, somewhen.

I understood, after one or two more of these terrible leaps. Access was random. There was no way to dial up a year, a day, a scene. The Park had supplied no program, none; the eight thousand hours weren't filed at all, they were a jumble, like a lunatic's memory, like a deck of shuffled cards. I had supposed, without thinking about it, that they would begin at the beginning and go on till they reached the end. Why didn't they?

I also understood something else. If access was truly random, if I truly had no control, then I had lost as good as forever those scenes I had seen. Odds were on the order of eight thousand to one (more? far more? probabilities are opaque to me) that I would never light on them again by pressing this bar. I felt a pang of loss for that afternoon in Ibiza. It was doubly gone now. I sat before the empty screen, afraid to touch ACCESS again, afraid of what I would lose.

I shut down the machine (the light level in the room rose, the Muzak poured softly back in) and went out into the halls, back to the display screen in the entranceway. The list of names slowly, greenly, rolled over like the list of departing flights at an airport: Code numbers were missing from beside many, indicating perhaps that they weren't yet in residence, only awaited. In the *D*s, three names, and DIRECTOR—hidden among them as though he were only another of the dead. A chamber number. I went to find it and went in. The director looked more like a janitor or a night watchman, the semiretired type you often see caretaking little-visited places. He wore a brown smock like a monk's robe and was making coffee in a corner of his small office, out of which little business seemed to be done. He looked up startled, caught out, when I entered.

"Sorry," I said, "but I don't think I understand this system right."

"A problem?" he said. "Shouldn't be a problem." He looked at me a little wide-eyed and shy, hoping not to be called on for anything difficult. "Equipment's all working?"

"I don't know," I said. "It doesn't seem that it could be." I described what I thought I had learned about The Park's access concept. "That can't be right, can it?" I said. "That access is totally random . . ."

He was nodding, still wide-eyed, paying close attention.

"Is it?" I asked.

"Is it what?"

"Random."

"Oh, yes. Yes, sure. If everything's in working order."

I could think of nothing to say for a moment, watching him nod reassuringly. Then, "Why?" I asked. "I mean why is there no way at all to, to organize, to have some kind of organized access to the material?" I had begun to feel that sense of grotesque foolishness in the presence of death, as though I were haggling over Georgie's effects. "That seems stupid, if you'll pardon me."

"Oh no, oh no," he said. "You've read your literature? You've read all your literature?"

"Well, to tell the truth . . ."

"It's all just as described," the director said. "I can promise you that. If there's any problem at all. . . ."

"Do you mind," I said, "if I sit down?" I smiled. He seemed so afraid of me and my complaint, of me as mourner, possibly grief crazed and unable to grasp the simple limits of his responsibilities to me, that he needed soothing himself. "I'm sure everything's fine," I said. "I just don't think I understand. I'm kind of dumb about these things."

"Sure. Sure. Sure." He regretfully put away his coffee makings and sat behind his desk, lacing his fingers together like a consultant. "People get a lot of satisfaction out of the access here," he said, "a lot of comfort, if they take in the right spirit." He tried a smile. I wondered what qualifications he had had to show to get this job. "The random part. Now, it's all in the literature. There's the legal aspect—you're not a lawyer are you, no, no, sure, no offense. You see, the material here isn't for anything, except, well, except for communing. But suppose the stuff were programmed, searchable. Suppose there was a problem about taxes or inheritance or so on. There could be subpoenas, lawyers all over the place, destroying the memorial concept completely."

I really hadn't thought of that. Built-in randomness saved past lives from being searched in any systematic way. And no doubt saved The Park from being in the records business and at the wrong end of a lot of suits. "You'd have to watch the whole eight thousand hours," I said, "and even if you found what you were looking for there'd be no way to replay it. It would have gone by." It would slide into the random past even as you watched it, like that afternoon in Ibiza, that party in Paris. Lost. He smiled and nodded. I smiled and nodded.

"I'll tell you something," he said. "They didn't predict that. The randomness. It was a side effect, an effect of the storage process. Just luck." His grin turned down, his brows knitted seriously. "See, we're storing here at the molecular level. We have to go that small, for space problems. I mean your eight-thousand-hour guarantee. If we had gone tape or conventional, how much room would it take up? If the access concept caught on. A lot of room. So we went vapor trap and endless tracking. Size of my thumbnail. It's all in the literature." He looked at me strangely. I had a sudden intense sensation that I was being fooled, tricked, that the man before me in his smock was no expert, no technician; he was a charlatan, or maybe a madman impersonating a director and not belonging here at all. It raised the hair on my neck and passed. "So the randomness," he was saying. "It was an effect of going molecular. Brownian movement. All you do is lift the endless tracking for a microsecond and you get a rearrangement at the molecular level. We don't randomize. The molecules do it for us."

I remembered Brownian movement, just barely, from physics class. The random movement of molecules, the teacher said; it has a mathematical description. It's like the movement of dust motes you see swimming in a shaft of sunlight, like the swirl of snowflakes in a glass paperweight that shows a cottage being snowed on. "I see," I said. "I guess I see."

"Is there," he said, "any other problem?" He said it as though there might be some other problem and that he knew what it might be and that he hoped I didn't have it. "You understand the system, key lock, two bars, ACCESS, RESET. . . ."

"I understand," I said. "I understand now."

"Communing," he said, standing, relieved, sure I would be gone soon. "I understand. It takes a while to relax into the communing concept."

"Yes," I said. "It does."

I wouldn't learn what I had come to learn, whatever that was. The Wasp had not been good at storage after all, no, no better than my young soul had been. Days and weeks had been missed by its tiny eye. It hadn't seen well, and in what it had seen it had been no more able to distinguish the just-as-well-forgotten from the unforgettable than my own eye had been. No better and no worse—the same.

And yet, and yet—she stood up in Ibiza and dressed her breasts with lotion, and spoke to me: *Oh, look, hummingbirds.* I had forgotten, and the Wasp had not; and I owned once again what I hadn't known I had lost, hadn't known was precious to me.

The sun was setting when I left The Park, the satin sea foaming softly, randomly around the rocks.

I had spent my life waiting for something, not knowing what, not even knowing I waited. Killing time. I was still waiting. But what I had been waiting for had already occurred and was past.

It was two years, nearly, since Georgie had died; two years until, for the first and last time, I wept for her—for her and for myself.

OF COURSE I went back. After a lot of work and correctly placed dollars, I netted a HAPpy card of my own. I had time to spare, like a lot of people then, and often on empty afternoons (never on Sunday) I would get out onto the unpatched and weed-grown freeway and glide up the coast. The Park was always open. I relaxed into the communing concept.

Now, after some hundreds of hours spent there underground, now, when I have long ceased to go through those doors (I have lost my key, I think; anyway I don't know where to look for it), I know that the solitude I felt myself to be in was real. The watchers around me, the listeners I sensed in other chambers, were mostly my imagination. There was rarely anyone there.

These tombs were as neglected as any tombs anywhere usually are. Either the living did not care to attend much on the dead—when have they ever?—or the hopeful buyers of the contracts had come to discover the flaw in the access concept— as I discovered it, in the end.

ACCESS, and she takes dresses one by one from her closet, and holds them against her body, and studies the effect in a tall mirror, and puts them back again. She had a funny face, which she never made except when looking at herself in the mirror, a face made for no one but herself, that was actually quite unlike her. The mirror Georgie.

RESET.

ACCESS. By a bizarre coincidence here she is looking in another mirror. I think the Wasp could be confused by mirrors. She turns away, the Wasp adjusts; there is someone asleep, tangled in bedclothes on a big hotel bed, morning, a room-service cart. Oh, the Algonquin: myself. Winter. Snow is falling outside the tall window. She searches her handbag, takes out a small vial, swallows a pill with coffee, holding the cup by its body and not its handle. I stir, show a tousled head of hair. Conversation— unintelligible. Gray room, whitish snow light, color degraded. Would I now (I thought, watching us) reach out for her? Would I in the next hour take her, or she me, push aside the bedclothes, open her pale pajamas? She goes into the john, shuts the door. The Wasp watches stupidly, excluded, transmitting the door.

RESET, finally.

But what (I would wonder) if I had been patient, what if I had watched and waited?

Time, it turns out, takes an unconscionable time. The waste, the footless waste— it's no spectator sport. Whatever fun there is in sitting idly looking at nothing and tasting your own being for a whole afternoon, there is no fun in replaying it. The waiting is excruciating. How often, in five years, in eight thousand hours of daylight or lamplight, might we have coupled, how much time expended in lovemaking? A hundred hours, two hundred? Odds were not high of my coming on such a scene; darkness swallowed most of them, and the others were lost in the interstices of endless hours spent shopping, reading, on planes and in cars, asleep, apart. Hopeless.

ACCESS. She has turned on a bedside lamp. Alone. She hunts amid the Kleenex and magazines on the bedside table, finds a watch, looks at it dully, turns it right side up, looks again, and puts it down. Cold. She burrows in the blankets, yawning, staring, then puts out a hand for the phone but only rests her hand on it, thinking. Thinking at four A.M. She withdraws her hand, shivers a child's deep, sleepy shiver, and shuts off the light. A bad dream. In an instant it's morning, dawn; the Wasp slept, too. She sleeps soundly, unmoving, only the top of her blond head showing out of the quilt—and will no doubt sleep so for hours, watched over more attentively, more fixedly, than any peeping Tom could ever have watched over her.

RESET.

ACCESS.

"I can't hear as well as I did at first," I told the director. "And the definition is getting softer."

"Oh sure," the director said. "That's really in the literature. We have to explain that carefully. That this might be a problem."

"It isn't just my monitor?" I asked. "I thought it was probably only the monitor."

"No, no, not really, no," he said. He gave me coffee. We'd gotten to be friendly over the months. I think, as well as being afraid of me he was glad I came around now and then; at least one of the living came here, one at least was using the services. "There's a *slight* degeneration that does occur."

"Everything seems to be getting gray."

His face had shifted into intense concern, no belittling this problem. "Mm-hm, mm-hm, see, at the molecular level where we're at, there is degeneration. It's just in the physics. It randomizes a little over time. So you lose—you don't lose a minute of what you've got, but you lose a little definition. A little color. But it levels off."

"It does?"

"We think it does. Sure it does, we promise it does. We *predict* that it will."

"But you don't know."

"Well, well you see we've only been in this business a short while. This concept is new. There were things we couldn't know." He still looked at me, but seemed at the same time to have forgotten me. Tired. He seemed to have grown colorless himself lately, old, losing definition. "You might start getting some snow," he said softly.

ACCESS RESET ACCESS.

A gray plaza of herringbone-laid stones, gray, clicking palms. She turns up the collar of her sweater, narrowing her eyes in a stern wind. Buys magazines at a kiosk: *Vogue, Harper's, La Mode. Cold,* she says to the kiosk girl. *Frio.* The young man I was takes her arm: they walk back along the beach, which is deserted and strung with cast seaweed, washed by a dirty sea. Winter in Ibiza. We talk, but the Wasp can't hear, the sea's sound confuses it; it seems bored by its duties and lags behind us.

RESET.

ACCESS. The Algonquin, terribly familiar morning, winter. She turns away from the snow window. I am in bed, and for a moment watching this I felt suspended between two mirrors, reflected endlessly. I had seen this before; I had lived it once and remembered it once, and remembered the memory, and here it was again, or could it be nothing but another morning, a similar morning. There were far more than one like this, in this place. But no; she turns from the window, she gets out her vial of pills, picks up the coffee cup by its body: I had seen this moment before, not months before, weeks before, here in this chamber. I had come upon the same scene twice.

What are the odds of it, I wondered, what are the odds of coming upon the same minutes again, these minutes.

I stir within the bedclothes.

I leaned forward to hear, this time, what I would say; it was something like *but fun anyway,* or something.

Fun, she says, laughing, harrowed, the degraded sound a ghost's twittering. *Charlie, someday I'm going to die of fun.*

She takes her pill. The Wasp follows her to the john and is shut out.

Why am I here? I thought, and my heart was beating hard and slow. *What am I here for? What?*

RESET.

ACCESS.

Silvered icy streets, New York, Fifth Avenue. She is climbing, shouting from a cab's dark interior. *Just don't shout at me,* she shouts at someone; her mother I never met, a dragon. She is out and hurrying away down the sleety street with her bundles, the Wasp at her shoulder. I could reach out and touch her shoulder and make her turn and follow me out. Walking away, lost in the colorless press of traffic and people, impossible to discern within the softened snowy image.

SOMETHING WAS VERY wrong.

Georgie hated winter, she escaped it most of the time we were together, about the first of the year beginning to long for the sun that had gone elsewhere; Austria was all right for a few weeks, the toy villages and sugar snow and bright, sleek skiers were not really the winter she feared, though even in fire-warmed chalets it was hard to get her naked without gooseflesh and shudders from some draft only she could feel. We were chaste in winter. So Georgie escaped it: Antigua and Bali and two months in Ibiza when the almonds blossomed. It was continual false, flavorless spring all winter long.

How often could snow have fallen when the Wasp was watching her?

Not often; countable times, times I could count up myself if I could remember as the Wasp could. Not often. Not always.

"There's a problem," I said to the director.

"It's peaked out, has it?" he said. "That definition problem?"

"Actually," I said, "it's gotten worse."

He was sitting behind his desk, arms spread wide across his chair's back, and a false, pinkish flush to his cheeks like undertaker's makeup. Drinking.

"Hasn't peaked out, huh?" he said.

"That's not the problem," I said. "The problem is the access. It's not random like you said."

"Molecular level," he said. "It's in the physics."

"You don't understand. It's not getting more random. It's getting less random. It's getting selective. It's freezing up."

"No, no, no," he said dreamily. "Access is random. Life isn't all summer and fun, you know. Into each life some rain must fall."

I sputtered, trying to explain. "But but . . ."

"You know," he said. "I've been thinking of getting out of access." He pulled open a drawer in the desk before him; it made an empty sound. He stared within it dully for a moment and shut it. "The Park's been good for me, but I'm just not used to this. Used to be you thought you could render a service, you know? Well, hell, you know, you've had fun, what do you care?"

He was mad. For an instant I heard the dead around me; I tasted on my tongue the stale air of underground.

"I remember," he said, tilting back in his chair and looking elsewhere, "many years ago, I got into access. Only we didn't call it that then. What I did was, I worked for a stock-footage house. It was going out of business, like they all did, like this place here is going to do, shouldn't say that, but you didn't hear it. Anyway, it was a big warehouse with steel shelves for miles, filled with film cans, film cans filled with old plastic film, you know? Film of every kind. And movie people, if they wanted old scenes of past time in their movies, would call up and ask for what they wanted, find me this, find me that. And we had everything, every kind of scene, but you know what the hardest thing to find was? Just ordinary scenes of daily life. I mean people just doing things and living their lives. You know what we *did* have? Speeches. People giving speeches. Like presidents. You could have hours of speeches, but not just people, whatchacallit, oh, washing clothes, sitting in a park . . ."

"It might just be the reception," I said. "Somehow."

He looked at me for a long moment as though I had just arrived. "Anyway," he said at last, turning away again, "I was there awhile learning the ropes. And producers called and said, 'Get me this, get me that.' And one producer was making a film, some film of the past, and he wanted old scenes, *old,* of people long ago, in the summer; having fun; eating ice cream; swimming in bathing suits; riding in convertibles. Fifty years ago. Eighty years ago."

He opened his empty drawer again, found a toothpick, and began to use it.

"So I accessed the earliest stuff. Speeches. More speeches. But I found a scene here and there—people in the street, fur coats, window-shopping, traffic. Old people, I mean they were young then, but people of the past; they have these pinched kind of faces, you get to know them. Sad, a little. On city streets, hurrying, holding their hats. Cities were sort of black then, in film; black cars in the streets, black derby hats. Stone. Well, it wasn't what they wanted. I found summer for them, color summer, but new. They wanted old. I kept looking back. I kept looking. I did. The further back I went, the more I saw these pinched faces, black cars, black streets of stone. Snow. There isn't any summer there."

With slow gravity he rose and found a brown bottle and two coffee cups. He poured sloppily. "So it's not your reception," he said. "Film takes longer, I guess, but it's the physics. All in the physics. A word to the wise is sufficient."

The liquor was harsh, a cold distillate of past sunlight. I wanted to go, get out, not look back. I would not stay watching until there was only snow.

"So I'm getting out of access," the director said. "Let the dead bury the dead, right? Let the dead bury the dead."

I DIDN'T GO back. I never went back, though the highways opened again and The Park isn't far from the town I've settled in. Settled; the right word. It restores your balance, in the end, even in a funny way your cheerfulness, when you come to know, without regrets, that the best thing that's going to happen in your life has already happened. And I still have some summer left to me.

I think there are two different kinds of memory, and only one kind gets worse as I get older: the kind where, by an effort of will, you can reconstruct your first car or your serial number or the name and figure of your high school physics teacher—a Mr. Holm, in a gray suit, a bearded guy, skinny, about thirty. The other kind doesn't worsen; if anything it grows more intense. The sleepwalking kind, the kind you stumble into as into rooms with secret doors and suddenly find yourself sitting not on your front porch but in a classroom. You can't at first think where or when, and a bearded, smiling man is turning in his hand a glass paperweight, inside which a little cottage stands in a swirl of snow.

There is no access to Georgie, except that now and then, unpredictably, when I'm sitting on the porch or pushing a grocery cart or standing at the sink, a memory of that kind will visit me, vivid and startling, like a hypnotist's snap of fingers.

Or like that funny experience you sometimes have, on the point of sleep, of hearing your name called softly and distinctly by someone who is not there.

JAMES PATRICK KELLY

Rat

James Patrick Kelly began contributing to magazines and anthologies in the late 1970s and quickly established a reputation as a writer of well-crafted stories that take a variety of approaches to an eclectic mix of themes. Much of his fiction is firmly grounded in social commentary. "Death Therapy" envisions a future justice system where simulated death is used to rehabilitate criminals. "Still Time" and "Crow" present opposing viewpoints on typical human behavior in the shadow of nuclear war. "Pogrom" presents the generation gap in terms of future civil war. "Big Guy" explores the breakdown of personal relationships and interactions coincident with the rise of rapid telecommunications and virtual reality. Kelly's best short fiction has been collected in *Think Like a Dinosaur and Other Stories*. His work as a novelist includes the diptych *Planet of Whispers* and *Look into the Sun,* concerned with life on the planet Aseneshesh, where political and religious strife replicates problems that cripple third world countries on Earth. His novel *Wildlife* explores the conflict between parent and offspring in the context of biogenetic engineering, with its tale of a young woman who rebels against the personality and destiny her father has engineered for her. He has also collaborated with John Kessel on *Freedom Beach.*

RAT HAD STASHED the dust in four plastic capsules and then swallowed them. From the stinging at the base of his ribs, he guessed they were now squeezing into his duodenum. Still plenty of time. The bullet train had been shooting through the vacuum of the TransAtlantic tunnel for almost two hours now; they would arrive at Port Authority/Koch soon. Customs had already been fixed, according to the maréchal. All Rat had to do was to get back to his nest, lock the smart door behind him, and put the word out on his protected nets. He had enough Algerian Yellow to dust at least half the cerebrums on the East Side. If he could turn this deal, he would be rich enough to bathe in Dom Perignon and dry himself with Gromaire tapestries. Another pang shot down his left flank. Instinctively his hind leg came off the seat and scratched at air.

There was only one problem; Rat had decided to cut the maréchal out. That meant he had to lose the old man's spook before he got home.

The spook had attached herself to him at Marseilles. She braided her blonde hair in pigtails. She had freckles, wore braces on her teeth. Tiny breasts nudged a modest silk turtleneck. She looked to be between twelve and fourteen. Cute. She had probably looked that way for twenty years, would stay the same another twenty if she did not stop a slug first or get cut in half by some automated security laser that tracked only heat and could not read—or be troubled by—cuteness. Their passports said they were Mr. Sterling Jaynes and daughter Jessalynn, of Forest Hills, New York. She was typing in her notebook, chubby fingers curled over the keys. Homework? A letter to a boyfriend? More likely she was operating on some corporate database with scalpel code of her own devising.

"Ne fais pas semblant d'étudier, ma petite," Rat said, "Que fais-tu?"

"Oh, Daddy," she said, pouting, "can't we go back to plain old English? After all, we're almost home." She tilted her notebook so that he could see the display. It read: "Two rows back, second seat from aisle. Fed. If he knew you were carrying, he'd cut the dust out of you and wipe his ass with your pelt." She tapped the Return key, and the message disappeared.

"All right, dear." He arched his back, fighting a surge of adrenaline that made his incisors click. "You know, all of a sudden I feel hungry. Should we do something here on the train or wait until we get to New York?" Only the spook saw him gesture back toward the fed.

"Why don't we wait for the station? More choice there."

"As you wish, dear." He wanted her to take the fed out *now*, but there was nothing more he dared say. He licked his hands nervously and groomed the fur behind his short, thick ears to pass the time.

The International Arrivals Hall at Koch Terminal was unusually quiet for a Thursday night. It smelled to Rat like a setup. The passengers from the bullet shuffled through the echoing marble vastness toward the row of customs stations. Rat was unarmed; if they were going to put up a fight, the spook would have to provide the firepower. But Rat was not a fighter, he was a runner. Their instructions were to pass through Station Number Four. As they waited in line, Rat spotted the federally appointed vigilante behind them. The classic invisible man: neither handsome nor ugly, five-ten, about one-seventy, brown hair, dark suit, white shirt. He looked bored.

"Do you have anything to declare?" The customs agent looked bored, too. Everybody looked bored except Rat, who had two million new dollars' worth of illegal drugs in his gut and a fed ready to carve them out of him.

"We hold these truths to be self-evident," said Rat, "that all men are created equal." He managed a feeble grin—as if this were a witticism and not the password.

"Daddy, please!" The spook feigned embarrassment. "I'm sorry, ma'am; it's his idea of a joke. It's the Declaration of Independence, you know."

The customs agent smiled as she tousled the spook's hair. "I know that, dear. Please put your luggage on the conveyor." She gave a perfunctory glance at her monitor as their suitcases passed through the scanner, and then nodded at Rat. "Thank you, sir, and have a pleasant . . ." The insincere thought died on her lips as she noticed the fed pushing through the line toward them. Rat saw her spin toward the exit at the same moment that the spook thrust her notebook computer into the scanner. The notebook stretched a blue finger of point discharge toward the magnetic lens just before the overhead lights novaed and went dark. The emergency backup failed as well. Rat's snout filled with the acrid smell of electrical fire. Through the darkness came shouts and screams, thumps and cracks—the crazed pounding of a stampede gathering momentum.

He dropped to all fours and skittered across the floor. Koch Terminal was his territory. He had crisscrossed its many levels with scent trails. Even in total darkness he could find his way. But in his haste he cracked his head against a pair of stockinged knees, and a squawking weight fell across him, crushing the breath from his lungs. He felt an icy stab on his hindquarters and scrabbled at it with his hind leg. His toes came away wet and he squealed. There was an answering scream, and the point of a shoe drove into him, propelling him across the floor. He rolled left and came up running. Up a dead escalator, down a carpeted hall. He stood upright and stretched to his full twenty-six inches, hands scratching until they found the emergency bar across the fire door. He hurled himself at it, a siren shrieked, and with a whoosh the door opened, dumping him into an alley. He lay there for a moment, gasping, half in and half out of Koch Terminal. With the certain knowledge that he was bleeding to death, he touched the coldness on his back. A sticky purple substance; he sniffed, then tasted it. Ice cream. Rat threw back his head and laughed. The high squeaky sound echoed in the deserted alley.

But there was no time to waste. He could already hear the buzz of police hovers swooping down from the night sky. The blackout might keep them busy for a while; Rat was more worried about the fed. And the spook. They would be out soon enough, looking for him. Rat scurried down the alley toward the street. He glanced quickly at the terminal, now a black hole in the galaxy of bright holographic sleaze that was Forty-second Street. A few cops with flashlights were trying to fight against the flow of panicky travelers pouring from its open doors. Rat smoothed his ruffled fur and turned away from the disaster, walking crosstown. His instincts said to run, but Rat forced himself to dawdle like a hick shopping for big-city excitement. He grinned at the pimps and windowshopped the hardware stores. He paused in front of a pair of mirror-image sex stops—GIRLS! LIVE! GIRLS! and LIVE! GIRLS! LIVE!—to sniff the pheromone-scented sweat pouring off an androgynous robot shill that was working the sidewalk. The robot obligingly put its hand to Rat's crotch, but he pushed it away with a hiss and continued on. At last, sure that he was not being followed, he powered up his wallet and tapped into the transnet to summon a hovercab. The wallet informed him that the city had cordoned off midtown airspace to facilitate rescue operations at Koch Terminal. It advised trying the subway or a taxi. Since he had no intention of sticking an ID chip—even a false one!—into a subway turnstyle, he stepped to the curb and began watching the traffic.

The rebuilt Checker that rattled to a stop beside him was a patchwork of orange ABS and stainless-steel armor. "No we leave Manhattan," said a speaker on the roof light. "No we north of a hundred and ten." Rat nodded and the door locks popped. The passenger compartment smelled of chlorobenzylmalononitrile and urine.

"First Avenue Bunker," said Rat, sniffing. "Christ, it stinks back here. Who was your last fare—the circus?"

"Troubleman." The speaker connections were loose, giving a scratchy edge to the cabbie's voice. The locks reengaged as the Checker pulled away from the curb. "Ha-has get a fullsnoot of tear gas in this hack."

Rat had already spotted the pressure vents in the floor. He peered through the gloom at the registration. A slogan had been lased in over it—probably by one of the new Mitsubishi penlights. "Free the dead." Rat smiled: the dead were his customers. People who had chosen the dust road. Twelve to eighteen months of glorious addiction: synthetic orgasms, recursive hallucinations leading to a total sensory overload and an ecstatic death experience. One dose was all it took to start down the dust road. The feds were trying to cut off the supply—with dire consequences for the dead. They could live a few months longer without dust, but their joyride down the dusty road was transformed into a grueling marathon of withdrawal pangs and madness. Either way, they were dead. Rat settled back onto the seat. The penlight graffito was a good omen. He reached into his pocket and pulled out a leather strip that had been soaked with a private blend of fat-soluble amphetamines and began to gnaw at it.

From time to time he could hear the cabbie monitoring NYPD net for flameouts or wildcat tolls set up by street gangs. They had to detour to heavily guarded Park Avenue all the way uptown to Fifty-ninth before doubling back toward the bunker. Originally built to protect U.N. diplomats from terrorists, the bunker had gone condo after the dissolution of the United Nations. Its hype was that it was the "safest address in the city." Rat knew better, which is why he had had a state-of-the-art smart door installed. Its rep was that most of the owners' association were candidates either for a mindwipe or an extended vacation on a fed punkfarm.

"Hey, Fare," said the cabbie, "net says the dead be rioting front of your door. Crash through or roll away?"

The fur along Rat's backbone went erect. "Cops?"

"Letting them play for now."

"You've got armor for a crash?"

"Shit, yes. Park this hack to ground zero for the right fare." The cabbie's laugh was static. "Don't worry, bunkerman. Give those deadboys a shot of old CS gas and they be too busy scratching they eyes out to bother us much."

Rat tried to smooth his fur. He could crash the riot and get stuck. But if he waited, either the spook or the fed would be stepping on his tail before long. Rat had no doubt that both had managed to plant locator bugs on him.

" 'Course, riot crashing don't come cheap," said the cabbie.

"Triple the meter." The fare was already over two hundred dollars for the fifteen-minute ride. "Shoot for Bay Two—the one with the yellow door." He pulled out his wallet and started tapping its luminescent keys. "I'm sending recognition code now."

He heard the cabbie notify the cops that they were coming through. Rat could feel the Checker accelerate as they passed the cordon, and he had a glimpse of strobing lights, cops in blue body armor, a tank studded with water cannons. Suddenly the cabbie braked, and Rat pitched forward against his shoulder harness. The Checker's solid rubber tires squealed, and there was the thump of something bouncing off the hood. They had slowed to a crawl, and the dead closed around them.

Rat could not see out the front because the cabbie was protected from his pas-sengers by steel plate. But the side windows filled with faces streaming with sweat and tears and blood. Twisted faces, screaming faces, faces etched by the agonies of with-drawal. The soundproofing muffled their howls. Fear and exhilaration filled Rat as he watched them pass. If only they knew how close they were to dust, he thought. He imagined the dead faces gnawing through the cab's armor in a frenzy, pausing only to spit out broken teeth. It was wonderful. The riot was proof that the dust market was still white-hot. The dead must be desperate to attack the bunker like this looking for a flash. He decided to bump the price of his dust another ten percent.

Rat heard a clatter on the roof; then someone began to jump up and down. It was like being inside a kettledrum. Rat sank claws into the seat and arched his back. "What are you waiting for? Gas them, damn it!"

"Hey, Fare. Stuff ain't cheap. We be fine—almost there."

A woman with bloody red hair matted to her head pressed her mouth against the window and screamed. Rat reared up on his hind legs and made biting feints at her. Then he saw the penlight in her hand. At the last moment Rat threw himself backward. The penlight flared, and the passenger compartment filled with the stench of melting plastic. A needle of coherent light singed the fur on Rat's left flank; he squealed and flopped onto the floor, twitching.

The cabbie opened the external gas vents, and abruptly the faces dropped away from the windows. The cab accelerated, bouncing as it ran over the fallen dead. There was a dazzling transition from the darkness of the violent night to the floodlit calm of Bay Number Two. Rat scrambled back onto the seat and looked out the back window in time to see the hydraulic doors of the outer lock swing shut. Something was caught between them—something that popped and spattered. The inner door rolled down on its track like a curtain coming down on a bloody final act.

Rat was almost home. Two security guards in armor approached. The door locks popped, and Rat climbed out of the cab. One of the guards leveled a burster at his head; the other wordlessly offered him a printreader. He thumbed it, and bunker's computer verified him immediately.

"Good evening, sir," said one of the guards. "Little rough out there tonight. Did you have luggage?"

The front door of the cab opened, and Rat heard the low whine of electric motors as a mechanical arm lowered the cabbie's wheelchair onto the floor of the bay. She was a gray-haired woman with a rheumy stare who looked like she belonged in a rest home in New Jersey. A knitted shawl covered her withered legs. "You said triple." The cab's hoist clicked and released the chair; she rolled toward him. "Six hundred and sixty-nine dollars."

"No luggage, no." Now that he was safe inside the bunker, Rat regretted his panic-stricken generosity. A credit transfer from one of his own accounts was out of the question. He slipped his last thousand-dollar bubble chip into his wallet's card reader, dumped $331 from it into a Bahamian laundry loop, and then dropped the chip into her outstretched hand. She accepted it dubiously: for a minute he expected her to bite into it like they did sometimes on fossil TV. Old people made him nervous. Instead she inserted the chip into her own card reader and frowned at him.

"How about a tip?"

Rat sniffed. "Don't pick up strangers."

One of the guards guffawed obligingly. The other pointed, but Rat saw the skunk port in the wheelchair a millisecond too late. With a wet *plot* the chair emitted a gaseous stinkball that bloomed like an evil flower beneath Rat's whiskers. One guard tried to grab at the rear of the chair, but the old cabbie backed suddenly over his foot. The other guard aimed his burster.

The cabbie smiled like a grandmother from hell. "Under the pollution index. No law against sharing a little scent, boys. And you wouldn't want to hurt me anyway. The hack monitors my EEG. I go flat and it goes berserk."

The guard with the bad foot stopped hopping. The guard with the gun shrugged. "It's up to you, sir."

Rat batted the side of his head several times and then buried his snout beneath his armpit. All he could smell was rancid burger topped with sulphur sauce. "Forget it. I haven't got time."

"You know," said the cabbie, "I never get out of the hack, but I just wanted to see what kind of person would live in a place like this." The lifts whined as the arm fitted its fingers into the chair. "And now I know." She cackled as the arm gathered her back into the cab. "I'll park it by the door. The cops say they're ready to sweep the street."

The guards led Rat to the bank of elevators. He entered the one with the open door, thumbed the printreader, and spoke his access code.

"Good evening, sir," said the elevator. "Will you be going straight to your rooms?"

"Yes."

"Very good, sir. Would you like a list of the communal facilities currently open to serve you?"

There was no shutting the sales pitch off, so Rat ignored it and began to lick the stink from his fur.

"The pool is open for lap swimmers only," said the elevator as the doors closed. "All environments except for the weightless room are currently in use. The sensory deprivation tanks will be occupied until eleven. The surrogatorium is temporarily out of female chassis; we apologize for any inconvenience . . ."

The cab moved down two and a half floors and then stopped just above the subbasement. Rat glanced up and saw a dark gap opening in the array of light diffuser panels. The spook dropped through it.

". . . the holo therapist is off-line until eight tomorrow morning, but the interactive sex booths will stay open until midnight. The drug dispensary . . ."

She looked as if she had been water-skiing through the sewer. Her blonde hair was wet and smeared with dirt; she had lost the ribbons from her pigtails. Her jeans were torn at the knees, and there was an ugly scrape on the side of her face. The silk turtleneck clung wetly to her. Yet despite her dishevelment, the hand that held the penlight was as steady as a jewel cutter's.

"There seems to be a minor problem," said the elevator in a soothing voice. "There is no cause for alarm. This unit is temporarily nonfunctional. Maintenance has been notified and is now working to correct the problem. In case of emergency, please contact Security. We regret this temporary inconvenience."

The spook fired a burst of light at the floor selector panel; it spat fire at them and went dark. "Where the hell were you?" said the spook. "You said the McDonald's in Time Square if we got separated."

"Where were *you?*" Rat rose up on his hind legs. "When I got there the place was swarming with cops."

He froze as the tip of the penlight flared. The spook traced a rough outline of Rat on the stainless-steel door behind him. "Fuck your lies," she said. The beam came so close that Rat could smell his fur curling away from it. "I want the dust."

"Trespass alert!" screeched the wounded elevator. A note of urgency had crept into its artificial voice. "Security reports unauthorized persons within the complex. Residents are urged to return immediately to their apartments and engage all personal security devices. Do not be alarmed. We regret this temporary inconvenience."

The scales on Rat's tail fluffed. "We have a deal. The maréchal needs my networks to move his product. So let's get out of here before . . ."

"The dust."

Rat sprang at her with a squeal of hatred. His claws caught on her turtleneck and he struck repeatedly at her open collar, gashing her neck with his long red incisors. Taken aback by the swiftness and ferocity of his attack, she dropped the penlight and tried to fling him against the wall. He held fast, worrying at her and chittering rabidly. When she stumbled under the open emergency exit in the ceiling, he leaped again. He cleared the suspended ceiling, caught himself on the inductor, and scrabbled up onto the hoist cables. Light was pouring into the shaft from above; armored guards had forced the door open, and were climbing down toward the stalled car. Rat jumped from the cables across five feet of open space to the counterweight and huddled there, trying to use its bulk to shield himself from the spook's fire. Her stand was short and inglorious. She threw a dazzler out of the hatch, hoping to blind the guards, then tried to pull herself through. Rat could hear the shriek of burster fire. He waited until he could smell the aroma of broiling meat and scorched plastic before he emerged from the shadows and signaled to the security team.

A squad of apologetic guards rode the service elevator with Rat down to the storage subbasement where he lived. When he had first looked at the bunker, the broker had been reluctant to rent him the abandoned rooms, insisting that he live aboveground with the other residents. But all of the suites they showed him were unacceptably open, clean, and uncluttered. Rat much preferred his musty dungeon, where odors lingered in the still air. He liked to fall asleep to the booming of the ventilation system on the level above him, and slept easier knowing that he was as far away from the stink of other people as he could get in the city.

The guards escorted him to the gleaming brass smart door and looked discreetly as he entered his passcode on the keypad. He had ordered it custom-built from Mosler so that it would recognize high-frequency squeals well beyond the range of human hearing. He called to it and then pressed trembling fingers onto the printreader. His bowels had loosened in terror during the firefight, and the capsules had begun to sting terribly. It was all he could do to keep from defecating right there in the hallway. The door sensed the guards and beeped to warn him of their presence. He punched in the override sequence impatiently, and the seals broke with a sigh.

"Have a pleasant evening, sir," said one of the guards as he scurried inside. "And don't worry ab—" The door cut him off as it swung shut.

Against all odds, Rat had made it. For a moment he stood, tail switching against the inside of the door, and let the magnificent chaos of his apartment soothe his jangled nerves. He had earned his reward—the dust was all his now. No one could take it away from him. He saw himself in a shard of mirror propped up against an empty THC aerosol and wriggled in self-congratulation. He was the richest rat on the East Side, perhaps in the entire city.

He picked his way through a maze formed by a jumble of overburdened steel shelving left behind years, perhaps decades, ago. The managers of the bunker had offered to remove them and their contents before he moved in; Rat had insisted that they stay. When the fire inspector had come to approve his newly installed sprinkler system, she had been horrified at the clutter on the shelves and had threatened to condemn the place. It had cost him plenty to buy her off, but it had been worth it. Since then Rat's trove of junk had at least doubled in size. For years no one had seen it but Rat and the occasional cockroach.

Relaxing at last, Rat stopped to pull a mildewed wing tip down from the huge collection of shoes; he loved the bouquet of fine old leather and gnawed and gnawed it whenever he could. Next to the shoes was a heap of books: his private library. One of Rat's favorite delicacies was the first edition of *Leaves of Grass* that he had pilfered from the rare book collection at the New York Public Library. To celebrate his safe arrival, he ripped out page 43 for a snack and stuffed it into the wing tip. He dragged the shoe over a pile of broken sheetrock and past shelves filled with scrap electronics: shattered monitors and dead typewriters, microwaves and robot vacuums. He had almost reached his nest when the fed stepped from behind a dirty Hungarian flag that hung from a broken fluorescent light fixture.

Startled, Rat instinctively hurled himself at the crack in the wall where he had built his nest. But the fed was too quick. Rat did not recognize the weapon; all he knew was that when it hissed, Rat lost all feeling in his hindquarters. He landed in a heap but continued to crawl, slowly, painfully.

"You have something I want." The fed kicked him. Rat skidded across the concrete floor toward the crack, leaving a thin gruel of excrement in his wake. Rat continued to crawl until the fed stepped on his tail, pinning him.

"Where's the dust?"

"I . . . I don't . . ."

The fed stepped again; Rat's left fibula snapped like cheap plastic. He felt no pain.

"The dust." The fed's voice quavered strangely.

"Not here. Too dangerous."

"Where?" The fed released him. "Where?"

Rat was surprised to see that the fed's gun hand was shaking. For the first time he looked up at the man's eyes and recognized the telltale yellow tint. Rat realized then how badly he had misinterpreted the fed's expression back at Koch. Not bored. *Empty.* For an instant he could not believe his extraordinary good fortune. Bargain for time, he told himself. There's still a chance. Even though he was cornered, he knew his instinct to fight was wrong.

"I can get it for you fast if you let me go," said Rat. "Ten minutes, fifteen. You look like you need it."

"What are you talking about?" The fed's bravado started to crumble, and Rat knew he had the man. The fed wanted the dust for himself. He was one of the dead.

"Don't make it hard on yourself," said Rat. "There's a terminal in my nest. By the crack. Ten minutes." He started to pull himself toward the nest. He knew the fed would not dare stop him; the man was already deep into withdrawal. "Only ten minutes and you can have all the dust you want." The poor fool could not hope to fight the flood of neuroregulators pumping crazily across his synapses. He might break any minute, let his weapon slip from trembling hands. Rat reached the crack and scrambled through into comforting darkness.

The nest was built around a century-old shopping cart and a stripped subway bench. Rat had filled the gaps in with pieces of synthetic rubber, a hubcap, plastic greeting cards, barbed wire, disk casings, Baggies, a No Parking sign, and an assortment of bones. Rat climbed in and lowered himself onto the soft bed of shredded thousand-dollar bills. The profits of six years of deals and betrayals, a few dozen murders, and several thousand dusty deaths.

The fed sniffled as Rat powered up his terminal to notify Security. "Someone set me up some vicious bastard slipped it to me I don't know when I think it was Barcelona . . . it would kill Sarah to see . . ." He began to weep. "I wanted to turn myself in . . . they keep working on new treatments you know but it's not fair damn it! The success rate is less than . . . I made my first buy two weeks only two God it seems . . . killed a man to get some lousy dust . . . but they're right it's, it's, I can't begin to describe what it's like . . ."

Rat's fingers flew over the glowing keyboard, describing his situation, the layout of the rooms, a strategy for the assault. He had overridden the smart door's recognition sequence. It would be tricky, but Security could take the fed out if they were quick and careful. Better risk a surprise attack than to dicker with an armed and unraveling dead man.

"I really ought to kill myself . . . would be best but it's not only me . . . I've seen ten-year-olds . . . what kind of animal sells dust to kids . . . I should kill myself and you." Something changed in the fed's voice as Rat signed off. "And you." He stooped and reached through the crack.

"It's coming," said Rat quickly. "By messenger. Ten doses. By the time you get to the door, it should be here." He could see the fed's hand and burrowed into the rotting pile of money. "You wait by the door, you hear? It's coming any minute."

"I don't want it." The hand was so large it blocked the light. Rat's fur went erect and he arched his spine. "Keep your fucking dust."

Rat could hear the guards fighting their way through the clutter. Shelves crashed. So clumsy, these men.

"It's you I want." The hand sifted through the shredded bills, searching for Rat. He had no doubt that the fed could crush the life from him—the hand was huge now. In the darkness he could count the lines on the palm, follow the whorls on the fingertips. They seemed to spin in Rat's brain—he was losing control. He realized then that one of the capsules must have broken, spilling a megadose of first-quality Algerian Yellow dust into his gut. With a hallucinatory clarity, he imagined sparks streaming through his blood, igniting neurons like tinder. Suddenly the guards did not matter. Nothing mattered except that he was cornered. When he could no longer fight the instinct to strike, the fed's hand closed around him. The man was stronger than Rat could have imagined. As the fed hauled him—clawing and biting—back into the light, Rat's only thought was of how terrifyingly large a man was. So much larger than a rat.

TERRY BISSON

Bears Discover Fire

Science fiction does not always mix well with humor or fantasy, but Terry Bisson has managed fusions of both in his novels and short fiction. His first novel, *Wyrldmaker,* published in 1981, puts a science fiction spin on a hackneyed theme from sword-and-sorcery fiction. *Talking Man* works elements of both fantasy and science fiction into a tall tale format. His alternate-history novel *Fire on the Mountain* wreaks an original and compelling variation on the familiar theme of a future in which the South won the American Civil War: here, a successful slave revolt leads to the creation of Nova Africa, a new republic in the place of what would have been the Confederate States. The humor in Bisson's stories ranges from slapstick to sly satire and invariably calls attention to the irrationality of increasingly complex worlds that simple humans are ill equipped to deal with. In his screwball adventure novel *Voyage to the Red Planet,* the first manned trip to Mars is a gimmick staged by a bumbling Hollywood producer banking heedlessly on a blockbuster to boost his sagging fortunes. *Pirates of the Universe* is a satirical space opera set in a future where Disney-Windows is the controlling corporate conglomerate. *The Pickup Artist* is a comic dystopia about a future where agents for the Bureau of Arts and Entertainment are charged with destroying artistic creations that the world has run out of room for. Bisson won the Nebula, Hugo, and Theodore Sturgeon Awards for the title tale of *Bears Discover Fire and Other Stories.* His other books include the short-fiction collection *In the Upper Room;* a posthumous collaboration with Walter M. Miller Jr., *St. Leibowitz and the Wild Horse Woman;* a sequel to the landmark novel *A Canticle for Leibowitz;* nonfiction books on Nat Turner and Mumia Abu Jamal; and novelizations of the films *Galaxy Quest* and *The Sixth Day.*

I WAS DRIVING with my brother, the preacher, and my nephew, the preacher's son, on I-65 just north of Bowling Green when we got a flat. It was Sunday night and we had been to visit Mother at the Home. We were in my car. The flat caused what you might call knowing groans since, as the old-fashioned one in my family (so they tell me), I fix my own tires, and my brother is always telling me to get radials and quit buying old tires.

But if you know how to mount and fix tires yourself, you can pick them up for almost nothing.

Since it was a left rear tire, I pulled over to the left, onto the median grass. The way my Caddy stumbled to a stop, I figured the tire was ruined. "I guess there's no need asking if you have any of that FlatFix in the trunk," said Wallace.

"Here, son, hold the light," I said to Wallace Jr. He's old enough to want to help and not old enough (yet) to think he knows it all. If I'd married and had kids, he's the kind I'd have wanted.

An old Caddy has a big trunk that tends to fill up like a shed. Mine's a '56. Wallace was wearing his Sunday shirt, so he didn't offer to help while I pulled magazines, fishing tackle, a wooden tool box, some old clothes, a comealong wrapped in a grass sack, and a tobacco sprayer out of the way, looking for my jack. The spare looked a little soft.

The light went out. "Shake it, son," I said.

It went back on. The bumper jack was long gone, but I carry a little quarter-ton hydraulic. I found it under Mother's old *Southern Livings*, 1978–1986. I had been meaning to drop them at the dump. If Wallace hadn't been along, I'd have let Wallace Jr. position the jack under the axle, but I got on my knees and did it myself. There's nothing wrong with a boy learning to change a tire. Even if you're not going to fix and mount them, you're still going to have to change a few in this life. The light went off again before I had the wheel off the ground. I was surprised at how dark the night was already. It was late October and beginning to get cool. "Shake it again, son," I said.

It went back on but it was weak. Flickery.

"With radials you just don't *have* flats," Wallace explained in that voice he uses when he's talking to a number of people at once; in this case, Wallace Jr. and myself. "And even when you *do*, you just squirt them with this stuff called FlatFix and you just drive on. Three ninety-five the can."

"Uncle Bobby can fix a tire hisself," said Wallace Jr., out of loyalty, I presume.

"*Him*self," I said from halfway under the car. If it was up to Wallace, the boy would talk like what Mother used to call "a helot from the gorges of the mountains." But drive on radials.

"Shake that light again," I said. It was about gone. I spun the lugs off into the hubcap and pulled the wheel. The tire had blown out along the sidewall. "Won't be fixing this one," I said. Not that I cared. I have a pile as tall as a man out by the barn.

The light went out again, then came back better than ever as I was fitting the spare over the lugs. "Much better," I said. There was a flood of dim orange flickery light. But when I turned to find the lug nuts, I was surprised to see that the flashlight the boy was holding was dead. The light was coming from two bears at the edge of the trees, holding torches. They were big, three-hundred-pounders, standing about five feet tall. Wallace Jr. and his father had seen them and were standing perfectly still. It's best not to alarm bears.

I fished the lug nuts out of the hubcap and spun them on. I usually like to put a little oil on them, but this time I let it go. I reached under the car and let the jack down and pulled it out. I was relieved to see that the spare was high enough to drive on. I put the jack and the lug wrench and the flat into the trunk. Instead of replacing the hubcap, I put it in there too. All this time, the bears never made a move. They just held the torches, whether out of curiosity or helpfulness, there was no way of knowing. It looked like there may have been more bears behind them, in the trees.

Opening three doors at once, we got into the car and drove off. Wallace was the first to speak. "Looks like bears have discovered fire," he said.

WHEN WE FIRST took Mother to the Home almost four years (forty-seven months) ago, she told Wallace and me she was ready to die. "Don't worry about me, boys," she whispered, pulling us both down so the nurse wouldn't hear. "I've drove a million miles and I'm ready to pass over to the other shore. I won't have long to linger here." She drove a consolidated school bus for thirty-nine years. Later, after Wallace left, she told me about her dream. A bunch of doctors were sitting around in a circle discussing her case. One said, "We've done all we can for her, boys, let's let her go." They all turned their hands up and smiled. When she didn't die that fall she seemed disappointed, though as spring came she forgot about it, as old people will.

In addition to taking Wallace and Wallace Jr. to see Mother on Sunday nights, I go myself on Tuesdays and Thursdays. I usually find her sitting in front of the TV, even though she doesn't watch it. The nurses keep it on all the time. They say the old folks like the flickering. It soothes them down.

"What's this I hear about bears discovering fire?" she said on Tuesday. "It's true," I told her as I combed her long white hair with the shell comb Wallace had brought her from Florida. Monday there had been a story in the Louisville *Courier-Journal*, and Tuesday one on NBC or CBS *Nightly News*. People were seeing bears all over the state, and in Virginia as well. They had quit hibernating, and were apparently planning to spend the winter in the medians of the interstates. There have always been bears in the mountains of Virginia, but not here in western Kentucky, not for almost a hundred years. The last one was killed when Mother was a girl. The theory in the *Courier-Journal* was that they were following 1-65 down from the forests of Michigan and Canada, but one old man from Allen County (interviewed on nationwide TV) said that there had always been a few bears left back in the hills, and they had come out to join the others now that they had discovered fire.

"They don't hibernate anymore," I said. "They make a fire and keep it going all winter."

"I declare," Mother said. "What'll they think of next!" The nurse came to take her tobacco away, which is the signal for bedtime.

EVERY OCTOBER, WALLACE Jr. stays with me while his parents go to camp. I realize how backward that sounds, but there it is. My brother is a Minister (House of the Righteous Way, Reformed) but he makes two-thirds of his living in real estate. He and Elizabeth go to a Christian Success Retreat in South Carolina, where people from all over the country practice selling things to one another. I know what it's like not because they've ever bothered to tell me, but because I've seen the Revolving Equity Success Plan ads late at night on TV.

The school bus let Wallace Jr. off at my house on Wednesday, the day they left. The boy doesn't have to pack much of a bag when he stays with me. He has his own room here. As the eldest of our family, I hung on to the old home place near Smiths Grove. It's getting run-down, but Wallace Jr. and I don't mind. He has his own room in Bowling Green, too, but since Wallace and Elizabeth move to a different house every three months (part of the Plan), he keeps his .22 and his comics, the stuff that's important to a boy his age, in his room here at the home place. It's the room his dad and I used to share.

Wallace Jr. is twelve. I found him sitting on the back porch that overlooks the interstate when I got home from work. I sell crop insurance.

After I changed clothes I showed him how to break the bead on a tire two ways, with a hammer, and by backing a car over it. Like making sorghum, fixing tires by hand is a dying art. The boy caught on fast, though. "Tomorrow I'll show you how to mount your tire with the hammer and a tire iron," I said.

"What I wish is I could see the bears," he said. He was looking across the field to I-65, where the northbound lanes cut off the corner of our field. From the house at night, sometimes the traffic sounds like a waterfall.

"Can't see their fire in the daytime," I said. "But wait till tonight." That night CBS or NBC (I forget which is which) did a special on the bears, which were becoming a story of nationwide interest. They were seen in Kentucky, West Virginia, Missouri, Illinois (southern), and, of course, Virginia. There have always been bears in Virginia. Some characters there were even talking about hunting them. A scientist said they were heading into the states where there is some snow but not too much, and where there is enough timber in the medians for firewood. He had gone in with a video camera, but his shots were just blurry figures sitting around a fire. Another scientist said the bears were attracted by the berries on a new bush that grew only in the medians of the interstates. He claimed this berry was the first new species in recent history, brought about by the mixing of seeds along the highway. He ate one on TV, making a face, and called it a "newberry." A climatic ecologist said that the warm winters (there was no snow last winter in Nashville, and only one flurry in Louisville) had changed the bears' hibernation cycle, and now they were able to remember things from year to year. "Bears may have discovered fire centuries ago," he said, "but forgot it." Another theory was that they had discovered (or remembered) fire when Yellowstone burned, several years ago.

The TV showed more guys talking about bears than it showed bears, and Wallace Jr. and I lost interest. After the supper dishes were done I took the boy out behind the house and down to our fence. Across the interstate and through the trees, we could see the light of the bears' fire. Wallace Jr. wanted to go back to the house and get his .22 and go shoot one, and I explained why that would be wrong. "Besides," I said, "a twenty-two wouldn't do much more to a bear than make it mad.

"Besides," I added, "it's illegal to hunt in the medians."

THE ONLY TRICK to mounting a tire by hand, once you have beaten or pried it onto the rim, is setting the bead. You do this by setting the tire upright, sitting on it, and bouncing it up and down between your legs while the air goes in. When the bead sets on the rim, it makes a satisfying "pop." On Thursday, I kept Wallace Jr. home from school and showed him how to do this until he got it right. Then we climbed our fence and crossed the field to get a look at the bears.

In northern Virginia, according to *Good Morning America,* the bears were keeping their fires going all day long. Here in western Kentucky, though, it was still warm for late October and they only stayed around the fires at night. Where they went and what they did in the daytime, I don't know. Maybe they were watching from the newberry bushes as Wallace Jr. and I climbed the government fence and crossed the northbound lanes. I carried an axe and Wallace Jr. brought his .22, not because he wanted to kill a bear but because a boy likes to carry some kind of a gun. The median was all tangled with brush and vines under the maples, oaks, and syca-mores. Even though we were only a hundred yards from the house, I had never been there, and neither had anyone else that I knew of. It was like a created country. We found a path in the center and followed it down across a slow, short stream that flowed out of one grate and into another. The tracks in the gray mud were the first bear signs we saw. There was a musty, but not really unpleasant smell. In a clearing under a big hollow beech, where the fire had been, we found nothing but ashes. Logs were drawn up in a rough circle and the smell was stronger. I stirred the ashes and found enough coals to start a new flame, so I banked them back the way they had been left.

I cut a little firewood and stacked it to one side, just to be neighborly.

Maybe the bears were watching us from the bushes even then. There's no way to know. I tasted one of the newberries and spit it out. It was so sweet it was sour, just the sort of thing you would imagine a bear would like.

*   *   *

THAT EVENING AFTER supper I asked Wallace Jr. if he might want to go with me to visit Mother. I wasn't surprised when he said yes. Kids have more consideration than folks give them credit for. We found her sitting on the concrete front porch of the Home, watching the cars go by on I-65. The nurse said she had been agitated all day. I wasn't surprised by that, either. Every fall as the leaves change, she gets restless, maybe the word is "hopeful," again. I brought her into the dayroom and combed her long white hair. "Nothing but bears on TV anymore," the nurse complained, flipping the channels. Wallace Jr. picked up the remote after the nurse left, and we watched a CBS or NBC Special Report about some hunters in Virginia who had gotten their houses torched. The TV interviewed a hunter and his wife whose $117,500 Shenandoah Valley home had burned. She blamed the bears. He didn't blame the bears, but he was suing for compensation from the state since he had a valid hunting license. The state hunting commissioner came on and said that possession of a hunting license didn't prohibit ("enjoin," I think, was the word he used) *the hunted* from striking back. I thought that was a pretty liberal view for a state commissioner. Of course, he had a vested interest in not paying off. I'm not a hunter myself.

"Don't bother coming on Sunday," Mother told Wallace Jr. with a wink. "I've drove a million miles and I've got one hand on the gate." I'm used to her saying stuff like that, especially in the fall, but I was afraid it would upset the boy. In fact, he looked worried after we left and I asked him what was wrong.

"How could she have drove a million miles?" he asked. She had told him forty-eight miles a day for thirty-nine years, and he had worked it out on his calculator to be 336,960 miles.

"Have *driven*," I said. "And it's forty-eight in the morning and forty-eight in the afternoon. Plus there were the football trips. Plus, old folks exaggerate a little." Mother was the first woman school-bus driver in the state. She did it every day and raised a family, too. Dad just farmed.

I USUALLY GET off the interstate at Smiths Grove, but that night I drove north all the way to Horse Cave and doubled back so Wallace Jr. and I could see the bears' fires. There were not as many as you would think from the TV—one every six or seven miles, hidden back in a clump of trees or under a rocky ledge. Probably they look for water as well as wood. Wallace Jr. wanted to stop, but it's against the law to stop on the interstate and I was afraid the state police would run us off.

There was a card from Wallace in the mailbox. He and Elizabeth were doing fine and having a wonderful time. Not a word about Wallace Jr., but the boy didn't seem to mind. Like most kids his age, he doesn't really enjoy going places with his parents.

ON SATURDAY AFTERNOON the Home called my office (Burley Belt Drought & Hail) and left word that Mother was gone. I was on the road. I work Saturdays. It's the only day a lot of part-time farmers are home. My heart literally missed a beat when I called in and got the message, but only a beat. I had long been prepared. "It's a blessing," I said when I got the nurse on the phone.

"You don't understand," the nurse said. "Not *passed* away, gone. *Ran* away, gone. Your mother has escaped." Mother had gone through the door at the end of the corridor when no one was looking, wedging the door with her comb and taking a bedspread which belonged to the Home. What about her tobacco? I asked. It was gone. That was a sure sign she was planning to stay away. I was in Franklin, and it took me less than an hour to get to the Home on I-65. The nurse told me that Mother had been acting more and more confused lately. Of course they are going to say that. We looked around the grounds, which is only a half acre with no trees between the interstate and a soybean field. Then they had me leave a message at the sheriff's office. I would have to keep paying for her care until she was officially listed as Missing, which would be Monday.

It was dark by the time I got back to the house, and Wallace Jr. was fixing supper. This just involves opening a few cans, already selected and grouped together with a rubber band. I told him his grandmother had gone, and he nodded, saying, "She told us she would be." I called Florida and left a message. There was nothing more to be done. I sat down and tried to watch TV, but there was nothing on. Then, I looked out the back door, and saw the firelight twinkling through the trees across the north-bound lane of I-65, and realized I just might know where to find her.

IT WAS DEFINITELY getting colder, so I got my jacket. I told the boy to wait by the phone in case the sheriff called, but when I looked back, halfway across the field, there he was behind me. He didn't have a jacket. I let him catch up. He was carrying his .22 and I made him leave it leaning against our fence. It was harder climbing the government fence in the dark, at my age, than it had been in the daylight. I am sixty-one. The highway was busy with cars heading south and trucks heading north.

Crossing the shoulder, I got my pants cuffs wet on the long grass, already wet with dew. It is actually bluegrass.

The first few feet into the trees it was pitch-black and the boy grabbed my hand. Then it got lighter. At first I thought it was the moon, but it was the high beams shining like moonlight into the treetops, allowing Wallace Jr. and me to pick our way through the brush. We soon found the path and its familiar bear smell.

I was wary of approaching the bears at night. If we stayed on the path we might run into one in the dark, but if we went through the bushes we might be seen as intruders. I wondered if maybe we shouldn't have brought the gun.

We stayed on the path. The light seemed to drip down from the canopy of the woods like rain. The going was easy, especially if we didn't try to look at the path but let our feet find their own way.

Then through the trees I saw their fire.

*   *   *

THE FIRE WAS mostly of sycamore and beech branches, the kind that puts out very little heat or light and lots of smoke. The bears hadn't learned the ins and outs of wood yet. They did okay at tending it, though. A large cinnamon-brown northern-looking bear was poking the fire with a stick, adding a branch now and then from a pile at his side. The others sat around in a loose circle on the logs. Most were smaller black or honey bears, one was a mother with cubs. Some were eating berries from a hubcap. Not eating, but just watching the fire, my mother sat among them with the bedspread from the Home around her shoulders.

If the bears noticed us, they didn't let on. Mother patted a spot right next to her on the log and I sat down. A bear moved over to let Wallace Jr. sit on her other side.

The bear smell is rank but not unpleasant, once you get used to it. It's not like a barn smell, but wilder. I leaned over to whisper something to Mother and she shook her head. *It would be rude to whisper around these creatures that don't possess the power of speech,* she let me know without speaking. Wallace Jr. was silent too. Mother shared the bedspread with us and we sat for what seemed hours, looking into the fire.

The big bear tended the fire, breaking up the dry branches by holding one end and stepping on them, like people do. He was good at keeping it going at the same level. Another bear poked the fire from time to time but the others left it alone. It looked like only a few of the bears knew how to use fire, and were carrying the others along. But isn't that how it is with everything? Every once in a while, a smaller bear walked into the circle of firelight with an armload of wood and dropped it onto the pile. Median wood has a silvery cast, like driftwood.

Wallace Jr. isn't fidgety like a lot of kids. I found it pleasant to sit and stare into the fire. I took a little piece of Mother's Red Man, though I don't generally chew. It was no different from visiting her at the Home, only more interesting, because of the bears. There were about eight or ten of them. Inside the fire itself, things weren't so dull, either: little dramas were being played out as fiery chambers were created and then destroyed in a crashing of sparks. My imagination ran wild. I looked around the circle at the bears and wondered what *they* saw. Some had their eyes closed. Though they were gathered together, their spirits still seemed solitary, as if each bear was sitting alone in front of its own fire.

The hubcap came around and we all took some newberries. I don't know about Mother, but I just pretended to eat mine. Wallace Jr. made a face and spit his out. When he went to sleep, I wrapped the bedspread around all three of us. It was getting colder and we were not provided, like the bears, with fur. I was ready to go home, but not Mother. She pointed up toward the canopy of trees, where a light was spreading, and then pointed to herself. Did she think it was angels approaching from on high? It was only the high beams of some southbound truck, but she seemed mighty pleased. Holding her hand, I felt it grow colder and colder in mine.

*   *   *

WALLACE JR. WOKE me up by tapping on my knee. It was past dawn, and his grand-mother had died sitting on the log between us. The fire was banked up and the bears were gone and someone was crashing straight through the woods, ignoring the path. It was Wallace. Two state troopers were right behind him. He was wearing a white shirt, and I realized it was Sunday morning. Underneath his sadness on learning of Mother's death, he looked peeved.

The troopers were sniffing the air and nodding. The bear smell was still strong. Wallace and I wrapped Mother in the bedspread and started with her body back out to the highway. The troopers stayed behind and scattered the bears' fire ashes and flung their firewood away into the bushes. It seemed a petty thing to do. They were like bears themselves, each one solitary in his own uniform.

There was Wallace's Olds 98 on the median, with its radial tires looking squashed on the grass. In front of it there was a police car with a trooper standing beside it, and behind it a funeral home hearse, also an Olds 98.

"First report we've had of them bothering old folks," the trooper said to Wallace. "That's not hardly what happened at all," I said, but nobody asked me to explain. They have their own procedures. Two men in suits got out of the hearse and opened the rear door. That to me was the point at which Mother departed this life. After we put her in, I put my arms around the boy. He was shivering even though it wasn't that cold. Sometimes death will do that, especially at dawn, with the police around and the grass wet, even when it comes as a friend.

We stood for a minute watching the cars and trucks pass. "It's a blessing," Wallace said. It's surprising how much traffic there is at 6:22 A.M.

THAT AFTERNOON, I went back to the median and cut a little firewood to replace what the troopers had flung away. I could see the fire through the trees that night.

I went back two nights later, after the funeral. The fire was going and it was the same bunch of bears, as far as I could tell. I sat around with them awhile but it seemed to make them nervous, so I went home. I had taken a handful of newberries from the hubcap, and on Sunday I went with the boy and arranged them on Mother's grave. I tried again, but it's no use, you can't eat them.

Unless you're a bear.

| JOHN KESSEL |

A Clean Escape

John Kessel's reputation as a writer of sophisticated, literary fantasy and science fiction is predicated on a handful of stories that frequently invade the territory of classic writers and use the lessons in their literature as sounding boards for contemporary values and social mores. The mock essay "Herman Melville: Space Opera Virtuoso" and the Nebula Award–winning riff on *Moby Dick*, "Another Orphan," both chart incongruous intersections of the period of Melville and modern times. "The Big Dream" tells of a private detective, on the trail of Raymond Chandler, slowly evolving into a character in a typical Chandler crime story. "The Pure Product" and "Every Angel Is Terrifying" both extend ideas in the southern gothic fiction of Flannery O'Connor. H. G. Wells is himself a character in the Wellsian tale "Buffalo." These stories, and Kessel's alternate-history tales "Some Like It Cold," "The Franchise," and "Uncle John and the Saviour," have been collected in his short-fiction compilations *Meetings in Infinity* and *The Pure Product*. The creative playfulness implicit in the "what-if" speculations of these stories extends to Kessel's work as a novelist. *Good News from Outer Space* sketches a satirical portrait of a dysfunctional America on the eve of the twenty-first century, obsessed with alien invasion and millennial irrationality. *Corrupting Dr. Nice* is a screwball time-travel story involving a father-daughter team of flimflam artists who traverse timelines and alternate histories in search of victims. Kessel has also written the novel *Freedom Beach* in collaboration with James Patrick Kelly.

> *"I've been thinking about devils. I mean if there are devils in the world, if there are people in the world who represent evil, is it our duty to exterminate them?"*
> JOHN CHEEVER,
> "The Five-Forty-Eight"

AS SHE SAT in her office, waiting—for exactly what she did not know—Dr. Evans hoped that it wasn't going to be another bad day. She needed a cigarette and a drink. She swiveled the chair around to face the closed venetian blinds beside her desk, leaned back and laced her hands behind her head. She closed her eyes and breathed deeply. The air wafting down from the ventilator in the ceiling smelled of machine oil. It was cold. Her face felt it, but the bulky sweater kept the rest of her warm. Her hair felt greasy. Several minutes passed in which she thought of nothing. There was a knock at the door.

"Come in," she said absently.

Havelmann entered. He had the large body of an athlete gone slightly soft, thick, gray hair and a lined face. At first glance he didn't look sixty. His well-tailored blue suit badly needed pressing.

"Doctor?"

Evans stared at him for a moment. She would kill him. She looked down at the desk, rubbed her forehead with her hand. "Sit down," she said.

She took the pack of cigarettes from the desk drawer. "Would you care to smoke?"

The old man took one. She watched him carefully. His brown eyes were rimmed with red; they looked apologetic.

"I smoke too much," he said. "But I can't quit."

She gave him a light. "More people around here are quitting every day."

Havelmann exhaled smoothly. "What can I do for you?"

What can I do for *you*, sir.

"First, I want to play a little game." Evans took a handkerchief out of a pocket. She moved a brass paperweight, a small model of the Lincoln Memorial, to the center of the desk blotter. "I want you to watch what I'm doing, now."

Havelmann smiled. "Don't tell me—you're going to make it disappear, right?"

She tried to ignore him. She covered the paperweight with the handkerchief. "What's under this handkerchief?"

"Can we put a little bet on it?"

"Not this time."

"A paperweight."

"That's wonderful." Evans leaned back with finality. "Now I want you to answer a few questions."

The old man looked around the office curiously: at the closed blinds, at the computer terminal and keyboard against the wall, at the pad of switches in the corner of the desk. His eyes came to rest on the mirror opposite the window. "That's a two-way mirror."

Evans sighed. "No kidding."

"Are you recording this?"

"Does it matter to you?"

"I'd like to know. Common courtesy."

"Yes, we're being videotaped. Now answer the questions."

Havelmann seemed to shrink in the face of her hostility. "Sure."

"How do you like it here?"

"It's O.K. A little boring. A man couldn't even catch a disease here, from the looks of it, if you know what I mean. I don't mean any offense, doctor. I haven't been here long enough to get the feel of the place."

Evans rocked slowly back and forth. "How do you know I'm a doctor?"

"Aren't you a doctor? I thought you were. This is a hospital, isn't it? So I figured when they sent me in to see you you must be a doctor."

"I am a doctor. My name is Evans."

"Pleased to meet you, Dr. Evans."

She would kill him. "How long have you been here?"

The man tugged on his earlobe. "I must have just got here today. I don't think it was too long ago. A couple of hours. I've been talking to the nurses at their station."

What she wouldn't give for three fingers of Jack Daniels. She looked at him over the steeple of her fingers. "Such talkative nurses."

"I'm sure they're doing their jobs."

"I'm sure. Tell me what you were doing before you came to this . . . hospital."

"You mean right before?"

"Yes."

"I was working."

"Where do you work?"

"I've got my own company—ITG Computer Systems. We design programs for a lot of people. We're close to getting a big contract with Ma Bell. We swing that and I can retire by the time I'm forty—if Uncle Sam will take his hand out of my pocket long enough for me to count my change."

Evans made a note on her pad. "Do you have a family?"

Havelmann looked at her steadily. His gaze was that of an earnest young college student, incongruous on a man of his age. He stared at her as if he could not imagine why she would ask him these abrupt questions. She detested his weakness; it raised in her a fury that pushed her to the edge of insanity. It was already a bad day, and it would get worse.

"I don't understand what you're after," Havelmann said, with considerable dignity. "But just so your record shows the facts: I've got a wife, Helen, and two kids. Ronnie's nine and Susan's five. We have a nice big house and a Lincoln and a Porsche. I follow the Braves and I don't eat quiche. What else would you like to know?"

"Lots of things. Eventually I'll find them out." Evans' voice was cold. "Is there anything you'd like to ask me? How you came to be here? How long you're going to have to stay? Who you are?"

His voice went similarly cold. "I know who I am."

"Who are you, then?"

"My name is Robert Havelmann."

"That's right," Doctor Evans said calmly. "What year is it?"

Havelmann watched her warily, as if he were about to be tricked. "What are you talking about? It's 1984."

"What time of year?"

"Spring."

"How old are you?"

"Thirty-five."

"What do I have under this handkerchief?"

Havelmann looked at the handkerchief on the desk as if noticing it for the first time. His shoulders tightened and he looked suspiciously at Evans.

"How should I know?"

HE WAS BACK again that afternoon, just as rumpled, just as innocent. How could a person get old and still be innocent? She could not remember things ever being that easy. "Sit down," she said.

"Thanks. What can I do for you, doctor?"

"I want to follow up on the argument we had this morning."

Havelmann smiled. "Argument? This morning?"

"Don't you remember talking to me this morning?"

"I never saw you before."

Evans watched him coolly. The old man shifted in his chair.

"How do you know I'm a doctor?"

"Aren't you a doctor? They told me I should go in to see Dr. Evans in room 10."

"I see. If you weren't here this morning, where were you?"

Havelmann hesitated.

"Let's see—I was at work. I remember telling Helen—the wife—that I'd try to get home early. She's always ragging me because I stay late. The company's pretty busy right now: big contract in the works. Susan's in the school play, and we have to be there by eight. And I want to get home soon enough before then to do some yardwork. It looked like a good day for it."

Evans made a note: "What season is it?"

Havelmann fidgeted like a child, looked at the window, where the blinds were still closed.

"Spring," he said. "Sunny, warm—very nice weather. The redbuds are just starting to come out."

Without a word Evans got out of her chair and went to the window. She opened the blinds, revealing a barren field swept with drifts of snow. Dead grass whipped in the strong wind and the sky roiled with clouds.

"What about this?"

Havelmann stared. His back straightened and he leaned forward. He tugged at his earlobe.

"Isn't that a bitch. If you don't like the weather here—wait ten minutes."

"What about the redbuds?"

"This weather will probably kill them. I hope Helen made the kids wear their jackets."

Evans looked out the window. Nothing had changed. She slowly drew the blinds and sat down again.

"What year is it?"

Havelmann adjusted himself in his chair, calm again. "What do you mean? It's 1984."

"Did you ever read that book?"

"Slow down a minute. What are you talking about?"

Evans wondered what he would do if she got up and ground her thumbs into his eyes. "The book by George Orwell titled *1984.*" She forced herself to speak slowly. "Are you familiar with it?"

"Sure. We had to read it in college." Was there a trace of irritation beneath Havelmann's innocence? Evans sat as silently and as still as she could.

"I remember it made quite an impression on me," Havelmann continued.

"What kind of impression?"

"I expected something different from the professor. He was a confessed liberal. I expected some kind of bleeding heart book. It wasn't like that at all."

"Did it make you uncomfortable?"

"No. It didn't tell me anything I didn't know already. It just showed what was wrong with collectivism. You know—Communism represses the individual, destroys initiative. It claims it has the interests of the majority at heart. And it denies all human values. That's what I got out of *1984,* though to hear that professor talk about it, it was all about Nixon and Vietnam."

Evans kept still. Havelmann went on.

"I've seen the same mentality at work in business. The large corporations, they're just like the government. Big, slow: you could show them a way to save a billion, and they'd squash you like a bug because it's too much trouble to change."

"You sound like you've got some resentments," said Evans.

The old man smiled. "I do, don't I. I admit it. I've thought a lot about it. But I have faith in people. Someday I may just run for state assembly and see whether I can do some good."

Her pencil point snapped. She looked at Havelmann, who looked back at her. After a moment she focused her attention on the notebook. The broken point had left a black scar across her precise handwriting.

"That's a good idea," she said quietly, her eyes still lowered. "You still don't remember arguing with me this morning?"

"I never saw you before I walked in this door. What were we supposed to be fighting about?"

He was insane. Evans almost laughed aloud at the thought—of course he was insane—why else would he be there? The question, she forced herself to consider rationally, was the nature of his insanity. She picked up the paperweight and handed it across to him. "We were arguing about this paperweight," she said. "I showed it to you, and you said you'd never seen it before."

Havelmann examined the paperweight. "Looks ordinary to me. I could easily forget something like this. What's the big deal?"

"You'll note that it's a model of the Lincoln Memorial."

"You probably got it at some gift shop. D.C. is full of junk like that."

"I haven't been to Washington in a long time."

"I live there. Alexandria, anyway. I drive in every morning."

Evans closed her notebook. "I have a possible diagnosis of your condition," she said suddenly.

"What condition?"

This time the laughter was harder to repress. Tears almost came to her eyes with the effort. She caught her breath and continued. "You exhibit the symptoms of Korsakov's syndrome. Have you ever heard of that before?"

Havelmann looked as blank as a whitewashed wall. "No."

"Korsakov's syndrome is an unusual form of memory loss. Recorded cases go back to the late 1800s. There was a famous one in the 1970s—famous to doctors, I mean. A Marine sergeant named Arthur Briggs. He was in his fifties, in good health aside from the lingering effects of alcoholism, and had been a career noncom until his discharge in the mid-sixties after twenty years in the service. He'd functioned normally until the early seventies, when he lost his memory of any events which occurred to him after September, 1944. He could remember in vivid detail, as if they had just happened, events up until that time. But of the rest of his life—nothing. Not only that, his continuing memory was affected so that he could remember events that occurred in the present only for a period of minutes, after which he would forget totally."

"I can remember what happened to me right up until I walked into this room."

"That's what Sgt. Briggs told his doctors. To prove it he told them that World War II was going strong, that he was stationed in San Francisco in preparation for being sent to the Philippines, that it looked like the St. Louis Browns might finally win a pennant if they could hold on through September, and that he was twenty years old. He had the outlook and abilities of an intelligent twenty-year-old. He couldn't remember anything that happened to him longer than forty minutes. The world had gone on, but he was permanently stuck in 1944."

"That's horrible."

"So it seemed to the doctor in charge—at first. Later he speculated that it might not be so bad. The man still had a current emotional life. He could still enjoy the present; it just didn't stick with him. He could remember his youth, and for him his youth had never ended. He never aged; he never saw his friends grow old and die, he never remembered that he himself had grown up to be a lonely alcoholic. His girl-friend was still waiting for him back in Columbia, Missouri. He was twenty years old forever. He had made a clean escape."

Evans opened a desk drawer and took out a hand mirror. "How old are you?" she asked.

Havelmann looked frightened. "Look, why are we doing—"

"How old are you?" Evans' voice was quiet but determined. Inside her a pang of joy threatened to break her heart.

"I'm thirty-five. What the hell—"

Shoving the mirror at him was as satisfying as firing a gun. Havelmann took it, glanced at her, then tentatively, like the most nervous of college freshmen checking the grade on his final exam, looked at his reflection. "Jesus Christ," he said. He started to tremble.

"What happened? What did you do to me?" He got out of the chair, his expression contorted. "What did you do to me! I'm thirty-five! What happened?"

Dr. Evans stood in front of the mirror in her office. She was wearing her uniform. It was quite as rumpled as Havelmann's suit. She had the tunic unbuttoned and was feeling her left breast. She lay down on the floor and continued the examination. The lump was undeniable. No pain, yet.

She sat up, reached for the pack of cigarettes on the desktop, fished out the last one and lit it. She crumpled the pack and threw it at the wastebasket. Two points. She had been quite a basketball player in college, twenty years before. She lay back down and took a long drag on the cigarette, inhaling deeply, exhaling the smoke with force, with a sigh of exhaustion. She probably could not make it up and down the court a single time any more.

She turned her head to look out the window. The blinds were open, revealing the same barren landscape that showed before. There was a knock at the door.

"Come in," she said.

Havelmann entered. He saw her lying on the floor, raised an eyebrow, grinned. "You're Doctor Evans?"

"I am."

"Can I sit here or should I lie down too?"

"Do whatever you fucking well please."

He sat in the chair. He had not taken offense. "So what did you want to see me about?"

Evans got up, buttoned her tunic, sat in the swivel chair. She stared at him. Her face was blank, pale, her thin lips steady. It was the expression of a woman terminally ill, so accustomed to her illness, and the necessity of ignoring it, that all that showed of the pain was mild annoyance. I am going to see this through, her face said, and then I'm going to kill myself.

"Have we ever met before?" she asked.

"No. I'm sure I'd remember."

He was sure he would remember. She would fucking kill him. He would remember that.

She ground out the last inch of cigarette. She felt her jaw muscles tighten; she looked down at the ashtray in regret. "Now I have to quit."

"I should quit. I smoke too much myself."

"I want you to listen to me closely now," she said slowly. "Do not respond until I'm finished.

"My name is Major D. S. Evans and I am a military psychologist. This office is in the infirmary of NECDEC, the National Emergency Center for Defense Communications, located one thousand feet below a hillside in West Virginia. As far as we know we are the only surviving governmental body in the continental United States. The scene you see through this window is being relayed from a surface monitor in central Nebraska; by computer command I can connect us with any of the twelve monitors still functioning on the surface."

Evans turned to her keyboard and typed in a command; the scene through the window snapped to a shot of broken masonry and twisted steel reinforcement rods. The view was obscured by dust caked on the camera lens and by a heavy snowfall. Evans typed in an additional command and touched one of the switches on her desk. A blast of static, a hiss like frying bacon, came from a speaker.

"That's Dallas. The sound is a reading of the background radiation registered by detectors at the site of this camera." She typed in another command and the image on the "window" flashed through a succession of equally desolate scenes, holding ten seconds on each before switching to the next. A desert in twilight, motionless under low clouds; a murky underwater shot in which the remains of a building were just visible; a denuded forest half-buried in snow; a deserted highway overpass. With each change of scene the loudspeaker stopped for a split-second, then the hiss resumed.

Havelmann watched all of this soberly.

"This has been the state of the surface for a year now, ever since the last bombs fell. To our knowledge there are no human beings alive in North America—in the Northern Hemisphere, for that matter. Radio transmissions from South America, New Zealand and Australia have one by one ceased in the last eight months. We have not observed a living creature above the level of an insect through any of our monitors since the beginning of the year. It is the summer of 2010. Although, considering the situation, counting years by the old system seems a little futile to me."

Doctor Evans slid open a desk drawer and took out an automatic. She placed it in the middle of the desk blotter and leaned back, her right hand touching the edge of the desk, near the gun.

"You are now going to tell me that you never heard of any of this, and that you've never seen me before in your life," she said. "Despite the fact that I have been speaking to you daily for two weeks and that you have had this explanation from me at least three times during that period. You are going to tell me that it is 1984 and that you are thirty-five years old, despite the absurdity of such a claim. You are going to feign amazement and confusion; the more that I insist that you face these facts, the more you are going to become distressed. Eventually you will break down into tears and expect me to sympathize. You can go to hell."

Evans' voice had grown angrier as she spoke. She had to stop; it was almost more than she could do. When she resumed she was under control again. "If you persist in this sham, I may kill you. I assure you that no one will care if I do. You may speak now."

Havelmann stared at the window. His mouth opened and closed stupidly. How old he looked, how feeble. Evans felt a sudden wave of pity and doubt. What if she were wrong? She had an image of herself as she might appear to him: arrogant, bitter, an incomprehensible inquisitor whose motives for tormenting him were a total mystery. She watched him. After a few minutes his mouth closed; the eyes blinked rapidly and were clear.

"Please. Tell me what you're talking about."

Evans shuddered. "The gun is loaded. Keep talking."

"What do you want me to say? I never heard of any of this. Only this morning I saw my wife and kids and everything was all right. Now you give me this story about atomic war and 2010. What, have I been asleep for thirty years?"

"You didn't act very surprised to be here when you walked in. If you're so disoriented, how do you explain how you got here?"

The man sat heavily in the chair. "I don't remember. I guess I thought I came here—to the hospital, I thought—to get a checkup. I didn't think about it. You must know how I got here."

"I do. But I think you know too, and you're just playing a game with me—with all of us. The others are worried, but I'm sick of it. I can see through you, so you may as well quit the act. You were famous for your sincerity, but I always suspected that was an act, too, and I'm not falling for it. You didn't start this game soon enough for me to be persuaded you're crazy, despite what the others may think."

Evans played with the butt of her dead cigarette. "Or this could be a delusional system," she continued. "You think you're in a hospital, and your schizophrenia has progressed to the point where you deny all facts that don't go along with your attempts to evade responsibility. I suppose in some sense such an insanity would absolve you. If that's the case, I should be more objective. Well, I can't. I'm failing my profession, I realize. Too bad." Emotion had gradually drained away from her until, by the end, she felt as if she were speaking from across a continent instead of a desk.

"I still don't know what you're talking about. Where are my wife and kids?"

"They're dead."

Havelmann sat rigidly. The only sound was the hiss of the radiation detector. "Let me have a cigarette."

"There are no cigarettes left. I just smoked my last one." Evans' voice was distant. "I made two cartons last a year."

Havelmann's gaze dropped. "How old my hands are! . . . Helen has lovely hands."

"Why are you going on with this charade?"

The old man's face reddened. "God damn you! Tell me what happened!"

"The famous Havelmann rage. Am I supposed to be frightened now?"

The hiss from the loudspeaker seemed to increase. Havelmann lunged for the gun. Evans snatched it and pushed back from the desk. The old man grabbed the paperweight and raised it to strike. She pointed the gun at him.

"Your wife didn't make the plane in time. She was at the western White House. I don't know where your damned kids were—probably vaporized with their own families. You, however, had Operation Kneecap to save you, Mr. President. Now sit down and tell me why you've been playing games, or I'll kill you right here and now. Sit down!"

A light seemed to dawn on Havelmann. "You're insane," he said quietly.

"Put the paperweight back on the desk."

He did. He sat.

"But you can't simply be crazy," Havelmann continued. "There's no reason why you should take me away from my home and subject me to this. This is some kind of plot. The government. The CIA."

"And you're thirty-five years old?"

Havelmann examined his hands again. "You've done something to me."

"And the camps? Administrative Order 31?"

"If I'm the president, then why are you quizzing me here? Why can't I remember a thing about it?"

"Stop it. Stop it right now," Evans said slowly. She heard her voice for the first time. It sounded more like that of an old man than Havelmann's. "I can't take any more lies. I swear that I'll kill you. First it was the commander-in-chief routine, calisthenics, stiff upper lips and discipline. Then the big brother, let's have a whiskey and talk it over, son. Yessir, Mr. President." Havelmann stared at her. He was going to make her kill him, and she knew she wouldn't be strong enough not to.

"Now you can't remember anything," she said. "Your boys are confused, they're fed up. I'm fed up, too."

"If this is true, you've got to help me!"

"I don't give a rat's ass about helping you!" Evans shouted. "I'm interested in making you tell the truth. Don't you realize that we're dead? I don't care about your feeble sense of what's right and wrong; just tell me what's keeping you going. Who do you think you're going to impress? You think you've got an election to win? A place in history to protect? There isn't going to be any more history! History ended last August!

"So spare me the fantasy about the hospital and the nonexistent nurses' station. Someone with Korsakov's wouldn't make up that story. He would recognize the difference between a window and a projection screen. A dozen other slips. You're not a good enough actor."

Her hand trembled. The gun was heavy. Her voice trembled, too, and she despised herself for it. "Sometimes I think the only thing that's kept me alive is knowing I had half a pack of cigarettes left. That and the desire to make you crawl."

The old man sat looking at the gun in her hand. "I was the president?"

"No," said Evans bitterly, "I made it all up."

His eyes seemed to sink farther back in the network of lines surrounding them. "I started a war?"

Evans felt her heart race. "Stop lying! You sent the strike force; you ordered the pre-emptive launch."

"I'm old. How old am I?"

"You know damn well how—" She stopped. She could hardly catch her breath. She felt a sharp pain in her breast. "You're sixty-one."

"Jesus, Mary, Joseph."

"That's it? That's all you can say?"

The old man stared hollowly, then slowly, so slowly that at first it was not apparent what he was doing, he lowered his head into his hands and began to cry. His sobs were almost inaudible over the hissing of the radiation detector. Dr. Evans watched him intently. She rested her elbows on the desk, steadying the gun with both hands. Havelmann's head shook in front of her. Despite his age, his gray hair was thick.

After a moment Evans reached over and switched off the loudspeaker. The hissing stopped.

Eventually Havelmann stopped crying. He raised his head. He looked dazed. His expression became unreadable. He looked at the doctor and the gun.

"My name is Robert Havelmann," he said. "Why are you pointing that gun at me?"

"Please don't," said Evans.

"Don't what? Who are you?"

Evans watched his face blur. Through her tears he looked like a much younger man. The gun drooped. She tried to lift it, but it was as if she were made of smoke—there was no substance to her, and it was all she could do to keep from dissipating, let alone kill anyone as clean and innocent as Robert Havelmann. He took the gun from her hand. "Are you all right?" he asked.

DR. EVANS SAT in her office, hoping that it wasn't going to be a bad day. The pain in her breast had not come that day, but she was out of cigarettes. She searched the desk on the odd chance that she might have missed a pack, even a single butt, in the corner of one of the drawers. No luck.

She gave up and turned to face the window. The blinds were open, revealing the snow-covered field. She watched the clouds roll before the wind. It was dark. Winter. Nothing was alive.

"It's cold outside," she whispered.

There was a knock at the door. Dear God, leave me alone, she thought. Please leave me alone.

"Come in," she said.

The door opened and an old man in a rumpled suit entered. "Dr. Evans? I'm Robert Havelmann. What did you want to talk about?"

| LISA GOLDSTEIN |

Tourists

Lisa Goldstein's fiction features motifs common to science fiction, including time travel, visits to exotic alien worlds, and future dystopia. In Goldstein's hands, however, these elements are usually means to literary ends that are more properly categorized as magic realism, mythopoeic fiction, and contemporary fairy tales. She achieved instant recognition in 1982, when her first novel, *The Red Magician*, an allegorical treatment of the rise of Naziism and the holocaust, won the American Book Award. Her next two novels are her most conventional excursions into science fiction. *The Dream Years* forges a link between the surrealist art movement of the 1920s and the French countercultural movement in 1968, through the adventures of a time-traveling novelist who finds the two eras more similar than not. *A Mask for the General* is set in a future America under the rule of a dictatorial soldier and explores ideological and social differences that have shaped different factions in the revolutionary subculture. *Tourists*, expanded from the novella of the same name, gradually eases its characters into Amaz, an uncharted third world country that serves as the setting for some of Goldstein's short fiction and runs on its own peculiar rules of logic. *Strange Devices of the Sun and Moon* presents the historical era just prior to the Enlightenment as one where fantasy and mythology are still accepted and thus regularly permeate daily life. *Summer King, Winter Fool,* set in a world where gods and mortals interact, is Goldstein's most overt detour into high fantasy. *Walking the Labyrinth,* in which a young woman comes into her heritage as the descendant of stage magicians who practiced real magic, and *Dark Cities Underground,* which deploys the familiar theme of the breakdown between reality and the world of a literary fantasy, are both examples of Goldstein's talent for conveying a sense of magic potential in the everyday through a slight, often imperceptible twist of ordinary events. Her short fiction has been collected in *Daily Voices* and *Travellers in Magic.*

HE AWOKE FEELING cold. He had kicked the blankets off, and the air conditioning was on too high. Debbie—Where was she? It was still dark out.

Confused, he pulled the blankets back and tried to go to sleep. Something was wrong. Debbie was gone, probably in the bathroom or downstairs getting a cup of coffee. And he was—he was on vacation, but where? Fully awake now, he sat up and tried to laugh. It was ridiculous. Imagine paying thousands of dollars for a vacation and then forgetting where you were. Greece? No, Greece was last year.

He got up and opened the curtains. The ocean ten stories below was black as sleep, paling a little to the east—it had to be east—where the sun was coming up. He turned down the air conditioning—the soft hum stopped abruptly—and headed for the bathroom. "Debbie?" he said, tentatively. He was a little annoyed. "Debbie?"

She was still missing after he had showered and shaved and dressed. "All right then," he said aloud, mostly to hear the sound of his voice. "If you're not coming I'll go to breakfast without you." She was probably out somewhere talking to the natives, laughing when she got a word wrong, though she had told him before they left that she had never studied a foreign language. She was good at languages, then—some people were. He remembered her saying in her soft Southern accent, "For goodness' sake, Charles, why do you think people will understand you if you just talk to them louder? These people just don't speak English." And then she had taken over, pointing and laughing and looking through a phrasebook she had gotten somewhere. And they would get the best room, the choicest steak, the blanket the craftswoman had woven for her own family. Charles's stock rose when he was with her, and he knew it. He hoped she would show up soon.

Soft Muzak played in the corridor and followed him into the elevator as he went down to the coffee shop. He liked the coffee shop in the hotel, liked the fact that the waiters spoke English and knew what an omelet was. The past few days he had been keeping to the hotel more and more, lying out by the beach and finally just sitting by the hotel pool drinking margaritas. The people back at the office would judge the success of the vacation by what kind of tan he got. Debbie had fretted a little and then had told him she was taking the bus in to see the ruins. She had come back darker than he was, the blond hairs on her arm bleached almost white against her brown skin, full of stories about women on the bus carrying chickens and temples crumbling in the desert. She was wearing a silver bracelet inlaid with blue and green stones.

When he paid the check he realized that he still didn't know what country he was in. The first bill he took out of his wallet had a 5 on each corner and a picture of some kind of spiky flower. The ten had a view of the ocean, and the one, somewhat disturbingly, showed a fat coiled snake. There was what looked like an official seal on the back of all of them, but no writing. Illiterates, he thought. But he would remember soon enough, or Debbie would come back.

Back in his room, changing into his swim trunks, he thought of his passport. Feeling like a detective who has just cracked the case he got his money belt out from under the mattress and unzipped it. His passport wasn't there. His passport and his plane ticket were missing. The traveller's checks were still there, useless to him without the passport as identification. Cold washed over him. He sat on the bed, his heart pounding.

Think, he told himself. They're somewhere else. They've got to be—who would steal the passport and not the traveller's checks? Unless someone needed the passport to leave the country. But who knew where he had hidden it? No one but Debbie, who had laughed at him for his precautions, and the idea of Debbie stealing the passport was absurd. But where was she?

All right, he thought. I've got to find the American consulate, work something out. . . . Luckily I just cashed a traveller's check yesterday. I've been robbed, and Americans get robbed all the time. It's no big thing. I have time. I'm paid up at the hotel till—till when?

Annoyed, he realized he had forgotten that too. For the first time he wondered if there might be something wrong with him. Overwork, maybe. He would have to see someone about it when he got back to the States.

He lifted the receiver and called downstairs. "Yes, sor?" the man at the desk said.

"This is Room 1012," Charles said. "I've forgotten—I was calling to check—How long is my reservation here?"

There was a silence at the other end, a disapproving silence, Charles felt. Most of the guests had better manners than to forget the length of their stay. He wondered what the man's reaction would be if he had asked what country he was in and felt something like hysteria rise within him. He fought it down.

The man when he came back was carefully neutral. "You are booked through tonight, sor," he said. "Do you wish to extend your stay?"

"Uh—no," Charles said. "Could you tell me—Where is the American consulate?"

"We have no relations with your country, sor," the man at the desk said.

For a moment Charles did not understand what he meant. Then he asked, "Well, what about—the British consulate?"

The man at the desk laughed and said nothing. Apparently he felt no need to clarify. As Charles tried to think of another question—Australian consulate? Canadian?—the man hung up.

Charles stood up carefully. "All right," he said to the empty room. "First things first." He got his two suitcases out of the closet and went through them methodically. Debbie's carrying case was still there and he went through that too. He checked under both mattresses, in the nightstand, in the medicine cabinet in the bathroom. Nothing. All right then. Debbie had stolen it, had to have. But why? And why didn't she take her carrying case with her when she went?

He wondered if she would show up back at the office. She had worked down the hall from him, one of the partners' secretaries. He had asked her along for companionship, making it clear that there were no strings attached, that he was simply interested in not travelling alone. Sometimes this kind of relationship turned sexual and sometimes it didn't. Last year, with Katya from accounting, it had. This year it hadn't.

There was still nothing to worry about, Charles thought, snapping the locks on the suitcases. Things like this probably happened all the time. He would get to the airport, where they would no doubt have records, a listing of his flight, and he would explain everything to them there. He checked his wallet for credit cards and found that they were still there. Good, he thought. Now we get to see if the advertisements are true. Accepted all over the world.

He felt so confident that he decided to stay the extra day at the hotel. After all, he thought, I've paid for it. And maybe Debbie will come back. He threw his towel over his shoulder and went downstairs.

The usual people were sitting out by the pool. Millie and Jean, the older women from Miami. The two newlyweds who had kept pretty much to themselves. The hitchhiker who was just passing through and who had been so entertaining that no one had had the heart to report him to the hotel management. Charles nodded to them and ordered his margarita from the bar before sitting down.

Talk flowed around him. "Have you been to Djuzban yet?" Jean was saying to the retired couple who had just joined them at the pool. "We took the hotel tour yesterday. The marketplace is just fabulous. I bought this ring there—see it?" And she flashed silver and stones.

"I hear the ruins are pretty good out in Djuzban," the retired man said.

"Oh, Harold," his wife said. "Harold wants to climb every tower in the country."

"No, man, for ruins you gotta go to Zabla," the hitchhiker said. "But the buses don't go there—you gotta rent a car. It's way the hell out in the desert, unspoiled, untouched. If your car breaks down you're dead—ain't nobody passing through that way for days."

Harold's wife shuddered in the heat. "I just want to do some shopping before we go home," she said. "I heard you can pick up bargains in leather in Qarnatl."

"All we saw in Qarnatl were natives trying to sell us decks of cards," Jean said. She turned to Millie. "Remember? I don't know why they thought Americans would be interested in their playing cards. They weren't even the same as ours."

Charles sipped his margarita, listening to the exotic names flow around him. What if he told them the names meant nothing to him, nothing at all? But he was too embarrassed. There were appearances to keep up after all, the appearance of being a seasoned traveller, of knowing the ropes. He would find out soon enough, anyway.

The day wore on. Charles had a margarita, then another. When the group around the pool broke up it seemed the most natural thing in the world to follow them into the hotel restaurant and order a steak, medium-rare. He was running low on cash, he noticed—he'd have to cash another traveller's check in the morning.

But in the morning when he awoke, cold sober, he knew immediately what he'd done. He reached for his wallet on the nightstand, fingers trembling a little. There was only a five with its bleak little picture of a shrub left. Well, he thought, feeling a little shaky. Maybe someone's going to the airport today. Probably. The guys in the office aren't going to believe this one.

He packed up his two suitcases, leaving Debbie's overnight bag for her in case she came back. Downstairs he headed automatically for the coffee shop before he remembered. Abruptly he felt his hunger grow worse. "Excuse me," he said to the man at the desk. "How much—Do you know how much the taxi to the airport is?"

"No speak English, sor," the man said. He was small and dark, like most of the natives. His teeth were stained red.

"You don't—" Charles said, disgusted. "Why in God's name would they hire someone who doesn't speak English? How much," he said slowly. "Taxi. Airport." He heard his voice grow louder; apparently Debbie was right.

The man shrugged. Another man joined them. Charles turned on him with relief. "How much is the taxi to the airport?"

"Oh, taxi," the man said, as though the matter were not very important. "Not so much, sor. Eight, nine. Maybe fifteen."

"Fifteen?" Charles said. He tried to remember the airport, remember how he'd gotten here. "Not five?" He held up five fingers.

The second man laughed. "Oh no, sor," he said. "Fifteen. Twenty." He shrugged.

Charles looked around in desperation. Hotel Tours, said the sign behind the front desk. Ruins. Free. "The ruins," he said, pointing to the sign, wondering if either of the men could read. "Are they near the airport?" He could go to the ruins, maybe get a ride. . . .

"Near?" the second man said. He shrugged again. "Maybe. Yes, I think so."

"How near?" Charles said.

"Near," the second man said. "Yes. Near enough."

Charles picked up the two suitcases and followed the line of tourists to the bus stop. See, he thought. Nothing to worry about, and you're even getting a free ride to the airport. Those taxi drivers are thieves anyway.

It was awkward maneuvering the suitcases up the stairs of the bus. "I'm going on to the airport," Charles said to the driver, feeling the need to explain.

"Of course, sor," the driver said, shrugging as if to say that an American's suitcases were no business of his. He added a word that Charles didn't catch. Perhaps it was in another language.

The bus set off down the new two-lane highway fronting the hotels. Soon they left the hotels behind, passed a cluster of run-down shacks and were heading into the desert. The air conditioning hummed loudly. Waves of heat travelled across the sands.

After nearly an hour the bus stopped. "We have one hour," the driver said in bad English. He opened the door. "These are the temple of Marmaz. Very old. One hour." The tourists filed out. A few were adjusting cameras or pointing lenses.

Because of the suitcases Charles was the last out. He squinted against the sun. The temple was a solid wall of white marble against the sand. Curious in spite of himself he crossed the parking lot, avoiding the native who was trying to show him something. "Pure silver," the small man said, calling after him. "Special price just for you."

In front of the temple was a cracked marble pool, now dry. Who were these people who had carried water into the desert, who had imprisoned the moon in pale marble? But then how much had he known about the other tourist spots he had visited, the Greeks who had built the Parthenon, the Mayans who had built the pyramids? He followed the line of tourists into the temple, feeling the coolness fall over him like a blessing.

He went from room to room, delighted, barely feeling the weight of the suitcases. He saw crumbling mosaics of reds and blues and greens, fragments of tapestries, domes, fountains, towers, a white dining hall that could seat a hundred. In one small room a native was explaining a piece of marble sculpture to a dozen Americans.

"This, he is the god of the sun," the native said. "And in the next room, the goddess of the moon. Moon, yes? We will go see her after. Once a year, at the end of the year, the two statues—statues, yes?—go outside. The priests take outside. They get married. Her baby is the new year."

"What nonsense," a woman standing near Charles said quietly. She was holding a guidebook. "That's the fourth king. He built the temple. God of the sun." She laughed scornfully.

"Can I—Can I see that book for a minute?" Charles said. The cover had flipped forward tantalizingly, almost revealing the name of the country.

The woman looked briefly at her watch. "Got to go," she said. "The bus is leaving in a minute and I've got to find my husband. Sorry."

Charles's bus was gone by the time he left the temple. It was much cooler now but heat still rose from the desert sands. He was very hungry, nearly tempted to buy a cool drink and a sandwich at the refreshment stand near the parking lot. "Cards?" someone said to him.

Charles turned. The small native said something that sounded like "Tiraz!" It was the same word the bus driver had said to him in the morning. Then, "Cards?" he said again.

"What?" Charles said impatiently, looking for a taxi.

"Ancient playing set," the native said. "Very holy." He took out a deck of playing cards from an embroidered bag and spread them for Charles. The colors were very bright. "Souvenir," the native said. He grinned, showing red-stained teeth. "Souvenir of your trip."

"No, thank you," Charles said. All around the parking lot, it seemed, little natives were trying to sell tourists rings and pipes and blouses and, for some reason, packs of playing cards. "Taxi?" he said. "Is there a taxi here?"

The native shrugged and moved on to the next tourist.

It was getting late. Charles went toward the nearest tour bus. The driver was leaning against the bus, smoking a small cigarette wrapped in a brown leaf. "Where can I find a taxi?" Charles asked him.

"No taxis," the driver said.

"No—Why not?" Charles said. This country was impossible. He couldn't wait to get out, to be on a plane drinking a margarita and heading back to the good old U.S.A. This was the worst vacation he'd ever had. "Can I make a phone call? I have to get to the airport."

A woman about to get on the bus heard him and stopped. "The airport?" she said. "The airport's fifty miles from here. At least. You'll never find a taxi to take you that far."

"Fifty miles?" Charles said. "They told me—At the hotel they told me it was fairly close." For a moment his confidence left him. What do I do now? he thought. He sagged against the suitcases.

"Listen," the woman said. She turned to the bus driver. "We've got room. Can't we take him back to the city with us? I think we're the last bus to leave."

The driver shrugged. "For the tiraz, of course. Anything is possible."

If Charles hadn't been so relieved at the ride he would have been annoyed. What did this word tiraz mean? Imbecile? Man with two suitcases? He followed the woman onto the bus.

"I can't believe you thought this was close to the airport," the woman said. He sat across the aisle from her. "This is way out in the desert. There's nothing here. No one would come out here if it wasn't for the ruins."

"They told me at the hotel," Charles said. He didn't really want to discuss it. He was no longer the seasoned traveller, the man who had regaled the people around the pool with stories of Mexico, Greece, Hawaii. He would have to confess, have to go back to the hotel and tell someone the whole story. Maybe they would bring in the police to find Debbie. A day wasted and he had only gone around in a circle, back to where he started. He felt tired and very hungry.

But when the bus stopped it was not at the brightly lit row of hotels. He strained to see in the oncoming dusk. "I thought you said—" He turned to the woman, hating to sound foolish again. "I thought we were going to the city."

"This is—" the woman said. Then she nodded in understanding. "You want the new city, the tourist city. That's up the road about ten miles. Any cab'll take you there."

Charles was the last off the bus again, slowed this time not so much by the suitcases as by the new idea. People actually stayed in the same cities that the natives lived. He had heard of it being done but he had thought only young people did it, students and drifters and hitchhikers like the one back at the hotel. This woman was not young and she had been fairly pleasant. He wished he had remembered to thank her.

The first cab driver laughed when Charles showed him the five note and asked to be taken to the new city. The driver was not impressed by the traveller's checks. The second and third drivers turned him down flat. The city smelled of motor oil and rancid fish. It was getting late, even a little chilly, and Charles began to feel nervous about being out so late. The two suitcases were an obvious target for some thief. And where would he go? What would he do?

The panic that he had suppressed for so long took over now and he began to run. He dove deeper into the twisting maze of the city, not caring where he went so long as he was moving. Everything was closed, and there were few streetlamps. He heard the sounds of his footfalls echo off the shuttered buildings. A cat jumped out of his way, eyes flashing gold.

After a long time of running he began to slow. "Tiraz!" someone whispered to him from an abandoned building. His heart pounded. He did not look back. Ahead was a lit storefront, a store filled with clutter. The door was open. A pawn shop.

He went in with relief. He cleared a space for himself among the old magazines and rusty baking pans and child's beads. The man behind the counter watched but made no comment. He took out everything from the two suitcases, sorted out what he needed and repacked it and gave the other suitcase to the man behind the counter. The man went to a small desk, unlocked a drawer and took out a steel box. He counted out some money and offered it to Charles. Charles accepted it wordlessly, not even bothering to count it.

The money bought a meal tasting of sawdust and sesame oil, and a sagging bed in an old hotel. The overhead fan turned all night because Charles could not figure out how to turn it off. A cockroach watched impassively from the corner.

The city looked different in daylight. Women in shawls and silver bracelets, men in clothes fashionable fifty years ago walked past the hotel as Charles looked out in the morning. The sun was shining. His heart rose. This was going to be the day he made it to the airport.

He walked along the streets almost jauntily, ignoring the ache in his arms. His beard itched because last night, in a moment of panic, he had thrown his electric razor into the suitcase to be sold. He shrugged. There were still things he could sell. Today he would find a better pawn shop.

He walked, passing run-down houses and outdoor markets, beggars and children, automobile garages and dim restaurants smelling of frying fish. "Excuse me," he said to a man leaning against a horse-drawn carriage. "Do you know where I can find a pawn shop?"

The man and horse both looked up. "Ride, yes?" the man said enthusiastically. "Famous monuments. Very cheap."

"No," Charles said. "A pawn shop. Do you understand?"

The man shrugged, pulled the horse's mane. "No speak English," he said finally.

Another man had come up behind Charles. "Pawn shop?" he said.

Charles turned quickly, relieved. "Yes," he said. "Do you know—"

"Two blocks down," the man said. "Turn left, go five blocks. Across the hospital."

"What street is that?" Charles asked.

"Street?" the man said. He frowned. "Two blocks down and turn left."

"The name," Charles said. "The name of the street."

To Charles's astonishment the man burst out laughing. The carriage driver laughed too, though he could not have possibly known what they were talking about. "Name?" the man said. "You tourists name your streets as though they were little children, yes?" He laughed again, wiping his eyes, and said something to the carriage-driver in another language, speaking rapidly.

"Thank you," Charles said. He walked the two blocks, turned left and went five blocks more. There was no hospital where the man had said there would be, and no pawn shop. A man who spoke a little English said something about a great fire, but whether it had been last week or several years ago Charles was unable to find out.

He started back toward the man who had given him directions. In a few minutes he was hopelessly lost. The streets became dingier, and once he saw a rat run from a pile of newspapers. The fire had swept through this part of the city leaving buildings charred and water damaged, open to the passersby like museum exhibits. Two dirty children ran toward him, shouting, "Money, please, sor! Money for food!" He turned down a sidestreet to lose them.

Ahead of him were three young men in grease-stained clothes. One of them hissed something at him, the words rushing by like a fork of lightning. Another held a length of chain which he played back and forth, whispering, between his hands. "I don't speak—" Charles said, but it was too late. They were on him.

One tore the suitcase from his hand, shouting "El amak! El amak!" Another knocked him down with a punch to his stomach that forced the wind out of him. The third was going through his pockets, taking his wallet and the little folder of traveller's checks. Charles tried feebly to rise, and the second one thrust him back, hitting him once more in the stomach. The first one yelled something and they ran quickly down the street. Charles lay where they left him, gasping for breath.

The two dirty children passed him, and an old woman balancing a basket of clothes on her head. After a few minutes he rolled over and sat up, leaning against a rusty car up on blocks. His pants were torn, he noticed dully, torn and smeared with oil. And his suitcase with the rest of his clothes was gone.

He would go to the police, go and tell them that his suitcase was gone. He knew the word for suitcase because the young thief had shouted it. Amak. El amak. And suddenly he realized something that knocked the breath out of him as surely as a punch to the stomach. Every word in English, every word that he knew, had a corresponding word in this strange foreign language. Everything you could think of—hand, love, table, hot—was conveyed to these natives by another word, a word not English. Debbie had known that, and that was why she was good at languages. He hadn't. He had expected everyone he met to drop this ridiculous charade and start speaking like normal people.

He stood up gingerly, breathing shallowly to make the pain in his stomach go away. After a while he began walking again, following the maze of the city in deeper. At last he found a small park and sat on a bench to rest.

A native came up to him almost immediately. "Cards?" the native said. "Look." He opened his embroidered bag.

Charles sighed. He was too tired to walk away. "I don't want any cards," he said. "I don't have any money."

"Of course not," the native said. "Look. They are beautiful, no?" He spread the brightly colored cards on the grass. Charles saw a baseball player, a fortune teller, a student, some designs he didn't recognize. "Look," the native said again and turned over the next card. "The tourist."

Charles had to laugh, looking at the card of the man carrying suitcases. These people had been visited by tourists for so long that the tourist had become an archetype, a part of everyone's reality like kings and jokers. He looked closer at the card. Those suitcases were familiar. And the tourist—He jerked back as though shocked. It was him.

He stood quickly and began to run, ignoring the pain in his stomach. The native did not follow.

He noticed the card sellers on every corner after that. They called to him even if he crossed the street to avoid them. "Tiraz, tiraz!" they called after him. He knew what it meant now. Tourist.

As the sun set he became ravenously hungry. He walked around a beggarwoman squatting in the street and saw, too late, a card seller waiting on the corner. The card seller held out something to him, some kind of pastry, and Charles took it, too hungry to refuse.

The pastry was filled with meat and very good. As though that were the signal, the other card sellers he passed began to give him things—a skin of wine, a piece of fish wrapped in paper. One of them handed him money, far more money than a deck of cards would cost. It was growing dark. He took a room for the night with the money.

A card seller was waiting for him at the corner the next day. "All right," Charles said to him. Some of the belligerence had been knocked out of him. "I give up. What the hell's going on around here?"

"Look," the card seller said. He took his cards out of the embroidered bag. "It is in here." He squatted on the sidewalk, oblivious to the dirt, the people walking by, the fumes from the street. The street, Charles noticed as he sat next to him, seemed to be paved with bottle caps.

The card seller spread the cards in front of him. "Look," he said. "It is foretold. The cards are our oracle, our newspaper, our entertainment. All depends on how you read them." Charles wondered where the man had learned to speak English, but he didn't want to interrupt. "See," the man said as he turned over a card. "Here you are. The tourist. It was foretold that you would come to the city."

"And then what?" Charles asked. "How do I get back?"

"We have to ask the cards," the man said. Idly he turned over another card, the ruins of Marmaz. "Maybe we wait for the next printing."

"Next—" Charles said. "You mean the cards don't stay the same?"

"No," the man said. "Do your newspapers stay the same?"

"But—Who prints them?"

The man shrugged. "We do not know." He turned over another card, a young blond woman.

"Debbie!" Charles said, startled.

"Yes," the man said. "The woman you came with. We had to convince her to go, so that you would fulfill the prophecy and come to the city. And then we took your pieces of paper, the ones that are so important to the tiraz. That is a stupid way to travel, if I may say so. In the city the only papers that are important to us are the cards, and if a man loses his cards he can easily get more."

"You—you took my passport?" Charles said. He did not feel as angry as he would like. "My passport and my plane tickets? Where are they?"

"Ah," the man said. "For that you must ask the cards." He took out another set of cards from his bag and gave them to Charles. Before Charles could answer he stood up and walked away.

By midday Charles had found the small park again. He sat down and spread out the cards, wondering if there was anything to what the card seller had said. Debbie did not appear in his deck. Was his an earlier printing, then, or a later one?

An American couple came up to him as he sat puzzling over the cards. "There are those cards again," the woman said. "I just can't get over how quaint they are. How much are you charging for yours?" she asked Charles. "The man down the street said he'd give them to us for ten."

"Eight," Charles said without hesitation, gathering them up.

The woman looked at her husband. "All right," he said. He took a five and three ones from his wallet and gave them to Charles.

"Thank you, sor," Charles said.

The man grunted. "I thought he spoke English very well," the woman said as they walked away. "Didn't you?"

A card seller gave him three more decks of cards and an embroidered bag later that day. By evening he had sold two of the decks. A few nights later, he joined the sellers of cards as they waited in the small park for the new printing of the cards. Somewhere a bell tolled midnight. A woman with beautiful long dark hair and an embroidered shawl came out of the night and silently took out the decks of cards from her bag. Her silver bracelets flashed in the moonlight. She gave Charles twelve decks. The men around him were already tearing the boxes open and spreading the cards, reading the past, or the present, or the future.

After about three years Charles got tired of selling the cards. His teeth had turned red from chewing the nut everyone chewed and he had learned to smoke the cigarettes wrapped in leaves. The other men had always told him that someone who spoke English as well as he did should be a tour guide, and finally he decided that they were right. Now he takes groups of tourists through the ruins of Marmaz, telling them about the god of the sun and the goddess of the moon and whatever else he chooses to make up that day. He has never found out what country he lives in.

GEORGE ALEC EFFINGER

One

George Alec Effinger cites the theater of the absurd as a major influence on his writing and refers to his style of multilayered, free-ranging fiction as "surreal fantasy." He first earned renown as a writer of stylish and challenging short stories in magazines and anthologies in the 1970s. His first novel, *What Entropy Means to Me*, is actually a quartet of linked stories that begin as a traditional quest fantasy but subtly transforms into a reflexive inquiry into family dynamics, political power struggles, and the act of artistic creation. Subsequent stories show a similar audacity of plotting and narrative structure. A number of his tales, notably "The Pinch-Hitters," "Naked to the Invisible Eye," "From Downtown at the Buzzer," and "Breakaway," draw on sports and games as their central metaphor. His novels *Death in Florence, Those Gentle Voices: A Promethean Romance,* and *The Wolves of Memory* evoke a sense of parallel realities and alternate worlds through their deployment of characters with the same names as those in short stories but with different personalities and motivations. Effinger has explored the intricate possibilities of time travel in his novels *The Nick of Time* and *The Bird of Time* and satirized heroic fantasy in *Maureen Birnbaum, Barbarian Sword-person*. His trilogy of novels featuring Marîd Audran (*When Gravity Fails, A Fire in the Sun,* and *The Exile Kiss*—all set in a future Middle East) is notable for its rendering of traditional Moslem culture receptive to the incursions of cyberpunk technology. Effinger's numerous stories have been collected in *Mixed Feelings, Irrational Numbers, Dirty Tricks,* and *Idle Pleasures*. He has also written a number of film novelizations; a roundrobin novel, *The Red Tape War; Nightmare Blue* (with Gardner Dozois); and the mainstream novel *Felicia*.

IT WAS YEAR 30, Day 1, the anniversary of Dr. Leslie Gillette's leaving Earth. Standing alone at the port, he stared out at the empty expanse of null space. "At eight o'clock, the temperature in the interstellar void is a negative two hundred seventy-three degrees Celsius," he said. "Even without the wind chill factor, that's cold. That's pretty damn cold."

A readout board had told him that morning that the ship and its lonely passenger would be reaching the vicinity of a star system before bedtime. Gillette didn't recall the name of the star—it had only been a number in a catalogue. He had long since lost interest in them. In the beginning, in the first few years when Jessica had still been with him, he had eagerly asked the board to show them where in Earth's night sky each star was located. They had taken a certain amount of pleasure in examining at close hand stars which they recognized as features of major constellations. That had passed. After they had visited a few thousand stars, they grew less interested. After they had discovered yet more planetary bodies, they almost became weary of the search. Almost. The Gillettes still had enough scientific curiosity to keep them going, farther and farther from their starting point.

But now the initial inspiration was gone. Rather than wait by the port until the electronic navigator slipped the ship back into normal space, he turned and left the control room. He didn't feel like searching for habitable planets. It was getting late, and he could do it the next morning.

He fed his cat instead. He punched up the code and took the cat's dinner from the galley chute. "Here you go," said Gillette. "Eat it and be happy with it. I want to read a little before I go to sleep." As he walked toward his quarters he felt the mild thrumming of the corridor's floor and walls that meant the ship had passed into real space. The ship didn't need directions from Gillette; it had already plotted a safe and convenient orbit in which to park, based on the size and characteristics of the star. The planets, if any, would all be there in the morning, waiting for Dr. Gillette to examine them, classify them, name them, and abandon them.

Unless, of course, he found life anywhere.

FINDING LIFE WAS one of the main purposes of the journey. Soon it had become the Gillettes' purpose in life as well. They had set out as enthusiastic explorers: Dr. Leslie Gillette, thirty-five years old, already an influential writer and lecturer in theoretical exobiology, and his wife, Jessica Reid Gillette, who had been the chairman of the biochemistry department at a large middle-western state university. They had been married for eleven years, and had made the decision to go into field exploration after the death of their only child.

Now they were traveling through space toward the distant limits of the galaxy. Long, long ago the Earth's sun had disappeared from view. The exobiology about which both Gillettes had thought and written and argued back home remained just what it had been then—mere theory. After visiting hundreds and hundreds of stellar systems, upon thousands of potential life-sustaining planets, they had yet to see or detect any form of life, no matter how primitive. The lab facilities on the landing craft returned the same frustrating answer with soul-deadening frequency: no life. Dead. Sterile. Year after year, the galaxy became to the Gillettes a vast and terrifying immensity of insensible rock and blazing gas.

"Do you remember," asked Jessica one day, "what old man Hayden used to tell us?"

Gillette smiled. "I used to love to get that guy into an argument," he said.

"He told me once that we might find life, but there wasn't a snowball's chance in hell of finding intelligent life."

Gillette recalled that discussion with pleasure. "And you called him a Terran chauvinist. I loved it. You made up a whole new category of bigotry, right on the spot. We thought he was such a conservative old codger. Now it looks like even he was too optimistic."

Jessica stood behind her husband's chair, reading what he was writing. "What would Hayden say, do you think, if he knew we haven't found a goddamn thing?"

Gillette turned around and looked up at her. "I think even he would be disappointed," he said. "Surprised, too."

"This isn't what I anticipated," she said.

The complete absence of even the simplest of lifeforms was at first irritating, then puzzling, then ominous. Soon even Leslie Gillette, who always labored to keep separate his emotional thoughts and his logical ones, was compelled to realize that his empirical conclusions were shaping up in defiance of all the mathematical predictions man or machine had ever made. In the control room was a framed piece of vellum, on which was copied, in fine italic letters and numerals:

$$N = R.f_p n_e f_l f_i f_c L$$

This was a formula devised decades before to determine the approximate number of advanced technological civilizations man might expect to find elsewhere in his galaxy. The variables in the formula are given realistic values, according to the scientific wisdom of the time. N is determined by seven factors:

$R.$ or the mean rate of star formation in the galaxy (with an assigned value of ten per year)

f_p or the percentage of stars with planets (close to one hundred percent)

n_e or the average number of planets in each star system with environments suitable for life (with an assigned value of one)

f_l or the percentage of those planets on which life does, in fact, develop (close to one hundred percent)

f_i or the percentage of those planets on which intelligent life develops (ten percent)

f_c or the percentage of those planets on which advanced technical civilization develops (ten percent)

L   or the lifetime of the technical civilization (with an estimated value of ten
     million years).

These figures produced a predictive result stating that N—the number of advanced civilizations in the Milky Way galaxy—equals ten to the sixth power. A million. The Gillettes had cherished that formula through all the early years of
disappointment. But they were not looking for an advanced civilization, they were
looking for life. Any kind of life. Some six years after leaving Earth, Leslie and Jessica
were wandering across the dry, sandy surface of a cool world circling a small, cool
sun. "I don't see any advanced civilizations," said Jessica, stooping to stir the dust
with the heavy gauntlet of her pressure suit.

"Nope," said her husband, "not a hamburger stand in sight." The sky was a kind
of reddish purple, and he didn't like looking into it very often. He stared down at the
ground, watching Jessica trail her fingers in the lifeless dirt.

"You know," she said, "that formula says that every system ought to have at least
one planet suitable for life."

Gillette shrugged. "A lot of them do," he said. "But it also says that every planet
that could sustain life, will sustain life, eventually."

"Maybe they were a little too enthusiastic when they picked the values for their
variables."

Jessica laughed. "Maybe." She dug a shallow hole in the surface. "I keep hoping
I'll run across some ants or a worm or something."

"Not here, honey," said Gillette. "Come on, let's go back." She sighed and stood.
Together they returned to the landing craft.

"What a waste," said Jessica, as they prepared to lift off. "I've given my imagination all this freedom. I'm prepared to see anything down there, the garden variety
of life or something more bizarre. You know, dancing crystals or thinking clouds. But
I never prepared myself for so much nothing."

The landing craft shot up through the thin atmosphere, toward the orbiting
command ship. "A scientist has to be ready for this kind of thing," said Gillette
wistfully. "But I agree with you. Experience seems to be defying the predictions in a
kind of scary way."

Jessica loosened her safety belt and took a deep breath. "Mathematically unlikely,
I'd call it. I'm going to look at the formula tonight and see which of those variables
is the one screwing everything up."

Gillette shook his head. "I've done that time and time again," he said. "It won't
get you very far. Whatever you decided, the result will still be a lot different from
what we've found." On the myriad worlds they had visited, they never found anything
as simple as algae or protozoans, let alone intelligent life. Their biochemical sensors

had never detected anything that even pointed in that direction, like a complex protein. Only rock and dust and empty winds and lifeless pools.

IN THE MORNING, just as he had predicted, the planets were still there. There were five of them, circling a modest star, type G3, not very different from Earth's Sun. He spoke to the ship's computer: "I name the star Hannibal. Beginning with the nearest to Hannibal, I name the planets: Huck, Tom, Jim, Becky, and Aunt Polly. We will proceed with the examinations." The ship's instruments could take all the necessary readings, but Gillette wouldn't trust its word on the existence of life. That question was so important that he felt he had to make the final determination himself.

Huck was a Mars-sized ball of nickel and iron, a rusty brown color, pocked with craters, hot and dry and dead. Tom was larger and darker, cooler, but just as damaged by impacts and just as dead. Jim was Earthlike; it had a good-sized atmosphere of nitrogen and oxygen, its range of temperatures stayed generally between − 30°C and + 50°C, and there was a great abundance of water on the planet's surface. But there was no life, none on the rocky, dusty land, none in the mineral-salted water, nothing, not so much as a single cyanobacterium. Jim was the best hope Gillette had in the Hannibal system, but he investigated Becky and Aunt Polly as well. They were the less-dense gas giants of the system, although neither was so large as Uranus or Neptune. There was no life in their soupy atmospheres or on the igneous surfaces of their satellites. Gillette didn't bother to name the twenty-three moons of the five planets; he thought he'd leave that to the people who came after him. If any ever did.

Next, Gillette had to take care of the second purpose of the mission. He set out an orbiting transmission gate around Jim, the most habitable of the five planets. Now a ship following in his path could cross the scores of light-years instantaneously from the gate Gillette had set out at his previous stop. He couldn't even remember what that system had been like or what he had named it. After all these years they were all confused in his mind, particularly because they were so identical in appearance, so completely empty of life.

He sat at a screen and looked down on Jim, at the tan, sandy continents, the blue seas, the white clouds and polar caps. Gillette's cat, a gray Maine coon, his only companion, climbed into his lap. The cat's name was Benny, great-grandson of Methyl and Ethyl, the two kittens Jessica had brought along. Gillette scratched behind the animal's ears and under his chin. "Why aren't there any cats down there?" he asked it. Benny had only a long purr for an answer. After a while Gillette tired of staring down at the silent world. He had made his survey, had put out the gate, and now there was nothing to do but send the information back toward Earth and move on. He gave the instructions to the ship's computer, and in half an hour the stars had disappeared, and Gillette was traveling again through the darkness of null space.

*   *   *

HE REMEMBERED HOW excited they had been about the mission, some thirty years before. He and Jessica had put in their application, and they had been chosen for reasons Gillette had not fully understood. "My father thinks that anyone who wants to go chasing across the galaxy for the rest of his life must be a little crazy," said Jessica.

Gillette smiled. "A little unbalanced, maybe, but not crazy."

They were lying in the grass behind their house, looking up into the night sky, wondering which of the bright diamond stars they would soon visit. The project seemed like a wonderful vacation from their grief, an opportunity to examine their lives and their relationship without the million remembrances that tied them to the past. "I told my father that it was a marvelous opportunity for us," she said. "I told him that from a scientific point of view, it was the most exciting possibility we could ever hope for."

"Did he believe you?"

"Look, Leslie, a shooting star. Make a wish. No, I don't think he believed me. He said the project's board of governors agreed with him and the only reason we've been selected is that we're crazy or unbalanced or whatever in just the right ways."

Gillette tickled his wife's ear with a long blade of grass. "Because we might spend the rest of our lives staring down at stars and worlds."

"I told him five years at the most, Leslie. Five years. I told him that as soon as we found anything we could definitely identify as living matter, we'd turn around and come home. And if we have any kind of luck, we might see it in one of our first stops. We may be gone only a few months or a year."

"I hope so," said Gillette. They looked into the sky, feeling it press down on them with a kind of awesome gravity, as if the infinite distances had been converted to mass and weight. Gillette closed his eyes. "I love you," he whispered.

"I love you, too, Leslie," murmured Jessica. "Are you afraid?"

"Yes."

"Good," she said. "I might have been afraid to go with you if you weren't worried, too. But there's nothing to be afraid of. We'll have each other, and it'll be exciting. It will be more fun than spending the next couple of years here, doing the same thing, giving lectures to grad students and drinking sherry with the Nobel crowd."

Gillette laughed. "I just hope that when we get back, someone remembers who we are. I can just see us spending two years going out and coming back, and nobody even knows what the project was all about."

Their good-bye to her father was more difficult. Mr. Reid was still not sure why they wanted to leave Earth. "A lot of young people suffer a loss, the way you have," he said. "But they go on somehow. They don't just throw their lives away."

"We're not throwing anything away," said Jessica. "Dad, I guess you'd have to be a biologist to understand. There's more excitement in the chance of discovering life somewhere out there than in anything we might do if we stayed here. And we won't be gone long. It's field work, the most challenging kind. Both of us have always preferred that to careers at the blackboards in some university."

Reid shrugged and kissed his daughter. "If you're sure," was all he had to say. He shook hands with Gillette.

Jessica looked up at the massive spacecraft. "I guess we are," she said. There was nothing more to do or say. They left Earth not many hours later, and they watched the planet dwindle in the ports and on the screens.

The experience of living on the craft was strange at first, but they quickly settled into routines. They learned that while the idea of interstellar flight was exciting, the reality was duller than either could have imagined. The two kittens had no trouble adjusting, and the Gillettes were glad for their company. When the craft was half a million miles from Earth, the computer slipped it into null space, and they were truly isolated for the first time.

It was terrifying. There was no way to communicate with Earth while in null space. The craft became a self-contained little world, and in dangerous moments when Gillette allowed his imagination too much freedom, the silent emptiness around him seemed like a new kind of insanity or death. Jessica's presence calmed him, but he was still grateful when the ship came back into normal space, at the first of their unexplored stellar systems.

Their first subject was a small, dim, class-M star, the most common type in the galaxy, with only two planetary bodies and a lot of asteroidal debris circling around it. "What are we going to name the star, dear?" asked Jessica. They both looked at it through the port, feeling a kind of parental affection.

Gillette shrugged. "I thought it would be easier if we stuck to the mythological system they've been using at home."

"That's a good idea, I guess. We've got one star with two little planets wobbling around it."

"Didn't Apollo have . . . No, I'm wrong. I thought—"

Jessica turned away from the port. "It reminds me of Odin and his two ravens."

"He had two ravens?"

"Sure," said Jessica, "Thought and Memory. Hugin and Mugin."

"Fine. We'll name the star Odin, and the planets whatever you just said. I'm sure glad I have you. You're a lot better at this than I am."

Jessica laughed. She looked forward to exploring the planets. It would be the first break they had in the monotony of the journey. Neither Leslie nor Jessica anticipated finding life on the two desolate worlds, but they were glad to give them a thorough examination. They wandered awe-struck over the bleak, lonely landscapes of Hugin and Mugin, completing their tests, and at last returned to their orbiting craft. They sent their findings back to Earth, set out the first of the transmission gates, and, not yet feeling very disappointed, left the Odin system. They both felt that they were in contact with their home, regardless of the fact that their message would take a long time to reach Earth, and they were moving away too quickly ever to receive any. But they both knew that if they wanted, they could still turn around and head back to Earth.

Their need to know drove them on. The loneliness had not yet become unbearable. The awful fear had not yet begun.

The gates were for the use of the people who followed the Gillettes into the unsettled reaches of the galaxy; they could be used in succession to travel outward, but the travelers couldn't return through them. They were like ostrich eggs filled with water and left by natives in the African desert; they were there to make the journey safer and more comfortable for others, to enable the others to travel even farther.

Each time the Gillettes left one star system for another, through null space, they put a greater gulf of space and time between themselves and the world of their birth. "Sometimes I feel very strange," admitted Gillette, after they had been outbound for more than two years. "I feel as if any contact we still have with Earth is an illusion, something we've invented just to maintain our sanity. I feel like we're donating a large part of our lives to something that might never benefit anyone."

Jessica listened somberly. She had had the same feelings, but she hadn't wanted to let her husband know. "Sometimes I think that the life in the university classroom is the most desirable thing in the world. Sometimes I damn myself for not seeing that before. But it doesn't last long. Every time we go down to a new world, I still feel the same hope. It's only the weeks in null space that get to me. The alienation is so intense."

Gillette looked at her mournfully. "What does it really matter if we do discover life?" he asked.

She looked at him in shocked silence for a moment. "You don't really mean that," she said at last.

Gillette's scientific curiosity rescued him, as it had more than once in the past. "No," he said softly, "I don't. It does matter." He picked up the three kittens from Ethyl's litter. "Just let me find something like these waiting on one of these endless planets, and it will all be worthwhile."

Months passed, and the Gillettes visited more stars and more planets, always with the same result. After three years they were still rocketing away from Earth. The fourth year passed, and the fifth. Their hope began to dwindle.

"It bothers me just a little," said Gillette as they sat beside a great gray ocean, on a world they had named Carraway. There was a broad beach of pure white sand backed by high dunes. Waves broke endlessly and came to a frothy end at their feet. "I mean, that we never see anybody behind us, or hear anything. I know it's impossible, but I used to have this crazy dream that somebody was following us through the gates and then jumped ahead of us through null space. Whoever it was waited for us at some star we hadn't got to yet."

Jessica made a flat mound of wet sand. "This is just like Earth, Leslie," she said. "If you don't notice the chartreuse sky. And if you don't think about how there isn't any grass in the dunes and no shells on the beach. Why would somebody follow us like that?"

Gillette lay back on the clean white sand and listened to the pleasant sound of the surf. "I don't know," he said. "Maybe there had been some absurd kind of life on one of those planets we checked out years ago. Maybe we made a mistake and over-looked something, or misread a meter or something. Or maybe all the nations on Earth had wiped themselves out in a war and I was the only living human male and the lonely women of the world were throwing a party for me."

"You're crazy, honey," said Jessica. She flipped some damp sand onto the legs of his pressure suit.

"Maybe Christ had come back and felt the situation just wasn't complete without us, too. For a while there, every time we bounced back into normal space around a star, I kind of half-hoped to see another ship, waiting." Gillette sat up again. "It never happened, though."

"I wish I had a stick," said Jessica. She piled more wet sand on her mound, looked at it for a few seconds, and then looked up at her husband. "Could there be something happening at home?" she asked.

"Who knows what's happened in these five years? Think of all we've missed, sweetheart. Think of the books and the films, Jessie. Think of the scientific discoveries we haven't heard about. Maybe there's peace in the Mideast and a revolutionary new source of power and a black woman in the White House. Maybe the Cubs have won a pennant, Jessie. Who knows?"

"Don't go overboard, dear," she said. They stood and brushed off the sand that clung to their suits. Then they started back toward the landing craft.

Onboard the orbiting ship an hour later, Gillette watched the cats. They didn't care anything about the Mideast; maybe they had the right idea. "I'll tell you one thing," he said to his wife. "I'll tell you who does know what's been happening. The people back home know. They know all about everything. The only thing they don't know is what's going on with us, right now. And somehow I have the feeling that they're living easier with their ignorance than I am with mine." The kitten that would grow up to be Benny's mother tucked herself up into a near little bundle and fell asleep.

"You're feeling cut off," said Jessica.

"Of course I am," said Gillette. "Remember what you used to say to me? Before we were married, when I told you I only wanted to go on with my work, and you told me that one human being was no human being? Remember? You were always saying things like that, just so I'd have to ask you what the hell you were talking about. And then you'd smile and deliver some little story you had all planned out. I guess it made you happy. So you said, 'One human being is no human being, and I said, 'What does that mean?' and you went on about how if I were going to live my life all alone, I might as well not live it at all. I can't remember exactly the way you put it. You have this crazy way of saying things that don't have the least little bit of logic to them but always make sense. You said I figured I could sit in my ivory tower and look at things under a microscope and jot down my findings and send out little announcements now and then about what I'm doing and how I'm feeling and I shouldn't be surprised if nobody gives a damn. You said that I had to live among people, that no matter how hard I tried, I couldn't get away from it. And that I couldn't climb a tree and decide I was going to start my own new species. But you were wrong, Jessica. You can get away from people. Look at us."

The sound of his voice was bitter and heavy in the air. "Look at me," he murmured. He looked at his reflection and it frightened him. He looked old; worse than that, he looked just a little demented. He turned away quickly, his eyes filling with tears.

"We're not truly cut off," she said softly. "Not as long as we're together."

"Yes," he said, but he still felt set apart, his humanity diminishing with the passing months. He performed no function that he considered notably human. He read meters and dials and punched buttons; machines could do that, animals could be trained to do the same. He felt discarded, like a bad spot on a potato, cut out and thrown away.

Jessica prevented his depression from deepening into madness. He was far more susceptible to the effects of isolation than she. Their work sustained Jessica, but it only underscored their futility for her husband.

"I HAVE STRANGE thoughts, Jessica," he admitted to her, one day during their ninth year of exploration. "They just come into my head now and then. At first I didn't pay any attention at all. Then, after a while, I noticed that I was paying attention, even though when I stopped to analyze them I could see the ideas were still foolish."

"What kind of thoughts?" she asked. They prepared the landing craft to take them down to a large, ruddy world.

Gillette checked both pressure suits and stowed them aboard the lander. "Sometimes I get the feeling that there aren't any other people anywhere, that they were all the invention of my imagination. As if we never came from Earth, that home and everything I recall are just delusions and false memories. As if we've always been on this ship, forever and ever, and we're absolutely alone in the whole universe." As he spoke, he gripped the heavy door of the lander's airlock until his knuckles turned white. He felt his heart speeding up, he felt his mouth going dry, and he knew that he was about to have another anxiety attack.

"It's all right, Leslie," said Jessica soothingly. "Think back to the time we had together at home. That couldn't be a lie."

Gillette's eyes opened wider. For a moment he had difficulty breathing. "Yes," he whispered, "it could be a lie. You could be a hallucination, too." He began to weep, seeing exactly where his ailing mind was leading him.

Jessica held him while the attack worsened and then passed away. In a few moments he had regained his usual sensible outlook. "This mission is much tougher than I thought it would be," he whispered.

Jessica kissed his cheek. "We have to expect some kind of problems after all these years," she said. "We never planned on it taking this long."

The system they were in consisted of another class-M star and twelve planets. "A lot of work, Jessica," he said, brightening a little at the prospect. "It ought to keep us busy for a couple of weeks. That's better than falling through null space."

"Yes, dear," she said. "Have you started thinking of names yet?" That was becoming the most tedious part of the mission—coming up with enough new names for all the stars and their satellites. After eight thousand systems, they had exhausted all the mythological and historical and geographical names they could remember. They now took turns, naming planets after baseball players and authors and film stars.

They were going down to examine a desert world they had named Rick, after the character in *Casablanca*. Even though it was unlikely that it would be suitable for life, they still needed to examine it firsthand, just on the off-chance, just in case, just for ducks, as Gillette's mother used to say.

That made him pause, a quiet smile on his lips. He hadn't thought of that expression in years. That was a critical point in Gillette's voyage; never again, while Jessica was with him, did he come so close to losing his mental faculties. He clung to her and to his memories as a shield against the cold and destructive forces of the vast emptiness of space.

Once more the years slipped by. The past blurred into an indecipherable haze, and the future did not exist. Living in the present was at once the Gillettes' salvation and curse. They spent their time among routines and changeless duties that were no more tedious than what they had known on Earth, but no more exciting either.

As their shared venture neared its twentieth year, the great disaster befell Gillette: on an unnamed world hundreds of light-years from Earth, on a rocky hill overlooking a barren sandstone valley, Jessica Gillette died. She bent over to collect a sample of soil; a worn seam in her pressure suit parted; there was a sibilant warning of gases passing through the lining, into the suit. She fell to the stony ground, dead. Her husband watched her die, unable to give her any help, so quickly did the poison kill her. He sat beside her as the planet's day turned to night, and through the long, cold hours until dawn.

He buried her on that world, which he named Jessica, and left her there forever. He set out a transmission gate in orbit around the world, finished his survey of the rest of the system, and went on to the next star. He was consumed with grief, and for many days he did not leave his bed.

One morning Benny, the kitten, scrabbled up beside Gillette. The kitten had not been fed in almost a week. "Benny," murmured the lonely man, "I want you to realize something. We can't get home. If I turned this ship around right this very minute and powered home all the way through null space, it would take twenty years. I'd be in my seventies if I lived long enough to see Earth. I never expected to live that long." From then on, Gillette performed his duties in a mechanical way, with none of the enthusiasm he had shared with Jessica. There was nothing else to do but go on, and so he did, but the loneliness clung to him like a shadow of death.

He examined his results, and decided to try to make a tentative hypothesis. "It's unusual data, Benny," he said. "There has to be some simple explanation. Jessica always argued that there didn't have to be any explanation at all, but now I'm sure there must be. There has to be some meaning behind all of this, somewhere. Now tell me, why haven't we found Indication Number One of life on any of these twenty-odd thousand worlds we've visited?"

Benny didn't have much to suggest at this point. He followed Gillette with his big yellow eyes as the man walked around the room. "I've gone over this before," said Gillette, "and the only theories I come up with are extremely hard to live with. Jessica would have thought I was crazy for sure. My friends on Earth would have a really difficult time even listening to them, Benny, let alone seriously considering them. But in an investigation like this, there comes a point when you have to throw out all the predicted results and look deep and long at what has actually occurred. This isn't what I wanted, you know. It sure isn't what Jessica and I expected. But it *is* what happened."

Gillette sat down at his desk. He thought for a moment about Jessica, and he was brought to the verge of tears. But he thought about how he had dedicated the remainder of his life to her, and to her dream of finding an answer at one of the stellar systems yet to come.

He devoted himself to getting that answer for her. The one blessing in all the years of disappointment was that the statistical data were so easy to comprehend. He didn't need a computer to help in arranging the information: there was just one long, long string of zeros. "Science is built on theories," thought Gillette. "Some theories may be untestable in actual practice, but are accepted because of an overwhelming preponderance of empirical data. For instance, there may not actually exist any such thing as gravity; it may be that things have been falling down consistently because of some outrageous statistical quirk. Any moment now things may start to fall up and down at random, like pennies landing heads or tails. And then the Law of Gravity will have to be amended."

That was the first, and safest, part of his reasoning. Next came the feeling that there was one over-riding possibility that would adequately account for the numbing succession of lifeless planets. "I don't really want to think about that yet," he murmured, speaking to Jessica's spirit. "Next week, maybe. I think we'll visit a couple more systems first."

And he did. There were seven planets around an M-class star, and then a G star with eleven, and a K star with fourteen; all the worlds were impact-cratered and pitted and smoothed with lava flow. Gillette held Benny in his lap after inspecting the three systems. "Thirty-two more planets," he said. "What's the grand total now?" Benny didn't know.

Gillette didn't have anyone with whom to debate the matter. He could not consult scientists on Earth; even Jessica was lost to him. All he had was his patient gray cat, who couldn't be looked to for many subtle contributions. "Have you noticed," asked the man, "that the farther we get from Earth, the more homogeneous the universe looks?" If Benny didn't understand the word homogeneous, he didn't show it. "The only really unnatural thing we've seen in all these years has been Earth itself. Life on Earth is the only truly anomalous factor we've witnessed in twenty years of exploration. What does that mean to you?"

At that point, it didn't mean anything to Benny, but it began to mean something to Gillette. He shrugged. "None of my friends were willing to consider even the possibility that Earth might be alone in the universe, that there might not be anything else alive anywhere in all the infinite reaches of space. Of course, we haven't looked at much of those infinite reaches, but going zero for twenty-three thousand means that something unusual is happening." When the Gillettes had left Earth two decades before, prevailing scientific opinion insisted that life had to be out there somewhere, even though there was no proof, either directly or indirectly. There had to be life; it was only a matter of stumbling on it. Gillette looked at the old formula, still hanging where it had been throughout the whole voyage. "If one of those factors is zero," he thought, "then the whole product is zero. Which factor could it be?" There was no hint of an answer, but that particular question was becoming less important to Gillette all the time.

AND SO IT had come down to this: Year 30 and still outward bound. The end of Gillette's life was somewhere out there in the black stillness. Earth was a pale memory, less real now than last night's dreams. Benny was an old cat, and soon he would die as Jessica had died, and Gillette would be absolutely alone. He didn't like to think about that, but the notion intruded on his consciousness again and again.

Another thought arose just as often. It was an irrational thought, he knew, something he had scoffed at thirty years before. His scientific training led him to examine ideas by the steady, cold light of reason, but this new concept would not hold still for such a mechanical inspection.

He began to think that perhaps Earth was alone in the universe, the only planet among billions to be blessed with life. "I have to admit again that I haven't searched through a significant fraction of all the worlds in the galaxy," he said, as if he were defending his feelings to Jessica. "But I'd be a fool if I ignored thirty years of experience. What does it mean, if I say that Earth is the only planet with life? It isn't a scientific or mathematical notion. Statistics alone demand other worlds with some form of life. But what can overrule such a biological imperative?" He waited for a guess from Benny; none seemed to be forthcoming. "Only an act of faith," murmured Gillette. He paused, thinking that he might hear a trill of dubious laughter from Jessica's spirit, but there was only the humming, ticking silence of the spacecraft.

"A single act of creation, on Earth," said Gillette. "Can you imagine what any of the people at the university would have said to that? I wouldn't have been able to show my face around there again. They would have revoked every credential I had. My subscription to *Science* would have been canceled. The local PBS channel would have refused my membership.

"But what else can I think? If any of those people had spent the last thirty years the way we have, they'd have arrived at the same conclusion. I didn't come to this answer easily, Jessica, you know that. You know how I was. I never had any faith in anything I hadn't witnessed myself. I didn't even believe in the existence of George Washington, let alone first principles. But there comes a time when a scientist must accept the most unappealing explanation, if it is the only one left that fits the facts."

It made no difference to Gillette whether or not he was correct, whether he had investigated a significant number of worlds to substantiate his conclusion. He had had to abandon, one by one, all of his prejudices, and made at last a leap of faith. He knew what seemed to him to be the truth, not through laboratory experiments but by an impulse he had never felt before.

For a few days he felt comfortable with the idea. Life had been created on Earth for whatever reasons, and nowhere else. Each planet devoid of life that Gillette discovered became from then on a confirming instance of this hypothesis. But then, one night, it occurred to him how horribly he had cursed himself. If Earth were the only home of life, why was Gillette hurtling farther and farther from that place, farther from where he too had been made, farther from where he was supposed to be?

What had he done to himself—and to Jessica?

"My impartiality failed me, sweetheart," he said to her disconsolately. "If I could have stayed cold and objective, at least I would have had peace of mind. I would never have known how I damned both of us. But I couldn't; the impartiality was a lie, from the very beginning. As soon as we went to measure something, our humanity got in the way. We couldn't be passive observers of the universe, because we're alive and we're people and we think and feel. And so we were doomed to learn the truth eventually, and we were doomed to suffer because of it." He wished Jessica were still alive, to comfort him as she had so many other times. He had felt isolated before, but it had never been so bad. Now he understood the ultimate meaning of alienation— a separation from his world and the force that had created it. He wasn't supposed to be here, wherever it was. He belonged on Earth, in the midst of life. He stared out through the port, and the infinite blackness seemed to enter into him, merging with his mind and spirit. He felt the awful coldness in his soul.

For a while Gillette was incapacitated by his emotions. When Jessica died, he had bottled up his grief; he had never really permitted himself the luxury of mourning her. Now, with the added weight of his new convictions, her loss struck him again, harder than ever before. He allowed the machines around him to take complete control of the mission in addition to his well-being. He watched the stars shine in the darkness as the ship fell on through real space. He stroked Benny's thick gray fur and remembered everything he had so foolishly abandoned.

In the end it was Benny that pulled Gillette through. Between strokes the man's hand stopped in mid-air; Gillette experienced a flash of insight, what the oriental philosophers call *satori,* a moment of diamond-like clarity. He knew intuitively that he had made a mistake that had led him into self-pity. If life had been created on Earth, then all living things were a part of that creation, wherever they might be. Benny, the gray-haired cat, was a part of it, even locked into this tin can between the stars. Gillette himself was a part, wherever he traveled. That creation was just as present in the spacecraft as on Earth itself: it had been foolish for Gillette to think that he ever could separate himself from it—which was just what Jessica had always told him.

"Benny!" said Gillette, a tear streaking his wrinkled cheek. The cat observed him benevolently. Gillette felt a pleasant warmth overwhelm him as he was released at last from his loneliness. "It was all just a fear of death," he whispered. "I was just afraid to die. I wouldn't have believed it! I thought I was beyond all that. It feels good to be free of it."

And when he looked out again at the wheeling stars, the galaxy no longer seemed empty and black, but vibrant and thrilling with a creative energy. He knew that what he felt could not be shaken, even if the next world he visited was a lush garden of life—that would not change a thing, because his belief was no longer based on numbers and facts, but on a stronger sense within him.

IT MADE NO difference at all where Gillette was headed, what stars he would visit: wherever he went, he understood at last, he was going home.

WITHDRAWN

Damage Noted